The Sweet and Simple Kind

YASMINE GOONERATNE

Little, Brown

LITTLE, BROWN

First published in 2006 by Perera Hussein Publishing House, Sri Lanka
First published in Great Britain as a paperback original in 2009 by Little, Brown

A CIP catalogue record for this book is available from the British Library.

ISBN 978-1-4087-0163-8

Typeset in Spectrum by M Rules
Printed and bound in Great Britain by
Clays Ltd, St Ives plc

Papers used by Little, Brown are natural, renewable and recyclable products made from wood grown in sustainable forests and certified in accordance with the rules of the Forest Stewardship Council.

Little, Brown
An imprint of
Little, Brown Book Group
100 Victoria Embankment
London EC4Y 0DY

An Hachette Livre UK Company
www.hachettelivre.co.uk

www.littlebrown.co.uk

ACKNOWLEDGMENTS

Seven tales which feature Tsunami and Latha Wijesinha and members of the Wijesinha family first appeared in *Masterpiece and Other Stories*, a collection published by Indialog Publications, Delhi, in 2002. My thanks to Indialog for this, and special thanks to Ananda de Alwis and the late Ian Goonetilleke, A.J. Wilson, and George Keyt, storytellers to whom I owe much that appears here as fiction; to the lively ladies who occupied rooms on the top floor balcony at Sanghamitta Hall from 1954 to 1958; to Lucy Hartland for the gift of a phrase; and to Lakshmi, Chandi, Brendon, Channa, Devika, Ameena and Sam, the friends who have read my manuscript at various times, and given me the priceless benefit of their encouragement and advice.

Yasmine Gooneratne
2006

For Brendon

I

I'm just an old-fashioned girl, with an old-fashioned mind
Not sophisticated, I'm the sweet and simple kind . . .

Marve Fisher, 'Just an Old-Fashioned Girl' (1954)
and Eartha Kitt, *In Person at the Plaza*

Of my two sisters, she proved by far the better actress, the more skilful dissembler, keeping the double handicap of an agile brain and an incisive tongue so well concealed that she quickly acquired an enviable image outside our household as 'a sweet, *simple* girl . . . though a little shy'.

Relative Merits: A Personal Memoir (1986)

1

LOYALTY

Loyalty (and the damnable lack of it in his wife) was the thought uppermost in the mind of Sir Andrew Millbanke as he looked down at Lady Alexandra's dead body, spread-eagled on the paved pathway of the Residency. She had let him down, as usual, during the entire week, making a god-awful fuss just because he had insisted on taking Brenda van Buren along as their guest on that trip to Bentot, so that the poor woman could get in a spot of sea-bathing. So what if, of the two of them, Brenda cut a far better figure in a bathing suit? Sir Andrew had a shrewd idea that his wife positively *enjoyed* finding things to complain about; but in choosing today of all days to leap out of her window and kill herself, Alexandra had excelled her own record. She knew better than anyone else (except his two A.D.C.s, of course) how important it was that he should be at the very top of his form today, when he was welcoming an important visitor. The Prince of Wales, presently touring the island, was due to arrive at the Residency gates at precisely eleven o'clock.

His Excellency was aware that he was being closely observed by the little group of people standing close by. They were all members of the household staff and, with one exception, were all British. The exception, a Sinhalese under-gardener, had been the first to see the body in the Residency garden, and report its presence there. Coming to work at six o'clock as he usually did, Alwis Appu had very nearly tripped over Lady Millbanke lying lifeless in the middle of the pathway. Although a native, Alwis had been well trained in the proper British way of doing things, and he did not, therefore, panic and run about shouting for help as an ordinary native might have done. Instead he had proceeded immediately to the Residency staff quarters, where he found James Burnett, his senior in the gardening hierarchy, enjoying an early-morning cup of tea. On learning of Alwis's discovery, Burnett, a dour Scot who was not easily ruffled, had set down his cup and alerted John Cole, the head gardener, who abandoned the newspaper he was reading and went in search of the (British) A.D.C., Nigel Marsh. This young man, although he had not been very long in his post, had the presence of mind to put on morning dress and a black tie before he ascended the red-carpeted stairway to the Governor's suite, knocked discreetly, and slipped a sheet of paper under the door.

Marsh had wondered briefly, while he was dressing, whether he should wake up his colleague Rowland Wijesinha, the Governor's other (native) A.D.C. He had decided against it. Wijesinha was a thoroughly decent chap, Cambridge and all that, and of course he would have to be told about the incident eventually but, all things considered, Wijesinha was a native after all. This was a situation that would call for the utmost discretion, and Marsh was not certain that a native could be relied on to be discreet. The four men stood outside the door of the gubernatorial suite in silence, waiting. Ten minutes ticked past by the A.D.C.'s watch, at the end of which time the door opened and Sir Andrew emerged, fully dressed and perfectly composed, his silver-knobbed walking stick in his hand.

'Good morning, your Excellency! This way,' said Marsh, and led the little procession out of the building by way of the garden door, Burnett and Cole following the Governor, and Alwis Appu bringing up the rear. Marsh remembered, as he went, how impossible it was that this morning could turn out to be a 'good' one for Sir Andrew; but it was now too late to retract his courteous greeting and substitute something more suited to the occasion. Sounds of activity drifted across to them from the kitchen quarters, and as he walked into the early morning sunshine Sir Andrew noted that Burnett and Cole had put on a frightfully good show of roses for the Prince's visit, and wondered automatically, as he always did, whether his breakfast eggs would be scrambled or poached.

In the garden, no one was about and everything was still. The body of Lady Millbanke lay as Alwis had found it, a braid of brown hair covering the face.

The old man's taking it well, Marsh thought.

He considered it really rotten luck that his first great occasion in his new job should have been clouded by such an accident. He supposed that it *was* an accident. It must be. Marsh had been a reluctant witness of the row at Bentot, but did not consider that His Excellency's obvious fancy for Mrs van Buren was sufficient reason for Lady Millbanke to kill herself.

'That blowsy bitch,' Lady Millbanke had said of her unwanted guest. But she had said it (Marsh thought) without much conviction. Sir Andrew possessed a wandering eye which tended to linger on amiable brunettes like Mrs van Buren, and his wife should surely, by this time, have learned to cope with it. So it must have been an accident: Her Excellency had been looking out of her window, she had leaned out too far, lost her balance and fallen. Although it was true that since Lady Millbanke occupied a suite at the opposite end of the corridor to her husband's, there was no way of knowing for certain whether her fall had been accidental or not, unless her ayah had been awake at the time the tragedy had occurred.

Marsh, a young man of romantic disposition who had read a novel or two, remembered Heathcliff's cry of 'Cathy! Cathy!' in *Wuthering Heights*, and waited expectantly for the Governor's matching cry of anguish. He supposed that at any moment Sir Andrew would fling his stick away, take his dead wife in his arms, and carry her into the house. He'll do it any minute now, Marsh said to himself, gazing absently at one of Lady Millbanke's bedroom slippers which had fallen among the pansies in the flower bed beneath the library window. More mundane matters occupied the minds of James Burnett and John Cole. The flowers for the Prince's reception in the Grand Ballroom had been selected and arranged by Lady Millbanke herself the day before: who would see to the flowers for her own lying-in-state? They noted that the sun had not yet touched her ladyship's body, but it would do so soon. They'd better get cracking on the arrangements for the funeral.

Alwis stood respectfully at a little distance from the others, and recalled what he had heard in the servants' quarters from Magilin, Lady Millbanke's ayah, of her employer's melancholy moods.

'Every evening, just sitting by the window,' Magilin had said. 'Nothing outside to look at, just the darkness, and only the sound of the owls in the trees, but Madam just sitting there thinking and thinking without speaking a word.'

Even as her name came into his mind, Magilin stepped out into the garden.

'Alwis aiya, Madam is not in her room, do you know where—'

She paused in mid-sentence at the sight of Alwis's cautionary hand upraised for silence, then, catching sight of the body on the pathway with the group of men around it, she cried out with horror.

'*Aiyo*, what has happened to Madam?'

'Oh, damn and blast,' the Governor muttered. 'It's all over now. The story'll be all around the town in half an hour.' He added irritably (for Magilin had flung herself down on the dew-sodden grass and had set up the ear-splitting keening that always accompanies a death in the village):

'Tell the woman to stop that bloody yowling.'

Alwis escorted the weeping Magilin back to the house, wondering as he went how the poor lady had met her end. Did she fall? Or had she been pushed? Would the police be summoned? The group of men continued to stand still, contemplating the dead Lady Millbanke, their minds occupied with the same thought. The silence in the garden was absolute.

With a start, Marsh pulled himself together. This was no time for idle speculation. He remembered with alarm the diplomatic minefield into which he would be propelled in the next few hours: upon him would fall the responsibility of somehow reconciling the pomp of a royal visit with the austere requirements of official mourning. One thing was certain: Sir Andrew would need his fullest sympathy and support. Marsh squared his youthful shoulders, and prepared to regard as his duty whatever the Governor required of him.

Sir Andrew looked up. He tapped his stick on the paving stones, and pointed it at the body of his late wife.

'Clean it up,' he said, and walked back into the house.

The death of Lady Alexandra Millbanke occurred, of course, many years before Independence: British Governors had not yet given way to home-grown Governors General, and the Residency itself was still a Government property. It would probably still be one, had not rumour and local gossip so dogged Sir Andrew after his wife's death that he put in for early retirement, and made as soon as he decently could for the safety of the British Isles. The rumours had been of a peculiarly damaging kind, and it was easy to see where they had sprung from. Alwis Appu and A.D.C. Wijesinha, though loyal servants of the Crown, were natives after all, and would not have been able to resist the temptation to gossip.

The Residency had been originally owned by a British planter named James Armitage Lucas who had made a substantial fortune from the planting of tea. Never having been one to hide his light under a bushel, Lucas had bestowed his own name on his magnificent hill country estate. An enthusiastic hunter and an excellent shot, Lucas thoroughly enjoyed the remainder of his life in Ceylon, but having no sons to inherit Lucas Falls and continue the planting traditions of the family, he had sold the property to the colonial Government, and returned with his wife Arabella and their daughters to England. Following Lady Millbanke's unfortunate accident, the house was put on the market again, and was purchased by a wealthy Sinhalese mudaliyar named Don Jeronis Wijesinha.

Tsunami and Latha Wijesinha were second cousins on their fathers' side, and descended from the very same Don Jeronis who had purchased James Lucas's tea estate. They were of the same age, having been born in the same year, with only three months between them. Although they belonged to the same clan, which is Anglican Christian by religion and consequently Westernized by background and education to the point at which some branches of it seemed more British than the British themselves, Latha's was a lowly branch of it, and Tsunami's an extremely privileged and superior one, high up on the Wijesinha family tree.

Tsunami's father, Rowland Wijesinha, was not only very wealthy in his own right, being the owner of extensive inherited estates, but possessed the height, bearing, and impressive profile that are often associated in the popular mind with aristocracy. As a barrister who had had the right sort of private school education (first at All Saints' College in Kandy, then at

King's College, in Colombo), going on from college to take a law degree at Cambridge, he was highly regarded in his profession. The cultivation, manufacture and marketing of tea grown at Lucas Falls was only one of his many spare-time agricultural interests: the others included the cultivation of rubber and coconut in the low country, and spices in the properties that he owned in between. It was very likely, the family thought, that Rowland would go into politics one day, as his grandfather (who had been an appointed Member of the old Legislative Council) had done before him. At the very least he would surely be elevated, as his father had been, to the Supreme Court bench.

Through three different phases of European occupation, the Wijesinha family had managed to keep close to the centres of colonial power. Its more responsible members took some pride in the fact that the respect in which the family was generally held derived from its record of proven service rather than from its wealth and means. By the 1940s they had all, responsible or not, come to regard their continued access to privilege as something that had been inherited rather than earned.

2

NAMES

The exotic and euphonious word *tsunami*, which bears such terrible significance for us today, had been chosen in 1935 as the baptismal name of Rowland and Helen Wijesinha's younger daughter. The second name they had chosen for her (though Latha didn't know that for some time, because Tsunami wasn't keen on publicizing the fact) was Alexandra. Rowland Wijesinha, whose branch of the family had served the British for generations, and who, as we have seen, held the position of (native) A.D.C. to the Governor of Ceylon at the time of Tsunami's birth, had followed family tradition by loyally bestowing on his daughter the name of the Governor's wife, Lady Alexandra Millbanke. Subsequent events had caused Rowland to regret this gesture, but by then it was rather too late for regrets.

Latha Wijesinha first met Tsunami at a family wedding in 1943, and was immediately fascinated by her, sensing from the beginning that there was something strange about her cousin's unusual name. The very next day she went into her father's study very quietly, so as not to disturb him, and looked Tsunami up in the *Shorter Oxford Dictionary*.

Tsunami. Names always mean something: Latha knew this, even at the age of eight, for her mother and her aunts had told her the meaning of hers often enough. Latha is a name intended to please and pacify, to soothe and solace. It carries calming associations of harmony and delight that the Sinhala poets of old must have loved to evoke, for they constantly used the word to describe their most decorative and sweetest-natured heroines. 'Latha' means 'a clinging vine'. Unasked, Latha's mother had told Tsunami this on the day the girls first met.

'Is your name a Japanese one, like mine?' Tsunami had asked Latha.

Soma Wijesinha had chipped in before her daughter could open her lips.

'Latha is not a Japanese name. It is a true *Sinhala* name, and I chose it for her myself.'

Latha felt her toes curling with embarrassment inside her new Clark's shoes, for she guessed what was likely to follow. She was not mistaken.

'*We* don't go in for meaningless foreign names,' her mother went on.

Soma, a Government school teacher, was always eager to make the point, even to the very young, and especially to an English-educated and excessively Westernized child like her husband's niece Tsunami, that a Sinhala heritage was something to be proud of. Soma had heard her husband's nieces and nephews calling their mother 'Mummy' and their father 'Pater'. She hesitated. Should she not seize the opportunity to give the child a proper perspective on the ridiculous affectations instilled in Sinhalese children by Western education?

Deciding that this was the right moment for it, and encouraged by Tsunami's wide-eyed, attentive gaze, she continued:

'A girl who is named Latha will grow up to be like a clinging vine. Not just because she will be graceful and lovely, but because she will be a perfect wife. She will cling to her husband as a creeper clings to a tree. His strength will support her, and her beauty will decorate his sturdy branches.'

Latha looked down at the floor, hoping by this means to avoid Tsunami's amused eyes. She wished Amma would stop giving her silly little lecture. It was unnecessary. It was unforgivable. She would never live it down.

'I understand, Auntie. A kind of parasite,' Tsunami said, and calmly changed the subject.

Soma was taken aback, and very much annoyed.

Parasite? She had chosen her daughter's name for its auspicious associations; she believed that it would shape, not only Latha's character, but her future. As for Tsunami, the child unsettled Soma, and had done so from the time she had called with her husband a few years previously on his cousin Rowland Wijesinha and his wife Helen, and found no one at home except the servants and Tsunami, then six years old. Most little girls of Tsunami's age would have hidden themselves shyly behind their ayah, and allowed the servant to tell the visitors that the master and mistress were out. Latha, a child of the same age, would most certainly have done so. Not so Tsunami, who had greeted her aunt and uncle with perfect ease and aplomb, and invited them to sit down in the drawing room. She had then rung the bell for Raman and asked him to bring in a soft drink each for Auntie and herself, and to ask Uncle what he would like to have.

'Very good, baba,' Raman had said.

While he carried out her orders, Tsunami had settled herself on the sofa beside Soma, and made polite conversation until Rowland and Helen returned. Herbert Wijesinha had been much amused by his niece's performance (which he recognized as modelled on her mother's manner), but Soma, who had married into the Wijesinha family from a very different background, had not been pleased.

'What a precocious child that is, Herbie,' she said now, in the car coming home from the wedding. 'And rude, when you say! Did you hear how she spoke to me just now?'

Diplomatically, Herbert Wijesinha concentrated his attention on negotiating the sharp U-turn into Dickman's Road, and made no reply. But Tsunami hadn't meant to be rude, she had merely asked a question and received an answer. Satisfied, she had turned to the next question on her agenda.

That next question, delivered with what Latha was soon to know as Tsunamian bluntness, was: please could Latha come and spend the next school holidays with us, Auntie? Please? Please? Please? Soma often regretted the fateful 'Yes' which had sent her daughter upcountry to Lucas Falls Estate that April with her husband's relations. She would have liked to say 'No,' and to make some excuse. But at that time she had been too much in awe of Tsunami's father to refuse the invitation.

So here was Latha Wijesinha, launching at the age of eight on what would become a lifetime's occupation, the pursuit of knowledge. To enter her father's study was always an interesting experience for Latha, because it was a room like no other in her family's small house. Entering it was like going on safari in a Tarzan movie: you never knew what you might discover each time you turned a corner. It was, in fact, not so much a room as a landscape, made up of pyramids and precipices of books, between which narrow chasms, winding canyons and occasional valleys led the visitor to different areas of recreation and interest.

The path to Herbert Wijesinha's writing table was a straight one, and resembled a chasm between two precipices, each of them half as tall as Latha herself, and made up of carefully stacked magazines, souvenirs of her father's bachelor days as a student in Paris and London. From this chasm certain narrow gorges (also lined with stacked books and magazines) led away in different directions: tributaries, as it were, of the main canyon. The visitor who followed them would reach either the window on one side of the room, or a set of bookshelves extending from the floor to the ceiling on the other side, or an alcove at the back leading to what had once been a gentleman's dressing room and was now a holding station for more books and magazines.

Herbert had had, as a child, a passion for green mangoes (eaten with chilli and salt in the company of like-minded classmates). He had been adept at bringing them down with a well-aimed stone from the branches of trees in the gardens of his parents' neighbours. His aim, thus developed, was exceptionally good, so good that he had bowled with distinction for St Alban's College in his schooldays. He now spent his working hours as a Customs officer in the Port of Colombo, and was in private life a collector; which is to say, he was a hoarder of memorabilia, accumulated and kept on the principle that it was likely to come in useful at some time or another. One part of his 'collection', an unfailing source of pleasure to its owner, consisted of quotations from cricket books and radio commentaries. A lover of fine language, Herbert was building a personal anthology on the subject of his favourite game, the centrepiece of which would one day be Neville Cardus's description of Frank Worrell's batting form in 1950: 'An innings by Frank Worrell knows no dawn. It begins at high noon.'

But that was still some time into the future: the year in which Latha met Tsunami being 1943, Herbert's cricket anthology was still in embryo, still more an idea than a reality. Leaving Soma fast asleep, he would tiptoe from the marital bed at three in the morning to switch on the ancient wireless in his study, stretch himself out on the sofa, and listen to Test Match commentaries broadcast by the BBC. The thwack! of bat on ball and the answering roar of the crowd which came to his ears across the world from England or Australia was to Herbert the sweetest sound in the world. In a country like Ceylon, which worshipped the sport, he had no lack of old school friends and drinking companions who shared his passion for that most satisfying of all varieties of discourse, 'cricket-talk'.

The other, larger, part of Herbert's collection could have been titled 'Ceylon/Sri Lanka: Politics, Aspects of': as freedom from colonial rule came into view in the late 1940s (Independence was granted in 1948), the ever-expanding subject of island politics would become the main focus of his non-sporting interest. While the new nation's leaders battled each other for supremacy, two shelves of buff-coloured manila folders came into being in Herbert's study, each folder bearing the name of a local politician. The folders contained Herbert's neatly written observations on the highs and lows of individual careers. Not that Herbert had any concept of himself as a political analyst: observing political parties being hastily cobbled together for the purpose of contesting the island's first General Election in 1947, and men of his own social class and background squabbling, pushing and shoving in their eagerness for office, the intensity of Herbert Wijesinha's feelings robbed him of the objectivity necessary for such a role. Keeping his mind clear of party politics and his records meticulously up to date would, as the years passed, become Herbert's antidotes for anger, despair, cynicism and irrational hope, the moods between which concern for his small but precious country kept his mind constantly on the move.

Nor would he ever regard his extensive collection as a preparation for 'going in for politics' himself: indeed, his wife Soma (who had already shown herself to be a woman of strong will and decided opinions) had stated flatly that she would divorce him if he did. But just as he had been thrilled as a schoolboy by the sheer unpredictability of cricket, Herbert was fascinated as an adult by the twists and turns of which the human mind is capable; and it did not take many years of observation and reading to convince him that the cream of his country's liars and lapdogs, its crooks and con-men, its time-servers, turncoats, thieves, and traitors was to be found in its Houses of Parliament.

'One day,' Herbert would sometimes say to himself, looking over the manila folders which he increasingly thought of as dossiers, 'one day, I'll write a book and document the doings of these scoundrels.'

This was the thought that gave shape and purpose to the hours he spent in his study. And until the day arrived when his book would become more than the gleam in his eye which it was in 1943, Herbert continued to add newspaper clippings to his collection, supplementing them occasionally with carbon copies of letters he had written to newspaper editors under the pseudonym of *Pro Bono Publico*.

To Soma Wijesinha, as a new bride, had fallen the task of enshrining in a leather-covered album paragraphs and pictures her sisters-in-law had clipped from the sports pages of newspapers that recorded their brother's early cricketing triumphs at St Alban's. Herbert's eldest sister Chloë in particular had been a keen follower of the game and of her brother's achievements. There were a great many newspaper clippings, stored neatly between sheets of tissue paper in a cardboard box marked 'Hirdaramani's for Glistering Saris', that Chloë had handed over to Soma to be pasted into the album. Soma herself had little understanding of cricket, but she knew where her duty lay. She read some of the reports as she pasted them in, and she found it hard to recognize in the 'hostile bowler' and the 'brilliant strategist' she encountered on the printed page the mild-mannered, easy-going Herbie she had married. Soma was thankful, especially after 1956 when every man and his dog appeared, as she said, to fancy themselves as politicians, that at least her Herbie did not imagine that he could serve his country by standing for election; for if he had, and if he had been successful in getting into Parliament, there would have been a great many more news reports to clip out, and more albums to fill.

Soma Wijesinha had long given up suggesting to her husband that he should sell or give away some part of his collection. Early in their marriage she had hoped that he would do so, if only to make room for the cricket books and sports magazines that continued to pile up on a trestle table outside the door of his study. Now, ten years into their happy relationship, she contented herself with entering the room once a week, accompanied by her domestic help. Armed with a long-handled duster, Soma would brush away the dust gathering on the tops of the book-precipices, while the servant would sweep out the chasms and gorges between them.

Like many English-speaking husbands of his generation, Herbert usually addressed his wife as 'Dear'. (Soma, for her part, generally called him 'Here', which could be variously interpreted, depending on the circumstances, as either 'Look here', or 'Did you hear me?') Their marriage had been – and still was, in the main – a love match but, although visitors were theoretically welcome to sit on Herbert's sofa, Soma did not linger to chat to her Herbie. A large pile of papers and books relating to State Council affairs of the 1930s and 1940s would have had to be moved from the sofa to the floor in order to permit such domestic exchange.

The only visitor whom Herbert really welcomed into his study was Latha herself, the child who, if she had been the boy born to Herbert and Soma Wijesinha on the very day in 1930 that Herbert's particular hero had landed in Colombo, and had captained Australia in a Test Match at the Tamil Union Sports Club grounds, would, without doubt, have been named 'Don Bradman'. Unfortunately, that first Wijesinha child had lived only fifteen minutes. Soma's sentimental thoughts of her lost son and Herbert's speculations as to what young Don Bradman Wijesinha would have done if he had lived (in addition to reading Classics at St Alban's, of course, playing cricket for Ceylon, and swimming the Palk Strait) had been part of Latha's growing years. She had never resented these flights of parental fancy. On the contrary, she indulged herself with speculations of her own. If Bradman Aiya had been around, Latha often thought, at different stages of those years, there were so many things they could have done together: he would have taught her to swim and to ride a bicycle, they could have gone on picnics, she would have gloried in his Captain's innings at the annual King's-Albanian match, she wouldn't have been so shy in the presence of 'boys' . . .

Arriving five years after her brother and growing up an only child, Latha had made her own niche in her parents' lives. Her confiding manner and her pretty face pleased Soma who, although a strong personality in her own right, would not have known what to do with an equally wayward daughter. Latha loved her mother, but her father was her hero. Herbert, for his part, enjoyed spoiling his little girl and buying pretty things to take her fancy. He appreciated, too, the respect with which she treated his books. Latha was too little, when she first visited her Thaththa in his 'office', to tip his book-precipices over and disturb its carefully ordered landscapes, and also too young to walk away with his treasured copies of *London Life* and *The Talk of the Town*. Even before she could read, Herbert allowed his small daughter the run of his study as long as she remembered to put books and magazines back in their right places, and refrained from dog-earing their pages, cutting pictures out of them for her school scrapbooks, and wasting his typing paper and ribbons. He did not mind her asking him occasional questions, but in order to encourage her to find answers to them herself he kept his largest reference books, mainly dictionaries and encyclopaedias, on the lower shelves of his book-case, so that she (and even the youngest of the brothers and sisters that he and Soma hoped would follow her in later years) would have no difficulty looking something up.

Latha took the *Shorter Oxford Dictionary* from its place on the lowest shelf of her father's book-case, and placed it carefully on the floor. She sat down cross-legged in front of it, and turned the flimsy pages until she came to the letter 's'. When she could not find Tsunami in the dictionary's long columns, she closed the book and attempted to replace it with another.

Her struggle to do this disturbed Herbert's concentration. He put down his pen, and looked up.

'What are you looking for, duwa?'

'Sunami,' Latha said. 'Can't find it, Thaththi.'

'Try looking under "T".'

Still no luck.

'Try the *Encyclopaedia Britannica*,' Herbert suggested. He placed a large volume on his writing table, and drew up a chair for Latha, opposite his own. She turned a page, and there it was.

Tsunami.

'Read it aloud,' Herbert said. 'I'll help you over any hard words.'

'"*After the earth-quake or other gen-e-rating impulse*",' Latha read, '"*a train of simple, pro-gres-sive ossi . . . ossi . . .*"'

'Oscillations? Oscillatory?' Herbert volunteered.

'"*Oscil-la-tory waves is pro-pa-gated great distances at the ocean surface in ever-widening circles, much like the waves produced by a pebble falling into a shallow pool*".'

Latha didn't know at that time what 'oscillatory' and 'propagated' meant, but she had learned something about earthquakes in her Geography class at school.

'"*In deep water*",' she continued, '"*the wave-lengths are e-nor-mous—*"'

Spelling out the English words and adding up the numbers with her father's help, she read the entry to its end, noticing as she persevered that reading the hard words became easier as she went on. A tsunami, Latha discovered, could make coastal waters rise as high as a hundred feet in ten minutes. She tried to visualize this, and failed; and yet, a tsunami that had hit Awa in Japan in 1703, said the *Britannica*, had killed more than a hundred thousand people. That was the most destructive tsunami to date. Latha knew what 'destructive' meant; and once, while on holiday with her family, she had been turned head over heels on the beach at Hambantota by a wave that her father had said at the time was 'enormous'.

'Why did Uncle Rowland and Auntie Helen name Tsunami after a wave?' Latha asked her father.

It seemed such an odd thing to do! Herbert explained that in 1935, when Latha and Tsunami were born, the old tradition of choosing children's names according to the auspicious syllable prescribed in their horoscopes had come back into style.

'Your syllable was *la*, and your cousin's was *su*. There are plenty of Sinhala names that begin with *su*—'

'Sunethra, Surangani, Sujatha, Sushila, Susima!' said Latha promptly. These were names she heard read out every morning in class, when Miss Perera took the Attendance Register for Standard Two. Her father nodded.

'That's right. Tsunami's parents wouldn't have had to look far for a name. But your Uncle Rowland thought those Sinhala names were too common.'

Herbert hesitated for a moment. He had learned early that his daughter had an acute ear, and had consequently become cautious about speaking his mind in her presence.

'That bloody fool of a minister,' he had said once in Latha's hearing, and a couple of days later had heard his daughter say of a small classmate:

'I don't like him, Amma. He's a buddy poo.'

So he added, in a tone so bland that Latha couldn't be sure whether her father was criticizing her uncle Rowland or praising him:

'Your Uncle Rowland has a well developed aesthetic sense, and he is attracted to the unusual. At the time your cousin was born he was going through what he likes to call his Japanese phase. He told me he liked the sound of *tsunami*. He said it reminded him of the sound of the sea.'

'But . . . didn't the *meaning* of the name bother Uncle Rowland?' Latha asked doubtfully. 'All those people dying?'

'Not a bit,' Herbert said cheerfully. 'Why should it? It didn't even bother your mother, and you know what she's like about the meanings of names. It's a Japanese word, you see, Latha, and what has a meaning in Japan – or anywhere else – is meaningless here. It's irrelevant. You'll find out as you grow older that you have the privilege of belonging to a society so advanced and civilized – or so damned obtuse – er, sorry – that it doesn't give a hoot about the world outside it.'

Latha took no notice of this last remark. She guessed it to be one of those observations her father sometimes made as he contemplated the world around him but, having no conception as yet of the uses of irony, she did not understand it. She continued to look puzzled, so Herbert approached the matter from a different angle.

'Would *you* have known or cared what Tsunami meant if you hadn't looked it up in an encyclopaedia?'

Latha said nothing, but she was not convinced; and from the day she read about her in *Britannica*, she regarded her cousin Tsunami with awe and not a little fear.

Names are fateful things. They set unseen forces in motion. They have the power to shape character. They can determine the course of a person's life. All this Latha had learned from the talk of the grown-ups around her: from her father who would have named an eldest son Don Bradman; from her mother who was always looking up names in her school registers for the benefit of young married cousins; but especially from her aunts, who were regarded by all as experts on the occult. Their own names, as they often said with pride, had been chosen after proper consultation with the stars.

Was Tsunami to be a victim of catastrophe, or a creator of it? Did she have any idea of what the future might hold for her? Latha never asked her cousin these questions, and she told no one, not even her beloved Thaththa who had helped her find Tsunami in *Britannica*, the terrible secret she had discovered. She thought over the problem all that night and most of the next day, too, and she made a decision.

Fear gave way to a sense of privilege. Latha felt very special, for the knowledge of Tsunami's dire fate had been disclosed to her, and to her only. Whatever fortune, good or ill, overtook Tsunami, whatever terrible crime she was predestined to suffer or commit, Latha would stand by her cousin. She would be loyal.

3

ROWLAND WIJESINHA

When the time came for him to think of marriage, Rowland Wijesinha, possessor of so many natural advantages and acquired qualifications, could have had his choice of brides from his own low-country Sinhalese community. His widowed mother had fended off many marriage proposals that arrived while her son was away in England, studying law at Trinity Hall. Some of these proposals had come from among their own relations, but there had also been a great many from low-country Sinhalese businessmen who had made money from arrack-renting and the manufacture of copra, and were now looking for well-connected husbands for their daughters. None of these in Mrs Wijesinha's opinion was good enough for her only son.

'After my Rowley was born,' she was fond of saying, 'Nature broke the mould.'

The Wijesinha family traced its origins to the hill-country, and old Mrs Wijesinha began looking speculatively at the pedigrees of some of the older Kandyan Sinhalese families. These, though somewhat impoverished after the Kandyan War of 1818 deprived them of a good deal of their land, had remained in their districts, and claimed to have retained their blood-lines intact. Before she could arrive at a final choice, however, Rowland sprang a surprise on her and indeed, on the entire family.

His choice had fallen unaccountably on a complete 'outsider' in the marriage stakes, the convent-educated youngest daughter of a prosperous Indian Tamil tea planter.

Mrs Wijesinha could *not* understand it. As she said (though not, of course, to her son), even one of her numerous nieces whose parents were so pitifully anxious that their daughters should catch Rowley's eye, would have been better than this. Wasn't it obvious, said those parents, that a powerful charm must be at work? Everyone knew that the charmists of India had all kinds of spells and devilish potions at their command. Clearly, one of them must have Rowland in its grip.

The truth was, however, that the only charm Helen Ratnam had employed to lure a Sinhalese husband to her side had been her beauty. Rowland Wijesinha had fallen, as deeply as it was possible for him to do, in love; and it had all been brought about without guile or deliberation, for Helen was not interested in love or marriage, but in art. Growing up in Delhi, Helen had acquired a name for herself as a talented child-artist. Her earliest work had been seen and warmly praised by no less a judge than the painter Jamini Roy himself, and although her themes and style altered as she grew up, she had been allowed by her parents to maintain her interest in art.

It was at an exhibition in Bombay of the work of young Indian artists that Rowland Wijesinha, then on a tour of the subcontinent, had seen the young painter.

'Your Uncle is attracted by the unusual,' Herbert was to tell Latha some years later. He had Helen in mind when he made this remark, and it was perfectly true. Rowland believed that he had an eye for beauty, and certainly he had been powerfully attracted; though whether he had been charmed by Helen's canvases or by the artist herself, no one could be quite sure.

Herbert, who knew that his cousin was proud of his reputation as a connoisseur of oriental art, believed that Rowland had acquired Helen Ratnam rather as he might have purchased an exquisite ivory figurine for the drawing room in his house at Lucas Falls. He was convinced of it when once, during a visit he paid the newly married couple, Helen (then eighteen) came running into the drawing room and flung herself into a chair, breathless and glowing from a walk with the dogs. Herbert had gazed at her with admiration, Rowland with silent disapproval. She met her husband's eyes, recollected herself quickly, and immediately sat up straight, her eyes lowered, and her delicate hands folded demurely in her lap. It was an attitude that Rowland obviously favoured, since he had had her portrait painted (by Mudaliyar A.C.G.S. Amarasekera, doyen of Ceylon's artists at the time) in that identical pose.

There was no doubt that Helen's striking beauty enhanced the beauty of her husband's beautiful house. It was one more proof of the fact that Lucas Falls (differing markedly in this regard from most Wijesinha houses, which were crammed from floor to ceiling with china dogs and cats, ornamented brass clocks, and naked green glass nymphs holding up lampshades and vases, souvenirs of visits to Brighton and Tunbridge Wells) owed its elegance to Rowland's good taste.

Rowland often said that the patronage of artists and poets was a duty which had from the earliest times accompanied the Wijesinhas' high station in life. Did he really believe this? Herbert was not certain. Rowland certainly behaved as though he did. Herbert (who irreverently regarded most of the family legends as based on pretentiousness and wishful thinking) had been present at a Lucas Falls dinner party during which, between the mulligatawny and the fish course, his cousin Rowland had related to some visiting Europeans a story about a Wijesinha ancestor, an eighteenth-century Gate Mudaliyar well known in his time for two things: his vanity, and his generous patronage of artists and poets.

A celebrated poet had arrived at the Wijesinha walauwa in Matara one day and made his obeisance (said Rowland), requesting permission to recite a poem he had composed for the Gate Mudaliyar's pleasure. He had been welcomed with enthusiasm, and allowed to proceed.

'Recite your poem. I am listening,' the Mudaliyar had said.

The poem had commenced in the traditional manner, with a formal invocation of the divine Sarasvati, goddess of Wisdom and Learning. This was an accepted convention of the form, for without the goddess's active assistance, what work of literary art could possibly succeed? The Gate Mudaliyar had nodded his approval of the graceful two-line benediction with which the poem began. When, however, the benediction was followed by the equally traditional *dahapadhasahaella*, ten lines of elaborate praise dedicated to the goddess, his smiling countenance clouded over. It seemed that he had expected the poet to break with tradition, and dedicate the poem to his prospective patron. When he had heard the poem to its end, and had heard no mention of his own name, his rage had been terrible to behold.

'Do you come crawling here on your belly to seek my patronage, and do you have the impudence to read me a poem dedicated to another person?' the Gate Mudaliyar had inquired icily. 'Out of my sight, dog! You can go to the goddess, and petition her for your reward.'

Rowland Wijesinha must have enjoyed observing the effect of this anecdote on his foreign guests, because he related it frequently. When they learned that the work rejected by the Gate Mudaliyar had later become (under different patronage) an epic in the canon of classical Sinhala poetry, his guests were always tremendously impressed; not only by the arrogance of the former leaders of the ancient country they were visiting, but by Rowland himself, the aristocratic inheritor of such fascinating traditions.

The tale didn't go down quite so well with the locals: most of Rowland's Ceylonese listeners smiled to themselves, and discreetly refrained from comment. It was left to Herbert to tell Rowland in private that he regarded their common ancestor's conduct as a prime example of small-minded vanity for which he should have been immediately sacked from his Government post. He did so, and was met with a tolerant smile from his cousin. The next time he attended a dinner party at Lucas Falls, he heard the story told all over again, in exactly the same manner.

The majority of Rowland's relatives did not care a jot then, nor do they care now, about the family tradition of patronage that Rowland made so much of, and had taken so much to his heart. They registered, of course, the obvious fact of Helen's beauty: they could hardly overlook *that*. With the Wijesinhas Rowland passed for an expert judge of beauty in sculpture, painting and architecture, and it was only to be expected, said his relations, that he would look for beauty in a wife. But they did not understand Helen's love of art, and they were completely uninterested in her talent. What they did have in good measure was a very proper respect for money: they consoled themselves at the time of Rowland's wedding with the knowledge that the Indian newcomer had brought a very large dowry to the marriage. And Helen was to prove herself a satisfactory wife to Rowland in other ways as well, for in the first eight years following their wedding in 1927 she bore him five children, three of them sons.

4

HOW LATHA DISCOVERED ENGLISH LITERATURE

Despite their shared family connections and the fact that he too had had (at St Alban's) the type of private school education which Rowland had had at King's, following this with a diploma acquired in England, Herbert Wijesinha had not, unlike his wealthy and glamorous cousin, attracted much attention in the marriage market. Herbert's branch of the family boasted no legislative councillors, Supreme Court judges or art patrons to establish any kind of an inherited tradition, and he had no personal ambitions beyond the conscientious performance of his duties as a Government servant. Herbert had eventually married a Government school teacher of Sinhala. The fact that Soma came from a Buddhist family did not ruffle the Anglican feathers of the Wijesinha clan too much: Herbert wasn't important in the family's scheme of things; nor, to tell the truth, was religion itself.

Latha's parents had started their married life moving from one set of Government quarters to another, usually outside the capital, Colombo. In terms of money and status there could be no comparison between the two families. But money and status, at least in the 1930s, were not as important in the island as they have now become. Family ties, on the other hand, were everything. From the time that he and Herbert were schoolboys together, Rowland had demonstrated his respect for such ties. Although a sportsman of only average talent himself, he showed up regularly at Albanian cricket matches, to cheer his cousin on with cries of 'Jolly good show!' and 'Well *played*, old boy!' and in later years, instead of patronizing Herbert or showing off his own wealth when weddings and funerals brought the two families together, Rowland generously overlooked Herbert's occasional acerbity, and treated him with an easy comradeship that did him credit.

Towards Latha's mother Rowland behaved with an elaborate, Western-style courtesy that at first disconcerted, but later came secretly to please her: he always addressed her in impeccable (if slightly accented) Sinhala, and she never discovered that as far as he was concerned, the Buddhist tradition in which she had been brought up was a form of primitive superstition which only peasants, domestic servants, and other illiterates took seriously. The families were not on visiting terms: both sides would have found such visits extremely embarrassing, for how could the grandeur of Tsunami's family have possibly been accommodated on the tiny veranda of the Government Service bungalows that Latha's family occupied, where the only domestic help available came from buxom, bossy young Kamala, who banged saucepan lids about exuberantly in her little kitchen and, uninvited, contributed opinions of her own to the conversation of her employers? And how would Latha's parents have coped with Helen's five-course dinners prepared by Vaithianathan, her chef, and served by a phalanx of men servants in silver-buttoned starched white jackets, supervised by Rowland's dignified steward and butler, the incomparable Raman?

There was no need to have such subtleties explained. Tsunami and Latha simply registered them without thought or question. When the two girls first met at that wedding in 1943, they had both just turned eight, and were attending a grown-up party for the first time. Latha had on a new dress for the occasion. It was made of rose-pink organdy, with a smocked bodice, white lace inserts threaded with pink ribbon, and a sash ornamented with rosebuds. Her shoes were shiny and new, and she wore a pink satin ribbon in her hair. Though Latha would forget the reason for the party, and the many, many parties that followed it, she always remembered the dress because her Aunt Helen commented on it.

'Now *that's* what I call a real party-dress!' Helen Wijesinha had said, admiring the smocking, the lace, and the sash with its rosebuds. 'A truly-ruly peach of a party-dress!'

Naturally, Latha had warmed to her from that moment. And then Tsunami stepped from behind her mother, and Latha's heart was lost for ever.

Each of the children had recognized immediately, with no need for speech, that in the other she had found a kindred spirit. Perhaps each also recognized the other's loneliness, for they were both isolated, although for different reasons: Latha as an only child, since the younger brothers and sisters her parents had hoped would arrive to keep her company never did, in fact, materialize; Tsunami as the youngest child in a family of five, with a sizeable gap between herself and her nearest sibling, her brother Colin. The instant attraction of the two little girls to each other greatly amused the grown-ups of both families, even Latha's mother. They referred to the two children as *amba yaluwo*, two mangoes growing on the same stem, and accepted the fact that at family parties Tsunami and Latha would wish, and should therefore be permitted, to sit together.

When they did so, they usually talked about books: both children had inherited a passion for reading from their parents. It was Herbert who had encouraged this interest in Latha: when he made his weekly trip to the Fort on Saturdays, he invariably took his daughter with him. She loved being 'parked' in the children's section of H.W. Cave's venerable bookshop on Prince Street while her father disappeared around the corner in search of freshly ground coffee from Cargill's or cigarettes and whisky from Apothecaries', Miller's, or Whiteaway's.

'Is there something you'd like me to buy for you?' Herbert would invariably inquire on his return; and Latha, who was growing into the kind of rapid reader who can zip through an entire story-book while standing up in the store, usually replied:

'Nothing, Thaththi.' (Which was a relief to Herbert, who sometimes found himself a little short of cash.)

On one occasion, however, the answer to her father's question was an emphatic:

'*This* one, please, Thaththi!'

Herbert put on his spectacles, took the volume from his daughter, and examined it curiously. There was nothing extraordinary, he thought, about its cover picture of an eighteenth-century belle dressing for a ball, her blonde hair piled on her pretty head and disposed on her neck in two shining ringlets. Except . . . Herbert looked at the cover more closely, and noticed that tending the young lady's elaborate coiffure, and positioned at intervals around her ice-blue skirts, the flounces and frills of which they were holding up (the better to reveal two tiny, satin-shod feet), were scores of delicate, moth-like creatures, their silken wings transparent in the sunshine streaming into the room through an open window. Latha had puzzled over the picture for some time.

'How could this possibly be?' she asked her father.

Latha liked things to be satisfactorily explained. She could not be happy until she had read the text, and found out who the young lady in the picture was, and by what kind of magic an ordinary mortal can command an army of fairy folk to adjust her hair and tend her dressing-table.

Herbert had noticed that the child was so enchanted by the book in her hands that she had even forgotten to perform her usual part in their weekly ritual: placing the fragrant packet of newly roasted Cargill's coffee to her face in order to feel its warmth against her cheek.

Latha's lifelong love affair with English literature began that morning, with her father's purchase of an expensive copy of *Stories from the Poets.* A child who had believed up to that time in Santa Claus and the Easter bunny, Latha encountered a different and potent magic in 'seeing' the sylphs of *The Rape of the Lock* prepare Belinda for her appearance at Hampton Court. The poems of Pope, Keats, Spenser, Tennyson, Scott, Macaulay and

Christina Rossetti fed her imagination: as she grew up, they became a part of her thinking. Herbert never knew that while he was away at work in the Customs office, his daughter often lay on the sacred sofa in his study, reading aloud to the empty room passages from the anthology he had bought for her.

Then out spake brave Horatius,
The Captain of the Gate:
'To every man upon this earth
Death cometh soon or late.
And how can man die better
Than facing fearful odds,
For the ashes of his fathers,
And the temples of his gods?'

Latha would recite, the toes of one small foot tapping out Macaulay's rhythms against the curved wooden arm of the sofa, her eyes filling with tears at the vision of generous, patriotic, heroic Horatius. Of all the narrative poems in her book, this was the tale that moved her most. She felt herself transported to ancient Rome, and in her ears there sounded the steady tread of marching feet as the legions of Lars Porsena converged on the beleaguered city. Latha was quite unaware that Macaulay had written his poem to inspire a generation of English public schoolboys in the age of Victoria, and not at all to enthral a little Sinhalese girl in a twentieth-century Asian city.

The books she read began from that time to occupy a large space in Latha's life. She was delighted to find that her new-found cousin was similarly devoted to reading. Tsunami, too, was moved by the romance of poetry, but she had read much more widely than Latha, and had developed a mind that was much more critical of what she read. Tsunami spoke with scorn of a poet named Patience Strong, whose verses Latha happened to know well, since her aunts on her mother's side collected them in the form of hand-painted bookmarks and booklets embellished with bluebirds, roses, and English country cottages which they insisted on giving her as birthday presents. Tsunami also lavished contempt on one Florence Barclay, the author of a novel titled *The Wall of Partition*. Latha had never even heard of it, but Tsunami's aunts, it seemed, greatly admired this book which, according to their niece, was a work of unparalleled 'soppiness'.

Since the two cousins attended different Colombo schools, and since Government servants' subsidized accommodation boasted no telephones (though Tsunami's home had a telephone, of course, with extensions on each floor of their two-storey house, and one in her father's study), daily meetings or conversations were out of the question for Latha and Tsunami.

But despite her dislike of the child, Soma Wijesinha had been quick to recognize that Tsunami was highly intelligent and exceptionally well read for her age. She didn't mind the large number of postage stamps Latha used up each month, writing to Tsunami about the film she had seen that week, the book she had finished reading that day, the dream she had dreamed last night.

'Writing to a cousin can't do any harm, Herbie,' Soma told her husband. 'Letter-writing can be very educational. As long as they don't write to each other about harmful matters.'

What her mother had meant by 'harmful matters' Latha did not know then – but she was right about the cousins' correspondence being educational. Looking up 'Tsunami' in the *Encyclopaedia Britannica* foreshadowed, in its way, the permanent effect her Uncle Rowland's family was to have on Latha's life. Every moment of that first holiday on their estate, every single little thing that was said and done in the company of her cousins on the many holidays that followed, was instructive in a thousand ways of which they, and Latha, were quite unconscious. She was taking in information all the time, absorbing instructions on ways of speaking, thinking, eating and behaving that were quite different from the ways in which these things were done in her own home.

Latha's mother disapproved of what she called 'Western ways of behaving'. Since these happened to include ballroom dancing, at which her husband had himself been, in younger days, something of an adept, marriage had called for a fair amount of adjustment from Herbert. People still remembered him nimbly dancing the Charleston at the Galle Face Hotel's weekly tea dances, and doing 'The Lambeth Walk' (*Oi!*). Soma's views extended to many matters outside the family home: she was, for instance, one among many parents at the Buddhist school for girls that Latha attended as a 'day-scholar' who objected vociferously to their daughters' wearing shorts or divided skirts for P.T., and who deplored the shameless kissing and fondling that were to be seen in American movies.

'But *why* doesn't Auntie Soma like people kissing?' Tsunami asked, when Latha mentioned this at Lucas Falls.

' 'Cos kissing's Western,' Latha explained. 'Amma says only a Neuropean person would go in for kissing.'

'What about Burgher people?' Tsunami said. 'All the Burgher people we know kiss everybody.'

To this Latha could provide no answer. Her experience of 'Burgher people' was limited, and she had certainly never seen any Burgher person kissing her mother. She offered an alternative suggestion.

'Amma says it's better for your health to bow down to the ground before people than to kiss them,' she said. 'She says it's more . . . more *hygienic*, and it's what Sinhalese people like us should always do. But only in the family, I think.'

'Well, *we* don't bow down to *any*one,' Tsunami said, in a tone which seemed effectively to close the subject. But then she added, after some thought:

'Anyway, nobody I know kisses properly, not real kisses. All our aunts just grab you and put their cheeks next to yours and take deep breaths.'

Latha nodded. Her aunts and her mother did exactly the same.

Despite her open contempt for all things Western, and her promotion of all things 'Sinhala' and Buddhist, Soma Wijesinha was intensely curious about the holidays Latha spent in the care of her Westernized Uncle Rowland and his Indian Christian wife on their tea estate at Lucas Falls. As a fourth-former, Soma had visited a tea plantation once as part of a school expedition, but she had never in her life actually lived on one. She questioned Latha closely about her Aunt Helen's management of the household. Were Helen's children, Tsunami's elder sister Tara and her three older brothers, kind to Latha? How were Tara and Tsunami getting on at Ashcombe School? How were the boys doing at King's? What sorts of games did the children play at Lucas Falls? How many indoor servants did Rowland and Helen employ? How many gardeners? Did Helen personally tend the roses? (The rose garden on the estate, established by Alexander Lucas's wife Arabella in the 1890s, was very famous, and people came from all over the island to see it.) Did Helen manage to speak to the servants in Sinhala, or did she employ Tamil servants only? No doubt, Soma speculated, the meals served were exclusively Western-style or Indian, and Sinhalese rice dishes and curries were banished altogether from the table?

Latha managed to avoid answering all these questions except the last. Vaithianathan, Helen's chef, a man whose art as a pastry cook came close to genius, liked his superlative skills to be appreciated. Since Latha, who was obviously going to be a frequent visitor, made it clear that she loved watching him at work, 'Vaithi' kept a special high stool for 'Latha Baba' to perch on in the Lucas Falls kitchen, and was happy to explain what he was doing as he went along. He allowed her to shape the puff pastry leaves that decorated the tops of his pies, and taught her how to make perfect ripples dance around the rims of rhubarb and pineapple tarts. (Since Latha was such a favourite with 'Vaithi', Tsunami and Colin too scored frequent invitations 'to come and taste'.) Latha was delighted to inform her mother that Sinhalese or Tamil dishes were a regular feature of midday meals at Lucas Falls, and that Western 'courses' were only served at dinner.

The behaviour of the domestic staff at Lucas Falls was a subject that was eagerly canvassed by Soma and her sisters. Since Latha stubbornly refused to satisfy the curiosity of her mother and her aunts, they had to substitute flights of fancy for what they had no way of knowing at first hand.

'It's shocking, the way Helen spoils those servants,' was the opinion of Latha's Aunt Caroline. 'I hear that at Lucas Falls the servants sleep on beds – *beds*, if you please, not mats! – *and* they have the same seer fish cooked for them that is served at the table. Fine doings! Helen's extravagance must be costing Rowland thousands of rupees – not to mention the fact that those servants of hers put on superior airs whenever they meet any of *mine*.'

'It seems Helen allows that woman servant of hers, Alice, to wear sandals in the house,' said her sister. 'Sandals! *In the house!* Next thing we hear will be that Alice is receiving visitors and sitting at the dinner table—'

'As for that driver of Rowland's, that Ali Cassim or whatever his name is, what they want an English-speaking driver for, I don't know. And a Muslim, too! Helen had better look after her daughters and her young women servants carefully, why, you must have heard what happened in Preethi's house last month—'

Deprived of gossip about happenings below stairs at Lucas Falls, Latha's aunts would move joyfully to their next favourite topic, the sexual peccadilloes of their own servants. One of Soma's sisters, awakened in the middle of the night by the sound of a gently closing door, had had to get out of bed and go all the way downstairs in her dressing gown to make sure that her ayah was sleeping on her own mat and not romancing in the moonlight with the cook. A second, hampered in her social activities by the failure of her children's ayah to return to work after the Sinhala New Year holidays, was preparing to dock the errant young woman's salary for a month. A third, discovering the loss of three saris and a pearl necklace, had called in the police, who had traced the missing items to the wedding trousseau of a servant who had gone home to get married; her theft discovered, the servant had threatened to throw herself under a train.

Herbert Wijesinha listened to the conversation of his wife and his sisters-in-law without comment. Speculations about the flirtations of ayahs and chauffeurs did not interest him, but everything relating to Helen Wijesinha most certainly did. It was his personal opinion that Helen was the best thing that had happened to his family in several generations. He thought his cousin Rowland extraordinarily lucky to have carried Helen off while she was much too young and inexperienced to compare him with other suitors, but he was too wise to say so in the hearing of his wife or her sisters. As the only member of the family who was admitted to Latha's confidence, however, Herbert had been amused to learn that the Lucas Falls children liked to people their lives with story-book characters. They had long ago bestowed on Alice, their mother's Indian ayah, the soubriquet of 'Old Nokomis', after the wise old woman in Longfellow's poem *Hiawatha*. P.G. Wodehouse, a great favourite with all the children, had inspired the renaming of Raman as 'Jeeves' and of Vaithianathan as 'Anatole'.

'What shall we call Ali?' Tara had asked Latha, who had been delighted to be consulted, and drawn into her cousins' game in this way. Ali

Mohamed Cassim, her uncle's debonair Muslim chauffeur, was an active participant in holiday cricket games organized by the boys.

'Abou,' said Ranil. '"*Abou Ben Adhem, may his tribe increase.*" Or maybe not. Abou may be a Jewish name, and Ali may not like that.'

'What about Phaeton?' asked Chris.

'I know,' Latha said. 'Apollo! After all, Apollo drove the horses of the sun, and Ali drives Uncle Rowland's car.'

After some discussion Chris suggested that Ali could be christened 'Alexander' after Alexander Pope, the writer of Latha's favourite poem. Hearing about the re-naming of the domestics at Lucas Falls, Herbert's amusement had given way to concern.

'May I ask what Alice and Raman and Vaithi and Ali think of being christened by you children in this way?' he had inquired mildly of Latha. 'They might object, you know. They've got names of their own, after all, and they're probably very proud of them.'

'Oh, they don't know about it,' Latha had replied airily. 'And even if they did, they wouldn't mind. It's like being given a pet-name.'

'Is that so?' said Herbert. 'Servants might not think of themselves as family pets.'

He said no more on the subject. He hoped that his daughter was not developing into a spoiled little brat of the type with which, having grown up in an old-style Sinhalese walauwa himself, he was all too familiar. He had observed Rowland and Helen's children as they were growing up, and he was ready to concede that they did seem to regard their servants with affection – quite as much affection, he reflected without irony, as they lavished on their pets. Which was a good deal more, after all, than servants received in other households of his acquaintance, in which he had seen mature women and aged men being ordered about imperiously by their small spoiled charges, and very young servants receiving slaps and blows for minor misdemeanours.

Latha told her mother a great deal about her visits to Lucas Falls, but she didn't tell her everything. She didn't tell her, for instance, about the magnificent bathroom with its English porcelain bath that she shared with Tsunami. (At home Latha bathed, like every other child whose home was in a suburb to which pipe-borne water had not yet been carried, at a well which was secluded from prying eyes by a thick hibiscus hedge). She didn't tell her mother that her bed at Lucas Falls had on it a green quilt with a pattern of roses, peach-blossom and lilies, so that lying on it or under it she could imagine that she was a mermaid swimming in a sea-green ocean, or a princess sitting under a flowering tree in a green meadow, her lap filled with peaches and apples; that when she was visiting at Lucas Falls she attended church service with her cousins every Sunday, and saw an American movie at least once a week. She didn't tell her that her cousins kissed their parents when they came home for the holidays, and kissed them again when the holidays were over and they were returning to boarding school in Colombo. She didn't tell her that she liked it very much when Aunt Helen kissed her goodnight. She didn't tell her she was falling in love with Tsunami's eldest brother, Ranil, and that in one of her favourite daydreams Ranil took her in his arms exactly as Clark Gable took Vivien Leigh in *Gone with the Wind*, and pressed his lips on hers.

And she certainly didn't tell her about either Mr Goldman or Mr van Kuyk.

5

MR GOLDMAN OF ROTHSCHILD'S

When the breakfast bell rang one morning during the first holiday Latha spent at Lucas Falls, she joined Tsunami's family in the dining room to find a stranger seated on her Uncle Rowland's right. He was tucking into porridge and scrambled eggs and toast with vigour and enjoyment. Latha could tell at once from his appearance and his bearing that he was a foreigner, but she had too little knowledge of the world to know what sort of a foreigner he was.

'Latha, this is our Visiting Agent, Mr Goldman of Rothschild's,' said her uncle. 'Franz, my niece Miss Latha Wijesinha.'

Mr Goldman half-rose from his seat at the table, and bowed politely to Latha. Instinctively, Latha curtseyed in return, as she had been taught to do by Mrs Ingleton, the dancing teacher at her school. The curtsey caused Rowland to look at Latha with surprised approval, and she sat down in a golden glow of satisfaction. Then her Aunt Helen came into the dining room, and Mr Goldman sprang instantly to his feet. He came right round the long dining table, drew out Helen's chair, and helped her take her place opposite her husband before returning to his own seat. Such gentlemanly behaviour – Uncle Rowland's formal introduction and Mr Goldman's bow – was a new experience for Latha. The finer points of such Western courtesies as the introduction of a gentleman to a lady (and not the other way round, even though the lady in question might be only eight years old), or getting up for a lady, or opening doors for her to pass through had no part at all in her family life at home. Although Latha's parents were, in their way, a loving couple, her father wouldn't have dreamed of getting up for his wife every time she came into the room, and she would have been quite perplexed if he had taken it into his head to do anything of the kind.

'Thank you, kind sir,' Helen said, and began pouring coffee from a tall silver coffee pot into delicate china cups. 'I hope you had a comfortable night: did you sleep well?'

'Excellently, dear lady,' said Mr Goldman. 'I know to whose thoughtfulness I owe the many little comforts I find in my room.'

Latha could see Aunt Helen was pleased, because she smiled warmly at Mr Goldman before turning her attention to the supervision of her children's breakfasts. Oatmeal porridge was an altogether new experience for Latha. She found she did not care for it. She looked about her for a plate of the roti or pittu that would have been part of a breakfast at home, but there was nothing of that sort in sight. Across the table from her, Tsunami was carefully building a little island of porridge in the middle of her plate. Latha watched, fascinated, as her cousin poured some milk around the mound she had made, then poised a sugar cube on the shore of her island. Latha had seen Tsunami do this before, and she knew that the cube represented a shipwrecked sailor looking vainly for a sail. Raising the milk jug in her right hand and pouring from a height, Tsunami sent a tidal wave of warm milk crashing down into her plate that engulfed the island, and swept the sailor right off his beach and into the ocean.

'Don't play with your food, Tsunami,' Tara said in her grown-up, elder-sister voice. 'You know it's not allowed.'

Tsunami smiled at Latha, crushed the melting sugar cube into the milk (thereby putting an end to any hope the sailor might have had of rescue), and began thoughtfully eating her porridge. Mr Goldman resumed his conversation with Uncle Rowland. Their talk concerned the weather, but there was nothing inconsequential about it, they were deciding on a suitable day for planting out new seedlings. He must, however, have been aware of what was going on at the other end of the table because once, as Latha's Aunt Helen buttered a slice of bread and spread honey on it, he bowed and said gallantly:

'Ah, your Majesty! The traditional breakfast!'

'Uncle Rowland,' said Latha later that day. 'Why did Mr Goldman call Auntie Helen "Your Majesty"?'

'Because,' her uncle replied, 'she likes honey on her bread.'

Latha thought this over, and a few breakfasts later during which she had had further opportunity to observe Mr Goldman, she asked her uncle how it was that Mr Goldman knew English nursery rhymes.

'The same way you do,' Uncle Rowland said. 'He heard them as a child.'

'But he's not English,' Latha said. 'He said yesterday that he comes from Australia.'

'Mr Goldman is German. He's a German from Australia. They speak English in Australia, Latha, didn't you know? But of course *you're* English, aren't you? And *you* come from *London*!'

The heavy sarcasm that Rowland Wijesinha regarded as wit was often directed at his wife and his children. Since Latha was a child who took everything she heard literally, most of her uncle's sarcasm, like her father's irony, went completely over her head. On this occasion, though Rowland's barb was aimed at her, she took no notice of it whatever because her attention had been caught by his mention of London. Latha knew a good deal about London, which figured in many of the books she was reading and the movies she was occasionally taken to see, as a magical place, a city to dream about. Like the heroines in the stories they were reading, Tsunami and Latha were planning to 'come out' in London when they were both sixteen.

Latha was fascinated from the start by Mr Goldman's courtly, old-world manners. He was even more polite than her Uncle Rowland, whom she had regarded until that week as the politest man she had ever met. She had not been at Lucas Falls for more than a few days when, passing by a side veranda where her Aunt Helen had set up her easel and was busy painting, she had overheard a remark from the Visiting Agent that seemed to her the prettiest speech she had ever encountered outside a book or a film.

'Now, where has my palette knife gone?' Helen had said softly to herself, quite unaware that she was not alone on the veranda. 'I had it a moment ago—'

'Here it is, ma'am, at your feet, where every man of sense must wish to be,' Mr Goldman said.

Rising from the depths of the planter's chair in which he had been enjoying a nap after lunch, he picked up the knife from the floor to which it had fallen, and handed it to her aunt. Such courtesy was of a kind Latha associated with 'London' and with 'England', and she therefore thought it was quite appropriate to her uncle, who everyone in her family circle said was 'England-returned'. She had been surprised to find it in someone who even she could tell was no Englishman. But now the mystery had been solved. Being a Neuropean, Mr Goldman would naturally know all there was to know about London. He would probably go in for kissing, too.

Mr Goldman was the *Periya dorai* (big boss) of the neighbouring Rothschild tea plantation, one of a group of estates owned by a member of the well-known family of international financiers. In his role as Visiting Agent for the Rothschild Group of sterling tea companies, Mr Goldman would visit Lucas Falls every three months, spend a week in residence while inspecting the work in field and factory, and write a report for the company. He had come to Rothschild's from, of all places, Australia, which Tsunami and Latha identified on the great globe in Rowland's office-room as shaped like the head of a Scotch terrier and located at the other end of the world.

'You wouldn't think a German from Australia would know much about tea-planting,' her cousin Christopher had told Latha. 'But Pater often says that Mr Goldman's the best V.A. the company's ever had.'

And that was another thing which amazed Latha – until she got used to it – about the Lucas Falls family: all the children, even Colin and Tsunami, addressed their father by the curious name of 'Pater', as if it were the most natural thing in the world for them to do. (They also called their mother 'Mummy', but Latha did not find that so curious: several of her classmates did the same.) She asked her parents once what 'Pater' meant. Herbert explained that the word was a Latin one which meant 'Father', and added that the boys had probably learned it at King's College, where the study of Latin and Greek was part of the curriculum. Soma audibly sniffed her disapproval of such nonsense. Rowland and Helen, she said acidly, were probably planning to send their sons to Eton or Harrow.

By the time Latha met him, Franz Goldman had long been a fixture at Lucas Falls. He remained one for almost all the time she knew him, and some of her happiest memories of holidays on the estate were lit up by his genial presence. If Tsunami and Latha were up early enough on the day of his arrival, they would wave to Mr Goldman as he drove up from Rothschild Estate in his big Humber and climbed the steps to the veranda in his khaki shorts, knee-socks and boots, his walking-stick in his hand and his ledger under his arm.

Franz Goldman's days at Lucas Falls followed a regular pattern, beginning at five o'clock each morning, when he and Rowland would be up before dawn for the morning muster on the estate. At that time of day, with dew still sparkling on the grass, the mist veiling the mountains and no sun as yet in the sky, there was no need for a solar topee. But Mr Goldman liked to protect his bald head from the damp mist, so he would place upon it a large white handkerchief with a knot tied in each corner. Later in the day when the sun was high in the sky, Mr Goldman would make another round 'in the field', this time without Rowland, and then his topee would be very much in evidence, and he would take his big bulldog Kaiser with him for company.

If Rowland happened to be away visiting one of his other estates at the time of the V.A.'s visit, Mr Goldman would attend the muster and do his field rounds alone, but he would always be back to the bungalow for breakfast with the family. Then he would visit the factory, supervise the tea-tasting, and watch the tea leaves being dried, powdered and packed. Then he would be back for lunch with Helen and the children, and enjoy a 'snooze' in the afternoons. Latha observed that her Aunt Helen always made careful preparations for Mr Goldman's visits to Lucas Falls, for it was up to her as the wife of the resident planter to make sure the V.A. took away with him a good impression of the day-to-day management of the bungalow. She spent days planning menus for breakfast, lunch, tiffin and dinner, and saw to it that the floors shone and the servants were at their well-trained best. Latha would always remember one Sunday lunchtime, when Vaithi had excelled even his own high standards. Fragrant yellow rice, studded with raisins and golden-brown nuts and wreathed with fine threads of omelette, was on the menu, together with curried chicken that melted in the mouth, crisp papadams, her Uncle Rowland's favourite mint sambol, and half a dozen salads and pickles calculated to thrill the tongue and please the palate. Among the latter was a bowl of the *achcharu* beloved of Tara, with its golden mustard sauce and tiny red onions gleaming on their wooden skewers among the green beans. But best of all were Vaithi's curried prawns, everybody's favourite, succulent in their glorious thick gravy.

'This prawn,' said Mr Goldman that day, spearing one on his fork, and gazing upon it with a respect that bordered on reverence, 'appears to have come down to me from Crustacean Heaven. It's probably sacrilege to eat him, but . . .'

He popped the prawn into his mouth. 'What a way to go!'

Halfway through his lunch, Mr Goldman paused. His bald head was aglow with moisture and his face was as red as a tomato. Everyone watched, fascinated, as he took his white handkerchief out of his pocket, tied a knot in each corner, and placed it on his head to absorb his perspiration. He had no idea how funny he looked; or if he had, he obviously didn't care a hoot. Tara, Tsunami and Latha giggled. Even dignified Rowland unbent enough to smile, and Helen began to shake with suppressed laughter. Latha knew she did, since she was seated next to her. Mr Goldman knew it too, because he smiled in Aunt Helen's direction and bowed.

'God's own food, dear lady, God's own food!' he said, and took up his spoon and fork once more.

Mr Goldman entered with great verve and zest into the spirit of all the games and entertainments at Lucas Falls. He was, the family had discovered, something of an actor, and he had a splendid baritone voice. He was always humming a tune under his breath and one day, when Latha asked him what the tune was that he was humming, the tune became a song.

There is a lady sweet and kind,
Was never face so pleased my mind;
I did but see her passing by,
And yet I love her till I die.

When Mr Goldman sang, he placed his hand on his heart, a gesture which Latha thought indicated a romantic and sentimental nature until Rowland informed her that it helped the notes to come out more strongly.

His enthusiasm infected them all, and brought out unsuspected talents in everyone. Helen looked for her sheets of piano music, long abandoned in favour of domesticity and motherhood, and she had a Mr Ephraums come all the way from Colombo to tune the piano in the drawing room. Mr Ephraums was blind, and Latha and Tsunami liked to stand beside him while he sat at the piano, his head cocked to one side and his blind eyes staring into space, listening intently to the sound of one piano key after another. Rowland, after a little coaxing by his daughters, confessed to a liking for Gilbert and Sullivan. He was even heard practising 'I am the very model of a modern Major-General' in the bath, while Tara, Tsunami and Latha, in embroidered silk kimonos borrowed from Helen's wardrobe, painted fans in their hands, and red geraniums in their hair, produced a very pleasing version of 'Three Little Girls from School'. Tara practised readings from the poetry of Tagore (a living, breathing writer whom Helen admired, but whose name Latha only ever heard mentioned at Lucas Falls). Even the boys joined in, with dramatized recitations from *The Idylls of the King*, dialogues from *Julius Caesar* and the occasional soliloquy from *Hamlet*.

Soon after Latha's first visit to Lucas Falls, a ritual gradually developed in which, under Mr Goldman's direction, a little concert was regularly presented in the drawing room to mark the last evening of the boys' school holidays. This was attended by neighbouring planters, with their wives and children, and members of the estate staff.

At the first such concert Latha attended at Lucas Falls, Tara and Tsunami presented a scene from *Snow White and the Seven Dwarfs*. Latha, who had been taken by her parents to see the Disney film at the Regal Cinema in Colombo, had been so terrified by the Wicked Witch that when the Queen metamorphosed into a toothless hag she had climbed down from her seat, knelt down in front of it with her back turned to the flickering screen, and placed her fingers over her eyes. Now, two years older, she watched, amazed, for her cousin Tara seemed to have undergone just such a transformation. White hair, a hooked nose, a toothless mouth, gleaming eyes beneath a ragged, black hood . . . Latha could not recognize her.

Crouched in the chimney corner of the Lucas Falls drawing room, clutching a basket of fruit and emitting a high-pitched cackle in the manner of Walt Disney's Wicked Witch, Tara twirled a shiny red apple temptingly before her little sister's eyes. Stop! Stop! Latha wanted to call out as Tsunami stretched out her hand for it. That's no magic wishing apple, it's poisoned! You'll die if you eat it! Don't do it, Tsunami!

But nothing could stop Tsunami/Snow White, intent on her dream of the Prince and his castle, moving headlong to disaster. She took the apple in her hand and Tara, watching her intently as she raised it to her lips, laughed a dreadful, malevolent laugh of triumph. The curtain fell to a storm of applause as Tsunami dropped lifeless to the floor, the half-eaten apple rolling out of her hand.

At the last concert Latha attended at Lucas Falls, she was to sing a duet with her cousin Chris. The rehearsals for this event, which were conducted by Franz Goldman in the spare room, caused general hilarity among the youthful spectators who turned up to listen and advise.

'No, no, no!' Mr Goldman cried. 'You do *not* see her, Christopher! Not at first. Remember, you are a huntsman, you are out hunting – here, imagine this is your bow' (and he put a ruler in the huntsman's reluctant hand) '– and it is only by chance, while pursuing some animal, a deer, perhaps, that you glimpse this lovely lady in the distance.'

'What distance, sir!' Chris had protested. 'Latha's practically standing on my foot.'

'She will not be standing on your foot when you sing this duet in the drawing room, Christopher. She will be at the other end of the room . . . Miss Latha, stand here by me, please, till I give you the word. Now, Christopher! Again.'

Chris leapt from the bed on to the floor and stamped about the spare room for a while, the ruler swinging in his left hand. He paused a moment, peered at Latha from beneath his right one ('Yes, yes! well remembered!' Mr Goldman cried. 'There will be much foliage between you on the day!') and gave tongue:

On yonder hill there stands a lady,
Who she is I do not know,
I'll go ask her hand in marriage,
She must answer Yes or No . . .

Mr Goldman gently pushed Latha forward. 'Go on, Miss Latha!'

Oh, no, John, no, John, no, John, no!

Chris flung away his ruler, fell on one knee, and placed his right hand on his heart:

O, I will give you gold and jewels,
I will make you rich and free,
I will give you silken dresses,
Madam, will you marry me?

In reply to which Latha, turning away from him according to Mr Goldman's direction, responded dolefully:

Oh, no, John, no, John, no, John, no!

The duet Chris and Latha were rehearsing came from one of Helen's music books, where it figured under the title of 'The Spanish Merchant's Daughter'. Tsunami didn't think the story made sense.

'If she's turned him down once already on sight, why does he think mentioning his money will make any difference?'

Latha didn't care whether the story made sense or not. She had discovered that she adored the stage, and although there was only one verse that the heroine was required to sing solo, that verse provided plenty of opportunity for dramatic action. Flinging her right arm out with such energy on the second line that Chris complained she very nearly put his eye out, and wistfully touching her fingertips to her cheek on the third, Latha gave the verse her all:

My father is a Spanish captain,
Went to sea a month ago,
First he kissed me, then he left me,
Bid me always answer No:
Oh, no, John, no, John, no, John, no!

Latha's melancholy rendering brought a round of enthusiastic applause from the audience gathered on the spare room bed to hear the rehearsal. Chris, who had risen from his knees during Latha's singing of the refrain, now appeared to be walking away in deep dejection. Suddenly an idea seemed to strike him, and he retraced his steps.

Madam, since you are so cruel,
And that you do scorn me so,
If I may not be your lover,
Madam, will you let me go?

In response to which the lady, smiling joyfully now, and assisted by a rousing chorus from the audience, cooed:

Oh, no, John, no, John, no, John, no!

Tsunami and Latha privately considered the ballad's huntsman hero not only soppy but extremely dim.

'He asks her to marry him twice, and it's only when she gives him a hint that he gets the point,' Tsunami said. 'What kind of a hero is that?'

Then I will stay with you for ever,
If you will but be my wife.
Or, dear madam, have you settled
To live single all your life?

Chris managed a courtly bow in mid-stanza, showing (as Mr Goldman told the little audience) an instinctive feeling for dramatic conflict admirable in one so young, before offering Latha his arm on which to sweep off the 'stage' after the final clinching refrain:

Oh, no, John, no, John, no, John, no!

Alice had made Latha a long dress to wear for the concert, imaginatively adding to it a fringed train in which she could sweep back and forth to good effect. '"Clothed in white samite, mystic, wonderful"!' said her cousin Ranil, when Latha made her appearance at the dress rehearsal, throwing her immediately into a fever of shy embarrassment. Helen curled Latha's straight hair into ringlets, and lent her a sandalwood fan behind which, as the heroine of the little musical drama, she was supposed to hide her blushes. Chris, for his part, was booted and spurred, and equipped with a magnificent hat adorned with a curling feather. Their duet, which was sung on the day of the concert amidst a forest of potted palms brought in from the veranda by the Lucas Falls gardeners, was duly praised. The entire concert, in fact, was a great success. Mr Goldman was especially pleased, and showed his pleasure next holidays (which happened to be the last Latha spent at Lucas Falls) by introducing the young people to the game of chess.

'You should all learn to play this game, and play it well,' he told them. 'Not only because it is a great game, not only because it concentrates the mind, but because, unlike most other games that are played in this world of ours, it has nothing to do with trade and it was not invented in England or America.'

This the children could hardly believe. Why, the boards for Lotto and Ludo and Snakes and Ladders had 'Made in England' printed all over them, and the Monopoly board, too, announced that its distinctive design, even its very name, were the trademarks of John Waddington, Ltd, copyright of Parker Brothers, Inc. Every game they had ever heard of had been invented in England or America. This was surely a universal rule: how could chess be an exception?

And yet it was, or so Mr Goldman assured them. Chess was a royal game, he said, which kings and queens had played in the palaces of ancient India thousands of years before the invention, even, of cricket. It was a game for warriors, in which Black battled White for supremacy in the field; it was a Game of Life (said Mr Goldman), meant to be played by the gallant and the wise. He reflected a moment, then recited:

'Tis all a Chequer-board of Nights and Days,
Where Destiny with Men for Pieces plays . . .

And here his hostess, who had slipped into the spare room unnoticed, and had been sitting in the big wing-chair beside the never-used marble fireplace, listening to the discussion while she worked at her embroidery, joined in:

Hither and thither moves, and mates, and slays,
And one by one back in the Closet lays.

Mr Goldman looked at her with admiration and clapped his hands. Helen blushed and looked down at her needlework, where a yellow silk thread, drawn double, was fastening satin-stitch hearts into the centres of blue forget-me-nots. After a moment's hesitation, everyone joined in the applause.

Latha would always remember the surprise she had felt that evening, for although her Aunt Helen loved plays – it was she who had devised the scene from *Snow White* in which her daughters took part – and often read stories to the girls before she tucked them into bed at night, she had never struck Latha before that afternoon as someone who either liked or recited poetry.

6

HOW THEY PLAYED MONOPOLY

In all aspects of her life in India, Helen Ratnam had learned early to adapt her own desires to the requirements of others. She had been brought up, like many Indian girls of her class and generation, to accept without question her parents' plans for her future, and she married at eighteen the husband they had chosen for her. She had spent several evenings in her fiancé's company before the wedding and, suitably chaperoned, had duly visited the caves at Ajanta and viewed the Taj Mahal by moonlight. She had imagined Ceylon as a holiday resort to the south of her own country, and had been told that its fabled beauty and romantic possibilities were comparable only to those of Kashmir. She knew, of course, that her parents were marrying her to a very wealthy man. She had been shown photographs of his house in the Ceylon hill-country, its surroundings and its staff. But having been born to wealth and comfort herself, Helen was not especially impressed by Rowland's fortune. It meant less to her than the future it seemed to guarantee of a tranquil and cultivated existence. Visualizing what marriage would be like, Helen had looked forward to hours of delicious solitude devoted to landscape painting, interrupted only by intimate moments with her cultured and sensitive husband.

Once she arrived in Ceylon, these dreams had had to be adjusted to reality. The island, and especially its hill-country, were everything she had hoped for in the way of spectacular beauty, and there were plenty of family retainers on hand to minister to her every wish, but she found that her role as mistress of Lucas Falls was to be from now on the most important aspect of her new existence. An establishment like Lucas Falls didn't run itself, administration and governance must be the full-time occupation of 'the lady of the house'. Her mother-in-law had told Helen so very firmly, the first time she had called on her son and his bride and found an easel and palette, together with brushes, oil, turpentine and canvases, set out on a side veranda.

'I hope you're not wasting precious time on painting useless pictures,

Helen, my dear,' Rowland's mother had said. (The old lady was a firm believer in the excellent principle of beginning as one meant to go on.) 'There's a great deal for you to do in the house and the garden. Once children arrive, you'll find your hands full, so you should practise now. In any case, there are plenty of pictures in this house already.'

Which was, of course, perfectly true. The house at Lucas Falls had no shortage of large framed sepia-tinted Victorian prints on its walls, with titles such as *Two's Company*, *Three's a Crowd*, *The Letter*, and *The Proposal*, in which young Englishmen and women posed in a variety of tableaux. Helen had obediently put her paints and brushes away and redirected her interest in art to practicalities, in particular to the maintenance of her husband's beautiful house and its magnificent garden.

In the early years of her marriage she would often play or sing after dinner. Rowland enjoyed hearing her sing, and so, later on, did the Visiting Agent Mr Goldman, whose big baritone voice she sometimes accompanied on her piano. When Latha came to visit, she looked forward to these evening entertainments, for there was nothing of the kind to be heard in her own home except her father's collection of jazz records, which she was allowed occasionally to play on an ancient gramophone in Herbert's study. Sometimes Helen and Franz Goldman sang duets, and, as the children grew up and developed an interest in joining in, they introduced into their repertoire such part-songs as 'Row, row, row my boat', or 'The Wraggle-Taggle Gipsies'.

Latha's romantic heart thrilled to this last ballad and its tale of a wealthy woman who abandoned the comforts of her home for a free and independent life.

> *It was late last night when milord came home,*
> *Inquiring for his lady, O*

sang Mr Goldman.

> *The servants cried, on every side,*
> *She's gone with the Wraggle-Taggle Gipsies, O!*

chorused Ranil, Chris and Colin.

> *What makes you leave your house and your land,*
> *What makes you leave your treasure, O?*

Ranil demanded.

> *What makes you leave your new-wedded lord,*
> *And off with the Wraggle-Taggle Gipsies, O?*

questioned Tara and Tsunami. To which Helen and Latha responded defiantly:

What care I for my house and my land,
What care I for my treasure, O?
What care I for my new-wedded lord,
I'm off with the Wraggle-Taggle Gipsies, O!

Latha was acknowledged by everyone to own the best singing voice of the party; and since the last two verses of the ballad were her special favourites, she was often permitted to sing the first one solo:

What makes you leave your goose-feather bed,
With the sheet turned down so bravely, O?
Tonight you'll sleep in the cold, open field,
Along with the Wraggle-Taggle Gipsies, O!

to be joined in singing the second by all the voices in triumphant chorus:

What care I for my goose-feather bed,
With the sheet turned down so bravely, O?
For tonight I'll sleep in the cold, open field,
Along with the Wraggle-Taggle Gipsies, O!

Alice, Helen's personal ayah – or 'Old Nokomis', as the Lucas Falls children called her – was a large, motherly woman who had accompanied Helen from India on her marriage to Rowland. In caring for her mistress's physical wellbeing, Alice scorned the imported creams, lotions, and skin tonics that were available at Cargill's and Miller's, the large department stores in Colombo, and turned instead to herbal and natural products. Proud of Helen's thick, dark hair, her soft skin, and her radiant complexion, Alice had been pleased to find that the garden at Lucas Falls produced a good supply of the avocados, cucumbers, tomatoes, limes, bees' honey and assorted herbs that went to make up what Tsunami and Tara privately called her witch's cabinet. Alice was also a skilled masseuse. She kept up the weekly massages with fragrant oil of sandalwood that had first begun when Helen was sixteen, and she saw to it that Helen slept undisturbed for two hours after her ministrations.

At fifteen years of age, Tara Wijesinha found herself the fortunate inheritor of Alice's expertise, sharing her mother's rituals of personal care and rest. It was not long before Tsunami and Latha, too, were initiated into the esoteric rites over which 'Old Nokomis' presided; but since they could not be relied upon to 'play quietly' during the rest periods, and were much too indisciplined to put up with an hour of massage without fidgeting, they were allowed as a special treat at these times to give each other a sandalwood face mask.

'Two drops of lime juice, two drops of honey . . .'

They watched, fascinated, as Alice took a small golden block of sweet-scented sandalwood and a sharp knife from her witch's cabinet, scraped sandalwood powder into a bowl, and mixed it with rosewater that she measured, drop by fragrant drop, into the bowl. Their hair was pinned back, their faces well scrubbed, and then they were each given a small saucer of thick, sweet-smelling liquid with which they were allowed to anoint each other. When the liquid was all used up, Alice spread two mats on the cool wooden floor, and commanded that the two girls lie flat on their backs without moving, until their face masks had dried.

The sandalwood smelled heavenly, Latha thought. She put a hand tentatively to her cheek, and felt a grainy surface, still slightly liquid, beneath her fingertips.

'Don't touch it, baba! And don't speak or smile,' chided Alice.

Latha hastily put her hand back on the mat beside her, shut her eyes tight, and tried to go to sleep as she knew Tara and her Aunt Helen had done in the next room.

'Breathe in, baba!' Alice told her. 'Now breathe out! Now in again! Now out! Don't move or speak, or all my good work will be undone.'

Latha's attempts to sleep must have succeeded, for she woke up with a start to find Tsunami looking down at her curiously, an unfamiliar Tsunami who seemed to have a face constructed of white cement in which three wide holes replaced her eyes and mouth.

'You look like a ghost, Latha,' Tsunami said, and giggled.

'Why not take a look at yourself, baba,' Alice chuckled, handing her Helen's tortoiseshell-backed hand-mirror.

Latha put her fingers warily to her face once again, and this time was appalled. The mask seemed to have set as hard as concrete. Would it ever come off?

Alice brought her a basin of cool water. Both children were relieved to find that their masks, when splashed with water, crumbled to bits and washed off quite easily. They emerged glowing from Alice's hands, and studied their reflections in the mirror.

'"One must suffer to be beautiful",' observed Tsunami, who had recently been reading *The Little Mermaid*.

Latha, who had heard herself described once as 'a comely child', and was beginning to take an interest in her own appearance, thought privately that it would be worth any amount of suffering to grow up looking like Auntie Helen. She added Alice's rites and rituals to the list of topics she didn't bring up at home: her mother did not go in for such wickedly self-indulgent practices as oil massages and sandalwood face masks.

'Latha Baba was so frightened, aiya, she thought we would have to send for you to bring a chisel to break the sandalwood mask I put on her face,' Alice told Raman over their cup of tea that afternoon.

Raman permitted himself a dignified smile.

Raman the butler had originally been his master's valet. Over the years he had come to exercise such influence over Rowland and over the household generally that Helen, fresh from her convent school in Delhi, had been warned by her mother-in-law at the time of her wedding that Raman was not to be crossed in any way.

'If any kind of dispute develops between you and Raman over the running of the household,' the old lady had said to the young bride, 'you will be the one to go, not Raman.'

A sinister statement, one might have thought, with which to begin married life! But there was, in reality, nothing in the least sinister about it. It was just a fact of life in the Lucas Falls household. Raman and Helen had got on well from the start. By the time Latha came to visit, he had become her aunt's adviser and friend as well as her uncle's, devising the menus in consultation with Vaithianathan who ruled over the kitchen, interviewing gardeners and chauffeurs, ayahs and dhobis, presiding over service in the dining room, and taking charge of the household keys when Helen and Rowland were away.

Vaithianathan was a great collaborator when Helen wished to devise special treats for her children and her visiting niece. (One of these was his *Crème Brûlée,* the recipe for which Rowland had brought back to Ceylon with him by exercising his persuasive powers on the Trinity Hall cook.) The children called it 'Glass Pudding', and loved smashing through its gleaming caramelized surface to the creamy custard beneath. But splendid as the meals were that were sent up from Vaithianathan's domain to the high-ceilinged dining room at Lucas Falls, it was Latha's childhood memory of picnic baskets packed by her aunt with Vaithi's assistance and advice, from which came delicious food to be eaten in the open air while wood-pigeons fluttered and called in the forested hills above, that stayed with her when Lucas Falls had been left behind and its happy company of cousins dispersed for ever.

Perhaps, Latha thought many years afterwards, it was because picnics by the waterfall had not been a daily occurrence that she remembered the details about them so vividly. Most times, the children would be driven back to Lucas Falls by Alexander quick smart, because Master wanted the car. And in any case, after the boys had been back home from the King's College boarding for a few days, such rural pleasures would begin to pall.

When that happened, the children would retreat to a huge four-poster bed that took up most of the space in a spare room which was set apart for Very Important Visitors. This bedroom and the dressing-room attached to it were kept ferociously tidy, their furniture and their old-fashioned brass fittings polished to a high gloss by the servants. But the bed itself was too wide, its rose-coloured quilted counterpane was too soft, and its canopy and lacy curtains offered hiding places too tempting to be overlooked by children who wanted a quiet place to play.

Under this magnificent bed, stored away in a chest which was pushed out of sight and forgotten for most of the year, were many things that were not in current use: these included some of Helen Wijesinha's painting materials, miniature clay pots for open-air cooking, and cardboard boxes containing the wooden counters for draughts, the white-spotted black rectangles for dominoes, and brightly coloured packs of cards for Snap, Happy Families, Patience and Beggar-My-Neighbour. The chest also contained jigsaw puzzles, and a number of board games that only came into their own during the holidays. In the long evenings, before dinner was served in the dining room, especially if his visit to Lucas Falls coincided with a time when the boys were home for the holidays, Mr Goldman would sometimes join the children in playing Scrabble and Ludo on the canopied bed.

The board game they all loved best came out of a rectangular cardboard box with three panels of red and white upon the lid, and eight red, black-edged letters stamped in the middle of the white panel in the centre that read M-O-N-O-P-O-L-Y. Inside the box was a bright red board which opened up on the bed to reveal a space as smooth and green as the lawns at Rothschild Estate, with rectangles all along its edges that bore panels of different colours: blue, brown, purple, green, yellow, red, orange and crimson. Each rectangle had a different name, and on each rectangle was stamped a different number with a squiggle beside it. The unfamiliar names puzzled Tsunami and Latha until Mr Goldman explained that they were the names of streets, squares and railway stations in London.

London again! Latha's attention was instantly captured. And as for the game itself – what could be more exciting than to actually be *in* the city of one's dreams? Pyramids of words could be constructed on the Scrabble board, and neighbours comprehensively beggared at cards, but in no other game could valuable real estate be so triumphantly acquired and so casually surrendered as in Monopoly. It was a game at which Latha's older cousins, especially Ranil and Tara, were particularly adept: they bought, sold, and rented properties so quickly and profitably that they made Latha's head spin. Money changed hands in sums that seemed huge to Latha. She and Tsunami were making good progress in arithmetic, but had only learned as yet to count up to one thousand.

'What's that squiggle, Mr Goldman?' Tsunami asked.

'That's the sign for sterling,' the V.A. replied. 'English people don't care for rupees and cents, they deal only in sterling; that is, in pounds, shillings and pence.'

Tsunami and Latha felt infinitely sorry for English people, who didn't know what a shiny fifty-cent coin looked like, and had to make do with a squiggle. Still, playing with their money was fun. What Tsunami liked best about Monopoly was the stack of money which came out of the red and white box, pretend bank notes of different colours with rubber bands around each denomination. With these notes, it seemed, you could buy title-deeds to any property on the board that you wanted, and also tiny wooden houses and hotels that you could build on the property you owned. Mind you, the money wasn't all income, for you had to pay rent if you landed on someone else's property, and an even higher rent if you stayed in one of their hotels. There were thirty-two bright green houses in all, and twelve red hotels. (Tsunami and Latha had counted them.)

'You must have been to England hundreds and thousands and millions of times, Mr Goldman,' Latha said once to their jovial companion who knew so much about Bond Street and Oxford Street, Whitehall and Liverpool Street Station.

'Trillions of times,' said Tsunami.

'No, young ladies,' Mr Goldman replied. 'As a matter of fact, I haven't been to England at all. Not once in all my life.'

They all, even the boys, looked at him in amazement.

'Do you mean to say you've never seen the white cliffs of Dover, sir?' asked Chris.

'No, never,' said Mr Goldman. 'Some members of my family did, though. They left Hamburg just in time, just before Britain closed her doors to people like us. But the ship my parents and I were travelling in was stopped by British Immigration when it reached Tilbury. There was talk among the passengers that we would have to go back to Hamburg. My mother began to cry. She had suffered and endured everything, everything, without a protest until that moment, but now she was shaking with fear. I know, because she had her arm around me, and it was trembling. My father comforted her. "Rachel," he said, "Rachel, trust me, trust God. He will look after us." But she had lost faith, it seemed. "There is no God," she said, "or else He has forgotten us." It was then that the captain gave an order and the ship turned around. He refuelled at Marseilles and again in Bombay, and he landed us in Perth, Australia. Luckily for us.'

A square in one corner of the Monopoly board carried a picture of a man in uniform with an upraised finger.

'Who's that man, Mr Goldman?' Latha asked.

The V.A., who had gone off into a little reverie, came out of it with a start and said:

'That? That's a Nazi. He'd send you to a concentration camp if he found out you were a Jew.'

He must have seen the surprised expressions on their faces, because he quickly corrected himself.

'Just a joke,' said Mr Goldman. 'Not a very good one, I'm afraid. Sorry about that. The man in uniform,' he went on, 'is a policeman, a true-blue British bobby who will send you to jail if you break the law.'

'What law?' asked Tsunami.

'Oh . . . there are so many laws in this world to be broken! More than any man can count. You are breaking the law if you drive your car too fast, or park it in a no-parking area. Or if you trespass on another man's property.'

That was more like it. They had all seen the signs around Lucas Falls Estate, warning that trespassers would be prosecuted. Even though, as Tsunami pointed out to Latha at Sunday service, Our-Father-who-art-in-Heaven-Hallowed-be-Thy-Name was supposed to be more inclined to forgive trespassers than to prosecute them. (Soma Wijesinha, who had learned to tolerate Herbert's attending church at Christmas and Easter, would have been very annoyed if she had known her daughter was attending an Anglican church service with Tsunami's family on every Sunday of the holidays, marking the hymns of the day in her Uncle Rowland's hymnal, and genuflecting with her cousins at particular points in the Communion service. Of course Latha didn't tell her about that, either.)

Monopoly seemed to be full of similar contradictions. When a fall of the dice landed Chris on the British bobby's square, he had to go immediately to jail, to languish behind bars until a lucky throw on the next round got him a double. Yet the square in another corner of the board was marked 'Free Parking', and the one opposite carried a red arrow and the word 'GO' in large letters. If you found yourself on the first you didn't have to pay anyone anything at all, and on the second the Bank actually paid you two hundred English pounds! This, Chris informed Latha (loftily, even though he was speaking from a jail cell), was her salary.

'Salary?' Tsunami wanted to know. 'What's salary?'

'A salary is what my company pays me when I submit my report,' was Mr Goldman's explanation.

'Does Pater have a salary?' Colin asked.

'Indeed he has a salary,' Mr Goldman replied. 'Although I understand he doesn't really need one. Unlike your obedient, humble servant.'

This, as Latha later discovered, was perfectly true. Her Uncle Rowland planted tea in a gentlemanly, rather than a professional way, as practice for the future. One day he would retire from planting for Rothschild's, and run the family estates he had inherited. His future was secure, a security that his children would inherit, along with his property. Meanwhile, the personal planting of tea was a game to Uncle Rowland.

Just as Monopoly was a game to his children. It was played, unlike most of their other games, with enormous concentration. Someone slithering down a snake might hiss with frustration, or one of the younger players, tired of continually losing at Ludo, might slide off the bed on to the floor and say:

'It's not fair! You're cheating! I've had enough, and I'm not playing with you any more.'

That sort of thing simply didn't happen when they were playing Monopoly, for it would have brought the game to an immediate end, and nobody wanted that: they all knew what would happen next.

Ranil, as the eldest member of the group and its permanent Master of Ceremonies, would signal his displeasure. Offenders would promptly be thrust out of the august company on the spare room bed, and Tara, as Ranil's auxiliary, would formally announce their exclusion from all future games. Ostracized by everyone, prohibited even from entering the spare room, and cast into the outer darkness of 'Coventry' (a place unrepresented on the Monopoly board, but only too well known to them all), it was the just punishment of such spoilsports to be totally ignored and isolated until they repented, apologized, and humbly sought readmission to the magic circle.

Franz Goldman was greatly amused when he first saw the Lucas Falls system of boycott and sequestration in action.

'So British!' was his comment.

It was a remark that Latha never really understood until much later, when Tsunami described to her the years she had spent at a private school for girls run by English nuns in Colombo.

Single-minded in her pursuit of knowledge, about London and everything else, Latha never once sabotaged a game in this way, and therefore never once required punishment. Guidance and financial advice were unfailingly provided by Christopher whenever she needed them and sometimes when she did not. As for Tsunami, Ranil and Tara particularly enjoyed having their little sister along when they played Monopoly, for then Tsunami (who hadn't a clue about the value of money, and in any case preferred giving things away to acquiring them) would have a special role to play.

'Me, me! I'll be Banker! Please let me be Banker!' Tsunami would cry happily.

Ranil or Tara, smiling, would lay out for her in neat little piles the paper notes in their various colours. Everyone would choose a token, Ranil would rattle the dice, and play would begin.

Latha would always remember a particular game of Monopoly that went on and on without stopping for two rainy weeks of the holidays (with intervals allowed when Helen sent Raman to call the children away from it to join the V.A. and herself at lunch, tea or dinner). The game went on so long because Tsunami as Banker could never harden her heart enough to declare anybody bankrupt or send them to jail. Loans are easy to wheedle out of a Banker who will accept title deeds for worthless property in Whitechapel or the Old Kent Road, in return for huge amounts of cash. Tsunami's rare generosity would enable desperate speculators not only to survive, but to go on to prosperous careers in real estate, building houses in Park Lane and hotels in the Strand.

'She has too kind a heart, she is too compassionate, this little Tsunami,' Mr Goldman said once. 'How will you ever survive real life, young lady?' (Ranil had just relieved his sister of five thousand pounds, in the form of a bank loan.) 'You must never again let any one do that to you, my dear.'

He looked round at the other players.

'It is lucky for her that Tsunami has her three strong brothers to protect her, a fine, sensible sister, and a loving cousin. You young people will have to look after this little girl. You must guard her interests, or she will be lost. For who can tell what disasters lie ahead?'

Latha, listening, wondered what he would say if she told him her secret. *Tsunami, Mr Goldman, doesn't need anyone's protection, mine or Tara's or yours. She's in no danger of being lost! She's an earthquake waiting to happen . . . and if I were you, sir, I'd get out of her way . . . Unless it's the other thing, and she's the one the earthquake hits . . .*

But of course Latha didn't say it.

7

SILENCE, SWEETNESS AND SIMPLICITY

There were so many things, Latha discovered, that couldn't be said. She had been gifted with a memory like blotting-paper, but a lot of what it absorbed could not be mentioned: not even at Lucas Falls, and certainly not at home. She would like to have discussed some of her puzzling discoveries with Helen, but there was a certain enigmatic remoteness about her aunt that discouraged confidences.

And yet, if Latha had only known it, Helen Wijesinha, who had left her sisters and school friends behind in India, and had found herself, after several years of marriage, the only adult woman in a family of four males, had learned to value female companionship. As a schoolgirl she had devoted her time to painting and reading. Her husband's reputation as a connoisseur of art and literature was one of the reasons why she had consented to marry him. But, once married, and reconnected with his busy life in Ceylon, Rowland did not seem to have much time for either of these interests. Helen yearned for congenial, intimate chat, of the kind she perhaps believed only daughters or sisters can supply.

On 1 October 1945 the Sinhala language was established throughout the island as the medium of education in all school classes below Standard V. Tsunami who, like Latha, had graduated to the first form that year, told her cousin that she knew now how a condemned prisoner must feel when a last-minute reprieve snatches him from the gallows.

'The poor things!' she said, of those among her classmates at Ashcombe who had failed to make the transition to the Upper School. 'Fancy having to study every single subject in Sinhala! Do you realize what a lucky escape we've just had, Latha?'

'We'll still have a Sinhala language class every day,' Latha pointed out mildly.

Privately, she wished very much that English lessons could be fitted into the slots assigned to Sinhala language classes in the Form I timetable, but the knowledge that the national language would continue to be taught in the Upper School caused her no distress. Her parents spoke Sinhala at home, and possibly as a result of this, she had a far greater command of the language than her cousin did.

'Oh, I can manage *that* all right,' was Tsunami's reply. 'Not sure I could have survived studying every subject in the wretched language, though. I *hate* it!'

Latha made no reply. She understood Tsunami's feelings though she did not share them; she also knew better than to express such a sentiment to anyone but her cousin. For like it or hate it, Sinhala still had to be kept up. Sinhala was the official language of the culturally resurgent nation, and it was only right that everyone should know how to speak and write it correctly.

To bring Tsunami's Sinhala up to standard, Rowland engaged a tutor. The young man he chose for this task, a tall, weedy individual whose snow-white national dress flapped, bat-like, around his lanky frame as he cycled twice a week up the drive of the Wijesinha home in Colombo, usually found when he got to the front door that his pupil had flown. Tsunami disliked being forced to do anything, and frequently arrived late for her lessons. Sometimes she managed to avoid them altogether, which poor Mr Gamalath pretended not to mind. Her indifferent attitude to the Sinhala language did, nevertheless, wound him to the quick, for he was devoted to his subject and besides, he had to travel many miles to his teaching appointments. When Helen reproached Tsunami for her behaviour to her Sinhala tutor, Tsunami shrugged, and apologized. She didn't want to upset him, she said, but she just wasn't interested. Sinhala was okay, she supposed, if you wanted to communicate with the servants – Mr Gamalath flinched when he heard her say this – but studying it was a complete waste of time.

At school one day, Tsunami lost her temper.

'Why do I have to waste my time studying Sinhala *kavi*, Miss?' she had asked her Sinhala poetry teacher at Ashcombe. 'Sinhala is a dead language. It's deader than Latin, and it isn't half so interesting.'

The teacher had been so upset by this statement that she had burst into tears. She was a highly strung young woman who had emerged from the University inspired by a desire to replace Ceylon's old society of brown sahibs and memsahibs with a brave new world populated by intelligent young people who valued their own culture and their ancient traditions. And here was Tsunami, whom she knew to be one of the brightest children in her class . . .

'How can you speak in this way about your own language, child!' she had scolded Tsunami. 'You'll regret one day that you ever said such a thing.'

Tsunami, unrepentant, showed no sign of contrition. She duly handed up her Sinhala homework to her teacher, and received good marks for it, but all the books she bought or borrowed from the College library for her own pleasure were English books. While Latha read the English classics and focused on romance, Tsunami's taste was directed to popular novels of action. For the duration of one entire holiday, she devoted herself exclusively to tales of the French Foreign Legion, and P.C. Wren became her favourite author.

Having no knowledge of written Sinhala herself, and being therefore in no position to act as Mr Gamalath's auxiliary at Lucas Falls, Helen concentrated instead on passing on to her daughters the domestic arts in which she took most pleasure. How else can one explain the phenomenon of The Quilt? While Tara and Tsunami were still quite young, their mother had them join her in the making of a patchwork quilt. Such work is not traditional to Sri Lanka, or to the Southern Province (where older women, such as Rowland and Herbert Wijesinha's great-aunts, still vied with one another in the art of lace-making). But quilting was at one time a popular craft among women in southern England, and Helen had been introduced to it by an English teacher at her Delhi school. Choosing quilting as a craft by means of which she could extend the beauty of her husband's ancestral home, Helen selected various fabrics, cut them out with care, and assigned to Tara the task of tacking the brightly coloured diamonds and hexagons in place and hemming them firmly together. It was Tsunami's task (and Latha's, too, for she had a standing invitation to join the quilters when she was visiting at Lucas Falls) to finish off each completed section with decorative herringbone stitch.

The quilt progressed rapidly. Tara, Tsunami and Latha were never bored by this task, no doubt because they were all too young at the time to have developed rival interests, but also because they were learning to share, as they sewed, Helen's tastes in literature. For as the girls sewed, Helen read aloud, chiefly from books, plays and poems she had loved as a schoolgirl in India. It was she who introduced them, almost before they could read, to *Hassan*, *As You Like It*, *David Copperfield*, *Wuthering Heights* and *The Merchant of Venice*. And it was Helen's voice that first let fall in her niece's receptive ear the three magical sentences spoken by Mr Darcy in *Pride and Prejudice* that were to shape Latha's future views on love and life: 'In vain have I struggled. It will not do. You must allow me to tell you how ardently I admire and love you.'

And so, while the Wijesinha boys were out playing football or cricket, Tara would hem and Tsunami and Latha herringbone to the rhythm of Emily Brontë's prose. While her male cousins followed the adventures of heroes and villains in the fiction of Robert Louis Stevenson, Captain Marryat, R.M. Ballantyne, Alexandre Dumas, and Arthur Conan Doyle, Latha compared Wickham with Darcy, and Edmund Bertram with Henry

every minute of the holidays she spent with Tsunami and her family on their hill-country estate. She didn't know how to explain it, but the very air one breathed felt fresher there, somehow, than it did at home. This cool change did not occur only in Latha's mind – the change from Colombo's sweltering days and stuffy, airless nights becomes immediately apparent as soon as travellers start the ascent, by way of a series of acute hairpin bends, to the mountains. Rowland's family would leave Colombo early in the morning, before dawn. As their big Chevrolet moved like a shadow through villages and small towns that were just waking to the new day, climbing higher and higher along steep macadamized roads edged with tea bushes, the air would become scented with pine and the heady fragrance of drying tea-leaves. The hill slopes on either side of the road would be covered with a close carpet of mossy green, tea bushes so skilfully planted, pruned and plucked that the soil between them was invisible to the eye.

The climate up-country is crisp and cold. When the wreaths of mist lift, leaving the grass wet with dew, mornings on the estate clink and ring with birdsong, sounding very much as if a crowd of children were jingling thin silver coins in their pockets, considering the possibilities. Sunshine slants through the treetops, flashing upon streams and waterfalls, striking the bonnet of the estate car as it makes its way down to the town, glancing off the glass bangles and gold earrings of the tea-pluckers as they walk with their baskets suspended from their foreheads to begin the day's work.

As the sun rises higher in the sky, the air loses its freshness and the rocky outcrops among the tea bushes grow warm first, then hot – hot enough to fry an egg on, according to Mr Goldman. And then comes evening, and with it the mist rolls in, rising in feathery wisps from the shimmering silver-blue expanse of an ancient reservoir that waters the rice-fields in the valley below, thickening as it climbs the mountainsides, swallowing up trees and shrubs and bushes as it advances, to lie at last, a blanket of white cloud, over the garden and grounds of Lucas Falls. If Raman did not close the doors and let down the shutters at half past six on February nights, the mist that had engulfed the garden would walk unbidden along the verandas of the house and come in at the windows, as much at home as any member of the family.

When the Wijesinha boys came home from boarding school, they introduced Latha and Tsunami to all kinds of interesting new ideas. Christopher and Colin led Latha one day into what they said was the oldest part of the house.

'Look! Look up, Latha!' Chris said.

Above their heads, on the white-painted ceilings of several rooms, Latha could make out large black lettering.

'What do the letters say?'

She learned that the ceilings of the house had been constructed from the material in which the first machines for the estate's tea factory had arrived, packed and wrapped for their long sea journey from England to Ceylon. Of more recent construction was the wing which, according to Colin, was the home of the resident ghost.

'*A ghost?*'

'All old houses are haunted,' Colin airily informed Latha. 'Our ghost is Lady Millbanke, a Governor's wife. I'll show you her room, and the window she jumped from.'

The window looked to Latha just like all the other windows in that part of the house, but if Colin was to be believed, a pale wraith-like figure was sometimes to be seen wandering beneath it on moonlit nights.

'And that's nothing,' Colin went on. He was enjoying the effect he was having on his impressionable cousin. 'Guests who've slept in that room have been wakened in the middle of the night by a *sound* . . .'

'A sound? What sort of sound?'

'The soft sound, Latha, of the brass knob on their door being *turned* by an invisible *hand* . . .'

'That's quite enough, Colin,' cut in Christopher sharply. 'Stop it. You're terrifying her.'

On one unforgettable occasion (Latha had been making her second visit to Lucas Falls), Chris and Colin showed the little girls a cardboard shoe-box, from inside which came the sound of a soft but distinct rustle.

'What's inside?' Tsunami asked, holding the box carefully to her ear.

She passed it to Latha, who was sure she could hear the whirr of fluttering wings. *Sylphs!* Latha thought. But she was too shy to say the word out loud in case Colin laughed at her. (She knew Chris was too kind to do anything like that, but she wasn't sure of Colin.)

'Butterflies,' Colin told her. 'We caught them yesterday, with my butterfly net.'

The gardens at Lucas Falls had, for several days, been swept by the breezes of the northeast monsoon, on the wings of which, looking for all the world like flower petals shaken from paradisal rose-bushes, floated clouds of white and yellow butterflies. Tsunami and Latha liked to sit on the veranda, and watch them drifting by like confetti on the wind, waves of butterflies rising and falling as the breezes strengthened or slackened. And Colin had put them in a shoe-box!

'But they'll die in there!' Tsunami cried. 'They won't be able to breathe or fly.'

'They'll never get to see Sri Pāda,' Latha said mournfully.

She had learned from Raman that the butterfly migrations to Ceylon's sacred mountain peak always occurred in the months of March and April.

'The butterflies are making their last pilgrimage, Latha baba,' Raman had explained. 'They are going to the top of Sri Pāda, to pay their last respects to the Lord Buddha's sacred footprint. And when they have done that, then—' he hesitated, but went on, 'then they die.'

'*Die?*' Latha was horrified. 'Why should they die?'

'Because they are tired,' Raman told her. 'It's a long, long journey, and they don't stop anywhere along the way, no, not even for a drink of water. But they are happy. They are satisfied. They know they have fulfilled their destiny.'

'Don't worry, Latha, it'll be okay,' Chris told her cheerfully. 'They may not make it to Sri Pāda, but their children will.'

He showed her tiny holes that he and Colin had bored in the top of the shoe-box with the points of the dividers in their maths instrument cases.

'Those holes are for the butterflies to breathe through,' he explained, and set the box carefully on the play-room window sill. 'Now, none of us must touch the box, or disturb them in any way. And Tsunami, please make sure that Jeeves doesn't throw the butterflies out.'

'And that Anatole doesn't cook them!' Colin amended.

During the previous holidays, an experiment in dissection undertaken by Ranil for which eight prawns fresh from the market had been laid out on a chopping board while he went to collect his instruments, had been whisked away by Vaithi, cooked a rosy pink, and served up with mayonnaise as an entrée at lunch. Nobody had warned the chef that a science experiment was in progress in the pantry.

In a few days, the flutter of wings inside the shoe-box had ceased.

'I'll bet they're dead,' Tsunami said accusingly. 'You've killed them, you two.'

But no, it seemed that the butterflies were not dead, they had just been replaced by something completely different: a score or so of bright green caterpillars, tiny creatures with huge appetites, who spent the whole day eating. The boys combed the estate for leaves with which to line the shoe-box. Tsunami and Latha watched, fascinated, as the caterpillars' jaws moved rapidly up and down, and from side to side across the surface of the leaves, consuming one leaf after the other. And then, all at once, their movements ceased, and one morning the children found that the caterpillars had disappeared completely, transformed into silvery globes that clung to the undersides of the leaves.

Latha tried to detach one of the shining globes with her little finger. It swung a little from side to side, but wouldn't come away from the leaf.

'That's a chrysalis,' Colin told the girls. 'It's hanging on there because its life depends on it.'

The pendant globes gleamed and shone. They were, Latha thought, very much like the silvery drops of mercury she had once seen during a spell in bed when her mother had broken a thermometer while shaking it down to take her temperature. The mercury drops had rolled about on the bed sheet, looking like water drops but moistening nothing.

All too soon, it seemed, the shining magical globes lost their shine, and became brown and dull.

'They've become cocoons,' Chris said. 'Now things are getting interesting!'

Latha couldn't see how the dull cocoons could be more 'interesting' than the mercury drops had been, but she understood Chris better when the cocoons split: produced, it seemed, by a different kind of magic, tiny bedraggled creatures crawled out of them. In seconds, or so it seemed to the fascinated children, they opened their wings, flapped them once or twice, then flew away from the box, into the garden. Butterflies!

'It's an experiment we did at school,' Chris said. 'It's really meant for silkworms, to show how silk is manufactured, but there aren't any mulberry leaves to be found in Colombo, and to rear silkworms you've got to have mulberry leaves. They won't eat anything else.'

That afternoon, Tsunami and Latha looked up 'silkworms' in Arthur Mee's *Children's Encyclopaedia* in the Lucas Falls library.

'"*Within the chrysalis a marvellous transformation takes place. Not always, for we do not permit it to happen with the majority of silkworm cocoons . . .*"'

'Stop!' said the listening Tsunami. 'Who's "we"?'

'It doesn't say. I expect it's the workers in the silk factories. It just goes on:

'"*This moth has become an entirely domesticated species, bred in captivity. The females do not seek to fly away, nor the caterpillars to wander, but rest in the place where they are hatched and fed . . .*"'

'It sounds awfully cruel to me,' Tsunami said thoughtfully. 'Fancy putting winged creatures in a place where they can't fly—'

'They don't *want to* fly,' Latha pointed out. 'Arthur Mee says they just want to stay where they are.'

'How does he know? Can he read a silkworm's mind?'

Latha did not reply. She continued to read aloud:

'"*Silk of unmatched quality is produced by these caterpillars, woven, scores and scores of yards of thread to a single cocoon, to form a rest and refuge while the change from grub to moth is achieved. Only a sufficient number to keep up stocks is permitted to undergo the complete change –*"'

'Oh, I see,' Tsunami said. 'They keep some silkworms to weave the silk, and let the rest fly away. Well, that isn't too bad. But I'm glad Chris and Colin did it with butterflies – they all flew away, didn't they? Come on, Latha, it's tea-time.'

Latha slowly shut Volume 9 of the *Encyclopaedia*, put it away, and followed her cousin out of the library. Her eye had moved further along the page while Tsunami was speaking, and she was horrified by what she had read.

The remainder [wrote Arthur Mee], *when the cocoons are spun and the caterpillar deeply entranced within, are steeped in hot water, which destroys life and leaves the human owner to unwind the silk and weave it.*

'Destroys life'? That meant killing.

Latha had learned from her mother, and in scripture classes at the Buddhist girls' school she attended, that the destruction of life was to be avoided at all costs. She was deeply distressed. So that was who 'we' were, not just factory workers in China, but everyone in the world who wasn't a silkworm but liked wearing silk. That included people like herself. People like herself put those lively little caterpillars in a box, tricked them into falling asleep, and then boiled them alive, killing them for the sake of the silk they had woven. And what about the little girl caterpillars who, according to Arthur Mee, 'did not seek to fly away'? Latha, one of whose favourite daydreams involved soaring over house-tops and hills on magic carpets like the princes and princesses in *The Arabian Nights*, could not imagine that there was anyone in the world who would say 'No, thank you,' if offered the chance to fly away from the cruelty of the world. Latha was glad she hadn't had to read that bit aloud to Tsunami, who always took things harder than she did.

Latha remembered the golden fawn Tsunami had 'adopted' as her special pet when one of the watchmen at Lucas Falls brought it to the house. A doe had been found dead among the forest trees near the falls, and the fawn, newly dropped, was so weak that it could barely stand. As she grew stronger under Tsunami's care, the little animal would come stepping delicately around the corner of the veranda where the children were playing table-tennis and, rising on her hind legs, would take tiny mouthfuls of grain from Tsunami's hand. She made friends with everyone in the household, from Vaithi in the kitchen (who put milk out for her in a little enamel bowl) to Helga, Tara's Alsatian, and her pups, with whom she would play on the lawn in front of the house. But one day the fawn, nearly full-grown, leaped over the garden wall. Nibbling at the lush grass that grew on either side of the road, she wandered towards the village below. When the village dogs saw her coming trustingly towards them, they immediately pulled her down and killed her.

'Don't cry, dearest,' Aunt Helen had said, comforting Tsunami. But Tsunami would not be comforted.

'She only wanted to play,' she said. 'Why couldn't they let her live? Why didn't they understand?'

When Latha reached the dining room, she found that everyone had gathered there for tea. A picnic by the Falls was being planned for the following day, and the memory of the caterpillars trapped in their 'trance' quickly vanished from Latha's mind. Picnics were among the special delights of the boys' holidays, for the children would usually spend their first days back swimming in the rock pools at the foot of the waterfall nearby. The water, which comes tumbling down from the mountain peaks above Lucas Falls, is icy and fresh. Black and grey monkey-faces sometimes looked out at them from among the branches of the tall trees that edge the pools, in the shade of which ferns flourish, and the white sheaths of arum lilies, and the soft, velvety green moss which Tsunami and Latha liked to take back to the estate for Helen's table arrangements. When they came out of the water, shivering with cold, the estate car would be waiting for them by the bridge above; and in its boot they would find a basket of pink guavas, rose-apples or mangosteens, and with it, hot and delicious, picnic parcels of rice and curries baked in banana leaves that Vaithi had sent along in the care of Alexander.

Tsunami's family called those leaf parcels *lamprais*. Later, when Latha read about an English king who had died of a surfeit of lampreys, she felt a sympathy for him that she had never felt for any historical personage excepting Madduma Bandara, the brave little boy she had heard about in her History class at school who had stepped forward to meet the executioner in his elder brother's place. It was a miracle, she reflected, that neither her cousins nor she had suffered King Henry's fate, for they must have come near it often enough. Especially Colin, whose appetite at any given moment was like something out of *The Jungle Book* or *The Call of the Wild*, and whom Latha had seen finish off three or four lamprais at a sitting. She was deeply disappointed to learn from her uncle Rowland that lampreys were merely a variety of fish, and had no connection with *lomprijst*, the Dutch original of Vaithi's picnic parcels.

Latha, who had quickly got over her initial awe of her uncle Rowland, and presented her questions to him as they occurred to her, absorbed with interest the history of lamprais as recounted by him at the Lucas Falls dining table.

'Lamprais,' Rowland had stated, leaning back in his chair at the head of the table and dipping his fingers fastidiously into a cut-glass finger-bowl in which floated a tiny purple orchid, 'are a Dutch creation, built on a local custom. They have evolved over the hundred and fifty years that the Hollanders ruled maritime Ceylon, and all the sambals and pickles Vaithi puts into them are from recipes the Dutch acquired during their sojourn in Java and Sumatra.'

Finding her way past her uncle's pompous way of turning the simplest answers into a lecture, Latha worked out that lamprais were essentially just a sophisticated, up-market version of the savoury parcel of boiled rice and curried vegetables which every farmer's wife in Ceylon baked in banana leaves for her husband or her sons to take with them to the rice fields. She repeated this information at home, adding:

'So you see, Amma, lamprais are centuries old, and we were eating them here years and years before the Dutch or anyone else came over to conquer us and please can I take some to the school picnic next month?'

Soma Wijesinha knew nothing of lamprais, nor did she want to know.

Her studied indifference towards anything she thought was 'alien' to local custom was a further manifestation of the enormous chasm that seemed to separate Tsunami's family from Latha's. The only reply Latha received was:

'Western rubbish! I don't know where the child picks up these ideas.'

A good many of the 'ideas' to which her mother objected – though not, of course, the history of lamprais – came from the movies Latha saw during the holidays she spent at Lucas Falls; for during the school holidays, her cousins went to the movies whenever they chose. On one occasion, when a circus from India came to town, and Hindi movies were shown in a closed tent in the field where the Sunday market was usually held, Tsunami, Latha, Chris and Colin paid twenty-five cents each at the tent-flap 'door' to sit cross-legged on the grass and watch the flickering screen on which heroines in gauze and jewels sang and swayed, flashed melting glances at mustachioed heroes, and fluttered unbelievably long lashes at their wildly enthusiastic, toe-tapping audience.

The local cinema house brought Latha a different experience altogether. The cinema bore a sign, '*Himalaya Theatre*', in coloured lights that flashed on and off during the evening hours. It stood in the centre of the small neighbouring town, next to the vegetable market, and was quite unlike the splendid picture palaces of Colombo with their gilt pillars and shiny, bright posters. It didn't matter to Latha, ardent movie fan that she was becoming, that the Himalaya was dark and dingy, and smelled of stale vadai and murukku. Changing its programme every two or three days, this unprepossessing place was to Latha a kind of paradise, offering a passage to strange and wonderful worlds full of fantasy and excitement.

At the Himalaya, where Latha saw movie after movie with her cousins, the price of a seat was one rupee and ten cents. For fifty cents you could have a place on a bench right under the screen, but for one-ten, cinemagoers were offered their choice of a seat in one of a dozen rows of cane-bottomed wooden chairs. In the crevices of those chairs there lurked, Aunt Helen said, generations of bed bugs. She warned Latha that as soon as the lights dimmed, those bugs would emerge and do their worst. The boys were all right, their trousers and shorts protected them, and Tara was old enough to wear some very smart slacks her mother had brought back for her from London. But Tsunami and Latha, in their short dresses, spent most of the time wriggling and squirming in their seats, their eyes glued to the flickering screen. Later, Aunt Helen would put calamine lotion on their bumps and weals, and suggest that next time the little girls might like to take a cushion each along with them.

Her Aunt Helen also armed Latha against another kind of predator, the two-legged kind. On an early visit to the cinema with her cousins – the film was *Samsara*, a Hindi movie epic which went on and on, as Ranil said, for several life-cycles, not just one – Tara leaned over to Tsunami and Latha just before the lights dimmed for the first part of the programme, and gave them each a large, wicked-looking safety pin.

'Here you are,' she said. 'If anyone bothers either of you while the film is showing, you can reach behind you with one of these, and let them have it!'

She had a similar safety pin in her own hand, and was prepared, it seemed, for any eventuality. The lights dimmed, and the newsreels began, followed by the trailers of films to come. Not knowing what to expect, Latha sat for a while wondering what Tara had meant. Nobody 'bothered' her, except of course the bugs. But as soon as the lights dimmed again for the main feature, and her attention, which had been temporarily distracted by vendors of devilled cashews and chocolates, was re-focused on the screen, Latha became aware that in the darkness of the theatre the empty seats in the row behind her had become occupied. Nothing untoward happened, so she forgot all about what Tara had said, and concentrated on the heroine's problems.

Until at last, very very quietly, a mysterious movement began at the back of her seat. The first touch, when it came, could have been accidental: people do put their feet on the seats in front of them, after all. Latha paid no attention, but after a while bare toes began to prod and tickle her in a way that could not by any means have been accidental. She turned her head sharply and looked over her shoulder. A man was seated directly behind her, his eyes fixed intently on the screen. Latha turned back to the movie. After a few moments, the prodding and tickling began again. She nudged Tsunami, and whispered her predicament to her.

'Sure it's him?' Tsunami whispered.

'Yes.'

'Okay.' She kept her eyes fixed on the screen. 'You know what you've got to do, Latha. Get your pin ready, don't let on you've noticed, then go ahead, and jab!'

Latha opened her safety pin and held it in position. The tickling and probing began again. She counted to ten while slowly, stealthily, she reached behind her. Suddenly, without any warning, she brought the pin down hard, and encountered bare flesh. A sharp intake of breath could be heard from the row behind her.

'Well done, Latha. You scored!' Tsunami said.

She turned round quickly in her seat. Latha was too frightened and shy to look, but Tsunami was just in time to see a shadowy figure jump up in the darkness, and make quickly for the exit.

'You drew blood that time,' Tara said with ghoulish satisfaction, on the other side of Latha. She sounded very pleased. 'It'll be a long time before he tries anything like *that* again.'

Tara and Tsunami called this kind of thing 'being bothered' or 'being interfered with'. Apparently it happened all the time at cinemas, though not to the boys. So if you were female and enjoyed going to the movies, you simply made use of the Safety Pin Strategy to deal with it.

Most of the American movies Latha saw during those holidays were Westerns and musicals. 'Remember the Alamo!' became a catchphrase for the three girls, while 'A man's gotta do what a man's gotta do' was practically done to death by Chris and Colin. Latha accepted everything she saw on the screen as part of the natural order of things. It did not, for instance, strike her as being in the least odd that Carmen Miranda should tape a bowl full of fruit to the top of her head, or that traffic in New York should come to a halt while Doris Day or Betty Grable (attended by a flock of chorus girls attired as bridesmaids) was wedded to Howard Keel or Gene Kelly in the middle of Fifth Avenue. What fantasies the boys entertained Latha never found out, but she and Tsunami longed to weave flower garlands like Dorothy Lamour, or surface smiling among floating waterlilies like Esther Williams.

A few American movies came to Ceylon by way of India, where they had been censored in accordance with the Government of India's strict standards of propriety. Even severer than Soma Wijesinha on 'harmful matters', the Indian censors cut every kiss out of every movie on principle: the result, Latha found, was extraordinarily frustrating – against a shimmering moonlit landscape the actors' hands would touch, their smouldering glances connect, and a thrilling dialogue would develop on the screen which was clearly leading to an embrace and a passionate kiss, and then – just at what Latha and Tsunami would, if they had known the term, have called the crucial moment – CUT! and the children would find themselves looking at a day-time view of the Grand Canyon or the Rocky Mountains.

Latha discovered that her cousins had turned this particular frustration into comic entertainment. She never forgot her first experience of this practice, which occurred during a showing of an India-censored version of *The Rains Came*, in which any symptom of tenderness between the Indian doctor and the English heroine had been sternly deleted for fear of giving Britain's Indian subjects inappropriate ideas and thereby undermining the authority of Empire. The wooden expression of the American actor playing the Indian doctor under a heavy layer of suntan make-up took on, in these circumstances, a permanent air of irritation. His feelings were entirely understandable, but they were certainly not reflected in the one-ten seats where, as soon as a kiss was obviously imminent, the six Lucas Falls children conducted an orchestrated count-down to the moment of non-consummation.

'Ten!' Ranil chanted *sotto voce*, giving the signal, and the rest of them took up the cry in a sort of whispered hiss: 'Nine-Eight-Seven-Six-Five-Four-Three-Two-One-Zero-CUT!'

Such excitements were notably absent when Latha was taken to see a movie in Colombo. Attending the three-fifteen show on a Sunday at the Regal Cinema, the Majestic, the Empire, the Olympia, the Savoy, or, later, the Liberty, was a regular part of her weekends as a child. (Cinema-going was not, of course, permitted during the school week, but Herbert Wijesinha, who adored the movies, saw a film every Sunday afternoon, and occasionally took Latha with him if the movie was judged by her mother to be harmless.) In the company of her father, her mother, or her aunts, Latha saw *Snow White*, *Bambi*, *Pinocchio* and *The Wizard of Oz*, films eminently suitable for children's viewing. Never, except at Lucas Falls, did she see a film unless an adult chose the movie and accompanied her to the cinema.

Once, and only once, Latha mentioned at home the Safety Pin Strategy she had learned at Lucas Falls. There was an embarrassed silence. No one explained the behaviour of the stranger in the cinema. Latha realized that she had encountered yet another topic one did not bring up in public, even in the privacy of one's own home. She concluded that this too, like the curious behaviour of plants, animals, and the stars of the silver screen, was connected in some unfathomable way with love.

There was no one at home that she could consult, for her mother and most of her aunts regarded ignorance about everything relating to love, sex or marriage as a positive virtue in young girls. Except that they didn't call it ignorance: they called it innocence, *lajjava* ('shame'), or simplicity. For a long while after seeing Disney's *Dumbo* Latha had believed that all babies were brought by storks, later adapting this belief to a theory of her own that puppies were probably 'laid' by their mothers, just as eggs were laid by hens. Before her regular visits to Lucas Falls began, one of Latha's favourite pastimes as a very small child had been the making of little nests from the crinkly paper in boxes of Cadbury's chocolates. Into each of these she would put three or four shiny white canna seeds, and hide the 'nests' among the leaves and branches of the hibiscus hedge in the garden, hoping to deceive small birds into laying eggs in them. No one enlightened her.

'So sweet! So innocent!' her aunts had chorused approvingly. 'Your daughter, Soma, is such a sweet, *simple* girl.'

As Latha grew older she learned that to be called 'simple' was the highest compliment a daughter could earn for her parents in her mother's family. It became clear to her that silence, sweetness, and simplicity were the virtues that were most highly valued in women and girls. She worked hard to achieve all three, learning early to keep strictly to herself any information on the subject of sex that came her way. And at Lucas Falls, plenty of such information did come Latha's way as she discovered that, like plants and trees, the animals on the estate had their 'seasons'. When

Tara's beautiful Alsatian, Helga, had her puppies, they arrived as a 'litter'. And as for eggs, Latha discovered that some were 'fertile' and others were not (a matter of some importance when vegetarians came to lunch). A papaya tree might not bear fruit unless a tree of the same variety was planted close enough to it to allow cross-pollination to take place. Colin's much-loved pet tortoise Peter was quite out of spirits until a female tortoise named Peach arrived to keep him company.

Latha had to speculate on such matters mostly on her own, for her cousin was simply not interested. Tsunami's knowledge of the climbing plants and vines that she had shocked her aunt Soma by referring to as 'parasites' was neither precocious nor pretentious. She was the kind of child who absorbs information effortlessly and naturally, and this piece of information had been taken on board by her in the same way that she and her siblings absorbed many different kinds of knowledge: by following their father around his various estates and listening to him talk with the managers of his nurseries and livestock.

Since information about the facts of life came to Tsunami in the natural way it did, she was much less disposed to dwell on matters of sex and love than Latha was, or to fantasize about their various aspects. It is hardly surprising that her understanding of the ways in which plants and animals reproduce their kind was much more advanced than her cousin's.

Another area in which Latha had a good deal of difficulty was in reconciling life as she encountered it at Lucas Falls with the traditional principle of *guru bakthi*, respect for the teacher, which governed her life at school. In Rowland Wijesinha's house most subjects were open to discussion, while at Amarapāli Maha Vidyālaya, the Buddhist school for girls which Latha attended, the questioning of a teacher's statement could be, and sometimes was, considered an act of disrespect and rebellion. When, during the relation of a *Jātaka* tale of the Bodhisattva's life, one of Latha's classmates had asked how a prince and princess wandering in the forest could have had a baby without getting married first, her question had been only answered with silence, pursed lips, and a frown of disapproval from the teacher.

At home, the silence on such subjects was even more intense, shrouding them in clouds as suffocating, Latha thought, as the mist that blanketed the garden and grounds of Lucas Falls in the month of February. The air was thick with questions unasked and unanswered. Latha was puzzled by the fact that she was expected to be ashamed of any knowledge she might have of the way her own body worked. She knew what the reaction would have been at home, in Colombo, to Tsunami's announcement (made casually at the breakfast table one fine sunny morning) that Tara's dog Helga was 'on heat again'.

'Did I hear right?' Latha's aunt Caroline would have said, gleefully affecting a highly artificial amazement.

'Shameless!' Soma Wijesinha would have responded with disgust.

And Latha's Auntie Bertha, who always went for the jugular, would have delivered the final damning condemnation against which there was no appeal:

'*Forced ripe.*'

8

MR VAN KUYK OF KANDY

During her second holiday with Tsunami's family at Lucas Falls, when Latha had just turned nine, a family party arrived on a visit. Uncle Rowland, foreshadowing the event at breakfast one morning in his best proprietorial manner, said that there would be two children in the party, daughters of Mr Gerard van Kuyk, his former classmate at All Saints' College, Kandy. One of the girls, Uncle Rowland said, was ten years old (or possibly eleven), her sister two or three years younger. Tara and Tsunami, of course, knew them well. So did their brothers. He was sure Latha would find them good company.

A second party of visitors, which was due to arrive after the van Kuyk family had left, consisted of only two people: an aunt of Rowland Wijesinha's, and her daughter Moira. Rowland told the girls that his cousin Moira was interested in art, so it was a great pity that the two visits were not to coincide, since Mr van Kuyk was an artist.

An artist! Latha, who liked to draw, and enjoyed watching her aunt Helen at her sketch-book, was excited by the prospect of meeting another real, living artist, and when breakfast was at an end, she and Tsunami withdrew to their favourite perch on the lowest branch of a sapodilla tree in the corner of the garden, so that Latha could ask her cousin for information.

'They're *both* artists,' Tsunami told her. 'Uncle Gerard and Auntie Estelle, I mean, not the children. At least, I don't think so, I can't remember much about Sylvia, the younger one, but Sybil, who's our age, reads all the time. When she was here last year, she ignored everyone and everything because she had started on a big book in Pater's library, and wanted to finish it before she left.'

'She doesn't *sound* like good company,' Latha said doubtfully.

'Oh, she is. Anyway, *I* like her, though the boys don't . . . much. Colin says she shows off too much – as if *he* doesn't! She's just too clever for him – wins all the board games whenever we get her to play – so he's quite happy to let her go on reading.'

'If Mr and Mrs van Kuyk are artists,' Latha said, 'they'll be good company for Auntie Helen. Does Mrs van Kuyk paint flowers?'

Helen Wijesinha no longer painted the large, colourful canvases of her girlhood. Her artistic vision, following her marriage, appeared to have been refined (some might have said 'narrowed') to accommodate smaller works. These were not the still-life compositions that Latha was constantly being set to execute at her school (consisting usually of a bisected papaw, two halves of a mangosteen, five rambutans and a plantain on a plate). Helen had directed her interest as an artist to translating the floral glories of Lucas Falls into embroidery she designed herself. Her contribution to the Lucas Falls milieu – one of which her mother-in-law approved – was to embellish the beauty of the house with art of a different kind. Her painting and needlework, reflecting the care for accuracy and proportion she had developed in her drawings of plants and flowers at her Delhi convent school, were now directed towards recording the loveliness of the Lucas Falls gardens. There were many evidences of her skill around the house, for the flowers she chose for Latha to draw would often become the subject, later, of an embroidery design of her own.

One such work of Helen's which was particularly admired when visitors came to the house was a firescreen she had embroidered for the drawing room, decorated with an unusual and original combination of indigenous wild flowers she had collected on the estate: sudu-mihiriya, golden kahanelu, keena, dathketiya, and wal-pichcha (the starry nine-petalled white jasmine), framed by the overarching bells of purple nelu. When showing visitors around his house or his estate, and introducing them to his dogs, Rowland never failed to point the firescreen out to visitors as the work of his talented wife.

'Yes, Mrs van Kuyk draws flowers and paints landscapes, and teaches art in Kandy. So does her husband.' Tsunami hesitated, then went on: 'But I don't think Auntie Estelle will be coming. They don't live together any more, you see. Sybil and Sylvia live with their aunt Mrs Rosemary Vanderzeil. Auntie Rosemary's awfully nice. You'll like her.'

Latha had never heard of parents who didn't live together, or of children who left home to live with their aunts. She decided to approach the subject from a different angle.

'What did you say his name was?'

'Gerard van Kuyk.'

'I've never heard of him.'

'Well, Mummy says he's the best artist in Ceylon. She made Pater buy some of Uncle Gerard's paintings at an exhibition in Colombo last November. Come with me, I'll show you.'

Tsunami showed Latha four colourful canvases that lay on a table in the living room upstairs. They were unframed pictures of village scenes, women standing at the gates of a Hindu temple with lotus flowers in their hands, women offering alms to a monk in yellow robes, women listening to a sermon, a boy playing with a kite.

'They're waiting for their frames,' Tsunami said. 'Carolis Baas promised to fit the frames last week, but his daughter fell ill, and he couldn't come. Pater says he hopes the pictures will be framed and hung before Uncle Gerard arrives, or he'll never hear the end of it.'

This piece of information made Latha very curious to see Tsunami's 'Uncle Gerard'. It seemed that he was someone who could actually boss her Uncle Rowland around. There must, Latha thought, be very few people in the world who could do that. Since Tsunami called him 'Uncle', he must be a member of Uncle Rowland's family: wouldn't he then also be connected to hers? She made a point of being on hand the morning he was expected, and was amply rewarded for Mr van Kuyk turned out to be a person such as Latha had never before encountered.

The first thing she registered about her Uncle Rowland's former classmate was that he could not possibly be a relative, since he had the pale skin of a Neuropean. He was not, on the other hand, in the least like Mr Goldman. Latha tried to puzzle it out.

'Is Mr van Kuyk a Burgher?' she whispered at last to Tsunami. Her cousin nodded.

'But you never said!'

'I thought you knew. Everyone knows Uncle Gerard is a Burgher, Latha.'

'*I* didn't!'

Tall, pale-skinned, and bespectacled, Mr van Kuyk's appearance was entirely un-Burgher-like. All the Burgher gentlemen Latha had ever seen – Mr D'Abrera the Post Master at the local post office, Dr Muller her family's regular doctor, Mr de Zylva who taught Zoology to the senior classes at her school, Mr Vandersmagt the auctioneer to whom had been entrusted the disposal of her grandfather's surplus furniture, Mr La Brooy who had been at University with her father, cricket-loving Professor Eustace Pereira who had been at school with her father and was now Professor of Engineering at the University of Ceylon, Mr Kelaart the husband of Aunt Helen's dressmaker in Colombo, Mr de Bruin who taught English and Mathematics at King's College, Mr Ephraums who tuned the Lucas Falls piano, Rev. Mr Toussaint the young curate at St Mark's Church, not to mention her father's sports club friends and Customs Office colleagues – they all dressed neatly in the 'British style'. This meant that they were generally to be seen in suits featuring trousers with turn-ups, buttoned-up shirts with stiff collars, neckties and, during the daytime hours, solar topees worn on hair that was clipped and trimmed in the mode the barber at Gabriel's Hairdressing Saloon in Colpetty called 'shote-back-an'-side'.

Mr van Kuyk's hair, however, looked as if it had never seen a pair of scissors or a razor – it was thin and lank, and so long that it hung almost to his shoulders. He was wearing a white cotton *dhoti* looped around his legs, open sandals on his pale feet, and a blue long-sleeved shirt with white thread embroidery on the collar and cuffs. Latha thought he looked very untidy, as if he'd just picked his clothes up and thrown them on, without thinking too much about them. ('Like a walking dhobi-basket,' her mother would have said, if she could have seen him.) Mr van Kuyk was talking as he got out of the car – a red Baby Austin – and was still talking as he loped, rather than walked, into the house, taking the front steps two at a time. His sister Rosemary Vanderzeil turned out to be a sedate Burgher lady wearing a floral patterned sari, instead of the dress Latha had expected her to wear. She was followed by two little girls in frilly dresses, with a Sinhalese ayah in tow. Raman brought up the rear of the procession, carrying in his own hands an artist's sketchbooks and painting materials, and directing the men servants to be careful with the suitcases as Appuhamy, Mr van Kuyk's driver, unloaded them from the car.

'Mummy's giving Uncle Gerard her studio to work in while he's here,' Tsunami whispered. 'He says he can only work in daylight, so she thinks that glass pane in the ceiling of her studio will be just the thing, 'cos it'll catch all the sunlight there is, and let it through.'

The four canvases had been framed and hung just in time for the van Kuyks' arrival, two in the hall, and two in the drawing room, where the family and their guests usually foregathered for drinks before lunch. The painter, who had been making for the drawing-room door with the assurance of one who knew the house well, stopped when he saw the two paintings in the hall. He spent some moments standing before them and gazing at them intently. After a while he nodded, and looked round at Rowland.

'You've put them in a very good light, Rowley, old boy,' were his first words to his host. 'Well done. Excellent.' He turned to his hostess. 'I know this man very well, Helen. Known him for years. To be frank, I honestly didn't think he'd get it right. Doesn't know the first thing about art.'

Latha had often heard her uncle speak knowledgeably about art and artists. She was astonished to see him take with a smile, and without any rejoinder, this casual insult to his good taste.

Mr van Kuyk looked around him.

'Where are Helen's pictures, Rowley?' he said. 'You had a very fine one hanging in the hall when I was last here.'

'Oh – I know the one you mean. It's been sent away for a new frame,' Helen said quickly.

Latha looked hard at her aunt. She knew where the picture was: it hadn't been 'sent away', it was in Helen's studio, with its face turned to the wall. Mrs Vanderzeil gave Helen's cheek a polite peck, and the two little girls shook hands with Rowland. Gerard van Kuyk's gaze, wandering around the hall, fell on Latha, who was standing with Tsunami and his daughters near the foot of the stairs.

'And whose fortunate face do you brighten, child?' he asked Latha.

Latha looked up at him blankly.

'He's just asking who your father is,' Tsunami whispered.

Latha was too embarrassed to answer. Turning to Rowland, the painter said:

'And who did you say this little beauty is?'

'This is my cousin Herbert's daughter,' said Rowland. 'You know Herbert Wijesinha, Gerard – he came with us to your house last year, and bought two of your paintings.'

Gerard van Kuyk threw back his unkempt head, and emitted a shout of laughter.

'Herbie! Good God, fancy my old friend Herbie fathering an infant Sakuntala! Or is she a Sita or a Savitri? Well, child,' he said to Latha, 'what do you think of my pictures, eh, the ones your Papa bought for you?'

Latha did not understand until she was much older (and had read a good deal more) that in comparing her to three famous heroines of Indian legend, the artist had paid her an unusual compliment. She didn't like hearing her father spoken of in van Kuyk's off-hand manner, almost as if he were some kind of joke.

'My name is Latha,' she said coldly. 'Not any of the ones you mentioned. And my Thaththa couldn't have bought any pictures of yours for me, Mr van Kuyk. I've never seen any at home.'

'No, I'll bet your dear mother took one look at them and threw them out of the house,' van Kuyk said. 'Well, sweetheart, would you do me a favour? When you get home just scout around and see if you can find them. I can promise you that if they are in the house, they'll be covered with sheets. Tell that Philistine, your father, that if he isn't going to put my pictures where people can see them, I'd like to have them back.'

It seemed as if he were joking, but Latha thought Mr van Kuyk sounded quite annoyed. Uncle Rowland intervened.

'Herbert's mother, my late Aunt Anne, was your first patron, Gerard,' he said. 'You told me the story yourself, don't you remember? That she bought some drawings you'd made of local personalities because she believed young artists must be encouraged and supported? As for Herbert, he said something very like that when he made his own purchases at your exhibition. "A young artist at the start of his career, struggling to make his name known, needs moral support" was how he put it to me. I thought it very decent of Herbert, since he's not a rich man.'

Latha looked gratefully at her uncle. Van Kuyk had the grace to look a little ashamed, but he was unrepentant.

'Doesn't make him less of a Philistine,' said he. 'Or that wife of his less of a Mrs Grundy.'

'There'll be heaps of time to get to know each other later, children,' Helen put in quickly. 'Let Tsunami show you to your rooms. We'll be having lunch in an hour, Rosemary – time for everyone to have a shower and a rest. It must have been a tiring journey.'

She departed, taking the ayah with her to entrust her to the care of Alice (who would see to it that Vaithi gave her a cup of tea), while everyone dispersed. Latha sought refuge in Rowland Wijesinha's library, her favourite place for private thought at Lucas Falls. This left Tsunami in sole charge of Sybil and Sylvia van Kuyk, for the boys had not yet come home for the holidays and Tara, who would as a matter of course have taken on the task of helping her mother entertain the van Kuyks, was visiting Helen's family in India.

Latha decided to avoid the visitors. She spent the remainder of the day following her Aunt Helen around like a shadow, with occasional visits to her uncle's library to read. She had decided that she did not like Gerard van Kuyk. He had hurt her feelings, and she did not want to provoke another display of his artistic temperament, especially if it involved insults to her parents. If those pictures are still in our house, she thought, I'll make sure I find them; and then I'll put them in the waste-paper basket, or give them to the bottle vendor.

Gerard van Kuyk painted, during that visit to Lucas Falls, like a man possessed. Helen informed the children that he was preparing for a major exhibition of his work, to take place in a few months' time, and he could think of little else. It was a surprise to Latha, therefore, to learn from her uncle and aunt a few days later that Mr van Kuyk had inquired for her. From his window he had glimpsed Tsunami and Latha sitting on the branch of their sapodilla tree, talking, and had expressed a wish to paint them in just that position, with his daughters' pretty ayah to make a third in the composition. Rowland explained to Latha that to his friend art was more than a hobby, more even than a means of livelihood.

'Now, take your Aunt Helen, for instance. For her, painting is just a hobby,' Rowland said.

Helen, who was sitting opposite her husband and listening to this conversation, was silent. Rowland continued:

'And so it should be. She has other responsibilities. She has domestic duties to think about. But for Gerard, it's a vocation. He has dedicated himself to art, and everything he does is connected to that.'

Rowland, who rather fancied himself in the role of art expert, was in an expansive mood. He spread himself on the subject of his distinguished friend's career.

'Until quite recently,' he said, 'all Gerard's friends feared that he was turning Buddhist. He was visiting temples and attending religious ceremonies practically every day, and conducting long conversations with Buddhist monks in his fractured Sinhala. Then it turned out that he was studying the temple murals, with the idea of doing something of that kind himself. And it wasn't just an idea or a whim, because he's done it. The next time we're in Colombo, Tsunami, I'll take the two of you to see the murals he has painted at Ananda Vihara.'

'What's a mural?' Latha whispered to Tsunami.

'It's a wall-painting,' Tsunami whispered back.

'The project,' continued Rowland, 'involved Gerard in a lot of unlikely activities. Offering trays of flowers at the shrines, for instance, bowing down to the ground in front of the chief priest . . . Fancy that, Helen! A good Dutch Burgher, an old boy of All Saints', no less, prostrating himself before the filthy unwashed feet of a yellow-robed charlatan—'

Rowland had completely forgotten that his niece, daughter of a Buddhist household, was present, and listening wide-eyed to the discussion. With a discreet lift of an eyebrow, which Latha did not observe, Helen stopped her husband in mid-sentence.

'Gerard has just returned from a visit to India,' she said. 'I wonder whether Tara happened to run into him?'

'I shouldn't think it likely, India's a big country,' Rowland said. But he must have taken his wife's hint, for nothing more was heard of van Kuyk's 'unlikely activities'.

Tara, who had been touring Kashmir in the company of one of Helen's married sisters with whom she was a great favourite, returned from India in time for the last days of the van Kuyks' visit. She exclaimed with delight when she saw the paintings hanging in the hall.

'Why,' she said, 'that one's just . . . *India*!'

Helen was pleased.

'Well done, Tara,' she said. 'Many people might have missed the difference.'

An earlier visit that Gerard van Kuyk had made to India, according to Helen, had brought about notable changes in his work. The artist's interest in Sinhalese village life, for instance, had been replaced by an infatuation with India and its rural culture.

'Look again at the four paintings of his that we've just got framed, Latha,' she said. 'They are all village scenes, but Tara was able to see that one of the four is an Indian village scene, not a local one. That's Gerard's interest just now. You, Tara, Tsunami and Ran Menikē could put on saris and paint a *pottu* on your foreheads, and anyone would mistake you for Indian girls.'

'Who's Ran Menikē?' Latha asked.

There was an uncomfortable silence.

'Ran Menikē is . . . a friend of the family,' Helen said at last. 'She often models for Gerard. You know, Rowland, I think Menikē must have modelled for Gerard in at least two of the pictures we have – and I'm sure she was the model for the paintings your Thaththa bought, Latha.'

'Well, I don't want to be painted by that man,' Latha said flatly. 'Not after all the things he said about Amma and Thaththa.'

'Don't you?' Aunt Helen said. 'I'd be flattered. I wish he'd ask me!'

'He'd never dare to ask you, Mummy,' Tara said. 'He knows Pater wouldn't like it.'

'Who says so?' her father replied. 'I'd be happy to buy a picture of your mother that had been painted by Gerard. I admit, Tara, that I wouldn't be over-enthusiastic about the idea of your mother acting as an artist's model, but I have a modern mind and, though I say it myself, I believe I have a liberal outlook.' He added expansively: 'Art, after all, is art, and must find patrons if it is to exist.'

Helen said thoughtfully:

'Gerard did ask me once to bring my sitar along to his studio one evening, and play to him while he painted. "You will be my inspiration, Helen," he said. "You will be my *shakthi*."'

'What's *shakthi*?' Tsunami wanted to know.

'Soul. It means a soul, a spiritual self,' her mother replied. '"You can leave that husband of yours at home," Gerard added. "I know him – he knows nothing about music."'

'And did you go?' Latha asked. 'Did you go to his studio, Auntie Helen?'

'No, of course not,' Aunt Helen replied. But Latha noticed that she smiled a little to herself as she said it.

'If he did take your picture' – Latha had not yet understood that posing for an artist was rather different from having one's photograph taken – 'would he ask you to take all your clothes off?'

One of the paintings in the hall, in which a naked golden-skinned girl with long black hair gazed thoughtfully at a half-open lotus flower, had caused her a fair amount of puzzlement.

'He certainly might, being Gerard,' Aunt Helen said, and laughed. 'But I wouldn't pose in the nude, not even for an old friend.'

Latha was relieved to hear this, and asked no more questions. Tsunami, however, seemed to feel some further discussion was necessary.

'Latha's never seen a nude before, Mummy,' she said. 'She's shocked.'

'I'm not!' Latha said.

'Oh, come on! You know you are!' Tsunami replied.

'Well, how could Latha have seen a nude?' Uncle Rowland asked. 'We don't see them often in Ceylon. They make most people uncomfortable. Er, that is – middle-class people, of course, not people like us.' He elaborated on the subject, for Latha's benefit:

'When people here have their portraits painted, Latha, they usually dress in their best clothes. But in Europe, artists' models are quite used to posing in the nude. Painters like to show they can do more than paint frills and flounces.'

'Even if you don't have your portrait painted by Uncle Gerard, you should get him to write in your autograph album, Latha,' said Tara. 'He's a poet as well as an artist. Mummy says he'll be very famous some day. Who knows? – his signature in your album may be worth a lot of money.'

9

LATHA'S AUTOGRAPH ALBUM

Latha's autograph album was her most treasured possession. It had been given her on her seventh birthday by one of her mother's many sisters, a serious-minded aunt who treated everything, even the giving of birthday presents, as an opportunity for moral education.

'Delightful task!' this aunt had written on the fly-leaf of the album, 'To rear the tender thought, to teach the young idea how to shoot.'

On its crimson cover, the word 'Autographs' was embossed in flowing gilt script. Beneath it, in matching script, was Latha's name, and on the first page her aunt had inscribed a verse that was much admired by everyone who saw it:

Go, little Book, and tell each valued friend
For whose prized autograph I now thee send,
Tell them their words will always treasur'd be,
Links in the Golden Chain of Memory.

The pages of the album were of varied pastel shades, all except the two middle ones, which were white, and on which her aunt had painted in watercolours a 'Wall of Friendship' on which two bluebirds perched, their wings curled lovingly about each other. Her aunt explained to Latha that her dearest friends could be asked to write their names on the bricks in the wall, and then invited to write a message to her on one of the coloured pages.

The messages in Latha's album, especially those contributed by her relations, were mostly quotations from English poets and philosophers. Latha did not quite understand what many of these messages meant, but she treasured them just the same. At school, nearly every girl in her class had an album very much like hers, but the contents of theirs were rather different. They were keen collectors of 'celebrity' autographs, and they vied with one another in capturing on the pages of their albums the signatures of eminent persons and distinguished visitors to the school. Only two pages of Latha's album carried signatures that Latha herself regarded as the insignia of the great: on one of them Paula Phillips, her English teacher at Amarapāli M.V., had signed her name; on the other Santa Claus, for whom she had left a slice of Christmas cake on the dining-room table on Christmas Eve, with her album open beside it, had written:

'Thank you very much for the delicious cake, Latha. Merry Christmas! With love from Santa Claus.'

Since the members of her family led quiet, conventional lives that were out of the public eye, and hardly took her anywhere unless it was to a relative's house or to the cinema to see a children's film, Latha was in no position to compete with her classmates in the matter of collecting celebrity signatures. But there came a day which miraculously changed all that, and it was Tsunami's eldest brother, Ranil Wijesinha, who wrought the miracle.

The annual encounter between King's College and St Alban's at cricket takes place in the March of every year. This most important of the island's sporting fixtures enjoys the status of a public holiday, and both schools being elite establishments, cabinet ministers and even Prime Ministers may be seen during the match in one or other of the school pavilions, chatting with other old boys and applauding balls that have cleared the pavilion roofs or gone to the boundary. Excitement, mounting steadily in the Colleges and their 'sister-schools' in the fortnight before the King's–Albanian, reaches fever-pitch on the morning of the match. Curious things begin to happen. Quiet, well-spoken youths from perfectly respectable families turn into packs of half-inebriated ruffians and roam the city streets in hired taxi-cabs, brandishing College flags and chanting their school songs. Some, carried away by their enthusiasm, shout *baila* obscenities at the tops of their voices and, if they happen to be passing a mosque, think nothing of snatching a fez from the heads of pious Muslim gentlemen who are on their way to Friday prayers. In sporadic bursts of heroism the youths attempt to scale the walls of women's colleges all over Colombo, aware that in those colleges wait scores of adoring schoolgirls who have for the past two weeks been indicating to all and sundry where their sympathies lie by sporting rosettes in the King's College colours of purple and gold or the Albanian colours of blue and white, and who are now trembling in pleasurable anticipation of an invasion of their school grounds.

In the year that Tsunami and Latha entered the first form at their respective schools, the Principal of Ashcombe decided to have the tall gates locked and barred as soon as school sessions began on the first day of the King's–Albanian match. This sensible precaution, far from acting as a deterrent, spurred the reckless invaders on to fresh deeds of derring-do.

Tsunami and her classmates at Ashcombe crowded to their classroom window in time to see bicycles being hoisted over the gates into the school yard. Schoolboys wearing purple and gold rosettes on shirts that had been picturesquely ripped to shreds, clambered over the gates in the wake of their bicycles, and rode them defiantly all over the College grounds until forcibly evicted; while a shocking rumour, strenuously denied by the Principal, claimed that senior boarders with Albanian sympathies had tied blue and white pyjamas – *pyjamas!* – to flagpoles and waved them from the dormitory windows. With so much going on, who could concentrate on class work? Irritated members of staff complained that it was quite impossible to keep the girls at their desks and their minds on their lessons while the King's–Albanian match was either in prospect or in progress. At last the Principals of Colombo's women's colleges bowed to the inevitable, and declared the first day of the match (traditionally a Friday) a half-holiday.

Every year, in the months of February and March, the national newspapers are devoted almost exclusively to sports news, and particularly to news of school cricket. Seventeen-year-old Ranil Wijesinha's photograph, dominating the sports page of the *Ceylon Daily News* one morning, showed a tall, handsome young man in cricket whites walking out to the crease at the Tamil Union Oval to open the batting for King's College. He was pulling on his gloves as he walked, his bat tucked stylishly under his arm.

'That's your cousin Ranil,' Herbert Wijesinha told Latha, showing her the newspaper photograph. He read aloud to his wife and daughter the sports reporter's description of Rowland and Helen's eldest son.

'"A batsman of exceptional elegance and accuracy" . . . H'm. I must say I'd like to see Ranil play, Soma. Latha, would you like to come and keep me company?'

Latha went to school that morning in a blissful daze, proud in the knowledge that she was a member of that elite group at Amarapāli M.V. whose brothers and cousins were playing in the Big Match. When a senior prefect condescended to cross the playground in order to speak to her as soon as she entered the school yard, Latha realized that something unusual was happening.

'Is Ranil Wijesinha your brother?' inquired the prefect.

'N-no,' Latha said.

'A cousin, then?'

'Yes.'

She found herself immediately elevated to star status. Ranil probably didn't even know at that time that she existed, but some of his glamour had rubbed off on his young cousin. Latha discovered that she was related to a superhero with whom most of the senior girls at her school were in love.

She now learned from his many fans in the school that the cousin she had never seen was also the handsomest, the tallest, and (said one lucky soul who had actually met this superman at an inter-College debate) the most charming of all the players in the King's College eleven. Ranil's younger brother, Christopher Wijesinha, was also in the team but, said the experts, there could be no comparison between the two. When she was told that several seniors had pestered their parents to let them attend the match that afternoon, entirely for the sake of watching Ranil Wijesinha play, Latha was able to say proudly that she, too, would be there.

The Tamil Union Oval was gay with flags and fluttering pennants when Herbert and Latha arrived. All around them the air rang with the shriek of whirling rattles through which could be heard the deafening strains of College songs, sung competitively and tunelessly by several hundred shrill boyish voices from opposite sides of the cricket ground. A very smartly dressed and polite prefect stationed at the entrance gates took their tickets and escorted them to seats in the Visitors' Pavilion. Latha looked around her. In the row behind her were several fashionably dressed ladies wearing dark glasses and fanning themselves, while their husbands explored the contents of picnic baskets and opened bottles of beer. Across the grounds, in the College tents, excitement was intense. King's won the toss, and to prolonged cheering from one side of the field and dead silence from the other, Ranil Wijesinha opened batting for his College, quickly chalking up a half-century that seemed to Latha's bemused gaze to consist entirely of sixes and fours. Every time he sent a ball to the boundary, the school's small fry who had been allocated places on the greensward in front of the King's College pavilion invaded the field whooping, cheering, and waving purple and gold flags.

'"The Assyrian came down like the wolf on the fold, And his cohorts were gleaming in purple and gold", eh, duwa?' Herbert said, prepared even to forgive King's its imminent victory over his old College in view of his nephew's brilliant performance.

During the lunch interval, parties of schoolgirls walked back and forth in front of the pavilions, pretending they didn't hear the long, low whistles that followed them as they tossed their heads and self-consciously showed off their pretty new clothes. This was also, it seemed, part of the King's–Albanian ritual. Latha recognized several familiar faces from her own school in the groups of preening girls.

Latha was pleased when Herbert, having consumed the fish cutlets and egg-and-tomato sandwiches Soma had packed for their lunch, announced his intention of strolling over to the King's College tent to congratulate his nephew. She accompanied her father, her autograph album clutched in one hand and a brand-new fountain-pen in the other. Too excited and shy to speak, she stood silent while Ranil, recognizing his father's cousin and acknowledging the family connection with a courteous 'How are you,

Uncle?', patted the top of her head in a dashing, big-brotherly way. Latha had hoped to obtain Ranil's autograph; but at the end of the day's play, she found herself the proud owner of much more than that, for her cousin, with the easy generosity of a god scattering largesse, handed her album to his brother Christopher and assured Latha that Chris would get her the signatures of the entire team.

When Latha returned from the match, she went straight to the kitchen and rescued the *Daily News* from Kamala, who had been about to use it to wrap up vegetable peelings. She cut Ranil Wijesinha's photograph out of the sports page, and pasted it carefully into the scrapbook she had begun to compile that year, titled 'Very Important Events in My Life'. And it was a very important event, for as a result of her cousin's kindness, Latha found herself the envy of the whole school following the King's College victory. Each player, it seemed, had his following of devotees, and the autograph album bearing the signatures of the heroes of the day was passed reverently from hand to hand. To Latha, of course, one page was sacred:

> *Grow old along with me!*
> *The best is yet to be.*

The two rhyming lines, she believed, contained a message that was meant for her, and for her alone. She did not know then that this verse of Browning's has been for many generations a perennial standby of those who are invited to write in autograph albums. But even if she had known, Latha wouldn't have cared. Autograph albums were to her the ultimate in sophistication, and she was suffering intensely, if secretly, from a severe attack of hero-worship. She slept that month, and for several months afterwards, with her album beneath her pillow, opened at the blue page sanctified by Ranil Wijesinha's handwriting.

Although, as a result of her regular visits to Lucas Falls, she was now in constant contact with her hero, nothing had occurred to shake her devotion to her handsome cousin. Should she offer the rude and unpleasant Mr van Kuyk an opportunity to write his name in the Sacred Book? If autograph albums were intended for the signatures, not only of friends, but of celebrities, a famous painter obviously qualified for inclusion. Aunt Helen had pointed out to her, too, that though Latha did not know any members of the King's College cricket eleven personally, she had all their signatures in her book. They had signed when requested to do so because, Aunt Helen said, they knew they were celebrities. Latha thought this over, and decided finally that she would invite Mr van Kuyk to write in her album. She also decided that she would place her hand firmly over the page carrying Ranil's message, so that Mr van Kuyk could contaminate it neither with his gaze nor with his touch.

But she would not call him 'Uncle Gerry' as Tsunami did. And on no account would she let him kiss her.

On the morning that the van Kuyk family was due to depart, while their luggage was being brought downstairs into the hall, Latha produced her autograph album at the breakfast table.

'Would you write in my book, please, Mr van Kuyk?'

Gerard van Kuyk, who was a spectacularly sloppy eater even when he was not in a hurry, wiped the coconut gravy from his lips with his starched white napkin, pushed his chair back from the table, and gave Latha's album his full attention. Her plan to place her hand over Ranil's message didn't work, since the painter took the book out of her hands, and began turning the pages.

'Interesting!' he said to Latha. 'Very interesting . . . Your friends, little girl, seem to be obsessed with desire . . . a desire to have you grow up pure and virtuous. Listen to this, Rowley. These people can't get "virtue" out of their minds. On page three we have this – "*Love Virtue, she alone is free.*" Who contributed that? One of your aunts, a regular Mrs Grundy, I'll bet?'

Mrs Grundy again! Latha didn't know who Mrs Grundy was, but she nodded: it was the work of her mother's sister Caroline.

'Typical,' said van Kuyk. 'And here's another—

'"*Be good, sweet maid, and let who will be clever . . .*"

'Tell me, Latha, are you really planning to be sweet and good? What a dull life you're going to lead! Wouldn't it be much more interesting – and much more fun – being clever and wicked?'

Latha made no reply.

'Let me see if I can remember a suitably moral message that I can write in your book. Hey, what about that little verse we used to repeat at All Saints', Rowley, how did it go?

> "*Thou shalt not covet thy neighbour's wife,*
> *His ox thou shalt not slaughter,*
> *But thank the Lord it isn't a sin*
> *To covet thy neighbour's daughter . . .*"

'That would be all right, wouldn't it? Moral enough for you, young lady?'

'Do stop teasing the poor child, Gerry,' said Rosemary Vanderzeil from her chair next to Rowland. 'Let me write in her album if all you're going to do is make fun of it. Come over here, child.'

Van Kuyk didn't seem to hear her.

'Oho, here's a good one!' he went on. '"*Loss of virtue in a female is irretrievable.*" Oh, very true, very true. Always keep those wise words in mind, child. They will guide you in your path through life. And also these:

'"*Who can find a virtuous woman?*"

'Who indeed! The person who wrote that seems to have abandoned all hope, because he follows it up with—

'"*Her price is far above rubies.*"

'Was that a bachelor uncle of yours, Latha?'

Latha said nothing. Did Mr van Kuyk have second sight? Or how ever could he have known it was her father's younger brother, her Uncle Peter, who wrote that message in her album the day his fiancée broke off their engagement?

'Well, don't expect me to produce gems from the Victorians for your album, Miss,' said van Kuyk. 'But if you will lend your book to me for half an hour, I'll see what I can do.'

'Hurry up, Gerry,' his sister called, after his retreating back. 'We're all packed and ready to go.'

This was indeed the case. Trunks and boxes were waiting in the hall, packed by the children's ayah, and carried downstairs under Raman's direction. Sybil van Kuyk was coaxed out of the library, where she was still reading, presumably intending to do so until the last possible moment. The van Kuyks' Austin had barely vanished through the estate gates when:

'Lucky you! What did he write in your album?' Tsunami wanted to know.

Latha held it out to her. Aunt Helen, who had been standing in the drive waving the van Kuyk family goodbye, paused on her way into the house to look over Tsunami's shoulder.

The artist had chosen a cream-coloured page for a pen and ink drawing of two sloe-eyed young girls in Indian dress, sitting astride the branch of a tree. *Latha and Tsunami, Lucas Falls 1944*, he had written at the side of the picture, and beneath it was his signature, 'Gerard van Kuyk'. At the foot of the page was a title: '*Radha and her Confidante await the coming of Krishna*'.

'You know, Latha, I would keep that drawing very carefully if I were you,' Aunt Helen said. 'One day you may be very glad you did.'

Latha had no idea who Radha and Krishna were, or why she would be glad at some time in the future, rather than now.

'Who knows?' her cousin Tara had said. 'His signature in your album may be worth a lot of money.'

Had Aunt Helen and Tara meant the same thing? They sounded the same, but Latha sensed that there was a difference, though she couldn't put her finger on exactly what it was.

In preparation for the van Kuyks' visit, Helen Wijesinha's flower drawings, her palette, brushes and tubes of paint had been stored in a corner of the studio, and covered with a linen sheet so that they would not prove a distraction to the artist. Helping her aunt to put her studio back in order the following day, Latha came upon a pencil sketch Mrs Vanderzeil had made of Helen gathering flowers in the garden, and presumably discarded since she hadn't taken it away with her. Latha propped the sketch up on the mantelpiece and looked at it. She wondered whether her aunt would have posed in the nude if Mrs Vanderzeil had asked her to do so. The girl gathering lotuses in Mr van Kuyk's painting must, obviously, have raised no objection. Did it make a difference if the artist was a man?

Latha decided that these were two more questions which she would have to put off asking for the present. The number of such questions seemed to be growing with every holiday she spent at Lucas Falls.

As she went upstairs after dinner that evening, Latha paused to look attentively at the paintings hanging in the hall. Lit from beneath, the flesh of the girl with the lotus flower seemed to glow with a golden light. She was, Latha thought, very beautiful, with her long eyes and delicate fingers. But hadn't she minded posing for a picture with no clothes on? However 'famous' an artist her friend Mr van Kuyk might be? For Latha was shocked, though she would never have admitted it to the blasé Tsunami. She was extremely thankful that Mr van Kuyk had not taken it into his mischievous head to draw Tsunami and herself with no clothes on. She would have had to cut the page out of her precious album before she went home, to prevent her mother seeing it.

10

ART, CRAFT AND POLITICS

Helen Wijesinha had been working for several years on an ambitious project: an embroidered tablecloth intended for the long dining table at Lucas Falls. Carbon-stamped with a pattern based on her own flower drawings, it would, when complete, be hem-stitched all round, strewn with tiny satin-stitch blossoms, and carry a broad border of roses, lilies and forget-me-nots. Like the 'daily embroidery' of Mrs Transome in George Eliot's novel *Felix Holt*, the tablecloth had become a constant element in Helen's life.

To this piece of embroidery Latha, who liked to sew and embroider, was sometimes allowed to contribute a satin-stitch petal or two or a veined green leaf. She would have liked to try her developing skills on a forget-me-not, though she was not very sure at that time, never having seen a forget-me-not, whether its centre should be embroidered in yellow or in silk of some other colour. She didn't even know, in fact, whether the flower should have been blue at all. She asked Helen about that, and she was told the point had been settled for her aunt once and for all, a long time ago, by Miss Celia Whitecliff, an Anglo-Indian lady who had been her teacher at her school in Delhi. Miss Whitecliff's antecedents came from Surrey, in England; and a forget-me-not, Miss Whitecliff had declared with all the authority conferred on her by her English ancestry, was blue.

Helen told Latha she had felt, instinctively, that the centre of a forget-me-not (of whatever colour) should be crimson. What, after all, could lie at the heart of a flower so romantically named but some bright memory that must never be allowed to fade? Left to herself to match the imagined brilliance of such a memory, Helen confessed that she would have chosen the crimson silk from among all the skeins in her work-basket.

'You see, Latha,' said Helen, 'I actually *preferred* the crimson.'

She sounded guilty, almost as if she were owning up to stealing a sugar cube from the Lucas Falls sugar bowl. For it was not in the nature of things that Helen should ever have been allowed as a girl to make her own choice, even of a skein of embroidery silk. And though the blending of blue and crimson made a pleasing contrast that was, besides, easier to work on without eye-strain, Miss Whitecliff had rejected her choice outright.

'No, Helen, that won't do, my dear,' Miss Whitecliff had said when she saw the first crimson drops forming under Helen's needle. 'It won't do at all. English flowers have soft, delicate colours – try this pale yellow.'

The pale yellow was tried, and pronounced suitable, first by Miss Whitecliff and then by Helen's mother, Tsunami's Indian grandmamma.

'Sweetly pretty,' Miss Whitecliff had said, and Mrs Ratnam had agreed.

And so Helen, whose earliest paintings had displayed a love of vivid colour and a free-flowing line which had attracted Jamini Roy's attention, had learned early to suppress her fondness for what her teacher called the ugly, brutal, *wild* colours of the local Indian flora in favour of the soft pinks and muted violets of refined good taste. This early education in English aesthetics and an interest in botany that she had developed while she was at school had served Helen well when she married Rowland and became the mistress, not only of a plantation home built on the lines of an English country house in Wiltshire or Sussex, but of the famous gardens that surrounded it.

These gardens had been the creation of Arabella Lucas, the young wife of James Armitage Lucas, the energetic tea planter who had bought the estate from the Crown when it was put on the market following Lady Millbanke's mysterious death. It was from J.A. Lucas that the district and its spectacular waterfall had taken their names. Arabella must have been one of those Englishwomen Latha would later read of who consider gardening an art form. She must have certainly taken her garden very seriously. According to Rowland Wijesinha, Mrs Lucas had made use of every holiday at 'home' to visit famous gardens in Britain and Europe, and bring back seeds and bulbs for the gardeners to plant and nurture at Lucas Falls.

Latha often wondered in later years at the energy Mrs Lucas had lavished on her garden. It seemed to her that there is something desperate about such energy, something not quite right when what should be a pleasure turns into an obsession. Wherever one looked at Lucas Falls, one saw vistas of Englishness: not merely the roses, the lilies, the pansies and hollyhocks associated with country gardens in Britain, and which had flourished in the cool, moist climate of Ceylon's hill-country but, taking advantage of the broad acres afforded by her husband's magnificent property, Mrs Lucas had created avenues and walks in the style of the English eighteenth century, varied by such features as a quincunx, a bower, a stream, and even a maze. It was almost, Latha heard Mr Goldman say once, as if Arabella Lucas had been building, not merely a garden, but a wall of Englishness between herself and the threatening tropical world beyond the boundaries of her husband's estate.

Helen did not make any important changes in Mrs Lucas's original design for the garden. It had been made very clear to her that her task as inheritor and successor was to keep things as they were, blooming and beautiful, and this task she performed to her own credit and her husband's, so that under her care Lucas Falls Estate maintained its reputation as a showplace. But she retained her love of wild flowers, and devoted a small section of the garden exclusively to their planting and nurture. This was entirely a personal and private interest of Helen's own. Neither Tara nor Tsunami shared it, but Latha did, and Helen often asked Latha to join her in this special section of the garden. She seemed to be happiest when, with a sketchbook and pencils in the pocket of her gardening smock, she was walking along the paths, choosing blossoms. When she had made her selection she would stand the flowers in a glass of water and set Latha to sketch them, seating herself opposite her niece at a little table in her studio that was specially dedicated to this activity. She taught Latha the Latin name of every indigenous plant and flower they drew together, writing beside it in tiny script in Latha's sketchbook the Sinhala or Tamil name for each.

Latha had noticed during her visits to Tsunami's family at Lucas Falls that not all her Aunt Helen's creations were intended for public display. Some of her aunt's artistic interests seemed to be pursued entirely for her private pleasure. One corner of her garden, for instance, was devoted to flowers she had imported from India. This 'Indian' section did not occupy a large area and, perhaps because it was not quite in keeping with the rest of the garden as planned by Arabella Lucas and maintained by her successors, it was screened from general view by a hedge of colourful crotons. Latha noticed that her aunt spent a lot of time there, and that she had had a wooden garden seat installed beneath a shady tree to which she often retreated with a book or some embroidery. Though small, the 'Indian garden' had a beauty of its own, and as Latha had many opportunities to notice, her aunt liked to be surrounded by beautiful things.

Some of the things in which her aunt seemed to take most pleasure were of her own devising, but Latha thought that every one of them, however insignificant, had something special and delicate about it. Even her fine cotton petticoats, which hung in a camphor-wood closet in her dressing room, were a wonder to behold, with double rows of lace inserted at knee and hem, and white silk flowers embroidered in between.

To Latha it seemed the ultimate in luxury that undergarments which no one but the wearer ever saw should be so lovely to look at and so delicate to touch. Her mother sniffed scornfully when Latha described her Aunt Helen's petticoats to her, and said they were a waste of money, typical of a woman who had her clothes made to order by a dressmaker. (Latha's petticoats, like her mother's, were made of serviceable poplin, and were sewn by her mother on an old Singer sewing machine that she had brought with her to her marriage.) When Latha said that the petticoats were made and embroidered by Aunt Helen herself, and not by a dressmaker, not even by Alice, Soma pretended not to hear.

What other aspects of her aunt's life were there, Latha sometimes wondered privately, which she kept entirely to herself?

The visitors who had been due to arrive a few days after the van Kuyk family's memorable visit did not appear after all: influenza, it appeared, had hindered their plans. It seemed to Latha that her Aunt Helen was not displeased by their failure to show up, even though one of them (Rowland's cousin Moira) was the aspiring artist he had described to her, whose watercolours were much admired in the extended Wijesinha family. Helen said nothing, however, on the subject. The visit was eventually paid, but it was paid quite a long time later, in 1946, a date Latha never forgot because the visit coincided with another of a quite different kind that was to bring about significant change in the household she had come to know and love.

A deputation of 'notables', influential persons of the district, visited Lucas Falls one morning, to call on Rowland Wijesinha. Latha heard later (from Tara and Chris) that they had come with a request: would the master of Lucas Falls allow his name to be put forward by them for election to Ceylon's new Parliament?

Helen was in the garden with Latha, Tsunami and Colin when this deputation arrived, but Moira Wijesinha, who had duly arrived with her mother to pay their long-deferred visit to Lucas Falls, had been on hand to welcome it. Moira's mother had been delighted with the proposal, and she had urged Rowland to accept it.

'Your mother would be so pleased to see you go in for politics,' she told Rowland. 'Ceylon needs people from families like ours to steer things in the right direction – and here is a chance for you to serve your country.'

Moira, one of the young women in Rowland's family whose hopes of marrying him had collapsed with the unexpected advent of Helen Ratnam, outsider from India, was equally enthusiastic.

'You are so talented, Rowland Aiya,' said she. 'Just see what a good brain you have, and such clever ideas. All the time, whenever you are talking, there is something everyone can learn. My word, Amma, you should have heard how Rowland Aiya was explaining to me yesterday about the paintings of De Gass, all this time I have been thinking De Gass just painted pictures of ballot dancers, but now I can really understand that there is a meaning behind them.'

Rowland bridled.

'Now, now, you mustn't feel shy to hear me saying so!' Moira gave her cousin's shoulder a playful push. 'It is the truth I am telling, isn't it, you are such an educated, such an intellectual person! What Amma is saying is quite right, Rowland Aiya, you really should go in for politics.'

'What you are waiting for, Rowland, I just don't know,' said her mother.

'Oh, come, Aunt Eliza, do you really think our parliamentarians would be interested in hearing me discuss the French Impressionists?'

But just as Rowland had not corrected Moira's pronunciation of 'ballet' or 'Degas' he had not disagreed with her estimate of his capabilities.

'Pater pretended he wasn't interested, but you could see he was most frightfully bucked by the invitation,' Chris reported to the others when the deputation had taken its leave. 'And he didn't seem to mind Auntie Moira and her mother gushing all over him, either.'

'Oo-ooh, Rowland Aiya, you *must* go in for politics, you simply *must*,' mimicked Colin, in a high falsetto, and was quelled by a glance from Chris.

'Mummy says people change when they take to politics,' Tara said. 'She says it happened in her own family: her favourite brother, Uncle Badrinath, joined the Congress Party because he admired Mr Gandhi and shared his ideals and philosophies. Well, Mummy admires Mr Gandhi too, but it wasn't Mr Gandhi who ran the Congress Party! And politics changed Uncle Badri from the person he'd been to someone Mummy says she no longer wanted to know.'

'*Pater* wouldn't change,' Tsunami said loyally. 'I know he wouldn't, not even if they made him Prime Minister.'

'Frankly, I didn't care for the person who led that deputation,' Chris said. 'He actually told Pater that it was a pity he happened to be married to an Indian lady, because this district is mostly populated by Sinhalese people, and Pater's having an Indian wife would substantially lessen his chances of being elected.'

Colin was furious.

'What cheek!' said he. 'Why didn't Pater tell him to push off? Fancy coming here, and parking himself on our veranda, and telling Mummy she's not wanted in her own house? And tucking into Vaithi's patties and sandwiches, too.'

'Mummy wasn't there,' Chris reminded his brother. 'She was in the garden with Latha, remember? When the deputation arrived, it was Auntie Moira and her mother who greeted them. They were sitting on the veranda, waiting for Alexander to bring the car round.'

'Yes, and I'll bet they stayed on to listen,' Colin said. 'And I'll bet they'll tell everyone in Colombo how that person insulted Mummy. Just wait and see. How could Pater let that man talk about her like that in front of them?'

'It wasn't quite like that,' Chris said. 'The man didn't insult anyone. In fact, he was very quiet, very well behaved. He told Pater he hoped no one would take offence, he was just stating facts. About the way people act

saying she had to discuss with Vaithi his preparations for the New Year celebration.

In the days that followed the two ladies' visit, everything seemed just the same as before, yet Latha sensed that something was amiss. Something had occurred within the family she loved that she could not understand. The very atmosphere in the house had distinctly altered, but whether this was due to the fact that the master and mistress of the house seemed to have little to say to each other these days, or not, Latha couldn't make out.

11

SEEING THE NEW YEAR IN

Turning the pages of her autograph album in later years, Latha found that her cousin Ranil's blue page was one among many in which different people at various stages of her childhood and adolescence had urged her towards a variety of contradictory destinies.

Only Tsunami (and Gerard van Kuyk), it seemed to her, hadn't urged her to do or be anything. Tsunami had simply contributed an observation:

In this world of froth and bubble,
Two things stand like stone,
Kindness in another's trouble,
Courage in your own.

Unlike most of the other contributors to Latha's album, her cousin had remembered to mention the source of her quotation.

'Who's Adam Lindsay Gordon?' Latha asked her father.

It was a name unknown to either of her parents. The appearance of an Australian poet's name in a Ceylonese child's autograph album in the 1940s says something about the wide range of books available to the children of the Lucas Falls household. The bookshelves in Rowland and Helen Wijesinha's library were open to anyone who wanted to read, the only rule being the same one Latha's father insisted on in Colombo with regard to reference books in his study: that a book, when borrowed, had to be put back in the precise place on the shelf from which it had been taken.

But there were some differences. Latha's aunts, and even her mother, did not encourage reading.

'Just look at this girl, always bent over a book! If you go on like this, child, you'll grow up chicken-chested!'

This was a comment with which Latha was very familiar. At Lucas Falls, however, her cousins read all the time, and nobody told them they should not. Besides, in that house ruled by a wealthy man who prided himself on his modern mind and liberal outlook, not only was the range of available books much greater, but nothing was forbidden. Nothing on Rowland and Helen Wijesinha's shelves, it seemed, was unsuitable for children to read. Herbert Wijesinha who, as a young man, had read *Lady Chatterley's Lover* and other novels by D.H. Lawrence in pirated versions, smuggled out to 'the East' by enterprising European booksellers, and now kept them in an obscure corner of his study shielded from disapproving eyes by protective precipices of *Punch* and *London Life*, would have been surprised to learn that well before she was twelve years old his daughter had encountered not only Lawrence but Oscar Wilde. (And not merely Wilde's *The Happy Prince* or *The Nightingale and the Rose* – though those had sent her to bed in tears – but the trial proceedings that had sent *him* to prison). Such reading went on entirely unsupervised at Lucas Falls: side by side with Agatha Christie and Dorothy L. Sayers and Edgar Allan Poe, Latha and her cousins read the *Decameron* and *Our Mutual Friend.*

Like its well-stocked library of imaginative literature, many of the things Latha most enjoyed at Lucas Falls were pastimes of which most of her relations would not have seen the point. Word-games, for instance, nonsensical rhymes, and her cousins' habit of capping quotations. The merest thing, it seemed, could set them off.

'Look at that jasmine creeper on the fence!' Tara said one day, raising her eyes from a book to look out of the drawing-room window. 'It's covered all over with red tips. The season must be changing.'

Behind her, Chris intoned instantly:

'"Tis springtime now, the festive cow . . ."'

And Colin completed the couplet with:

'"Hilarious, leaps from bough to bough."'

'Oh, do shut up, children,' Tara said in her most grown-up voice. 'You're being very silly.'

Whereupon everyone within earshot had shrieked with laughter. What would Latha's mother have made of that? Tsunami and Latha had their favourite rhymes, too, and took turns reciting them.

Tsunami: 'One for sorrow, two for joy.'
Latha: 'Three for a wedding, four for a boy.'
Tsunami: 'Five for silver, six for gold—'
Both, together: '—Seven for a story never told!'

P.G. Wodehouse, Ogden Nash, Harry Graham, everything the Lucas Falls children read – and they read a great deal – was grist to their mill. Latha's cousins had developed a way of talking that was made up almost entirely of quotations and amounted to a private code. A visiting aunt whose tight corsets tended to bring on fainting spells that she invariably described in graphic detail when she called on Helen, was once addressed to her face by the poker-faced Colin (recruited to help hand round sandwiches and cakes) as 'Auntie Mabel'.

'Why do you call me Auntie Mabel, dear, when my name is Clarissa?' she inquired mildly.

'Because you faint a lot, Auntie,' he replied.

The aunt, though somewhat mystified, let this explanation pass. When, after her visitor had left, his mother reproached him for his rudeness, he replied that his remark hadn't been rude at all, since Aunt Clarissa didn't understand jokes anyway, so couldn't possibly have understood him.

'Whereas,' he added, after Helen had gone upstairs, 'she'd have understood me all right if I'd asked her if Uncle Tom was keeping pretty fit these days, because—"'

'"Uncle Tom and Auntie Mabel",' Tara chipped in, '"fainted at the breakfast table . . ."'

'"Children! You must take this warning",' Chris continued; and Ranil finished it for him –

'"Never do it in the morning!"'

Latha and Tsunami, quite as puzzled as their aunt, gazed wonderingly at Ranil.

'Never do what?' they asked him in chorus.

'Why, never faint of course.'

When Latha came up to Lucas Falls for the first time, she found herself in Ranil's godlike company practically every day. She was apt to become silent and abstracted if he were anywhere near; thankfully, nobody seemed to notice that at least one little girl in the household was living in a world of wishes and golden dreams. If there were a new moon in the sky, Latha would be the first to hold up her gold bangle to it and make a wish. Every time a kingfisher flashed past in a brilliant blue blur, Latha made a wish. Each wish, naturally, related in some way to the object of her devotion.

One of Latha's favourite fantasies had her walking up the nave of St Mark's Church in a cloud of white tulle, towards Ranil handsome in naval uniform, with Tsunami bringing up the rear as bridesmaid while an angelic choir trilled tunefully in the background. In another, she was aboard a slow boat to China on the deck of which heroic Captain Ranil lay helpless and unconscious, while a gash on his noble brow was tenderly and efficiently bandaged up by Nurse Latha in Red Cross uniform. The fact that the hero of her daydreams took hardly any notice of her except to pass her the butter-dish at breakfast time, or remind her that it was her turn to throw the dice for Ludo, mattered not at all to Latha. She went on dreaming.

Latha's adoration of her personable cousin was an entirely different thing from her affection for his younger sister. Her dreams of him occupied nearly every waking moment. And a few days before her twelfth birthday, an incident occurred which invested Ranil's image with an aura of gallantry in Latha's mind that it never quite lost, despite everything that happened afterwards.

It is a tradition in the Westernized branch of Latha's family that New Year's Day is celebrated as 'open house'. From around two o'clock in the afternoon, the long table in the dining room at Lucas Falls would be set with crystal, silver, and lace-trimmed linen, and laden with traditional savouries, cakes and sweets. A steady stream of visitors would call on Rowland and Helen Wijesinha until well past eleven at night. Latha's parents would not, of course, be observing the ritual in Colombo. Since her mother observed the 'open house' tradition only at the Sinhala New Year in April, and did so then on much less grand a scale, Herbert would have to content himself with calling on his relatives on the first of January, to drink their health in arrack and imported whisky.

New Year festivities as they were observed at Lucas Falls demanded a good deal of organization. Her Aunt Helen had, Latha knew, spent days in consultation with Raman, and she had that very day been personally supervising preparations in the kitchen.

For it was New Year's Eve, and the Lucas Falls household, having finished dinner, was talking about going early to bed. Rowland looked at his watch, remarked that it was nine o'clock, and stated that he expected everyone in the family to attend church in the morning, and be on hand to greet guests in the afternoon. This was bitterly disappointing to Latha. She would be twelve years old on the fifteenth of January, and there were all kinds of grown-up things she had been secretly planning to do at the stroke of midnight on New Year's Eve, resolutions she wanted to make, romantic wishes she wanted to write on pieces of paper and send whirling up the drawing-room chimney as heroines did in books (there was no such thing as a drawing-room chimney in Herbert and Soma's house in Colombo).

'Aren't we going to stay up to see the New Year in, Uncle Rowland?' Latha asked.

'Oh, I don't think so, Latha,' replied her uncle. 'I want an early night: New Year's Day or not, there'll be the estate muster in the morning.'

Aunt Helen, too, didn't intend to stay up. Nor did Latha's cousins, not even Tsunami. Tara wanted to finish sewing coffee-coloured lace trimming on to the green silk dress she planned to wear next day to church: she needed to use her mother's sewing machine, and the machine was upstairs. Chris and Colin had been on a hike, and said they were too dead tired to do anything but drop into bed. Ranil was nowhere to be seen.

'All right, then,' Latha said with reckless daring. 'I'll stay up by myself.'

Rowland looked sharply in her direction, and she added hastily: 'If Auntie and Uncle don't mind.'

'I should warn you, Latha, that the estate generator stops working at ten o'clock,' Rowland said. 'All the lights in the house will cut out automatically. How will you cope with that?'

'I can get the child some candles,' Helen suggested. 'But . . . do you think you'll be all right, Latha? Are you sure you won't be frightened, all by yourself?'

'The ghost of Lady Millbanke will float through the drawing-room wall, Latha, and bite off your fingers, one by one,' Colin said. 'Did you know she walks at midnight on New Year's Eve? And her spectral voice will sound in your terrified ears: *Oo-oo-oo-oo, ah-h-h-h . . .*'

'Quite sure, Auntie,' Latha said.

'Bet she'll be scared stiff,' Colin said. 'Bet that when Jeeves comes in to draw the curtains and open the windows tomorrow morning, he'll find Latha stretched out on the rug, dead with fright. Or else, she'll be dead asleep.'

'You're wrong,' Latha said.

'Okay, bet you ten rupees I'm not.'

It was too late to retract. She was in for it now, whether she liked it or not. Though very nearly twelve years old and practically grown up, Latha was afraid of the dark; and the more she thought about Lady Millbanke's ghost and the lonely hours that she would have to pass all by herself in that big drawing room in a dark and silent house, waiting for her to appear, the less she liked it. But she was certainly not going to admit it.

Without a word to anyone, Tsunami left the room and returned with her teddy bear, Frederick. Latha made a place for Frederick beside her on Aunt Helen's Chesterfield sofa, glad that he was so big and soft and warm. She was aware that Frederick had never been known to spend a night apart from his owner, and she appreciated Tsunami's gesture.

'Here, Latha,' Chris said, 'this will help pass the time.'

He put *The Adventures of Sherlock Holmes* on the table near the fireplace, and on it his copy of *Gulliver's Travels.*

'You needn't bother,' Colin told his elder brother. 'She won't get beyond page six.'

'Shut up, brat,' Chris said. 'I'll bet you another ten chips she will. *And* I'll expect you to pay up on the dot, tomorrow morning before breakfast.'

He gave Latha an encouraging pat on the shoulder, and went off to bed.

'Har, har,' Colin said, undeterred. 'Poor old Chris! A gallant knight, withal – but he's lost his money. Latha'll come screaming up the stairs in half an hour.'

'What's all this? What's all this?'

It was Ranil, overflowing with self-confidence, positively glowing with energy. (Latha wondered what on earth her cousin had been doing: climbing? playing tennis? swimming by the Falls?) He was late for dinner, but in no doubt, obviously, that everyone would be delighted to see him. He pulled out a chair, flung himself into it, and declared that he was famished. His father looked severely at him over his spectacles.

'And where were you this evening, may one ask?' Rowland inquired. 'Your mother had dinner put back by half an hour, entirely on your account.'

Ranil looked suitably abashed.

'I'm sorry, Pater.'

He had, he said, been spending the evening with a group of College friends in town.

'You could have telephoned us, Ranil,' Helen said gently.

'Sorry, Mummy. Just didn't think of it. You know how it is when pals get together. Hey, Raman! Any pudding left?'

Helen rang the bell for Raman. While Ranil wolfed down what was left of dinner, Colin told his brother all about his bet with Latha and Chris. Feeling extremely foolish, Latha tried to make herself invisible beside Frederick in her corner of the sofa. Ranil heard Colin out attentively. Then:

'So you want to see the New Year in, Latha?' he said. 'And not one of these miserable rascals will help you to do it? Well, I think that's just too bad. Give me a minute to get changed, and I'll keep you company.'

Her cousin was certainly in towering spirits, Latha thought. She could hardly believe her ears. All year she had been dreaming up romantic scenarios in which she and Ranil would walk alone in the moonlight or swim lazily among water lilies in tropical lagoons. In between these blissful interludes, she would dazzle him with the brilliance of her witty small talk. Latha had read *The Importance of Being Ernest* in the Lucas Falls copy of Wilde's works, and she had her answer ready for the moment when Ranil would ask her if she kept a diary.

'Of course,' she would reply carelessly. 'I take my diary everywhere with me: one must always have something sensational to read in the train.'

Now, however, now that the moment had actually arrived in which she would be spending three whole hours alone in the company of her idol, Latha didn't know whether to be happy or terrified. She wondered what she could possibly find to do or say that would interest and amuse her sophisticated cousin. Helen, for her part, was relieved that Latha would have some company in her lonely vigil. She gave her son a grateful look before she set some tall white candles in the candelabra, placed a matchbox beside them, wished the young people a happy New Year, and followed her husband upstairs.

'Now, Latha,' Ranil said, when they were alone in the drawing room, 'you and I are going to play cards.'

He wheeled the card-table nearer to the fire, opened it up, drew up three chairs, and sat Frederick in one of them.

'There,' he said, 'Frederick can keep score.'

He glanced at his wrist-watch and handed Latha the cards.

'Which game shall we start with?'

Latha hesitated. Beggar-My-Neighbour? No. Old Maid? Definitely not!

'I'd like to play Snap,' she said.

'Okay. Snap it is. Why don't you shuffle those cards while I get a couple of candles lit? Then I'll cut.'

Latha was so nervous that she dropped the cards on the green baize table-top instead of shuffling them. Ranil didn't seem to notice. While she was retrieving them, he placed the candelabra on the table between them.

'Fine,' he said. 'Now deal.'

Latha obeyed. As she did so, the clock in the hall struck ten. Every note seemed to reverberate through the silent house.

'Deal, Latha!' commanded Ranil.

As Latha placed the fourth card on the baize cloth, all the lights in the drawing room went out. She was very conscious of the darkness surrounding the little pool of candle-light in which they sat playing cards, but Ranil paid no attention.

Two more hours, Latha thought. How ever shall we get through them? It was not that she dreaded falling asleep, for she was wide awake and alert to every sound. It was just that she had never been alone with a young man before. Whatever would her parents say when they came to know about her midnight tryst with Ranil? For they would be bound to find out. Sooner, rather than later, one of Latha's cousins – Colin, for sure – would be bound to mention it.

'Oh, did you know, Auntie, that Latha saw the New Year in with Ranil . . . ?'

Better to tell them herself, Latha thought.

'Amma, Ranil Aiya did such a kind thing last holidays, he offered . . .'

No, that wouldn't do, Amma would see through it at once. Latha decided to swear Tara and Tsunami to secrecy: the boys were unlikely, after all, to get chatting with her mother.

'What's the matter?' Ranil asked. 'Cat got your tongue?'

Latha abandoned her thoughts of home and concentrated instead on the cards. Her feelings about this incident were hers alone, she decided, and she would never reveal them to anyone, not even to Tsunami. As the minutes ticked slowly by and they went from Snap to Rummy to Beggar-My-Neighbour to Patience, and finally to whist and the rudiments of bridge, Latha occasionally stole a glance at her cousin.

Ranil was indeed very good-looking – like Gregory Peck in *The Keys of the Kingdom*, Latha thought – and he had a trick of furrowing his brow in concentration which was very much like his little sister's. With only two players, their choice of games was restricted, but still they did well. She was left wondering at the number of games people played with an ordinary pack of cards – although the pack with which she and Ranil were playing was by no means ordinary. The cards in Latha's hand carried a picture on their backs of a lady in a pale blue dress, with a great deal of lace and transparent gauze at her neck and wrists, and silver-white curls piled high on her head. Many years later, in a London art gallery, Latha saw the picture again in a portrait by Gainsborough.

The pinewood logs glowed red in the fireplace, and one of them fell apart with a sudden burst of sparks and a bang that made Latha jump.

'Did you know it's five minutes to midnight?' Ranil asked.

They put the cards away, folded up the table, and pushed their chairs back. When Latha stood up, her knees were stiff and painful. She realized that her head had begun to ache. Ranil snuffed out the candles, they walked out of the drawing room, and stood together in front of the grandfather clock at the foot of the staircase in the hall, where a single petrol lamp was kept burning all night.

Neither Ranil nor Latha said a word. The hands of the clock came together as they watched, there was a kind of whirring sound that seemed to come from deep inside the works, and slowly, very slowly and almost meditatively, the clock began to strike twelve. One, two, three, four, five, six, seven . . .

'Happy New Year, Latha,' Ranil said.

He put his hand under her chin, and looked reflectively for a moment into her upturned face. Latha instinctively shut her eyes and waited for whatever would happen next. When she opened them, he was still looking down at her.

'You're a very cute kid,' he said and then, inexplicably: 'We should think about putting a Ten Year Plan in place.'

He seemed about to say something more, but appeared to change his mind. He hesitated for a long moment, then placed an arm around Latha's waist, bent down and kissed her on her forehead.

'Happy New Year, my beautiful cousin,' Ranil said.

Colin was the first person down to breakfast the following morning. By the time Latha and Tsunami came in, early morning sunshine was streaming through the windows, and the festive meal was well under way.

Ranil came in, and surveyed his younger brother's loaded plate.

'Left anything for the rest of us?' he inquired.

When Colin nodded, his mouth full, Ranil affected amazement. He lifted the silver dish covers on the sideboard, and helped himself to the milk-white, diamond-shaped pieces of milk rice and to its seven traditional accompaniments.

'Genius, pure genius!' he said, and on the other side of the hatch, Vaithi, who was supervising service in the pantry, smiled with pleasure.

'By the way, putha,' Ranil added, seating himself next to Colin, 'you've lost your bet. Latha didn't doze off once. Did you, Latha?'

'No,' said Latha. She found it impossible to look at Ranil. Following his kiss, she had gone off to bed in a daze of happiness, and had found sleep long in coming. 'Lady Millbanke didn't turn up, either.'

The truth was, that she had forgotten all about Lady Millbanke until this moment. She added:

'But I'm very sleepy now. And I forgot all about making my resolutions, Auntie, and sending my wishes up the chimney.'

'Never mind, dear,' Helen said from her place behind the coffee-pot. 'You can do that next year.'

Ranil's kiss was one among many unexpected things that happened during that holiday season at Lucas Falls. The events which followed soon afterwards were so remarkable, and they cast such long shadows over the lives of everyone in the household that they obliterated everything else. No one ever remembered to mention New Year's Eve, 1947, to Latha's mother or to anyone else.

But Latha never forgot it. Nor did she forget the fragrance the pine logs yielded as they crackled and glowed in the marble fireplace, the soft rustle of cards being shuffled and dealt in the silent drawing room, or the golden glow of candle-light in which she had sat with her cousin Ranil on the night he tutored her in the games that grown-ups play.

12

FALLING FROM GRACE

'Latha baba, Tsunami baba, where are you? Madam is calling for you.'

Alice, who was on her way to check the dhobi's laundry list, looked in at Rowland's library door to deliver this message. She knew the girls must be in the library because she had already looked everywhere else, but she did not see them at first, since Tsunami and Latha had each appropriated one of the two large leather chairs that stood on opposite sides of the fireplace. The wings of the chairs completely hid them and the books they were reading from view, an advantage of which both were well aware, and of which Tsunami in particular made good use when she knew she was being summoned to do something she did not particularly like doing.

'Why?' Tsunami inquired.

She was absorbed in *The ABC Murders*, and her thoughts were focused entirely on Agatha Christie.

'Visit to aunties,' returned Alice, and did not stay for an answer.

'Oh, goody,' said Tsunami, temporarily shelving Poirot. 'Come on, Latha, let's go.'

During the many holidays she spent at Lucas Falls, Latha was to accompany her aunt on several such visits, most times with Tsunami for company and once without (Tsunami being on that occasion in bed with a cold). On this, her first such excursion, the big car, with Tsunami seated at the front, Helen and Latha in the back, and a uniformed Alexander at the wheel, negotiated the curves of the winding estate road with ease. They soon left the trim tea bushes of the estate behind, to head for more open spaces. The road grew rockier, and the trees disorderly. Latha had expected that their destination would be yet another tea plantation, containing yet another 'Auntie' – a pretty lady like her Aunt Helen, except that quite unlike Aunt Helen who had plenty to occupy her and never complained about anything, the first thing their hostess would do would be to exclaim that she had been 'dying for company'.

'Aiyo, child, it's so nice of you to come and see me . . . I am all alone all day with nothing to do when Annesley is in the field,' was the burden of frequent appeals to her aunt from the wives of tea planters employed on St Cloud, Dambatenne, Glenanore, Golconda, Craig and other neighbouring estates. But the car descended to the main road, and travelled a good thirty miles away from the tea district before it entered a small town and came to rest in front of a house with a little patch of garden at the front of it and a hint of a washing line at the back.

Sure enough, there was an 'Auntie' waiting on the front steps to greet Aunt Helen. But unlike the trim and elegant planters' wives who usually visited the Wijesinhas, and were visited by them, this one was a plump auntie in a rather grubby housecoat, with her hair lying loose and untidily on her shoulders. She looked to Latha as if she had just got out of bed. Two of the buttons on the front of the housecoat were, Latha noticed, undone. The two ladies greeted each other affectionately, and kissed with enthusiasm.

'How nice! You've brought the children!' said their hostess as Latha and Tsunami emerged from the car.

She enveloped first Tsunami, then Latha in a warm, somewhat sticky embrace, from which they emerged slightly dazed from the pressure, and also from a powerful scent of lily-of-the-valley. Helen shrugged her shoulders expressively, and the 'Auntie' smiled a smile of perfect understanding.

'We must find something really interesting for you to do, darling,' she said to Tsunami. 'Would you like to play in the garden?'

Tsunami, who hated being addressed as 'darling', shook her head, and politely said:

'No, thank you.'

'There's a swing in the garden,' coaxed the 'Auntie'. 'Why don't we ask your driver to give you a push . . .?'

Tsunami, at her most blasé, said:

'It's too hot to go outside in the garden, Auntie. Both Latha and I would rather be inside, in the shade.'

There was no disputing such an argument. Everyone knows children must not be permitted to play in the sunshine, for fear of 'getting sunstroke'. The two ladies exchanged glances.

'I've brought some books along,' Helen volunteered. 'Latha's a great reader, aren't you, Latha?'

'Just like her cousins, no?' said the Auntie, whose home (as far as Latha could see) was entirely innocent of either books or bookshelves. 'Always with their noses buried in a book!'

Tsunami shot her a look of hatred, looked meaningfully at her cousin, and shook her head imperceptibly. Latha, who had been about to say 'Oh, yes!' and reach for one of the proffered books, remained silent while Tsunami looked critically through the books Alexander brought from the car.

'They're all baby books, Mummy,' said she with scorn.

'But you were reading Wren and Andersen only the other day, Tsunami,' Helen reminded her. 'You didn't say *Beau Geste* was a baby book then?'

Tsunami did not reply.

'Oh, dear,' Helen said, and turned to her friend. 'I had no idea they wouldn't settle down . . .'

Eventually the two ladies sat down together at one end of the small sitting room, and Tsunami and Latha were persuaded to begin a game of chess on the veranda, on a board which the Auntie, in a sudden fit of inspiration, produced from a cupboard.

Latha wondered why Tsunami had urged her to come all this way merely to be bored. She would have much preferred the leather chair in her uncle's library. Tsunami, as usual, read her cousin's thoughts.

'Just wait a bit, Latha,' she said. 'Wait until they get going.'

A great virtue of the game of chess is that it is played in perfect silence. In the sitting room the two ladies communicated in whispers. Aunt Helen's friend got up from time to time and looked into the veranda, where both children were obviously deep in concentrated thought. She went to the kitchen door, gave orders to an invisible person that tea should be brought without delay, and returned to the sitting room. She drew her cane-bottomed chair so close to Helen's that their knees were practically touching.

'So then,' said she to Aunt Helen, 'he shut the door, and locked it. What could I do? But I had no time even to say anything, aney, or call out to the servant, because then he threw me backwards onto the bed—'

Latha was soon to discover that her Aunt Helen knew several 'Aunties' plump of figure and slightly haggard of face, who lived alone with one or two servants in tiny suburban houses very like this one, and could usually be found in the daytime hours dressed in kimonos or housecoats with their long hair unbound, or untidily swept into buns or nets. They tended to smell heavily of stale scent, read soppy novels with well-thumbed, dog-eared pages, and had tales to tell of their sexual experiences that were occasionally sentimental and invariably graphic. They were all unfailingly delighted to see Helen. Latha discovered that accompanying her aunt on these expeditions paid off handsomely, since the visits invariably involved a sumptuous tea featuring patties, ham sandwiches, cream buns, a luscious fruit or lemon cake, and chocolate éclairs. Their surroundings might be slovenly, and their persons dishevelled, but the 'Aunties' certainly did themselves well in the food department. As Tsunami said, the chocolate éclairs alone were worth coming for; on top of which, as she pointed out, there was all the valuable information to be carried away from these 'visits'.

Latha puzzled over Aunt Helen's visits (and the assorted information to be gained therefrom) for some time before she asked her cousin who exactly these mysterious 'Aunties' were, and why they never paid return visits to Lucas Falls.

Tsunami's answer was more puzzling than the mystery itself.

'Oh, they're mistresses,' she said airily. 'And don't say anything about them at home, because Pater's forbidden Mummy to have anything to do with them.'

'Mistresses? But Auntie Helen is a mistress. She's mistress of Lucas Falls, isn't she?'

'Not like that, silly,' replied Tsunami. 'These Aunties are *people's* mistresses. Mummy and Pater used to know them a long time ago, when their husbands were alive, before Colin and I were born. Then their husbands died, and they didn't have as much money to entertain with as they'd had when their husbands were still around. So people they knew stopped being keen on inviting them to their parties and dinners, because they couldn't return invitations. And after a bit they fell from grace.'

'*Fell from grace?* What does that mean?'

'It means they did something which stopped anyone wanting to have anything more to do with them. Like being sent to Coventry.'

'What did they do?'

'Oh, I don't know . . . Different things . . . Well, for a start, that Auntie we visited yesterday had a baby years after her husband died. It's something you mustn't do, because after you've done something like that, you don't get asked anywhere, and people stop visiting you.'

'Oh, I see,' Latha said. 'It's like when you have measles.'

She'd had measles the previous year, and the enforced isolation that measles brought with it had caused her to suffer dreadfully.

'Well, yes, I suppose it is, a bit,' Tsunami said doubtfully. 'Except that some people visit them all the time. Especially the people they're mistresses of . . .'

'And Auntie Helen,' Latha said thoughtfully.

'Yes, Mummy visits them regularly. She has four friends she used to know when she first married Pater, and they were all great friends, played bridge together at the Planters' Club, and tennis, and mahjong. Then their husbands died—'

'Of what?'

'Oh, *I* don't know. Heart attacks and strokes and things, I suppose. And after that they fell from grace.'

'It's pretty nice of Auntie Helen to keep on visiting her friends when everybody else has sent them to Coventry,' Latha said after some reflection.

'Well, Mummy must be the only one who does it – I've never met anyone else visiting them, when we visit. Because I always go, you see. Mummy always takes me with her.'

'Like she took me,' Latha said. '*Why* does she take us with her?'

'Oh, Alexander told me once it's because of gossip,' Tsunami said. 'Alexander admires Mummy like anything. He says everyone is jealous of her because she's so pretty and clever, and he says he hopes I'll always go visiting with her when she asks me to, because no one can ever say anything really unkind about a lady who goes visiting with her daughter.'

And her niece, Latha thought. She felt very proud that she had been invited to act as a shield for her beloved aunt when she was going sick-visiting.

'Does Tara go?'

'Don't know,' Tsunami said. 'Maybe Mummy's never asked her.'

After a while, during which Latha turned over and over in her mind the information Tsunami had provided –

'Tsunami, don't the Aunties ever get well?' she asked.

The measles had not, after all, lasted for ever.

'No, never.' Tsunami was quite certain about that. 'Once it happens, it happens for always. Like the prison sentence in *The Man in the Iron Mask*. But don't look so worried, Latha, they're quite happy. Some of the people-they're-mistress-of are quite important people, and rich, too. The one who belongs to that last Auntie we visited – the Auntie with a bit of a squint – he's a Minister in the State Council, Alexander says. And he adores chocolate éclairs, so she has them ready for him every time he comes to see her, even though he's getting awfully fat, and they're not at all good for him. He's a bachelor, so she says it's up to her to provide him with all his home comforts . . .'

'What's a bachelor?' Latha asked.

'It means he's not married.'

'You mean, most of them are married?'

'Oh, yes. There's an Auntie who lives in Bandarawela, the person-she's-mistress-of is married, and has three children. But he's got heaps of other girlfriends, too, and he gets a terrific kick out of telling Auntie all about them. All the details. What they do together, and so on. Then she tells Mummy . . . When Mummy goes to see her, you can hear shrieks of laughter coming from the sitting room all the time—'

'Do you always listen in?'

'Always,' Tsunami said. 'If you don't listen in, how would you ever know what's going on?'

Her Uncle Rowland, Latha noted, did not accompany her aunt on her sick visits. Latha had wondered at the beginning why this should be so, especially since the Aunties always inquired after the welfare of 'dear Rowley'. They spoke most affectionately of him, and regularly asked Aunt Helen to give him their regards. She decided that her uncle's absence was inevitable since Aunt Helen's visits to the Aunties were invariably made when her uncle happened to be visiting one of his properties elsewhere. Later, reflecting on Tsunami's warning against mentioning the Aunties to Rowland, and the fact that she never heard them or their good wishes mentioned to him, Latha realized that the visits were a secret between her aunt, her cousin, herself, and Alexander, a secret that was never to be revealed to anyone. Especially not to Uncle Rowland.

It seemed, Latha reflected, that there were many things Uncle Rowland didn't like Aunt Helen doing. Latha was, as her mother said, 'a noticing child', and she often noticed much more than her mother ever realized she did. She noticed, for instance, that despite the luxury in which she lived, her Aunt Helen was not happy. She became aware of this when she observed that in an existence which appeared to be wholly dedicated to pleasing her husband and her children, her aunt managed to reserve some small areas that were for herself alone. These areas were tiny, as tiny as her aunt's 'Indian garden' which, Latha thought, must itself be certainly one of them. The beautifully embroidered underclothes in her aunt's closet were, she felt, probably in the same category. And visiting the Aunties, Latha decided, must definitely be another.

For the first time Latha became aware that husbands and wives sometimes had secrets from one another. She wondered what her Uncle Rowland would do if he ever got to know about Aunt Helen's sick-visiting. And one Sunday afternoon, after Moira and her mother had left for Colombo, and everyone at Lucas Falls was enjoying an after-lunch siesta, she found out.

Latha was in the library, reading *Peter Pan*, and sitting in her favourite leather-covered chair by the fireplace, when she heard voices raised outside the library door. Or rather, she heard her uncle's voice, since her aunt seemed to be saying nothing at all.

'How dared you do it, Helen?' Uncle Rowland demanded.

Latha heard them come into the library, and made herself as small as possible in her chair. The door shut with something of a bang.

'Against my express orders—'

'Your request,' Helen put in quietly.

'What was that? What did you say?'

'Your request. It was something that you *asked* me not to do. You didn't order it.'

'Well, I may have put it to you as a request, out of courtesy, and consideration for you. But you knew very well that in going to visit that – that low-class tart, you were dragging my name in the mud as well as your own.'

'She is an old friend, Rowland. A friend of yours as well as mine.'

'She is no friend of mine. You know that very well. I have nothing to do with her. I have had nothing to do with her for years. Not since Cecil died, and she produced that illegitimate brat two years afterwards, and gave it his name. And as my wife, I forbid you to have anything to do with her either.'

There was a pause, during which Latha sat very still.

'Rowland,' began Helen gently, 'Surani is quite alone in the world these days. Almost all her old friends have dropped her—'

'Yes, it seems they have more sense than my brainless wife, who thinks she can do anything she likes because my name protects her reputation. Helen, you know nothing of this country, you have no idea how gossip gets started and how it spreads—'

'I have lived here nearly twenty years, Rowland,' Helen reminded him. 'I don't think you can say that I am a stranger to the way—'

'To the way people talk? Then why, for God's sake, do you take my car, which is very well known everywhere in the district, and use it to visit a well-known prostitute?'

'Surani is *not* a prostitute,' Helen said. 'You and I know plenty of people whom we both visit – and whom you welcome into this house – who could better be called that than Surani.'

Instead of calming her uncle down, Latha thought, Helen's quiet tone seemed to make him even angrier. His voice became very loud.

'Now, you just listen to me, Helen. As you are well aware, I cannot afford to have my name and yours linked to women of easy virtue, women who have kicked over the traces, disreputable women whose very presence in the neighbourhood is a disgrace to the district I hope to represent—'

'But *I* am not standing for election, Rowland,' Helen said, her voice still gentle and low. 'Why should what I do affect your chances of being elected?' She added: 'As that . . . associate of yours who came here recently reminded you in front of the children and your own relations, I am only an outsider. Why should anyone care what I do, or what I think?'

'*Everyone* cares what you do and think, Helen, and everyone makes it a point to inform themselves on the subject because you are my wife. And since I don't care to continue this discussion any further, I am telling you, once and for all, that you will not see anything more of that woman. And if you still don't know why, it's because I will *not have it*!'

Latha thought she felt a sneeze coming. To make it go away, she focused her mind on speculating as to what 'kicked over the traces' could possibly mean. She decided eventually that it must mean something like 'falling from grace'.

'And another thing,' continued the angry voice of her uncle. 'I have been informed that you are in the habit of taking Tsunami with you on these . . . these clandestine expeditions of yours. Let me remind you, Helen, that that child is quite old enough to know what's going on, she's old enough to know the difference between right and wrong, and – listen to me carefully – if I find that this ever happens again, it is Tsunami who will suffer for it. She will get a whipping from me that you and she will never forget.'

Latha heard the library door open and shut again. She was about to get up and creep back upstairs and into her own room when she realized that Aunt Helen had not left the library, and that she was crying.

Well, she could hardly get up and go out of the room now, Latha thought, Auntie Helen would know she had heard the whole awful exchange. She might even suppose she had been spying on her and on Uncle Rowland. Latha prayed that her aunt would not think of finishing her crying in the chair on the opposite side of the fireplace. If she did, Latha decided, she would find her niece fast asleep.

As it turned out, Latha was spared this last deception, for Raman's voice made itself heard outside, asking Alice whether she had seen the mistress. After a moment or two, during which Latha visualized her aunt drying her eyes and summoning up a smile, Helen rose and left the room. Latha counted slowly to three hundred, then strolled out of the library as casually as she could, *Peter Pan* in her hand.

Just outside the library door, she ran full tilt into Colin. He was cautiously walking towards her, holding on to the upper railing of the banisters, his eyes tight shut.

'What's the matter, Colin?' Latha asked. 'What are you doing?'

Colin opened his eyes.

'I'm practising,' he said, and immediately shut them again. Still holding on to the banisters, he began descending the stairs.

'Practising? For what?'

'For when I go blind,' Colin replied.

'*What?*'

It was the first Latha had heard of any belief on her cousin's part that he was losing his sight, and she didn't believe a word of it. She wondered how much he had heard of his parents' conversation in the library; he'd obviously been listening in. Then,

'Look out!' she cried, as Colin very nearly cannoned into a little table at the corner of the landing, on which stood a portrait of their common ancestor, Gate Mudaliyar Wijesinha.

'You didn't need to worry, I knew all the time that the old boy was there,' Colin said nonchalantly. 'I've been up and down the stairs a dozen times, and I haven't bumped into him *once*.'

He stopped when he was halfway down the lower flight of stairs.

'By the way, where have *you* been, Latha?' he asked. 'Didn't you know Vaithi was making Bombay Toast for afternoon tea?'

Latha didn't tell Tsunami what she had heard that afternoon, but she thought often and sadly about it. Despite his sarcasm, she had come to like her Uncle Rowland, and she respected him; the sudden switch he had

'He likes me to look like his own people. Like your people, Latha.'

'Should I take mine off too?'

'You don't need to,' Aunt Helen said. 'For you, wearing a *bindhi is* only a game.'

That was the first and the last time that Latha ever saw her aunt wearing a *bindhi*. She wondered whether her aunt found many things in Ceylon unfamiliar or strange, and whether Uncle Rowland had had to explain them to her when she first came to live in the island.

As time went on, Latha grew gradually wiser and less naïve, partly under Tsunami's tutelage, partly as a result of her own observation of the people around her. One Vesak day she learned, for instance, something of the deathly cold currents that can flow beneath the surface of an outwardly respectable marriage.

Taken along on a Vesak visit to relatives on her mother's side of the family, Latha and her parents had found the house in comparative darkness. This created a shadowed and desolate patch in a street that was otherwise brightly illuminated, for in every other house the birth of Lord Buddha was being celebrated with enthusiasm. As darkness fell, cloth wicks had been lit in the rows of tiny oil lamps placed along verandas and up flights of steps, so that they shone like stars and made normally humble homes look like palaces. From every tall tree brilliant paper lanterns swung in clusters, one large lantern glowing in the centre of each group, with six or eight miniature lanterns (the *pattow*, or 'babies') bobbing about around it.

The afternoon heat had ebbed away, and the clusters of shining lanterns swayed and bobbed in a gentle evening breeze. The effect was breathtakingly beautiful. The street was filled with people who had come out to admire the festive lights and enjoy the coolness of the evening, families walking along hand in hand so that children did not get lost in the crowd. Latha would have liked to have stayed out in the garden to enjoy the Vesak lights, but her mother hurried her up a flight of dark steps and on to a gloomy veranda.

At the sound of the doorbell an unshaded electric light snapped on in the hall. Soma Wijesinha's niece and her husband were evidently at home. The Vesak visitors were invited in, and the usual soft drinks were brought out on a tray and served to Latha and her parents by the two young daughters of the house.

Conversation did not go well. After the health of everyone in both families had been duly inquired into, and the children asked if they were studying well at school, it became evident that no one had anything more to say. It was Soma, inevitably, who broached the question that was on everyone's mind.

'No Vesak lights this year, child?' she said to her niece. 'What happened?'

No one answered her. After a moment, her niece Rohini said:

'I told Ravi, "Why go to the trouble of hanging up lanterns this year? Better that you and I buy some rope and hang ourselves from the rooftop of this house as Vesak decorations."'

Her voice was quite clear, and as cold as the mountain stream which fed the pool at Lucas Falls.

'Then our two *pattow* could hang on either side of us.'

The unfortunate Ravi flinched, and the two children looked at the floor. Their mother glanced at her husband, then at her aunt's startled face.

'Why, what's the trouble, Auntie? Why do you look so surprised? Everyone knows what things are like in our house. Why pretend?'

Soma said afterwards that she could not understand it: her niece's marriage, arranged according to strictly traditional Sinhala pattern, should have been a happy and successful one, for the horoscopes had agreed, the young people's planets had been safely in the right astrological houses, the wedding date had been guaranteed one hundred per cent auspicious, and the coconut which was ritually split at the wedding ceremony had fallen into two exact halves. What could possibly have gone wrong?

That something had indeed gone very wrong was proved a year later when Latha learned (though not from her mother) that Ravi was a compulsive gambler. His wife surprised him one day, rifling her jewel case for items she did not often wear: his intention had been to pawn them. She foiled his plan by pre-empting it: that very afternoon she wrapped up her jewellery in a bundle, and gave it to her mother for safe-keeping. When Ravi found out what she had done, he got very drunk, and beat her in front of their children and several inquisitive neighbours who, hearing her screams, rushed over to 'help' with their opinions and advice.

'He has never raised his hand to Rohini before this,' Latha's informant – an aunt – told her; she was apparently lost in wonder at Ravi's restraint and forbearance.

Relations between husband and wife deteriorated sharply following this incident, as Ravi gradually stripped the household of every saleable item he could find – his wife could not, after all, take *everything* to her parents' house.

It happened that Ravi – this same Ravi whom Latha and her parents had visited that Vesak evening (and for whom his horoscope had foretold a long and prosperous life) – died that same year. ('Of cirrhosis of the liver,' said the family grapevine.) Tsunami and Latha were taken along by their respective parents to the funeral. It was the first funeral either of the two girls had ever attended, so the white flags fluttering at the entrance to the house were quite new to them, and so was the oppressive silence that seemed to hang over everything.

They found Ravi, clad in a dark blue business suit with his hands folded neatly over his stomach, and his feet encased in white silk socks, laid out in a coffin that was lined with white satin and sprinkled with fresh rosebuds. His eyes were closed, and the skin of his face and hands had darkened to a muddy grey colour. Latha found it hard to recognize in the corpse the easy-going character she remembered from their Vesak visit, casually dressed in a sarong and shirt, and leather sandals, pouring out generous tots of arrack for himself and 'Herbie Uncle'.

Occasionally a suppressed sob broke the silence as some kinswoman arrived and was conducted to the side of the coffin to pay her last respects. The menfolk, on the whole, wore expressions of great solemnity, but said nothing, not at any rate until they had made their escape from the house to chairs placed beneath the shade trees in the garden, where they could loosen their neckties, relax, and comfortably discuss politics: they certainly did not weep.

When Tsunami and Latha came into the funeral house with their parents, they found Rohini seated in the hall, beside the coffin. Her children, who were seated on either side of her, got up at her prompting, and kissed Tsunami and Latha perfunctorily on each cheek before returning to their places. It was difficult to know what to do next, except to watch people move back and forth before the coffin, speaking to Rohini or to each other with lowered voices. But they didn't have to wonder long about that. Tsunami and Latha stared at each other with astonishment as an ear-splitting shriek from the opposite side of the room ended the silence. Tacitly encouraged by her siblings encamped on the other side of the coffin, Ravi's younger sister had begun performing her duty of ritual mourning.

'Oh, why did you leave us, Ravi Aiya?' she wailed. 'Why did you desert us? If only you had listened to my advice, if only you had stayed with us, among the people who love and respect you as you deserve, such a tragedy would never have occurred. I would have looked after you, *I* would have prevented it . . .'

'*Sh! Sh! Sh!*' whispered her siblings in soothing chorus. 'Don't say such things, child, you mustn't let your feelings run away with you . . .'

Thus encouraged, the mourner continued:

'Oh, what a tragic life he has led ever since, among hard-hearted people who have never valued his fine qualities of character! What is my life worth now, without your presence, dearest Aiya! What can be the point of living, for an unfortunate woman like myself, deprived by fate of the most loving and loyal brother the world has ever seen? Oh sad and melancholy day, that saw my dear brother thrown among ravening jackals!'

Hearing this, Soma Wijesinha's niece, stung by her sister-in-law's rhetoric (which she rightly interpreted as calculated personal insult rather than lamentation for the dead), jumped to her feet. Fearing the worst, onlookers instinctively stepped forward to separate the two women: emotions were clearly running high.

Luckily the widow was of a gentler nature than her tormentor; and the coffin, too, heaped with garlands and wreaths, stood massively in her path. Frustrated, she resorted to alternative tactics. Calling out her dead husband's name, and declaring that all that was left to her now was to accompany him to the grave, Rohini attempted to fling herself into the coffin. A squadron of her own relations promptly swung into action, almost as if they had expected such an emergency. Crying 'No, no! That's enough!' and 'Don't do it, Akka!', they forcibly held her back.

Was this the same young woman who had offered a few months ago to hang her husband, their children and herself from the rooftop of her house? Latha couldn't believe what she was seeing and hearing. Tsunami looked at her cousin, raised an eyebrow ever so slightly, and inclined her head, an invitation to her to step outside into the garden. When they reached the shade trees at the far end of the lawn, they found that Chris had anticipated them.

'Getting rather hot in there, what?' Chris said, an understatement typical of his general style.

'Isn't it,' Latha replied, with equal casualness; and added:

'Do you think she's really going to do it?'

'Do what?' Chris asked.

'Have herself buried in Ravi Uncle's coffin?'

'Nonsense! There isn't room for two in the coffin, anyway.'

'It was just like a play,' said Tsunami.

Latha agreed.

She knew Tsunami was thinking of *kolam*, the song-and-dance melodramas they had seen performed at Lucas Falls by strolling players. The last time Latha had seen such a play was during the festival of Diwali, when the players had presented their songs and dances for the entertainment of the workers on the estate. Neither Tsunami nor Latha were old enough at the time to have encountered more sophisticated theatre. It was only many years later, at a performance of *Oedipus Rex* in London, that Latha recognized in the unnaturally bright, tearless gaze of Jocasta, the expression she had seen in her Uncle Rowland's eyes when he called all the children together in the drawing room at Lucas Falls to tell them that Helen had gone away and would not be coming back.

'Ah Love!' Mr Goldman had remarked one day, quite without warning and in the middle of a game of Monopoly, while the trading value of stocks and shares trembled beneath the canopy, the price of property rose and fell, and the business of bargaining continued to swirl furiously around him on the pink quilted counterpane,

Ah Love! could thou and I with Fate conspire
To grasp this sorry Scheme of Things entire,

Would we not shatter it to bits – and then
Remould it nearer to the Heart's Desire!

To which Helen, re-threading her needle, and not looking up once, had responded:

Alas, that Spring should vanish with the Rose!
That Youth's sweet-scented Manuscript should close!
The Nightingale that in the Branches sang,
Ah, whence, and whither flown again, who knows!

Leaning over her aunt's shoulder to admire her embroidery, Latha had caught a delicate turbulence of lavender water and sandalwood-scented powder around the movements of her wrist that remained for ever in her memory, and came immediately to her mind whenever she thought of her.

And Latha thought often of Helen in later years, for although it caused a good deal of talk at the time (in the planting community, and also in the families of the clan where the women, especially, had a great deal to say on the subject), her aunt's decision to go away with the V.A. in his big Humber, very early one day in 1947, before the morning muster, never altered in any way the affection and the high regard Latha always had for her.

14

AFTERSHOCKS

Rowland Wijesinha and his children met with studied calm the crisis that had occurred in their lives. Their composure (which was much remarked upon by Latha's aunts) underlined, more emphatically than anything else Latha had observed up to that time, the difference between Tsunami's family and her own. Her mother thought their calmness indecent, even unnatural. In Soma Wijesinha's family, death or divorce was invariably accompanied by hysteria and hostility on a heroic scale.

The stoic dignity with which Rowland met the situation created by the elopement of his wife was typical of those aspects of his character that Latha most admired. A lesser man might have paraded his loss, demanded the sympathy of his friends, and drowned his sorrows in drinking sessions at the Club. Rowland acted as if nothing of importance had occurred, a stance which effectively discouraged inquisitive relations (such as Latha's mother) from asking impertinent questions.

'Fine goings-on in Rowland Aiya's household! I wonder what the children think of their mother's doings? That poor little girl . . .'

Soma was very pleased to be in a position to pity Tsunami.

'Fancy Helen just walking out of the house and leaving those poor children motherless! Just wait and see – she'll suffer for it some day. And,' Soma added, with every sign of satisfaction, 'she'll never be able to come back to Ceylon, that's for sure. People will never forget what she did.'

Latha made no reply to this, and after a pause of a few moments her mother continued:

'So? So how is Rowland keeping the household going?'

Latha shrugged, and picked up a book. Her father unfolded his newspaper.

'I see they've shifted the General Election to a new date,' he remarked. 'It seems the first date the Government chose is not auspicious enough.'

'Auspicious enough for whom? Not the Opposition!'

Soma prided herself on her knowledge of national politics. She didn't notice that she had been successfully side-tracked. But only for the

the afternoon helping Soma make sweets for the Sinhala New Year (though she tasted more than she actually made), never disagreed with her sister.

'Quite right, Nangi, you can't be too careful these days,' she said, and reached for another piece of *kalu dodol*.

15

A STONE IN THE POOL

Latha, whose enjoyment of English books had grown by the time she was thirteen or fourteen into a major obsession, discovered early in her school career that her knowledge of English authors and her ability to quote from them could get her through tight situations in almost every subject. Miss Joan Muller, who taught her class History, had been so impressed by Latha's vivid account of the heroic manner in which Horatius Cocles defended the Sublician bridge against the massed Etruscan armies led by Lars Porsena of Clusium that she awarded a rare ten marks out of ten to her essay on Ancient Rome. When Miss Mabel Christoffelsz, her Geography teacher, set the class to write an account of Deserts in Africa, Latha, who didn't care much for Geography or for the way Miss Christoffelsz taught the subject, prepared for this unwelcome task in an unconventional way: she re-read *Beau Sabreur*, a novel that had been a favourite of hers ever since she first read it in the library at Lucas Falls. Walking again beside the debonair Henri de Beaujolais along the rue des Enfants Abandonnés, Latha thrilled as she searched with him for the Paymaster's Office so that he could enlist in the French Foreign Legion. Why? To pursue his country's interests. Where? In the deserts of Africa. So the book could be justifiably regarded as being within the purview of her Geography essay. Latha smiled as she indulged herself in this piece of self-indulgent sophistry, recalling as she read that *Beau Sabreur* had been a favourite of Tsunami's too. She wondered, as she followed the exploits of the gallant Major as he fought off militant Touareg raiders and licentious desert sheikhs, whether Tsunami still read P.C. Wren and thrilled to *Beau Geste*.

The two families had been out of touch for nearly two years, and whatever Latha knew of her uncle and her cousins since Helen's departure now reached her second-hand, through family gossip. Rothschild's couldn't very well keep Mr Goldman on as *periya dorai*, said her relations, not after all the scandal caused by the elopement. He'd had to give up his appointment as V.A., too, since as a 'bounder' and a 'cad' he would have been blackballed or cut dead in every Planters' Club in the country. Nor was comment restricted to the family or to the island's planting community. Although Wijesinha influence kept it out of the newspapers, Rowland's branch of the family was so socially prominent that his wife's elopement with a 'European' V.A. had become the subject of common gossip. It had even generated a scurrilous *baila* ballad that was sung at every street-corner to the undisguised merriment, said Soma Wijesinha furiously, of every ruffian and ragamuffin in the country.

Marriage fashions changing, getting like the U.S.A.,
Planter Wijesinha giving wife to the V.A.,
Who says Ceylon out of date?
Dowry giving tea estate,
V.A.'s going Yoo-rup to invest his severance pay . . .

So Mr Goldman, disgraced and ostracized in Ceylon, had gone overseas, and had taken Helen with him. That much was known for certain, but little else.

The postman rang his bicycle bell, and Latha put her book down and went to the door. All the letters were, as usual, for her father, and she very nearly missed an envelope addressed to herself. It was sheer coincidence, of course, but it seemed to Latha that some kind of sympathetic magic was at work when she opened her letter, for it turned out to be from the very person Soma Wijesinha insisted on describing in conversation as 'that poor Abandoned Child'.

'Dear Latha,' Tsunami wrote, 'I hope you are well. We are all well too.'

This was the *mantra* with which, Latha and Tsunami had been instructed at an early age, all proper letters began. (Although, if Rowland Wijesinha was to be believed, there had been a johnny at King's in his time who had come to the College from some provincial school in the back of beyond, who had been taught a different *mantra*: 'Dear – I hope you are well. I am also in the same well.')

'We were hoping,' Tsunami went on, 'to go to L. Falls as usual these hols, but our plans are changed now, as Pater is getting married again.'

So casually was the stone dropped into the still pool of Latha's childhood experience that was to change her life for ever. She could not understand her cousin's matter-of-fact way of referring to her father's remarriage. Didn't Tsunami *care*? Latha did not see how anyone else could take Aunt Helen's place. Didn't Tsunami feel the same way? What about Tara and the boys? Most important, what about Uncle Rowland?

Latha put *Beau Sabreur* back on the shelf, took down her father's copy of Matthew Arnold, and re-read 'The Forsaken Merman', a poem over which she and Tsunami had shed sympathetic tears when they read it together long ago in *Stories from the Poets*. Matthew Arnold, Latha felt, had described Uncle Rowland's tragic situation exactly. Those English romantic poets like Arnold and Keats had really understood the anguish of the sorrowing heart. What had changed Uncle Rowland? She could not understand how her uncle could bear to live with anyone else, after having once been married to Aunt Helen. For him, it seemed to Latha, the sedge should have withered permanently from the lake below Lucas Falls, and all birds ceased to sing.

But it seemed that Latha was the only person in the family who thought so. Neither affection nor love appeared to enter into the matter when Rowland's plans to remarry were mentioned by anyone else, even by her father. It was only to be expected, said Herbert, that Rowland would marry again sometime. And with his new responsibilities as a Member of Parliament and a family of young children to bring up, Soma added, he was likely to marry sooner rather than later.

When the news became official and engraved invitations arrived in little embossed envelopes, no one in the family had any illusions about the reasons for Rowland's remarriage; indeed Herbert Wijesinha said he felt sorry for the poor chap, forced to go through all that rigmarole of having a second marriage arranged for him so that his household could continue to run as smoothly as it had in Helen's time.

Rowland's second marriage took place in Independence year, 1948, before the world had had time to catch up on the progress of 'the runaways', as Soma Wijesinha euphemistically referred to Mr Goldman and Helen Wijesinha in her daughter's hearing. Their fortunes were energetically discussed wherever clan members met – they were discussed and speculated upon, Latha suspected, even when the clan met in force at her uncle's wedding to his new wife, his cousin Moira. It was presumed – indeed, hoped – that they were married, and that Mr Goldman had made an honest woman of Helen. People were a bit vague about the present whereabouts of the couple, although, as the popular *baila* averred, the former V.A. had gone into property development. Some people thought they must have fled to Australia, well known as a land in which convicts, criminals, and other miscreants frequently disappeared without trace, others said they must have gone into hiding in Britain or America.

All were agreed that his abrupt change of profession would have been a big change at first for Mr Goldman, wherever he was. But then, he had been well known in the planting community as an efficient and resourceful individual. Assuming that he was also adaptable, and that his wife continued to be the charming and delightful person she had been in Ceylon, most people (except Soma Wijesinha and her sisters who seemed determined to think otherwise) were satisfied that, wherever they had ended up, the Goldmans must be reasonably happy.

The rest was a bit blurred, and grew even more so with the passing of time; mostly, Latha realized, because once the Goldmans had left the island, they ceased to be interesting to anyone who lived there.

'You'll find out as you grow older,' Herbert had once told Latha, 'that you belong to a society so advanced and civilized that it doesn't give a damn about the world outside it.'

Latha was discovering for herself the truth of this statement. By leaving Ceylon, her aunt and Mr Goldman had made themselves not only invisible, but irrelevant. Politics had become the focus of interest of the island's post-war society, and gossip that was unrelated to the doings of politicians held no one's attention for very long.

Having entered the world of national politics, Rowland Wijesinha continued, therefore, to interest the public, though his former wife did not. Herbert and Soma's domestic help, Kamala, who followed the election news with close attention, had taken a week's leave to go home in order to vote. When she returned, she was elated.

'No wonder our Rowland *hamu* has the largest majority in the country,' she said. 'On Election Day, I impersonated *three times* at the voting booth!'

Herbert was profoundly shocked. He had not realized that Kamala's village was in Rowland's electorate of Dikgala. The girl had probably thought that in breaking the law she had his own tacit approval.

'Kamala,' he began helplessly, 'you should never—'

'And I would have impersonated a fourth time for our Dikgala *deviyo*,' Kamala told Herbert proudly. 'But my father said, "No, no, duwa, that's enough, if you do it once more, we will all end up in the police".'

Soma was indignant.

'*Deviyo*, indeed! Since when has your cousin Rowland become a god? These ignorant villagers!'

The second 'Mrs Rowland', wife of the new Member of Parliament for Dikgala, was kindly regarded and warmly received in the Wijesinha family: she was, after all, 'one of their own'. But that approval was by no means general.

'Fat, fair and probably flatulent,' Herbert had said dismissively, when Latha asked him on his return from Rowland's wedding, what the bride was like. He and Soma had attended the wedding, but although Latha had been included in the invitation, and although she was eager to see Tsunami again, she had refused to accompany them. She could not bear to think of the Moira she had once met taking Helen's place at Lucas Falls.

For Soma Wijesinha, Rowland's second wife represented a continuation of the Westernized world she envied and professed to despise, with little of the personal charm that had mitigated and sometimes even excused Westernization in Helen. The wedding reception, she reported on her return, had been very grand, as befitted an M.P. whom everyone expected soon to see in the Cabinet. It had been held at the Galle Face Hotel, in a blaze of manufactured feudal splendour.

The register had been signed by the Prime Minister himself. That dignified personage had arrived at the ceremony flanked by two senior members of his Cabinet who were well-known to be rivals for his position whenever it should happen to fall vacant. The sight had entertained Herbert, but only for a moment. Amusement gave way to profound irritation when he saw his cousin, the bridegroom, desert his post by his bride's side at a crucial point in the ceremony in order to make sure that the P.M. was comfortably seated.

'What's that ass Rowland doing?' Herbert had muttered to Soma: 'Making sure he'll be ranked No. 3 in the Premier Stakes?'

His disgust kept him silent for the rest of the evening, and Latha learned the details of the occasion from her mother and from one of the weekend newspapers which celebrated it in a double-page article titled 'The Wedding of the Year!'

The newspaper article carried pictures of the bride, her mother, and Tara and Tsunami (as bridesmaid and flower-girl respectively, among a flock of other bridal attendants), and gave details of the wedding clothes. Latha cut the article out of the newspaper, and pasted it, column by column, into her scrapbook, together with the wedding invitation and the gold-paper wrapping of the piece of wedding-cake her mother had brought home with her from the reception. She studied Tsunami's face in the newspaper picture carefully, but could not see that she looked any different from the other flower-girls. The newspaper columnist described them as dressed alike in gold organza, and carrying identical, gold-painted baskets filled with crimson anthuriums, but the speckled grey newspaper pictures, entirely devoid of colour, made them look like dreary carbon copies of one another.

Soon the newspaper clipping in Latha's scrapbook was surrounded by others:

'Mrs Rowland Wijesinha attends a cocktail party at the Grand Oriental Hotel', 'Mrs Rowland Wijesinha turns heads at the Governor's Cup Meet', 'Mrs Moira Wijesinha opens the new wing of the Lady Stanley Hospital', 'Mrs Moira Wijesinha collects donations on behalf of the Red Cross' . . .

Moira was clearly enjoying her new life as the wife of an M.P., said Soma acidly.

It was certainly obvious that she adored being part of Colombo's social scene, for she was often photographed attending charity events. Her saris and accessories were regularly described in detail in the fashion pages of the weekend papers, and the value of her jewellery assessed to the nearest rupee. The family telephone lines buzzed with gossip about the sums of money 'Mrs Rowland' was said to spend on clothes. Such was the excitement her extravagance aroused that even Soma, when comparing 'Mrs Rowland' with her predecessor, forgot all about the 'runaway' Helen's failings and misdemeanours.

'I must say, Helen never went in for such nonsense in her time,' Soma said. 'Show your father that picture, Latha. Just see, Herbie, the border on that sari is all done in gold beads and silver threadwork. And with shoes and handbag to match! Must have cost Rowland thousands.'

'Hmm? Well, he can afford it. And it will last her for years, probably.'

Herbert, who had the racing pages of *The Searchlight* open in front of him, was not really paying much attention.

'What are you saying, Herbie! I don't understand you. Last for years? Those Colombo dress-designers make each outfit specially, one for each occasion. When she has worn it once, Moira must be giving it to the cook-woman. Those dress-designers make a packet out of silly, stupid women like Moira.'

'Maybe so. But they've got to live too, haven't they?'

To mark the occasion of his cousin's entry into politics, Herbert had taken out a new manila folder, written 'Rowland Wijesinha, M.P.' neatly across the top, and placed it on the shelf in his library which would thereafter become a rich resource of information about the doings of the island's men of power and influence. Herbert also brought home from Cave's Bookshop for his collection the official biography of the new Member of Parliament, a glossy publication in the Party colour of green, with a photograph of Rowland in snow-white national dress on its cover. Soma read extracts from it aloud at breakfast, punctuating her reading with sour comments.

'I'm willing to bet Rowland Aiya has never worn national dress in his life before now,' said she. 'He doesn't look very comfortable in it, does he? Moira must have pinned him into it with safety pins. And just look at all these photographs of *her*!'

There were, indeed, many photographs of Moira Wijesinha in the book, flamboyantly dressed and hung about with expensive jewellery.

Latha could not help noticing that the official biography made no mention of her uncle's first marriage. There was a large coloured family group photograph in the book, in which Rowland and Moira, flanked by the five Wijesinha children, posed on the front steps of their Colombo house and smiled at the camera; and there were several pictures of Ranil, Chris and Colin accompanying their father on walks around Lucas Falls Estate.

Latha noticed that Chris was almost as tall as Ranil. She also noticed, somewhat to her surprise, that Colin was wearing spectacles.

'I'm practising,' Colin had told her once, fumbling his way down the staircase at Lucas Falls with his eyes tightly shut, 'for when I go blind.'

Had his game become a reality? She remembered guiltily that she had not believed him at the time.

A great deal was made in the biography of the beauty of the famous grounds at Lucas Falls ('cared for and maintained by generations of garden lovers in the Wijesinha family') but Helen herself, it seemed, had been effectively erased from the record.

Later that year, 'Mrs Rowland' duly performed what Latha suspected to have been a duty pointed out to her by her husband as a family obligation: Latha was invited (on imported pale green writing paper with the letters R and M entwined in gold in the top left-hand corner) to Lucas Falls for the holidays. By chance both Herbert and Soma were out when the invitation arrived, and since it was addressed to herself, Latha did not feel that she was obliged to mention its arrival to her parents.

She wrote back with a polite refusal, making no excuses for her inability to accept the invitation. Next morning, she tore up the sheet together with its envelope, and dropped them both in the classroom waste-paper basket at school.

16

FRENCH LESSONS

Buddhan saranam gachchami . . .
Dhamman saranam gachchami . . .
Sanghan saranam gachchami . . .

Eight o'clock. The year is 1951. Two hundred and twenty girls in snow-white school uniforms, their hair neatly plaited and tied with black ribbons, are lined up in the shady playground of Amarapāli Maha Vidyālaya, and are being led through their morning devotions by Miss Sriyani de Zoysa, the school's Deputy Principal.

One of the girls engaged in invoking the protection of Lord Buddha, of his teaching, and of the community of monks he established in the sixth century before Christ, is Latha Wijesinha, now sixteen years old and a Fifth Former. Amarapāli M.V., the school for girls that Latha attends, is a part of her family tradition on her mother's side. Latha's grandmother had been one of a group, the friends and supporters of the devout Buddhist lady who had founded the school in 1917 in memory of her son. Their aim had been to ensure that their daughters received a sound Buddhist education, and received it through the Sinhala language. Soma Wijesinha and her sisters had all attended Amarapāli, and Soma's had been the deciding voice when the time came for her to choose with her husband the school their daughter would attend as a day-scholar.

'What about Ashcombe?' Herbert had tentatively suggested.

Ashcombe School, the Anglican college for girls which his nieces Tara and Tsunami Wijesinha attended, was the sister institution of Herbert's own St Alban's, and he had happy memories of past occasions on which he and his classmates had attended Ashcombe's fêtes and fairs, and flirted decorously with the school's pretty students under the watchful eye of their Principal, a nun.

'Who can pay such high fees?' Soma said at once. 'Anyway, it's much too far away.'

Herbert disagreed, but he did not insist. He knew that his wife's chief objection to Ashcombe was that, being a Christian school run by an order of English nuns under the patronage of the Anglican Bishop of Colombo, she thought it unfitted to impart the proper moral values that should guide Ceylonese children through life. Quite the contrary. Soma Wijesinha was convinced that by introducing Ceylonese children to the arts and sciences of the West through the English language, schools such as Ashcombe, St Alban's, and All Saints' were subtly undermining the traditional values of the nation.

If the truth were to be told, Herbert hadn't really cared much, either way. He would probably have moved heaven and earth to obtain for any son of his the best education money could buy (which, for him, at that time, would have meant sending the boy to St Alban's or King's). But since his only child happened to be a girl, the question did not arise. Herbert, like most other Ceylonese men of his class and generation, believed that daughters do not require any kind of education other than a training in the domestic arts. Traditionally, this was provided for them by their mothers, but since Soma, a full-time Government school teacher herself, had neither the time nor the inclination to teach her daughter how to cook, sew, and play the piano, Amarapāli M.V. seemed the rational choice.

Pleasantly located in the city's residential quarter, women's colleges generally prided themselves on developing obedience, good manners, and ladylike deportment in their students. In laying particular emphasis on the concept of *guru bakthi*, unquestioning acceptance of the teacher's word (the traditional principle that had governed educational practice in ancient Ceylon), the founders of Amarapāli, however, had been confronted with something of a problem: social custom had for generations denied education to Sinhalese, Tamil and Muslim women of good family, and as a result, there were few female teachers available in the school's early years to undertake the proper education of Buddhist girls.

And yet, suitable teachers had to be found, for it is only *guru bakthi*, firmly inculcated in the young, that can create docile daughters, those bringers of joy to parental hearts. Soma's years at the school had been years of compromise. The staff of Amarapāli had been mostly made up at that time of elderly Burgher single ladies of unimpeachable character. It might have been expected that as Christians teaching in a Buddhist establishment they would experience some conflict of conscience: surprisingly, they did not. It was made clear to them from the start that the students' religious development would be no concern of theirs. Regular visits to the school by Buddhist monks and nuns, and regular attendance by the girls at ceremonies in the neighbouring temple on festival days, looked after the religious side of things. Soma's teachers were dedicated to creating replicas of themselves from the materials that came into their hands. Except, of course, that their girls would not remain single, but develop into the good wives and mothers of the future.

Miss Mabel Christoffelsz, who had taught Geography to Soma's class, and was still teaching when Latha was enrolled in the Junior School, was a great believer in the virtue of the girls' keeping their voices down and saying 'Good morning!' and 'Good afternoon!' to teachers at appropriate times. 'Her voice was ever soft and low, an excellent thing in woman', Miss Christoffelsz would quote, sitting up straight in her chair at the same time to demonstrate that a nice girl's knees should always be firmly pressed together on every occasion that did not actually involve walking. Years later, these were mainly what Latha remembered about Miss Christoffelsz's teaching: voices and knees. About Geography, her official subject, 'Chrissy' knew little that was not in the class textbook, but under her kindly eye Latha learned how to draw artistic maps of the British Isles, their coal and steel towns marked with neat red dots, and the ocean surrounding them edged with dark blue crayon which was then painstakingly smudged with bits of blotting paper to create an illusion of blue space.

The department of Domestic Science had been ruled in Soma's time by a Mrs Emma Durrant, the genteel widow of an Anglican clergyman, whose idea of teaching her subject had been to involve her class in the making of the cakes and puddings that had delighted the heart (and eventually ruined the digestion) of her late husband. When Latha came to Amarapāli and joined the Domestic Science class in Form I, Mrs Durrant was still teaching there. Latha looked forward to Mrs Durrant's classes, since they were scheduled for the afternoons, the hungriest time of the school day, and tended to end as pleasant little parties at which students had a chance to taste the products of their labour.

Herbert, who enjoyed his food, and cherished memories of meals he had consumed as a student in France, took a great interest in Latha's Domestic Science studies. Soma was much too busy to take an interest in planning menus and trying out new ideas. Her domestic help, Kamala, had left to get married, and the repertoire of Kamala's replacement (her younger sister Podina) was neither large nor subtle. Herbert had secretly hoped that culinary standards in his household would improve sharply as his daughter learned to cook. Much, therefore, was expected of Latha by her father. Latha, who adored Herbert, did her best to oblige him.

'What are we having for dinner tonight, duwa?'

'Apricot Pudding, Thaththi,' would be the reply. (Or Apple Crumble, or Stewed Pears, or Spotted Dick, or Peach Melba, whatever Mrs Durrant had taught her class to cook that week.)

'Bloody English cooking,' Herbert would grumble to himself, but he did not say it aloud for fear of hurting his daughter's feelings.

Since apricots, apples, currants, pears and peaches were only to be had in tropical Ceylon in their imported form, dried or tinned, Latha's demonstrations at home of what she had learned in school frequently turned out to be very expensive. Besides, as Herbert told Soma when they were balancing the weekly budget, what was wrong with the local product, in a country where every market stall in town and village overflowed with fresh fruit in season, pineapples, mangoes, oranges, papaya and mangosteens? When he realized that Mrs Durrant, though doubtless a good and well-meaning woman, saw herself as a kindly aunt handing down family recipes rather than as instructor of his daughter in any kind of structured study, Herbert took time off in his lunch hour to seek assistance at his favourite bookshop, Cave's in the Fort of Colombo.

Looking through a shelf of cookery books at Cave's, Herbert's eye was caught by a black and white line drawing of a kitchen interior that reminded him of the farmhouse in the Loire Valley where he had boarded as a student. Like the kitchen pictured in the book, the kitchen he remembered had been hung with shining copper pans, its rafters garlanded with strings of garlic. On the top of its massive stove, a huge pot of soup redolent of herbs had been perpetually simmering. From this domestic shrine had come the meals Herbert remembered: delicate omelettes stuffed with mushrooms and served with tender, garden-picked peas, crisp onion rings, golden-brown oven-roasted potatoes, a cream-cheese mould in the shape of a heart and topped with fat, juicy strawberries . . .

Herbert's mouth watered at the memory. He had never heard of Elizabeth David, but the prose that accompanied the drawing sounded to him very much like poetry:

Those who care to look for it [advised Mrs David] *will find the justification of France's culinary reputation in the provinces, at the riverside inns, in unknown cafés along the banks of the Burgundy canal, patronized by the men who sail the great petrol and timber barges to and from Marseilles, great eaters and drinkers most of them, in the hospitable farmhouses of the Loire and the Dordogne, of Normandy and the Auvergne, in sea-port bistros frequented by fishermen, sailors, ship-chandlers and port officials . . .*

Herbert didn't know cooks could write atmospheric prose. He rolled the words *Loire*, *Dordogne*, *Auvergne* on his tongue several times: they had the authentic sound of music.

'A present for you, duwa,' he told Latha, and put the book in her hands.

It was as much a present for himself as for his daughter, but Herbert was delighted with the way Latha responded to it. The stories Mrs David related in *French Country Cooking* of chefs and their specialities read to her like fairy tales with happy endings – there was the Abbé Chevrier, a Prince of the Roman Catholic Church who had coaxed a pound of spinach to absorb ten ounces of butter over five tender daily cookings; there was the elegant Paris model who adored garlic and risked her career by indulging her passion for the herb over a whole, heavenly week of eating practically nothing else; there was Catherine, a provincial cook, a 'strapping young woman of thirty-four', the fame of whose cooking spread so widely throughout her province that the greatest ladies in the land tried in vain to lure her away from her employer . . .

Cooking with wine and herbs such as basil and marjoram is not part of island tradition, and Herbert had to search far and wide for the ingredients that would allow Latha to experiment. When Elizabeth David's *Boeuf en daube* called for the delicate browning of meat in olive oil before it was permitted to link up with wine and selected herbs and simmer to a melting tenderness in a casserole, Herbert bargained with the Muslim butcher in the Colpetty market for the best piece of 'undercut', searched the Wines and Spirits department at Cargill's for a full-bodied red, hunted out tiny bottles of brandy and Armagnac, and contrived to persuade the vegetable-seller who came round daily with his brimming baskets to bring him parsley, basil and chives grown in the market gardens of Nuwara Eliya. Garlic, a staple of the Ceylon cuisine, was available everywhere, but olive oil was not to be found on the shelves of any Colombo grocery. After days of patient exploration, Herbert ran a bottle of olive oil to earth in a pharmacy. He kept it under lock and key in his drinks cabinet, out of the reach of Podina who might well, in extremity, have used it to fry *papadams*.

On Fridays, when Latha returned from school and there was no need to think about homework until Sunday evening, Herbert and his daughter would spend time together in companionable cooking, then reverently put the lid on whatever poetic ensemble they had concocted according to Mrs David's sage advice, and allow it to simmer for several hours. And then they would feast on the results.

Soma Wijesinha, who had no interest in 'Western' cuisine, but recognized the importance of bringing up a daughter who could cook, observed their experiments in the family kitchen with tolerant amusement: which was a good thing, and led to peace in the home. But Latha and Herbert did not really need a companion to share their passion. A pair of conspirators, they read Elizabeth David aloud to each other and, casting Mrs Durrant's recipes for stodgy suet puddings into the waste-paper basket in Herbert's study, they drew up elaborate shopping lists and laid delightful culinary plans for weekends and holidays.

With her father's encouragement, and her memories of Vaithianathan's expertise as demonstrated at Lucas Falls to give her confidence, Latha became skilled, as she grew up, at translating theory into practice, and the unfamiliar into the everyday.

'What's an aubergine, Thaththi?'

Herbert was stumped. His memories of France, though they remained a source of pleasure, were somewhat short on detail.

'I'll find out for you.'

But Latha discovered the answer for herself. The problem was solved the following weekend, when Claire Henriet, the elegant wife of a friend of Herbert's at the newly established French Consulate, took Latha to the market with her to translate unfamiliar terms.

'*Regarde*, Sylvie!' exclaimed Madame Henriet to her daughter, delighted by the sight of wicker baskets spilling over with fresh greens and juicy vegetables of every vibrant colour under the sun. '*Des courgettes! Des citrouilles! Des aubergines!*'

Aubergines? Latha looked in the direction in which Madame Henriet's index finger with its brightly varnished nail was pointing, and saw a basketful of the familiar purple brinjals that she, like every Sinhala speaker, knew as *vambotu*. She bought a pound of 'aubergines' and three fat bulbs of garlic at the market stall, asked for bacon at the Ceylon Cold Stores, and when she got home, announced to the household:

'Guess what we're having for dinner? *Aubergines en Gigot*, from the Catalan coast of France!'

'Aiyo, Madam, I was planning to make yellow rice tonight,' Podina complained to Soma. 'I told Latha baba, "Why not let me put that nice vambotu you bought into a pickle?" And you know what she told me? "My book says oberjing anjigo is the best way in the world to eat vambotu!" Oberjing anjigo! What kind of a dish is that? How can it be better than vambotu pahi? The master should never have given Latha baba such a book.'

Podina sulked for days, since her own skills, it seemed to her, were being overlooked and undervalued. Everyone knew men were above entering a kitchen: so why else should the master – a man, after all! – act like a wife (or a domestic servant), and take a cooking spoon into his hand? Her territorial instincts were outraged by Herbert's unwarranted invasion of her personal space.

Their differences of opinion could have become a major source of friction in the household, had not Latha calmed Podina down by suggesting to Herbert that the maid-servant should join them in their shopping expeditions. Latha had gathered through her reading, and through Vaithi's example, that expert chefs prefer to buy the day's provisions early in the mornings, when the fresh produce is just being brought into the markets. Podina quickly gained status as the family's expert on the freshness of fish, and the crispness or otherwise of greens, and she soon earned a reputation among the *mudalalis* in the market stalls as a knowledgeable young woman who knew the value of things and could not be cheated. Any fish *mudalali* who surreptitiously threw a handful of wet sand into the scales when he was weighing prawns received so sharp a tongue-lashing from Podina that he didn't try it a second time. Under her guidance, learning to check eggs for freshness by floating them in cold water, learning to substitute local produce for imported or prohibitively expensive products, Latha learned also that not all wisdom is to be found in books.

Herbert was delighted by the success of this first attempt. Before long he presented Latha with a second gift, *The Good Housekeeping Book of Picture Cookery*. What it lacked in elegance and literary charm, *Picture Cookery* made up for in accuracy. On page after page, illustrated with photographs in black and white and full colour, were step-by-step instructions in dozens of culinary processes. These were merely the basics of Western cuisine presented in an orderly and scientific manner, but they seemed to Latha, reading about them in Ceylon, both delightful and exotic. She read both books over and over again, and could have recited a good deal of Mrs David's text from memory.

Another part of Latha's education for life at this time consisted, unexpectedly, of lessons in French language and culture. Herbert's memories of his idyllic student days in France had led him to suggest that Latha attend classes in French language with Madame Michelle Feuillard, an expatriate resident in Colombo. Soma hadn't seen the point of this idea. She reminded him that they were already spending more money than they could afford on Sinhala tuition: for with all the changes that were taking place in the country, and Latha so obsessed with English language and literature, it was essential that she should maintain proficiency in her own language. On this point, however, Herbert had not given in.

'French is an international language,' he said. 'You never know when or how it might come in useful.'

Soma had sniffed a little at the word 'international', but she had given way, and Latha's experience of French culture, which up to that time had been restricted to her reading of Elizabeth David and the short stories of de Maupassant which she had encountered at Lucas Falls, was expanded considerably as a result.

Michelle Feuillard, largely self-educated, claimed Parisian origins. She was not a qualified teacher of language. She had arrived in Ceylon soon after the end of World War II in the company of her protector, a rich Muslim businessman, and when he decided to establish his family and his business in Oman, she had decided to stay on in the island. Madame was a practical woman. Her liaison with Ismail had accustomed her to the good things of life, and she realized that she could live very comfortably for very little in Colombo, where servants abounded and her name was known. Hers had been a familiar face in Colombo society in her good years, and she was still on the French Embassy's invitation list. She had occasionally lent her services free of charge to the local branch of the Alliance Française, and now that she had to actually work for a living, the Ceylonese friends she had made in more prosperous times stood by her, and sent their daughters to her for the extra 'polish' that a little French vocabulary could add to their conversation.

Madame Feuillard's reputation as a teacher was based partly on her old friends' good will (Herbert had learned of her abilities through a former admirer of hers) and partly on her own sound common sense. She realized, for instance, that the spelling of French words would only further perplex students who were already coping with the idiosyncrasies of English, and she urged them to listen carefully to what she was saying, and to take down her words in their own Sinhala or Tamil script. This practical application of phonetics worked amazingly well. Madame's reputation grew as her best students demonstrated their ability to cope satisfactorily with the demands made on them at cocktail parties by their parents' European friends – no one expected from them, after all, a discourse on Sartre.

Latha enjoyed her after-school sessions in Madame Feuillard's little house. She liked dogs, and not having one of her own, was greatly entertained by her teacher's four black poodles who leaped with joy at the sight of her, shed their hairs all over Madame's chintz sofa, and resembled no dogs she had encountered anywhere else.

'Zey feel zis heat so terribly,' Madame Feuillard would say. 'Don't you, Schopie, my precious?'

And lifting her still-blonde curls from her plump neck so that she could wipe away the perspiration that was collecting there, she would welcome Schopenhauer (named for the philosopher who had famously adored poodles) into her capacious embrace and check up on whether the time had come to have his woolly coat clipped for the annual Kennel Club show. The silver cups and trophies she had won with Schopenhauer, Annabelle, Chérie and Alphonse were on display in a glass-fronted cabinet in her living room, compensating in some measure for the absence of a framed language diploma from the Sorbonne.

Madame was devoted, she said, to the wisdom of Schopenhauer (the man, not the dog), and she owed her contentment and prosperity to his views on Love and Happiness. Her life had been spent in enjoyment of one and pursuit of the other. The secret of a good life, she advised her pupils, was to avoid confusing the two. Occasionally she would take a break from teaching to get out a pack of Tarot cards and read her pupils' fortunes.

'Oo, zaire is coming soon a truly wonderful man into your love life,' she told Latha once. 'He ees not young, but he is oh, so reech . . . so generous . . . and I can see in the cards that he adores you. He will do anysing, everysing for you, if you will only be kind to heem. That ees all you have to do, to keep him beside you for ever, just be kind to heem . . . But what ees this? Zaire ees a wicked woman that I see also, she is working against you, laying her plans, plotting and scheming. *Why* is she so angry weeth you? Have you been flirting with one of her lovers, you naughty girl?'

Latha's eyes opened wide. She was unaware that she *had* a 'love life', and had met only one woman whom she might conceivably have considered 'wicked': Miss Jean Robinson, a teacher at her school who made a point of humiliating one of Latha's classmates, a girl whose school uniforms were invariably grubby at the collars because, as everyone knew, her parents couldn't afford a good dhobi and her mother did the household laundry herself.

Madame Feuillard, perceiving that her invitation to a confidence had missed its mark with this innocent, turned up another card and sighed with relief.

'But zaire is no need to worry, everysing will be all right. He will come back to you, and you will triumph.'

She changed the subject, put her cards away, and made tea for herself and her pupil.

There were other students who came to Madame for French lessons who were much more aware than Latha was of all that their teacher had to offer. One student in particular, the sophisticated daughter of a Colombo physician, whose lesson usually preceded Latha's, would generally be leaving as Latha arrived. Beside Irangani de Silva, who was already 'in sari', and whose choli blouses were skilfully fashioned by a tailor (recommended to her mother by Madame's own tailor in the Pettah) to emphasize the nipples of her pouting breasts, Latha in her shapeless white school uniform, white socks and hair-ribbons, looked and felt the child she was. Madame would often be putting the cards away as Latha arrived, indicating that a fortune-telling session with Irangani had just ended. The satisfied smiles of teacher and pupil showed that the fall of the cards had predicted something of riveting interest, perhaps an imminent meeting with an ideal husband – 'such an 'andsome, rich young man, who is oh, so crazy for you—', but Irangani, being quite as much interested in present enjoyment as in future bliss, would use Madame's telephone to arrange additional meetings with a series of current boyfriends on her way home.

'At the Savoy, then, the three-fifteen show,' she would whisper softly into the receiver and disappear into the depths of her father's car, while Latha took her exercise books out of her satchel so that Madame could check her homework.

On one occasion, Latha's lesson with Madame Feuillard was interrupted by a visit from a stranger.

'Come and join us, sweetie,' the newcomer was told. 'Come over here, and meet one of my very, very best students!'

Madame's visitor was a gentleman in his forties, well groomed and smartly dressed if somewhat portly. He was carrying several large packages in his arms, which he smilingly deposited on chairs in Madame's living room.

'You have left us nowhere to sit, you naughty boy!' exclaimed Madame.

This was true, and Latha shyly made room for him on the sofa.

'And you are early, too, Armand,' chided their hostess. 'What's this you have brought me? Such beautiful French champagne!'

'Some little presents from Paris, only,' said her guest, 'to thank you for all your gracious help.'

'Mr Armand de Silva is also a student of mine, just like you,' Madame explained to Latha, while her visitor unwrapped one of the packages. 'He has had such a success – and he says he owes it all to me, the dear, sweet boy!'

Fending off Chérie and Schopenhauer, who were so excited to see Mr de Silva that Latha wondered whether he had gifts in his pockets for them in addition to the packages he had brought for Madame, her fellow-student told Latha that he owned an import-export business which was going international, and doing very well. He had just pulled off, he said, a very profitable deal in French chiffon saris – it would be the first time ever that these desirable items appeared in Colombo shops – and the packages contained samples of his wares which he intended as gifts for Madame and her friends. Madame Feuillard fell with cries of delight on the saris he had brought with him, and immediately draped two of them over the backs of her chairs for Latha to admire. They were indeed very pretty.

'All the ladies here will be crazy for them,' said Madame. 'So soft! So delicate! I shall have mine made into an evening dress.'

She selected a black chiffon strewn with camellias shading in colour from crimson to the palest rose, and held it against herself.

'Everyone will want one like it. *Down*, Schopie, good boy! Now, *this* one,' she added, 'would be perfect for you, Latha.'

She flung several yards of soft, flowered chiffon over Latha's shoulders.

'What do you think, Armand?'

'*Très charmant*,' he replied, looking admiringly at Latha. 'Take it, take it!'

Latha had caught a glimpse of herself in the large oval mirror on Madame's wall, and it was with some regret that she folded the sari, and put it back with the others.

Madame consoled the disappointed Armand.

'I am sure she will choose one later,' she said. 'Latha is a good girl. She is also very shy. Meanwhile,' she added, 'I am so glad to see that you have been practising your French conversation.'

'It was very useful to me in Paris,' replied he, and laughed reminiscently. 'Very useful. *Voulez-vous faire une promenade avec moi, Mademoiselle?*'

It seemed to Latha that the words were accompanied by a wink, but she could not be sure. His enthusiasm was certainly not damped in the least by her own apparent lack of it. He was in a mood to celebrate, and said he hoped Latha would join him. At Madame's request he opened the bottle of champagne he had brought her, and they both laughed when the pop of the cork startled Latha.

'You are not used to champagne, Miss?' inquired Armand de Silva.

'No,' Latha said.

'But I have just poured out three glasses,' said he. 'And if you don't join in our little celebration, one glass will go to waste. It will be such a pity.'

He appealed to Madame Feuillard.

'A small glass like this one won't affect the French lesson, will it, Madame? Surely those bubbles won't go to her pretty head?'

He placed a pudgy hand on Latha's knee.

Madame did not seem to have heard Armand's question, nor, it seemed, had she observed Latha's involuntary recoil. She patted Schopenhauer's black head, sipped from the glass she held in her hand, and said appreciatively:

'Oh, this is *wonderful*, Armand. You have such excellent taste.'

'One harmless little glass of champagne only,' said the gentleman on the sofa, gazing reproachfully at Latha, 'and just see, what a fuss you are making about it! Don't be alarmed, little girl, we won't tell Mummy, it will be a secret, just between the three of us. Now, what do you say?'

Latha was silent.

'You are spoiling my celebration, you know . . . Didn't you hear our teacher say what good champagne it is? Come, let me tempt you.'

He held out the brimming glass, and looked annoyed when Latha shook her head.

'*Tiens!*' said Madame Feuillard, looking out of her window. 'Perhaps this is not quite the moment, Armand. Let us put it off for another time. Latha, *votre papa est arrivé, ma chérie*.'

She smiled and waved to Herbert from her window. He saluted her politely in return, but he did not get out of the car. Herbert made a point of personally escorting Latha to her lessons with Madame Feuillard, and he was always at the garden gate to take her home again when her lessons were over, but he never went into the house himself.

'Why don't you ask the French lady to lunch on Sunday, Latha?' Soma had suggested once. 'You could make her your Rata Twee.'

The suggestion represented a concession on Soma's part: she did not care for *ratatouille* herself – there were so many ways of cooking vegetables that were much more interesting – but she did not want her daughter to grow up thinking she disapproved of everything Western. To her surprise, Herbert had discouraged the idea. He suspected, as Soma did not, that Madame Feuillard's life still had its seamy side, and he did not want Latha to encounter her as a teacher of anything other than French conversation.

17

A CAREER FOR LATHA

When Independence came to Ceylon in 1948, it was received by local people with mixed feelings of satisfaction and foreboding. Herbert Wijesinha, who drank beer and ate devilled cashews and potato chips while playing bridge every Saturday afternoon with colleagues in the Customs department, found that the subject came increasingly under discussion between rubbers. His own attitude was noncommittal, since he did not foresee that there were any great changes in the offing. The British sahibs would be replaced, smoothly and without fuss, by their brown-skinned counterparts: 'public school' and university men, the majority of whom belonged to Herbert's own class and community, now staffed the civil and judicial services. They had been trained by the British, and could surely be trusted to do things right. Life would go on much as it had done before Independence.

In some respects, Herbert thought, life might be positively improved by the departure of their former overlords. Soma Wijesinha, who had often been annoyed by the obsequious readiness of counter clerks at Cargill's, Miller's and Whiteaways, Colombo's large department stores, to serve English women expatriates ahead of herself, looked forward to a future in which shopping would be a pleasure rather than an irritation.

Others thought differently.

'This country is going to the dogs,' stated Mr Benjamin Ferdinands, a leading light of the island's Dutch Burgher Union, with whom Herbert had a slight acquaintance since Ferdinands was occasionally invited by a Burgher member of his group of card-playing cronies to make a fourth at bridge.

Mr Ferdinands had read the writing on the wall and had realized that it would no longer be in English.

'In a land where the English language will have no place,' he said, 'there can be no place for *me*.'

Herbert became aware for the first time of certain gaps that had begun to show themselves in the society he knew. Many of his Burgher friends were preparing to 'go abroad'; but it soon became evident that they were not going abroad on holiday, but leaving the country for good. They were bound, it seemed, for Britain, Canada and Australia, countries in which English was spoken, and where they could be sure that their children received an English education. Herbert was somewhat offended by their attitude which, in his view, betrayed a mistrust of his own community. Anyone would think that Sinhalese people couldn't be trusted to be fair to minorities, he said to Soma. People like the Burghers, who had lived so long among the Sinhalese, should know us better than *that*. Characteristically, he channelled his wounded feelings into jest.

'Burghering off to bloody Australia,' he grumbled, and recorded with bitter humour in one of his manila folders of 1952 that a new Burgher art form was developing in the island as Burghers whose families had married into local communities and could not, as a result, offer the proof of European origin which Australia demanded of would-be immigrants, were constructing new family trees to replace the old ones that were stained by a Sinhalese, Tamil or Muslim connection.

Although Herbert insisted on satirizing the claims of departing Burghers to unblemished Dutch descent, the prospect of emigration from Ceylon caused some members of that community a good deal of heartbreak. Denial of their roots does not come easily to people who have lived and loved for several centuries in a land they have come to regard as 'home'. Most Burghers showed their resilience of spirit and settled energetically into their new homelands, making a virtue of necessity. Others packed their bags in resentful silence and made a vengeance of it.

The aforementioned Mr Benjamin Ferdinands, who had become expert while in Ceylon in constructing and reconstructing family trees, avenged himself by establishing a genealogical society in the Australian state of Victoria and publishing under its imprimatur a genealogical guide titled *Australians! Meet Your Ancestors!* which omitted any mention of the country he had left behind him. Herbert ordered a copy from Cave's Bookshop for his own library, and discovered fresh cause for satire when he found that the book advised Burghers who had settled in Australia to search for their origins in Holland, Germany, France and Switzerland.

'Not a mention from old Ferdie, even in passing,' he told Soma, 'of the three hundred years his own family spent in Ceylon. Have you seen his sister? Black as a boot.'

In the somewhat fraught atmosphere that surrounded the granting of Independence to Ceylon by the British, the elderly Burgher teachers at Amarapāli Maha Vidyālaya began, one by one, to retire, leaving the island to join members of their families who had emigrated to the West soon after the General Election of 1947. (They were doing the same at

Ashcombe.) The most cursory glance at the school registers revealed that the numbers of Burgher students enrolled were shrinking each year. By the time Latha reached the first form, almost all her Burgher friends, the classmates with whom she had sat in class all the way up the Junior School, had vanished, and by the time she reached the Fifth Form, her class was almost one hundred per cent Sinhalese by race and Buddhist by religion. The few exceptions were Tamil and Muslim.

The teachers who had retired or emigrated were replaced by a new breed of youthful graduates of the University of Ceylon. Idealistic and purposeful, these energetic young women came into the teaching profession with ideas very different from those that had been held by Miss Christoffelsz and Mrs Durrant. Proud of their hard-won degrees, they looked forward to preparing their pupils for a university education.

It came as a considerable shock to a good many of them, therefore, to discover that they were not expected to prepare their students for any career other than marriage. One of these disillusioned young teachers was Paula Ferdinands, who taught English to the middle and senior school at Amarapāli. Paula, a niece of Herbert Wijesinha's acquaintance Mr Benjamin Ferdinands, had chosen, unlike her disgruntled elder relative, to stay on in Ceylon when most members of her family were filling out Australian immigration papers. Her reason for doing so had not endeared her to her uncle.

Pretty Paula Ferdinands had fallen in love while at University with a most unsuitable young man – unsuitable, that is, from the point of view of the Ferdinands family, which claimed descent from an ancestor who had 'come over' to Ceylon in the entourage of a seventeenth-century Dutch governor. Rajan Phillips, two years older than Paula, a brilliant (if unorthodox) idealist, had arrived in the island from the opposite direction. He had been born and educated in Malaya, and had been sent to Ceylon for his university education while the rest of his Tamil family remained in Kuala Lumpur.

Rajan had made an instant impression on Paula when they met on campus at Thurstan Road. She had never in her life met anyone remotely like him: the young men of her own community, solid, stalwart members of the Burgher Recreation Club, played rugger and cricket, and never, if they could help it, opened a book. Sitting with Rajan in the university canteen, gazing into his deeply intelligent dark eyes while he described to her his vision of a world in which concepts such as those of race, class and caste would disintegrate totally, and interpersonal relationships take priority above everything else, Paula's defences had melted like butter on oven-warm *breudher*. Rajan quoted Keats to Paula as they walked to the Thurstan Road bus stop, and taught her, from the eclecticism of his Malayan experience, how to choose the most delicious items on the menu of the Modern Chinese Restaurant without breaking their budget. They had to watch the rupees and cents, for neither of them had much money to spend on entertainment: Paula was on an allowance from her father, and Rajan, who boarded with other students at a guest-house near the campus, had to economize on every aspect of his living. (Asked once why he didn't think of shaving off his beard, Rajan had replied that he was saving on the purchase of razor-blades.)

Paula was one of the few persons outside her family whose signature figured in Latha's autograph album. This was partly because Latha regarded Miss Ferdinands as a true 'celebrity', and looked forward with the deepest pleasure to her English classes each week. But it was also because Latha was powerfully attracted to anything in her unremarkable world that represented romance. Paula certainly represented romance.

Her marriage to Rajan, like everything else about them, had been wildly romantic: gossip was rife at Amarapāli that Rajan had called one afternoon at the Ferdinandses' house to find Paula weeding flower-beds near the front porch. Entirely on impulse ('She went when he called her, *with the earth still on her hands*!' one of Latha's school friends informed her class with awe in her voice; 'can you *imagine* it?'), Paula and Rajan had rustled up a classmate to act as a witness to their marriage, and had then taken a bus to the nearest registry office to emerge from it as Mr and Mrs Phillips. They had set up their first home in a friend's garage – *a garage!* said the girls at Amarapāli – from which, after graduation from the University, they had moved, on the money they earned from teaching, to a tiny cottage by the sea at Mount Lavinia. This was convenient for Rajan, who had joined the teaching staff of St Alban's College, located in the same seaside suburb. It was not so convenient for Paula, for whom each day's teaching at Amarapāli involved bus travel to Colombo and back, since they could not afford a car, even on their joint salaries. But she never complained, nor did she wish herself back among the comforts of her parents' house in respectable, conservative Spathodea Avenue.

The Phillipses' neighbours were Sinhalese villagers, illiterates for the most part, who kept pigs, goats and chickens that frequently strayed into their tiny garden. Paula and Rajan didn't mind: this was, after all, the beginning of Rajan's 'New World Order', a community of people of all walks of life, in which people valued one another as friends and fellow-workers.

The socialist theories according to which young Mrs Phillips was living her married life were not known to the Board of Governors at Amarapāli M.V. What they did know, and greatly respected, were Paula's solidly respectable Dutch Burgher background, her first-class degree in English, and her ability to secure outstanding examination results. Following her arrival at the school, the reputation of Amarapāli M.V.'s English teaching had soared. These things cancelled out the Tamil background and somewhat dishevelled, Byronic appearance of Paula's husband. Wisely refraining from discussing anything in class but the literary uses of the English language, and anything in the staff room but the price of groceries, Paula got on very well with everyone. She was popular with her younger colleagues, and was hero-worshipped by at least one of her students.

Frustrated by her failure to get a love of literature past the closed minds of the young ladies of Amarapāli, Paula Phillips thought she saw in Latha a glimmer of hope for the future. The essays Latha submitted as she moved through middle and senior school cheered Paula's heart and uplifted her spirits. She congratulated herself on having discovered a student who responded to literature, a child who was unusually well read, and excelled in composition. Was Latha Wijesinha university material? Why not? Latha had just acquitted herself with distinction in the Senior School Certificate examination. And in the middle of Composition one day, when Latha had just turned sixteen, Paula posed a fateful question to her class.

'Well, girls, have you given any thought to what you will do in two years' time, when you leave school?'

The class giggled. Why was Mrs Phillips asking such a silly question? Of course they knew what they would do when they left school. They would get married. Marriage was the occupation for which their parents and Amarapāli M.V. had trained them. Was there any other?

One student put up her hand.

'Miss, yes, Miss.'

'Well, Malini?'

'I'll be getting married, Miss. To my cousin Ananda.'

The giggles swelled into a wave of laughter. Everyone knew all about Malini's cousin Ananda, now in his final year at Medical College. One talented artist in the class had offered to design Malini's wedding sari, another had promised to organize delivery of baskets of flowers from her father's rubber estate to decorate the dais on which the bride and her groom would stand during the ceremony. Although not all of them were conveniently supplied with eligible cousins, marriage had been the constant subject of their thoughts and conversations throughout the past year. Why, it was only that very afternoon that they had been regaling one another during the lunch interval with descriptions of 'inspection visits' paid by 'prospectives' to their homes.

'He has coconut property in Chilaw,' one girl had said, 'and his father owns plumbago mines. The marriage broker says the family's very rich. The moment Amma was informed that he was calling with his parents to inspect me, she sent the drawing-room curtains off to Burtol's to have them dry-cleaned, and insisted on beating every carpet in the house.'

'That's nothing: our entire house was colour-washed, when one of my prospectives came calling,' said another. 'And all the chairs in the sitting room were re-upholstered in red plush.'

'My father ransacked Blooms for carnations and roses to plant an instant garden outside the dining room. Can you beat that?' said a third.

'What was the poor man coming to inspect, the curtains, the carpets, the garden, or you?' their friends had wanted to know.

'That's just what I asked Amma. She told me not to be cheeky, and sent me off with the ayah to get my hair done at Elegance. No one's told me yet if any proposal came for me, but who's complaining? I got a new sari out of it, with a handbag and embroidered shoes to match, designed specially for me by Kirthi, so it wasn't a complete waste of time.'

Had they known of these lunch-time conversations, Latha's mother and her aunts would have frowned on such casual hilarity. They knew what their daughters did not: that marriage in Ceylon is not a laughing matter, but an extremely serious business. Marriages are – or, at any rate, they were in the 1930s – negotiated at 'top level' between parents, elders and go-betweens with due attention to considerations of caste, religion, status and dowry. Only when all have agreed, and only then – provided, of course, that the astrologers judge the stars of the young couple to be in appropriate and auspicious relationship to one another – is the proposal permitted to filter down to the 'lower level', i.e., to the young man and woman most intimately concerned. Once that point is reached, it only remains for the pair to meet, suitably chaperoned, and the arrangements which have already been made on their behalf by the family to be confirmed and ratified. The young couple, assured of their elders' support in their new life together, obediently prepare themselves to . . . do what? To fall in love? Not quite. 'Falling in love', parents such as Soma Wijesinha said, was an idea imported from the West, and nourished by sentimental novels and romantic films. Much more realistic, as she and her sisters knew well, is the ancestral wisdom that distinguishes between marriages arranged by elders and marriages undertaken for 'love' alone:

A pot of cold water placed on a hot fire will eventually come to the boil, but a pot of boiling water placed on cold ashes will inevitably grow cold.

Latha's Aunt Caroline would quote the Sinhala proverb sententiously whenever the subject of marriage came up in general conversation, and everybody would nod their heads in agreement.

Timing, however, is everything. The parents of Latha's classmates had been growing increasingly worried as their daughters approached the crucial age of eighteen. For after that point, the presence of an unmarried daughter in a Ceylonese household becomes a daily reproach. The world begins to say that the poor child's family have obviously not tried hard enough to 'find someone' for her to marry, or that they are too poor to offer a dowry large enough to attract a proposal. With every passing day, the search for a suitable son-in-law was becoming more and more desperate, even as, like silk moths stirring their wings, ready to take flight, the hearts of their daughters were beginning to flutter excitedly, pleasurably, at the prospect of marriage. Not only would marriage give them households of their own, but it would free them from the irksome presence of the chaperones and ayahs who presently accompanied them on every outing on the strict instructions of their parents.

'Any other career plans?'

The class looked blankly back at Paula Phillips.

A hand went up in the third row.

'My mother wants me to take classes in shorthand and typing, Miss. Until I get married.'

Mrs Phillips wrote this information down.

'Other careers that anyone has in mind?'

Her pencil moved down the list, and stopped.

'Latha Wijesinha: have *you* any thoughts about a future career?'

When the school bell rang at the end of the morning, Paula Phillips came into the Staff Room, slammed her books down on a table, and threw herself into a wicker chair. Her colleagues looked at her inquiringly. They knew her to be a quiet young woman, not given to making overly dramatic gestures.

'I need this,' Paula said, pouring herself a cup of tea. 'I've just had a nasty shock. If there were any brandy in that staff room cupboard, I'd be adding it to the tea. Let me warn you, you'll be needing some too.'

Latha Wijesinha, said Paula, one of those four really bright girls in VIB whom they were all doing their best to get into University, had just informed her that she had her future all planned, and that it had nothing to do with university studies.

'Next year,' Latha had stated, 'I want to enrol for the Diploma in Domestic Science at the Good Housekeeping Institute in London.'

'Just think about that,' Paula said, sipping her tea. 'As calm as you please. You'd imagine she'd never heard of university studies, never heard of Peradeniya.'

Latha had, as a matter of fact, heard herself answer Mrs Phillips's unexpected question with almost as much surprise as the teacher herself. She had never actually put her half-formed ambition into words before. But now that the words had been spoken, Latha grew more confident. Yes, she had said to herself: that's what I want to do.

Some moments had passed before Mrs Phillips responded.

'An interesting idea, Latha,' she had said at last. 'Did your parents suggest this as something they would like you to do?'

'No, Mrs Phillips.'

'Where did you hear of this Institute?'

'I read about it. There was an article about it in the newspapers. It said the Institute is the best place in Britain for proper Domestic Science training. When I have my diploma, I'd like to enrol for a *Cordon Bleu* in Paris. What I'd *really* like,' Latha had added, warming to her theme, 'is to do the *Cordon Bleu* first, but it's sure to be more expensive than a British diploma, and they may be more willing to enrol me in Paris if I already have a qualification—'

'And what will the Institute in London and the cookery school in Paris train you for, Latha? Is it your life's ambition to teach Domestic Science at Amarapāli?'

With surprise Latha detected sarcasm in the voice of her favourite teacher. Mrs Phillips sounded like her Uncle Rowland in one of his meanest moods. What could she have said to annoy her so much?

But she decided that she was not going to retreat from her chosen position. In frequent re-readings of the text of her beloved *Picture Cookery*, she had unconsciously registered more than processes of food preparation, and an answer to this new question floated into her head with no need for any rehearsal.

'Oh, no, Mrs Phillips. I'm hoping, if I'm good enough, to succeed Miss Phyllis L. Garbutt as Director of the Institute.'

It was this remark, seemingly symptomatic of thought and prior planning on the part of her best student, that had upset and annoyed Paula Phillips.

'We simply cannot stand by and let this happen,' she told her colleagues. 'It's up to us to do something about it.'

'I don't see why *we* should get involved,' the Assistant Librarian said doubtfully. 'Not if Latha has made up her mind. And if she does decide to come back and teach here, she'd certainly do a much better job running Domestic Science than dear old Ma Durrant.'

Everyone agreed that it was certainly time Mrs Durrant retired. They also advised their colleague against interference in Latha Wijesinha's plans.

'Believe me, Paula, you don't want to get into an argument with that mother of Latha's,' said one of them. 'I met Mrs W. at the last P.T.A. meeting. A strong resemblance to a bulldozer. If she's the person who has put the idea into Latha's head, you haven't a hope of bringing her round to any other point of view.'

'I don't know,' Paula said thoughtfully. 'Latha didn't say it was her parents' idea. I asked her that very question, and she said she'd read about the Institute in a newspaper article. Besides, she strikes me as an original child, with a mind of her own—'

Her colleagues looked at Paula with amused concern.

'Friends, did you hear that?' the Assistant Librarian asked of the world in general. 'Paula, Paula, this is the real world you're living in. A young woman with "a mind of her own"? In this country? What are you talking about?'

Paula told her colleagues about the first English composition Latha had handed her in class. She had been so delighted with it that she had copied it for her personal file.

'I'd asked the first-formers to model their compositions on Addison's *The Adventures of a Shilling*,' she said. 'You remember the essay – a coin minted in the reign of Queen Elizabeth travels from hand to hand and from generation to generation, gets locked up for years in a miser's hoard, then is spent with all its companions by the miser's spendthrift son . . . Well, everyone in the class wrote their compositions to the Addisonian pattern. They were so boring and predictable that I practically fell asleep reading them. Then I read Latha's. It was only one page long, and it was titled *The Adventures of a Prawn*. Her composition had that prawn hatched with millions of its brothers and sisters in the warm waters of the Indian Ocean. After several exciting adventures, in which the prawn escapes from a shark and encounters a pussycat, it ends up in Crustacean Heaven – a wedding luncheon in Paris – nestling in a cream sauce flavoured with garlic and basil, on a bed of saffron rice. I've never had anything like it from any of the classes I teach. Certainly not from a first-former. The way that child writes! She'd be wasted doing a Domestic Science diploma. *That's* what I'm talking about.'

'Well, she's obviously passionate about food,' the Assistant Librarian said. 'Is she passionate about anything else? Literature, for instance?'

'She's the best student in my Literature class,' Paula said simply. 'I cannot – *will not* – lose her to Domestic Science.'

'That composition of hers has made me hungry,' said another teacher. 'I don't know whether you are aware of it, folks, but it's time for lunch.'

'Well, Paula,' the Assistant Librarian said, as they left the Staff Room. 'What are you going to do about this student of yours?'

'I don't know yet,' Paula replied. 'But I'll work something out.'

18

A SWEET, SIMPLE GIRL

'Herbie,' Soma Wijesinha said the following evening. She sounded puzzled. 'I had a telephone call at the school today, from one of Latha's teachers at Amarapāli. She apologized for ringing in school hours, but she doesn't have a phone at home.'

'Well, neither do we,' Herbert said reasonably. 'Who was she, and what did she want?'

'She said she was a Mrs Phillips,' said his wife. 'From the name, can't be Sinhalese, must be Burgher or Tamil. The voice sounded Burgher.'

'Well, what did Mrs Phillips want? Has Latha got a problem at school?'

'No, no! In fact, just the opposite – wait till you hear! But this Mrs Phillips didn't ring to talk about Latha's school work, she rang to ask me a question. Did I know, she said, that Latha was planning a career in Domestic Science?'

Herbert considered this.

'First I've heard of it,' he said. 'Has Latha said anything to you about it?'

'No, Herbie. But it sounds as if she said quite a lot about it to Mrs Phillips. She says Latha told her she has her future all planned: first, a diploma in London, then training in a cookery school in Paris, and then a career in Domestic Science. She sounded quite upset about it. Well, I didn't see that this teacher had any reason to be annoyed about Latha's choosing a career like that – it isn't as if she'd said she wanted to be a circus performer or a film actress – so I told her no, I didn't know about it, but if that was what Latha would like to do, we had no objection.'

'Quite right,' said Herbert.

'Then she asked me another question. Didn't we think, she said, that Latha should give up this Domestic Science idea entirely, and go to University instead? She says that if you and I give our permission, she is willing to give Latha special classes to prepare her for the Scholarship Examination.'

'What Scholarship Examination?'

‘A scholarship to the University, Herbie. To Peradeniya. Mrs Phillips says Latha is the best student she has ever had. Now, what do you think of *that*?’ Soma’s voice was full of pride. ‘She says she would have a very good chance of winning the scholarship if she put her mind to it. What do you think?’

University? It had never been Herbert Wijesinha’s intention to send his daughter to University. When a girl’s schooldays came to an end, what was there for her to do but get married? And now this teacher had told Soma that Latha should go to University instead. Obviously, Soma was pleased to hear such praise of their daughter’s intelligence. Well, so was he, more pleased than he cared to admit. (After all, girls were not meant to be brainy, were they?) But are we pleased *enough*, Herbert asked himself, to actually send her to University? He wasn’t sure about that. He tried to imagine what Latha would say if he and Soma were to suggest the possibility of a university career to her. The matter had never been discussed in their family before now, but then, it had never come up.

The costs of special tuition were likely to be high, of course . . .

‘Soma,’ he said, ‘what kind of person is this Mrs Phillips? Did she strike you as someone who wants to make money out of parents? We may not be able to afford tuition. Why don’t we ask her what her charges would be?’

‘Did you think for one moment that I would forget to ask her that question?’ said his wife. ‘Of course I asked her! And that’s another funny thing – she doesn’t intend to charge anything at all. She said she would be teaching Latha out of interest. I told her I’d talk to you and ring her back. What shall I say, Herbie?’

‘I think we should ask Latha what she wants to do, before you speak to Mrs Phillips,’ Herbert said. He tried to sound as casual as possible. ‘She may not be interested at all in going to University.’

The question was accordingly put to Latha at dinner that evening. To Herbert and Soma’s surprise, it was answered with complete silence.

‘You don’t have to tell us right away, duwa,’ Herbert said at last. ‘Maybe tomorrow or the day after would be all right. But your mother tells me that Mrs Phillips needs to have a firm answer soon.’

In bed that night, Latha tried to calm her restless thoughts. Some of her classmates, she knew, were already preparing for the university entrance examination. She had not put her name down for it. What was the point? She would inevitably have to do as her mother decided, and she had learned while growing up that her wishes did not always coincide with her mother’s decisions. Why hope for something, and then be disappointed? Latha had contented herself with hoping that her parents would come to a decision one way or another before it was time for her to sit the Higher School Certificate exam.

Latha knew that the H.S.C. was combined with the university entrance examination: if you passed one, you automatically passed the other. She had done well in the S.S.C., so why not the next one up, the H.S.C.? A University sounded, she thought, very much like a grown-up version of school; and Latha certainly enjoyed her school life, so why should she not enjoy going to University?

When she said so to her parents at dinner the following night, Soma pursed her lips and looked meaningfully across the dining table at Herbert. She said nothing, however, and the next day she rang Mrs Phillips to say that she and her husband agreed to the proposal of extra classes for Latha with the possibility – Soma would not concede that it was more than the merest possibility – of a university career in mind. But she was not happy about it.

On the first Tuesday that Herbert took his daughter along to the Phillipses' home, he received something of a shock. The readiness of a school teacher to forgo a tuition fee had led him to think that Mrs Phillips must live in comfortable, if modest, surroundings. He had certainly not expected squalor. A large sow with several piglings in tow had run, grunting and squealing, across the dirt road that led to the cottage, practically under the wheels of his car. A woman dressed in a cloth and a soiled jacket had come running out of the hut next door to the Phillipses' little house, waving a towel, and had chivvied the pigs into their pen. She had smiled at Herbert, showing him a row of betel-stained teeth, and thanked him: presumably, Herbert thought, for not destroying her means of livelihood. She had then called out to Paula Phillips that she had visitors.

At the sound of the woman's voice, the occupants of the neighbouring huts and houses had come to their doorways. By the time the Phillipses' front door opened and Rajan Phillips emerged, the Wijesinhas had been thoroughly inspected.

'Do come in,' Rajan said, holding the door open for Herbert and Latha. 'Paula won't be a minute.'

Herbert's first thought as he surveyed the Phillipses' minuscule front room was that he was in familiar territory. Books were stacked on the floor and along the walls, journals and still more books covered the surface of every available table and occupied every chair. Apart from his own, he had never seen so large a private library. Rajan removed some books from two of the chairs so that Herbert and Latha could sit down, and, leaning against a window-sill, offered them tea.

'Not for me, thanks,' Herbert said. 'I must be on my way. I'll be back at . . . when would Mrs Phillips wish to end the lesson? In an hour's time?'

'Make it two,' Rajan said, pouring Latha a lemonade.

'Wonderful collection you've got here,' Herbert said as he left.

He had just spotted on the dining table a book by Arthur Koestler that he had seen reviewed the previous week in the *Daily News*, but had rejected the thought of buying because it was so expensive. Phillips must spend a fortune on books, he thought. Why doesn't he get himself some bookshelves?

Latha hadn't known what to expect of her lessons with Mrs Phillips, but to be on the safe side had brought along an exercise book and several pencils.

Mrs Phillips opened a book, and laid it on the table between them.

'*The Village in the Jungle*,' she said. 'By Leonard Woolf. Have you ever heard of Leonard Woolf, Latha? Or of his wife Virginia Woolf?'

Latha had heard the name of Virginia Woolf, but not that of Leonard. She now learned that Virginia, who was dead, and Leonard, who was alive and living in England, were famous authors. Paula informed her that some respected critics thought Virginia Woolf the greatest writer of the present day.

'But Leonard has a special importance for us in Ceylon,' she continued, 'because he lived here for many years, and after he returned to England, he wrote a novel about this country. This is the novel he wrote.'

Latha looked at the book with interest. It was covered in green cloth, with its title stamped in black on the front and on the spine. She had, without thinking about it, assumed that all novels, especially novels by English authors, were about English shires and cities: Yorkshire or Hampshire, or Derbyshire (home of Mr Darcy in *Pride and Prejudice*), and of course London.

'I'd like to hear you read the first few pages aloud, Latha,' Mrs Phillips said.

> *The village was called Beddagama* [Latha read], *which means the village in the jungle. It lay in the low country or plains, midway between the sea and the great mountains which seem, far away to the north, to rise like a long wall straight up from the sea of trees. It was in, and of, the jungle; the air and smell of the jungle lay heavy upon it – the smell of hot air, of dust, and of dry and powdered leaves and sticks. Its beginning and its end was in the jungle, which stretched away from it on all sides unbroken, north and south and east and west, to the blue line of the hills and to the sea. The jungle surrounded it, overhung it, continually pressed in upon it . . .*

And so began Latha's first lesson with Paula Phillips, and her first encounter with the idea that her own country could inspire poetic English prose, the most poetic prose, Latha thought, that she had ever read in her life. That first chapter was a long one, but Latha read on, uninterrupted by either Paula or Rajan (who passed silently through the front room once, and refilled Latha's empty glass as he did so), until she had finished it.

'I'm lending you the book, Latha,' Mrs Phillips said. 'It's my only copy. As you can see, its spine is a little worn, so treat it carefully, read it, and bring it with you when you come to see me next Tuesday. Then we'll talk about it.'

Their sessions together followed the same pattern each week, varied only by the variation in the books Paula Phillips introduced to Latha, and in the music Rajan Phillips played on an ancient gramophone that stood on a small table near the window. Conrad's *Heart of Darkness*, Katherine Mansfield's *The Garden Party* and *Miss Brill*, D.H. Lawrence's *The Rocking Horse Winner* – some of these titles Latha had seen at Lucas Falls, she had even looked into some of them, but she had never read them in quite this way, as objects for analysis, thought and discussion. She enjoyed the music Rajan chose, which was new to her: Bach, Beethoven, Handel, Mozart. 'Extension sessions' was the term Rajan used for the Tuesday classes: he seemed as pleased as his wife was, that there was so much already in Latha to extend. The range of her reading surprised them both, and they learned with interest of her holidays at Lucas Falls, and the library where she had spent so many hours undisturbed.

'But Thaththa's got a library too,' Latha said. 'Only, it's mostly cricket. And politics.'

Rajan was very interested.

'Oh, yes? What kind of politics?'

'Ceylon politics,' was the answer. 'But he doesn't buy as many books nowadays as he used to. He buys mostly magazines.'

When Rajan invited Herbert on his next visit to spend some time looking at his books, and to borrow any that he might like to read, Herbert hesitated at first, then accepted with pleasure.

'Your friends the Phillipses' house is like a lending library,' Herbert told Latha.

Not infrequently, while Paula Phillips and Latha talked books and music inside the tiny cottage, Rajan Phillips and Herbert Wijesinha talked books and politics outside it, as they strolled along the railway line, and gazed out over the sea at the setting sun.

It was inevitable that, along with a deeper appreciation of the way words worked, Latha would absorb from her visits to the Phillipses at Mount Lavinia, something of their way of looking at life. She noticed that their relationship with their pig-rearing next-door neighbour Seelawathie was very different from everything she knew at home or anything she had encountered at Lucas Falls. Raman, Vaithi, Alice – what had been required of them by her uncle was service, not friendship. She tried to imagine her parents – even her father – speaking to Podina with the easy comradeship she saw demonstrated between Rajan and Seelawathie, and failed. Podina and her kind would have been regarded by Tsunami's family, and even by her own, as servants, not friends.

At home Latha talked only about the English literature texts she was reading with Mrs Phillips. This was wise: Soma Wijesinha would have been greatly disturbed if she had had any inkling that a quiet revolution was taking place in her daughter's mind. Latha went to Mrs Phillips for lessons in English, after all, not for indoctrination into a value system alien to all proper thinking. Soma had not, as it happened, actually seen the neighbourhood to which Herbert took Latha every Tuesday. But she was aware that Mrs Phillips was a Burgher (of good family) and her husband a Tamil. Theirs were communities of which Soma knew little and about which she cared less. It was nice of Mrs Phillips to give time to Latha free of charge, but then, why shouldn't she? It must be a pleasure to her to teach an intelligent girl like Latha; and anyway, Mrs Phillips probably realized that Latha (being a member of the Wijesinha family) was conferring honour and dignity on the Phillips household by the mere act of visiting it.

Soma, who had always resented Latha's affection for Helen Wijesinha, had been secretly relieved when Helen's elopement with Franz Goldman removed her from the family circle as a source of unsuitable values. She had no idea that Latha had begun to replace the single image of her Aunt Helen with the double image of Paula and Rajan Phillips. Latha looked forward to her weekly visits, not only because she always carried away from them some new way of looking at the literature she loved, but because she felt herself growing as a person from the moment she entered their house at Mount Lavinia, and took her accustomed place among the Phillipses' piles of books and journals. Without their ever saying so, it was clear that Rajan and Paula were unimpressed by the things that constituted her selfhood outside their home: her status as the daughter of her parents, as a Sinhalese, even her status as Paula's pupil and a student at Amarapāli M.V., receded into insignificance. It seemed to Latha that in their company she became a person in her own right, a person of value for what she was in herself, not for what she represented. This was a completely new idea to her, and it took her some time to get used to it.

Herbert, for his part, found Rajan Phillips stimulating company, if somewhat extreme in his theories about Ceylon's place in the world and its political future as an independent nation. Their views on most things to do with politics were almost diametrically opposed: Rajan, for example, resented the presence in Ceylon of a British Governor-General, Herbert (who had met the monocled Lord Soulbury at his cousin Rowland's house) rather liked the old boy.

'He's a witty man, has a nice turn of phrase and an eye for a pretty girl,' he told Rajan, who was not amused.

Herbert believed that with D.S. Senanayake, the country's first Prime Minister, at the helm of affairs, things could not go too far wrong. Rajan, convinced that the 'Grand Old Man' was grooming a son of his to succeed him in a dynastic succession, while continuing to talk about democratic elections, thought this view extremely naïve.

One evening Herbert broached a subject with Rajan that he had, from a sense of delicacy, hitherto avoided. But it had been on his mind for some time, and he felt that Rajan, who had been born and brought up outside Ceylon and, furthermore, was a partner in a 'mixed marriage', might produce an objective, because distanced, opinion on it.

'What do you think, Mr Phillips,' inquired Herbert, as the two men took their now familiar path, stepping across the railway sleepers to the beach on the other side of the railway line, 'of the direction in which race relations are moving in this country? I'm asking you this question because you and your wife seem to achieve a balance in your attitude which I don't see in many of the people I meet. And especially not in our politicians.'

Rajan Phillips smiled.

'Paula and I are people without power in this society, Mr Wijesinha,' he said. 'We belong to minority communities so small that they are insignificant in the scheme of things, so we can afford to take a balanced view: we stand to gain nothing, whatever view we take. Your position is very different, is it not? Your community is, overwhelmingly, the majority community in this country. Whatever your personal view might be, you would, if pushed to make a decision in a crisis, think and act as your community does. Is that not so?'

'Not a bit of it!' returned Herbert warmly. 'I think as an individual. Always have.'

'But you are not in politics, Mr Wijesinha. Several of your relations are: and that makes a difference, you know. You don't need to think about the next election, except to hope that a party will win power that has the nation's welfare at heart. *They* cannot think about the next election except in terms of getting elected. When they have to make a decision, that objective would take priority over all other considerations. It must.'

'All considerations except race,' Herbert said. 'I have a cousin who is a politician, and I am quite certain that he would never let race become an issue. No gentleman would. I don't know how much you know of this country, Mr Phillips, but when I was a boy, people of different cultural and religious backgrounds appreciated each other. Mixed marriages such as yours were rare – they still are – but they did occur; my cousin – this same cousin – married a Tamil from India. The point I wish to make is that close friendships across race lines were a fact of ordinary life. But when I read the papers today, especially the speeches of politicians, it seems to me that we are losing the ability to understand and appreciate one another.'

As soon as he had said this, Herbert felt embarrassed. He was not accustomed to talking so openly about his inmost doubts and fears. He remembered how, as a young man returning by P&O from Europe, he had sometimes found himself confided in by perfect strangers on board ship. They seemed driven to reveal their most private concerns: as the ship entered the Red Sea, all manner of details about breaking marriages, spendthrift sons and wayward daughters were recounted to the sympathetic young Ceylonese who was such a good listener. He wondered whether Phillips was amused by this version of a shipboard confidence. He glanced covertly at his companion's face, and could detect no sign of amusement there.

'You're right to be concerned, Mr Wijesinha,' Rajan said at last. 'If people lose the ability to communicate with each other and they are divided by politics or language—'

'The politics *of* language, rather,' interrupted Herbert.

'Certainly: the politics *of* language, we will be entering upon a dangerous period in the country's history. On the other hand, change, of one kind and another, has to take place, as you know. That's part of life. So we have to remember that when you talk of close friendships that were established across race lines, you are talking, not only of the past, but of the educated elite to which you and your cousin belong. You know what it was to sit in the same class room with students of other communities, you conversed in English and played cricket and football with them, you visited their homes and were treated to their mothers' cooking. Later, you went to University with them, today you probably play bridge with them—'

Herbert laughed.

'Quite right,' he said. 'How did you know?'

'It figures,' Rajan replied simply. 'That's the way our societies developed under the British: it's very much the same in Malaya. The question that is probably troubling you is: how long will it last, this pleasant state of affairs that you remember, now that the British have left?'

'I tell myself,' Herbert said, 'that it's lasted five years. I see that as a good augury for the future. Don't you? Why should it not continue?'

'Oh, it should. We must all hope that it will. But not everyone belongs to your educated elite, Mr Wijesinha. Beneath you and your educated friends and relations are many thousands of people who have never known the rapport with other communities that you describe. I don't mean that they are hostile to them, not at all. But tolerance is what I see and feel around me, not friendship and shared experience. Not yet. By choosing to live here, Paula and I have deliberately engaged in an experiment. I suppose you must have surmised that by now. It's not a complicated experiment, it's quite a simple one, in fact. We just try – in our dealings with our neighbours, for instance – to substitute friendship for tolerance. Because tolerance can evaporate when hard times come, or when politicians play on the emotions of uneducated people.'

The sea had become turbulent. Large waves had begun to roll towards the sea-shore, and the crash of the breakers against the rocks bordering the far side of the beach almost drowned his words.

'That,' Herbert said, raising his voice in order to be heard by his companion, 'is exactly what I'm afraid of. I suppose you will think I've got a lively imagination, but some of the things I hear people say are making me very uneasy.'

Herbert wondered whether Rajan had heard him. His next words showed that he had.

'There are cranks in every society, Mr Wijesinha,' Rajan said. 'Don't let them discourage you, sir! From what I've seen of this country, cranks get short shrift from the sensible people here. I'm teaching my students at St Alban's – which I understand from Latha was your old school – literary criticism by asking them to analyse paragraphs from political speeches taken from the daily papers. How many genuine ideas does a typical speech contain? How much does it rely on emotional language? That sort of thing. You'd be cheered by the results I'm getting. I have every confidence in the intelligence and good sense of your daughter's generation. It's getting very windy. Shall we turn back?'

Soma Wijesinha, meanwhile, did not cease to worry. She believed that every woman must equip herself to earn a living, even if her position in life did not require her to do so. A product of Ceylon's Teachers' Training College, Soma was proud of her contribution to the family's income. Thinking on these lines, she was well in advance of her own times, and certainly in advance of most of the women in her husband's family. A cousin of Herbert's, asked by the editor of a newspaper's Women's Page for her views on university education for women, had replied flatly:

'Nice girls don't go to University.'

But there were matters on Soma's mind that went far beyond her belief in female independence. She wondered whether she and Herbert had done right to mention university studies to Latha at all. The new University established at Peradeniya, seventy-two miles from Colombo, was not only residential but, unlike the sedate private school to which she and Herbert had sent Latha, it was co-educational. In that seemingly simple fact lurked all manner of horrors. What if Latha, having been allowed to go to Peradeniya, far removed from parental supervision and control, were to meet some thoroughly unsuitable young man and elope with him? Or, worse still, come back home unmarried and pregnant? The very thought of that was enough to keep Soma up all night, worrying.

She did not communicate these ideas directly to Latha. But she discussed her fears privately with Herbert in Sinhala, and although she veiled them in euphemisms, and avoided using proper nouns, it was not difficult for Latha listening attentively when her parents believed her to be asleep, to work out exactly what they were talking about.

'Suppose, Herbie,' Soma said one night, 'just suppose that as a result of going up there, and *falling into trouble*, the child ends up *smearing charcoal on our faces*, what shall we do? What will people think of us?'

Decoded from the Sinhala, this translated – for Latha, at sixteen, was by no means as innocent as her mother believed her to be – as a very real fear of the public disgrace that would inevitably follow the pregnancy of an unmarried daughter; and worse, of ostracism within the family circle. On no account, she decided, should her mother's fears be given food on which to grow. Not if she wanted to be allowed to go to University. Because, from the moment that Peradeniya had been mentioned by her father over the dinner table as a real possibility, Latha had secretly decided that a cookery diploma and a *Cordon Bleu* could wait. She and Tsunami had dreamed as children of 'coming out' in London, but those dreams had disappeared long ago, and 'Abroad' had no charms for her. What she wanted now – though she was reluctant to admit it to herself – was a life removed from the home in which she had grown up, a yearning for privacy and independence which had sprung from a sudden, sharp awareness that there were many pairs of eyes watching her, and judging her every move. Could she achieve such a life within the island? Perhaps Peradeniya might be the haven she was looking for.

Perceiving that her parents had not yet made up their minds on the subject of a university education, Latha wished that her aunt Helen were at hand to discuss the problem with her. Or her cousin Christopher. If only she could ask Chris for advice! Tsunami, of course, was her kindred spirit, but Christopher, of all the Lucas Falls family, had been Latha's particular guide and friend in moments of doubt and worry.

In the absence of the support she needed, Latha went instinctively on defence alert. She enjoyed the intellectual exchanges that were possible with her father, but she had long learned the wisdom of never appearing 'forward' or 'advanced' in the presence of her mother and her aunts: in their vocabulary these were capital crimes. Quiet and reticent by nature, Latha now became particularly cautious in her behaviour towards any male with whom she found herself in company. In the presence of a man – any man – she barely raised her gaze from the floor, and never on any account did she catch a masculine eye, not even that of an elderly uncle.

Her efforts were rewarded when, towards the end of the school year, her mother raised no objections to Latha's eventually sitting the Higher School Certificate examination with the rest of her classmates. An H.S.C. certificate, Soma had reasoned, would after all be an even better passport to employment than the S.S.C. qualification, a Teachers' Training College diploma like her own, or a certificate from the Colombo Polytechnic. And Latha had shown herself to be a sensible girl, modest and restrained in her behaviour, even in the company of men. Soma judged her as unlikely to be distracted from her studies by the presence in her class of 'boys'.

'A sweet, simple girl, your Latha,' said Soma's sister Caroline approvingly. 'And a good heart. More important, in the end, than all the university education in the world.'

Soma gloried in this accolade.

She might have felt a good deal less pleased, had she been able to see into her daughter's secret thoughts. For as the months passed slowly by, what had been a general feeling of discontent in Latha sharpened into an intense longing to escape. The slightest reference to the University at Peradeniya in a newspaper or in general conversation secured her immediate, if covert, attention, for it had become clear to her that the University of her imagination, with its carefree undergraduate community, its learned dons, and its famously beautiful hill-country setting was the place for her. She maintained a careful silence at home and at school on the subject of her hopes regarding Peradeniya, aware that if she showed too much enthusiasm, her mother and her aunts would be bound to interpret her eagerness as a desire to get away from home.

Admitting to herself that they would be partially right in thinking so, Latha's mind was flooded with guilt. How disloyal she was being to her parents! Especially to her father who, she told herself, had always been her friend, not her enemy. There were many, many times when Latha came very near confiding in Herbert. In this important matter, surely he would be on her side? What held her back from pouring out her heart to him was her suspicion that her father had no secrets her mother could not wheedle out of him. And even if it meant treating her beloved father as a spy, she was determined not to provide, by the smallest false step on her part, an excuse for her family to forbid her taking her one chance of a freer life.

Latha occasionally wondered whether Tsunami, with whom she had had no contact for several years, was developing similar strategies of deception. She decided that it was most unlikely: liberal-minded Uncle Rowland, and probably Aunt Moira too, would surely be much less critical of Tsunami than her mother was of her. She thought many times of writing to Tsunami – but what if 'Mrs Rowland' opened her letter?

The events of the next few months increased Latha's feelings of guilt. Her mother fell ill, and her aunts took turns tiptoeing about the house, addressing each other in whispers, and giving Latha daily lists of instructions to be carried out and medicines to be brought home from the City Dispensary. Latha often lay awake in the midnight hours, wondering whether she was experiencing the working-out of a hostile *karma*. Could her mother's illness be a form of cosmic punishment for her unfilial thoughts? Was her mother about to die? Latha was glad now that she had not confided in her father, and thereby added to his unhappiness, but in nothing else could she feel that she had done right. She had successfully hidden her disloyal feelings from her parents but, as she had often been told as a little girl at dhamma class, every evil thought and action is followed inevitably by reaction.

'Cause and effect, action and reaction,' the graduate in Buddhist philosophy who taught Religious Studies at Amarapāli had said. 'These are the principles that govern human behaviour. When we think evil, evil follows, as surely as the rut in the road follows the wheel.'

Latha, struggling with her feelings of guilt, wondered what more could possibly happen to make her feel worse than she was feeling now.

Soma's health improved, but Latha's conviction that fate's vengeful eye was fixed upon her was confirmed when, following her illness, her mother was advised to retire from teaching. Like all long-term teachers, Soma retired on a Government pension, but the family income took a sudden sharp fall. It now became very clear that Latha must work for her living after she left school, so that she could make a contribution from her salary to the household income. The University at Peradeniya, which had once seemed so near that Latha sometimes fancied she could reach out and touch it, had suddenly become a golden castle hidden somewhere up above the clouds, well beyond her reach. The Government's Free Education policy had opened up university studies to financially disadvantaged students. But even if, with the help of Mrs Phillips's tuition, she passed the Higher School Certificate examination for which she was to sit in her last school year, she knew that she could not burden her parents with the extra expense involved in the purchase of textbooks and the payment of the residential fees at Peradeniya.

It was a source of great consolation to Latha at this time that, due to the fact that they cost her parents nothing at all, her private lessons with Paula Phillips continued.

'What's the harm, Herbie?' Soma said. 'She won't be going to University, but no harm in learning.'

Herbert found himself looking forward to his discussions with Rajan as they walked along the seashore; he had, before the year was over, completely forgotten the unattractive surroundings of the Phillips house that had so surprised him on his first visit. On his many subsequent visits he frequently encountered Seelawathie's pigs, together with goats, ducks and squawking chickens, but now he hardly noticed them.

Not so his wife.

One Tuesday afternoon, Herbert was delayed in the Fort, and for the first time since Latha's visits to Mrs Phillips had begun, Soma drove her daughter in the family car to the house in Mount Lavinia. As they turned off the main road on to the dirt track that led to the cottage, Latha saw the neighbourhood as it must look to her mother's eyes, and her heart sank as she realized that she had grown oblivious to the squalor amidst which Mrs Phillips and her husband had established their tiny island of civilized values. For yes, there were the pigs, the chickens and the goats, there were the snotty-nosed children in their dirty shorts and ragged frocks, staring at the familiar car with the unknown lady at the wheel. Paula appeared at her door, and waved a greeting, thereby removing any hope Latha might have entertained that her mother might believe they had somehow got into the wrong street.

'Good afternoon, Mrs Wijesinha,' Rajan called, materializing beside the car with a small basket of eggs and okra purchased from Seelawathie. 'Won't you come in?'

'Thank you, no,' Soma replied.

She dropped Latha at the gate with her books and pencils, and drove off, managing to smile bravely until she knew she was safely out of sight.

'My goodness, Herbie,' she said, later that evening, when she thought Latha was safely asleep. 'What a miserable dump! Mrs Phillips comes from a respectable Burgher family, she must be used to the best of everything. How can she stand living in a wretched place like that?'

19

DAUGHTERS IN THE HOUSE

'So . . . so, what are you doing about Latha?'

Such a question, so direct and uncompromising, can only be asked by one sister of another. Soma Wijesinha's sister Bertha had dropped in for an afternoon of leisurely gossip, and to tell her about a 'prospective' she had found for her niece.

For at seventeen, Latha had very nearly reached the age at which mothers begin to look about for 'someone suitable' for their daughters to marry. Match-making aunts are informed that formal approaches might now be made. Soma was well aware that this was the traditional way to find a bridegroom. But her sisters informed her that there were others.

'Get that husband of yours to give up reading the racing results in the newspapers,' her sister Bertha had instructed Soma. 'It's time he concentrated on speaking to people.'

In the early 1950s, Sunday newspapers had not yet become the market places of the nation, and professional marriage brokers had not yet gone out of fashion. Mothers who dreamed of capturing husbands for their marriageable daughters, or brides for their well-qualified sons, still turned for assistance to those respectable middle-aged gentlemen attired in tweed cloth and coat, with gleaming watch-chains attached to their waistcoats and long ledgers under their arms, whose rickshaws pulled up by invitation outside the garden walls of families that were on the hunt for brides and bridegrooms.

Thirty years earlier, the brokers had ruled the marriage market, an institution which had swung smoothly into action as soon as the results of Final Examinations in the University or in the professional colleges were published in the national press. Every broker's ledger had carried entries on each of the young men who topped the lists in Medicine, Law and Engineering (universally recognized as the best 'prospectives'). The family histories of such young men were exhaustively researched, findings regarding property noted, and contacts discreetly made. But times were changing, and parents who knew what was what now looked for help to mutual friends, frequently specifying the extent of the dowry they were prepared to offer.

Herbert enjoyed reading the miscellaneous information provided by the 'people' his wife was discreetly interviewing. It appealed to his sense of the ridiculous. He could not afford to offer any young man a dowry with his daughter, but he took a perverse pleasure in reading that Mr X or Mrs Y were eager and willing to bestow house property, estates, sovereign gold jewellery, one or more cars, and a negotiable number of lakhs of rupees on the civil servant, doctor, lawyer or engineer who came forward to take a daughter off their hands.

When the engagement of Tara Wijesinha (to a lawyer in Rowland's branch of the clan) was announced in the newspapers, Soma chose to forget that the two families had been out of touch for several years, and looked forward to having her own daughter figure prominently at what would surely be a high-society wedding. She went so far as to believe that 'Mrs Rowland' would invite Latha to be one of Tara's bridesmaids. Here would be the perfect opportunity to introduce Latha to the world, to bring her pretty face, her graceful figure, her domestic skills and, above all, her gentle, docile nature to the attention of mothers of eligible sons.

'Just wait and see, Herbie,' said she to her husband, 'I am sure we will find the right person for Latha among the guests at that wedding.'

Alas, how disappointing was it to Soma, then, that no message arrived from Rowland Wijesinha or his new wife, inviting Latha to join her cousin Tara's bridal procession! Soma's irritation was great indeed.

'Hardly worth the trouble of going to the wedding at all,' she grumbled, as she carefully filled in the acceptance card which had been enclosed with Tara's pretty white and silver invitation.

'Couldn't Rowland find someone better for that daughter of his than a briefless barrister?'

Soma was convinced that a marriage was being arranged for Tsunami, too.

'Such things always happen in pairs,' said she, invoking the knowledge imparted to her by her sisters. 'And Rowland Aiya being a cabinet minister now will bring all the young men flocking.'

The family had done without a telephone for years, but one was now installed on which Soma made daily calls to her sisters and her match-making friends. To Latha's intense discomfort, her mother began to talk of nothing but the pressing need to get her married as soon as possible. Meal-times at home became a daily ordeal, as her mother reported on the progress that was being made with one match-maker or another. Their domestic help Podina, who was herself considering marriage with a stone mason from her village whose family had sent a proposal to her parents, would call out from the kitchen suggestions of her own. An unpleasantly competitive spirit began to enter Soma's meal-time reports.

'Leave the child alone,' Herbert occasionally said in private to his wife. 'Latha will marry when she wants to.'

Soma regarded this attitude as the height of irresponsibility.

'"*When she wants to*"? What are you talking about, Herbie? Do you realize that if she doesn't get married next year, or at least get engaged, she will lose her chance for ever?'

'You're exaggerating, my dear. Latha has plenty of options. In the first place, we haven't even asked her if she *wants* to get married.'

'What is there to ask? Of course the girl wants to get married. Have you bothered to ask yourself what she will do if she *doesn't* get married?'

To which, as there was no answer, Herbert didn't attempt to make one. His own mind was preoccupied with selfish thoughts that had never struck him before, of what life would be like for *him*, should Latha marry and leave home.

Latha, for her part, counted herself lucky that at least it hadn't yet occurred to her parents to consult her horoscope. The peaceful home-life of Srimani Laksapathiya, a classmate, had been thrown into turmoil after an astrologer had warned her parents that all her chances of getting married would end in six months' time, when her birth planet entered the house of Saturn. On hearing this dire prediction, Srimani's father (a senior civil servant with an Oxford degree) had promptly abandoned all good sense and dignity in a desperate hunt for a husband – any husband – for his daughter. Srimani herself, until then a happy, carefree teenager with nothing on her mind beyond improving her tennis handicap at the Women's International Club courts and clipping pictures of Errol Flynn and Robert Taylor out of *Photoplay Magazine*, had immediately been put, first, on a diet, and next on the marriage market. In tears, she had confided to Latha between classes that every marriage broker in Colombo was carrying about in his ledger a description of her cookery skills, gentle temperament, clear complexion and substantial dowry.

At least, Latha thought, *she* had not been put up for sale.

One afternoon, as she was shuffling through papers on Soma's writing table to find a library card, Latha came upon a hand-written list headed *Marriage Proposals*. It was adorned with a drawing of two love-birds holding up a heart between them, and carried a subheading: *Brides Wanted*.

So Amma has taken to interviewing brokers, Latha thought. She read through the listed entries with amusement.

A partner is sought for up-country, Radala, handsome, well-mannered 34-year-old son owning properties worth rupees twenty-five lakhs; horoscope essential.

Christian Govi father from south seeks a convent-educated beautiful bride for 28-year-old only son from a respectable family, army lieutenant, Kuja 7 in horoscope. State dowry, send photograph.

Sister invites proposals for 29-year-old Karava Buddhist doctor brother, presently working in USA . . .

Fascinated, Latha now examined a second page that she found pinned to the first. At least, she thought, her mother was not yet desperate enough to put her into a *Bridegrooms Wanted* list in a newspaper! Fancy figuring in an entry like the one which read:

A partner is sought for 25-year-old 5′ 4″ tall good-charactered educated daughter. Owning land and other assets.

Latha smiled to herself as she read this. She knew very well that in her case there were no 'land and other assets' owned, and none to be offered.

Then, abruptly, she stopped smiling. She noticed for the first time that some of the entries in each column had a pencilled tick beside them. Could her mother have answered some of these advertisements? The implications of a 'yes' answer to this question took a few moments to sink in. When they did, Latha realized with horror that people she had never met might already know her name, they might be scrutinizing her photograph, and assessing her 'assets' and 'qualifications'. The very thought of such an invasion of her privacy was like a needle piercing her skin.

Why did people make such a fuss of daughters when they were little? Latha reflected angrily. Why did they dress them up like dolls and take such pride in their appearance, if all they wanted to do with them when they were grown up was to get rid of them as quickly as possible? She longed to talk to Tsunami. Was she being subjected to the same humiliation? And if so, what was she doing about it? Once Latha went so far as to pick up the shiny new telephone in the hall and dial her uncle Rowland's Colombo number. She heard a ringing sound as the call connected, but she lost her nerve and replaced the receiver before her call was answered.

The following week, just as Latha had succeeded in regaining her normal happy frame of mind, she learned that her parents had been invited to dine with old friends at one of Colombo's most exclusive clubs, the Capri. Here it comes, Latha thought: the first of the 'prospectives' in the brokers' lists. But it seemed she was mistaken. The 'old friends' were genuine, a physician and his wife whom her parents had known well in the early years of their marriage: Dr Siri Munasinghe and his wife Annabelle had, in fact, introduced Herbert and Soma to each other. Having settled in Britain, they were now back 'home', on holiday with their children. Latha had been included in the invitation, her mother said: Auntie Annabelle and

Uncle Siri were very keen to meet the young lady they had last seen as a five-month-old baby.

'They're just being polite, Amma,' Latha said. 'They wouldn't want to meet me – and you know you and Thaththi won't be able to talk about anything interesting while I'm around. I don't want to go.'

'But, duwa. It's the *Capri*!' Soma replied. 'Your father and I can't afford membership, but the Munasinghes obviously can. Surely you'd like to see what it's like? We've all heard so much about it.'

The newspapers had certainly had a great deal to say about this recently established club, its elegant decor, its exclusive clientèle, its unobtrusive orchestra, its imported wines, above all its sophisticated European menus. And her mother was right: Latha was curious to see the Capri for herself, and experience her first taste of authentic Italian cuisine. At the same time it was odd to hear her mother, usually so prejudiced against all things 'Western', advocating a Western-style restaurant. It was very rarely, too, that her mother addressed Latha as *duwa*, daughter. Her manner was uncharacteristically gentle, her voice almost pleading in its tone. Latha thought it all rather strange, but in the end she gave in. As usual, when dealing with her mother, it was easier that way.

'Will this do?'

She took out of her almirah a pretty embroidered cotton sari that she liked, and shook out the folds before hanging it up. Her mother was horrified.

'Do? Of course it won't do! You must wear silk, child, a Kanchipuram at the very least; and I'll ring Elegance to make an appointment for you to have your hair done on Monday afternoon.'

'What on earth for, Amma? We're not going to a wedding. It's just dinner with your old friends!'

But now that the invitation had been accepted and the evening was definitely on, there was no stopping Soma. When the two ladies alighted at the entrance to the Capri, to wait in the porch until Herbert had parked the car and rejoined them, Latha was resplendent in a kingfisher-blue Indian silk sari, her mother's pearl pendant and earrings very much in evidence, gold bangles on both wrists, and her hair in a bunch of tiny curls at the nape of her neck, each curl embellished with a jasmine blossom in its centre. She looked very pretty, but also as much unlike her everyday self as her mother and the hairdresser at Elegance could make her. The multitude of sharp little pins that held her curls in place jabbed painfully into Latha's scalp, and a single strand of hair, stiffened with enough hair spray to withstand a stormwind, had been trained to fall in artistic disarray to her shoulder.

All this fuss, Latha thought, for a mere dinner at a restaurant!

'*Apoi*, Latha baba is looking very beautiful today,' Podina said admiringly as they set off from the house. 'Just like a film star.'

'I'm sure I look a perfect fool, Amma,' Latha whispered. 'Shall I take off the pendant? Or some of the bangles? It's too much.'

'Nonsense!' Soma hissed back. 'You look perfectly lovely. Just put your shoulders back, hold your head up, and smile. Oh, and remember: *don't talk about books*! Here they are.'

And there, indeed, they were. Her father's tall, dark-suited friend, consultant paediatrician at Great Ormond Street Hospital in London, his slim, elegantly coiffured and carefully made-up wife, and three sophisticated young people, whom they introduced as their children, Anupam and Shalini, and Anupam's school and university friend, Sujit Roy. Herbert Wijesinha arrived in the portico, perspiring slightly in the lounge suit he hadn't worn for years. While the two men shook hands heartily and slapped each other on the back, the ladies went through the ritual of touching cheeks and inhaling as they embraced, and the young Munasinghes and Latha looked warily at each other. Sujit Roy, immaculate in a dinner jacket, and quite at his ease, was the first to speak.

'It's very good of you, sir, to ask me along to a family party,' said this young man to Dr Munasinghe. 'I must admit I was feeling slightly lost until Anupam rang the office. I don't know many people here yet.'

'Not at all, not at all, Sujit,' said Dr Munasinghe genially. 'We're delighted that you could join us. Colombo is a friendly place, you'll find. After you, ladies.'

He stepped back, and let the women in the party precede him into the Capri's dining room. Shalini Munasinghe was wearing a suit – presumably bought in London, Latha thought. Her hair was short and, even to Latha's inexperienced eye, most beautifully cut. She had smiled at Latha during her father's exchange with their guest. Her brother, a tall and very good-looking young man – Latha, who instinctively measured every man she met against certain standards that had been set in her childhood, noticed that he was even taller than her cousin Ranil – now held out his right hand to her and said:

'Good evening, Latha!'

Seized by a sudden impulse, Latha made no reply; instead, she took a step back, brought her palms together, and bowed politely in the Munasinghes' general direction. She didn't know what had made her do it, *Ayu bowan*, the traditional greeting, had never come naturally to her. Thinking about it later, she concluded that she must have done it to see how these England-returned Ceylonese would react to a Sinhala greeting. Shalini's eyes widened, but Anupam didn't react at all. He merely withdrew his hand, smiled slightly and devoted himself to admiring the decorative moulding on the dining-room ceiling.

Mrs Munasinghe, however, seemed most impressed by Latha's 'traditional' manners. She regarded her with approval.

'What a beautiful young lady our little baba has become!' she said, kissing Latha delicately on each cheek. 'I used to carry you in my arms, child, when you were so tiny that you could be placed on a pillow!'

Oh, God, Latha thought. Well versed in the conversation of her aunts, she waited in dread for the moment when Mrs Munasinghe would begin to recall changing her diapers. Fortunately, Mrs Munasinghe broke off her reminiscences at this point to bring her son into the picture.

'I asked Anupam if he remembered the curly-headed little girl whom we all made such a fuss of when we lived next door to each other,' said she. 'Why, do you remember, Soma, the first time he was given an *appa* to eat with butter and jaggery, Anupam liked it so much that he jumped up from the table and ran next door to share it with your baby girl?'

Everyone at the table smiled indulgently at this evidence of boyish chivalry.

'I'm afraid this will be a dreadful disappointment to you, Mother, but I just can't remember that incident,' said the hero of her story, quite unperturbed. 'But then I believe I was only two and a half at the time.'

His voice, Latha thought, was pleasant enough, quiet and well modulated, but his accent! It was so *English*! Anupam Munasinghe's speech sounded so affected to Latha's ears that she wondered whether he was putting it on for her family's benefit. She glanced at her mother, who appeared to have noticed nothing unusual. Soma Wijesinha apparently remembered the incident well, for the two ladies laughed in unison.

Anupam Munasinghe and Sujit Roy made a formidable pair. Their manners were as English as their accents, Latha thought, their perfectly tailored dinner jackets as faultless as Cary Grant's. She hadn't seen or heard anything so impressive since her holidays at Lucas Falls, when she had observed her Uncle Rowland at breakfast, lunch and dinner. Roy anticipated the waiter in pulling back Latha's chair, and Anupam listened with what seemed to be genuine interest to her father's anecdotes about his Government Service experiences. When Latha's table napkin slipped from her lap on to the floor, both young men dived with one accord to retrieve it. Maybe this was what an education in England did for Asian men, Latha thought. It appeared that Anupam and his friend had first met as schoolboys at Harrow. They had continued their friendship at Cambridge, even though their paths had taken different directions after graduation.

'Didn't want to follow his papa into medicine,' Dr Munasinghe said. 'Anupam wanted to make his own way in the world, and do his own thing.'

'Oh?' Soma said.

She sounded distinctly disappointed, and Latha suddenly recalled the tick she had seen placed beside an entry advertising a 'prospective' who was a doctor working in the United States.

'So what did you decide to do, putha?'

Stop it, Amma! thought Latha. You're already talking to him as if he were your son-in-law!

'He has entered the diplomatic service,' Mrs Munasinghe replied proudly. 'In fact, he's just received his first . . .'

'I'm a glorified office-boy at our Embassy in Bonn, Auntie,' Anupam interposed quickly. 'Maybe things will become a bit more interesting next year.'

With his sister's help, he managed to change the subject, but his parents had made their point. It was a point that Latha was able, despite her inexperience, to grasp. The Munasinghes were looking out for a bride for their brilliant diplomat son. It was quite likely, she thought, that Shalini too was on the marriage market. (Accidentally catching that young woman's self-assured glance, Latha decided that if *she* were being bargained for, it must definitely be happening without her knowledge or consent.)

What concerned Latha most at that moment, however, was neither Anupam's situation, nor his sister's, but her own. She realized now in all its shaming awfulness what her mother had been up to. Anyone less naïve than I am would have worked it out long ago, Latha thought, furious at her own simplicity. All that insistence on my joining this silly party, all that fuss about silk saris and flowers in my hair. Latha felt over-dressed, self-conscious and angry. What was this sophisticated young man with his Harrow education and Cambridge background thinking of her family – and of her? Latha didn't know, but she thought she could guess. She wondered whether she was the only girl his parents had arranged for him to inspect, or the first of a long string of would-be brides, all young, beautiful, 'convent-educated' and plentifully provided, no doubt, with 'land and other assets'.

No one subjected Sujit Roy to any interrogation, not even her mother. That's because he's obviously from India, and therefore doesn't count, Latha thought. So they've ruled him out of their calculations. As a marriage partner, that is. Well, *she* would ask him a question or two.

'Are you a diplomat too, Mr Roy?'

'Oh, no,' the young man replied. 'I just mess around a boat-builder's yard in Portsmouth. Learning how to build boats. And do call me Sujit.'

'Boats? What sort of boats? Does your family own a shipping line or something?'

'No such luck,' he said. 'It's just a private passion. I've been crazy about sailing boats since I was a kid, so it seemed the natural way to go. Remember *The Wind in the Willows*?'

Latha nodded.

'Well, I subscribe to Ratty's philosophy: "There is *nothing* – absolutely nothing – half so much worth doing as simply messing about in boats."'

'Our friend Sujit has a life plan which involves living in a Mediterranean paradise,' said Anupam. 'Building boats in which he'll take American millionaires around the Greek islands . . .'

'And make so much money that he'll become a millionaire himself . . . but one who sleeps beneath the open skies at night . . .' Shalini put in.

'. . . And feasts all day on calamari and crayfish washed down with retsina,' finished her brother.

Latha's eyes began to sparkle.

'You're not serious!'

'Dead serious. Why, don't you believe us?'

'It's just the most romantic thing I've ever heard of,' Latha breathed. 'What do your parents think about it, Sujit?'

'I don't suppose my father would have approved . . . much,' Sujit replied. 'But he isn't around any more to express an opinion. Died last year.'

He did not seem especially distressed by this fact.

Dr Munasinghe had been studying the Capri's wine list with close attention.

'What do you think of the menu, son?' he asked Anupam.

'They seem to have quite a good range, sir,' came the reply. 'I think we should have an enjoyable evening.'

Fancy calling one's thaththa 'Sir', Latha thought. Sir, to one's father? It was even stranger than Ranil and Chris at Lucas Falls calling their father 'Pater'. What kind of world did boys enter when they went to England for their education? Even Herbert Wijesinha looked somewhat surprised.

It was inevitable, of course, that while the elders in the party reminisced about past times, recalling camping trips to Yala and April holidays spent in hill-stations, their Indian guest should talk chiefly to Shalini, leaving Anupam to entertain Latha. Unwillingly Latha conceded (privately) that Anupam did this very well. Most of the young men she had met socially up to that time had had only one topic of conversation: the food on the plate before them, the food they had enjoyed at the Mount Lavinia Hotel the previous week, and the food they were looking forward to enjoying at the G.O.H. buffet in the week to come. Duty done, they would then completely ignore Latha, and lean across her to engage the man on the other side of her in a discussion of cricket or rugger that lasted the rest of the evening.

In a happier mood Latha would have appreciated Anupam's attentiveness. But she was not in a happy mood that evening. She regarded him with thinly veiled hostility. He didn't seem to notice, and inquired what she would like in the way of wine to accompany the entrée she had chosen. Latha was encountering both for the first time, but was certainly not going to admit it.

'Why don't you choose for me?' she said.

She had meant this to sound detached and indifferent, but she realized, too late, that she should have phrased it more carefully. Contrary to her intention, her words conveyed the impression that she was deferring to Anupam's superior knowledge and experience. Soma Wijesinha, who had overheard their little exchange, looked at her daughter with approval. Latha's mind, however, was travelling in a direction that Soma did not detect. She was wondering whether Anupam remembered any Sinhala at all. Probably not. She decided to go on the offensive; and when, having ordered on Latha's behalf, Anupam leaned back in his chair, smiled at her and said, 'Tell me all about yourself,' she refused to co-operate.

'No,' she replied. 'I'm curious about you. Tell me about your name. I've never met anyone named Anupam before.'

'It's a Bengali name,' he said. 'Sujit will bear me out, he's the genuine Bengali article. My name's pure accident. Mother had been to see a romantic Bengali movie that was showing in Colombo the week before I was born.'

'Does it mean anything special?'

'I'll say it does!' Roy said, and grinned mischievously. Anupam shot him a warning look, and he said no more.

'It means something very special,' smiled Dr Munasinghe, who had been listening in from the other side of the table. '*Anupam* means "The Incomparable".'

He immediately received the complete and undivided attention of everyone at the table. Latha's parents – even her mother – were silenced. Latha glanced at the face of the young man beside her, and was amused to note that he looked thoroughly embarrassed. Quite as embarrassed as they made me feel a little while ago, she thought darkly. But he recovered quickly.

'Who could possibly live up to such a name!' he said. 'And I've never tried to do it.'

'Perhaps you succeed without trying!' said Latha's mother.

Oh, Amma, Latha thought angrily. *Stop it!* You're making your hopes for me so obvious. She looked very hard at her mother across the arrangement of purple orchids and gold and white araliya in the centre of the table, but she failed to catch Soma's eye. *The Incomparable*, indeed! Latha thought. She sat up straight in her chair. This was no time to brood. She should let this self-assured and probably very conceited young man know, without delay, exactly where he stood: with her, if not with her family. She opened her mouth to speak, but Shalini Munasinghe anticipated her.

'Oh, look, they've got a dance floor,' she said.

On a tiny floor among the tables, a few couples were already dancing. Sujit Roy looked across at Shalini and inclined his head.

'Shall we?'

She rose to her feet at once, and followed him. They moved to the music with the practised ease of accomplished dancers who also know each other very well. The tempo quickened, and while some of the dancers immediately left the floor as if to say that too many demands were being made of them, Sujit and Shalini moved seamlessly from the slow beat to the fast one, their feet in perfect harmony to a complicated Latin rhythm. Latha watched them admiringly.

'Your sister dances so well,' she told Anupam.

'She should,' he replied. 'And so should Sujit. They're both silver medallists, you know. They partner each other at Dancing School exhibitions in London. Shali could probably do Sujit's steps in her sleep.'

'About Sujit,' Latha said. 'Is that really true? About building boats in the Mediterranean? I don't have any brothers, but if I had, and if one of them had suggested such a thing, the skies would have fallen. In our family, I mean.'

'Oh well, Sujit pre-empted that. His father left a large fortune – he was a very successful Bombay businessman – most of it going to his only son, with a life-interest for Sujit's mother, and money set aside for substantial dowries for the girls in the family. There are three of them, and it would have been Sujit's duty to see them well married. Which would not have been a problem, of course, they're all nice girls, and they've been well provided for by their father. However, once all the funeral ceremonies were complete, Sujit informed his mother that he was giving up any claim he might have to the family fortune. It could all be divided up and his share given to his sisters. He was going to follow his dream . . . Now, could they refuse such an offer?'

Latha made no reply.

'"The isles of Greece!",' she said to herself. '"The isles of Greece! Where burning Sappho loved and sang . . ."'

Her mind filled with images of golden sand and bright sunshine, and beautiful white houses with vine-covered walls that would look out over water of an unbelievable blue.

'What it must be,' she said softly, 'to have a dream like that, and be able—'

'And to be able to fulfil it? Yes. But it takes nerve, don't you think? Sujit's an unusual character. He's also very determined. He knows that fishermen here have been building catamarans all along our west coast for centuries, and he's here because he wants to find out how it's done, and do it better.'

The music came to a stop, and the dancers came back to the table.

'Perhaps you'd care to dance the next one with me,' Anupam said.

Latha hesitated. How could she possibly confess, in the company of such sophisticates, that she could not dance, and had never been in a ballroom in her life?

'You needn't worry,' Shalini told Latha. 'I assure you that my brother and Sujit, unlike most men, can be trusted on a dance floor. They won't tread on your toes, they won't puff whisky fumes in your face, and they won't ring you up tomorrow morning and suggest that you sleep with them.'

Soma Wijesinha, who had been eavesdropping shamelessly on the young people's conversation, appeared to have upset her glass of wine. In the general flurry of mopping up the spills and slipping a side-plate beneath the table cloth to help it dry out, Latha was saved from having to give Anupam an answer.

'May I ask my question again?' he said, when the tumult caused by this accident had subsided. And to Latha's surprise he added, under his breath, 'At least it'll be a change of subject.'

For the first time, Latha felt rather sorry for him. Perhaps Anupam, despite his sophistication, was as much a lamb being led to the slaughter as she was. But she had made up her mind, and was not to be moved.

'And what question was that?' she asked. 'I'm afraid I've forgotten.'

'I asked you to tell me about yourself.'

'Why ever would you want to know?' Latha countered. 'It's not as if we're at all likely to meet again.'

Their conversation, which their respective mothers had doubtless hoped would flow easily and naturally, had been moving – if it moved at all – in a series of jolting stops and starts. This, Latha admitted to herself, was entirely her doing and not Anupam's, for he was making every effort to get it back on course. Shalini and Sujit, on the other hand, were doing much better, but then they were already old acquaintances. Latha's off-hand response did not, however, succeed in discouraging Anupam Munasinghe.

'Why would you think we shall not meet again? My parents are here on holiday – now – but they are considering a permanent return to the island next year. If they do return – or if your family decides to visit Europe – I should think we most certainly *will* meet again. I, for one, would be very disappointed if we do not.'

Oh, very prettily said. Full marks for courtesy.

But she could not make the man out. Did he mean what he had just said? If he were trying out on her what her school-friends called a 'line' – and Latha suspected that he was – she decided she would cut it short decisively, there and then.

'Next year?' she said. 'I don't expect to be around next year.'

Soma Wijesinha was thunderstruck. She gazed in dismay across the table at Latha. Was it for this, said the expression in her eyes, that your father and I have just spent hundreds of rupees at Elegance? Latha didn't care. For the first time in her life, she had been handed the power to control events, to decide the shape of her own existence.

'Well, not in Colombo, anyway,' she said. 'I'll be at University by then. That's seventy miles away from Colombo. It's quite a distance.'

Anupam smiled.

'Peradeniya, eh?' he said easily. 'I was up there only last week, visiting an old friend. A wonderful place. And remember, I grew up in England. Seventy miles doesn't seem any kind of distance to me.'

For two weeks following the evening at the Capri during which her daughter had been 'inspected' by the Munasinghes' diplomat son, Soma jumped up and rushed eagerly to the telephone every time it rang. When two more weeks passed without any further word from the Munasinghe family, it became obvious, even to Soma, that Anupam Munasinghe, of whom she had entertained high hopes on Latha's behalf, must have returned to Britain at the end of his holiday. No proposal had been sent to Herbert and Soma by his parents.

Soma made it clear to Latha that this was all her fault. She hadn't done justice to the wonderful opportunity fate had presented to her at the Capri.

'Fancy letting a catch like Anupam Munasinghe slip through your fingers!' she said irritably.

Her recent illness had not improved her temper.

'I warned you, Latha, to stay off the subject of studies when he was talking to you. But no, you always do what you want, not what I say.'

She looked across the table at her husband for support.

'*Won't* listen. She never does. And see now, what has happened? They lost interest. *He* lost interest. No man wants to marry a bookworm.'

There was a sting in her mother's words that Latha had never heard before. It made her feel as if she had walked blindly into a nest of scorpions. Why does she want to hurt me? she asked herself. They *both* encouraged me to read and study, it wasn't only Thaththa. She made up her mind that she would not lose her temper.

'He never had any "interest" in me, Amma,' she said. 'And anyway, what's he doing in the diplomatic service if he doesn't like educated women? In a job like that, he must be meeting them every day.'

'You're talking about two entirely different things,' her mother retorted. 'Being a diplomat is a profession. Choosing a wife is a personal matter. No man, however intelligent, wants a wife who is cleverer than he is.'

'Thank you for that, my dear,' said Herbert, looking up from his paper. 'So tell me, did I prove my super-intelligence by wanting to marry you, or have you been acting stupid through twenty years of married life, just to spare my feelings? Only joking,' he added, and smiled sympathetically at his daughter.

'Here, don't you encourage her, Herbie, please. You know perfectly well that I'm right. Anyway,' and here she turned back to Latha: 'You're wrong about the Munasinghe boy. You cut him down every time he asked you a question. I heard you, so don't try to deny it. Anyone could see that he liked you.'

'Is that so?' Latha replied. 'Well, *I* didn't like *him*. I think he's insincere and affected—'

This was not at all true, for Latha had liked young Munasinghe. Her conscience pricked her as she spoke, but she ignored it, and continued:

'—and so's his sister. I thought their Indian friend was much more interesting.'

Soma shot her daughter a nervous glance.

'A very peculiar young man,' she said. 'And thoroughly irresponsible, if you ask me. He's making a virtue out of ducking his family duties, isn't he?'

'Amma! How can you say that? He's given up every cent his father left him to his sisters. I don't know a single person here who would have done such a thing. As for "making a virtue" out of anything, I think you're being very unfair – he didn't even know he was being discussed—'

'Didn't he? Well, all I can say is that if your brother had lived, he would never have left you to find a husband on your own. He might not have been a Bombay millionaire, but he would have been properly brought up, and known where his responsibilities lay—'

'Well, at least we all had a pleasant evening,' interrupted Herbert. 'And if Latha didn't care for the Munasinghe children, there's no more to be said, is there?'

This appeared to effectively close the discussion. Latha looked gratefully at her father. It was good to know, she thought, that she could rely on some support from him in a crisis. Her mother, however, continued to complain.

'Quite so. What's the good of talking about it now? Latha has lost her chance.'

Soma drew a deep breath, and let it out again forcefully.

'It's obvious what *you* need to do now, madam,' she said, turning on her daughter. 'You'd better stop being so choosy – and as soon as you leave school, you'd better start looking for a well-paid job.'

Latha had, as it happened, already begun attending classes in shorthand and typing. What else could she do, she thought gloomily, with no money and no university degree, but train to be someone's secretary or personal assistant? She looked about her, at young women she knew who were already filling that role, and decided that, whatever happened, she was not going to limit her horizons to Pitman and a filing system.

She applied for library cards at the British Council and the U.S. Educational Foundation and enrolled, without telling her parents of it, in a ballroom dancing class run by Mrs Marjorie Sample which her school was offering to its seniors that year, free of extra charge. Anupam Munasinghe had mentioned that his sister was a ballroom dancing silver medallist. He was probably one himself, though he hadn't said so. Latha had no aspirations in that direction, but maybe, she thought, if she could master some basic steps and become more sure of herself on a dance floor, she too might achieve something like Shalini Munasinghe's self-confidence.

'Oh, he's perfectly S.I.T.,' Shalini had said of a colleague at her place of work in London: a casual remark, but evidently intended as a compliment. Latha, mystified, had learned on inquiry from an amused Anupam that 'S.I.T.' was England-speak for 'Safe in Taxis'. The phrase, and its context, spoke of a measure of worldly sophistication far beyond her own reach.

Mrs Sample told Latha she was making good progress, and had a natural sense of rhythm. Was there someone at home with whom she could practise her dance-steps? Latha wished very much that her answer could have been 'yes'. If only her brother could have been around! Her family on her mother's side was short of young men with an interest in anything but sport, or Latha could, she thought, without too much comment from her aunts, have requisitioned one of them.

Latha surveyed the possibilities on her father's side. Her cousin Ranil, of course, would have been perfect. She had marvelled at the way Shalini Munasinghe had looked her brother's friend Sujit Roy directly in the eye, the way Shalini had made, with perfect freedom and with no reproaches from her mother, outrageous remarks which echoed Latha's own thoughts, but which she could never have brought herself to utter out loud. She pictured herself boldly meeting Ranil's challenging gaze and holding it while their bodies bent and swayed to the rhythm of the tango. Her fantasizing about Ranil did not last long: what she needed, she sensibly reminded herself, was someone whose company would carry no romantic complications, someone who could be 'trusted on a dance floor', someone with whom she could relax and be her natural self.

Someone like her cousin Chris, for instance.

But of course Chris, like Ranil, was no longer within her reach. Nor was Colin. Reading novels borrowed from the British Council, discussing them with Paula Phillips, and learning how to do the quickstep and the waltz did not lessen Latha's feelings of depression. What was happening to her? She could not understand it, she could not understand herself. How could she feel like this, especially when her mother had been so recently ill, and needed her constant companionship? Outwardly, Latha gave nothing away, but the strain of hiding her inmost thoughts from parents whom she loved was beginning to show.

Herbert Wijesinha, who hated to see his daughter unhappy, came home early one afternoon from the city and asked her to accompany him to a movie.

'They're showing *Casablanca* at the Regal,' he told her. 'Wouldn't you like to see it again?'

Casablanca was Herbert's favourite film. He had watched it many times with the greatest enjoyment, and could have repeated most of the script from memory. A sonnet he had once begun writing, addressed to the angle of Ingrid Bergman's hat in the film's final scene, was the nearest he had ever come to writing poetry.

'No, thank you, Thaththi.'

Disappointed, Herbert tried again. He put a small cardboard box into Latha's hand.

'Remember these?' he said. 'Santa Claus brought one just like this for you one Christmas, when you were five years old. All the way from China.'

Inside the box were a dozen small scallop shells. Latha turned them over and looked up at him, perplexed. Remember? What was there to remember?

'Podina,' Herbert called to the servant girl in the kitchen. 'Bring me two glasses of water.'

Podina, curious, lingered to watch as Herbert dropped one of the shells into a glass. Instantly, the two halves of the shell sprang apart. From its centre a bright green stem unfurled itself and spread the petals of a brilliant red camellia on the surface of the water.

'*Apoi*, magic!' Podina breathed.

'Thaththa,' Latha said. 'I've grown up a bit, I'm not a five-year-old any longer.'

She was not going to let on that at the sight of the opening petals, memory had brought back to her a vision of that wonderful Christmas when she was five and still believed in the existence of Santa Claus. She remembered the sharp scent of pine needles on the Christmas tree beneath which Andrew Lang's twelve *Coloured Fairy Books* had been left in a wooden book-case of their very own, and with it two other magical gifts: a kaleidoscope which yielded, every time you shook it, a window of brilliant, changing colours, and a little box just like this one, with a message on it in fluorescent ink. *To Latha, with love from Santa Claus.* Years had passed before Latha had recognized the handwriting on the box as her father's.

Herbert looked hurt.

'Don't you like them any more?' he asked. 'You loved them when you were little. I haven't seen one of these for years, thought we'd stopped importing them.'

Hopeful, he tried yet again.

'Drop in another shell, the colours may be different.'

'What's the matter with this child, I don't know,' Soma remarked. 'Won't talk, won't eat, mopes around the house with a long face . . . Better take her to see Dr Lucien, Herbie, and get him to prescribe a tonic.'

Obediently, Latha swallowed glassfuls of Dr Lucien Gunasekera's pink mixture, but did not tell the family physician what was amiss. What was the point of confiding in him? Dr Lucien Gunasekera, who had known her from the time she was a child (his distinguished father Sir Frank Gunasekera had, in fact, brought Latha into the world), would immediately tell her parents that she was pining to escape, escape from a situation in which her days were being shaped by nothing but her mother's endless criticism, the watchful observation of her family circle, and the impudent comments of a domestic servant. And then – for Latha had no illusions about that – her life would simply close down.

The efforts she was making to achieve an escape were small ones, but there was beginning to be something desperate about them. She practised her shorthand exercises ceaselessly, and whenever she had the house to herself (which was not often, since her mother had been advised to get as much rest as possible, and so was usually at home), Latha put one of her father's Victor Silvester records on the gramophone turntable, and waltzed or quick-stepped around the tiny sitting room. She told herself (though without much conviction) that she was beginning to make progress.

Not for the first time, Latha wished she had obeyed her first impulse and waited until her call to Tsunami had been answered. Isolated and depressed, she needed to confide in someone who would not betray her feelings to the world.

At Rowland and Moira Wijesinha's Colombo house, meanwhile, matters were not proceeding smoothly either. It had always been obvious to them both that they would have no trouble finding a suitable match for Tara, but after a time they had begun to worry about Tsunami, whom nothing and no one seemed to please. What would become of the child? Moira asked. Regular visits to aunts and cousins were the means by which marriages were made, and the Wijesinha clan was based in Colombo. Marriageable girls must be seen and admired by relations who would spread the word, Moira said. Why, then, did Tsunami avoid their relations whenever she could?

Moira, who was generous-hearted in her own way, and wished to see her husband's daughters as happily and prosperously settled as she was herself, urged her nieces to join the Women's International Club in Guildford Crescent. The Club, she said, welcomed young newcomers. (She was, of course, a popular member of the Club herself, and had already served once as its honorary secretary.) Tara obediently joined up, played tennis, and showed off her culinary skills by contributing meringues and iced cakes to the Club's lavish teas and luncheons. Tsunami, on the other hand, stubbornly refused to join.

When the time came for serious plans to be made for the girls' marriages, it seemed that no young man whose name was tentatively proposed could please Tsunami: one was conceited, she told Moira, a second stupid, a third thought money was everything. This last complaint would have puzzled Rowland, had he been told of it by his wife, for Rowland had always had a well-founded respect for wealth, and believed in acquiring as much of it (by honest means, naturally) as he possibly could.

Life went on, however, and if there was a stream of dissidence in Tsunami's soul that ran counter to the mainstream of Wijesinha existence, she kept it to herself. The first time her family had any real inkling that all was not well with her was on the great occasion of her brother Ranil's twenty-first birthday. Tsunami, having dutifully danced once with every young man on the Wijesinha invitation list, sat down at last, out of range of the music, and determinedly unstrapped her high-heeled shoes.

'I'm not dancing with any of *them* again,' she said. 'Morons, one and all. "Slim" Kodikara, that idiot friend of Ranil's, trod on my toe, then discovered I had nine others and trod on each of them in turn.'

Moira regarded her anxiously.

'You shouldn't talk like that about your brothers' friends, Tsunami,' she said.

'*You* don't have to dance with them, Auntie Moira,' said Tsunami crossly. '*You* don't have to talk to them.'

'What do they talk about?'

'Cars. Sport. And books.'

Moira was puzzled.

'Books? But you would enjoy that, surely!'

'Enjoy it?' snapped Tsunami. 'The only thing "Slim" Kodikara ever reads is *Reader's Digest*.'

'So, what's wrong with *Reader's Digest*?' asked her brother Colin, appearing unexpectedly on the veranda and immediately making the heart of one of his juvenile female cousins beat faster by throwing himself into a chair beside her. 'I read it every month. It's okay. It's good.'

'Nothing's wrong with *Reader's Digest*,' Tsunami said, 'except that your friends – and you – will have to wait until your next birth to understand what good books are really like. You haven't evolved far enough yet.'

She stalked off, her shoes dangling from her hand, leaving Colin gazing after her, puzzled by the insult.

'Just listen to her, Auntie,' he said. 'Who does she think she is?'

II

O brave new world,
That has such people in't.

William Shakespeare,
The Tempest (1611) Act V, Scene 1

1

TARA'S WEDDING

Four weeks before the date of Tara Wijesinha's wedding, Soma and Herbert received a request from Rowland's wife. Would Latha be able to join the bridal party as one of Tara's six bridesmaids? Soma was so delighted by the invitation that she decided not to waste time resenting its late arrival. Instead, she made excuses for it.

'There are so many nieces in Herbie's family,' as she told her sister Caroline. 'How to please everyone? Latha is only distantly related . . . Or maybe someone got measles or mumps, and had to drop out . . .'

Caroline wasn't convinced. Under normal circumstances, she would have pointed out the last-minute nature of Moira's invitation, and suggested to Soma that she had been slighted. But she was a practical woman, and she recognized the importance of the event.

'Good chance for Latha,' she said.

Any fears that Herbert and Soma might have had that Latha's debut as a society bridesmaid would involve the family in inordinate expense were immediately put to rest by Moira Wijesinha. She would see to everything – indeed, she had already seen to everything, she assured them. Appointments had been made with the dressmaker, the hair stylist, the shoemaker and the florist.

'My car will come for Latha at nine o'clock sharp tomorrow morning,' she instructed Soma. 'Please tell her to be ready. This will be for preliminary measurements only. The first fit-on will be in two days' time.'

On the following day, Alexander drove up in Rowland Wijesinha's big car. Latha's expectation that she and Tsunami would be visiting the dressmaker together was abruptly dashed. The car was empty. She went alone to her appointment at Mrs Kelaart's dressmaking establishment in Cotta Road, and returned home alone.

'So, how was Auntie Moira?' her mother asked.

'I didn't meet her,' Latha said. 'I think she had to go to an appointment of her own.'

'And Tsunami?'

'She wasn't there either.'

'You know what? I think I had better come with you for the fit-on,' her mother said. 'These things can't be done by proxy.'

At the fitting of Latha's sari-blouse and petticoat, two days later, she and Soma met two of the five other bridesmaids, both of them young sisters of Tara's fiancé. Soma attempted to extract information from them about the wedding arrangements, but got nowhere: both girls appeared to be dumbstruck with wonder at their own good fortune in being part of Tara's wedding party, and could talk of nothing else.

'Does the young lady want her sari-blouse made bracket style?' asked Mrs Kelaart's assistant, her mouth full of pins.

Bracket-style? Latha looked questioningly at Soma.

'"Bra Cut",' explained Mrs Kelaart, intercepting the look. She was supervising the fitting from an armchair near the mirror.

'We put a pleat here, and here, and another one here, and even girls with nothing at all up here look as if they have plenty . . .'

'Like nice, juicy mangoes!' the assistant put in, smiling.

Latha blushed.

'What about the bra?' Soma inquired.

'With a nice figure like hers,' the assistant said, 'no bra needed at all, easily can do. She's not stout, no? Very nice. Bracket easily can wear.'

Well, that's something! At least I'm not stout. Wonder what the hairstylist will have to say? 'Very nice. Not bald, no? Curls easily can wear?'

'Are you coming for the night before, Akka?' asked one of the bridesmaids.

The night before?

It's as if we're speaking different languages, Latha thought. But on this point Soma was able to discourse with authority.

'Yes, she is,' she replied on Latha's behalf 'We are all coming. We're all invited.'

It was the first Latha had heard of it.

'It's the party Tara will have on the night before the wedding,' Soma explained. 'All the wedding gifts will be on display. And the trousseau.'

Latha's hopes rose again as she remembered something from past days with the Lucas Falls family.

'It's Tara's birthday, too,' she said, and added hopefully: 'Maybe Tsunami will be there!'

'No, Tsunami won't be there,' said her fellow-bridesmaid. 'She won't be back in time for the wedding.'

Back? From where?

The bridesmaid added:

'Fine thing, no? Not even coming for her only sister's last maiden birthday!'

Last maiden birthday?

Latha deeply regretted having mentioned Tara's birthday, if it was going to cause resentment to be directed at the mysteriously absent Tsunami. So that was the reason for the late invitation, she reflected sadly. At the last minute, Tsunami had had to drop out of her role as bridesmaid at her sister's wedding. Well, she was not going to humiliate herself by asking why.

No such inhibitions held her mother back, however.

'Where is Tsunami?' Soma inquired.

'Why, Auntie, Tsunami's gone to Oxford. Didn't you know?'

From that moment on, Latha lost all interest in the wedding. She obediently kept all the appointments Moira Wijesinha had made for her, but her heart wasn't in them. On a day when the major task to be checked off on Moira's list was the wrapping of wedding-cake, she went dutifully, but without enthusiasm, to the Wijesinha house and met there, once again, only her fellow-bridesmaids. Moira Wijesinha sat the girls down together around a table piled with tiny empty boxes printed with two entwined Ts (Thank goodness, no hearts and bluebirds, Latha thought), and to the accompaniment of *Housewives' Choice* on Radio Ceylon's Commercial Service, they wrapped squares of wedding-cake in silver foil, and placed them in their boxes.

'Very nice, very pretty,' said the bridegroom's mother who, as Moira's lieutenant, had been asked to supervise the execution of this essential task.

On the following day, Moira took the flower-girls out after lunch to Mrs Kelaart's for the fitting of their beaded and embroidered blouses and chiffon skirts, and then she accompanied the bridesmaids to Gemrich in the Fort for a final fitting of their specially made shoes. Somehow, in the midst of all this activity, Latha learned from one of the other bridesmaids that Tara had wanted to have her reception at the Galle Face Hotel, but 'Mrs Rowland' had insisted that it be held in the Wijesinha house.

'According to Auntie Moira, Uncle Rowland's position in politics makes it essential that he must be seen welcoming guests to his ancestral home,' Latha informed Herbert, her face impassive and her voice carefully neutral. 'A hotel would have been too impersonal. So Tara didn't insist.'

A week later, Latha accompanied Tara to Bloom's to choose the wedding flowers.

'I want something very simple and not too expensive,' Tara told Miss Gwenda Cooke, the proprietress of Bloom's, a woman with the build of a grenadier guardsman, who wore mannish suits and court shoes, cropped her dark hair as short as a boy's, and had a half-smoked cigarette dangling permanently, it seemed, from the corner of her mouth.

Miss Cooke snorted.

'So who's paying for these flowers? Isn't it the bridegroom?'

Tara blushed and bridled. The florist surveyed her unsympathetically.

'My dear girl, you don't imagine he'll be buying you flowers *after* the wedding, do you?' she asked. 'You should sting him for a whacking sum while you have the chance.'

The cynicism of this remark had shocked Latha. If it distressed Tara, she soon got over it.

Latha had initially thought of refusing Tara's invitation as she had, several years previously, ignored her stepmother's invitation to visit Lucas Falls. Now that she had committed herself to it, and resigned herself to the fact that Tsunami would not be present, each day that brought the wedding closer made her more philosophical. Ultimately, she even found herself looking forward to the event. It was the first family wedding in which she had ever been closely involved, and although she was not to share the occasion with Tsunami, the fact that she would be once again part of the Lucas Falls family gave her special pleasure. As it turned out, of the three Wijesinha boys only Colin was occasionally in evidence when Latha visited the house: Tara's wedding day, which coincided with his school holidays from Eton, had brought him home early. Latha did not allow herself to think too much about Ranil. He and Chris were not expected to arrive from overseas until the day before the wedding.

On the morning of the wedding, Latha arrived at her uncle's house, and found it filled with flowers. Baskets of lilies, dozens of red roses, sprays of white jasmine and what seemed like forests of asparagus fern had been sent down by train from Lucas Falls for the decoration of the church, the house and the bridal dais, and now elaborate floral arrangements decked every room of the house. The veranda was filled with chattering and gossiping ladies fanning themselves and drinking iced coffee who looked Latha up and down as she descended from Herbert's little car. With relief she escaped from their scrutiny into the house, where she found her bridesmaid's sari laid out for her on Tsunami's bed.

'How are you, Latha baba?' said a familiar voice.

There was Alice, very much older than Latha remembered her, and seemingly a little shrunken with the passing of time. ('It's just that I've grown taller,' Latha consoled herself, unhappy at the change in someone she remembered as an impressive presence in her childhood years.) Alice was still as indispensable as ever, it seemed: in her hands were six clothes hangers, from which were suspended the six sari-blouses made by Mrs Kelaart's indefatigable sewing ladies, now perfectly pressed and ready to wear.

Latha's duties as a bridesmaid were simple and straightforward. Moira Wijesinha had the whole event organized from start to finish, and Latha found that there was very little for her to do, apart from looking her very best, seeing to it that the flower-girls didn't mislay their sprays of carnations, and stayed in line as the bridal party preceded Tara and Rowland up the nave of St Mark's Church, and handing round silver-sprayed baskets of wedding-cake at the reception. Moira's astrologer had advised that the auspicious time for the wedding ceremony was at one-fifteen in the afternoon, so at eleven o'clock on the morning of the wedding, an expert arrived to dress the bride – 'You'd think Tara hadn't been putting on her own clothes all her life,' Soma said acidly later – and Salon Elegance sent their best stylist round to the Wijesinha house to arrange the flowers in Tara's hair. This was done in Tara's bedroom, where the three mirrors of her dressing-table permitted each detail of the elaborate process to be viewed from every angle by Moira, who was seated on Tara's bed, with one of her cousins (a mother of five married daughters) to assist and advise. When she had finished with Tara, the stylist bestowed her expertise on the bridesmaids and the flower-girls. She was midway through her task when there was a discreet knock on the door of Tara's bedroom.

A portly middle-aged gentleman, impeccably attired in a pale grey suit and an elegant silk tie, with a white rosebud in his button-hole, stood in the doorway.

'Uncle Eric!' Moira cried joyfully.

'Uncle Eric', Latha learned, was the Mr Fix-It of Colombo's female social world, and anyone or anything he didn't know in connection with weddings was not worth knowing. He was not, as far as Latha could ascertain, actually related to any member of her family; yet, if pressed, he could always trace a relationship, mention some marriage he had brokered, or some family will in which he had been left a legacy. Not that it mattered at all, really, for everyone addressed him as 'Uncle Eric' anyway. Moira was delighted to see him, as well she might, for it seemed that no wedding in Colombo could be deemed a success unless 'Uncle Eric' had been called in to advise and supervise proceedings. Moira had solicited his advice on everything from the flower arrangements in the church to the menu of the wedding buffet. He had arrived at an early hour in order to do her make-up and the bride's. This was especially important because, for the first time in Ceylon, a movie was being made of a wedding. Tara and Tissa would exchange their marriage vows to the sound of whirring cine-cameras, and in the glare of flash bulbs. Bright lights would illuminate the church ceremony and the reception, so that the make-up had to be professionally perfect.

But Mr Fix-It's expertise didn't stop there.

Latha marvelled later that day, when Tara's wedding veil of fine net caught on the coir matting on the floor of the nave at St Mark's, and threatened to slip away from the coronet that held it in place. With 'The Voice that Breathed o'er Eden' sounding in their ears, urging speed, Latha and her fellow-bridesmaids found 'Uncle Eric' at hand, dapper and reliable, ready to spring to their aid. With a touch as delicate as a woman's, he rescued the veil, re-adjusted it, and even administered the gentle nudge that started Tara and Rowland on their way to the altar.

Herbert had been invited by his cousin Rowland to sign the register as an attesting witness at his eldest daughter's wedding. Accordingly, as bride, groom, and wedding party vanished into the vestry, Herbert rose from his seat beside Soma and followed them. He was amused to find when he got there, however, that his responsibility had been usurped: one of Rowland's cabinet colleagues had preceded Herbert into the vestry, had taken it for granted that he was expected to sign the register, and unasked, had proceeded to do so. Immediately assessing the situation, Herbert courteously stepped back, but the incident had not escaped Moira Wijesinha's watchful eye.

'Poor dear man – he goes to so many weddings and he signs so many registers!' she cooed to Herbert, laying a beringed hand on his arm and looking up into his face in an attempt to coax her husband's cousin into overlooking what she knew very well could be interpreted by him as a personal slight.

'Who can blame him if he makes an occasional *fox pass*?'

'No one,' Herbert returned. 'By now it must be automatic. He probably makes *fox passes* in his sleep.'

The reception, at which the Prime Minister toasted the bridal couple, was much like other wedding receptions of its time, but it earned a special place in Herbert Wijesinha's manila folders because the P.M., his mind presumably on other matters, had forgotten the names of both bride and groom.

'To Sriyani and – er – Lalith?' the Prime Minister had said uncertainly, raising his glass to the couple on their flower-decorated dais.

'No, sir, it's Tara and Tissa,' an aide had hissed, under cover of a ripple of laughter from the assembled guests.

Moira, determined that Tara's marriage should be remembered as 'The Wedding of the Year', just as her own had been, had ensured that caterers, musicians, photographers and florists were in constant (and expensive) attendance. Her craze for publicity had resulted in invitations being extended to the fashion editors of all the island's principal magazines and newspapers. Tara herself seemed perfectly unfazed by it all; in fact, Latha noted with surprise, she seemed to be actually enjoying it.

The serving of alcoholic drinks, Moira had said firmly, could not be left to the caterers. It had to be supervised, preferably by a member of the family, or all kinds of unpleasant things could happen. Whole cases of imported Scotch had been spirited away at some weddings she had attended, at others fights had broken out among guests who had had too much to drink. To prevent such excesses occurring at Tara's wedding,

Colin had been entrusted with the responsibility of supervision. He, in turn, had enlisted the help of able and knowledgeable friends of Christopher's and his own whom Latha now saw fanning out on the other side of the ballroom, a party of elegant young men in grey suits with red rosebuds in their button-holes, who were assisting with the serving of champagne and whisky to Rowland's male guests.

On the whole, as Herbert and Latha agreed afterwards, Tara's wedding had been a lot of fun. It was the first time that Latha, as an adult, had encountered her father's family in force, and she had been impressed, despite the undoubted eccentricity of some individuals, by the Wijesinha clan's serene confidence regarding its own place in the world. They are rather impressive, even if it's in an odd kind of way, Latha thought, and decided that she preferred their conversation, despite all its occasional arrogance and Philistinism, to the grubby gossip which formed the staple of conversation among her aunts on her mother's side. For the first time Latha realized that her father's family constituted that very segment of society which her mother's family obsessively discussed, yet pretended to despise – a patrician elite in which old money and privilege had frequently joined forces with political power. She had the intelligence to perceive also that, whether she liked it or not, she was part of them both.

Latha did not, of course, say anything at home about these discoveries. Discussion of the wedding with her parents confined itself to safe subjects, of which there were many. There were amusing incidents to talk over, such as the Prime Minister's bumbling toast to the bride and groom, and the Minister's *fox pass* in signing the marriage register. There had been moments of high drama, too, as when the bridegroom discovered at the last moment that he had misplaced the ring; and the page-boy, refusing to walk down the aisle without a bribe, had had to be coaxed by Latha with the aid of lemon drops administered one at a time. And there had been the incident of Auntie Ivy and the Wedding Cake.

'Keep an eye open for Auntie Ivy, girls,' Moira Wijesinha had warned the bridesmaids. 'Don't let her grab all the wedding-cake in your basket. Most people will ask whether they can take a piece home for someone in the family who couldn't attend. That will be quite all right. But Auntie Ivy . . .'

Latha, who had never met Auntie Ivy, had duly 'kept an eye open' as directed, but had noticed nothing untoward until Herbert captured her attention with a discreet wink. Latha looked questioningly at him. Seated on one side of her father was her mother, deep in conversation with the guest seated beside her in the circle. On the other side of him was a sweet-faced old lady, dressed in the fitted skirt and lace-edged blouse that was still worn by women of the older generation. Gaze as she might, Latha could see no one in their group who looked remotely like a cake-thief. What was she to do? Moira had issued no instructions.

Latha avoided revisiting Herbert's group with her basket of wedding-cake, and was amused to discover a fortnight later that the miscreant had been caught in the act. At Tara and Tissa's homecoming, a social event almost as gigantic as their marriage, the movie *Our Wedding* (directed and edited by Moira) had its first showing. The camera had lingered a while during the reception on the group in which Herbert and Soma had been sitting, and had focused on Herbert's white-haired neighbour. And there was Auntie Ivy, who had apparently brought the business of filching wedding-cake to a fine art, talking animatedly to the guest seated next to her, while shovelling a dozen pieces of cake into a large handbag held conveniently open on her lap. Auntie Ivy's weakness for wedding-cake was well known, and the movie, which always provoked gales of laughter when it reached this point, was shown at every family gathering for the rest of the year.

The dancing at the reception had been a revelation to Latha, not least for what it taught her of her country's history, and the Wijesinha family's place in it. The rhythm of *baila* and *kaffringa*, Latha found, was yet another of those traditions of the maritime provinces, inherited from the island's European conquerors, that had been hidden from her by her mother's prejudice against all things 'Western'. Far from having been relegated to a museum which, Soma had suggested, was the proper place for all colonial legacies, it showed itself at Tara's wedding to be part of a living culture.

For as soon as the speeches had been done with, and the formal English-style wedding waltz completed, the orchestra had turned with gusto to the real business of the evening. As the first seductive notes of the *baila* were heard, Rowland's relations threw decorum to the winds and made for the dance floor. All around the room the most dignified of men and prudent of women were rocking within seconds to the energetic, compelling beat of *baila* and *kaffringa*, the men in mock-amorous pursuit, the women flashing coy, sidelong glances while pretending to retreat. Now and then the dancers paused in their lively game of advance and withdrawal to beckon to the elders sitting quietly by, and to the children gazing open-mouthed and large-eyed at the unusual spectacle of their parents apparently indulging in public dalliance. Soon nearly everyone, old and young, had joined in and the floor was crowded.

Latha watched, fascinated, as hitherto unsuspected sides of her own parents' personalities were revealed. For no sooner had those opening notes signalled the beginning of a *baila* session than Herbert Wijesinha was immediately on the floor, dragging Soma, volubly protesting, helplessly behind him. The irresistible call of the music soon overcame Soma's reluctance, and Latha caught a memorable glimpse of her mother through the throng of dancers, as she affected to reject Herbert's vigorous advances, turned away from him in simulated scorn and swished the pleats of her sari from side to side as though they were the petticoats of a sixteenth-century Portuguese señorita. Latha was astonished: she was not used to thinking of her father as conquistador or her mother as conquest, yet here they both were, shamelessly flirting in public – and doing it to the rhythms of the West, too! From time to time, Soma would give her husband a glance of awed admiration which was not pretended, for the *baila* had the effect of transforming Herbert, generally so quiet and self-controlled, into a lion on the dance floor, where he pawed the ground with such ferocious energy that the other dancers formed an applauding circle around him, to give him the space he required.

Even Rowland, who was much too self-conscious and dignified to participate in such uninhibited display, beamed genially on the antics of his usually sedate relations.

'The *baila*,' he explained in his best lecturing manner to one of his European guests, the Yugoslavian Ambassador, 'is a dance of Spanish-Portuguese origin, so we may surmise that it was brought to Ceylon by the Portuguese invaders of the sixteenth century . . .'

'Ja, ja, Minister,' the Ambassador replied, and added (for he had been in the country some time):

'Along with that other delight, the lamprai, eh?'

Rowland was startled, but recovered his poise sufficiently to say:

'Er, not quite. The lamprai was invented by the Dutch, not the Portuguese. But you are right, Ambassador! Like the lamprai the *baila* is quite delightful, though it is not, of course, native to this country. It never can be, since it is a foreign import.'

All around him, even as he spoke, Rowland's relatives were contradicting this statement, demonstrating with stamping feet and shining eyes their uninhibited surrender to the call of the music, and the enthusiasm with which they had taken possession of this 'foreign import'.

'An early example of foreign aid, you might say?' Rowland continued, smiling.

But there was no one to applaud his witticism, for the Ambassador had not waited for Rowland to end his little lecture on the origins of *baila*.

'This wonderful music will not last for ever – would you care to dance with me, Madame?' he said, and hurried Moira on to the floor.

Although Latha had never danced to *baila* or *kaffringa* rhythms before – they were so very different from the Victor Silvester records to which she had become accustomed – the opening bars of the *baila* caused her spirits to rise and her toes to tap. Without warning of any kind, she found her hand seized by 'Uncle Eric'. She was pulled from her seat and hurried in the direction of the dancing couples.

'But I don't know how to do it!' Latha cried.

Her protest went unheard: the dancers had joined their voices to the drums and strings of the orchestra, and the rafters of the Wijesinha mansion resounded to their joy.

Once on the dance floor, Latha responded so enthusiastically to the beat of the music that she was disappointed when the session came to an end. The dancers would not hear of an ending, however. No one left the floor. Instead, everybody stood still and applauded until the orchestra, taking this broad hint as a compliment, went seamlessly into another part of its repertoire with 'Yes, Sir, That's My Baby'. Hearing a familiar voice, Latha turned her head. It was Herbert, singing lustily as he steered Soma around the floor. Catching sight of Latha, he waved cheerily as they galloped past.

'Your father's a fine dancer,' bellowed Latha's elderly partner. 'I'm sorry – was that your toe?'

'My turn, Uncle Eric.'

Miraculously, Chris Wijesinha had replaced 'Mr Fix-It'.

'Just got here,' he shouted over the music, by way of explanation. 'Plane was delayed as usual . . .'

The rest of the sentence was lost.

'What did you say?'

'Flew B.O.A.C. You know how it is – Better On A Camel . . .'

'Oh.'

Tara descended on them, briefly enveloping her cousin in a cloud of white tulle and perfume.

'Darling Latha! How sweet of you to help!'

She was about to pass on to the next bridesmaid when she saw her brother.

'Welcome home, Chris! You made it!'

Radiant, her veil tucked under her arm and her bridegroom in tow, Tara kissed her brother.

'Oh, isn't it just like the old days? Where's Colin? Where's Ranil?'

'Right here beside you, ma'am.'

Latha had, of course, known that Ranil would be at the wedding: he had arrived as planned on the previous afternoon. As the bride's elder brother, as handsome as ever, and 'England-returned' as his father had been in his day, Ranil had attracted all eyes at the church. But though Latha had glimpsed him from time to time during the reception, she had not actually met him. Constantly at Rowland's right hand, being introduced by his father to politicians and business magnates as 'My eldest son, who is practising law in London', and being continually asked by his father's associates when he was planning to go into politics himself, Ranil had had little time to spare at the wedding for his relatives.

But now, at last, here he was.

This was the moment of which Latha had dreamed for years. She raised her eyes shyly to Ranil's, hoping she was not too late to catch the glow that would surely light up his eyes as he saw her for the first time as an adult and a woman. Ranil greeted her with a brotherly peck on the cheek.

'Heavens, kiddo, haven't you grown up!'

Latha, shattered, made a half-hearted attempt at conversation, but quickly found that Ranil's attention was focused upon the far end of the reception hall, where Rowland Wijesinha was greeting his cabinet colleagues and political supporters.

'Excuse me, Latha,' Ranil said. 'Catch up with you later, okay?'

Latha nodded, and turned away. She decided that she didn't care, and concentrated on what Chris was telling her.

What *was* he telling her? The music was too loud for her to work it out. She looked vaguely up at him, and hoped that her answers were making sense. The orchestra stopped for refreshments, and Latha returned to her duty of handing round the wedding-cake as instructed by Moira. From time to time she smiled dutifully down at assorted aunts who insisted on patting her cheek and asking her when her own big day was coming round. At last, after the newly-weds had departed in a flurry of confetti and rose petals for their honeymoon in Kashmir, Chris drove Latha and her parents home.

'Well, what an evening that was!' Soma said, as they locked the house up for the night. 'Did you hear, Herbie, what everyone was saying about our Latha? How beautiful she looked?'

'Yes,' replied her husband. 'I heard. Where *is* Latha?'

Herbert was probably the only person present at the wedding who had perceived that all was not well with his daughter.

'She told me she was going to bed,' Soma said. 'The poor child has a headache.'

But one cannot take refuge in a headache for ever. On the following day, and for several weeks afterwards, Latha had to hear Tara's wedding talked over by her relations. Soma's sisters (who had not been invited) found the subject endlessly interesting. Latha's Auntie Bertha had a good deal to say about the extravagance of Moira's attire as reported in the fashion pages, and nobody, it seemed, could get over the fact that on the day after her wedding, Tara had appeared at the Colombo Race Course on Governor General's Cup Day.

'*Chi*, child,' Bertha told Soma, arriving at the Wijesinha home with a clipping from the Sunday papers in her hand. 'Just look at this, your Herbert's niece must be made of iron. Fancy going to the Races on the day after her wedding! You and I, Soma, could we even bring our legs together and walk three steps on the day after our wedding night?'

Soma made no reply to this. The previous evening's flush of enthusiasm had worn off, and she now claimed to have been disappointed by Tara's wedding. She regarded Moira's neglect of Herbert's prior claim to sign the register as a deliberate slight, and chose to believe that the insult extended to herself.

She had not been able to discover a single young man at the wedding who could be considered suitable for Latha. Mr and Mrs Munasinghe had been among the wedding guests, but there had been no sign of either Anupam or Shalini. On inquiry, it appeared that they had returned to London.

'And Latha was looking so pretty,' Soma sighed crossly to herself. 'But what's the use of looking pretty, when there's no one around to admire?'

'It's a good thing Tsunami couldn't be there,' she said aloud. 'Those bridesmaids' saris suited Latha and the other girls very well, but they wouldn't have suited Tsunami. She's much too thin for sari, anyway, arms like match-sticks.'

Herbert said:

'That was a fine set of musicians Moira had rounded up. And it was good to see the boys again. Ranil seems to be doing well, doesn't he?'

'Horrible wedding-cake,' Soma said. 'Tasted like *poonakku*. Moira should have asked me to make it.'

Poonakku. Cattle-feed. Latha changed the subject.

'I loved the music,' she said. 'I didn't know you both dance so well, Thaththi! And I really liked "Uncle Eric". Such a character! He's a true guardian angel, always around when he's needed. I can't make out how he anticipates things so accurately.'

'Experience,' said Herbert who, attentively observing the scene, had taken note of Uncle Eric and his manifold activities. 'He's been doing it for years. And if he's being paid by Rowland and Moira for his services, I'm sure they consider it money well spent.'

Bloody pervert! God knows what he's up to, hanging around women from morning till night, adjusting their saris and helping them slide their bangles on and off their wrists . . . I'll never let him anywhere near my little girl again . . .

'I thought I saw What's-his-name at the reception,' Herbert said aloud. 'You know who I mean – Anupam Moonesinghe's friend, the Indian lad. Did you see him, duwa?'

Latha too thought she had glimpsed Sujit Roy's tall figure among the guests at the reception, but it would never do to say so in her mother's presence. Aloud, she said:

'Who, Thaththi?'

It was at this low point in Latha's life that there arrived in the mail an envelope addressed to her, with the crimson and gold crest upon it of the University of Ceylon. Inside was a letter, summoning her to an interview with the University's Board of Examiners.

'What's the point in Latha going for an interview?' her mother wanted to know. 'It's not as if she's ever going to the Varsity.'

Herbert downed his tea and reached for a cigarette. (The family's straitened circumstances had not resulted in his cutting down on his cigarettes. A tin of Capstan Navy Cut was always within his reach.)

'Let her go anyway,' he said. 'Nothing lost – you never know what might happen.'

The interview was to take place in the Council Room of the University of Ceylon in Colombo. On the day before the interview a card arrived in the mail for Latha from Rajan and Paula Phillips. Slightly cheered by the sight of it, she put it into her handbag as a kind of good-luck charm, and approached the entrance to the University. She had never entered those sacred portals before, and she was very nervous. She had expected the university grounds to be filled with laughing, chattering students, but the corridor in which she was seated was deserted except for five other people. They were seated in a row and looked extremely nervous. Perhaps, Latha thought, they're also students waiting to be interviewed. Sitting very still in her pale pink voile sari and new, rather squeaky sandals, her eyes directed at a slight crack in the cement floor, she resisted the temptation to jump up and run home.

A door opened into the corridor.

'Miss Wijesinha?'

Six dignified gentlemen in suits and national dress and four ladies in sari seated in a semicircle around a large oval table interrupted their conversation to look Latha up and down as she entered the room.

'Please sit down, Miss . . .Wijesinha.'

Latha noticed for the first time that the speaker, who occupied the central place in the half-circle of interrogators, and must therefore, Latha thought, be the person who was chairing the meeting, was a foreigner. He had hesitated over her name, but had pronounced it correctly, with only a slight (British?) accent.

One of the ladies, whose fair skin and dark brown hair identified her as a Westerner although she was wearing a sari, smiled encouragingly at Latha, and she began to feel better. The lady's face seemed familiar: had she seen her before? Latha sat down, and balanced her handbag on her knees. The handbag was a present from her father. Finding that her fingers were clenched around its handle, she unclenched them one by one, took a deep breath, and tried to relax.

'An extremely impressive all-round performance in the examination,' remarked the Chairman. 'I would like to congratulate you on it. Your mark sheet—' here he held out his right hand, and a neatly dressed young man seated behind him got up at once, and with a quiet 'Here it is, Sir Ivor,' took a sheet of foolscap paper out of a folder and handed it to him.

The Vice-Chancellor scanned the sheet before him, nodded, and then looked up at Latha.

'English is your best subject,' he said. 'That's quite obvious from your marks. But Professor van Loten here has made a note that you write as if it's also the love of your life.'

His colleagues smiled.

'Is it?'

Latha didn't know what to say. Nothing her teachers or her father had told her had prepared her for Sir Ivor Jennings's relaxed Cambridge style.

'I do like to read,' she said at last; and added: 'My mother says I read too much.'

'Oh? And what do you read, Miss Wijesinha?'

The person the Vice-Chancellor had identified as 'Professor van Loten' had spoken for the first time.

'Novels and poetry, mostly.'

The professor opened his lips as if he were about to ask another question, but found himself pre-empted.

'Not, perhaps, so keen on local history, Miss?' said a gentleman in national dress who was seated on the Vice-Chancellor's right.

Latha made no reply, and he continued:

'I noticed that there was some . . . vagueness in your answer in the Ceylon History paper . . .'

Latha's mind became a blank. Vagueness?

'. . . regarding the identity of the statue that stands at the side of the Parakrama Samudra.'

Identity? What identity?

Latha's school's History Society had visited Polonnaruwa a few months before the entrance examination, and the history teacher had informed her class that the massive figure which dominates the giant water reservoir there, the 'Sea of Parakrama', was the statue of an Indian sage, holding a roll of parchment in his hands. Latha hadn't realized that there were any further questions to be asked or answered about its identity.

She passed on her history teacher's statement on the subject. It seemed to annoy her interrogator a good deal.

'Perhaps, Miss, you take your information only from your teachers? Don't you read the newspapers?'

For the first time Latha looked directly at the questioner. To her great surprise, she found that she could put a name to his face. It was a face that had appeared frequently in the newspapers of late, in connection with a controversy that had raged recently in the newspapers, involving scholars across the island. She hadn't paid much attention to it at the time, but now the memory of it came back to her, and she identified her interrogator as a professor of nationalistic views who had advanced the theory that the statue immortalized the royal builder of the reservoir. She knew now what the problem was.

'I – I believe it's also thought to be . . . a statue of King Parakrama Bahu,' she said, and saw him smile triumphantly. 'But I'm not very sure.'

His smile vanished.

'"Not very sure"? What is there to be unsure about? Are you equally unsure about the identity of the author of Shakespeare's plays, Miss, whether Marlowe wrote them or Bacon?'

Latha made no reply. Professor van Loten hummed quietly to himself and looked dreamily out of the window at a gardener who was watering a bed of cannas in the broiling sunshine. Latha's questioner turned to his colleagues, shaking his head in apparent despair.

'These ignorant teachers in our schools! What nonsense they are passing on to these children!'

The lady who had smiled at Latha earlier now intervened. She said she had a question to ask.

'Please go ahead, Mrs Motwani,' Sir Ivor said courteously.

The name rang a bell in Latha's mind. Mrs Clara Motwani, the American principal of Musaeus College (and a former principal of Visākha Vidyālaya, the country's most respected Buddhist school for girls), had been a distinguished guest at her own school prize-giving two years previously. Mrs Motwani's innovative promotion of Domestic Science as a scientifically taught subject at Visākha had very nearly inspired Herbert to suggest that Latha should abandon Mrs Durrant and change her school.

'I was interested by what you had to say in your Botany paper about indigenous plants of the hill-country,' said Mrs Motwani. 'Most students take their drawings from Joshua and Pulimood, and reproduce them in their answer papers. But it seemed to me that you have a detailed, first-hand knowledge of up-country wild flowers. May I ask if you have any thoughts about studying science at the University? Botany, for instance?'

'My home is in Colombo, but I've spent many holidays up-country,' Latha said. 'I have an aunt who loves flowers, and I think I learned a lot from her.'

'Is she a professional botanist?' Mrs Motwani inquired.

'I don't think she would have called herself that. She is – she was – an artist.'

Perhaps Latha had given the impression that her artistic aunt was no longer alive, for the sympathetic woman professor immediately abandoned this line of questioning and reverted to her earlier one.

'And do you have any plans for studying Botany, Miss Wijesinha?'

She obviously expected an affirmative reply. She had been Latha's only supporter at the interview so far, apart from Professor Loten, and in disappointing her Latha saw all her chances slipping away from her. But what point was there in pretending? She wasn't going to Peradeniya anyway.

'No, it has to be Arts for me,' Latha said; and added, to her own amazement: 'I would die if I couldn't do English.'

This time her questioners actually laughed out loud. (Except for the Vice-Chancellor, who smiled behind his moustache.) The English department in the University of Ceylon, as Latha was later to discover – and tremble at the memory of her temerity – was the University's elite department, well known in both Europe and Asia for the brilliance of its star academics and the excellence of its graduates. One did not, as an insignificant first-year undergraduate at the University of Ceylon, *plan* to study English there. One hoped and prayed, read widely and worked hard, and then, at the end of that first year, if one were extraordinarily lucky, one might find oneself called to the study of English Language and Literature, as to a sacred vocation. Latha had made the mistake of speculating about the unthinkable.

'Thank you, Miss Wijesinha,' the Vice-Chancellor said. 'You will hear from the University within the next two weeks.'

He has a kind smile, Latha thought.

But what's the use of kindness? I've failed the interview.

She got up from her chair and went to the door. The neat young man, evidently Sir Ivor Jennings's secretary, held it open for her, and she passed through. Outside, the sun was shining brightly, but Latha felt her skin prickle. She felt cold all over.

'Well?' her mother said, when she arrived home. 'What happened?'

In the silence that followed, Soma Wijesinha looked closely at Latha, and thought she detected tears on her daughter's cheeks. Suddenly the tears became a flood.

'Amma, I honestly don't know,' Latha wailed. 'I gave all the wrong answers. I made a complete fool of myself. I'm sure I failed.'

For once her mother asked no further questions. ('Who knew she cared so much about it?' she said to Herbert later that evening.)

'Eat your dinner, Latha baba, you'll feel better tomorrow,' called Podina from the kitchen. 'I've made your favourite, *vatalappam*.'

She was pleased to see Latha's tears cease to fall and her woeful countenance gradually brighten. Vatalappam, that Malay sweet rich with palm sugar and cinnamon, and perfumed with the fragrance of cardamom, was Latha's favourite dessert, as it was Herbert's also. Father and daughter were in complete agreement that vatalappam left even Elizabeth David's wonderful confections for dead.

The following day found Latha, fortified by vatalappam and soothed by a good night's rest, firmly determined to forget about the interview and all that she had hoped from it. She went as usual to her short-hand and typing classes, handed in the required exercises, and attended a farewell party for final-year students at her school. When a second letter arrived for her, once again bearing the University of Ceylon's crest, Latha put it aside.

After that terrible interview, why bother opening it? It would contain nothing but a polite rejection.

Eventually, it was her father who opened the letter. He read it through to the very end in silence, while Soma waited beside him without saying a word, Latha looked at him in dread, and Podina put her head around the door, anxious to know what was going on.

'News!' Herbert said at last; and added, teasingly:

'Whether good or bad, who can tell?'

'Here, stop your jokes, Herbie,' Soma said. 'We are all waiting.'

'You, my dear child,' Herbert told Latha, 'have been awarded an Exhibition in English on the results of the entrance examination. You have also been offered a bursary, which would support you for three, or possibly, four years at—'

He pretended to be overwhelmed by the hug Latha gave him. She snatched the letter out of his hand.

'Amma! They want to know, do I wish to accept the bursary!' she said. '"If you do not wish to accept it, kindly inform the University immediately, so that an offer may be made to another deserving student."'

She did not know whether to laugh or to cry.

'Four years! Four whole years at Peradeniya! And they ask me: Do I wish . . .?'

2

TRAVELLING FIRST

All the way from Colombo to Peradeniya, Latha thought about her good luck. If it weren't for the trunk on the swaying luggage-rack above the seat in front of her, stamped with her name and labelled 'Sanghamitta Hall, University of Ceylon, Peradeniya', in her father's neat black lettering, she would not have believed she was actually on her way to the place she had dreamed about for so long.

Three other students had entered the University from Amarapāli Maha Vidyālaya, and the girls had arranged to look out for each other at the Fort Railway Station. Latha duly scanned the platform for her classmates when she arrived there with her father, and was distressed when they did not appear. Where were they? If they got any later, they'd miss the train altogether. Until the moment at which a bell rang and the uniformed guard signalled the imminent departure of the 8.15 to Peradeniya and Kandy, Latha continued to gaze hopefully up and down the station platform. At last the train gave its first lurch preparatory to leaving, and she abandoned hope. She guessed that her former classmates, together with most of the young people she had glimpsed at the station and identified as her future fellow-students because they had trunks and luggage like her own, were crowded happily into the third-class carriages.

Herbert had insisted on Latha's travelling first-class:

'For safety, since your mother and I cannot come with you ourselves.'

So here she was, travelling in state and comfort, her companions three matrons in sari, two of them with families of small children. Seated between one of the mothers and her teenage daughter (who had clearly decided that reading her copy of *Picture Show Magazine* was more important than helping her mother cope with a crying sibling), Latha tried not to mind her isolation too much. She had, after all, a great deal to think about. Outside the carriage windows the landscape changed dramatically as the train began its long climb into the hill-country, but Latha hardly noticed.

'You are travelling alone, child?'

Surely that's obvious?

Latha nodded pleasantly.

'Going to Kandy?'

'Peradeniya.'

'Oh, you must be one of this year's new students. I thought so! You looked much too young to be married . . .?'

To the question implicit in this statement, Latha returned no answer. She wished she had a magazine in her hand, like her teenage neighbour. Her father, she recalled, was accustomed to make a joke of the national habit of asking personal questions out of idle curiosity.

'It's not a case of "Who are you?" on our trains,' Herbert liked to say. 'It's a case of "*Whose* who are you?"'

Latha was not sure she could survive three hours of cross-examination without being extremely rude. Fortunately, she was spared any further questioning. The ladies in the carriage and their children, all of whom had presumably made a very early start in order to catch the 8.15, had a three-hour journey before them. The sway of the train had a soporific effect that was hard to resist, and very soon, with the sole exception of the student of *Picture Show*, Latha was the only person awake in the carriage.

She wondered how her classmates were getting on in Third Class. As the train rounded the curve of a hill, she saw handkerchiefs waved from some of the carriage windows, which were answered by waves from carriages further along the train's long body. She wished she had a window seat, so that she could wave back too, but to get to the window she would have to stumble over the feet of several snoring ladies, and Latha decided against it.

Just as the train, having made a brief halt at Polgahawela Station, set off on the second stage of its journey, two persons burst noisily into the carriage. They were arguing vehemently. One of them, the conductor of the train, seemed to be requesting the other, presumably a passenger, to hand over his train ticket: the passenger was refusing to do so. His movements seemed uncoordinated, and he was so agitated that Latha wished yet again that she was travelling Third: the carriage she was in seemed to have shrunk suddenly in size (or else there seemed suddenly to be too many people in it). She felt very uneasy, not least because both powerfully built men were towering above her and obstructing any chance she might have had of changing her seat.

Asked yet again by the conductor for his ticket, the passenger announced that he had just been discharged from the Mental Hospital at Angoda. Everyone in the carriage promptly woke up. The children fixed their wide-eyed gaze on the speaker, and all the adults gave him their full attention. Encouraged, he began to talk without pause, his theme the injustice of the world.

Some people (like the conductor) had Government jobs, he said, others were lawyers, doctors, priests and cabinet ministers, while he, who was infinitely superior to any of them, was unemployed. He had been on a pilgrimage to Sri Pāda –

('Good, good,' interjected one of the ladies in the carriage. 'Did you make a vow?'

'Yes.'

'That is very good.')

– and he had told all this to the priest in the temple there, who had said: 'Gat out, gat out from here, you're mad,' but he had kept his temper and controlled himself in time, or he would have hurled that priest down the Peak –

(Sharp intake of breath on the part of an aged lady seated next to him.)

– he was about to commit suicide, for as everyone knew, you could do it quite easily if you just stopped breathing –

(Everyone in the carriage tactfully averted their eyes while the passenger held his nose for a few seconds, but eventually seemed to think better of killing himself and resumed his diatribe.)

– The whole world was crazy, it needed reform. The judges on the Bench, the Ministers in their grand houses – (is this a Government? he inquired of his fellow-passengers) – should all be lined up and shot – and he would be delighted, personally, to do the shooting. As for the doctors, what need had they to meddle with things they did not understand? The whole world knew that the medicine given out in hospitals was intended to weaken the body, so that when electricity was injected into you, you died, and then they did not need to look after you any more. We had our ancient Sinhalese systems of medicine, we had our powders and our ointments and our herbal remedies for every illness under the sun – what need had we for this new-fangled, much-vaunted 'science'? There were medicines distributed in the hospitals that thickened, blackened, and burned up the blood in the body, and the whole world should know it –

('*Apoi,* sin,' said the aged lady sympathetically. 'Quite right.')

– For the world needed reform – look at that Buddhist temple outside the train window, look at that Hindu *dévale* next to it, look at that church and the mosque over there, where did all the money they made there go? Not into *his* pocket, no fear – and did this cursed conductor have the nerve, the impudence, to ask him for a train ticket? Why did he not ask the people who had taken work from him, who had injected electricity into his blood, he was not going to travel with any bloody ticket –

(At this point the conductor departed in despair, and a small boy with a laden wicker basket on his shoulder passed through the carriage, which instantly filled with the delicious scent of hot masalavadai.)

– Here, *kolla*, how much are those vadai?

('Fi' cents for one,' replied the boy. The passenger took two and ate them.)

– It was only a fool who gave a cent to any of these rascals on the Ceylon Government Railways, in the train or out of it –

('You owe me ten cents, *mahattaya*, please,' the small boy said. Latha found ten cents in her purse, and gave them to the boy, who grinned at her and left.)

– For the whole world needed reforming, and he would surprise it with the deeds he would perform one day . . .

When the train arrived at New Peradeniya Station, the passenger was still talking. But by this time, sensing that they were being harangued by a conman rather than a lunatic, his fellow-travellers had relaxed. Some of them had even gone back to sleep. Latha herself had begun to feel a good deal better. She wondered briefly whether the passenger would go on talking to the end of the line, but had no time to speculate further, for she knew that her own journey had reached its end, and she must make sure she left none of her luggage behind her on the train.

The platform at New Peradeniya Station was crowded. The tiny station, built before Independence and the establishment of the University, had not been intended by the British to do anything more than serve the small, select staff working in the Botanic Gardens nearby. Now, every train was bringing students in from the outstations, young men and women with trunks and bags and boxes of books, who were deposited on the platform looking rather doubtful about what they should do next. Everyone asked everyone else in their immediate vicinity if *they* knew. In the resultant hubbub, Latha looked around again for her three schoolmates, but could see them nowhere on the platform.

A tall, soldierly-looking individual in khaki uniform marched up through the groups of chattering students, called firmly for silence, and introduced himself as the University of Ceylon's Chief Marshal. Transport, he said, had been arranged by the University in the form of coaches that would take the students to their respective halls of residence. He and his fellow Marshals would help them get themselves and their luggage into the right coaches. He knew, he said, that most of the young people on the platform were first-year students. The University of Ceylon, the country's premier institution of learning, welcomed them. He and his colleagues wished them all a happy and rewarding period of study at Peradeniya.

Once inside the coach marked 'Sanghamitta Hall', her trunk safely stowed with others on the top, Latha had time to look around again for her classmates. She could see no one she knew. It seemed that they had decided to come up to Peradeniya by later trains, or else had opted for other halls of residence. Latha had not expected this, and for the first time she felt lonely and insecure. A young woman seated next to her had her hair plaited in two stiff braids, and Latha tried not to notice that she smelled strongly of coconut oil. Glancing sideways, she observed that her neighbour was wearing a brightly flowered skirt and a cotton blouse. A printed cloth bag with a thermos flask in it and a paper parcel with oil stains on it that smelt of stale masalavadai lay in her lap. Looking down, Latha perceived that she was wearing rubber slippers, the cheap kind one bought on the Pettah pavements. Could this young woman possibly be a university undergraduate?

It appeared that she was, for it was not long before Latha heard her neighbour chattering gaily in Sinhala to students in the seats in front of her and behind her, quite as if she had known them all her life. Perhaps she had, Latha thought. Perhaps they had all gone through school together. Nobody spoke to Latha.

What does it matter? I don't care.

As the coach moved away from the station and began its journey to the halls of residence, Latha turned around in her seat, and looked out of the open window. It was eight years since she had last travelled out of Colombo and the south to spend a holiday at Lucas Falls. She had forgotten the enchantment of the hill-country. The landscape of Peradeniya opened before her, lush and green with the freshness of springtime, an undulating valley in the lap of wooded mountains which stretched away before her eyes, folded in line after line of subtly shaded blue, until they merged with the sky.

Latha thought she had never seen anything so beautiful. Massive old māra trees rose on either side of the road, spreading their great branches in an arch of welcome, and as the coach took a sharp turn to the right she caught her breath with excitement and wonder. From the branches of the trees swung strands of flowers, cascades of golden ehela, which spilled their bounty on the green grass beneath. A heady fragrance drifted in through the windows of the coach, and the chattering ceased beside her.

'*Deiyange pihitai!*' breathed Latha's neighbour.

Latha glanced at her with new respect. It's true, she thought. We are moving together, this stranger and I, and all of us in this coach, through a shower of gold.

It's like a miracle out of the old poetry books, a promise, a blessing, a gift from the gods.

3

HERBERT HAS A VISITOR

The Fort Railway Station had been very crowded that morning, and Herbert Wijesinha had some difficulty dodging toffee-vendors and fruit-sellers on his way back to his car. One of the toffee-vendors was, he noticed, selling Hamindagoda's jaggery toffee, a sweet of which Latha was extremely fond. He wished now that he had noticed that particular vendor a little earlier: he could have bought his daughter a bag of toffee, rich with chopped cashew nuts, to take with her on the train.

Herbert wondered whether he had done the right thing in buying Latha a first-class train ticket. He had wanted to show her how much he and her mother cared for her comfort. He now recalled that one of the peons in his office, a regular commuter, had mentioned that women travelling alone in first class sometimes regretted it.

'Not many people going first class these days, sir,' the peon had said. 'Ladies all by their self in a compartment, with no one nearby to hear them calling for help, so bad people taking advantage. I'm always sending my wife and daughter Third. Even my mother-in-law I am sending. Crowded—' he shrugged – 'but safe. Many children also going.'

Herbert had noticed numbers of young people, evidently students, crowding into the Third Class carriages. Perhaps Latha would have been happier – and safer, too – with them, despite the discomfort of an overcrowded compartment. However, it was too late to do anything about it now. Herbert decided that he would telephone Sanghamitta Hall that night or early the following morning, to make sure Latha had been all right.

He reflected, somewhat wryly, that he had already begun missing his daughter. Funny thing, that. The child had been in the house, year in, year out, throughout her childhood and adolescence, but he had hardly noticed the fact until she went away. He remembered how eagerly Latha had looked forward to her holidays with Rowland and Helen at Lucas Falls. During her absences Herbert had found himself quite glad of his wife's combative spirit: he didn't like getting into arguments, but at least it was better than silence in an empty house.

He also remembered how radiant Latha had always looked when she returned from those visits. It was partly the up-country air, of course. And the company of young people. Especially Christopher and Tsunami, whom he liked better than Ranil and Tara. Well, naturally, she would enjoy herself up at the Falls – her life with Soma and himself didn't have much variety or excitement to offer a bright, intelligent girl like Latha.

Negotiating the traffic, Herbert remembered a book he had given his daughter for Christmas when she was nine years old, *A Hundred and One Things a Bright Girl Can Do*. It was a book by a British author, published in England, and obviously intended for British children, but Latha had been delighted by it. Until she began to try out some of its suggestions.

> *Buy a return ticket by bus or train to an interesting place a few miles away from your home* [the book's author advised in her first chapter]. *Choose a place you have never visited before. Pack a sandwich, a nice, rosy apple, and some fruit-juice in your rucksack, get yourself a map from the train or bus station, and prepare to have an exciting day, all by yourself, EXPLORING!*

This idea had appealed strongly to Latha, who had promptly asked her mother if she could go 'exploring' the following Saturday. She had worked it all out: her school satchel could do double duty as a 'rucksack', and a couple of plantains could substitute for the apple. Soma hadn't given the proposal even five minutes' consideration. Nine-year-old Latha travel alone by bus? Out of the question. 'Exploring', indeed! What was there to explore? Where was she hoping to spend her day?

'Kandy?' Latha had said tentatively. She knew Kandy was a historic city.

'*Kandy?*' her mother exclaimed.

She sounded as surprised as if Latha had announced a decision to travel to Timbuctoo.

'A good seventy-two miles from Colombo, with a three-hour journey each way? Ridiculous!'

Perhaps Kamala could go with her? Latha had made the suggestion reluctantly. In the face of her mother's reaction she had decided to abandon the delicious thought of solitary travel which held (for her) half the charm of the adventure.

'What?' Soma said. 'A nineteen-year-old like Kamala, who has to be scolded twice a day for making eyes at the driver next door, what kind of chaperon would she make for you? Kamala would need a chaperon herself.'

Herbert, accused of putting unsuitable ideas into the child's head, had retreated guiltily to a card-playing session with his friends to escape his wife's reproaches.

Of all the suggestions in the book, only one was eventually judged to be feasible:

Why not ask a schoolfriend to tea? Here is the recipe for a delicious fruit cake that you can make yourself . . .

Latha, asked for the name of a friend she would like to invite to tea, had found her first choice rejected outright. Sundari Appadurai, a boarder at her school to whom Latha had taken a liking, and whom she knew to be homesick for her home in Jaffna, was unsuitable. She was Tamil for one thing. She might have been forgiven this lapse if her father had been a barrister with a house in Kynsey Road, or a physician with a surgery in Ward Place. Unfortunately, Sundari came from a provincial family in far-off Kankesanturai that the Wijesinhas had never heard of.

Sheila Christoffelsz, an active, energetic child who had invited Latha to partner her in the three-legged race at the school's Junior Sports Meet, was also unsuitable. She was a Burgher, and was therefore judged by Soma to be very probably both 'boy-mad', and a likely source of unsuitable ideas. Eventually Latha's third choice had been accepted: Preethi Wickremesinghe, a dull little girl who spent most of her time curling her hair and pasting pictures of the British royal family into an album, and whose reading had not progressed beyond the works of Enid Blyton, was judged suitable because she came from a 'good', respectable Sinhalese family that Latha's parents had already met socially the previous year.

The afternoon tea-party suggested in *A Hundred and One Things a Bright Girl Can Do* had not been a success. For one thing, the author's recipe for fruit cake turned out to be a flop. Latha had insisted on following it in preference to the recipe in her mother's standby, the *Daily News Cookery Book*, since it was the one thing she had been permitted to salvage from the original concept. All the fruit in the cake sank to the bottom, and the cake itself was as heavy as lead, something Latha herself pretended not to notice, but to which her little guest drew attention as soon as she put a piece of it in her mouth. For another, Preethi's elaborate taffeta party dress (which could not on any account be permitted to become soiled or crushed) ruled out any games after tea. The two little girls sat side by side on the drawing-room sofa, looking at corgis and coronets in Preethi's album until it was time for her to say goodbye, and Latha, who had spent the morning in a fever of anticipation, baking her cake and rehearsing her role of gracious hostess, went to bed in tears.

Herbert had sympathized with his daughter in her disappointment. He wished heartily that he had had no part in causing it. Typically, he bought her a bottle of Pascall's barley sugar to cheer her up. But he recognized, on reflection, the correctness of his wife's judgment in the matter. Ceylon was not Britain: Ceylon was Ceylon. Latha, who had to grow up in Ceylon, must come to terms with the rules that governed the society of which she was a part, and the earlier she learned to do that the better.

Picking his way among taxis and bicycles on the Galle Road, Herbert recalled their evening at the Capri. He had observed his daughter closely during what he now privately thought of as 'the Munasinghe fiasco'. He had refrained from attempting to influence Latha or thwart his wife's plans in any way, but he had sympathized with his daughter's point of view. Anupam Munasinghe, although he was certainly presentable, a career diplomat, and the son of an old friend, had not impressed him. Why not? Was he not intelligent enough for Latha? No, he was bright all right. A clever, well-educated young man. Was he too sophisticated? Too much a man of the world? Herbert remembered Anupam's formidably well-groomed appearance, and the ease with which he had ordered from a Western-style menu. 'The Incomparable', eh? He certainly appeared to live up to his name. But perhaps all that sophistication would be too much for his inexperienced, shy daughter. No, the main question that must concern him, as Latha's father, was whether young Munasinghe was good enough, *reliable* enough to make a life partner for his only child. Not immediately, of course, he reminded himself quickly. Not for many years: and certainly not until she had graduated.

Herbert smiled to himself at the thought of his daughter as a university graduate. Was *anyone* good enough for her?

'I'm biased, of course,' he told himself.

He remembered an English friend from his university days, the father of a beautiful and talented musician, who had telephoned him long distance from London to invite him to his daughter Sophie's wedding. Herbert, concerned at detecting a melancholy note in his old friend's voice on what should have been a joyful occasion, had inquired whether anything was the matter.

'Herbert,' Dr Robertson had said dolefully, 'Sophie is marrying an American.'

'Well?' Herbert asked. 'You should be very pleased, surely—'

'You have no idea what this means to me, Herbert,' his friend had interrupted him. 'I feel as if I were . . . as if I were handing a Stradivarius to a gorilla.'

Were fathers who loved their daughters ever entirely satisfied with their sons-in-law? Well, Herbert concluded, as he brought his car to a stop beneath the little portico of his house, let's see what Latha makes of Peradeniya. She said she didn't care for the young Munasinghes' Westernized manners, and thought them affected and insincere. She'll meet with any number of the home-grown variety at the University: let's see whether she likes them any better.

Unlike his wife, Herbert entertained no fears of a spinster's fate for their daughter. It was only a matter of time before some sensible young man, recognizing Latha's obvious attractions, showed up on the doorstep to ask for her hand in marriage. And if, by some unlikely chance, he failed to do so and Latha didn't find anyone who suited her, Herbert decided, she'll always have a home with us . . . if she wants one, that is.

There appeared to be no one at home. Soma had probably gone shopping, and taken the maid-servant with her. Herbert let himself into the house. Inside, it was dark and slightly stuffy, but it was cooler and much pleasanter than the bright glare of the veranda. He switched on the overhead fan in the dining room, took a bottle of beer from the refrigerator, and looked around until he found a bottle opener.

'There, that's better,' he said to himself.

Good old Beck's. Herbert liked the good things of life, and regarded German beer as definitely one of them. He kicked off his sandals, and leaned back comfortably, glass in hand. Regarding with a cheerful eye the bubbles of golden foam rising in his glass, he felt his spirits lift with them. No doubt about it, today was a special occasion, even though it was not (from his personal point of view) exactly a happy one.

He glanced at his watch. Eleven o'clock. In a couple of hours, Latha would be arriving in Peradeniya. He wished he could have done more to make this first flight from the family nest pleasanter for her. He would have liked to have driven her up to Peradeniya in the car, for instance. If they had made an early start, they could have stopped at some of his favourite spots *en route*, enjoyed a snack of hot *mas paan* and milky coffee at Kegalle, followed by an early breakfast at Peradeniya Rest House, where the Rest House keeper was an old acquaintance; and they could still have arrived in good time. Unfortunately, there were several ships due in that afternoon, and he could not very well absent himself when he knew how short-staffed they were just now at Customs.

Soma, he recalled, had made almost as much of a fuss over fitting Latha out for University as she might have made if the child had been getting married. She'd enjoyed herself shopping for saris, and embroidering 'L.W.' in cross-stitch on sheets, towels, pillow-cases and petticoats. Typical of women: it was the social and frivolous, not the intellectual side of Latha's future university experience that occupied her mother's thoughts.

Herbert, in contrast, had bought his daughter a dozen Monitor exercise books, a portable Olympia typewriter, and a supply of ruled paper. ('For your lecture notes, duwa,' he had said, hoping privately that some of it would be used for letters home.) He also presented her with a Parker pen, and a brand new bottle of Quink. Choosing the typewriter and the pen had given him a great deal of pleasure. The typewriter was a cheerful tangerine in colour, and the pen was dark blue.

His mind turning from study to creature comforts, Herbert had next invested in a small saucepan with a lid, six china cups and saucers, and six teaspoons. He had also filled a cardboard box with jars of Sanatogen, Horlicks malted milk, and Kepler's cod liver oil, together with tins of Milkmaid condensed milk, Nestlé's Milo, and Cadbury's cocoa. Remembering what institutional food in Britain had been like, Herbert was convinced that the meals in Sanghamitta Hall would be spartan. He was glad to be doing his bit to help Latha ward off starvation.

Remembering next how miserable his daughter had been as a child when she had a cold in the head, Herbert had got Podina to bottle a supply of powdered coriander, which he added to the essential items in the cardboard box. Latha could now brew her own cups of *koththamalli*, he said to himself: coriander tea was always such a comfort when one was far from home and feeling 'flu-ey'. Remembering how Soma had been accustomed to shake a few drops of eucalyptus oil on to a knot in Latha's handkerchief before pinning it to the child's uniform and sending her off to school, Herbert added to his store a small bottle of eucalyptus oil (bought from the City Dispensary) for Latha to use on 'cold days'.

Piling his purchases on his daughter's bed, ready for packing and transport, Herbert had said with assumed casualness:

'A few small things here for you, duwa, just see if there's space for some of them in your suitcase.'

Latha had been amazed.

'You've thought of absolutely everything, haven't you, Thaththi!'

When she examined his gifts closely, and discovered the coriander and the eucalyptus oil she had looked ready to cry: instead, she had put her arms around his neck as she had not done since she was a little girl, and kissed him on both cheeks. Well, Herbert thought, hastily leaving the room, if she needed anything else, she had only to let him know.

When the time came for Latha to say goodbye, Soma's final words to her daughter took the form of a reminder that there were two woollen cardigans in her suitcase, one of which she must not fail to put on when the Peradeniya weather turned wet and windy. Herbert's farewell, somewhat oddly for him, was a plea that she should avoid politics. Surprise must have shown in Latha's face, for her father elaborated:

'Campus politics, girl, campus politics. You'll find yourself besieged by people – mostly young men – wanting you to join one political party or another. Especially the Marxists. Not that I have anything against Marx, but his ideas as translated on the campus will only be a half-baked imitation of the original. None of its promoters will be looking to bring about genuine social change, they'll be campaigning to get into the Students' Union committee because it'll look good on their job applications. Take my advice, Latha. Stay away from politics, and concentrate on your studies.'

Promising faithfully to wear her cardigans and ignore campus politics, Latha had asked Podina to remember her to her married sister Kamala when she next went home to their village, and bidden her parents a tearful farewell. Herbert, recalling his last glimpse of his daughter at the train window, surrounded by strangers, wished yet again that he had managed somehow to make the trip to Peradeniya. A ring on the door-bell made him start. He went to the door and opened it, to find a stranger wiping his shoes on the mat.

'Please sit down, I'll be with you in a minute,' Herbert said, preparing to go indoors for his spectacles.

No doubt this would be someone pestering him for a subscription to a charity, and Herbert always liked to make sure that the appeal was a genuine one.

'Good morning, Uncle,' said a familiar voice.

Taking a closer look, Herbert recognized a family resemblance.

'Good heavens! Ranil?'

'No, Uncle Herbert. It's Christopher.'

'Of course. Good God, boy, you're as tall as your brother. I couldn't make you out at first.'

'Many people fail to do so, Uncle. I'm often mistaken for Ranil – oddly, not the other way about.'

'Come in, come in, Chris. Delighted to see you. Care for a beer? I've got some cold beer in the fridge.'

'Thank you. Let me help you find another glass.'

'Well, this certainly is an occasion,' Herbert said when they had settled down comfortably together, one on each side of the dining table. 'What brings you home? I thought all three of you boys are studying in England.'

'Well, two of us are over there. Ranil sat for his finals two years ago, and he's practising now in London. He's thinking of coming home, though, to take a job as Pater's private secretary. Colin's in accountancy.'

'And you?'

'I'm in Australia, Uncle Herbert, finishing a science degree in Sydney, and planning to get back here as soon as I can.'

'Glad to hear it. There's plenty here to keep a scientist busy.'

'And a lawyer, I hope. I've decided to earn my living in the law, and to do it in my own country.'

'Well, well, well! I had no idea,' Herbert said. He added:

'We haven't been in touch with your family for some time, I'm sorry to say.'

'Yes, I know that,' replied his nephew. 'That's partly why I'm here.'

He took a small package from his pocket, and placed it on the table between them.

'Is Latha at home, Uncle Herbert? I have a present for her. It's from my mother.'

The words came out quite casually and matter-of-factly, almost as though it wasn't the first time any of Rowland's children had talked to Herbert of Helen after her elopement with the Visiting Agent. Herbert decided to match, if he could, his nephew's remarkable poise.

'And how is your mother, Chris?'

'She's very well, Uncle Herbert. Australia seems to suit her.'

'So they decided on Australia, eh? I thought they'd settled in England.'

'I believe that England was part of my mother's original plan. But the first winter was a very cold one – the water froze in the pipes, it seems, which burst. Her flat was completely flooded . . .'

Herbert tried to imagine Helen, with or without Franz Goldman, coping with burst water pipes in the depths of a British winter, and failed. Soma would most definitely say, if she heard the story, that it was the judgment of Heaven on an adulterous woman. Herbert, who had always cherished a fondness for Helen, decided that Soma would never hear the story from him.

'So Franz advised her that Australia, where the climate, he said, was sane and civilized except for the odd flash flood or bush fire, would be the place for her. He said—'

'So you're in touch with him?'

'Oh yes,' Chris said cheerfully. 'I see him most weekends – most weekends, that is, when he's not driving my mother out of Sydney to visit some garden or other. Franz has gone into landscape gardening, you see, and she loves the life he's created for her.'

Herbert was glad to hear that Helen was happy. Had 'the life Franz Goldman had created for her' included marriage? Chris's account gave nothing away. Herbert would have liked to ask more questions, he would have liked to ask *that* question, and he knew that Soma, had she been present, would most certainly have asked it. But Chris did not seem to be especially forthcoming, and Herbert thought better of it.

'Well, here's to them both,' he said, raising his glass. 'I'll tell Latha you called – she'll be really pleased to have news of Helen.'

'My mother often talks of Latha,' Chris said. 'When she heard that Pater had married again, one of her big worries was that Latha would lose touch with us – with Tsunami especially.'

'Well, putha, I'm sorry to say they have lost touch, rather,' Herbert told him. 'Your Aunt Soma didn't take too kindly to the new Mrs Rowland. Nor, I suspect, did Mrs Rowland particularly want to keep up the contact with us. We aren't quite her cup of tea.'

'Aunt Moira's not too bad, you know,' said Chris. 'She means well. She's just a bit hard to take, especially after our mother and especially after Pater went into politics. I suppose I should mention that Colin and I invented a new version of Scrabble around that time which we called *MoiraSpeak* – not in her hearing, of course. The words we put on the board were limited to words that were in Aunt Moira's vocabulary: 'motorcade' in the place of 'cortège', 'rally' instead of 'crowd', 'fundraiser' instead of 'social', 'gift' instead of 'bribe', 'masses' instead of 'poor' – I'm sure you get the picture . . .'

'A political picture,' Herbert said.

'Yes. My sisters couldn't stand her at first, especially Tsunami, but they're getting on better now, I believe. She's grown on all of us. Ranil regards himself as her right-hand man, a sort of courtier, I suppose—' Chris smiled wryly as he said it – 'and Tara has actually become very fond of her.'

'Something I'd really like to know,' Herbert said, 'and I hope you won't mind my asking, is: how does your Aunt Moira get on with Raman and Vaithianathan?'

Chris looked at him with surprise, and Herbert hastened to assure him that his question was not prompted by mere curiosity.

'I'm hoping,' he said, 'that they're looking for other jobs. Raman is much too grand for us, of course, but Vaithianathan might be able to help me out. For old time's sake, since I certainly can't match the salary he must be getting from your father.'

'As far as I know, both of them have made the transition fairly smoothly,' Chris said. 'After Pater joined the Cabinet, Aunt Moira's life's become a round of luncheons and dinner-parties. She's a great one for entertaining, anyway, so Raman, being the perfect butler, is in his element. She'd be unlikely to let either Raman or Vaithi go unless things really reach crisis-point with them. I'll check discreetly with them both and let you know.'

Herbert looked at Chris with gratitude. 'You'd be doing me a great kindness, putha,' he said. 'It's not that our present lady can't cook, but we think that any moment now she'll be telling us she's leaving to get married. Soma says all the signs are there – including a tendency to collect soap.'

'*Soap*, Uncle Herbert?'

Herbert sighed.

'You haven't been back long enough, I think, Chris, to know about the Great Lifebuoy Happy Families Sweep? No, I thought not. Well, let me tell you, it's making my life sheer hell over here. Some sadistic fiend in the marketing department at Lever Brothers, reverting to his misspent childhood, has had the bright idea of getting the nation to play Happy Families. Every cake of Lifebuoy Soap you buy today carries a picture of a happy dad, a happy mum, a happy son or a happy daughter, all scrubbing themselves vigorously with Lifebuoy Soap. But the picture's inside the wrapping – please take careful note of that, *inside* the wrapping, not outside, where you can see it – so you have to buy a cake of soap if you want to know which picture's inside. The lucky customer who collects all four members of the happy Lifebuoy Family can claim a necklace, earrings and bangles, all made of guaranteed 22 carat sovereign gold. The catch, of course, is that while the shops and stores are flooded with cakes of Lifebuoy Soap carrying pictures of dad, mum and daughter, no one has yet been lucky enough to buy a cake of soap that carries a picture of the son. And do you know why?'

'Because there *are* no pictures of the son?'

Herbert regarded his nephew with approval.

'Dead right. Every servant girl in the land is spending her salary stocking up on Lifebuoy, hoping to find the cake of soap that will make her fortune. And our Podina is no exception. Every time Soma or I go out, there's Podina, standing at the door reminding us to buy some cakes of Lifebuoy. Then, as soon as we get home, she's into them like a hurricane, tearing through the wrapping papers, scattering them everywhere, driven by futile hope. I can tell you, Chris, I'm sick of it. Each time she's disappointed – which is every time she goes marketing, of course, or Soma does – she bangs about in the kitchen, taking out her fury on the pots and pans. I can't stand this, I told Soma last week. I want a change. What about getting a man, a male cook, to replace Podina? Soma's not too keen on the idea, but I'm all for Vaithianathan's dignified, quiet efficiency. A steady husband and father isn't he? Good – no chance of him wanting to get married again and contracting Lifebuoy disease . . .'

Chris was amused. 'Highly unlikely, I'd say. But if he ever did, I'm sure he'd pass on his skills . . .'

'And make the whole world a happier place. By the way,' Herbert said, 'didn't you kids call him Jeeves at one time?'

'No, it was Raman, being our butler and Pater's valet, who was the "inimitable Jeeves" in the P.G. Wodehouse books. Vaithi was christened Anatole after the French chef who worked for Bertie Wooster's aunt, Mrs Dahlia Travers. Fancy your remembering that, Uncle Herbert. Do you know, I'd forgotten all about it, but obviously you haven't.'

Chris looked at his watch and rose to his feet.

'I'm sorry I've missed meeting Auntie and Latha, but I'm due at home for dinner tonight.'

'Why don't you have dinner with us?' Herbert said.

'I'd really like to, Uncle Herbert, but it's my first night back in Colombo, and it wouldn't do to be late. You know what Pater's like about punctuality.'

'Who's at home today?' Herbert inquired.

'Everyone. That is, everyone except Colin. It'll be good to meet the girls again. Tara's coming, with Tissa. I haven't had a chance to talk to her since she got married. And Tsunami, of course, never writes.'

He paused as he reached the door.

'Would Auntie Soma and Latha be at home tomorrow, Uncle? I'd really like to see them. If Auntie doesn't object.'

'Women,' said Herbert, 'are entirely unpredictable. You're aware of that, aren't you? But I can't think of a single reason why your aunt could possibly object to seeing her nephew again. I think she'll be very pleased to know you're back in touch – in fact, she'll be very annoyed that I didn't persuade you to stay to dinner. As for Latha,' he added, remembering for the first time the reason for his earlier depression, 'she's at University, you know.'

'At *University*?'

'Yes.' Herbert swelled with pride, but tried to make himself sound as casual as possible. 'I saw her off this morning on the train to Peradeniya.'

After Chris had left, Herbert put the empty glasses on the kitchen table for Podina to wash up. He was about to pick up the phone, then remembered that Latha would still be on the train. Oh well, he would ring her tonight. After he'd told Soma about his visitor.

He wondered when Chris would make the trip to Peradeniya. He'd do it pretty soon, Herbert reckoned. For on hearing that Latha had left for the University, his nephew had hastily picked up the little package that had provided a reason for his visit, and dropped it back into his pocket.

'Don't worry about this, Uncle Herbert, I'll give it to Latha myself,' he had said. 'I've got to be in Kandy next week – I'll stop by Peradeniya and see her. My mother would like to know that I delivered her present just as soon as I could.' He had paused at the top of the veranda steps. 'And I won't forget your question about Vaithi.'

Herbert opened the evening paper, and gazed at the headlines without seeing them. Of course. It all came back to him now: it was from Latha that he had heard about the literary characters with whom Tsunami, Tara and their brothers had peopled Lucas Falls. Besides Jeeves and Anatole, there'd been an Old Nokomis . . .

'I wonder . . .' Herbert said to himself, but did not complete the thought.

Sitting alone in the silent house, missing his daughter, and thinking about the pleasant times they had had together, Herbert recalled how Chris's face had fallen at the news that Latha was on her way to a destination seventy miles away from Colombo. Chris and Latha. Latha and Chris? They were cousins, of course, but not so closely related that marriage couldn't be on the cards.

Chris and Latha.

It occurred to Herbert, although the visitation of the idea was a very brief one, that here indeed might be something that his bright girl could do.

It was a happy notion, if unexpected, but after contemplating it for a moment Herbert put it firmly away and picked up the newspaper. The child was being plagued enough by her mother's anxieties, and he did not wish to burden her with any of his own.

Glancing through his paper, Herbert wondered what would be on Podina's menu tonight. Something indescribably boring, no doubt: she did not possess the skills of her elder sister Kamala. He listened for the sound, either of Soma's key in the lock, or the thuds and bangs that generally accompanied Podina's return, soapless, from the market. All was quiet.

Should I ring Latha at Sanghamitta Hall, or let Chris's visit come as a surprise?

Herbert turned a page of his paper without making much sense of the headlines.

4

SETTLING IN

The chairs in the Warden's sitting room at Sanghamitta Hall were upholstered in rose-patterned chintz, comfortable English furniture of a type Latha had last seen at Lucas Falls. There were pale, pastel rugs on the floor, and pretty locally embroidered cushions on the single sofa, but the pictures on the walls were watercolours of landscapes unfamiliar to her. A Kandyan silver bowl filled with white and yellow daisies stood on a book-case beneath the long window. Sunshine streamed through that window on to Dr Springdale's possessions, glinting off the silver of the bowl and throwing a clear reflection of the flowers in it on to the polished floor. The bowl was flanked by two photographs, one of a small fair-haired child playing with a puppy, the other of three smiling young English girls in academic dress, standing in the archway of a Cambridge college.

Latha had time to look around the room and take in details of this kind because, as she was informed by a young woman in a neatly draped white sari who greeted her at the door, 'Warden Missie' had not yet returned from a University Council meeting on campus. Latha walked to the window and looked out at the drive. The coach had brought her earlier that day along that wide, curving sweep, depositing her with her fellow first-year students at the foot of a flight of polished red steps. At the top of those steps, waiting to greet the new batch of students, had stood Dr Joan Springdale, Warden of Sanghamitta Hall, then in her penultimate year of service to the University of Ceylon.

On sight of the Warden, the chatter in the coach had come to an abrupt stop. Many of the new students, who came from provincial schools which had no British or Burgher teachers on their staff, had never spoken to a 'foreigner' before. Meeting Dr Springdale, slight, silver-haired, English to the core, was the first of a series of new experiences that were to make up their first year at Peradeniya. Latha was perhaps the only student in the coach who had encountered a 'European' before that moment, and she owed it to Franz Goldman that she could meet the Warden's faded blue eyes without shyly looking away. Perhaps Dr Springdale sensed this somehow, because she smiled warmly in Latha's direction before speaking a few words of welcome to them all.

The Wardens of the women's halls of residence each had her personal style. Dr Springdale of Sanghamitta, as Latha was soon to find out, liked getting to know her students individually rather than *en masse.* Loud-voiced, brash Mrs Lobelia Raptor, Warden of Sir James Peries Hall, enjoyed addressing hers from the rostrum provided by the dais in the refectory of her Hall, while Dr Mohini Pathmanathan, a soft-spoken, dignified philosophy professor who filled the role of Warden at Lady Hilda Obeyesekere Hall, preferred to communicate with students chiefly – so Latha was told by friends at 'Hilda' – by way of messages pinned up on the notice board in her Hall's main lobby.

Latha was waiting in Dr Springdale's study because she had received a message, brought to her room by one of the Hall servants, that the Warden would like to see her as soon as she had 'settled in'. That process had not taken long, for Latha had only a single trunk to unpack. Her room was on the third floor of the Hall, and was simply but adequately furnished, with a coil-spring bed, a wardrobe with hanging space inside it and removable shelves, a dressing-table, a writing desk with four drawers, and a solid article of wooden furniture intended, according to the framed inventory that hung on the inside of the door, for soiled laundry.

The temporary nature of her occupancy was emphasized, Latha found, in the introduction to the inventory: this informed her that her room and its contents were meant to be used with care, and passed on in pristine condition to the next comer. (Well, Latha thought, looking around her and noting that the mattress and pillows on the bed were spotlessly clean and that everything in the room looked as bright and new as if it had just left the furniture-shop, the student who had this room before me has certainly looked after it well.) The inventory further stipulated that no nails were to be driven into the walls, no meals were to be cooked on the little electric hotplate in the room (since all meals were provided in the refectory on the ground floor of the Hall), the room itself was to be swept with the broom provided, and all sweepings, together with the waste-paper basket provided to receive them, were to be placed in the corridor each morning, to be disposed of by 'a member of the Hall staff'.

The person thus referred to turned out to be Mutthulakshmi, a tall, brightly clad young Tamil girl with the face and figure of a Paris model, who arrived on Latha's corridor at nine o'clock the next morning with her buckets and her *ekel* broom. Mutthulakshmi's rage for cleanliness kept the Hall corridors and bathrooms spotless, and discouraged untidiness in even the most spoiled and shiftless among the undergraduates whose sweepings and waste paper she efficiently 'disposed of'.

The window of the room and the door beside it gave on to a balcony from which the view, of a green, tree-filled valley backed by line upon line of distant blue mountains, was breathtakingly lovely. A sudden flash of brilliant blue among the tops of the trees told of the presence of kingfishers in the valley. Latha stepped out on to the balcony, with the childish desire of making a wish if the bird appeared again, and realized that there were five other doors opening on to the balcony besides her own. So there were to be six students sharing this balcony. She wondered whether they were all first-year students, and whether any of them had been in the coach which had brought her to the Hall.

Latha now became aware that she was not alone: the room two doors away from hers appeared to be occupied, for although the door was closed, from behind it came the clink of china and the scrape of furniture being pushed about on a cement floor. Should she tap on the door and make herself known, Latha wondered. But only for a moment. She felt suddenly shy. It would be best to get on with 'settling in'. Introductions could wait until later.

Latha's textbooks and the Monitor exercise books her father had bought for her lecture notes didn't take long to set out. Her prize possession, the Olympia typewriter, pleased her by sliding neatly into the top drawer of the writing desk, almost as if her father had measured the drawer before buying the machine. Family photographs and a framed snapshot of Paula and Rajan Phillips in the doorway of their home (taken by Herbert on the day of Latha's last visit to Mount Lavinia) went on the top shelf of what the inventory termed the 'cupboard fitment'. The provisions supplied by her father were rapidly arranged on the lower shelves, and the saris her mother had chosen for her, with their carefully matched jackets and petticoats, were soon hung up in the wardrobe. What else needed to be done? Nothing, really. When she had rearranged her books and papers for the third time, Latha realized that she was merely marking time, putting off the moment of her interview with the Warden. The large alarm clock her mother had given her with a peculiarly shrill ring ('in case you oversleep and miss your lectures') told her the time was half past twelve. Lunch in the refectory would be taken at one o'clock. She had better go down and get the interview over.

Dr Springdale walked into the room, folding up a sunshade which she gave into the charge of the young woman in sari, and came towards Latha with her right hand outstretched.

'I am so very sorry you were kept waiting,' the Warden said. 'Please, do sit down. Did you find your room without difficulty?'

Latha replied that she had, and added that her balcony commanded a wonderful view of the campus.

'Isn't it splendid!' said Dr Springdale. 'My own quarters don't have anything like as good an outlook – but there isn't much choice about that: I have to be reasonably close to the Hall administrative office. Which reminds me,' she added, 'of what I especially wished to consult you about, Miss Wijesinha.'

Consult? The Warden of Sanghamitta Hall *consult* a 'fresher'? Latha's surprise must have shown clearly on her face, because Dr Springdale smiled.

'Let me explain,' she said. 'It is Sanghamitta Hall tradition to appoint a student sub-Warden for each year. This is a little hard on a first-year sub-Warden to whom everything on campus is new, but the task gets easier with each year. I asked you to come and see me because I want to invite you to take on the sub-Wardenship for your fellow first-year students.'

Latha didn't know what to say. Dr Springdale waited a moment or two, then went on.

'Many of our students are from the provinces,' she said, 'and they are very uneasy and uncomfortable when they have to deal with me. They think of me, you see, as a foreigner. At any rate, for the first six months, or until they've got to know me better, and discover I'm human and I don't bite. Student sub-Wardenship is simply a matter of personal relations: you would be the main channel for communication between the students and myself on day-to-day matters, and if you run into any difficulties when I'm not around, Miss Seneviratne, the sub-Warden, is there to consult. Not to mention the two senior student sub-Wardens. You will probably be meeting all three at dinner tonight. Any questions?'

Latha hesitated.

'Yes,' she said at last. 'I'd like to know why you asked me, Dr Springdale, and not one of the other students?'

'I know something of your academic record,' said the Warden. 'Prefectship and House Captaincy in your last year at school, isn't that so? And Mrs Clara Motwani, Principal of Visākha Vidyālaya, who was present at your interview in Colombo, is a personal friend of mine. I have to make many snap judgments in this job, you see, and I don't often get a chance to study a student's personality or background until she has been resident in the Hall for a while. But I admit that I was actually looking out for you this morning, and when you arrived, I said to myself: "There, Joan, you've found your student sub-Warden!"'

Her smile was charming.

'Dr Springdale,' Latha said. 'Suppose I take on the sub-Wardenship, and then find, after a few weeks, that I cannot do it and keep up with my studies at the same time. What shall I do then?'

'Come straight to me,' the Warden replied. 'We'll deal with that problem when – if – it comes up. Quite frankly, I don't think it should.'

She paused a moment, then added:

'There is a small emolument, by the way, which goes with the position.'

The crunch of tyres on the gravel outside took her to the window.

'Here comes our last consignment of first-years,' she said. 'Just in time for lunch! Poor dears, they'll have to have it rather late.'

She rang a little silver bell on her desk, and the young woman in sari came in again.

'Prema, would you please let them know in the kitchen that there will be a second sitting for lunch today?'

Prema nodded and went out. Dr Springdale came away from the window.

'Well, my dear, I had better go and say my piece to this group. Just remember, dinner tonight is at half-past seven. You will be sitting with me and the other sub-Wardens at High Table. Enjoy your lunch, we'll talk again later.'

Alone in the empty room, Latha considered Dr Springdale's proposal. The Warden hadn't seemed to register the fact that Latha had not actually accepted the position she had been offered. Of course she hadn't actually refused it either, so maybe the Warden was justified in taking her acceptance for granted.

A burst of excited conversation outside made Latha cross to the window and look out. Students were descending from the coach, and identifying the pieces of luggage that three male Hall servants were lifting down from the top of it. Pandemonium reigned, everyone was talking at once. In the first stage of her new role of sub-Warden, Latha looked attentively at them, trying to work out from details of their appearance and such scraps of conversation as came drifting up to the window whether they were from city schools or from the provinces.

This Holmesian exercise was brought abruptly to an end by a vision that now came into view. Up the drive to the Hall came walking a short, fat sari-clad figure. With a multicoloured Fair Isle cardigan over her sari, multicoloured shoes on her plump feet, a gaily beribboned blue bonnet on her head, the whole topped off by a bright yellow parasol of the type carried by Buddhist monks to ward off the heat of the sun, the Warden of Sir James Peries Hall made a startling and memorable sight.

'*Une vache festive*, in very truth, don't you think?' said a quiet voice at her elbow.

Latha turned around.

It was Tsunami.

5

THE BALCONY

Mrs Lobelia Raptor had chosen to call on her fellow-Warden at the busiest moment of the academic year. Latha, who later had many opportunities to observe both ladies over an extended period of time, separately and together, was never able to settle to her own complete satisfaction whether this choice had been accidental or the result of carefully thought-out strategy. It is possible that the University's most unpopular Warden wished to discover the secret of her colleague's success; but one might have thought that after two years of continuous association with the Warden of Sanghamitta Hall, there were no more secrets left for Mrs Raptor to find out.

'Ah, ha, Joan, there you are!' bellowed Mrs Raptor cordially, standing four-square in the middle of the driveway. Dr Springdale, poised as if for flight on the topmost step at the entrance to her Hall, flinched visibly, then smiled a brave, resigned smile.

'Good afternoon, Lobelia,' she replied. 'How very kind of you to call.'

The glance she then gave Tsunami and Latha was friendly, but it was one of dismissal. Get along with you, said the glance, run away to your lunch in the refectory as quickly as you can: how I wish I could come with you!

Latha did not, of course, know then who the apparition in the bonnet was, and neither did Tsunami, who had arrived at the Hall half an hour before her cousin. Nor did they care. Having just rediscovered each other, they had thoughts for nothing and no one else. All Latha recalled in later years of those first moments of their meeting was that after the first delighted embrace, they found themselves walking side by side down the long corridor leading to the refectory. Latha had often wondered what a reunion with her cousin, if it ever took place, would be like. Would they find each other so changed that they would have nothing to say? Her joy on discovering that they were immediately on what her father would have called 'the same wave-length' was indescribable.

It's as if we've never been apart.

A bell had begun to ring somewhere, and from behind each of the doors they passed, girls emerged in response to its call, joining streams of other girls hurrying down the staircases placed at each corner of the main quadrangle, meeting other streams flowing into the Hall from the grounds.

Caught up in the mass of eager femininity, Latha and Tsunami found themselves entering, through one of three tall open doorways, a high-ceilinged room filled with long tables. Here several neatly dressed women in white saris were ladling lentil soup into bowls for the hungry crowd that already half-filled the refectory benches.

'I believe I'm going to enjoy this,' Tsunami remarked thoughtfully. 'Not just the dhal soup – though that smells good, too – but the whole bit. University and all that. I like the atmosphere. What about you?'

'I'm not sure yet,' Latha replied. 'There's something on my mind—' and Latha told Tsunami about the Warden's invitation.

'I sincerely hope you're not going to turn down the offer,' was her cousin's immediate response. 'I'll bet there are all sorts of perks that go with the job. And think about me – how nice it'll be for me, having a friend at court!'

'Have you settled in yet?' Latha asked.

'Not quite. I was halfway through unpacking when I remembered I had a message for Dr Springdale from an old Cambridge buddy of hers. A friend of Pater's. They were all up at the same time, apparently. I came haring downstairs with his letter, hoping to catch her before she went to lunch with the V.C., or whatever it is that Wardens do on the first day of an academic year. And there you were, Latha! Instantly recognizable, I might say.'

'Do you mean,' Latha asked in wonder, 'that you already know the Warden, Tsunami?'

'Oh lord, yes,' Tsunami said. 'We've known her for years. She's Colin's godmother, didn't you know?'

Why didn't Dr Springdale invite Tsunami to be her student sub-Warden, instead of an unknown quantity like me?

'And if you're wondering,' Tsunami said, demonstrating that the years of separation had not dimmed her talent for reading Latha's mind, 'why she didn't pick me for the job she offered you, let's just say she probably knows me a little too well.'

By this time Latha and Tsunami had found seats opposite each other, at one end of a long table; and now, for the first time since they had met, Latha took a covert look at her cousin. The first thing that struck her was that Tsunami had grown into a beauty. The second, that she looked very much like her mother. The same fine features, the same glowing complexion, the same quick smile, the same cloud of luxuriant black hair. But something was different. Latha tried to make out what it could be, and came to the conclusion that the difference between mother and daughter hinged partly on matters of personality. Where Aunt Helen, as Latha remembered her, had been tall and stately, and seemed a little remote until one got to know her well, Tsunami was rounded and curvy, and exuded a physical energy so potent that Latha's aunts would have disapproved of her on sight.

A second difference, Latha decided, was in their eyes. She remembered Aunt Helen's eyes as large, long-lashed and trusting as regards their expression, while the pair of eyes that gazed into hers across the refectory table were almond-shaped, and set at a slight angle in her cousin's smiling face. The expression in them seemed to change by the second. At the moment it was mischievous.

'So, Latha . . . have you quite finished looking me over?'

Latha felt intensely embarrassed.

'I'm sorry, Tsunami. I just couldn't help it. I haven't seen you for such a long time.'

'And what's your verdict?'

'Your photographs don't do you justice.'

'My . . .?'

Tsunami stared at her, then laughed out loud.

'Oh, you've been reading the newspapers! Those idiotic photographs in the fashion pages? They are entirely my dear Aunt Moira's doing.'

'Amma's often wondered how it's done,' Latha confessed. 'She says she'd like to get me into the fashion pages.'

'I suppose she wants to get you married,' said Tsunami. 'Well, at least she's doing it for your sake. Auntie Moira does it from vanity, plain and simple. As soon as she got engaged to Pater she put a tame dress designer, a jeweller, and two photographers on retainer, and now Tara and I are included in the monthly tariff.'

'I suppose you and Tara have huge dress allowances,' Latha said. She thought wistfully for a moment of her own small wardrobe, and the single silk sari she had brought to Peradeniya with her for a special occasion. 'You'd need it, wouldn't you, to have new things for every social event?'

'It's not the newness of the clothes that matters,' Tsunami informed her. 'I've worn the same thing heaps of times, and each time I do the fashion writers carry on as if it's high fashion, and pretend to be thunderstruck by its elegance and its originality. Most of the clothes in the fashion columns aren't worth looking at, anyway, and some are just plain awful. It's getting your picture in the papers that counts, sweetie, and anyone can do it if they have the money. Your mother's got the right idea, you know: it's the way things are done – Tara was photographed at every party she went to all the way up to her wedding day. Aunt Moira even goes to the extent – ugh! – of inviting that creepy little designer of hers to dinner parties at home. He writes it all up in his newspaper column afterwards, you see.'

'Well, my mother seems to think she's not doing right by me if she doesn't succeed in pushing me out of the house before I'm nineteen.'

Latha hadn't meant it to sound quite like that, but Tsunami – never slow-witted – was quick to pick up the bitterness in her cousin's voice.

'It's not really Auntie Soma's fault, Latha,' she said. 'I'll bet all your aunts are telling her she's failing to do her duty by you, and she's getting desperate.'

'It makes life pretty terrible at home,' Latha said. 'We seem to talk of nothing else but prospectives and proposals.'

Though she was, she realized, already feeling much better. It was a relief to actually say out loud at last what she had been brooding over in private for months.

'I can imagine. Well, you can tell Auntie Soma from me that getting your picture into the Sunday papers is no big deal, apart from the expense, which is fairly steep. It's just a question of money. Someone I know who once edited the fashion pages in the *Observer* told me she never had to waste any time talent-spotting at a public function. In fact, she didn't have to do a thing, or ask anyone anything. She would just get herself a soft drink and a plate of sausage rolls and sandwiches, and park herself at a table behind a potted palm with her notebook and pencil. Every woman in the room would come up to her at some point, and tell her exactly what she was wearing – that the lace had been bought in Paris, the rubies came from Bangkok, the shoes from Bond Street, etc., etc. All she had to do was to write it all down, point the photographer in the right direction, make sure he got the captions right, and file the whole thing for publication in the Sunday papers.'

Latha laughed.

'You can't be serious, Tsunami,' she said. 'You're exaggerating.'

'It's a fact,' replied her cousin. 'Cross my heart and hope to die. Ask Auntie Moira. She's right in there with the best of them, adores the competition. And then she puts on this big act – shock surprise amazement – "Heavens, they've put my picture in the papers . . . *again!*"' She paused. 'I can give Auntie Soma the telephone numbers of two fashion reporters who'll do exactly what she wants for a fee – if that's what *you* want.'

Latha wondered whether to take up her cousin's offer and relay this information to her mother in her first letter home. She decided that she would not.

'It sounds awfully simple,' she said at last. 'But I think I'll keep those telephone numbers to myself for the moment.'

'Suit yourself,' Tsunami said carelessly. 'It's often quite useful, you know, just to be aware exactly what's what. You don't have to use the information. But, Latha—' and here her tone changed – 'if you don't want to be put on the marriage market, you can say so, can't you? Surely that's your decision?'

'Not really,' Latha admitted. 'It's hard to keep saying No to Amma. I'm sure you remember what she's like. In fact, this will probably sound disloyal, but I've been longing to get away from home. Peradeniya, to me, is a godsend.'

'A passport to freedom, eh?' Tsunami said. 'Well, that's what it is for me, too. But not for the same reasons. This may come as a surprise to you, but I want to do more than just buy time. I want to *do* something with my life, something that would be really worth doing . . . I don't want to be like Tara.'

'But Tara *is* doing something worthwhile,' Latha protested. 'I'm sure my parents think getting married and bringing up a family is the best career anyone could have.'

'The trouble is,' Tsunami said, 'it's a career that doesn't leave space for anything else. I want the right to choose for myself. I want to make decisions, without every member of the family telling me what I should do, and what I should be. For that I need a degree. I need to be able to earn my own living.'

'Why can't you combine marriage and a career?' Latha asked, genuinely puzzled. 'Lots of people do.'

'Like who?'

'We-ell . . .'

Latha was about to say 'Your mother did,' but stopped herself in time, remembering how her marriage had ended Helen Wijesinha's artistic career. She said instead:

'Mrs Phillips, my English teacher at Amarapāli! *She's* done it.'

'School-teaching's not for me, Latha,' her cousin said. 'I'm not the type. I don't have the patience.'

'So what do you want to do?'

'Would it surprise you to know,' Tsunami asked, 'that I'm writing a novel?'

'Tsunami! How *wonderful*!'

'It may never come to anything,' Tsunami said. 'And I know I'll never be an Emily Brontë or a George Eliot. But there's no harm in trying, is there? I don't know whether I've got any talent or not. Probably not – every time I get something down on paper, it reads like an imitation of some writer I admire. I don't want to write imitations. That's why I gave up Oxford, and came here.'

'I'm sorry,' Latha said. 'I don't understand. You gave up *Oxford*?'

'It was Pater's idea that I put in an application,' said her cousin. 'I actually went up to Somerville for an interview. That's why I didn't make it to

Tara's wedding, you know. But then I decided – at the last moment, really – that Oxford wasn't for me.'

'Whatever made you do that?'

'I ran into a girl I know in the lobby,' Tsunami said indifferently. 'Her parents are friends of Pater's. She's only in her second year at Oxford, and she's already developed an accent. You'd have to hear it to believe it, Latha. And apparently you can't avoid it, the accent just grows on you. What would I ever create, after three or four years of *that*, but another Zuleika Dobson? I turned tail, and ran for my life. Luckily, I found when I got home that my enrolment at Peradeniya was still valid. So here I am.'

'Well, thank goodness you are,' said Latha with feeling. 'Your being here will make all the difference to *me*!'

'Why?' Tsunami inquired with interest. 'You've met our future classmates, have you? A wild and woolly lot, are they?'

'N-not exactly,' Latha answered. She remembered her first reaction to the student who had sat beside her in the coach. 'It's just that – they might be very different from what you were used to at Ashcombe.'

'Well,' said Tsunami cheerfully. 'I'll keep an open mind. Peradeniya people might turn out to be just what I'm looking for – as material for fiction, I mean. Maybe the next three years will help me find out.'

Latha told her of her own earlier ambition to direct the Good Housekeeping Institute in London. To her surprise, Tsunami laughed.

'You weren't serious?'

'Yes, I was,' Latha said. 'I might still do it!'

'Well, Latha,' her cousin said. 'Good luck to you if you do. But for the present, I'm glad you came out with that idea when you did, and startled the socks off your teachers. Or you wouldn't be here, would you, and we would have missed each other. Doesn't bear thinking about . . .'

She put her spoon down, rose to her feet, and picked up Latha's soup plate and her own. The refectory had filled up around them, and every place at their table had been taken. The air buzzed with conversation.

'I wonder whether we are meant to stick to these places for the rest of term,' Tsunami said, returning with well-filled plates for them both. 'Or does Dr Springdale want us to circulate?'

'She didn't say. All she told me about meals in the refectory was that at dinner tonight I'd be joining her at High Table.'

'Oh, well, that answers my question. No doubt you'll be up there with the gods in future, so I'll have to look around for congenial companions.'

There was a slight pause. Then:

'Since we've been talking photographs, yours don't do you justice either, Latha.'

'What photographs? I've never—'

'Oh, damn,' Tsunami said. 'Forget I said anything. By the way, I just love the hair.'

Latha, who had worn her long hair in two plaits almost all the way through school, had put it up on her sixteenth birthday, when she wore a sari for the first time. Tsunami, who had never seen her cousin in this new, grown-up mode, gazed at her approvingly.

'And you've got so tall, Latha. Anything would look good on you!'

But Latha was not to be distracted.

'What did you say about photographs?'

'A slip of the tongue. Sorry, I should never have mentioned them. These things are supposed to be done in deepest, darkest secrecy. But a friend of Auntie Moira's showed Tara a photograph of you. She said she knew we're related, and asked for background information.'

Latha tried hard to remain calm, since Tsunami apparently considered the matter too trivial to take seriously.

'Who was the friend? Do I know her?'

'No reason why you should. When marriages are being arranged, they don't usually tell you until the last moment.'

'Tsunami,' Latha said. 'I want to know. And you are going to tell me.'

'No, I'm not. I've been sworn to secrecy.'

'But—'

Lunch was at an end, and the tables were being cleared.

'Where's your room?' Latha asked.

She was determined to have her questions answered.

'Top floor,' said Tsunami. 'Two flights of stairs, and there's no lift, but it's a gorgeous view when you get there. Well worth the climb.'

'Mine's on the third floor, too. What's your room number?'

It turned out that they had been allocated rooms on the same corridor, and were to share a balcony.

'Oh, goody,' was Tsunami's first reaction to this discovery. Then:

'Wonder whether Dr Springdale did it on purpose. Just the sort of thing she might do. Hoping you'd be a good influence on me.'

'I'm wondering who our balcony-mates will be,' Latha said.

She followed Tsunami into her room, and stopped short on the threshold in amazement. Although the walls of Sanghamitta Hall were painted throughout in a light cream, the walls of this room had been painted the palest possible shade of sea-green. Frilled lace-edged curtains of an exactly matching shade had been hung in the window. Identical drapes surrounded the edge of Tsunami's dressing table, and masked the shelves attached to her 'fitment'. Although the room was identical with Latha's as regards its size, its shape and its furniture, its overall effect was quite different.

'I thought you said you'd moved in half an hour before I did,' Latha said.

'Would I tell a lie?' Tsunami replied. 'What you see before you is the handiwork of Mrs Moira Wijesinha. She "dropped in" on Dr Springdale a month ago, to inspect the students' rooms, picked out this one for me because of the view, and measured it for curtains. What she didn't tell Dr Springdale was that the day she came in to hang them up, she brought Girigoris Baas from Lucas Falls with her, and got him to do a quick colour-wash job on the walls . . . Dr Springdale was not pleased when she found out.'

'I shouldn't think she would be,' Latha said, remembering the inventory hanging in her own room. 'I don't want to criticize your aunt, Tsunami, but it seems pretty high-handed to me. After all, the Halls are Government property, and there are rules about the use of Government property . . .'

'My, my, what a law-abiding creature you've become!' Tsunami seemed amused. 'It's only a coat of paint, after all.'

Bravely, Latha continued.

'Paint's expensive. Only students from wealthy families like yours would be able to afford such a luxury,' she said. '*I* certainly couldn't afford it. Many of the girls here are even less well off than I am. They'd regard you, just on the basis of your painted room, as ostentatious.'

'Well, you don't, do you?'

'Of course not. I know that it was your aunt's idea, not yours. The point is, what do *you* think about it?'

'I quite like it,' her cousin said. 'I don't usually like the things Auntie Moira does, but do admit, Latha, that the room looks better – much better – this way.'

'No one's saying it doesn't. I like it too,' Latha said. 'But that doesn't alter the fact that other people – our fellow-students – won't think so.'

She heard her own words with astonishment.

Other people. What other people would think. Is this Amma speaking, or myself? Have I already started thinking like a student sub-Warden?

Tsunami was defiant.'

'Which would only prove their lack of imagination,' said she. 'Maybe I'll present everyone who criticizes my room with a pot of green paint and a paint brush.'

'I hope you're not serious,' Latha said. 'You'd be asking for trouble. The few who didn't dislike you would probably think you just silly. And spoiled.'

'Instead,' Tsunami said, 'of seeing me as the poor little darling I really am, put-upon by a wicked stepmother?'

Latha was relieved to find that Tsunami appeared to have taken her plain speaking in good part.

'Oh, forget it,' she said. 'What's done is done. After all, you don't have to ask every student in the Hall into your room!'

'Oh, Latha dear, but wouldn't that ruin my social life?'

Latha examined her cousin closely, but she seemed quite serious.

'Not half so much, I'd say, as inviting a kid from a provincial school to coffee in your under-sea boudoir.'

'Latha, you're so cruel,' Tsunami complained. 'Whoever would have thought you'd grow up to be such a hard-hearted Hannah?'

'Stop it, Tsunami. Be sensible. Entertain on the balcony,' Latha said. 'And if you absolutely positively *must* have someone to tea – someone who wouldn't understand what it means to have an Aunt Moira, and have to paint everything in one's father's party colours, I mean – you may have the loan of my room.'

She was pleased to see she had embarrassed Tsunami by her reference to Rowland Wijesinha's politics. The embarrassment lasted, however, only for a moment.

'Okay, let's make a start right now.'

Tsunami ducked behind her pale green curtain, and emerged with a tray on which she placed three sea-green cups and saucers.

'I hope you're impressed, Latha! I'm colour-coordinated to within an inch of my life . . . Aunt Moira again. What a woman! Thinks of everything. I vote we ask our next-door neighbour to join us for coffee.'

Before Latha could stop her, Tsunami had gone out into the corridor, and tapped on the door between her room and her cousin's. Latha followed her. After a moment or two, the door opened. The girl who stood in the doorway was certainly no sophisticated city student. Her sari, worn in the Kandyan manner, was of flowered cotton, her blouse was obviously home-made, and its sleeves were puffed, a style that Latha had only seen in her parents' wedding photographs. What was immediately obvious to both Latha and Tsunami, however, much more so than any shortcomings in dress or appearance, was the fact that their neighbour had been crying.

Latha's first impulse was to apologize for intruding, and to go away immediately. Not so her cousin.

'Hello,' Tsunami said cheerfully. 'You don't know us yet, but we're your neighbours. I'm Tsunami, and this is Latha. What's your name?'

'Amali,' was the whispered reply.

'Well, Amali, we thought we'd ask you to sit out on the balcony with us and enjoy the view before it gets too dark to see it. We thought we might have some coffee—'

'Or tea, or cocoa, if you'd prefer that,' Latha put in hastily.

'—So would you like to join us?'

Amali looked at them and said nothing.

'You needn't come out right away,' Latha said. 'We'll take a few minutes to find out whether my hot-plate works. When the water boils, I'll tap on your door.'

The door closed.

'She could have asked us in,' Tsunami said.

'Oh no, she couldn't,' Latha replied. 'Didn't you see the state of her room? Her trunk still unopened, her books all over the place. I think she must have been in the middle of settling in, then had a sort of wave of homesickness.'

'That would certainly explain the tears. Do you think she'll join us when we call her?'

'Who knows? We can but try.'

Tsunami and Latha pushed two chairs out on to the balcony. Latha filled her shiny new saucepan with water from the bathroom, and switched the hot-plate on. Almost immediately, the ring glowed red.

'Everything's so fresh and new,' Tsunami said. 'Isn't it wonderful? And aren't we lucky! You should hear what Ranil has to say about outmoded gas-fires in Britain, and the one-bar electric heater in his college room that doesn't work.'

She looked critically at Latha's saucepan.

'If we're going to make a habit of this kind of thing, I'd better ask Pater for an electric kettle,' she said.

She brought her cups and saucers out on to the balcony, and Latha opened a packet of biscuits.

'Your turn this time,' Tsunami said.

Latha tapped on the balcony door. After a moment, Amali came out. She appeared to have dried her tears. In her hand was a plate, on which, in a green banana leaf wrapping, were dhel chips in palm honey, a delicacy Latha remembered eating as a child in her grandmother's house in her ancestral village. She had not tasted it in years.

'I'll bring my chair out in a minute,' Amali said, in Sinhala. 'Meanwhile, you might like to have some of these. Amma made them.'

6

THE WARDEN BREAKFASTS IN HALL

Looking round the Sanghamitta Hall refectory, filled to capacity with laughing, talkative students bolting down their breakfasts before attending the first lectures of the 1954 academic year, Joan Springdale noted that her new first-year sub-Warden was seated at a table halfway down the long room, between two of the girls to whom she had allocated study-bedrooms on the same balcony. One of Latha Wijesinha's companions was that quiet Kiriella child from Kurunegala who had been too downcast and shy, when addressed by her the previous morning, to say a word in reply. The other, she was pleased to see, was Tsunami Wijesinha, younger sister of her godson Colin. Dr Springdale had wondered briefly whether the two Wijesinha girls were related, and had concluded that they might well be, but probably not very closely, since she had never encountered Latha at Lucas Falls.

She buttered a slice of toast and wondered how life at Peradeniya would affect Rowland and Helen Wijesinha's daughter. The wayward child of such a conservative family, educated at a single-sex school like Ashcombe, now set free for the first time among young people of her own age and interests, and in a particularly beautiful, sensuously appealing setting like that of the Peradeniya campus . . . Joan Springdale had vivid recollections of her own undergraduate life at Cambridge, and knew what it was to be stimulated at an impressionable age by the twin experiences of first love and new intellectual ideas. She gave the matter careful consideration as she reached for the marmalade, and decided that the odds were definitely against Tsunami Wijesinha's leading a tranquil, untroubled life at University.

Whether she did or not, however, was not Dr Springdale's immediate concern, for while she recognized that the area of university life which impinged on Romance was necessarily one of importance to Wardens who stood *in loco parentis* to the inmates of the Halls they governed, she always tried to remain constant to her decision never to interfere. She knew what many of her more naïve charges never suspected as they floated on the surface of their new and wonderful life at Peradeniya, that the period of their freedom was limited. Three, or at best four, years were all they would have, Dr Springdale reflected, before the conventions of caste and class-distinction which governed the larger society asserted their hidden power, inhibited a free choice of marriage partner and occupation, and rigidly limited the range of such choice.

What interested her more at the moment than Tsunami's romantic life in the months to come was her potential, if any, to become a useful member of the Sanghamitta Hall student community. Dr Springdale was aware that many sophisticated young women who came to Peradeniya from private schools like Ashcombe and privileged backgrounds like Tsunami's knew little of the villages in which the great majority of the nation's population lived. She had not met Rowland and Helen Wijesinha's younger daughter for some time, but knowing as she did that it was from the provinces, and not from the cities, that most of Peradeniya's students were currently being drawn, she hoped that Tsunami would not prove to be one of those spoiled little darlings from privileged backgrounds who had been taught in their homes and in their expensive city schools to look down upon country manners and provincial life, and who brought their prejudices with them to Peradeniya.

Observing her deep in animated conversation with Amali Kiriella and Latha, Dr Springdale was pleased: it was obvious that those three had taken to one another, and she rather thought they would be good for one another, too. The allocation of first-year rooms, a task to which she always attended personally, was part of her policy of getting to know her students individually and pointing them in directions she hoped would be potentially useful, not only to themselves but to the University. One of her greatest enjoyments was to find her little arrangements, however tentative or minor, working out according to plan.

Joan Springdale had now served two years as Warden of Sanghamitta Hall. With two more years to complete before she retired to live with her bachelor brother in Sussex, she was well placed to 'look before and after' in considering developments that had taken place in university education, especially the education of women. Joan had graduated in Classics from Cambridge with a First and the Caldecott-Moore Scholarship in 1938. She had begun research for a doctoral degree, but when her work on Livy manuscripts had been interrupted by the outbreak of World War II in 1939, she had lectured briefly in Classics at Reading before going with a relief team to Greece. She had returned to Girton when the war ended, and in 1946 had been offered, and accepted, a position as Inspector of Schools in Ceylon.

In this way she had discovered where her true vocation lay. A dedicated educationist, she had contributed in a major way to the deliberations that had led to the establishment of a fully residential campus in the hill-country town of Peradeniya. Personnel drawn from every significant educational institution in the island had debated the pros and cons of one location after another before making their final decision; and when the University of Ceylon established its second campus at Peradeniya, Dr Springdale had accepted appointment as the first Warden of Sanghamitta Hall.

Well, she had no reason to be dissatisfied with the Hall's achievements over the past years, and she had every hope that, following her own retirement in two years' time, it would continue to do well. Her gaze travelled from face to face along the refectory tables. Her reflections on what she saw before her were quietly content.

On her last visit 'home', Dr Springdale had revisited Cambridge, where a contemporary of hers ruled as Mistress of Girton College. Janet Wheelwright, B.A., Ph.D., D.Sc., one of the brightest products of the Persse School and a mathematician of international reputation, had distinguished herself early in her Cambridge career, and chosen an academic life for herself rather than the comfortable family life her parents, though proud of their brilliant daughter's achievements, would undoubtedly have preferred. Joan might have been Dr Wheelwright's sister-in-law, had not the war closed off all such delightful hopes and expectations by snatching away her fiancé Roger Wheelwright, Janet's elder brother.

Joan, two years into her time as Warden of Sanghamitta, had looked forward to observing how her friend Janet, formerly famous among Junior Common Room friends for her untidiness (except, of course, in the area of mathematics), managed her life as Mistress of a Cambridge College. An elderly maid in a black dress, starched white apron and frilled cap had greeted her on the front steps of the College and shown her into a room of fiercely ordered elegance that exactly matched the appearance of its occupant.

Goodness, Janet's turned into the perfect academic, Joan Springdale thought, remembering the shapeless hand-knitted woollies, hideous boots and ragged gown, frayed at the shoulders into thin black straps, in which her friend had been wont to come in to Hall on winter nights at Girton. Janet's hair, once a curly brown tangle, was now arranged in a neat silvery roll, her shoes were spotless, her clothes impeccable.

'Thank you, Muriel,' Dr Wheelwright said, as her maid wheeled in a trolley set with china cups and saucers, plates of scones and sandwiches, and two kinds of cake. 'We won't need to trouble you again.'

The maid vanished, closing the door behind her, and Dr Wheelwright lifted a silver cover.

'Oh good, Muriel remembered,' she said. 'Chelsea buns, from Fitzbillie's, Joan. I hope you still like them. I do. Nothing can beat a Chelsea bun on a winter afternoon.'

Halfway through tea, in search of a book that she wanted to show her friend, but which she could not find on the neat shelves beside her impressively tidy desk, Dr Wheelwright crossed the room, placed her hand on an almost invisible door-handle, and pulled it sideways. Joan Springdale caught her breath. On the other side of the room divider, familiar chaos reigned. Piles of books and papers cluttered the writing table, ash trays around the room were full to overflowing, coffee mugs littered the floor. Her gaze took in a carpet that had seen better (and cleaner) days, and an elderly, battered sofa over the back of which had been thrown a hand-printed raw cotton shawl that she was sure she recognized . . .

Isn't that the shawl Roger brought back for his sister from India?

It's the old days all over again, she hasn't really changed at all, thought Dr Springdale with relief.

'This,' said Dr Wheelwright with perfect seriousness, 'is where I really work. Muriel's itching to get her hands on it, but I don't allow it. No, Muriel, I tell her politely, you've got plenty to do already, I'll tidy things up myself when I need to. She doesn't approve, but she's too scared of me to say so.'

Joan Springdale had laughed.

'You *are* rather terrifying, Janet,' she said. 'Just a little. To anyone who doesn't know you.'

Their conversation had ranged over many things, going far beyond academic interests and the old days. Dr Springdale had taken the opportunity to discuss with her friend the responsibilities they had taken on, each in her own way and in two very different societies.

'Of the two of us, you've got the tougher job, Joan,' Janet Wheelwright had said. 'It must be such a complex society over there . . . All kinds of things must go on beneath the surface, of which people like us are hardly aware. Like one of those under-sea earthquakes . . . what do they call them? Invisible above the surface until they erupt, and when they do, they cause absolute havoc, lay waste in all directions.'

She paused, then went on:

'But you've just got to do the best you can, and hope that it's the right thing. It's a marvellous chance, of course, to make a difference.'

At this, Dr Springdale had shaken her head very firmly.

'I try to avoid thinking on those lines,' she said. 'It's so easy to misread situations, Janet. And when you're in a position of authority, dealing with young people who you know look up to you, because that's what tradition has taught them to do, trying to "make a difference" could turn out to be quite damaging. Damaging to them, I mean, though you can forget about it and try to do better next time.'

Joan Springdale had thought long and often about her meeting with Janet Wheelwright in her curiously partitioned Cambridge sitting room. A strong believer in the power of personal relations, Joan's long residence in Ceylon had given her a good knowledge of its people, but it had also stripped her of illusions. Unlike the many English visitors she entertained from time to time, she could never again, for instance, regard the island, despite its beauty, as a tropical paradise. Also, despite her affection for the country, and for the many friends she had made there, she knew she was still regarded as a foreigner in Ceylon. She sometimes found that knowledge hurtful, but it had been extremely valuable to her as an educationist. It had kept her from voicing her opinions until she was asked for them, and ensured that she was listened to when she did.

She had, of course, been present on the historic day on which the proposals for the Peradeniya campus had been formally signed and sealed in an office in the Ministry of Education. There had been many speeches made: in a land that prided itself on its silver-tongued orators, that was inevitable. Joan helped herself to a cup of her Hall's excellent coffee, and remembered with an inward smile the address with which her old friend the Professor of Western Classics had honoured the occasion.

'I am proud to think,' Professor Ribeira had told his colleagues as the documents were being circulated for the signatures of the Board, 'that we are ushering in today a period of profound and significant change, not only in the sphere of education, but in the country as a whole.'

Everybody had nodded, and one or two voices had been heard to say 'Hear, hear!'

'The first group of students to reside in our beautiful new campus,' continued the speaker, 'will have been drawn from our finest schools. They will represent the best values of our new nation. As pioneers, it is they who will establish the traditions that will shape the coming generations. What did Seneca say in his letter to Lucilius, commending the manner in which he treated his slaves?'

He paused, and looked around, as if awaiting an answer, but Joan did not give him one, nor did anybody else. Professor Lucius Catullus Ribeira's style was well known. Everyone around the table knew perfectly well that the question was purely rhetorical and would therefore be answered by the speaker himself.

'Seneca said:

> *Let some eat at your table because they deserve the honour, and others that they may come to deserve it. For if there is anything crude about them that has resulted from their low birth, it will be shaken off by keeping company with the distinguished.*

'Weighty words, my friends, weighty words. But much, much more than words. For in the course of the next twenty years, we shall see Seneca's prophecies fulfilled. I will not be around to witness it,' Professor

Ribeira had added regretfully, 'but I am confident that in the years to come, Peradeniya will have earned its right to be called a veritable home of the Muses.'

Recalling dear Lucius, Joan Springdale thought:

Oh, how very sure we all were about what we were doing! So confident! So *Oxbridge*!

L.C. Ribeira had been up at Oxford at the time she'd been reading Classics at Cambridge. They had met as members of I.U.S.P., the Inter-University Speakers' Panel, and she remembered him from their university days as a dear boy, somewhat pompous perhaps, but so well intentioned that one had to overlook his inclination to quote at length and pontificate a little. His efforts in initiating Ceylonese undergraduates into the mysteries of Latin and Greek poetry had made Western Classics the elite department of the University of Ceylon in its early days. Classics had held unquestioned sway over oriental studies, the indigenous arts, and even the sciences, before Everard van Loten's return to the 'University College' from Cambridge had raised English to the same level. Joan Springdale possessed a well-developed sense of irony, and it occurred to her that, preoccupied with past glories rather than with present realities, it might have slipped Lucius's mind that the 'crude' and 'low-born' persons to whom he referred in his speech were free citizens of a modern democratic society, and not the slaves of Ancient Rome.

When the question arose regarding the establishment of a residential campus at Peradeniya, the majority of the University's founders, Lucius Ribeira, Everard van Loten, Eustace Pereira and herself among them, had dreamed of an Oxford and Cambridge reborn, reconstituted in this most beautiful of tropical settings. Being themselves Oxbridge-educated, they were convinced that the residential experience to which they owed so much and which they valued so highly would act for good on the great mass of the island's population. Who could possibly doubt that 'good manners' and 'civilized values' would gradually filter down from the privileged students at the top of the social scale to the disadvantaged at the bottom, ultimately creating an ideal society? Well, Lucius was gone now. And he had been right: the University had certainly brought about significant social change. Although whether that change was quite what he and his fellow-founders had intended, Joan was not sure. Had their hopes for the new institution worked out exactly according to plan?

She rather thought not.

To her disappointment, Joan Springdale found that the ideal society they had dreamed of creating was still a long way off. From her vantage point at High Table, the Warden of Sanghamitta Hall had had many opportunities to observe how the 'filtering' process of social education envisaged by Professor Ribeira and her other colleagues, so smooth in theory, was in practice frequently impeded by snobbery and prejudice. Class- and caste-consciousness had come unexpectedly to the fore among the student population on campus, as well-heeled, self-confident young people amused themselves at the expense of classmates they regarded as their social inferiors by forming exclusive cliques, sitting together ostentatiously at meals, giggling at private jokes, and talking to each other in code, deliberately excluding awkward and dowdy 'provincials' from their exalted company. Childish but cruelly effective tactics, thought Dr Springdale, who had seen more than one young woman turn and walk disconsolately away from a refectory table that had been appropriated by a large and noisy group of Colombo students who were making it painfully clear that they had nothing in common with her, and that her presence at 'their' table was not wanted, even for the short space of a meal.

Dr Springdale had seen this kind of behaviour before, at her old school in England, but never at University, and not on such a scale. Girls could be so cruel! Some of the worst offenders, she knew, would never get over their early social conditioning. (Some would not even attempt to do so.) Not all 'provincials' at Sanghamitta who were humiliated in this manner reacted mildly, however: there had been some unpleasant incidents that had split the student body into hostile groups, one of them so bad that news of it had travelled beyond Sanghamitta, resulting in militant processions and crude posters which had done serious damage to the reputation of the Hall.

Joan Springdale winced at the memory. She hoped with all her heart that such distressing incidents would not recur during her last two years in office. Whenever she became aware that something of the kind was going on, she dealt with it quickly and effectively in a manner that was peculiarly her own. No punishment was administered, no threats were made. Instead, she invited the ringleaders to her office to afternoon tea. No other staff members or sub-Wardens were present to witness their humiliation as she spoke briefly, but scathingly, of the disgust she personally felt at their behaviour, and the disgrace they had brought upon the Hall, and upon themselves.

By the time she pointed out that although they might do well, even excel, in their studies, and even graduate with honours, they would have cheated themselves of the unique opportunity that the University had provided for their cultural and emotional growth, they were ready to die of shame. (This, she sometimes told herself, with some amusement, was when her 'foreignness' really paid off.) Her mild manner and soft voice masked an iron will, and though it might take a little time for her message to sink in, it had invariably done so long before the interview ended. Rarely did anyone who had once seen Joan Springdale's gentle blue eyes grow steely with anger, or experienced the lash of her scorn, repeat the offence or need a second invitation to 'afternoon tea with the Warden'.

These incidents caused Dr Springdale acute private distress, however, for she cared deeply about the Hall and, without being aware of it, had identified with Peradeniya. She sometimes came close to despair, especially when she became aware that some members of the academic staff were capable of fomenting class hatred among students for political reasons. What carried her through these disappointments and provided hope for the future was that in each of her years as Warden, a few students had been sensitive enough to grasp what she had come to think of privately and personally as the *point* of Peradeniya. Their influence had played an important part in establishing good relations throughout the Hall community.

Next week, she reflected, would be the week of the University Rag. Although the annual 'ragging' of first-year students was one of the campus 'traditions' that in Joan Springdale's opinion Peradeniya could do very well without, and she did not look forward to it with pleasure, she had no doubts that the Hall would acquit itself creditably. Avoiding the crude and even brutal excesses that were known to be practised in other Halls in the name of 'ragging', the Sanghamitta version of the University Rag often ended in students making new friends from backgrounds that would have remained entirely unknown to them, had they not come up to Peradeniya. Her student sub-Wardens, she reflected with satisfaction, had learned the importance of moral authority and knew how to exercise it.

They could be trusted to make sure that ragging did not go too far.

7

A BRAVE NEW WORLD

Like all their fellow first-years, Tsunami and Latha had heard plenty of horror stories about the University Rag. When, and what form, the Rag might take this year were as yet unknown, but stories were rife on campus about rags in the men's halls of residence that had deteriorated rapidly from good-humoured ridicule to physical brutality, stories of violence that were calculated to spread fear and unease. One such rag, it seemed, had ended in a terrified student jumping from a second-floor window to escape from his tormentors.

Could such a thing possibly happen at Sanghamitta?

Late at night on the Saturday of her first week at Peradeniya, there was a knock on Tsunami's door. Outside stood three Hall students whom Tsunami recognized as seniors, one of them a fourth-year who had been a classmate of her sister Tara's at school. They walked past her into her room without waiting for an invitation, and took their time looking around at her belongings before deigning to address her. When they did, it was in tones of the utmost hostility and contempt.

'Stand up when we speak to you, fresher! Is your name T. Wijesinha?'

'Yes.'

'Where's L. Wijesinha's room?'

'Further along this corridor.'

'Go along there, fresher, and bring her here.'

Tsunami did not move.

'Are you deaf, fresher? Didn't you hear what I said?'

'I only hear requests,' Tsunami replied. 'I don't hear orders. And kindly leave my room. I didn't invite you to come in.'

The visitors looked at each other, and there was a moment's silence before one of them spoke. When she did, it was to address the other two in a high falsetto.

'*Please leave her bee-yootiful green-painted room. The little darling never asked you yakkos in!*'

'I noticed she didn't ask us to sit down, either,' replied one of the group. 'Very rude, very rude, they don't seem to teach good manners in those Colombo schools. But we're going to sit down, aren't we?'

Two of the girls plumped themselves down on Tsunami's green coverlet, while the third perched on her desk and sat there, swinging her legs.

'All right, fresher. Let's start again. Where are you from?'

'Matalē,' Tsunami said calmly.

'Trying to be smart, ah? Not your hometown, fresher, your school.'

'Ashcombe School, in Colombo.'

'That's better. She's getting the point. This fresher isn't quite as dumb as she looks . . .'

'Her hearing's improved, too.'

'Now, listen to us, fresher! When you answer a question, answer it in the proper way. Say: "Great and respected seniors, august representatives of the Sanghamitta Hall Rag, I am a humble fresher from Ashcombe School, in Colombo." Got that? Okay, now say it!'

I'll see you fry in hell first, Tsunami said to herself. *You can't possibly hit me or burn my books, so what else can you do?*

She stood perfectly still and silent, in the middle of the room, and looked at the wall in front of her.

'You made a mistake, Sumana! This fresher *is* dumb . . .'

'May be deaf, too.'

'Poor child.'

Tsunami did not move, and after a moment or two the seniors decided that a judicious retreat would be the best way to save face.

'All right, fresher, in view of your severe disabilities, we'll let you off the hook.'

'Especially as we have a few more calls to make.'

'But before we go, we have a sacred duty to perform.'

The speaker got up from the bed, and flung open the door of Tsunami's wardrobe. All three crowded round, to examine the clothes on the hangers.

'Ooh, nice, *very* nice . . . Dadda's got heaps of big bucks, hasn't he? Look at this . . . and this! Never mind, *we'll* choose your wardrobe for Monday's lectures.'

That evening, Tsunami, Latha and Amali inspected the 'wardrobes' that had been selected by the Hall seniors for their first public appearance at lectures on campus. The 'august representatives of the Sanghamitta Hall Rag' had decreed that Latha's sari was to be worn at knee-length, and her hair fastened with a table fork. Amali was commanded to wear a petticoat instead of a sari, and had been ordered to walk barefoot to the Arts Building, with her shoes suspended from shoelaces around her neck. Surveying the wardrobe chosen for Tsunami, even Latha and Amali had to smile. A pale green sari, with the elegant bedside rug her aunt Moira had chosen worn as a shawl around her shoulders, her hair in tight plaits tied with green butterfly bows . . .

'They must really loathe me,' Tsunami said.

'Not at all,' Latha said. 'They think you're privileged, and can do with being taken down a peg or two. So they're trying to make you look comic and silly.'

'Well, I'm not going to wear this stuff,' said her cousin.

'You're not?' Amali was astonished. 'But you must, Tsunami. They'll never forgive you if you don't.'

'So what? I'll survive.'

'Just think of me,' Latha said. 'Walking into my first lecture at Peradeniya with a sari up to my knees, and a fork in my hair. I ask you! Could anything be worse?'

'And it's only for that one day,' Amali put in. 'The one morning, really. We can change after lunch.'

With great difficulty, Latha and Amali managed to talk Tsunami into a more amenable frame of mind. As they left Sanghamitta Hall after breakfast, clad in their prescribed attire, they passed a group of their fellow first-years, who were being compelled to do P.T. exercises on the front lawn under the watchful eye of two seniors.

Oh, the poor things, Latha thought. And in their beautifully pressed new saris, too . . .

The girls' progress to the lecture halls was impeded by groups of senior male students, whose amused smiles they pretended not to see. But they had still to run the gauntlet of Arunachalam Hall, from the lawn of which came the hoots and catcalls that they were to know from then on as the signature of the Peradeniya male.

'Ado, sweetheart!'

'Look at me, darling! Why so shy?'

'Wait a little, honey, not so fast! I'll keep you company . . .'

A young man ran full tilt down the steep slope of Arunachalam Hill, and fell prostrate at Amali's feet.

'Marry me, darling,' he said, his hand on his heart.

A group of his classmates surrounded the pair, and encouraged his wooing with enthusiastic cheers and boos. Cars passing by on the Galaha Road slowed down to a crawl, the better to observe the legendary Rag.

'Keep walking, Amali,' said Tsunami, through gritted teeth. 'Take no notice.'

They reached the Arts Building at last, and found their way to the lecture hall. A burst of applause greeted their entrance through the swing doors. All the seats in the first eight rows were occupied by grinning male students, and the three girls had to climb up a seemingly endless flight of steps to find seats. To their relief the dais was unoccupied. They had evidently arrived early, and their lecturer had not yet put in an appearance.

'Well, thank goodness for that,' breathed Latha.

She took her satchel from her shoulder, and opened it to take out of it the first of the Monitor exercise books her father had given her. An arm reached over her head and a hand snatched the satchel from her grasp. In a moment, she saw it tossed high in the air by one student, and caught by another. Helpless, she watched her property passed from hand to hand down the rows of laughing and cat-calling students, until, when it reached the front row, a student grabbed it and leaped with it on to the dais. To prolonged applause, he offered his prize to the audience for auction.

'Ladies and gentlemen, I have been offered ten rupees for this extremely elegant handbag. Ten rupees! Ten rupees! Any advance on ten rupees?'

'Nine-fifty.'

'Eight.'

'Fifty cents!'

'Any advance on fifty cents? Going, going . . .'

The doors swung open, and Dr Ian Vanden Driesen walked in, his black academic gown flapping behind him, to deliver the first first-year lecture in Economics. As Dr Vanden Driesen ascended the steps on one side of the dais, the auctioneer jumped down the steps on the other side, and took his place innocently in the front row. Taking no notice whatever of him, and ignoring the welcoming cheers of the front rows, Dr Vanden Driesen adjusted his gown and set his notes and books before him on the lectern.

Latha, thankful that at least the contents of her satchel had not been auctioned in individual lots, resigned herself to the loss of her property, and borrowed paper and a pencil from Tsunami. The lecture began, continued, and ended without further incident. At its close, Latha rose from her place, and looking neither to left nor right, descended the steps with dignity. A group of male students pushed past her, and as if by magic, her satchel was returned to her hand.

Once outside the swing doors, she opened it. The little money purse inside was intact, and pinned to her exercise book was a note.

Thank you for being such a good sport.

After dinner that evening, the seniors of Sanghamitta Hall held an elaborate initiation ceremony at which, to the accompaniment of a chanted mantra, a bitter concoction of *vanivalgata*, the medicinal preparation brewed by ayurvedic physicians, was ladled into beakers from a cauldron and administered to the first-year students. Latha had just concluded that things couldn't possibly get any worse than this, and had begun to wonder whether relations between freshers and seniors would ever improve, when a massive bowl of ice cream, bought at the seniors' expense, was brought into the Hall ('to sweeten your memories of the Sanghamitta Hall Rag'). The ice cream, when it came the way of Latha, Tsunami and Amali, was brought to them by the seniors who had terrorized them in their rooms at the start of the Rag. It was distributed with handshakes all round, and the evening ended with everyone called out for a session of *baila* singing in the courtyard.

Sitting at High Table the next night with Dr Springdale, her sub-Warden, and two other student sub-Wardens, Latha noticed that, following the amiable conclusion of the Rag, seniors and first-year students no longer sat in separate groups, but mingled freely together. From her point of vantage, high above the student tables, Sanghamitta presented a lively scene, the atmosphere in the refectory seeming entirely different from that of the school hall she had known. A buzz of female conversation filled this room too, but the tone of the talk that drifted up to her was more varied, more complex, and for those reasons much more interesting to her.

Nearly everyone at Amarapāli M.V. had belonged to the same social class and had tended to talk in much the same way, of much the same things. Their mothers had attended the same or similar schools and now, in middle age, were members of the same social set. Their fathers, who had formerly opposed each other at the cricket matches or athletics meets of rival Colleges, now amiably played golf and tennis together after office or business hours, and enjoyed a drink or a game of bridge together at 'the Club'.

The contrast with the stiflingly close family circle Latha had left behind her in Colombo could not have been greater. Here was a milieu in which the sophisticated products of private schools or well-endowed Government schools in the cities sat side by side at the same refectory tables with diffident young women from the provinces who had been educated at schools the names of which Latha had never even heard. At lectures, tutorials and seminars, at concerts, plays, and in the gymnasium, students from wealthy families would be meeting, for the first time in their privileged existence, students on Government grants who had pursued their studies by the light of flickering kerosene lamps in overcrowded village homes, and had known no social life beyond what could be wrung from the family circle and the local temple.

Latha realized, with something of a shock, that she was looking at a totally new world, a world that her own generation was, even now, in the process of shaping. She found this idea, which had never before occurred to her, extraordinarily exciting. She was glad that Tsunami had, at the last moment, abandoned the idea of going to Oxford as her father had wanted her to do. What luck, she thought, that we are sharing this moment in our lives, living in a free and independent country, at the beginning of a new age, in which every possibility is within our reach, in which nothing exists that youth, energy and idealism cannot achieve! What bliss . . .

Bliss was it in that dawn to be alive,
But to be young was very heaven.

That was Wordsworth, young and in Paris at the start of the French Revolution.

Those Romantics, Latha thought affectionately, had, as usual, got it exactly right.

8

ON THE ROAD TO KANDY

Chris Wijesinha pushed back the passenger seat of his sister Tara's Peugeot to accommodate his long legs, and sighed with contentment. It was good to be home, he thought; good to be back on the Kandy road again. Cricket matches with All Saints' College, Kandy, had often made journeys between Colombo and the hill capital necessary in Chris's schooldays, and the landscape was a familiar one to him. What was special about this trip, Chris told himself, was that he was being driven once again by Alexander, his father's chauffeur.

Tara had warned Chris that it was difficult to get Alexander's assistance these days. The chauffeur, who had been the childhood companion of the Lucas Falls children, with plenty of time to spare to play cricket with the boys, now spent his entire day driving Rowland to political meetings, or waiting for sessions to end at Parliament House. Rowland, rather grandly, had declined to use the ministerial car, except for official occasions. The ministerial car was one of the perks of his new office: his cabinet colleagues were only too glad to make use of theirs, and they made no fine distinctions between official and unofficial occasions. Which was why, as Rowland told Moira, ministerial cars were so frequently to be seen taking Ministers' children to school and back, or parked in the Fort while Ministers' wives did their shopping. He was above all that sort of thing, he said: unlike his colleagues, he could afford to run his own car, and did not need to do it at Government expense.

Alexander (whose name, it may be remembered, was Ali Mohamed Cassim, but who had been christened 'Alexander' years previously by the Lucas Falls children) had been on the point of leaving Rowland's service following the arrival of the second Mrs Wijesinha.

'What will I be doing,' this devoted admirer of Helen had inquired irritably of Tara, Tsunami, Christopher and Ranil, 'but driving Madam to the shops and to her bridge club, and waiting with the car until she is ready to leave some party?'

The combined efforts of the children had persuaded Alexander to stay on. And now he was certainly proving his worth, for although Rowland had forgone the use of a ministerial car, his cabinet status required a discreet, reliable and presentable English-speaking chauffeur. Alexander unquestionably filled the bill on all four counts.

He had, however, got married in Chris's absence, and was now the proud father of a six-month-old son, Jehan Mohamed. All of which meant, as Tara said, that his time was not his own these days. On this particular weekend, however, Moira had declared that as she and Rowland would be using the ministerial car to attend an investiture at Queen's House, Alexander could be spared to drive Chris up to Kandy.

'Although . . . since you say you might stop at Peradeniya to see how Tsunami's getting on, why don't I come too?' Moira had suggested at the last minute.

Luckily, a pressing appointment with her hairdresser had made her change her mind, and Chris had Alexander and the car to himself.

'So we are going to visit Tsunami baba, are we?' Alexander asked.

Tsunami had always been a great favourite with him, and the thought of seeing her again so soon gave him a good deal of pleasure. He hummed a tune. Alexander was definitely in holiday mood, Chris decided: it was highly unlikely that this degree of relaxation was possible when he was chauffeuring the Minister. Not to mention the Minister's wife. In fact, in his perfectly creased trousers and cream-coloured bush shirt, Alexander looked more like Chris's elder brother than his chauffeur.

'We are going to visit Tsunami baba . . . and also our cousin Latha,' Chris told him. 'She's at Peradeniya too, and she's in the same Hall.'

'Is that so? Madam didn't mention that. Does she know?'

'I don't really know whether she does or not,' Chris said. 'I never thought of asking her.'

Or of telling her!

'Why don't we stop at Kegalle, then, and buy some *mas paan* and fruit?' Alexander suggested. 'We could have a picnic, just like in the old days. My wife comes from Kandy, and I know a nice place for a picnic, by the river at Teldeniya—'

'I don't want to make too many plans,' Chris said. 'Who knows? Tsunami and Latha may not be in the Hall when we get there, or they may have other ideas about lunch.'

'What, when you and I come to pay a visit?' Alexander said. 'I don't think so!'

The landscape was as lovely as ever, Chris thought, as the car left the lowlands for the hills, and they began the steep climb to Kadugannawa.

'There was a time,' Alexander told him, 'when this journey could not be made without stopping for water. Up on the mountainside, just before we reach the Kadugannawa Pass, there's a waterfall which used to flow as a small stream into the ditch here. So some mudalali put a *pihilla* in there, a pipe made out of bamboo, to channel the water. "Why waste good water?" he said. He knew something about cars, and he knew that not a single one could make the climb without that stop, because by the time they had done the first part of the climb, their radiators would be burning like fire. All the cars would stop there for water, and the mudalali stationed a couple of lads by the roadside, with instructions to help the motorists. Free of charge, you understand: he was just demonstrating his good will. But then, with all the cars queuing up for water, that mudalali thought up another scheme: he put a soft-drink stall and a tea boutique next to the *pihilla*. He's made a lot of money out of that little stream. You can see his big sign when we round the next corner. Though now, of course, with cars like this one, we can do the whole trip in two hours and a bit, with not a single stop . . . What news, Master Chris, of your brother Colin?'

'He's fine,' replied Chris, rather taken aback by this abrupt change of subject. 'He went to college in England, you know. My father must have told you. The Institute of Chartered Accountants. A very good college.'

'Is that so?'

Alexander didn't sound convinced.

'Not as good as King's College, I think. He didn't get into any trouble in that English college?'

'Trouble?' Chris asked, astonished. 'What trouble?'

'Ho, ho,' said Alexander, much amused. 'So the young master didn't tell you? I don't think he told anyone.'

'Come on, Alexander, you can tell me. I promise I won't pass it on to anyone. Not even to Tsunami. Not even to Latha.'

'We-e-ll . . .'

Alexander always loved a story.

'At one time your small brother was getting up to all kinds of pranks at King's, so much so that your Principal started writing letters to the Master, telling him that the teachers were complaining about his son's bad behaviour. Except that the Master didn't get to read the Principal's letters, because your brother got them first and tore them up. At last, your Principal had had enough of it. He wrote again, asking the Master to kindly come and see him. In his office, at the school.'

'Good Lord!'

'Yes, good lord it is,' Alexander agreed. 'Now something had to be done. When he read that letter, your brother – I'll say he's a smart one! – asked me to come with him to the Principal's office on the day that had been suggested. "You can pretend to be my father, Alexander," he said. "I promise I'll give you fifty rupees if you put on your good suit and shoes and socks, and speak in English to the Principal on my behalf. I'll get you one of my father's ties. Old Silva has never met Pater, and he'll never know the difference."'

'And did you go?'

'How to let your small brother down, Master Chris! It was a desperate situation. He was really scared, not so much of the Principal as of what the Master would do to him if all his misdeeds came out . . . so I agreed.'

Chris visualized the scene in the Principal's office at King's College, a scene he knew only too well. 'Old Silva' was a tartar, wielder of a cane that was greatly feared by all the boys except the Prefects, who were presumed to have outgrown chastisement. Colin, well scrubbed and brushed, and very neatly dressed, had accompanied his 'father' into the office, and had stood meekly by while the Principal welcomed 'Mr Wijesinha', offered the elegantly outfitted Alexander a chair, and apologized for intruding on his valuable time.

'When did all this happen?' Chris interjected. 'Pater could not have been a Minister at the time, or the Principal would have instantly spotted that something was up. He'd have known Pater's face from press photographs, at least. You couldn't have got away with it.'

'It happened while your dear mother was still in Ceylon,' Alexander said. 'The Master had not taken to politics then. All I had to do was to imitate his way of speaking. Which, of course, I know very well. Very polite and gentlemanly, with an English accent. I didn't have to say much. The Principal did all the talking.'

The Principal, Chris learned, had spoken at length on the subject of Colin's crimes. Alexander had listened intently to the charges, his baleful gaze fixed on the villain.

'He has, Mr Wijesinha, broken just about every school rule there is, and my staff are at their wits' end to know how to control him. I want to discuss with you the possibility of withdrawing your son from the school—'

'*What is the meaning of this?*' Alexander had inquired of Colin, in a voice of thunder. Colin had looked down at his perfectly polished shoes and said nothing.

'Is this true?'

Colin nodded silently.

'I got up, went across to where my "son" was standing, looking as if butter wouldn't melt in his mouth, grabbed him by the ear and fetched him a thundering slap on the side of his head. I got, as you might say, carried away by the excitement of the moment, Master Chris.'

'It certainly sounds like it.'

Alexander told Chris that he had been about to administer a second slap when the Principal intervened.

'Now, now, Mr Wijesinha, you mustn't take it too badly,' Mr de Silva had said hastily, doubtless fearing a further show of violence from this incensed parent. 'I am sure we can sort things out. The boy has a great deal of good in him, we are all aware of that. You must not let a few boyish pranks disappoint you too much . . .'

'You should have heard the Principal begging me to overlook the young master's crimes. He said he was sure that he had been taught a lesson, and would mend his ways in the future. So I allowed myself to be persuaded.'

'And what did my brother do while all this was going on?'

'He said "*Ow!*", and rubbed his ear, and kept his eyes on the ground. You never saw such a penitent, not even in the mosque on Fridays. And after that, it was all over. The Principal showed me round some new buildings in the school, and thanked me for the contribution I had made to the College building fund. And after that I took my leave of him, and asked him to kindly keep me informed about my son's conduct. Once we were back in the car, I told your brother: "Okay, fifty rupees, please." "What fifty rupees?" he said. He was still rubbing his ear where I had twisted it. "How dared you give me a slap, Alexander!" "Would you rather I hadn't?" I asked him. "By now it would be your father who would be giving you a belting, not me!"'

Chris pondered the nature of a society in which a well-spoken chauffeur could masquerade as a gentleman, and not be found out. He wondered whether his father could, with equal success, have passed for Ali Mohamed Cassim.

On the whole, he rather thought not.

'Yes, it's a very good school, your King's College,' Alexander said, giving the Peugeot a free rein, now that the steep climb up the Pass was behind them. 'I had a good look around it that day. I'm thinking of putting Jehan's name down for King's College Primary, as soon as he's old enough.'

9

UNDER THE STARS

One of her responsibilities as a student sub-Warden, Latha found, was the job of taking 'Common Room Duty'. Rules at Sanghamitta Hall regarding the entertainment of male visitors were strict in the early 1950s. No male visitor was permitted to venture at any time beyond the Sanghamitta Common Room on the ground floor, where a student sub-Warden was expected to be on duty from 3 pm to 7 pm.

On arrival at Sanghamitta in the 1950s, a visitor would give the sub-Warden the name of the student he had come to see, and seat himself in the Common Room to wait while a message was relayed to her. If he were wise, he would not mention his own name, thus avoiding the embarrassment of hearing it called repeatedly across the quadrangle and echoed from floor to floor, as often as not bringing a crowd of inquisitive young women out of their rooms to hang mischievously over parapets and balconies to see what their Hall-mate's visitor looked like. Coming to the campus as they did from very conservative homes, and having nothing to compare it with, most women undergraduates at Peradeniya were delighted to find that men were permitted to visit at all. If their visitors found the system irksome, they did not say so but complied with it readily enough. (After all, the campus offered beautiful walks in all directions, which could be taken if the Common Room became too restrictive.)

Latha and her fellow sub-Wardens took turns at 'Common Room Duty'. At seven o'clock sharp, they had to ensure that all male visitors had left the Hall. If they had not, some sub-Wardens had been known to actually walk lingerers to the door.

Years later, when a spell in a women's college at Cambridge permitted her to make a comparison, Latha learned to her amazement that at Girton women undergraduates were permitted to entertain male visitors in their study-bedrooms in the College until 11 p.m. During her time at Cambridge, students succeeded in negotiating an extension of this time limit to midnight.

Latha's tutor at Girton, Miss Susan Gilchrist, had acquainted her at their first meeting with some interesting aspects of the College system.

'There's an old rule, which was instituted in the time of our founder, Emily Davies,' Miss Gilchrist had volunteered, offering Latha another slice of lemon cake as she spoke, 'that you couldn't have a male friend visit your room if there was a mattress in it. This meant that when your guest arrived, he generally found you wrestling your mattress out of your room and into your neighbour's. He would naturally offer to help – which, as you can imagine, rather tended to focus his mind on precisely the matter from which the College had hoped to distract it. Things are very different now, of course,' Miss Gilchrist added with a particularly sweet smile. 'I believe there are times – late at night especially – when there are more male students in the College than there are women . . .'

'Latha Wijesinha! A visitor for you!'

Latha, lost in the tumultuous emotional landscapes of *Jane Eyre*, did not hear the call from the quadrangle. It was Mutthulakshmi, passing along the corridor with her brooms and brushes, who tapped on Latha's door and relayed the message in Tamil.

'*Latha Missieyai santhika oru visitor!*'

Latha had been expecting her father to pay her an early visit ('Just to see how you are settling in, duwa'). She flew down the two flights of stairs and arrived breathless on the ground floor. She looked about her, but her father was nowhere to be seen though several students were entertaining visitors in the Common Room. Latha turned, and was about to go back to Charlotte Brontë, when a tall figure seated at one of the Common Room tables rose to greet her.

'Hello, Latha!'

Latha's first reaction was one of perplexity. And then, as he came towards her, she recognized him and her heart turned over. Ranil! *It's Ranil, come to see me!*

'Why, Latha! you look as if you've seen a ghost!'

The looks were Ranil's, but the voice was not.

It was only when he said, 'It's Chris, Latha,' and held out his hand for hers that she realized the mistake she had made. She smiled quickly, searching her mind for something to say. She was suddenly aware that their meeting was attracting curious glances from students at the other tables.

'Tsunami isn't here, Chris,' she ventured at last. 'But' – and she looked at her watch to gain time – 'she should be along in about ten minutes. Her tutorial ends at one o'clock.'

'Good,' Chris said. 'Let's wait for her. But I'm really here to see you. Did Uncle Herbert tell you that I missed meeting you in Colombo?'

Latha shook her head.

'When was that?'

'Three weeks ago.'

'Thaththa telephoned me on Sunday, but he never said a word.'

'Oh, well, maybe he didn't want to spoil the surprise. And tell the truth, you *were* surprised to see me, weren't you? You looked as if you were about to faint.'

By now, Latha had recovered her poise.

'Of course I was surprised! I thought you were all of you in England.'

'Well, the others are. I'm in Australia, though. I mentioned that at Tara's wedding, but maybe you didn't hear it, with that orchestra playing. Yes, I'm in Sydney. And so are a few other people you know. Including my mother.'

'Australia!'

Latha could not hide her astonishment.

'I'd always imagined Auntie Helen and Mr Goldman in England . . . Somewhere on the Monopoly board, in some suburb in London, from which Mr Goldman would commute every day to his city office via King's Cross or Liverpool Street Station.'

'They did go to England first,' Chris said, 'but after that I think Australia was a natural choice. Franz grew up there. He knows the country like the back of his hand. Anyway, where else would they go?'

'What about India?' Latha said. 'What about Aunt Helen's family in Bangalore? I remember Tara paying them a visit, so your mother must still be in touch. Wouldn't India have been her first choice?'

'Not with Franz Goldman in tow, no fear,' Chris said, smiling. 'Her family is very conservative. They would have been . . . well, very upset to see her come home with an Australian. And he wouldn't have let her make the trip alone – he's very protective.'

'Australia,' Latha said thoughtfully. 'It's a big country. Amma says bankrobbers and murderers are always disappearing there, and nobody seems able to trace them.'

She regretted this speech as soon as she had made it. She'd put Mr Goldman and her beloved aunt in the criminal class! But Chris didn't seem offended.

'Tsunami would agree with your mother,' he said. 'She doesn't have a high opinion of Franz. Has she said anything to you about him?'

'No, she hasn't,' said Latha. 'And I haven't brought up the subject either.'

'Very wise,' was the reply. 'Best to avoid it, I'd say. Which is a pity, considering the fact that he has very kindly thoughts about her, and about all of us.'

He brought a small package out of his pocket, and placed it on the table between them.

'Here's a gift for you from your Aunt Helen,' he said. 'Please write and tell my mother you have received it, or my life won't be worth living when I get back to Sydney.'

'May I open it now?'

'Why not?'

Inside the package was a small leather-covered box. Latha clicked the clasp open, and exclaimed with delight. Inside, on a bed of blue velvet, was a pair of earrings. They seemed to be made of black crystal, and on the curved surface of each were embedded three tiny white flowers that resembled miniature daisies.

'May I have a look?'

Chris turned one of the earrings over in his hand.

'These are wild flowers, Latha,' he said. 'Australian wild flowers. And I know now when and where she bought these earrings for you. We visited Old Government House in Sydney last summer, specially to see the garden and grounds, and she found the earrings in the souvenir shop. "That's for Latha!" she said.'

'It's kind of Auntie Helen to think of me,' Latha said. 'I wouldn't have been surprised if she'd forgotten me altogether. It's been so long . . .'

Latha's voice trailed away, and stopped.

'Now then, Latha,' Chris said hastily. 'There's nothing to be sad about. She's fine. Keeping well and all that, and happy in her new life. Franz is good company, you know, though she misses the family. Look, she's written her address on the back of the box.'

Latha looked. There, in Helen's handwriting, was a Sydney address.

'It must mean she wants me to write back,' she said.

'Definitely.'

'But she's still "Mrs Wijesinha",' Latha observed.

'No reason why she shouldn't be,' was the reply.

'I wish I could see her again,' Latha said. 'Tell me, Chris, does Mr Goldman still call Auntie Helen "dear lady"?'

Chris laughed.

'Franz doesn't call her "dear lady" any more: he's changed it to "Your Ladyship",' he said. 'Good Lord, Latha, what a memory! As good as Uncle Herbert's. So you remember that, do you?'

'Do I remember? I remember everything,' Latha said. 'Every single thing about Lucas Falls. Your family gave me the happiest time of my life.'

'You must come up again, Latha.' Chris paused. 'Though you may find things a bit altered. Aunt Moira does things differently, you know. And now, of course, with Pater in the Cabinet—'

He stopped, puzzled. Latha had averted her gaze.

'What's the matter?' Chris asked. 'Don't you want to see Lucas Falls again?'

'Not really,' Latha said. 'It wouldn't be the same.'

'Well, of course it wouldn't,' Chris said. 'We're not kids any longer – in fact, the only child there would probably be Tara's—'

'And Tooty's!' said Tsunami, who had just come in, unnoticed by both Latha and Chris. 'Don't forget Tooty, Chris!'

She turned to her cousin.

'What do you think of that, Latha? Our brother-in-law, who has a perfectly good name of his own, is called "Tooty" by his devoted wife. Apparently Tara started the habit while they were on their honeymoon. (Don't ask me why, it's not a subject I really want to explore.) And when they came back to Colombo for the homecoming party, my sister was heard to say to a bunch of our assorted aunts, "My Tooty is so *sweet* to me, he won't even let me lift a *cup*!"'

Latha couldn't help smiling. Tsunami's imitation of Tara was wickedly accurate.

'It sounds as if your sister's very much in love,' she said.

'Oh, no doubt about that!' retorted Tsunami. 'But she doesn't have to be so sickeningly sentimental about a perfectly ordinary guy with nothing on his mind but making money out of his law practice. Outside that, his only concern is rugger, and which team last won the Bradby Shield. Until he met Tara, that is. And even then, he had no idea whatever of getting married until Auntie Moira turned him around and pushed him in the right direction . . .'

'That's enough, Tsunami,' Chris said quietly. 'Let Latha make up her own mind about Auntie Moira, and Tara, and our brother-in-law. You don't have to do it for her.'

He turned to Latha.

'And the rest of us, too, will come under your microscope, I suppose, Latha, for I'm sure you will find us very much changed.' He paused a moment, then added:

'I wonder what you'll make of Ranil.'

'Oh, yes! Ranil . . .' Tsunami began, then stopped as Chris glanced at her.

'Well,' Latha replied, choosing her words carefully, 'I had a glimpse of Ranil at Tara's wedding. He seemed very busy.'

'He's busy, all right,' Tsunami said. 'Busy getting established. Busy meeting people, busy making himself indispensable to Pater, busy making up to Auntie Moira. And he's encouraging Pater in some *very* odd ideas—'

'Be fair, Tsunami. As the family's future head, he sees himself as the guardian of its traditions.'

Tsunami, now in full flight, took no notice.

'. . . I saw Pater the other day, posturing in front of his dressing-room mirror in the costume of an eighteenth-century *mudaliyar*. He told me it was a present from Ranil, specially made to order, the idea being that Pater should wear it for official functions. Official functions, I ask you! I must say Pater looked the ultimate grandee, but I didn't tell him that, I told him I didn't know official functions had become fancy-dress parties. Pater must have passed this on to Ranil, because Ranil's gone all cold and stiff on me. Obviously, he hasn't taken my comments at all well . . . Although, to be quite frank, I'm finding *Ranil* hard to take at all these days. In fact, if you really want to know, Latha, I'm finding my whole family hard to put up with.'

After a slight pause, Latha said to Chris:

'You and Tsunami seem quite unchanged to me. You're exactly what you always were. I'm sure it will be the same with every one of you.'

Chris looked at his watch.

'Are meals in Hall compulsory?' he asked. 'If not, why don't I take you both out to lunch at the local Chinese?'

'Ooh, Christopher W., you're such an angel,' his sister replied. 'How did you read my thoughts?'

'Alexander's here too, Latha,' Chris said. 'And he's looking forward to seeing you.'

Alexander was beaming when the girls came down the front steps of the Hall.

'Picnic?' he asked. 'Are we going on a picnic?'

'Maybe not,' said Chris. 'The East China Restaurant, we thought. I'm told it's Kandy's favourite place for a Chinese meal . . .'

Alexander frowned.

'There will be pork in everything,' he said.

'And Allah would not approve?'

'No.'

'A picnic sounds wonderful,' Latha said. 'I'd prefer it to a restaurant. Out in the open air, we can all sit together. We couldn't do that at the East China, Chris. Alexander would have to have his lunch somewhere else.'

'Can you organize *biryani* for four, Alexander?' Tsunami asked.

'No problem, Tsunami baba. The Muslim Hotel makes the best *biryani* in town.'

'And vatalappam to follow,' Chris said. 'Is it still your favourite dessert, Latha?'

Latha laughed.

'Good Lord, Chris!' she said. 'What a memory!'

The picnic spot at Teldeniya of which Alexander had spoken so highly to Chris turned out to be an enchanting place, a grassy dell by a gently flowing stream. Beside a smooth, grey rock that was exactly the right shape to lean against, cool water ran into a little creek that was shallow enough for Alexander to stand bottles of ginger beer and lemonade upright in the clean river sand. The chauffeur had his lunch at a discreet distance from the cousins: he wanted, he said, to smoke a cigarette. That was, if nobody minded. Nobody did.

The afternoon drifted by in quiet conversation. Nobody noticed when the golden afternoon turned into evening, and birdsong gradually ceased in the trees by the river. A cool breeze sprang up. Soon the sky above them would be glittering with pinpoints of light.

Ah, God! to see the branches stir
Across the moon at Grantchester!
To smell the thrilling-sweet and rotten,
Unforgettable, unforgotten
River smell, and hear the breeze
Sobbing in the little trees . . .

'Rupert Brooke,' Latha said, but she said it very quietly so as not to disturb whatever mood had tripped off Chris's recollection.

'Yes . . . Do you think it unsuitable? Lines written about another country, another University. Nothing at all to do with us, really. And as a matter of fact, I wasn't thinking of Cambridge at all. It's just that there's something about those lines and this place that reminds me of the picnics we used to have at home.'

Home? Unforgettable, unforgotten . . . Latha realized that Chris's mind had unexpectedly filled, as hers so often did, with images of Lucas Falls.

'Look, I have a question for you both,' she said. 'Don't answer it if you don't want to. Did Auntie Helen ever let on to any of you that she was thinking of going away?'

In the weeks that had passed since Latha and Tsunami met in Peradeniya, neither of them had brought up the subject of Helen's elopement. Perhaps Tsunami did not want to talk about it: Latha, who did, had not succeeded in finding the right moment. She knew, too, that there were other things to be talked of. But an opening had now been provided, and she should not, she thought, let this precious day with her cousins come to an end without the question being asked.

Tsunami seemed quite unruffled by Latha's question.

'We've gone over and over those last weeks and months, asking ourselves the same thing,' she said. 'At least Chris, Tara, Colin and I have. We didn't include Pater in the discussion – in fact, we went right away, out of the house where he couldn't hear us – and Ranil said he wasn't interested.'

'Not *interested*?'

'Don't ask me why,' Tsunami said. 'He just went right off the subject, didn't want to hear any discussion about Mummy and Mr Goldman, just didn't want to know. I thought, maybe being the eldest, he may have felt Pater's situation more than the rest of us did.'

Latha remembered the long, lonely walks along the estate roads that had taken Ranil away from the family during the days following his mother's departure from Lucas Falls, and she was filled with compassion for her beloved cousin. She wished that he had confided in her. He would have found a ready source of sympathy. Even, perhaps, of love (if that was what he needed).

'What do you think, Chris?' Tsunami asked. 'Hey, *Chris*!'

But Chris appeared to be asleep. He was lying back against the rock, with his head on one of the car cushions, and Tsunami's sun hat over his eyes.

'Anyway,' Tsunami went on, 'none of us can remember that Mummy ever said a word. Oh, except for one time, when she was reading Colin and me a bedtime story about children at a boarding school in England. Mummy stopped reading in the middle of it, and she asked me whether I would like to go to a school like the one in the story. She asked me. Me, specially, not Colin.'

'And what did you say?'

'I said yes, if it was only for a short time, and not for always. And only if Chris and Colin could come too.'

'That was nice of you, little sis,' Chris said, from the depths of what appeared to be a dream. 'Much appreciated.'

Latha gently lifted the brim of the sunhat and looked underneath it. Her cousin's eyes were still closed.

'Oh, so you're awake, are you? Well, Latha, the school in the story was a co-ed school, and it would have been a nice change from those ghastly nuns at Ashcombe. Then I remembered that the heroine of the story has a hard time at the school until she settles down to being a good class monitor, then a prefect, and eventually Captain of the school. I couldn't see myself doing any of that, so I said no, I didn't want to go. I don't remember that Mummy ever asked me anything like that again.'

'I wonder,' Latha said meditatively, 'if Auntie Helen thought at one time of taking you with her to England.'

She remembered Tsunami as she had been at eleven years old, with her big, serious eyes and her confiding air, and she had a sudden, heart-stopping picture of her aunt in those last weeks, torn between her lover and her youngest child.

'No way,' Chris said. 'Tsunami would only have added to her problems. Fancy coping with frozen pipes *and* my sister! Hey, that hurts, Tsunami.'

Latha now learned that things had become very difficult all round after Helen had left.

'Pater became security-mad in the strangest way,' Chris said. 'It was almost as if he thought Franz Goldman would come back and steal us all away, just as he'd stolen our mother. He had the locks changed on the doors in both houses, Colombo and Lucas Falls, and padlocks placed on all the gates. We all had to report to him personally before dinner every night, and show up every morning at breakfast. It was very hard on Ranil – no more spur-of-the moment evenings out with his College pals. You can imagine how wild he was about that.'

Latha could imagine.

'As for poor Tara!' Tsunami said, 'Pater started checking up on her friends and monitoring her telephone calls. She couldn't make a phone call or receive one without Old Nokomis hanging over the banisters asking her whom she was talking to, so the name could be reported back to the Master. I never imagined Alice would turn out to be such a traitor . . .'

Latha remembered now how surprised she had been at the time that Alice had not accompanied Helen on her flight. She had read *The Barretts of Wimpole Street*, and the question uppermost in her mind when she pondered the circumstances of her aunt Helen's elopement was: Hadn't Elizabeth Barrett taken her maid with her when she ran away with Robert Browning? Not to mention her dog Flush? She had decided that maybe Alice had become attached to Tara and Tsunami, and had opted to stay on to look after them.

'She probably thought she was doing it for Tara's good,' she suggested.

'*Good?* Tara was in floods of tears most of the time,' Tsunami said, 'and there were endless arguments. Then, for a while, Great-Aunt Eugene came to stay.'

'Great-Aunt Eugene,' Latha said thoughtfully. 'Isn't she that nice old dear who always wears white voile saris and smells of Vinolia soap and violet powder? I remember her. She's my great-aunt too.'

'Was, Latha, was. She's dead now. Probably it was coming to stay with us that killed her, poor thing. She was summoned by Pater, because he said we needed someone dependable besides Mrs Nathanielsz to look after us, especially Tara. Being old enough to go to parties on her own, Tara needed a chaperon who was a member of the family. Well, Aunt Eugene turned out to be absolutely useless from every point of view, and especially as a chaperon. Tara ran rings round *her*.'

Tara would go with her aunt to some function, Tsunami said, with Alexander to drive them there and bring them back, then Aunt Eugene would catch sight of an old school chum and the two elderly ladies would settle down to gossip in a corner. Tara would bring them a glass each of iced coffee or orange cordial and a plate each of sandwiches and patties. She would then make herself scarce until it was time to go home. It was not long before interfering relatives had informed Uncle Rowland that Tara was being allowed to run wild.

'But Rowland,' Aunt Eugene had said plaintively, when her nephew, shaking with barely controlled anger, asked his elderly relative what the hell she thought she was about, 'Tara was as good as gold. The dear child was sitting beside me all the time.'

Another problem, Chris said, was that Aunt Eugene had been a devoted member of the Pentecostal Church.

'Pater would become very irritated when his dinner-table conversations with us were punctuated by exclamations of "Praise the Lord!" from the other end of the table—'

'Oh, didn't she just love her food!' said his sister. 'No wonder she praised the Lord for having provided it. One mustn't speak ill of the dead and all that, but there's no denying that she was a greedy old thing. Whenever she found any of Anatole's dishes especially toothsome, she'd praise God for it – aloud. And then there was the day – remember, Chris? – Pater came back unexpectedly from visiting the Matara estate to find Aunt Eugene entertaining strangers.'

'Strangers?'

'Members of Aunt Eugene's church,' Chris said. 'Pentecostals. Americans. Pater walked into the hall and heard the most awful racket going on in the drawing room. Aunt Eugene's Pentecostal pals were down on their knees on the carpet, each of them kneeling before one of our calamander chairs. They had their hands clasped and their eyes tightly shut, and they were praying out loud in their American voices. After that, Pater said, Aunt Eugene had to go.'

'And so,' Tsunami continued, 'with many tearful farewells, she went. Then Pater decided to get married. Well, that was no go, either.'

'What do you mean, "no go"?' Latha said.

'I mean Auntie Moira wasn't up to doing the chaperon bit. Pater didn't know it when he married, but Auntie is into fortune-tellers and horoscopes. Her pet astrologer cast a horoscope for Pater, and told him that his elder daughter's stars were fighting with his, and that they should be separated from each other—'

'What?' Latha could hardly believe her ears.

'—Oh, just until Pater's unlucky period was over. So Tara and I were sent as boarders to Ashcombe.'

'You don't mean your father *believed* this nonsense?'

Uncle Rowland of all people! The sceptic, the rationalist, the cynic of the family – more so even than her own father – falling victim to an astrologer's tall story!

'Of course he didn't,' Tsunami said loyally. 'He's not crazy. But you don't know what Auntie's like, Latha. A steam-drill, just goes on and on, till there's no one left talking. Especially when it comes to astrologers.'

'Your Auntie Moira would get on well with my mother,' Latha said. 'Amma's got an astrologer she consults about everything – he's half-blind, and I swear he's drunk or high on ganja most of the time, but she believes every word he says.'

'Oh, your mother's astrologer doesn't sound a bit like Auntie Moira's,'

Tsunami said. '*She* wouldn't waste a cent on anyone like that. She'd call him a racketeer. *Her* astrologer wears a suit and a tie, and he advertises himself in the papers and in the in-flight magazines as a "Government-Registered Charmist". He has an office with astrological charts and framed degree certificates on the wall, most of them from America, and a special chair with a cushion on it that's embroidered with the signs of the zodiac, on which the P.M. sits when he comes in for a consultation. His fees are huge, only ministers and permanent secretaries and people like Auntie Moira can afford him. He cast a horoscope for Tara, and now Auntie's getting him to do Ranil's and Chris's and mine.'

Latha hesitated.

'*You* don't believe in horoscopes, do you, Tsunami?' she asked. 'And you, Chris? Thaththa says Amma's astrologer is an out-and-out charlatan.'

'Of course I don't believe in horoscopes,' Chris replied. 'Neither do Ranil and Tsunami and Colin. What did you think?'

'Well, it's been a long time,' Latha said defensively. 'You might have changed in six years. How should I know?'

'There are some things,' Chris said, 'on which I'll never change.'

Tsunami laughed.

'Oh, Latha, can you just imagine *me* with a horoscope!'

'Then why didn't you tell your aunt you didn't want one done?' Latha asked.

Even as she spoke, she remembered how she had herself given in to her mother's urging, and consented to meeting Anupam Munasinghe and his family at the Capri. She put the memory away and asked another question.

'Why did Uncle Rowland allow you and Tara to be sent to boarding school? After all, he has a house in Colombo.'

Tsunami looked at her pityingly.

'When you get to know Aunt Moira better, you'll know why,' she said. 'He probably wanted peace and quiet. We all know it's easier to let her have her own way.'

'Well, as long as Uncle Rowland doesn't actually *believe* in horoscopes, I suppose it's all right,' Latha said doubtfully.

She was thinking of her mother, and of the horoscope she had had cast for her that year without consulting her or her father. Latha's stars, the astrologer had told Soma Wijesinha, were in a very unusual combination, and it would be hard to find someone suitable whose horoscope matched hers. His inability to predict her future had made Latha extremely glad. She had, she was quite certain, long got over her childhood crush on Ranil, but no one else had yet replaced him in her thoughts and dreams, and she had no idea how she would feel about it if 'someone suitable' turned up. Latha knew only that as far as she was concerned, 'suitability' would involve a lot more than matching star signs.

'Of course it's all right!' Tsunami said. 'Who'd take horoscopes seriously?'

'Only about ninety per cent of this country's population,' Latha retorted. 'If Uncle Rowland doesn't believe in them, he and my father are in a tiny minority.'

'Well, he doesn't,' Tsunami said cheerfully. 'Pater may have gone nuts about security for a while, and he might have some peculiar ideas about what he calls "tradition", but he hasn't lost his marbles. He thinks the same as we do. Horoscopes? They're just a game.'

'What about Tara and Ranil?'

'I really think,' Tsunami said thoughtfully, 'that Tara would go along with most things, however silly they are, as long as she's sure they'd pay off.'

She saw Latha's expression change, and hastily amended her statement.

'Look, that probably sounds awfully mean to you, but what I'm trying to say is that our elder sister's attitude to life is . . . well, practical. Pragmatic. Wouldn't you agree, Chris?'

Chris said lazily:

'If you mean that Tara knows what she wants, and makes sure that she gets it, well, yes, I suppose I would agree with that.'

'Oh, it's much more than that!' said Tsunami. 'I saw her in action at boarding-school, and you didn't. They had a rule at Ashcombe, Latha, that presents of food from home had to be shared with everyone at your table. Tara really resented that. And when a big jar of Anatole's *achcharu* arrived for us, with all the red onions threaded on little *ekel* sticks, the way only he can do it, she stuck a label on the jar that said "All onions in this jar are reserved for Tara Wijesinha ONLY". And surely, Chris, surely you remember how she kept Auntie Sharma from us all until the old lady died?'

'Auntie Sharma? Who's she?'

'She was Mummy's elder sister. You must remember her, Latha. She visited us at Lucas Falls when you were there . . .'

'No,' Chris said. 'You've got it wrong, Tsunami. *Latha* was at Lucas Falls with *us* when Tara was in India, visiting Auntie Sharma. I was at school, but I heard all about it from Mummy. It was the time Gerard van Kuyk came on a visit, with his sister and the children.'

'Anyway,' Latha said, 'I'm quite sure I've never met your Indian aunt. So I don't know anything about it. What do you mean, Tsunami, by saying that Tara kept your aunt to herself? And what did your aunt have to do with Tara being practical?'

'Everything,' Tsunami said. 'I don't suppose anyone ever told you, but Mummy's sister Sharma was rich. Very, very rich. Rolling in it. She'd married into one of those princely families, and lived a luxurious life, six months in Switzerland, six months in India, a holiday house in Simla which was more like a palace than a house . . . You can imagine. Tara loved going to stay with her. She didn't have any children, and Tara was her special favourite. Tara used to send Auntie Sharma cards and presents for birthday and Christmas – "To Dearest Darling Auntie with love and kisses from her loving niece Tara", etc., etc. The cards made no mention of us – she didn't let any of us into the friendship, maybe she didn't want one of us to say the wrong thing and annoy Auntie Sharma. Sometimes I used to wonder whether Auntie Sharma even knew we existed! Once Ranil asked Tara point blank whether she was hoping Auntie Sharma would leave all her money to her when she died. I suppose he meant it as a joke, but Tara took it seriously, and she replied: "I think it's quite possible."'

'And did she? Leave Tara her money, I mean?'

'No, she didn't,' said Tsunami. 'She became rather batty in her last days, and left almost everything to a cats' home in Bangalore. Tara tried to look as if she didn't care, but she did. In fact, she was pretty cross about it. All that sweet talk, all that effort she'd invested in the friendship, just wasted! I don't suppose she believes in horoscopes, or auspicious times, or any of that mumbo-jumbo that the astrologer pulls on Auntie Moira, but she's quite happy to invest in it, if you see what I mean. It's not a question of faith, or religion. Tara would get her horoscope cast in the same way that she'd take out an insurance policy before travelling overseas. That's why, when she got married last year, she had the whole works: horoscopes, auspicious times, the lot. Aunt Moira, as you can imagine, was frightfully pleased with Tara. Felt she'd found an ally in the family.'

'And Ranil?'

Latha tried to make her question sound casual, and believed she had succeeded.

'Oh, Ranil . . . Who can tell with Ranil? He's a law unto himself. I expect that if a marriage were to be arranged for him, and they wanted the horoscopes compared, he'd fall into line. Most people do, Latha.'

Above their heads, the stars winked and glittered.

Do they really control our lives? Tsunami's and Tara's? Ranil's? Chris's? Mine?

10

TSUNAMI'S CONFESSION

During the days that followed Chris's visit, Latha found it difficult to rid her mind of the thought of Ranil conforming to a horoscope. She could understand a family like Amali's, old-fashioned and superstitious, its roots buried deep in provincial rural life, believing that its fortunes were written in the stars, and allowing those fortunes to be interpreted by unscrupulous astrologers. But not, surely, her free-living, free-thinking cousins at Lucas Falls? She reflected that her Uncle Rowland's 'unlucky period' must have lasted a long time, for she discovered that Tsunami had been still at boarding school when she turned seventeen.

'It wasn't too bad, you know,' Tsunami said carelessly. 'At least Ashcombe gave us occasional relief from home and Auntie Moira. Though I must say I found the routine of morning prayers, breakfast, evening prayers, homework, dinner and bedtime pretty irritating. And loyalty to one's House was supposed to occupy every waking moment that wasn't dedicated to God: House meetings, House matches, House sports, House rivalry, just as it was with my brothers at King's.'

She shuddered at the memory.

'I loathed that part of it, never saw the point of all that fervour. But Tara fitted in all right. And there were some interesting distractions.'

Amali, who was sitting with the two cousins on their common balcony, had just returned from a visit to the temple at nearby Hindagala. She had not yet changed out of her white sari, and her face was still lit, Latha thought, with a glow that it did not owe entirely to the light of the full moon shining above the clouds.

'You should come with me to temple next *poya* day,' Amali said.

Her visit had been arranged by the Buddhist Brotherhood on campus. ('Why no mention of a sisterhood in your organization's handout, Amali?' Tsunami had inquired mischievously: 'Doesn't the Brotherhood recognize the existence of women?')

‘To hear *pirith* chanted under a full moon, with all the oil lamps lit on the temple steps . . . it’s really inspiring. Will you come?’

‘What’s the resident monk like?’ Tsunami wanted to know.

‘He is a truly pious person,’ Amali said. ‘He sits absolutely still while he meditates and delivers his sermon – not every monk is able to do that, you know, some are quite restless; and it gets in the way of your own concentration when you see their eyes wandering here and there . . .’

Tsunami and Latha exchanged covert glances. Everyone on campus knew that some of the senior undergraduates, presumably lacking other means of financial support, had taken to the yellow robe as a means of putting themselves through University. Observant Latha and well-read Tsunami, well aware that strict rules regarding conduct and appearance govern the behaviour of Buddhist clergy, had noted with amusement that some of the yellow-robed seniors occasionally sported smart wrist-watches which assorted ill with their monkish attire, and that three days’ growth of stubble frequently adorned faces that should, according to the rule, have been close-shaven. (‘*Not* a pretty sight,’ as Tsunami dryly remarked of the stubble, though not, naturally, in the hearing of their devout and serious-minded friend.) The roving eyes of such undergraduate ‘novice monks’ were not unfamiliar to first-year students on the Peradeniya campus, and it was no surprise to Latha or Tsunami that an emissary of the ‘Brotherhood’ had called on pretty, shy Amali in her first week at Peradeniya with an invitation to join the organization.

‘We’ll come with you next month,’ Latha assured their friend.

She added, since no support seemed to be forthcoming from Tsunami: ‘At any rate, I will.’

‘It may interest you two to know that we had a clerical gentleman with a roving eye at Ashcombe,’ Tsunami offered.

‘But you said your school was run by nuns!’

‘Oh, it was. But even a nunnery has to have a chaplain, you know. And our chaplain was a fascinating guy.’

Ashcombe, the exclusive private school for girls in Colombo that Tara and Tsunami had attended, had been established in the 1870s by an order of Anglican nuns. It had acquired a new chaplain in Tsunami’s last year. The Reverend Andrew Clifton, vicar of neighbouring St Mark’s Church, was (according to Tsunami) an extraordinarily handsome Englishman with black hair, brown eyes, a beautiful tenor voice, and an Oxford degree in Divinity. Father Clifton also had a pretty young wife and two little boys who attended Ashcombe’s kindergarten. With a talent for delivering emotional and highly charged sermons, and for making friends wherever he went, this charismatic clergyman had promptly become the darling of both the Mothers’ Union and the Ladies’ Guild at St Mark’s. The members of the Ladies’ Guild embroidered for him the most glamorous set of vestments that ever was seen, in which he looked handsomer than ever.

So, at any rate, thought Ashcombe's young ladies, gazing up at their pastor from beneath their snow-white veils when, with a silver censer that dispensed deliciously fragrant incense swinging before him, Father Clifton followed the choir up the aisle and down the nave on festivals and holidays. The processions at St Mark's on Palm Sundays, and at Christmas and Easter were especially impressive, providing plenty of opportunity for a vicar with a sense of the dramatic. Father Clifton was frequently asked to tea by his adoring parishioners, and plied with sandwiches and cake. He never refused an invitation from a hostess to sing, and the voice that so thrillingly intoned the Lord's Prayer and the Nunc Dimittis in church, and delivered a sermon on St Crispin's Day which moved everyone who heard it to tears, was often heard at Lady de Soysa's and Mrs Fernando's tea parties, rendering 'O Sole Mio' and Toselli's 'Serenata' above the chaste tinkle of silver teaspoons in delicate bone china cups.

At Ashcombe, which he visited every week on Tuesdays in order to take morning prayers, and give a scripture class to senior students, Father Clifton was no less successful. A former chaplain of the school, the Reverend Oswald Bertram, a deeply spiritual individual who had been somewhat handicapped by adenoids and a constantly runny nose, had had the greatest difficulty in attracting an audience from among the senior girls to hear him deliver his weekly scripture lesson. Father Clifton, on the other hand, had no difficulties at all. The seniors not only flocked to his lectures on such topics as 'The Drama of the Mass' and 'What the Passion Means to Me' but they enrolled in force in St Cecilia's Guild, a group which was in the special care of the chaplain. Unlike the Roman Catholic Church, Anglicanism does not emphasize the confession of sins, and there was no pressure exerted on anyone to go to confession. Despite this, nubile young women with prayerbooks in their hands and deeply serious, sorrowful expressions on their faces lined up every Tuesday in the chapel pews, eager to confess their sins to the handsome chaplain and receive his absolution.

It was hardly to be expected that a spiritual force which appealed so strongly to the school's student population would fail to exert its power over their elders. There was a perceptible flutter in the voice of the Sister Superior, Reverend Mother Charlotte, when she introduced the chaplain to the assembled school at Tuesday morning prayers. Sister Elizabeth, a novice nun with a skill in puppetry acquired in her earlier lay life, shyly invited Father Clifton to write a little playlet for her student puppeteers to put on for the end-of-term celebrations: something he most willingly did, and helped Sister to rehearse it with them too.

But it was the response to Father Clifton's presence of Sister Margaret,

Vice-Principal, that had really intrigued (and eventually annoyed) Tsunami. Sister Margaret was tall and strikingly beautiful, with a fresh complexion, piercing green eyes, and an aquiline nose that was evidence, Tsunami's Aunt Moira insisted, of aristocratic connections. (It was rumoured that the nun was the niece of a Scottish peer, a former Viceroy of India, something that no one was supposed to mention, but of course everybody knew.) The black and white habit worn by the nuns at Ashcombe, which made Sister Superior look dumpier than ever, became her Vice-Principal exceedingly. Sister Margaret's good looks were greatly admired by such connoisseurs of feminine beauty as Rowland Wijesinha, who claimed to be drawn to Sunday service at St Mark's entirely by the anticipated pleasure of viewing the nun's profile as she chivvied his daughters and their white-veiled fellow boarders into their pews.

Sister Margaret was very advanced for the times, with modern views about literature and life. She encouraged her girls to read widely, and discussed with them the books they read, whether they were on spiritual subjects or not. It was this liberality of outlook that had drawn Tsunami to her, an interest which the nun (perceiving, no doubt, an unusual sensibility in this particular student) warmly returned. With Father Clifton's arrival in the parish, however, Sister Margaret seemed to have much less time to devote to her pupils. Instead, she snapped her bright sea-green eyes at the chaplain, and spent many hours on Tuesdays walking with him in the cool of the evening on the far side of the netball court, while Sister Elizabeth was dispatched to supervise the boarders' homework. No doubt the pair was discussing the state of Sister's soul or the prospects of the school choir, but Tsunami found her idol's defection hard to forgive.

Tsunami told Latha and Amali that Father Clifton sometimes lingered after the Tuesday scripture class was over, to talk informally with the students. On one occasion he had admitted, with a modesty especially disarming in one so learned, that he was finding it difficult to get his English tongue around some of the long Sinhalese surnames of his parishioners. A dozen eager voices offered to help him with theirs.

'My surname is "Premaratne", Father,' said one girl. '"Pray-mer-rut-ner". It means "Jewel of Love".'

She blushed prettily.

'Pray-mer-rut-ner,' intoned the Chaplain in his splendid voice, as solemnly as if he were reciting the Magnificat. He ignored the blush, and listened with pleasure to the applause that greeted his scrupulously correct pronunciation. Tsunami had watched the scene (and the enthusiastic hubbub that followed) from the sidelines. At last she stepped forward.

'I can teach you to say "Good morning" and "Good evening", if you like, Father.'

'That's very kind of you,' Father Clifton said.

'To say "Good morning" takes only three words: *Mama loku gembek.* Repeat it after me, Father: "Mummer lo-koo gem-bek". And "Good evening" is just as simple. You only have to say *Oomber loku gembek.* Do you see? Only one word changes, just as in English.'

'Mummer lo-koo gem-bek,' Reverend Clifton repeated thoughtfully.

'Very good,' Tsunami said approvingly. 'And—?'

'Oomber lo-koo gem-bek.'

'Oh, excellent! Well done!'

Torn between amusement and horror, Latha and Amali listened to this revelation.

'You didn't play a joke like that on the poor man! Tsunami, you *couldn't*!' they exclaimed.

'I could, and I did,' returned Tsunami calmly. 'I had this overwhelming vision of Father Clifton greeting Lady de Soysa or Lady Obeyesekere at one of their tea-parties with the words "You are a fat frog" – which, of course, they unfortunately are, rather – or, better still, greeting Sister Margaret one Tuesday morning before prayers with "I am a fat frog". It was too good an opportunity to pass up.'

'But surely someone must have laughed and given the game away. Or someone must have warned him?'

'You bet. A loyal member of the Andrew Clifton fan club rushed to tell him he was the victim of a practical joke, and so he never once used his lovely new vocabulary. A darned shame. After all my hard work.'

Following the failure of her first attempt to get her own back on the Chaplain for stealing away Sister Margaret's heart, Tsunami had become an ardent member of St Cecilia's Guild. The girl who had never shown any interest in her own spiritual advancement now regularly joined the queue on Tuesdays for confession.

'What on earth did you do that for?' Latha asked. 'Did you have anything to confess?'

'Of course I did . . . I confessed, frankly and freely, every single thing that was on my conscience . . . I told him that I had played a practical joke on him (which, of course, he knew already), and that I was forgetting to say my prayers . . . And once he had accepted me as a reformed character and truly penitent, which took him two or three Tuesdays to do, I got on to the serious stuff. I confessed with shame and sorrow that I was allowing my attention to wander during Holy Communion in church on Sundays, that I was harbouring lascivious thoughts and desires—'

'Lascivious?' Latha said.

'Yes,' Tsunami said. 'A lovely word, isn't it? I thought you'd appreciate it.'

'That wasn't what I meant,' Latha said, 'and you know it, Tsunami. Whom were you harbouring lascivious thoughts about, for heaven's sake?'

'About the prefects at St Alban's, of course. We were taken to S.A.C. every

Thursday afternoon for swimming lessons. Their pool was supposed to be available to us from 3.15 pm every Thursday, but somehow there always seemed to be some boys about when we arrived, still swimming final laps. The fellows who weren't still in the water were standing around showing off, strutting about beside the pool and flexing their muscles.'

'Only about the S.A.C. prefects?'

'Well, I confessed that I had lascivious thoughts about him, too.'

'*Tsunami!* Was that true?'

'Of course it was true. I told you – he was awfully good-looking, smashing, quite like a film star. Like Laurence Olivier, whom you admire so much, Latha. And one's only human.'

She hesitated, then added:

'Maybe I exaggerated things a bit.'

Shortly after she had made her confession, Tsunami went on, Father Clifton asked her to come up and kneel on the cushion beside him, so that he could give her absolution. He had gazed down at her with his beautiful brown eyes, placed a fatherly hand on her hair, and then had put his other hand down the front of her school uniform and squeezed her breasts.

On hearing this, Amali's eyes grew wide. Latha, for her part, was appalled. She did not believe what she was hearing.

'Clergymen don't do such things,' she said firmly.

Tsunami took a small packet of slim, cardamom-scented cigarettes from her writing-table drawer, lit one and inhaled pleasurably.

'I'm afraid they do, Latha,' she said. 'Or at any rate, and on this occasion, our chaplain did.'

Amali now spoke for the first time:

'Whatever happened after that?'

'Well, the story kind of . . . got about.'

'*How* did it get about?' said Latha fiercely. 'Did you tell anyone?'

'Well, Latha, it was on my conscience. I felt I was guilty – because I quite enjoyed what he did, I have to say. I had to tell someone – you do see that, don't you? And there was no point in going to *him* to confess my guilt, because of course he was guilty, too. So I told my best friend in the boarding-school about it. In confidence. And she promised she wouldn't tell a soul.'

Latha said:

'She can't have been a good friend, because she obviously told someone else about it.' As an afterthought, she added reproachfully:

'You should have told *me*, Tsunami. You should have written to me. I would have kept my promise. I wouldn't have told anyone.'

'I know. But, darling Latha, it'd been so long since we wrote to each other, I didn't know what you would think of me. Especially if I'd told you that I'd enjoyed it. You might have been shocked, you might have done a Sister Margaret on me.'

For when the story reached the ears of the Sisters, Tsunami said, all hell had broken loose. She was summoned to Sister Superior's office where an inquisition was immediately held. While little Sister Elizabeth and three other nuns cowered and huddled in the background ('like wounded doves in a dovecote,' Tsunami said), Sister Margaret, her eyes glittering with anger, advised Sister Superior that Tsunami should be placed on a diet of bread and water for a fortnight, and her mouth washed out with carbolic soap to prevent her telling such wicked, shameless lies in future.

'That's how they punish girls in Scottish schools, apparently,' Tsunami said airily.

'Did they do that to you?'

'Of course not.'

And though they threatened to expel her, Tsunami said, they didn't do that either.

'Fancy expelling me! Pater's one of Ashcombe's biggest benefactors.'

'What happened to your . . . your chaplain?' Amali asked.

The word was an unfamiliar one to her, but she had learned that it had religious significance, and she didn't know whether it was correct to apply it to a person who seemed to be both dangerous and unprincipled.

'Oh, it was all very sad,' Tsunami said cheerfully. 'Though the nuns refused to believe the story, all the ladies' groups at St Mark's Church did. Father Clifton was promptly ostracized by the Mothers' Union, and some members refused to accept Holy Communion at his hands. Old Lady Peries was the first to say she wouldn't step into St Mark's until that wicked, lecherous devil was sent away, and they all followed her example, like sheep. In the end the Bishop had to send Father Clifton back to England.'

'Tsunami,' Latha said, after a long pause. 'You *wanted* that story to get about, didn't you?'

Tsunami shrugged.

'Of course not,' she said. 'I just wanted to tell it to someone. It was on my mind. Like King Midas and the ass's ears. How was I to know that telling something to that particular girl was as good as placing an ad in the *Daily News*?'

She did not sound very convincing, and must have known she did not, because she added:

'I obviously didn't know her as well as I thought I did.'

On the contrary, you knew your friend only too well, Tsunami!

'What happened to the beautiful nun?'

To Amali, the situation Tsunami had described was so strange as to be almost beyond belief.

'Sister Margaret was sent to Ashcombe's sister-school in Darjeeling,' Tsunami told her. 'That's a resort in India, in the hills, more or less like Nuwara Eliya. The British used to flee to the hill-country stations when the weather became too hot for them in the plains. Well, Sister remained there several months: she'd been overworking, Sister Superior said, and needed to rest her nerves in a cool climate. When she came back, she had grown rather pale and thin, and she'd lost her lovely fresh complexion in spite of having been in Darjeeling. But she began to spend more time with us again, which was a good thing. Though all the books she discussed were religious books, *Lives of the Saints* and so on. Awfully dull.'

'Poor Sister Margaret,' Latha said.

And poor Reverend Clifton. A moment's weakness had brought about the collapse of a potentially brilliant career.

'Oh, I don't know. Why should you feel sorry for her?' said her cousin. 'Being a nun was her vocation, after all. She'd chosen to be wedded to Christ. All I did was remove a distraction, a barrier to the development of her spiritual life. So it all ended happily, all round.'

Happily? All round?

'Hardly a happy ending for Mrs Clifton and the children, Tsunami,' Latha said. 'His wife—'

'And those two little boys?' Amali added.

'Oh, they left the island with him. I'm sure they all got used to it in the end.'

'Used to what?'

'Oh, used to knowing what parents are really like. What they're capable of. We had to get used to knowing that, didn't we, Latha, when Mummy ran off with that bastard Goldman?'

Tsunami didn't seem to register the shock on Amali's face. She lit another cigarette, leaned back on her cushions, and expelled a stream of delicate cardamom-scented smoke.

A train of simple, progressive oscillatory waves is propagated great distances at the ocean surface in ever-widening circles . . .

Now where did I read that?

11

A NEW VOCABULARY

The acquisition of a new vocabulary is an important part of an undergraduate's university education in Arts anywhere in the world.

In the first term at the University of Ceylon at Peradeniya in the mid-1950s, a female student's first teachers used to be her male classmates, and the lessons she learned began in the moments preceding the lectures in Economics and History which, being prescribed courses for the General Arts Qualifying examination, all Arts students were expected to attend.

Latha had thought the noisy reception she had received at the Economics lecture at which her handbag was 'auctioned' was merely part of the University Rag. She believed that, following the Rag, lectures would immediately resume a normal, civilized pattern. She found that she was mistaken. On their second day at Peradeniya, she, Tsunami and Amali entered the 'B' Room five minutes early for their first lecture in History to an orchestrated clamour of wolf-whistles and catcalls. They were not the only women students so honoured: every female undergraduate was subjected to the same treatment as she came through the swing doors, and any unwary fresher who, taken by surprise, glanced up when she heard her name called, was greeted with redoubled hoots and jeers.

It was a pity, as Tsunami said, that the first lesson they'd had to learn at University was the art of ignoring every man in the room.

The second part of the vocabulary lesson taught at Peradeniya was verbal. When it became clear to the male students that their catcalls had ceased to win a reaction or response from their female classmates, they would begin to call loudly across the room to one another, using the language that Latha had heard her father describe once as 'blank prose'. The innocent and inexperienced among the women undergraduates were startled at first by what they were hearing, but the more sophisticated were not.

'Showing off, as usual,' Tsunami said scornfully on that first occasion, clearly enough to be heard, and to have the remark repeated. 'Just to show us they know some naughty words – I wonder if they can spell them too?'

Once the initial shock of the unfamiliar wore off, women students would replace it with unassailable composure. The noise, of course, was deafening, and could usually be heard down two corridors and outside the building.

But then the lecturer would make his entrance, and a pin-drop silence ensue.

Latha found that her duties as first-year sub-Warden did not interfere unduly with her schedule of lectures and tutorials, which fell quickly into a regular pattern, varied by sessions in the University Library. She had imagined that lectures would involve exchanges of views on the various points made, but it was immediately obvious to her that this would be impossible, given the numbers of students involved. Discussion, she found, took place in tutorials. These were held on the second floor of the Arts Building, and in each tutorial, student numbers were mercifully limited to ten.

The three girls walked together every day to their lectures. Since they were taking the same subjects for the G.A.Q., they could also attend the lectures together. Each of them had been assigned to a different tutor, however, so the times of their tutorials varied. Which was just as well, thought Latha, who enjoyed the evening conversations on the third floor balcony to which everyone brought a new and different point of view. Amali's bashfulness tended to prevent her making friends quickly among her fellow-students, but Latha and Tsunami were constantly discovering 'new people' in tutorials or in the Library, and inviting them up after dinner to their study-bedrooms or on the balcony, where quiet discussion could go on until late at night without disturbing anyone.

Two of the 'new people' Latha and Tsunami brought into their group of three were two girls who had been assigned rooms at either end of the third-floor balcony: a cheerful first-year named Sriyani de Alwis, who had the room next to Latha, and whose every waking thought was almost entirely given up to sport, and a third-year, Swarna Wijewardene, who had been a student sub-Warden in her first year, but had put in a special request to the Warden for a room at the very end of the third-floor balcony, where she would be free from chattering students on either side and could therefore concentrate on studying for her General degree. It was from Swarna that Latha received her second lesson in the new vocabulary.

'Sriyani, would you mind very much if I brought my books into your room while you're at the gym?' Swarna had asked, when term was in its third week. 'I can't take in a single thing I read while Hema and the rest of her O-Fac crowd are making that awful racket next door.'

The student who occupied the room between Swarna's room and Tsunami's was Hema Gikiyanagē, a second-year student with ambitions to make a career for herself as a play-back singer for the Sinhala cinema, who had already earned herself a reputation among her peers as the Songbird of the Oriental Faculty. Hema had ignored all friendly overtures attempted by Tsunami and Latha, and had made it abundantly clear, without actually saying so, that she wished she could have been assigned a room in some other part of the Hall. Latha, who had hoped that the last remaining room on their balcony could have been assigned to someone congenial, eventually stopped trying to make friends with Hema. As Tsunami said, Dr Springdale seemed to have slipped up on that one.

'No problem,' Sriyani answered. 'I'll exchange rooms with you, if you like, it makes no difference to me. I can study through anything.'

'You and I could just tell Hema to shut up, Swarna,' Tsunami suggested. 'I'm suffering too, remember? I've got her on the other side of *my* room.'

'You can't do that,' Latha said. 'We haven't any right to prevent her singing.'

'D'you call that nasal screech "*singing*"?' her cousin replied.

'Whether you like it or not, what we're hearing *is* the current style of Sinhala film music,' said Latha. 'Hema could just as well object to Sinatra on your record-player.'

'Well, couldn't she go away and sing somewhere else?' inquired Tsunami. 'Or at some other time, like when we're not in? I sympathize with Swarna. If I were studying for my Finals, the racket would drive me nuts.'

Latha wondered at first whether the situation merited a discussion with Dr Springdale. On further consideration, she decided to try resolving the matter herself. Having worked out what she intended to say, and choosing her time carefully, she invited Hema Gikiyanagē to her room for coffee after dinner. Hema surprised her by accepting her invitation. When she arrived, she did so with a friend in tow whom she introduced as a classmate. Latha had planned a tête-à-tête, and was taken aback by the presence of the uninvited guest, but she controlled her irritation, welcomed both girls politely, and set out chairs for them on the balcony.

'I'm so glad you could come,' she said, pouring out three cups of the excellent coffee she had borrowed for the occasion from Tsunami's supply. 'We're all so busy, aren't we – this term will just rush by, and we wouldn't have had a chance to get to know one another. I thought we should do something about it. Milk? Sugar?'

This effort was met by a silence that was broken only by the clink of coffee-spoons in the cups. It was obvious to Latha that her guests were not at ease. Quite understandable, she told herself: they were, after all, in unfamiliar surroundings. She decided to try again.

'Look, I have some lovely milk-toffee here, a present from Amali's mother in Kurunegala. Would you like some?'

Her offer was accepted, and the milk-toffee duly taken, but then silence fell once more, a silence so profound that Latha could hear the blast of a horn as the car to which it belonged rounded a bend on the Galaha Road. To her great relief, however, the mention of Amali's name appeared to have started a train of thought. Hema's friend put down her coffee cup and remarked on the fact that Amali and Tsunami were not present.

'You all go around so much together that I also thought they would be here,' Hema said, in support of this observation. She added:

'I suppose they don't want to meet us. That Tsunami Wijesinha can't speak a word of Sinhala, and she doesn't like my singing.'

Well, she's certainly direct!

Latha rallied gamely.

'Sinhala is certainly not Tsunami's best subject,' she agreed, 'but I didn't know anyone dislikes your singing, Hema.'

Liar! Liar!

'Amali and Tsunami wanted to see a film in Kandy, or they would probably be here this evening.'

Well, that was true, at least the first part of it was.

'But, yes, we are *all* spending less and less time after dinner on the balcony just now because our chatter must be so distracting for Swarna Wijewardene. She's busy writing the essays that will count towards her Finals, you see.'

Hema did not seem in the least interested in Swarna or her essays, but Latha continued:

'She's in her room right now, you know, working! I haven't asked her to join us because I don't want to disturb her.'

'*She* doesn't like me either,' Hema said.

'Oh, surely *not*?' Latha exclaimed. 'You must be mistaken!'

'Only yesterday,' Hema said plaintively, 'we were in the Common Room downstairs, listening to Sinhala film music on Radio Ceylon, and that Swarna girl walked in and switched the radio off. She said she wanted to know who had torn pieces out of the newspaper, so that no one else could read it. She was very angry, and very rude. Someone *had* torn pages out of the paper, but was that any reason to switch the radio off?'

'Maybe,' Latha hazarded, 'the radio was on so loud that she couldn't make herself heard unless she switched it off?'

There was no reply to this, so she reverted cautiously to the main issue.

'We all chatter so much and we never realize how every sound carries, don't you find?' she said gaily. 'Well, *we've* all decided to be very quiet on our balcony so that Swarna can get on with her reading! We're doing our best not to talk too loudly when we come up after dinner. We're not even playing any music . . .'

She was about to add: 'Maybe you'd like to do the same?' when Hema's uninvited friend said irritably:

'Yes, but Hema has to *practise*.'

Hema said nothing, and her friend continued:

'Where else can she practise but in her room?'

'Yes, I was wondering about that,' Latha said. 'And I think I have a solution. There's a Common Room on the ground floor which nobody uses after dinner. I can mention the problem to the Warden tomorrow, and I'm sure she'd be happy to let you have the use of it for your practices.'

An idea struck her.

'You could probably have that Common Room every night if you like, Hema, as long as you reserve it ahead of time, and put a notice on the door. Would one-hour blocks of time be enough, or would you like to make it two hours?'

Hema and her friend looked at each other with surprise, and finally gave grudging consent to this scheme.

After the two girls had left, Latha tapped on Swarna Wijewardene's balcony door.

'Success!' she said, smiling. 'But, do you know, I think they felt quite cheated, at having no further reason to complain!'

'There are *some* people,' said Swarna darkly, 'who aren't happy unless they can find something to complain about. They don't need a reason. But seriously, Latha, I'm very grateful you spoke to her about it. If I'd tried to reason with her myself, I'd have been in danger of starting World War III.'

'You? What can they possibly have against you?'

'Oh, lots of things! I've been getting on their nerves lately. I play tennis – a Western sport – and they don't. I read the English newspapers, and they don't. I go hiking with the Geography Honours lads, and they think that's immoral. I love dancing, and they disapprove of that, too: they think ballroom dancing's a sign of Western decadence. I think it was pretty heroic of you to ask them in for coffee. They probably can't stand you, Latha, with your English Literature fixation, and I'll bet they loathe Tsunami. It's the O-Fac mentality. *We* are Kultur, you see.'

'O-Fac? Kultur? What are you talking about?'

'O-Fac's campus-speak for Oriental Faculty. We're too Western-educated, too darned uppity for their taste. They think of us as "Kultur". They're okay with Sriyani, mainly because she's out on the cinder track most of the time, so they hardly see her, and they're okay with Amali because – well, could anyone possibly dislike Amali?'

Latha mentally reviewed the interview she had just had with Hema and her friend.

'There was a moment,' she said, 'while I was trying to make Hema feel at home, when I considered bringing out cushions and mats, so that we could all sit together comfortably on the floor rather than sit on chairs. How do you think that would have gone down?'

'Like a ton of lead,' Swarna said crisply. 'An O-Fac like Hema would have seen that as patronizing, the supreme insult. Especially coming from the Queen of Kultur.'

She laughed at the expression on Latha's face.

'Didn't you know that's what they call you?'

'I give up,' Latha said. 'It's all *so petty*, Swarna!' She thought for a moment, then added:

'But if there's a problem, it's their problem, not ours. And at least we've got them to concede our right to peace and quiet on the balcony!'

Latha knew, however, that the matter could not be dismissed so casually. The division of the Arts community into hostile factions of O-Fac and Kultur which she and her fellow first-years had inherited was not 'our' problem or 'their' problem, it was everyone's problem. And it was a problem that had to be solved. Swarna, with her senior status and her years of experience, seemed quite resigned to the division as a reality that had to be lived with. But Latha could not accept it. Where was the unity and wholeness she had expected to find in university life? The world seemed suddenly to have grown narrower and colder.

When Tsunami, Sriyani and Amali came upstairs and heard about Latha's diplomatic victory, they sat out under the stars and drank her health in hot chocolate.

In her next letter home, Latha made an amusing story out of her coffee party for the Songbird of the Oriental Faculty. But Herbert, who knew his daughter well, could read between the lines of her letter and he could not find it in his heart to laugh.

He saw only too clearly (and pitied) the disillusionment that had accompanied her triumph.

12

EXTRA-CURRICULAR ACTIVITIES

First-year life at Peradeniya for Latha, Tsunami and Amali fell rapidly into a pleasant pattern. Lectures and tutorials, coffee at the university canteen, study in the University Library, and walks in the evening hours along the shady avenues of the campus filled the weekdays. A Saturday would often see them on the bus to Kandy, where Latha had discovered that K.V.G. de Silva's bookshop in Trincomalee Street had canvas prints of French Impressionist paintings for sale which (if you saved your allowance and counted your rupees and cents carefully) were affordable, even by undergraduates.

She bought a Renoir print for Paula and Rajan Phillips there, *Woman with a Parasol in a Garden.* Tsunami bought a print for her Aunt Moira, a picture of ballet dancers in white tutus.

'Remember the "ballot" dancers of "De Gass", Latha?' she asked. 'But Auntie Moira's come on a lot since those early days. You'd never catch her saying "De Gass" now.'

Shopping on her own behalf, Tsunami had discovered a shop, also on Trincomalee Street, that specialized in cotton saris dyed in the brilliant colours beloved of tea pluckers on up-country estates.

'Just look at this wonderful coolie sari, Latha!'

The assistant had flung six yards of rust-red cotton bordered in emerald green across the counter.

'Isn't it *heaven*?'

And Latha had had to agree that it was, for she, who had come up to Peradeniya with a wardrobe of saris in pale pastel shades chosen for her by her mother, was discovering in herself under Tsunami's tutelage an unsuspected delight in contrasts of bright colour. She had, however, some reservations of her own about Tsunami's purchases.

'Tsunami,' she said as her cousin paid for her sari and had it put into a paper bag, 'isn't the word *coolie* an insult? Tea pluckers are estate workers, not *coolies*, surely!'

She ventured this statement cautiously, since she didn't want to be laughed at, or to sound over-critical.

'Does it matter?' Tsunami inquired.

The question appeared to bore her.

'From the point of view of economics, they're all "labour" aren't they? Why split hairs?'

Buying and wearing 'coolie' saris, Tsunami explained to Latha over ice cream sundaes at Elephant House, was a progressive thing to do, for the owner of a coolie sari showed the world that she was willing to flout expensive high fashion and dress like the commonest of ordinary folk. Who could be more common and ordinary than a tea-plucker on an estate? A second point in favour of 'coolie saris' was their straightforwardness and honesty: they were hand-woven from pure cotton, and didn't pretend to be silk or satin or anything else. A third point which was, of course, obvious: they were inexpensive—

'Eight rupees each, Latha! They're so cheap, no wonder the . . . estate workers buy them.'

In fact, said Tsunami, it could be said that the purchase of such saris actually struck a blow on behalf of the working classes: the mere act of buying such clothes and then wearing them – especially when those who bought and wore them were people everyone knew didn't have to count their rupees and cents, people such as Latha and herself – could only do good, for they cut right across the class lines which dictated who should wear what and when.

'Like Mahatma Gandhi's campaign to get everyone in India to wear home-woven *khadda*.'

Latha nibbled at the wafer that had arrived with her chocolate ice cream and puzzled for a while over Tsunami's reasoning. She wished she could talk the matter over with Paula and Rajan Phillips: would they agree with it? It seemed to her that something was definitely wrong with her cousin's thinking, but she was not sure what it was.

'Tsunami,' she said at last, 'to which social class do you belong?'

'The working class, of course,' returned her cousin lightly, and without hesitation. 'Ever seen anyone – even Mutthulakshmi – work as hard as I do?'

Latha laughed, and allowed herself to be persuaded. 'Coolie' saris were, she found, well within her budget: at a mere eight rupees each, why not give in to a little harmless temptation? Especially when one's spending money was limited to fifty? She had never cared much for buying pretty clothes: now – perhaps there was adventure in the Peradeniya air – she was developing a taste for them.

Unlike Latha, Tsunami didn't really have to think about keeping within a budget ('Pater's got deep pockets,' said she nonchalantly), but she seized the opportunity presented by 'coolie' saris to develop Latha's taste along lines that she said were 'interesting' because they were unconventional.

And besides, nobody could deny that the saris were stunningly beautiful.

Their dazzling new wardrobes – an emerald-green sari bordered with scarlet was Latha's favourite, and a honey-gold edged with blue was Tsunami's – could not fail to attract notice. Among the undergraduates threading their way into lectures, the two girls in their brilliantly coloured saris stood out like exotic tropical birds among a flock of drab doves.

'Your Catholic friends are very pretty,' observed one of Amali's associates in the Buddhist Brotherhood, 'but they seem to be a little frivolous.'

'They're not Catholics,' Amali had replied. 'They're Christians.'

'Catholics or Christians, what's the difference?' he had retorted. 'All the same – Methodists, Anglicans, Baptists, Pentecostals, high church, low church – they all believe in the same superstitions.'

'"Pretty"?' Tsunami had snarled, when news of this exchange came back to her via Amali. 'What does he mean, *pretty*? You'll need to expand that lad's vocabulary, Amali. As well as his general knowledge.'

Not all the three young women's weekends, of course, were devoted to sari-shopping. Most Sundays saw one or another, and quite often all three of them, involved with their fellows in extra-curricular activities of various kinds. Latha and Tsunami had joined the English University Dramatic Society ('the DramSoc') in their first week at Peradeniya; and in their third had found themselves assigned roles in Professor van Loten's forthcoming production of *A Woman of No Importance*. Amali had joined the DramSoc's Sinhala equivalent, which was currently involved in auditioning for some short plays by Dr Sarachchandra, Professor of Sinhala Literature. Tsunami and Latha both became members of a choir for unaccompanied voices instituted by a young Englishman who was teaching in the English Department.

Ronald Marchmont was the English Department's current import from Cambridge University. Every two years, a bright young doctoral student from a British University arrived in Ceylon, having been invited to spend two years teaching at Peradeniya. In theory this invitation was extended to women scholars too, and to all British universities; but in practice all such visitors in the University's first nine years had been male, and they had all come either from Oxford or Cambridge. By special arrangement with his home University, the two years spent in Ceylon were counted as one of the three expected of a doctoral candidate. This arrangement, the brain-child of Professor van Loten, himself a Cambridge man and the current departmental head, suited both sides very well: the Britisher pursued his research and accumulated teaching experience in one of the Commonwealth's most advanced universities on the salary of a Visiting Lecturer, while the Department that hosted him was given an opportunity to keep up to date with new trends in British literary studies.

The current holder of the Visiting Lectureship was proving a tremendous success. Ronald Marchmont's reputation as a disciple of the great F.R. Leavis and as a contributor to *Scrutiny* had preceded him to Peradeniya, where the Leavisites already teaching there regarded him with awe. He was, besides, an asset to the University as a whole. For not only was he devoted to the study and teaching of literature, a skilled exponent of the art of 'practical criticism', and a speaker who prepared and delivered his lectures with a precision that encouraged the most casual student to transcribe them *verbatim*, but he was interested in music, which had hitherto been an undeveloped area at Peradeniya.

If Peradeniya appreciated Marchmont, there was no doubt that he appreciated being in Ceylon. As innumerable foreigners have done from the sixteenth century on, he had fallen in love with the island at first sight. Marchmont had never been out of England before: the striking beauty of Ceylon's landscapes and the charm of its people, both male and female, delighted his aesthetic senses. He had been given to understand by his predecessor in the Visiting Lectureship that he would find congenial company among the staff on the Peradeniya campus, and students who were as good, if not better, than those he had been teaching part-time in Cambridge. Both these predictions had been proved true, and the end of the first year of his appointment had found Marchmont putting in an application for an extended term.

He had no idea how the Peradeniya community would react to his plan to set up a choral group on campus. Some people, responding to the cultural resurgence that had followed Independence in 1948, might regard his group as 'Westernized' and reactionary, because it focused on Western music and English lyrics. Who could tell? He was prepared to work hard to make the idea a success. Dr Joan Springdale, Warden of Sanghamitta Hall, had encouraged Marchmont in his initiative and lifted his spirits by offering him the use of space in her Hall for his choir practices.

'I'm sure you'll be able to get a good group together,' she had told him. 'There are plenty of talented young people here, eager to make the most of Peradeniya's possibilities. And you're offering them one that will delight them, and ultimately delight us all.'

Still, he could not be certain, and so he was very pleased to see so many of his own students turn up for his first audition. Especially Latha Wijesinha, the tall, graceful girl who attended his lectures on the Romantics in G.A.Q. English, and clearly enjoyed them. He did not know her lively little friend, but he had seen the two girls together on campus, and thought them an attractive pair. He hoped they had good voices, as well as good looks. They had the same surname, he noticed, looking down the attendance list, and wondered whether they were related.

'Right, who's next? Miss Latha Wijesinha? Fine. Any musical experience, Miss Wijesinha?'

Latha shook her head. She could hardly cite a few Christmas concerts under the direction of Franz Goldman as 'musical experience'.

'All right. You just enjoy music, and like listening to it, eh? Well, from tomorrow you and everyone else here will have the pleasure of *making* music . . .'

By 'everyone else', Ronald Marchmont meant a group of about twenty individuals, all that was left of some thirty or forty students and staff members who had come up to Sanghamitta Hall's second-floor Common Room in response to his call for recruits to the 'Varsity Voices'. Marchmont had been ruthless in weeding out the people who merely wanted to find out what *a cappella* meant, and others who had come along because a musically inclined sweetheart had expressed a desire to join 'Mr Marchmont's Group'.

'Okay. Miss Wijesinha, what will you sing for us?'

Latha had thought about this moment with some trepidation. She, who had thrilled as a child to Macaulay's story of Horatius and his two companions on the bridge, defending Rome against the massed armies of Clusium, had chosen for her 'audition' Thomas Moore's lyric, 'The Minstrel Boy'. She had first encountered it as a poem in one of her father's anthologies.

The Minstrel fell, but the foeman's chain
Could not bring his proud soul under,
The harp he lov'd ne'er spoke again,
For he tore its cords asunder,
And said: 'No chains shall sully thee,
Thou soul of Love and Bravery!
Thy songs were made for the pure and free,
They shall never sound in slavery!'

Ronald Marchmont was certain he had glimpsed tears in the eyes of the young singer, and wondered a little at such depth of feeling for the predicament of a country not her own. He led the applause of the choir as Latha returned to her seat.

'Well done, Miss Wijesinha, well done! Very good indeed. And now, what about you, Miss – er – Tsunami Wijesinha? By the way, have I pronounced your names correctly? You must both tell me right away if I have not.'

Latha only nodded her 'Yes'; but Tsunami said 'Quite right', and rewarded

Marchmont for his thoughtfulness with a smile of such surpassing sweetness that he went brick-red and dropped his music notes.

'And what are you going to sing for us?'

'"The Spider and the Fly", Mr Marchmont.'

'I don't think I know that one,' the choirmaster said.

But Latha did. She had seen the musical score at Lucas Falls, in one of her aunt Helen's music books, where it had been embellished with a line-drawing of a spider weaving a gossamer curtain for a tiny four-poster bed. She had heard Tara sing the song occasionally, accompanying herself on the piano, but never Tsunami.

Come to think of it, Latha recalled having only heard Tsunami in part-songs, with everyone else at the Falls joining in under Franz Goldman's direction: she had never heard her cousin sing solo. She hoped all would go well – there were some tricky moments in the song, she remembered, when the Fly returned for a second taste of the Spider's flattery . . .

Alas, alas, how very soon this silly little Fly,
Hearing all his flattering speeches,
Came quickly buzzing by!
On gauzy wing she hung aloft,
Then near and nearer drew,
Thinking only of her crested head,
And gold and purple hue,
Thinking only of her brilliant wings,
Poor silly thing at last,
Up jumped that wicked Spider,
And fiercely held her fast—

Latha need have had no fears on her cousin's behalf. What Tsunami lacked in sweetness of tone, she more than made up for with her feeling for dramatic timing and with the wicked glint in her almond-shaped eyes.

He dragged her up his winding stair,
Into his dismal den,
Into his little parlour –
And she ne'er came out again . . .

Ronald Marchmont gazed at Tsunami in amazement. Pure theatre, he said to himself. He had heard a lot about the shyness of Ceylonese girls: yet this one had transformed a moral fable into a sinister little drama of seduction.

'Excellent!' he said aloud.

He looked at the amused faces around him, then glanced at his watch.

'Next Sunday will be our first choir practice proper, ladies and gentlemen. I'll see you here at 5.30 pm sharp, and thank you very much for coming along this evening.'

As the members of the newly constituted Varsity Voices went down Sanghamitta Hill, humming cheerfully to themselves like a flight of contented bees, Marchmont climbed into his little car, which he had parked beneath Dr Springdale's sitting-room window by special dispensation of the Hall porter, and congratulated himself in advance on the triumphs to come.

For success could hardly be in doubt, when he had such talent at his command.

13

LOBELIA RAPTOR'S WORLD VIEW

April had come to the hill-country, and the jacaranda trees around the Peradeniya campus were coming into full bloom. With half an hour to spare before Professor van Loten's lecture began, Latha had decided to give herself the pleasure of a solitary walk through the University Park on her way to the lecture hall. This path was a little longer than the other, more usual, route, but spring had dressed a jacaranda tree in the park in such extravagant purple splendour that Latha and Tsunami, looking down at the massed blossom from the upper road two days before, had planned to take this very walk before the flowers were past their season.

Latha regretted Tsunami's absence, but it could not be helped: her cousin had left Sanghamitta immediately after breakfast, declaring that she had a full day of tutorials and library work ahead of her. Latha walked down the stairway that had been cut into the hillside, and entered the Park. She found the grassy verge of its ornamental lake thickly carpeted with purple petals. 'Keep off the grass,' cautioned a notice beside the path, but Latha decided that any rule would be worth breaking for the sensation of walking barefoot on that purple carpet. She put her books down beside the notice, and was about to slip off her sandals when the flash of a pair of binoculars in the green shade made her aware that she was being observed.

'Miss Wijesinha! Stop a minute! Not so fast! I want to talk to you!'

The Warden of James Peries Hall had a reputation for loud and brash behaviour: staff and students who liked peace and quiet tended to step discreetly aside when they saw or heard Mrs Lobelia Raptor coming. But there was no escaping that stentorian bray. It was too late for Latha to pretend she had not heard it.

'Good morning, Mrs Raptor.'

The Warden was taking her morning constitutional among the jacaranda trees. The binoculars in her plump hand were for watching birds, a favourite hobby of hers; or so she had told Latha when they had met at a dinner party given by Dr Springdale for her fellow Wardens at

Sanghamitta, to which the Hall sub-Wardens had also been invited. An alternative theory regarding those binoculars existed at Peradeniya: that the Warden of Peries Hall liked to train them on certain vantage points along 'Lovers' Lane' or on the slopes of Hantane Hill, where students occasionally lingered to admire the natural beauty of the campus in the company of their sweethearts.

'Nature is my delight,' Mrs Raptor had boomed across the table at Dr Springdale's dinner party. 'Not a furred or feathered creature, but is as dear to me as my own child.'

'Miss Wijesinha!' she shouted now. 'A moment or two earlier, and you could have had a glimpse of a pair of golden orioles in full flight.'

Latha resigned herself to her fate, picked up her books, and fell into step beside the Warden.

'I am told you enjoy the beauties of Nature too, Miss Wijesinha,' said her companion. 'Only the other day, wasn't it, that you and the other Miss Wijesinha were having a picnic on the river bank with two smart young gentlemen?'

Latha could hardly hide her astonishment.

The Warden's binoculars might be very powerful, but surely they cannot reach as far as Teldeniya?

'Ah, yes,' she replied, with carefully assumed casualness. 'That would have been the weekend that Tsunami's brother came up to visit her—'

'Doesn't Sanghamitta Hall provide lunch on the weekends? My Hall does.'

'Yes, the Hall does provide lunch, Mrs Raptor. And Dr Springdale always makes visitors welcome. But the weather was so beautiful that we thought it would be a pity to stay indoors.'

'Oh, and so one of the young men was Miss Tsunami Wijesinha's brother, was he? I see. And the other one?'

Latha thought rebelliously:

I don't have to put up with this inquisition!

But she responded to the question with her usual politeness.

'Oh, he's an old friend of their family. They've known him for years.'

'I hope her parents approve,' said the Warden. 'The campus is a very small community, you know. People talk. News gets about.'

I'll say it does, you inquisitive, interfering bitch!

Latha was surprised by the ease with which the word *bitch* had come so naturally to her mind. There was no doubt about it, Mrs Raptor brought out the worst side of her nature. *Bitch* was not a word she had ever used before to describe a person, not even in her thoughts. Unlike Tsunami, whose language, even as a child, verged so often on the picturesque that she had once voluntarily given up swearing for Lent. ('For the good of my sinful soul, Latha,' Tsunami had said at the time. 'But alas, my good intentions didn't last.')

'You should come up and join our sub-Wardens and myself at lunch in the Hall one day, Miss Wijesinha. It would give you an idea of how things are done in *other* halls of residence.'

'That's very kind of you, Mrs Raptor, but—'

'I have never seen you up at Peries Hall. What about Thursday this week?'

'I'd love to, but—'

'Good, that's settled, then. Twelve o'clock on Thursday. Don't be late: we are very punctual at Peries Hall. And you may bring Mr Rowland Wijesinha's daughter with you.'

The invitation gave neither Latha nor Tsunami any pleasure.

'It's a bit of a shame, really,' Latha said to Tsunami over dinner that evening.

'What is?'

Tsunami had just made it into the Hall as the dinner bell rang, and she didn't seem to be concentrating.

'Oh, that Mrs Raptor's manner is so embarrassing, and her voice so loud. I've heard that in her time she was something of a star in the Philosophy department in Colombo. She would be interesting to meet—'

'Not on your life!'

Tsunami sounded very definite.

'I wasn't quick enough about getting out of her way last week, and she cross-examined me – at the top of her voice, and in the middle of the Library, if you please, with signs everywhere saying "Silence" – about a rumour that Pater is to be our next Ambassador to Washington.'

'Odd how she gets to know everything about everyone,' Latha said thoughtfully.

'Not just odd,' replied Tsunami. 'It's weird. Sinister old cow. I wonder how much she knows about us!'

'Anyway,' Latha pleaded, 'you will come, won't you, Tsunami?'

'Nothing doing,' Tsunami said. 'The invitation was for you. Asking me along was just an afterthought.'

'Please, Tsunami, say you'll come. You wouldn't let me ride alone into the jaws of death, now, would you? Please!'

Tsunami hesitated.

'Oh, all right,' she said at last, reluctantly. 'But just remember you owe me something for this, Latha. There are ten million things I'd rather be doing than lunching with Mrs Raptor.'

The refectory at James Peries Hall was filling up with students when Latha and Tsunami knocked at the Warden's door and heard the command, '*Enna! Enna!*' Mrs Raptor was seated at her desk at the far end of a large rectangular room, with a telephone to her ear. She motioned to them to sit down.

They found themselves seated on either side of the open jaws of a snarling leopard. Its curling tongue was blood-red, Latha noticed, and its fangs, though yellow, looked very sharp. Golden glass eyes glared from the head attached to the beast's magnificent hide which, cured and mounted, was being used by Mrs Raptor as a floor rug.

'The jaws of death, in very truth,' Tsunami whispered. 'Do you suppose Mr R. is a big-game hunter?'

Mrs Raptor's husband, a tall, quiet Englishman who occasionally accompanied the Warden on her expeditions around the campus, was generally considered so unlikely a candidate for Mrs Raptor's tender regard that he could, Latha thought, have been almost anything. She thought over Tsunami's suggestion, and rejected it as improbable.

'It's much more likely he's a philosopher,' she said.

'He'd need to be, to cope with Mrs R.,' said Tsunami.

From a bracket on the wall nearest to Latha, a carved image of the meditating Buddha looked reflectively down on Mrs Raptor and her leopard. It was one of several images of the Compassionate One which had been placed around the room, on occasional tables, on the shelves of book-cases, and surmounting window frames. Since the room also contained two ivory elephant tusks on elaborate ebony pedestals, one at each side of the Warden's desk, and a waste-paper basket constructed from the massive foot of an elephant, Latha wondered whether Mrs Raptor's philosophical mind was not disturbed by surroundings that were so much out of step with the Buddha's message of non-violence. She leaned towards Tsunami, but before she could convey this observation to her cousin, Mrs Raptor finished her telephone conversation, replaced the receiver, and rose to greet her guests.

'Welcome, welcome to James Peries Hall!' said she, smiling broadly.

Tying the strings of her bonnet under her chin, and sweeping the two girls before her, the Warden sailed along the corridor, into the refectory, and up to the High Table. Latha and Tsunami, who were given places on either side of her, watched with interest as the students came in and took their seats at the tables in the body of the hall. They occasionally recognized a familiar face from one of their own classes, but resisted any temptation to wave or smile. It was well known that Mrs Raptor discouraged what she called 'fraternization' between staff and students, and both Latha and Tsunami were conscious that as the Warden's guests they were officially, even if only temporarily, 'staff'.

'See that girl who is just coming in?' Mrs Raptor said. 'She's from a village near Kandy. A very respectable old Sinhalese family.'

The student to whom she had referred, a slender young woman in sari, her hair gleaming with oil and combed into a thick plait, glanced up at the High Table, smiled shyly and put her hands together in the traditional gesture of respect before seating herself.

Mrs Raptor graciously acknowledged the greeting. The little exchange was surely, Latha felt, an indication that the Warden of Peries Hall maintained good relations with the students in her care. Had popular gossip on campus maligned Mrs Raptor?

Platters of steaming rice and bowls of curried vegetables were placed on the tables, and the Warden continued to talk, effortlessly achieving audibility over the clatter of serving spoons and an escalating buzz of conversation as more and more students entered the refectory.

'Now, that student over there, just coming in at the far end of the room – please have a good look at her, Miss Wijesinha.'

Latha and Tsunami obeyed the order. The student they were looking at seemed a little confused, Latha thought. She had come to a stop in the middle of the refectory with her back to the High Table, and was turning her head vaguely in different directions, as if she were listening for something rather than seeking a place to sit.

'She's one of our low-caste students,' the Warden said. 'In the old days, that type of person would not have been allowed even to read a book. This one got into Peradeniya on a bursary, and now she is in her second year. History Honours, if you please. And just you wait and see. By next year she will be standing for election to the Union, and after that, when she has graduated, who knows where her ambition may not take her?'

Latha was puzzled.

Does Mrs Raptor approve of the student she's singled out for our attention, or doesn't she? Does she approve of the way things were done in 'the old days' or doesn't she? How can one be sure?

The allusion the Warden had made to caste in the course of a casual conversation was unexpected and startling. Although Latha was aware that caste distinction had been the basis of the social structure of Ceylon in medieval times, she had conceived the idea – from where had it come? from her father? from Rajan Phillips? – that nowadays it was education, not caste, that determined a person's status.

Latha leaned forward in an attempt to see how Tsunami was reacting to Mrs Raptor's remark, but the Warden's bonnet blocked her view of her cousin.

'After a while,' their hostess continued, 'you get to know, almost by instinct, the background from which every student comes. I don't even have to hear their names now, I can tell with one glance at a student, or after hearing one word she utters, whether she belongs to an inferior caste, or comes – as we do – from a high-caste background. With so much talk of democracy in the air these days, everyone who isn't high caste pretends to be, and everyone who is high caste thinks it's bad form to talk about it at all. Absolute nonsense. Caste counts. And I'll give you a useful tip: the surest way to tell a person's caste is from the way that person smells. Haven't you noticed, you girls, that low-caste people *smell*?'

Latha looked down at her plate. She could not bear to gaze out over the refectory, for fear that her eyes might meet those of one of the students the Warden claimed to know so well.

Could they hear what Mrs Raptor was saying?

She was certainly making no effort to keep her voice down. Tsunami, for her part, said not a word.

Has Tsunami been deprived, for once in her life, of the power of speech?

She caught a glimpse of Tsunami as the blue bonnet ducked sideways, its owner having bent to pick up a table napkin which had slipped to the floor. Her cousin was gazing wide-eyed at the Warden, her expression unreadable.

Mrs Raptor seemed pleased by the silence that had greeted her remarks on the subject of caste.

'These are valuable facts about our people, Miss Wijesinha,' she continued, turning to Latha, 'which may be very useful to you sometime as a Hall sub-Warden, so you should take careful note of them.'

She helped herself liberally to the curries on the table and, beckoning a maid, ordered that the rice platter be refilled.

'And Mallika, some curd too, please.'

She resumed her instructional tone.

'When you have had more experience, you girls will find that what I have said is the truth. It is very important that people like us should know the facts about those among whom we are living, because in a year or two we will be outnumbered on campus and everywhere else in this country. Then we will need all the wisdom we can muster to deal with the situation.'

The curd which the Warden had asked for now arrived, carried in by one of the maids in a clay pot.

'However, as good high-caste Sinhala people, we must do our best for our inferiors, whatever their background or their politics,' Mrs Raptor went on, while beside her, Latha seethed with fury.

Who exactly did the Warden mean by 'we'?

'For instance, I have curd served in this Hall at lunch time every day, specially for the Tamil students from the north because, as I am sure you know, they require a full vegetarian diet and some of them don't even eat fish or eggs. Why, I don't really know,' Mrs Raptor added reflectively, 'Hindus are not forbidden to eat fish, only beef. Still, that is the way they do things in Jaffna. Curd, however, is a milk product, and it is full of vitamins, so I see to it that curd is served to them every day . . . You are very quiet, Miss Tsunami. Are you always as quiet as this?'

'I was thinking about what you have been saying, Mrs Raptor.'

The Warden smiled approvingly.

'I see you are an intelligent young lady. With many young people these days, advice from elders goes in at one ear and comes out the other. But you can always tell with young people from good families, that they will give thought to what is said by their elders. Now Tamils,' she continued, 'might seem to you to be an entirely different set of people. They are black-skinned, for one thing, which makes it easy to recognize them. That's not always so easy with low-caste Sinhalese. But in the case of Tamil people, too, smell counts. Tamils, even high-caste Tamils, smell of gingelly oil, it comes of the kind of food they have been eating all their lives long, up there in Jaffna. And of course, they don't keep themselves clean, which is not surprising when you consider that they are basically coolies used to living in mud huts, who were brought here by the British as labour for the estates. You must have observed it at Sanghamitta, Miss Wijesinha? I noticed when I was at dinner with your Warden last month that the Tamil students have grabbed all the ground-floor rooms. We guests had to walk along that corridor on our way to your refectory, and the whole place stank like Sea Street.'

'I'm sorry, Mrs Raptor, but I've never noticed any sort of smell along the ground-floor corridor,' replied Latha coldly. 'And I assure you that all the rooms at Sanghamitta are allocated by the Warden herself, nobody can "grab" them.'

'People like us', indeed! How dared this woman include me in her own warped view of the world?

Latha felt that she could have wrung the Warden's plump neck. She knew Sea Street well, a colourful thoroughfare in Colombo's Pettah district where there was a cluster of sari shops owned by Indian Tamils. She decided that she could not allow these statements to pass unchecked, the Warden must somehow be answered, and her benighted opinions challenged. If Tsunami remained silent, it was up to her to break into her monologue.

But how was it to be done?

Latha considered the problem for a moment or two, then spoke.

'Do you know Sushila Ramanathan, Mrs Raptor?' she inquired. With seeming casualness, she added helpfully: 'I'm told she was last year's Campus Queen.'

Mrs Raptor frowned slightly. Who did not know Sushila, a spectacularly beautiful Tamil law student in her second year at Peradeniya? The daughter of C.P. Ramanathan, a Colombo Q.C., Sushila was not a member of Sanghamitta Hall, but both the Wijesinha girls knew her by sight and, like everyone else on campus, had heard the story – no doubt exaggerated, but still in vigorous circulation – that her good looks had the entire population of the men's halls of residence clutching their pillows to their chests and murmuring '*Sushila! My darling!! Sushila, my love!*' in their dreams.

'I have not spoken to Miss Ramanathan, but I have seen her . . . about,' said Mrs Raptor. Her voice was icy, and conveyed the impression that the less she saw of Sushila Ramanathan, the happier she would be.

'Well, I was just thinking,' said Latha carefully, 'that Sushila must be the exception that proves your rule. The one about skin-colour, I mean. She's a very fair-skinned girl, isn't she, much fairer than Tsunami or me?'

'Burgher mother, Burgher mother,' said Mrs Raptor with dismissive assurance. 'That Ramanathan girl's mother was a Miss Herft. Very few pure-blood people about these days. Even among the Tamils. And now, with this campus opened to people from anywhere and everywhere, the situation is bound to get worse. I do my best, for my part, to discourage any kind of . . . *mingling*.'

As she spoke the last word, her face took on an expression of the strongest distaste.

'People should stay in their own communities, and these leftist parties which give our low-caste students ideas above their station in life should be banned from campus. I told the Vice-Chancellor so, only last week. After all, Miss Wijesinha, we Wardens and sub-Wardens are here, as the late Professor of Classics used to say, *in loco parentis*. We have a duty to watch over our students as if we were their own father and mother.'

Heaven help Tsunami and me, with Mrs Raptor as a substitute for our parents!

Latha made no reply.

'I love curd, but I like to have it with sugar,' Tsunami said, suddenly breaking her silence. 'May I ask for some, Mrs Raptor?'

'Certainly, certainly,' said the Warden hospitably. 'Here, Mallika, bring some sugar for Miss Wijesinha. Unless,' she added, 'you would prefer jaggery? I bought some excellent *kitul hakuru* in the Kandy Market yesterday, and told the kitchen to reserve it for High Table guests.'

'*Hakuru* would be lovely,' said Tsunami. 'Thank you very much.'

The jaggery arrived, finely scraped, in a china dish, and Tsunami sprinkled it on her curd. Latha, who adored curd and jaggery, was too annoyed with her cousin and with Mrs Raptor to ask for any.

'Do you know, I have a confession to make, Mrs Raptor,' Tsunami said, between mouthfuls of curd and jaggery.

Mrs Raptor was all attention.

'At lunch time in our Hall,' Tsunami went on, 'I sit with the Tamil students, mostly because some of them are in my class and are friends of mine, but also because they always offer me some of their curd. I suppose you would think that very wrong, wouldn't you?'

Few people meeting Tsunami for the first time could ever resist her appeal, and Mrs Raptor was no exception. The Warden gave this delightful, diffident young woman a smile of understanding and forgiveness. Latha tried to control her own anger.

Why, why, why is Tsunami directing all her charm, not to mention that innocent, childlike gaze, at this unspeakably horrible woman?

'But it's a strange thing,' Tsunami went on, 'though I sit with the Tamil students so often, I've never noticed that anyone smelled of gingelly oil! That's really odd, isn't it? And I met Sushila Ramanathan only last week – she's a member of Mr Marchmont's group, Varsity Voices, like the two of us – and she smelled absolutely wonderful – sandalwood, I should think it was. Of course, it might have been Chanel Number Five. I've been wondering just now whether the fact that I never seem to notice any bad smell around the people I meet is maybe because my mother is Tamil?'

As the girls left James Peries Hall and took the campus road to their afternoon lectures, Latha was the first to speak.

'I owe you an apology, Tsunami,' she said. 'I was thinking all sorts of horrible things about you for encouraging Mrs Raptor. You certainly had me fooled.'

Tsunami smiled wickedly.

'Did you see how her jaw dropped when I mentioned Mummy?' she said. 'She clearly hadn't done her homework on my family. Probably assumed Auntie Moira is my mother.'

'You've got to be careful, Tsunami, about misleading people,' Latha said. 'That quiet surface can be very deceptive . . . calm, peaceful, and then, without any warning, crash! Devastation! Take me today, for instance. I mean, I've always believed I knew you pretty well, but for a minute there you really had me thinking I was fighting the battle with Mrs Raptor on my own.'

Tsunami paid her no attention. Her thoughts were still on the final moments of their visit to Peries Hall.

'She'd be a good subject for satire,' she said reflectively. 'I wonder whether I could create a fictional character like Mrs Raptor . . . Not that I believe for a moment that anything I write about her could ever change the wretched woman's way of thinking! But with any luck, Latha, it'll be a long time before she tries anything like that again. "Tamil mother, Tamil mother!" she's probably saying to herself – that would explain everything satisfactorily. It would explain *me*.'

'Mrs Raptor's no fictional character, Tsunami! She's real, and she's a menace to campus society,' Latha said. 'If she is so prejudiced against some of the students in her Hall, she shouldn't be employed as a Warden.'

'Well, she certainly wasn't putting on a special performance for our benefit,' said Tsunami. 'She said all that because that's the way she thinks. Full stop. Also because she believed she was on safe ground, that we have the same attitudes that she does. All girls together, you might say.'

'She's got to be stopped,' Latha said.

'Latha! What's happened to your sweet temper and your famous kindly nature? My sister Tara's been telling me for years that she'd swap me for you any day, and here you are, talking about stopping people doing what comes naturally to them! You'd better watch out, or you'll end up like Mrs Raptor.'

'Maybe you're right,' Latha said. 'Maybe I can't stop Mrs Raptor judging her students by race and caste. But I can certainly make some rules for myself, and keep to them.'

They walked on in silence until Latha spoke again.

'Here's the first of my rules,' she said, 'and I don't care what you say, or what convincing reasons you produce, Tsunami, but I hereby give you notice: from now on, I'm deleting the phrase *coolie sari* from my vocabulary. I shall never again use the word *coolie* myself, and I don't want to hear it ever again, even from you.'

Tsunami stared at her.

'But, Latha,' she said. 'It's only a word! You know what Arnold Castilian says on the subject: you can't legislate for language – language is like the wind, "it bloweth where it listeth"—'

'*Especially* from you!' Latha said.

They walked on for a while, side by side, in a silence which Tsunami finally broke.

'That student, Latha,' she said. 'The one who's here on a bursary, the one Mrs Raptor said comes from a low-caste background?'

'Well, what about her?' Latha replied.

'She must be absolutely outstanding in the brains department.'

'How do you work that out?'

'Well, she'd have to be, wouldn't she, to get into second-year Honours? Didn't you notice something about her?'

'Sorry, Tsunami. I didn't get close enough to her to inhale.'

Latha was still angry, and her thoughts were so firmly fixed on Mrs Raptor's opinions that she could think of nothing else.

'Come off it, Latha. That isn't what I mean at all. You did notice, didn't you, that she's totally blind?'

14

APPEARANCE AND REALITY

'Do either of you believe,' Latha said slowly, 'that there will ever come a time in our country when race and caste will actually cease to matter?'

Tsunami and Amali looked at her anxiously. The three friends were in their favourite place for private discussion, the balcony they shared on the topmost floor of Sanghamitta Hall. Tsunami seemed to have already forgotten Mrs Raptor and her opinions, but she was aware that her cousin had not. Try as she might, Latha could not rid her memory of the stain left by the afternoon's exchange. She turned the Warden's words over and over in her mind, doing her best to grasp their implications.

'My English teacher's husband, Mr Phillips, believes such a time will come,' she said. 'A time when people will be honoured and rewarded for their merit and their intelligence rather than because they have the "right" connections or know how to parrot a superior's opinions.'

'What an idealist!' Tsunami said. 'Sorry, Latha, but the man's a dreamer.'

'I don't think he is, you know,' Amali said thoughtfully. 'I too believe such a time will come. Already, things are changing, ordinary people feel they have a say now in the way the Government is run. Don't you feel it?'

'Yes, I do,' Latha said. 'With the change of Government and everything being done now in the national language, our people are happy, they're content. What worries me is that the thinking of people like Mrs Raptor could spoil it all. It could set one community against another, and eventually it could ruin the whole society. Especially when such people are in powerful positions and if, like Mrs Raptor, they wield a lot of influence.'

'My answer to Amali's question, I'm afraid, is: frankly, no,' said Tsunami. 'Okay, I'm in a minority of one on this balcony, and maybe I shouldn't be the one to say this, with my father in the Cabinet, but the truth is that Pater doesn't care a hoot for what you call "ordinary people", Amali. I was at home when his election speeches were being written for him – they had to be written by someone else because he can't read or write Sinhala. His election speeches were all about "the common man" and "the down-trodden masses" and "we, the people". Auntie Moira put his English tweeds away in mothballs, and had national dress outfits tailored for him. And of course he got into Parliament, didn't he? And now he's in the Cabinet. Don't get me wrong, you two. I love my papa very dearly, he delivers stirring speeches, and he's getting to be a terrific actor. But when it comes to politics, I don't believe a single word he says.'

Silence followed her words. It was broken by Amali.

'If that is true, Tsunami,' she said, 'and you aren't saying these things for entertainment's sake – I know you like to do that sometimes, just to shock Latha and me! – well, then, we cannot say, as Latha just did, that our people are "happy", that they are "content". Maybe they seem to be so at the present moment, maybe they even think they are; but how long can that last? Our people will wake up one day to reality. They will have to face the knowledge that they have been deceived by . . . by actors like your father, and the results may be terrible. Worse than anything we can even imagine now.'

Tsunami made no reply. Amali said:

'If I've offended you by describing your father as an actor, please forgive me. I should never have said such a thing.'

'It's all right, Amali,' said Tsunami. 'I did it first! And it's no more than the truth.'

'In any case,' Amali continued, 'this is all speculation and theory. I am sure there are some people in the Government who sincerely intend to fulfil the promises they have made. *They* will make the difference. I'm convinced of it. Besides, there's a factor beyond politics and politicians; and as long as that exists – and it does – nothing really bad can happen to our country.'

'And what's that factor?' Latha asked.

'We're protected,' Amali said. 'This is a country that is under the special protection of the Gods who revere Lord Buddha.'

If she observed Tsunami's involuntary smile, she ignored it and continued:

'What happened here in 1942? Singapore fell to the Japanese, but nothing happened to Ceylon. Why was that? My father says the Japanese flew their planes over Colombo, but were turned away from their original intention. By what? Only the influence of Lord Buddha, emanating from the sacred Relic in Kandy, could have done it, he says.'

She paused, and then added:

'Whatever happens, whatever mistakes politicians make, this country will go on.'

How I wish, Latha thought, that I had Amali's conviction! I did once, but I don't now: maybe Thaththa's scepticism has rubbed off on me!

She looked at her friend's shining eyes, and wanted to speak in support of what she was saying, but could find no words. Just as well, she thought, recalling her father's advice that she should stay away from political discussions.

'All governments,' he had told her once, 'are flawed. Sooner or later, they all become corrupt and greedy. "Put not your trust in princes", Latha.'

How wise Thaththi is! And how cynical!

'My, my, how serious we're getting!' Tsunami said. 'I was hoping for some constructive advice from you two this evening about the play, and here we are, debating the state of the nation.'

Tsunami had been asked to direct a one-act play that Sanghamitta Hall was presenting for the annual DramSoc Inter-Hall Drama competition. She had immediately accepted, even though she knew it would mean spending three evenings a week in rehearsals. Latha pulled herself together, abandoned her thoughts about the chances of national survival, and focused instead on the problems of play-directing.

'I meant to ask you how rehearsals were going,' she said apologetically, 'but I was side-tracked by Mrs Raptor. Well, tell us: how *are* they going?'

'Fine . . . Paul is coming on very well.'

Paul Jayasinghe had been an early recruit to Tsunami's army of silent admirers, a tall, quiet youth who had, from the moment he had seen her in first year, devoted all his time to assisting her in whatever she wanted to do. Latha and Amali privately called him Tsunami's 'knight errant', and observed with amusement the regularity with which 'Sir Paul' happened to be lingering by the Arts Building exit at the very moment that a lecture Tsunami was attending was due to come to an end, and the alacrity with which he would offer to carry her books back to the Hall. Paul had been the first male volunteer to join the Sanghamitta Hall cast of the drama Tsunami had chosen for the Inter-Hall competition, and he now attended every rehearsal, having been given the role, essential to a Chinese folk play, of the Property Man.

'We rehearsed the scene in which the poor widow prays to the Buddha to rescue her family from their poverty. And there was Paul, standing in full view of the audience, but so impassive and expressionless that he didn't seem to be there at all, stalking forward from the wings to drop a cushion on the floor in front of Indrani just before she fell on her knees – and then a smaller cushion for each of the daughters just before they followed suit. Perfect timing, you'd think they'd been rehearsing for weeks. But we have a problem, Latha . . . we haven't yet found our Emperor of China. And we *must* find our Emperor soon, or we'll have to choose another play.'

Latha mentally reviewed the male members of the Sanghamitta Hall group. 'What about Sarath?'

'Not impressive enough.'

'Gamini?'

'Too scraggy. An Emperor should be a fine figure of a man!'

'Francis?'

'Baby-face! Not the type. Somewhere, out there on campus, the perfect Emperor awaits us. Latha, Amali, you'll have to help me find him.'

'Who, me?'

Amali, who had had strict instructions from her mother that she should not speak to a male student on campus for more than the space of one minute, was appalled.

'Yes, you,' Tsunami told her. 'Just look around you when you're in class, or in the Library, and when you think you've spotted talent, walk up to him and ask him if he'd like to audition for the part of the Emperor in our play.'

But it was Tsunami herself who eventually found 'the perfect Emperor', and she found him in the campus church the following Sunday, singing in the choir and reading one of the lessons.

'Who's that?' Tsunami whispered to the student kneeling beside her in the pew.

'Kenneth Fernando, third-year history,' said her neighbour.

'Nice voice,' Tsunami said. 'I'd like to meet him. Do you know each other?'

Her neighbour stared at her, astonished.

'Yes. Well, a bit . . . He's President of the S.C.M. on campus. Didn't you know?'

'No,' Tsunami said. 'Should I have?'

'Well, he's engaged to Chitra, that final-year student at Sanghamitta who leads the prayer meetings. She's the S.C.M.'s treasurer.'

Tsunami, who was not a member of the Student Christian Movement, and had never attended its prayer meetings, immediately enrolled. She thought her five-rupee subscription was money well spent on the play's behalf: when his fiancée introduced her to young Fernando the following week, he turned out to be even more impressive at close quarters, and perfectly amenable to the idea of play-acting.

'Though I should warn you right away that I've never taken part in a play before,' he said.

'Oh, you'll enjoy this one,' Tsunami assured him. 'I've been to the rehearsals, so I can tell you that you won't have many lines to learn, the girls do most of the talking.'

Tsunami was pleased with her find. Rehearsals went well, and Dr Pa Chow, Professor of Chinese, who had been charmed by Tsunami into sitting in on some of them in an advisory capacity, offered to paint two paper screens as a backdrop to the action. Offers of help came from other directions too. Some Hall students lent silk kimonos, Chinese embroidered slippers, and artificial flowers for the widow and her daughters to wear; Surya Wickremesinghe, a third-year, lent two superb yellow silk banners that her father had brought back with him from a conference in Peking, and two of the men in the cast constructed *papier mâché* 'wheels' for the Emperor's coach.

'What do you think of this sunshade?' Latha asked. 'It's not quite right for our play – it comes from Burma – but it's so pretty that it would be a shame to let it go.'

The sunshade in question was painted in shades of pink and mauve, with a scattering of flower petals across the surface. Amali's brother, a student in Rangoon, had brought it for her on his last visit home.

'We'll use it,' Tsunami said at once. 'Peach Blossom can be carrying it when the Emperor sees her for the first time. Meanwhile, just step back and have a look at Dr Pa Chow's screens!'

She leaned two hand-painted screens reverently against the Common Room wall.

'"I have painted them in the tradition of Sino-Japanese art, Miss Wijesinha," he told me. "According to the play, your Emperor is a scholar, not a warrior. So you see painted here a pine tree, a plum tree, and a bamboo. In the art of Japan these three stand for longevity, perseverance and integrity, the innate virtues of the gentleman-scholar." What does it matter if Peach Blossom's parasol isn't authentic, our screens most definitely are! And aren't they beautiful? Dr Pa Chow's such a pet, Latha! So helpful.'

Everything was going well. Too well, as Tsunami told Latha. It was obvious that some disaster was around the corner. And in the final week of rehearsals a problem arose, of so momentous a nature that it threatened to capsize the play altogether.

'But it's only a *little* kiss,' Latha heard Tsunami say pleadingly one evening, as she stopped by the Common Room in which a rehearsal was in progress.

'Little kiss or big kiss, I'm not doing it,' said Peach Blossom flatly. 'My whole family's going to be in the audience, my parents, my aunts and uncles, even my grandmother – she's coming down specially from Chilaw to see me act in the play. And what is she going to see? She'll see Kenneth Fernando kissing me, and that'll be the end of university studies for me . . . I tell you, Tsunami, Achchi Amma will have a heart attack, and it will be your fault—'

The problem, as Tsunami told an amused table at dinner the following evening, was that there were any number of male volunteers ready to take Kenneth's role as Emperor if it meant rehearsing with (and, hopefully, kissing) Sita Cooray who was playing Peach Blossom, but there wasn't a girl in the whole of Sanghamitta Hall who was prepared to risk her reputation and her family's good name by replacing Sita herself.

At the last moment Latha came up with a solution.

'Look,' said she to the Emperor and his reluctant bride. 'I think I can see how we might do this. Try turning your back to the audience, Kenneth. Now, take Sita's hand, and lean sideways. Like this. And you, Sita, stand where I am, and lean sideways in the opposite direction, so that Kenneth's head is between you and the audience. See? Now you're holding hands – that can't be helped, if you don't support each other you might lose your balance – but everyone on stage can see there's at least a foot of space between the two of you. And everyone in the wings can see it too.'

Latha was struck by a second idea.

'Tsunami, why don't you ask one of Sita's sisters to come backstage and help dress Peach Blossom for the play? Then she can stand in the wings, and watch the performance. She'll be able to tell your Achchi Amma and the rest of the family, Sita, that it may have *looked* like a kiss but it definitely wasn't.'

'Latha, you're a genius,' Tsunami said three evenings later, when the cast was celebrating Sanghamitta Hall's victory in the Drama Competition with a special dinner provided by the Warden. 'You made it all possible. Sita was getting set to back out, you know, when you came up with your strategy—'

'Ah, the illusion of the theatre!' remarked Dr Pa Chow, who was attending the celebration dinner as the Hall's special guest. 'It can be so effective. And the play was, indeed, very good. My sincere compliments to all concerned.'

Tsunami regarded him suspiciously.

'Something was wrong, wasn't it?' she said. 'I know it. I can see from your face that you're amused by something, Dr Pa Chow. Where did we go wrong?'

Dr Pa Chow shrugged.

'It was not important,' he said. 'Nothing anyone in the audience would have noticed. Except me.'

'Well, that's just too bad,' Tsunami said. 'This should have been such a happy day for us all, and now I won't be able to sleep tonight for worrying and thinking about it . . .'

Eventually, after much coaxing, which both Tsunami and Dr Pa Chow greatly enjoyed, the truth came out.

'It was the moment of your Emperor's first appearance,' he said. 'Young Fernando made such a grand entrance, with court officials walking before him and behind him, and the wheels of his carriage turning . . . and the banners on each side proclaiming the greatness of His Medieval Majesty . . . As of course they should . . .'

Dr Pa Chow could hardly contain his mirth.

'So?' Tsunami said. 'What was wrong with that? Everyone in the audience said afterwards that Kenneth looked superb.'

She was right: he had. Years later, his former campus mates would remind the Right Reverend Kenneth Fernando, Anglican Bishop of Colombo, that the dignity with which he carried himself when walking in Cathedral processions derived from an early appearance on the University DramSoc stage as an Emperor of China.

'Exactly,' said Dr Pa Chow. 'Everyone in an audience that can't read Chinese. Because if they could, they would have read the characters on those splendid banners on either side of the Emperor . . .'

'And?'

'And – you will kindly pardon me for saying this – they would have died laughing.'

Latha decided to intervene.

'The banners were absolutely authentic, Professor,' she said. 'I can assure you of that. They came direct from China.'

'I do not doubt it,' Dr Pa Chow said. 'Indeed, it was obvious that they did. *But what did the Chinese characters on those banners say?*'

Tsunami and Latha looked at each other blankly.

'I see that you don't know,' he said. 'If you had shown the banners to me before the performance, I would have told you. Well, I will tell you now. One banner – the one on the Emperor's right hand – said: "WORKERS OF THE WORLD, UNITE!" The other – the banner on his left – said "LONG LIVE CHAIRMAN MAO!"'

Dr Pa Chow looked with great amusement at the two crestfallen faces before him.

'We should have guessed,' Tsunami said. 'Surya's father's in the Opposition. Of course – it must have been a Communist Party conference he'd been attending in Peking.'

'You should not let this knowledge spoil your happiness in your achievement,' said Dr Pa Chow. 'It will be a secret between us three. You have presented a highly entertaining play and you have won a prize for your Hall. Best of all, you have learned an important lesson about the difference between appearance and reality, have you not? And next time, you will be on your guard.'

'I'm wondering,' Latha told Amali and Tsunami a few days later, 'whether there was something wrong with our play. No, I don't mean the banners, I mean something *seriously* wrong. I ran into Mrs Raptor today, and she told me she enjoyed the play. If *she* thought it was good, don't you think there must have been something wrong with it somewhere?'

'Look on the bright side,' Amali said. 'She's a scholar of Pali, and has a degree in Buddhist Studies. We must have got the Buddhist references right. Perhaps that's why she praised the play.'

'But what's her praise worth?' Latha said with scorn. 'We know she doesn't live by her own principles.'

She spoke lightly enough, but the others perceived that she was still disturbed by her afternoon as the guest of the Warden of James Peries Hall.

'Well?' Tsunami said briskly. 'What's the problem? Lots of people don't. Look at me: I should be getting up early in the morning and putting in an hour's study before breakfast, or else joining Sriyani in her hamstring stretches and running on the cinder track. Aunt Moira presented me with a large alarm clock to wake me up in the mornings. But do I get up when it rings?'

'No,' Amali said, smiling. 'It rings in my ear, waking me up, but you seem to sleep right through it.'

'Amali,' Latha said later, 'I know I shouldn't let it worry me so much, but . . . do you think most people in our country think like Mrs Raptor?'

What a nuisance I'm being! If Amali told me to shut up, and stop worrying myself and everyone else about Mrs Raptor and her wretched prejudices, I'd deserve it.

But after a few moments' reflection, her thoughtful friend attempted an answer to the question.

'Not everyone,' she said. 'Most people in our country, the majority in fact, are Buddhists. Lord Buddha opposed the caste distinctions that ruled Hindu society in his time. He said that it was neither birth nor outward appearance that denoted a true Brahmin, but the quality of a person's life and actions. Mrs Raptor lectures in Buddhist Philosophy, so she must know that very well. But when she spoke in that way about low-caste students and Tamil students she wasn't thinking about the Buddha's teachings, or expressing a Buddhist point of view, but a personal one. Therefore I'd say the answer to your question is "No". Most people in our country do *not* think like Mrs Raptor.'

Latha knew she should let the discussion rest there, but she could not.

'So you are suggesting, Amali, that though Mrs Raptor *claims* to be a Buddhist, though her office is so crammed with Buddha images that there's hardly any room to move around in it, she doesn't represent a majority opinion in this country? Are you saying that most Buddhists wouldn't think that way, wouldn't dream of thinking that way?'

Amali hesitated.

'Maybe I shouldn't have brought Buddhism into the argument at all,' she said. 'It's probably irrelevant. What was it Mrs Raptor said? "In a year or two people like us will be outnumbered on campus and everywhere else in the country." Have I got it right?'

'Yes. And she added: "Then we will need all the wisdom we can muster to deal with the situation." It sounded as though she was talking about a war that's about to break out.'

'Well, perhaps she was,' Amali said. 'By "people like us", I believe she meant *Sinhalese* people like us. Perhaps she thinks some kind of war's begun already, and that everyone who isn't Sinhalese must be regarded as "the enemy". It seems to me she was talking about survival—'

'But that doesn't make sense,' Latha said. 'This is not a country at war. People have never been happier than they are today.'

'Is that so?'

Tsunami, who had been silently listening to the conversation, spoke for the first time.

'*Are* people happy? What about the Tamils? How can Tamil people possibly be happy about what happened in 1948? Don't give me that blank look, please, Latha! 1948, since you seem to have forgotten it, was the year that they passed a Citizenship Act which changed the status of thousands of Indian Tamils in this country. I was only thirteen at the time the legislation was passed, but it was being discussed all the time by our planter friends, and I still remember thinking it was very unfair. Didn't *you* think it was unfair, Latha?'

'I wasn't there to hear the discussions—'

'Oh yes, I forgot. 1948 was the year my mother went away, wasn't it! And you deserted us too.'

'I *didn't* "desert" you, Tsunami! I tried again and again to come up to Lucas Falls, but each time I asked, my parents – Amma, really – seemed to have other plans . . .'

'Oh, never mind. It all happened a long time ago, didn't it, so there's no point in discussing it now.'

Her distress was obvious, and her tone belied the casualness of her words. Latha said nothing.

'What were we talking about?'

'The Citizenship Act of 1948,' Amali said quietly.

'Yes. Well, maybe you two didn't think about it because it didn't affect you, personally! But *we* couldn't shut our eyes to its implications. The labour force working on the tea plantation at Lucas Falls is nearly a hundred per cent Indian Tamil, and they were all affected. Just think about it: at one moment they were part of our society, making a *massive* contribution to our major industry, the next moment they found themselves stateless!'

If Auntie Helen had been in Ceylon at the time, she might have felt excluded, too.

It was very evident to Latha that this was no moment to bring up Helen's name, and she kept the thought to herself.

'And now,' Tsunami went on, 'what about Sinhala being declared the official language? Isn't that discrimination against everyone who doesn't speak and write Sinhala? Tamils, Muslims, Burghers – everyone who communicates in English. When you practise wholesale discrimination against people, the result *is* war.'

'I really don't think Mrs Raptor was talking of war,' replied Amali patiently. 'She was talking of an issue she considers more important than war – maybe she thinks it more important even than Lord Buddha's teaching – the survival of the Sinhalese race. I know many people who would think and even speak like Mrs Raptor, when it comes to an issue like that.'

'Do you?' snapped Latha. 'Well, *I* don't. My father, for instance, thinks of himself as Ceylonese first. The fact of being Sinhalese comes a good way behind, though he's proud of that too. Anyway, he would *die* before he'd allow himself even to *think* any of the rubbish Mrs Raptor was talking so loudly about—'

'What about your mother?' Amali asked. 'She's the true Buddhist in your family, isn't she? And you, Tsunami, what about your father?'

'Hmm?'

Tsunami, who had relapsed into her role as silent listener to the argument, her thoughts a hundred miles away, was startled by the question. Indeed, what about her family and Latha's? Following Mrs Raptor's discourse on the subjects of race and caste, she had realized that there must have been many occasions on which Latha had had to fend off or ignore dismissive remarks made by Auntie Soma and her sisters about her own mother's Indian Tamil background.

Her Christianity, too.

And her father? Tsunami suddenly remembered a remark her father had made years ago about his friend Gerard van Kuyk the artist, who, he declared, had 'prostrated himself before the filthy, unwashed feet of a yellow-robed charlatan' for the sake of an artistic project. That was prejudice too, wasn't it?

Except that it was aimed in a different direction.

'It seems to me,' she said slowly, 'that we're going through some kind of transition, like what happens when the planets seem to change their places in the sky. Maybe our politics, which have up to now been based on social class, are changing into something else . . . race politics.'

'But that would be unbearable!' Latha exclaimed. 'That's what happened in Germany, when the Nazis began persecuting Jews and sending them to gas chambers in concentration camps. It couldn't happen here, our Sinhalese people wouldn't allow it—'

'Wouldn't they, Latha? *Wouldn't* they? I'm not so sure.'

The moon was high in the sky before the three of them went to bed. It was some time before Latha let sleep overtake her restless thoughts. She told herself firmly that she must learn not to take her cousin's angry remarks to heart, she must learn to keep in mind the reasons for her insecurities.

She looked at her watch. It was three o'clock in the morning. In the evening there was to be a Hall meeting at which her presence as sub-Warden would be required. The agenda, which had been sent to her by the Hall president, was long, and discussion of some of the items on it threatened to be acrimonious. Latha sighed. She wished that some of the Hall's committee members would stop bringing politics into Hall affairs. Setting up the University at Peradeniya would have been a complete waste of time and money, she thought, unless that type of thinking could be changed.

Could it?

'It seems to me,' Latha said to herself as she switched off her bedside light, 'that it's up to our generation to change it.'

15

A COURSE IN ENGLISH STUDIES

'Any idea what our new neighbours are like?' Sriyani inquired of Latha. Of the students who had shared their balcony in the previous year, Hema Gikiyanagē and Swarna Wijewardene were no longer at Peradeniya. Both had sat successfully for their Finals, and would return to the campus in a few months' time to graduate at the coming Convocation. Hema's study-bedroom and Swarna's had been assigned by the Warden to two first-year students from Jaffna.

'Shy. Studious. Quiet. *Very* polite. You'll have to be on your best behaviour, Sriyani! Set a good example, keep regular hours, and show them we're not barbarians . . .'

'What do you mean, "regular hours"? Just because I come in late *occasionally* from the gym? I don't stay up till dawn, solving the problems of the nation! With any luck, one or both of them might have an interest in sport. We badly need some new people for the Hall athletics team. I'll sound the two of them out at the Hall meeting tonight.'

Students who attended the meeting that night had, however, other matters on their minds than recruitment to Sanghamitta's athletics team. Early in the meeting (which was conducted in the refectory), a bitter argument started up, initiated by a group of second-year Marxist students who, with no prior warning whatsoever, charged the sitting president with mismanaging Hall funds. The two first-years Sriyani had hoped to canvass on behalf of Hall sports listened wide-eyed as open insults and accusations of theft and misappropriation flew back and forth across the refectory.

'I won't be surprised if neither of them attend another Hall meeting,' Latha whispered to Sriyani. 'They look like terrified rabbits.'

Following Independence in 1948, and the division of popular opinion into two camps, the conservative Right and the Marxist Left, politics had become an important issue on campus. Charismatic individuals of leftist views became extremely popular with students. Candidates for election to the Students' Union and to Hall committees declared their views passionately and vociferously at open-air public meetings, and expected to be elected on the basis of their party affiliations.

Latha had accepted Dr Springdale's invitation, at the end of her first year, to stay on as a student sub-Warden in her second. She had no time for political involvement, even if she had had interests in that direction. Work seemed to have escalated sharply with the start of the new academic year. She and three of her balcony mates had qualified for Special Arts and were reading for Honours degrees: Amali in Economics, Tsunami in History, Sriyani in Geography, and Latha herself in English. Sriyani admitted to Latha and Tsunami that she wondered whether she had been wise in opting for Honours. She had managed, she said, to scrape into the second year of Geography Honours while collecting University Colours in nearly every sporting activity Peradeniya offered, but she would have to fit her studies into her sports programme somehow in the next two years if she hoped to graduate at the end of it.

As the argument in the Hall showed no sign of reaching a peaceful conclusion, Latha eventually used her authority as student sub-Warden to intervene during a pause in the debate, and suggest mildly that the president (who was, by this time, close to tears) should be given a chance to defend and explain herself before being removed from office. She did not expect that her words would have much effect on the accusers, whose blood was obviously up. The majority view had been that dismissal should be immediate. The president's removal seemed to be a foregone conclusion.

But a vote had yet to be taken on the matter; and since Latha, following her father's advice, had never before taken part in a Hall dispute, her quiet intervention on this occasion took her fellow-students by surprise. They listened to her, and to her own amazement her words carried the day. The president was voted time to answer the charges; she did so two days later, and survived in office. The incident was over: or so Latha thought.

A few days later, however, she was asked by one of her English tutors to stay back in class after the Linguistics tutorial was over. The tutor who detained her was Arnold Castilian, a senior member of the English Department staff. Castilian's brilliant mind and charismatic personality attracted many students, including Latha, who looked forward to his Language classes. She was aware, however, like everyone else on campus, that he conducted classes in Marxist theory off campus for the benefit of politically inclined students. Keeping her father's advice in mind, she avoided having much to do with him outside the walls of the Arts Building.

The revolutionary ideas generated in Castilian's Marxist theory classes – and the individual who generated them – had about them an exciting aura of cloak-and-dagger secrecy which added to their attraction. Tsunami, who enjoyed the thrill of experimenting with new ideas and new experiences, regularly attended his classes, feeling that she was doing something extremely daring by doing so. She was amused by her cousin's refusal to join her.

'You're so timid, Latha!' she said once. 'Come on, be adventurous, brave a little danger, just once in your prim and proper life!'

'Danger!' Latha had retorted crossly. 'What's so dangerous about Castilian's classes? He takes care to hold them off-campus and outside teaching hours, so no one's breaching university regulations by attending them.'

This was perfectly true; and once Latha had assured herself that Tsunami was not heading for trouble with the university administration by attending Dr Castilian's classes, she had not laboured the point. Her own encounters with him took place only in class, and his request on this occasion puzzled her. What could he possibly want to speak to her about?

Arnold Castilian came to the point straight away.

'I am very concerned to hear that you have been involving yourself in Hall politics, Miss Wijesinha,' he said.

His eyes behind his rimless glasses were unusually severe.

'You should understand that such an involvement is a complete waste of your time.'

Latha stared at him, and was silent.

Involving myself in Hall politics? What can he possibly mean?

'Next year will be your third year in English, and it is a period in your academic career that requires self-discipline, not self-indulgence.'

Latha could hardly credit what she was hearing. It was obvious to her, after a few moments' thought, that he must be alluding to the recent Sanghamitta Hall meeting at which she had intervened to keep the president in office.

News certainly travels fast at Peradeniya! But how can he have heard of it? Only Hall residents had been present at the meeting, and who could have possibly thought such a trivial incident important enough to tell Mr Castilian of it?

Besides that, the warning he had thought fit to give her astonished her, coming as it did from Arnold Castilian of all people.

If he regards Hall politics as a waste of time, why doesn't he tell Tsunami to stop attending his classes on Marxist revolutionary theory and concentrate instead on her History studies?

'We all expect a First Class from you in your Finals, Miss Wijesinha. I hope I shall not need to speak to you again on this subject.'

Latha left the tutorial room in a daze. None of her teachers at Peradeniya had ever spoken to her in such a tone; but, more than that, they had never spoken to her on such a subject.

A First Class degree in English? Can Dr Castilian really have meant what he said?

She went to the reference library, found herself a desk by a window, and tried to collect her thoughts.

Arnold Castilian's statement that she was expected by her teachers to graduate with First Class Honours (well known to be a rare occurrence at Peradeniya, but especially so in the elite Department of English) was the first of many unwelcome intimations which had recently been reaching Latha from other sources, that her progress was being monitored by others, and carefully assessed. Well-meaning friends like Sriyani had occasionally conveyed to Latha certain opinions of her classmates. These were intended to encourage her, but they had succeeded only in destroying her peace of mind.

'Merrick was saying at the track the other day that when it comes to the Finals, Latha, yours will be a "class war"! Not a "pass war", as it's going to be for the rest of us poor benighted souls. He's in English, and everyone thinks *he's* in line for a First, so he should know.'

Latha had managed, with some difficulty, to smile. The good opinion of Merrick Seneviratne was worth having: he had earned her respect as well as everyone else's by combining an interest in track and field with sound and well-written English essays. But the knowledge that so much was expected of her by others confused Latha, and made her apprehensive. She had begun English studies because she loved literature, but remarks like Merrick's and Dr Castilian's made her aware for the first time that loving literature and qualifying for a degree in the subject can be two entirely different things.

From the day of her interview with Arnold Castilian, the reading of literature, once her greatest pleasure, became an interest that she could no longer indulge for her own enjoyment.

Merrick's objective, Latha knew, was to top their Honours class in English, and use his results in the Finals as a passport to the Ceylon Civil Service. Others had taken that path before him, and the details of their achievements were well known among the students: the prizes they had won in their first and second years, the number of A grades they had obtained in their Final papers. Merrick was not alone this year in his ambition, and he had an eager competitor in Irwin Fernando, a bright young man from an obscure provincial college who had emerged from among the also-rans to win the Fort Library Prize for English at the General Arts Qualifying examination.

Unfortunately, this early success had gone to Irwin's head. He had begun in second year to absent himself from the classes of the teachers he considered boring. The Honours class was a small one, and Irwin's repeated absences had been noted and reported to the Dean of Arts by Professor Titus Dupré, an old-fashioned pedagogue for whose intellectual abilities Irwin had the greatest contempt, and whose classes he had consistently avoided. Irwin had very unwisely made his opinions of some of his lecturers known among his friends at the Union canteen, and Professor Dupré, furious at learning from a mischief-making associate of Irwin's that a second-year student had described him as a pedestrian mediocrity, had insisted on immediate expulsion.

Dismissal from the University would most certainly have been Irwin's fate (and probably the end of his career), had the Dean not taken a more liberal view of the young man's excesses. The Dean was a kindly individual. He had heard young Fernando acquit himself eloquently in Union debates, and believed he had a brilliant future ahead of him if he would only curb his intellectual arrogance. With Everard van Loten's assistance, the Dean had managed to smooth their colleague's ruffled feathers, and Irwin was permitted to remain at Peradeniya.

Latha liked Irwin Fernando very much. She enjoyed his brand of wit, and though she sympathized sincerely with him in his predicament, she could not quite suppress a smile when she learned the details of the conditions on which his reprieve had been granted.

'My God, Latha!' Irwin groaned. 'They've doomed me to show up at every bloody English class until the end of next term. If I miss a single one without an adequate reason, the Dean says, it'll be all up with me. Not that I'd care, mind you, it wouldn't be a punishment if they were Castilian's classes that I was being forced to attend, or van Loten's, or Marchmont's. But you remember, don't you, what's on our timetable next term?'

She did.

The major course that Irwin would be forced to attend next term in obedience to the Dean's ruling was Titus Dupré's famously tedious series of lectures on Milton. Irwin winced at the thought of the hours of boredom that awaited him. But he did what the Dean had asked him to do, and did it with commendable grace, so that nobody could have cause for complaint. And with humour, too: at one of Professor Dupré's classes on *Paradise Lost*, when Latha happened to be Irwin's neighbour, her classmate's open textbook came sliding gently towards her along the top of her desk. A pencilled note at the foot of the printed page expressed his anguish:

Milton! Thou shouldst be living at this hour!

Latha knew that to be able to print the magic letters C.C.S. after his name was Irwin Fernando's dream, just as it was Merrick Seneviratne's. To enter the Ceylon Civil Service was the dream, in fact, of every talented male university student who was not qualifying to enter the legal or medical professions. Irwin had confided to her once, over tea and cutlets at the canteen, that success in the Finals was for him a matter of life and death, since his father was elderly, his family was not well off, and he had two younger sisters whose future would one day be his responsibility.

By implying that Latha, as a woman, was free of such pressures, and that she should, in fact, take other things – and other people – into consideration besides herself and her love of literature, he had succeeded in making her feel extremely guilty. Perhaps, she thought, it had been unintentionally done, perhaps he wasn't aware that she was in Peradeniya on a bursary. Knowing that she was Tsunami's cousin, knowing that Tsunami's father was a prominent politician, Irwin probably thought her own family was as wealthy and influential as Tsunami's. Latha was too proud to give Irwin details of her own financial situation, and her good manners kept her from reminding him that as the Ceylon Civil Service was not open to women, he would be facing no competition from her.

While Arnold Castilian was holding one section of the undergraduate population in thrall with the fascination of his lectures on Marxist theory, Ronald Marchmont was entrancing another by introducing its members to the writing of the English Romantics. Marchmont was responsible for involving Latha in what she would always remember as the part of English Studies which she had most enjoyed at Peradeniya. The historical period allotted for special study to her year extended from 1796 to 1832, and among the authors nominated for detailed study were some of her personal favourites: among them Wordsworth, Byron, Keats, and Jane Austen. At the end of the term a long essay would be expected of each student, an essay that would cover the entire *oeuvre* of their chosen author.

Marchmont, who enjoyed teaching the Romantics, had read the poetry of Wordsworth and Byron aloud in class with verve and passion, delivering lectures that should really, Latha told Tsunami with enthusiasm, have been in print. She was certain that one day they would be. Knowing, however, that Marchmont regarded himself above all, as "an Austen man", Latha was convinced that his lectures on the incomparable Jane would be for her the supreme treat in a feast of delectables. She knew very well that by making Austen her choice for her long essay, she would involve herself in the reading and analysis of six long novels and a plethora of critical studies, but she looked forward joyfully to re-reading the novels she loved, and talked so much to her closest friends about Ronald Marchmont's skills as a teacher that she infected them all with her own mood of eager anticipation.

'Would you object, Dr Marchmont, if three of my friends attended your Austen lectures?' she asked Marchmont at the conclusion of his classes on Wordsworth's poetry. 'They're not studying English literature – Shirani Pathirana and my cousin Tsunami are in second-year History Honours, and Amali Kiriella's reading Economics – but they've all three read all six of the novels, and this may be the only chance they'll ever get of hearing them properly discussed.'

Far from objecting to this proposal, Marchmont had been delighted by it. He immediately granted Latha's request. As she thanked him and prepared to leave, he added:

'Miss Wijesinha, I do wish you'd stop calling me "Dr Marchmont"! I haven't got my doctorate yet, you know. Why not just call me "Ron"?'

Latha had smiled, and had made no reply. Marchmont shrugged. He had learned that a smile like that meant a polite but firm 'No, thank you'; and he had learned it from experience. Enchanted by the beauty of the campus, he had suggested to his Honours students during his first term at Peradeniya that an occasional class should be held out of doors.

'Just think,' he had said to them, 'what it would be like to read Keats's 'Ode to a Nightingale' beneath one of those magnificent trees in the University Park . . . "I cannot see what flowers are at my feet, nor what soft incense hangs upon the boughs . . ."'

He had confided to them that some of his own happiest hours at Cambridge had been passed on the banks of the Cam, in the company of a book or a like-minded friend.

His Honours class had gazed at Marchmont in astonishment. Beneath a *tree*? On the banks of a *river*? When there were perfectly good classrooms that had been specially designed to facilitate tutorials? Marchmont was wiser now, and he knew that such informality was more than he could ever hope for at Peradeniya. Give it up, Arnold Castilian had advised him, our students are conditioned to think in squares and straight lines.

But Marchmont still tried, occasionally.

The only student who thoroughly appreciated his relaxed, informal approach, and showed him clearly that she did, was Tsunami Wijesinha. She was not one of 'his' students, having elected to read History and not English, but she regularly attended choir practice with Marchmont's Varsity Voices, and had done what no other student was prepared to do: she had allowed him to put their relationship on a first-name basis. When Marchmont asked her, in exactly the way he had asked Latha, 'Why not call me Ron?', she had replied with perfect aplomb, 'Certainly, if you'll call me Tsunami.'

Latha had been startled when she first heard her cousin and her tutor address each other with such unheard-of informality.

'You actually called him "Ronald", Tsunami!'

'Why not? He asked us all to call him Ronald, at the very first Varsity Voices meeting, remember?'

'Yes, but nobody else uses his first name when they speak to him.'

'That's their problem, not mine. We have a lot in common, Ron Marchmont and I! Did you know he's writing a novel? Besides, anyone can see he's happier when things are kept informal.'

That was perfectly true. But Latha's awareness of campus convention was increasing daily, and her first instinct had been to advise Tsunami to go back to formal terms, in her own interests and Marchmont's. Tsunami flatly refused to do so, and eventually Latha had had to be content with advising her not to make a habit of such informality in public.

The knowledge that his classes were attracting students from other disciplines put the young Englishman on his mettle. His lectures – which had always been good – became better, wittier, more carefully structured. They became so satisfying, in fact, that Latha, who generally took the briefest of notes in class, used her knowledge of Pitman to set down each sentence that Marchmont uttered *verbatim*, and then sat up late at night transcribing his lectures into Monitor exercise books. Marchmont's approach to the subjects he taught appealed to her, and her enjoyment of Jane Austen in particular was increased tenfold by her realization, as he took the class step by step through the novels, that he was proposing conclusions similar to those she had reached during her unsupervised reading of them throughout her adolescent life. She looked forward eagerly to the last lecture in his Austen series, which was to be on *Persuasion*. Hearing him on the subject would be, she thought, like unwrapping a bonbon at the end of a feast. *Persuasion* was Latha's favourite among the Austen novels: gentle Anne Elliot, constant in love during eight years of separation and disappointment, was a character with whom she found it easy to identify.

But literary studies had ceased to be, for Latha, a simple matter of *liking* one character or *identifying* with another. Her English studies at Peradeniya had caused her to grow as a critic, and *Persuasion* for her was, above all, the work in which Jane Austen, nearing the end of her life, had moved away from satire and entered fully into the creative world of the true novelist.

How disappointing was it then for her to discover that Peradeniya's 'Austen man', far from regarding *Persuasion* as a supreme (if unfinished) achievement, one which would have led its creator in new directions, had she only lived long enough to pursue them, presented the novel in his lecture as a mere sentimental exercise! Latha could hardly believe her ears when Marchmont described her beloved Anne Elliot as driven by self-pity and old-maidish primness, and declared that the novel's conclusion – which had moved Latha to sympathetic tears – turned entirely on the restorative effects of sea air on a young woman's complexion.

'What am I going to do?' Latha asked her balcony mates. 'I agree with the man on every detail of the other five novels, and I disagree with him on every single thing he's said about *Persuasion*. How can I write an essay – my final essay for the term, everything depends on it – in which I challenge every word of the teacher's lecture?'

'Pick another topic,' Shirani Pathirana suggested. She looked down the lecture list on Latha's desk. 'Write on Keats instead. You know you adore Keats. And so does Mr Marchmont. Abracadabra! Exit problem.'

'Too late,' Latha said. 'Irwin Fernando has opted for Keats. He told me straight out that he'd have preferred to write on Jane Austen, but he didn't want the two of us to be in competition.'

'Compromise,' Amali advised. 'Sit on the fence.'

Latha shook her head.

'Not possible,' she said. 'Mr Marchmont's left no space for compromise. If I didn't know better, I'd say he's deliberately trying to provoke someone in the class to take issue with him on *Persuasion*.'

'Can you blame him?' Sriyani asked. 'The poor man must be sick to death of *guru bakthi*.'

'Maybe, maybe not,' said Latha. 'But, whatever may be in *his* mind, *I* cannot compromise – not on this. I – I just cannot agree with what he says about this book. I shall have to say so in my essay. And the moment I do, I'll lose marks.'

'Relax,' Tsunami said. 'It's only a book, after all.'

As Latha turned on her, she put her hands up and pretended to cower in terror.

'Okay, okay, don't shoot! But remember, I know Austen too. Maybe not as well as you do, granted, but I understand the way you feel about her. However, we're talking here about your degree, Latha, not Mr Marchmont's. *He* can say what he likes in class, and no one can question it: but your essay grade is what they'll look up when all the lectures are over and they're handing out degrees. So be careful.'

She smiled at Latha.

'And Jane, bless her soul, is dead. She'll never know you betrayed her.'

'Tsunami,' Latha began, then stopped herself and began to laugh.

How foolish of me to care so much about an author who's been dead for nearly two centuries!

She changed the subject.

It was not the first time that she had recently found herself and Tsunami on opposite sides of an argument, and she had decided some time ago that it would be best to avoid direct confrontation with her cousin if she possibly could. Until very recently, she had assumed that Tsunami's thoughts on most important subjects were identical with her own. She valued the understanding – often unspoken – that had united them as children, and her unexpected reunion with her cousin a year and a half ago had been until now the great joy of Latha's life. In recent weeks, however, they seemed to have grown apart. Her cousin seemed ready to fly into a state of prickly hostility to everything Latha valued or took for granted. Their balcony discussions often found the two of them combatively at odds; not, as before, affectionately seeking areas of mutual agreement.

A further development complicated the situation for Latha. As the weeks passed, a succession of classes, essays and seminars bringing ever closer the examination that would end their second Honours year, she discovered that Amali often seemed to understand her better than Tsunami did. The discovery surprised her, for she and Tsunami had their family ties, their long friendship, and their experience of city life in common, while Amali, recently met and quite unrelated to Latha by blood, had grown up in a provincial Sinhalese world that was quite unaffected by the changes taking place outside it. In Kandyan families like Amali's, as Latha knew, social life was conducted within a close-knit racial, religious, and caste group. In matters relating to marriage, especially, anything else was unthinkable.

When Amali discovered, for instance, that Tsunami's father, the head of a Sinhalese family, had married a wife from India, she was deeply shocked.

'However could such a thing have happened?' she asked Latha when Tsunami was not by to hear her.

Latha had appreciated her friend's restraint: from Amali's point of view, Rowland Wijesinha might just as well have married a Zulu, a Chinese, or an Eskimo. Latha did not attempt to explain the circumstances of her uncle's marriage. It was a subject on which she had very hazy ideas herself. Amali had eventually rationalized Rowland Wijesinha's union with Helen Ratnam by saying that it must have been unique even in a Westernized family, and had been accepted by Sinhalese society because the person who made the choice, being rich and male, could act with a freedom denied to those who were neither.

Well, life at Peradeniya certainly gives us freedom, Latha reflected. We can choose our friends here, we can choose whom we'd like to spend time with. This was something she appreciated, though the easy comradeship that marked Tsunami's friendships with her male classmates, and even with her tutors, was beyond her.

Such casualness epitomized the dangerous freedom which Soma had feared so much on behalf of her daughter. It's a good thing, Latha sometimes thought, that Amma doesn't get to see the campus at evening! For she knew that all around her at Peradeniya, her contemporaries were eagerly exploring the geography of love. In the flowery glades of the University Park, in the shadows of the pillars of the University Library, in the twilit moments that followed Peradeniya's magnificent sunsets, sweethearts walked and whispered. ('One Faculty that's certainly thriving on this campus is the Faculty of Love,' the professor of Dentistry had famously remarked one evening, as the headlights of his Austin Healey startled lovers lingering on the slopes of Hantane, causing them to spring apart and turn away from the light so that they could not be identified.)

Latha was aware that her mother scrutinized her behaviour carefully each time she went home on vacation, doubtless dreading the changes she might discover in her manner or mood. At first this had amused her, but now it was a cause of annoyance and irritation.

I need someone to talk to, someone I can trust.

She thought of her father, seated among his books and papers, and she poured out her worries to him in a long letter. How should she deal with Ronald Marchmont and his dismissal of *Persuasion*? Would it be misguided and foolish on her part to pin her academic career on her faith in the quality of a single work of fiction? Was Tsunami right in saying that Marchmont, merely by virtue of his position as teacher, 'can say what he likes in class, and no one can question it'? Should a teacher's judgment ever be challenged by a student? And how should she deal with a classmate's hints that she ought to have other things on her mind than studies – especially studies that might rob him of a livelihood?

Latha decided that while she was waiting for her father's reply, she would seek refuge and inspiration in the University Library. She would draw on the well-known erudition of Mr Ivan Ganesan, the Librarian, and methodically fill the pages of the exercise books her father had given her with the remarks made on Jane Austen's novels by scholars and critics over the hundred and fifty years that had passed since the author's death.

Was this the way to proceed?

It would certainly give her some idea of the thinking of other readers besides Marchmont and herself. The mental exercise would do her good: at the very least it might still her mind while she waited for Herbert's reply to her letter, and give it something useful to do instead of running round in circles like a squirrel in a cage.

16

A BLAST FROM THE PAST

Her reference notes completed, Latha began the second part of her preparation for writing her essay on *Persuasion.*

She decided that she would now put Ronald Marchmont's opinions and the views of all the critics she had read entirely out of her mind; and although she had read Jane Austen's last novel countless times for pleasure, and knew it almost by heart, she would re-read the book slowly, methodically, word by word, making a note whenever she came upon anything that looked like a clue to Anne Elliot's character.

For after much deliberation, Latha had decided that it was on the personality of Anne Elliot, the central intelligence and emotional heart of the novel, that her essay must focus. If, after such a close study as Latha was preparing to give her, Anne failed to satisfy as a complex, living personality, then everything else must fail, and Marchmont would have been right.

Latha sat in her study-bedroom at Sanghamitta, with her copy of *Persuasion* open at Chapter One, page one, and nothing else on her desk but a folder full of ruled paper. Around her, the Hall was silent. Every student on Latha's corridor was at a lecture or a tutorial, or working in the Library. On the page before her, Sir Walter Elliot had just opened his favourite book, *The Baronetage*, and was re-reading his favourite part of it: the history of the Elliot family, culminating in the account of his own life and career. (Just like Uncle Rowland! Latha thought, remembering how often a simple inquiry directed to her uncle had been rewarded with a lecture on the subject of Wijesinha ancestry and achievements.) So deeply engrossed in Sir Walter's vanity was Latha that she heard neither the click-clack of high-heeled shoes along the corridor nor the knock on a distant door.

'Miss Wijesinha?' said a female voice.

Latha was about to get up and go to her door when she heard the same voice again, speaking this time in Sinhala.

'Is Tsunami *hamu* in?'

Who could this be? And which of the Hall servants could she possibly be addressing? The honorific *hamu*, used in feudal households of the past, was surely inappropriate to Peradeniya's democratic halls. To her dismay, Latha heard Amali's voice responding politely in Sinhala.

'I think she's in. Let me try her door for you.'

There was a gentle tap on Latha's door.

'Latha?'

'Latha! I don't want any Latha!' said the voice irritably, in English. 'It's Miss Tsunami Wijesinha that I want to see.'

Latha opened her door.

Outside it, in the corridor, stood an elegant apparition in flowered chiffon, dark glasses and pearls. Becoming a cabinet minister's wife, even for a short period, had certainly wrought a remarkable change in Moira Wijesinha's appearance. Latha remembered the 'Mrs Rowland' who had fussily supervised Tara's wedding, and that earlier incarnation in which, resplendent in juvenile flounces and frills, she had visited Lucas Falls with her mother when Latha and Tsunami were children. At any moment now, she'll recognize me, Latha thought, she'll remember me as one of Tara's bridesmaids. But she was mistaken. It was soon evident that 'Mrs Rowland' had forgotten her completely.

Moira looked Latha up and down, and tapped her foot impatiently.

'Tsunami!' she said. 'Where's Tsunami?'

'She's at a class just now,' Latha said, consulting her wrist-watch. 'But she should be along at any moment. Please come in.'

Amali, who had a wicker basket filled with ironed cotton saris in her arms, excused herself politely, and walked on along the corridor. Moira Wijesinha watched her go.

'That ayah doesn't seem to know anything,' she said. 'Why does Dr Springdale employ a second-rate servant who can't speak English?'

'Amali is not a servant. She is an Honours student here, like Tsunami and myself,' Latha said.

'So why doesn't she speak English?'

'Amali is bilingual,' Latha explained, 'and speaks both English and Sinhala. But English, for her, is an academic language, so she prefers to use Sinhala which is the language she speaks at home.'

Moira Wijesinha did not look as though any part of Latha's explanation was registering with her.

'Well, she doesn't seem to read the Sinhala newspapers, or she would have known who I am.'

Like Emma Woodhouse, Latha could not resist.

'Oh?' she said. 'And who *are* you?'

She regretted her rudeness as soon as she had uttered the words. Moira Wijesinha was, after all, Tsunami's stepmother, and as such she deserved politeness, if not necessarily respect. Astonishingly, her visitor's next words indicated that her feelings had not been hurt.

'I am Mrs Rowland Wijesinha,' Moira stated with dignity. 'I am often in the newspapers, in connection with cultural events. My husband, Tsunami's father, is – or was until recently – the Minister for Cultural Affairs.'

She removed her dark glasses, presumably to facilitate recognition, and resumed her scrutiny of Latha.

'And who are *you*, may I ask? Haven't I seen you somewhere before?'

Latha ignored the question. As a sub-Warden of Sanghamitta, she held a master key with which she could have opened Tsunami's room had she wished to do so, but she knew that it was only in a crisis that the key was intended for use in that way. She did not regard Tsunami's failure to meet her stepmother as a crisis.

'Please sit down. Or you're welcome to wait for Tsunami on the balcony, if you like.'

She opened the door leading on to the balcony, and put a cushion in place in the chair she usually occupied. Her visitor leaned on the parapet, and examined the view through her dark glasses.

'It's very glary out here,' said she after a few seconds. 'I shall come in.'

Latha resigned herself to the inevitable, and put *Persuasion* away. Moira Wijesinha sat down, and looked about her.

'Tsunami shouldn't be long now,' Latha said. 'Would you like a magazine to read while you are waiting for her?'

Her visitor paid her no attention. Her gaze had settled on a framed photograph that stood on Latha's shelf. It was a holiday snapshot, taken on the sands at Arugam Bay. A young couple, leaning against a beached catamaran, looked cheerfully out of the frame. Between them stood a little girl, her skirt filled with sea-shells. Her mother's long hair was lifted by the sea-breeze. Latha, who adored that photograph, had insisted on Herbert's taking it out of the family album and framing it for her.

'Who's this?'

'My parents and myself.'

'H'm. I am sure I've seen them before. And I'm sure I've seen you before, too. But I don't know you. Who are you?'

'I'm Latha Wijesinha,' Latha said quietly. 'Tsunami's cousin.'

'Herbert Wijesinha's daughter?'

Latha nodded. 'And Soma's.'

Moira Wijesinha smiled in triumph.

'Oh, *now* I know you,' she said. 'You were one of Tara's bridesmaids. Why didn't you remind me?'

Latha made no reply.

'In any case, child,' Moira went on, 'you should remember me from the wedding – why, it was I who took you to Mrs Kelaart's, to have your sari blouse fitted, for goodness' sake!'

Latha smiled with deliberate vagueness.

'Oh . . . oh, yes . . . Of course, I remember now, we met during Tara's wedding, didn't we! I'm very happy to see you again, Mrs Wijesinha. Welcome to Sanghamitta.'

Round One definitely to me!

But if she had expected Moira to retire defeated from their little exchange, Latha was mistaken. Moira didn't even seem to realize that war had been declared. Her questions continued.

'Why didn't Tsunami tell us that you are at Peradeniya? Christopher was up here recently, wasn't he? Did you meet him? He didn't mention you either.'

'I've no idea why they didn't tell you,' Latha said. 'Maybe they didn't think it important enough to talk about.'

'Tsunami has told us nothing, absolutely nothing, about her friends on campus. I have asked her so often, but she never says a word. A very secretive girl, Tsunami, not like her sister Tara. Wait till I meet her!'

Quick footsteps were heard in the corridor and Tsunami arrived, breathless, at Latha's door.

'Sorry, sorry, sorry!' Tsunami said. 'Apologies, Auntie, for keeping you waiting. And apologies, Latha, I never expected the lecture to run over time, or I'd have mentioned that my aunt was coming to see me this morning.'

She dumped her bag of books on Latha's bed.

'Amali just told me you were waiting for me, Auntie. Sorry I took so long – it's two flights up, you know.'

'Yes, I know,' Moira Wijesinha said, extending a cheek to be kissed. 'I've just walked up those horrible stairs. Why doesn't your Warden have some lifts put into this building?'

Tsunami did not answer her question. Instead, she asked one of her own.

'Well, Latha's been looking after you very well, I see?'

'Tsunami! What is the meaning of this? Your cousin doesn't seem to know anything about me.'

Tsunami shot Latha a look of surprise. 'But, surely—'

'I think our conversation got off on the wrong foot, Tsunami,' Latha said evenly. 'Your aunt has just been telling me that Amali and I should read the newspapers.'

Tsunami glanced from one to the other. Then she changed the subject.

'What are we doing about lunch? It's nearly one o'clock, you must be starving, Auntie.'

Latha had by now begun to regret her momentary rudeness to Moira. She decided to make amends, and re-establish good relations. Recalling, with something of a start, that she was herself a person of some consequence in the Hall, she said:

'Please join me at High Table, Mrs Wijesinha. I'm afraid the Warden will not be with us – she's in Colombo today – but two of the other sub-Wardens will be there, and you would be very welcome.'

When Moira walked into the refectory and up to the High Table, she was recognized immediately, her appearance causing a sensation among the students and the maids. Moira was pleased: she flashed smiles graciously in every direction, and basked happily in her husband's reflected glory when three students seated in different parts of the refectory came over during the meal to introduce themselves respectfully to her as daughters of Rowland Wijesinha's constituents. Well, everyone *here* seems to read the newspapers, Latha thought, so that should make her happy! She listened, amused, as the buzz of comment rose higher.

'I noticed that you had some interesting prints on your wall. You are interested in art?'

Latha started, and recalled her wandering thoughts.

'Yes.'

'Do you know Gerard van Kuyk's work?'

'I've seen some of his paintings.'

'Very good. Well, I can introduce you to the artist himself this afternoon, if you like. I'm in Kandy today on a cultural mission – you might say as a sort of unofficial ambassador – to buy pictures for the Art Gallery in Colombo. I thought I'd take Tsunami with me to see Gerard. He adores pretty young girls, especially when they tell him what a great painter he is. It makes him feel young, I suppose.'

She looked Latha up and down.

'You can come along too, if you wish.'

Her manner was extremely grand. Latha hesitated. Her childhood memories of van Kuyk were still fresh in her mind. Though he had presumably mellowed with age, she was not sure that she wanted to meet him again, especially as a member of Moira Wijesinha's entourage. She was about to refuse the invitation when Tsunami, joining them as lunch ended, caused her to change her mind.

'Say "yes", Latha! Do say "yes"! Latha met Uncle Gerard years ago, Auntie,' she added, turning to Moira. 'We were both tots at the time, and he was much taken with our friend here.'

'Oh, really?' Moira did not sound convinced.

'Yes, really. Latha, you should show Auntie the picture he made of you.'

'It's at home,' Latha lied. 'And in any case—'

'*Gerard van Kuyk has painted this girl's portrait?*'

'Well, not exactly,' Latha said quickly. 'All he did was to draw a picture . . .' But Moira was not really listening.

'Excellent!' she said. 'In that case, you *must* come with us, it could make all the difference. And do you know what, Tsunami? I believe Gerard is going to ask me to sit for him! Rowland says he might – he says Gerard has always had an eye for the ladies. Though, if he did ask me,' she added, looking extremely coy, 'I – I don't know whether I would consent.'

'Oh, come off it, Auntie Moira! Of course you would!' Tsunami said.

'It might mean taking all your clothes off, Mrs Wijesinha,' Latha said, straight-faced. 'Are you willing to do that?'

'Well . . . he's a great painter . . . and in the interests of Art, I suppose I . . .'

A gleaming black limousine was waiting for them in the drive, with Alexander, smart in a dark blue uniform, at the wheel. His smile, as he caught sight of Tsunami and Latha, was warm, but he vouchsafed nothing beyond a respectful greeting. Latha inquired after his wife and son. They were in good health, Alexander replied, and said no more: it was evident that further conversation between her chauffeur and her guests would not be encouraged by the Minister's lady.

All the way from Peradeniya to Sapumalwatte, a rural hamlet near Kandy to which van Kuyk had apparently withdrawn to court his Muse, Moira Wijesinha talked of the painter, his career, and the close relationship that existed between the painter and herself.

'Gerard is so fond of me,' she said. 'People of artistic temperament can always sense a feeling for art in others, don't you think? And people with that kind of feeling must be as rare in a place like Sapumalwatte as rosebuds on a cactus. Besides, he's not only an artist, the man is a poet, a Sanskritist, a true intellectual. "Talk, Moira, talk," he said to me once; "I love to hear you talk while I'm painting!"'

Failing to see Latha's involuntary look of disbelief, Moira continued:

'And so one day, when it had become obvious to me that all this village cooking he is getting is ruining his health, I took the bull by the neck and offered Gerard the use of a little house we have in Guildford Crescent. Rent-free, of course. "Take it, Gerry, take it," I told him. "You can live there for as long as you like, and everything will be done for you. It's just round the corner from our place, you would be right in the middle of our very own neighbourhood!"'

In the pause that ensued as Moira was recovering her breath, Latha said composedly:

'How nice for him!'

'Yes. Of course, his living there would only enhance the area's reputation as the favourite haunt of artists and writers. Already, with Rowland and me in residence, and the Museum and the Art Gallery so close by, Michelle Feuillard said to me the other day that our neighbourhood is becoming a second Bloomsbury.'

In her effort to restrain her merriment at the thought of Moira 'taking the bull by the neck', Latha nearly missed her mention of Michelle Feuillard. It was quite some time since she had heard the name of her former French teacher. During that interval, it seemed, Madame Feuillard had progressed from tutoring Moira Wijesinha in French to becoming her intimate friend and confidante. It seemed that she shared Moira's devotion to art and music, accompanied her to art exhibitions and concerts when Rowland was unavailable, and advised on the menus for ministerial dinner parties. Above all, she shared Moira's passion for the paintings of Gerard van Kuyk – '*un artiste si spirituel*', Madame had declared – and by introducing his work to her diplomatic friends, she had helped his reputation to grow beyond all imagining.

In the years that had passed since Latha's meeting with van Kuyk at Lucas Falls, two books had been published on his work, and any number of articles had appeared in local and foreign magazines, all of them written by British and American art experts who vied with one another to pay homage to a great creative spirit. Van Kuyk had, it seemed, become a figure of international importance, and his rural retreat was now a kind of shrine, to which art-lovers and art-dealers came all the way from Europe and America to worship. As for Ceylon, Moira said, anyone who was anyone in Colombo – or hoped to be – had a van Kuyk painting, or two, or three, on their drawing-room wall.

'I have only one,' Moira told Latha and Tsunami. 'But then, I'm very choosy. I'd just bought a new carpet from Theo Jonklaas for the drawing room, and I wasn't going to have any pictures on my wall, or books on my book-shelves, that didn't match the colour of the carpet perfectly – and the settee and chairs, too, of course.'

Such restraint was not, it seemed, typical of Colombo's art-lovers. As Michelle Feuillard was fond of saying, most of the fashionable women who queued up to buy van Kuyk's paintings didn't care *what* they hung on their walls as long as it was recognizably from van Kuyk's brush and easel. They didn't mind the long journey they had to make in order to pay their respects to him, they tottered in their high-heeled shoes along the suspension bridge slung across a rapidly flowing river which connected the reclusive artist, serenely painting in his rustic surroundings, with the busy, sophisticated world of city life. That was because they hoped to bring back, in addition to paintings and drawings that would become the envy of their guests, an authentic story or two about the painter himself and his eccentricities that could provide a talking-point at cocktail parties.

The oddest of these eccentricities, Moira told the girls, as the ministerial car purred along the leafy roads outside the city of Kandy, was Ran Menikē. Had Latha heard of Ran Menikē? No? Well, that was not surprising. She was a nobody, a domestic servant, a Sinhalese woman who had been employed by Gerard and his wife as an ayah for their baby daughters. Gerard, believe it or not, had eloped with this young woman, who was obviously no better than she should be, and who couldn't, incidentally, speak two words of English, so goodness only knew how they had communicated, one could only guess . . . It had caused a great scandal, of course. In Colombo people talked of nothing else. Well, that was what had happened: leaving respectability and every moral consideration behind him, turning his back on civilized society, Gerard had made his home in Ran Menikē's village.

Where was that? At Sapumalwatte, where they were now going to visit him. In Sapumalwatte, as in all Kandyan villages, morality was of course completely unknown, so nobody had made a fuss.

'*Come, live with me and be my love,*' Latha said dreamily, half to herself. '*And we will all the pleasures prove that hills and valleys, dales and fields*—'

'What?' Moira didn't like being interrupted. 'What was that you said?'

'Nothing important,' Latha said hastily. 'Sorry.'

Intellectually and spiritually, of course, Menikē was far beneath Gerard, and it was a sad thing, an absolute *tragedy*, to think of this great artist marooned in a cultural desert with nobody to talk to about the things that interested him: poetry, the philosophy of art, its history, its techniques . . . Who was there in Sapumalwatte with whom he could commune on such matters? Nobody. Nobody at all. It was pitiful to see how eagerly he looked forward to Moira's visits, how regretful he was when duty called her back to Colombo.

She had often asked Gerry to take up permanent residence in Colombo. But Gerry, it seemed, was not yet ready for such a move. His roots were in the Kandyan district, he had told her – which was utter nonsense, he was a Burgher, after all, wasn't he? Whoever heard of Burghers putting down 'roots' among Sinhalese villagers! (Latha, remembering Paula Phillips, smiled to herself but said nothing.) Gerard had told Moira that he did not want to leave Ran Menikē and Sapumalwatte, which were the sources of his inspiration. And that was nonsense again, because what was there that a woman like Ran Menikē and a place like Sapumalwatte could possibly give Gerard that Moira – and Rowland, too, of course – could not provide?

Especially, Moira said earnestly, intellectual stimulation, and artistic inspiration. Drowning in a bucolic backwater like Sapumalwatte, Gerard had no idea of what was going on in the world's art centres, in New York, in Paris, in London. His painting revealed this lack very clearly by taking rural life as its only inspiration. Moira's friend Michelle Feuillard had warned that Gerard's horizons needed to be broadened for his own good and the good of his art. His genius needed stimulation, he needed to be put in touch with beautiful, vibrant young people who would inspire and invigorate him, he needed to be put in touch with a whole world of art and letters outside Sapumalwatte, indeed outside Ceylon itself. She, who counted some of the island's most attractive and intelligent young people among her students, and moreover, was familiar with the art centres of Europe, would advise Moira how she could introduce him into that world.

In Ran Menikē's village, Moira went on, Gerard had built himself a studio where he painted all day, stopping only when the light failed. He did nothing *but* paint. He did not, like other eminent artists, attend public functions, and was uninterested in giving interviews to journalists who would promote his reputation, or in meeting the dealers who were clamouring to set up outlets for his paintings. This was a great pity, because the time was exactly right for Gerard to establish himself as the great Asian genius that he was. He was quite willing (unlike Justin Deraniyagala, his nearest rival) to sell his paintings, but as he retained no agent to inform him as to the state of the market, the prices Gerard put on his paintings were often unrealistically low. Not that he should price them so high that only the gem merchants of Ratnapura or financial pirates from Canada or the U.S.A. would be able to afford them, no, but he should accept expert advice, and put his work on a proper business footing.

Michelle Feuillard's advice and Moira's blandishments had failed so far to lure Gerard to Colombo, so as the Art Gallery wanted to add some representative works by van Kuyk to its collection, a knowledgeable person had to be sent to meet the painter in his studio and negotiate a price.

Moira, it appeared, was the knowledgeable person on whom this responsibility had fallen.

The car slowed down, and slid to a stop beside a wayside stall on which fruit and vegetables were on display.

'Why are we stopping, Cassim?' Moira asked irritably.

'You told me you wanted to buy some fruit, Madam. As a present for Mr van Kuyk.'

'Oh . . .? Oh, yes.'

Moira lowered the car window and inspected the display through her dark glasses.

'Some of those mangoes, Cassim, some papaw, and a comb of plantains.'

'Van Kuyk *mahatthaya* has a great liking for curd, Madam. Shall I see if they have curd that is fresh today?'

While Alexander was making his purchases from the stall-keeper who was supervising the loading of the weighing scale, two young women came into view, walking towards them along the road. They were barefoot, and carried clay pots on their hips. On seeing Alexander, they giggled, glanced down self-consciously, looked up again, and went on their way. Occasionally, they turned their heads to look back at him.

'Just see how nicely village girls walk!' Moira said. 'And when they come back from the well with those pots full of water, they will be balancing them on their heads. It's so good for their figures. Not to mention their complexions and their general health – all that walking makes the sweat stream from their poreses, and flushes the whole system. But is it any good telling them so?'

There was no reply, and she continued:

'I'm on a committee working for Village Rehabilitation, and I can tell you that all we hear from the villagers from morning till night is a clamour for pipe-borne water. Why, they say, should we walk three times a day to the well for water, when in the towns all people need to do is to turn on a tap? We have children to look after, they say, meals to cook, and clothes to wash: can we be fetching water as well? I'm sorry to say our villagers are getting thoroughly spoiled, and all our traditional values are being destroyed . . .'

She paused, took a breath, and went on.

'Pipe-borne water, indeed! When Rowland went to the village we adopted just before the last by-election, he had to give his speech in a school hall because they didn't have a suitable place in which to welcome him. So the last time our committee took a vote on the matter, I voted against the installation of a water service in that village. Instead, we built a beautiful prayer-hall for *pirith* ceremonies which will double as a venue for public meetings. Some people criticized me, they said that clean water for our villagers is more important than *pirith* ceremonies and public meetings. I took no notice. At least, I felt, I've done my bit to preserve our ancient culture and keep our village women looking good.'

With Moira's purchases stowed in the boot of the car, they resumed their journey. Fifty yards along the track, as the car passed the girls with their clay pots, Alexander tooted the car horn gently twice, and Latha saw the girls wave at him and smile. She was about to say something when she felt Tsunami nudge her gently, and she remained silent. The city of Kandy was soon left behind, and they found themselves driving through a series of small villages fringed with coconut palms and edged with fields in which the rice stood lush and green. Sapumalwatte, Moira said, was one such village. It was now quite near, but to reach it they would have to cross a river by means of a suspension bridge.

'Cassim, you may park the car here, in the shade of these trees,' Moira said as they came to the riverbank and its bridge.

'Yes, Madam.'

'Once you have taken the fruit and the curd across to the house, you can get back to the car. Get yourself some lunch at that boutique over there, and wait for us. We should not be very long, but we'll need you when we return. You can see the other side of the bridge from here, so keep a lookout for Tsunami *hamu* while we're gone – she will wave to you from the other side if there is anything to be carried across. So make sure the boot is cleared: there may be some big pictures to take back to Colombo.'

'Very good, Madam.'

Alexander touched his peaked cap, and if he smiled to himself at Moira's imperious tone, he hid the smile very well.

'I have been told to remind you, Madam, that the Minister *hamuduruwo* has an appointment at Temple Trees in the evening. At six o'clock.'

'I'm aware of that. I shall be accompanying him.'

'Very good, Madam.'

Alexander parked the car as directed, escorted Moira and her nieces across the swaying bridge, then returned for Moira's gifts. Soon, with Alexander bringing up the rear, they were walking down a tiny street edged with small, well-tended houses, before the open entrances of some of which lace curtains had been hung in lieu of a front door. Each house had a small flower garden at the front, and a vegetable plot at the back, beyond which could be glimpsed trees heavy with limes, dhel and jak. It was a prosperous, well-kept, and friendly village. Women came out of their houses to stand in their doorways, comb their long hair, and smile pleasantly at the visitors passing by. Moira returned the smiles graciously, her hands folded in the traditional greeting. Latha had to concede that Tsunami's stepmother was performing her role of parliamentarian's wife admirably.

Gerard van Kuyk's neat, white-painted house stood in the midst of a small grove of coconut palms. Behind it paddy stood tall in the rice-fields. In the doorway of the house was a middle-aged Sinhalese woman dressed in a simple cotton osariya who smiled gently at them, and greeted Moira with folded hands.

'Please come in. He is waiting for you.'

Latha had formed an idea during the journey of what the painter's legendary lover would be like. Looking past the woman in the doorway, her eyes sought the siren who was doubtless reclining voluptuously in the room beyond. It took her a moment or two to realize that they had just been greeted by Ran Menikē herself. So this quietly spoken, hospitable, quite ordinary-looking woman, Latha thought with wonder, had been the girl at the centre of romance and scandal! This was the girl whose beauty glowed from canvases that were even now lighting up the walls of museums and living rooms from New York to Tokyo, the girl who had captured an artist's imagination and had carried him away with her from the city to live, Gauguin-like, in a world of simple rustic pleasures and amorous delight!

She longed to speak with Ran Menikē. Would her voice be soft and low, 'an excellent thing in woman'? How should the mistress of a genius be addressed? What would she say?

As it happened, there was no opportunity for Ran Menikē to say anything at all, even if she had wanted to, for Moira Wijesinha took command of the air-waves from the moment of her entrance into the house.

'So here I am at last, Gerry,' she called coyly, stopping outside a half-open door. 'Had you given me up for lost?'

17

PERSUASION

They entered a long, whitewashed room flooded with sunshine and light, its walls a kaleidoscope of colour.

At the far end of the room stood an easel, and from behind it strode Gerard van Kuyk, palette in hand, and looking very much as Latha remembered him. He put his painting materials down and came forward to greet his visitors, arms outstretched. He seemed glad to see them, Latha thought, but you could never tell. She took care to stand behind Tsunami and Moira, hoping by doing so to escape the painter's particular notice. He embraced Moira, and kissed her on both rouged cheeks before turning to the two girls and patting Tsunami's wrist in an avuncular manner.

'This ravishing young woman I know,' said he. 'But the other?'

'Guess, Gerry!' Moira said playfully. 'You've met her before.'

Van Kuyk looked Latha up and down, through spectacles that seemed even thicker than Latha remembered them, while Latha, for her part, wished that Tsunami had not told her stepmother the story of the autograph album.

Well, at least he's not kissing me – that's something to be grateful for!

She noticed a small stool by the door and sat down on it, thereby removing herself from the group surrounding the easel.

'Very appealing,' van Kuyk said at last, turning from his appraisal of Latha. 'It must have been a long time ago, or I could not have forgotten her.'

'Now, isn't that just like a man!' Moira said. 'Flatters a girl, and makes her think she's Sakuntala herself, and then forgets all about her, just like that!'

She snapped her fingers, and the tinkle of her laughter echoed in the long room.

Her words had sparked recognition in the painter's eyes.

'Not Sakuntala,' he said. 'No, it was not Sakuntala but Radha, wasn't it? At Lucas Falls? In Helen's time.'

The mention of Helen caused Moira to bridle somewhat, but she recovered her poise quickly, and continued to smile. It must happen all the time, Latha thought: she's probably used to it by now.

The gift of curd earned Gerard van Kuyk's warm approval.

'An auspicious present!' was his comment.

To Moira's solicitous hope that it would not be too rich for his digestion at that time of the day, he replied:

'But curd, Moira, is the king of desserts. And as you must surely know, there's always room for the king!'

But it seemed that Moira did *not* know. She said so, and the painter enlightened her.

'Sit down, Moira, and I will tell you a story . . . Long ago, in the time of the Kandyan kings, there lived a court jester and *bon vivant* whose name was Andarē . . .'

The story van Kuyk related was a folktale well known to Latha: she had heard it from an ayah who had looked after her as a child. Moira, it appeared, was hearing it for the first time.

Andarē, said van Kuyk, had arrived one day at the Kandyan court to call on the King, just as his royal patron's midday meal was drawing to a close.

'Stay, and have something to eat, Andarē,' the King had said to his favourite.

'No thank you, sire,' Andarē had replied, patting his stomach. 'My wife has just cooked me such a delicious meal that there is no room here for anything else.'

Just at this moment, the cooks brought in a pot of curd and a jar of honey.

'Wait a moment, wait a moment!' Andarē called as they were leaving, after they had served the King: 'What about me?'

'But you have told us all that there is no room in your stomach for any more food,' said the King.

'Ah, your Majesty,' replied the quick-witted jester, 'curd is the king of desserts, and there is always room for the King!'

'Is that so?' said the King. 'You will have to prove that statement, or the Royal Executioner will have your head!'

'No objection, your Majesty,' replied Andarē, 'but please let me finish my dessert first.'

Moira's veneer of sophistication seemed to have vanished completely. The painter told the story well, and she leaned forward eagerly, taking in every word.

'Do you think she really didn't know that story?' Tsunami asked Latha afterwards. 'Of course I didn't know it either, but then I heard my bedtime stories from Alice and Mummy, so I was up on Indian legends, stories from the *Ramayana* and so forth, Latha, while you, lucky thing, were absorbing Andarē tales at every pore. But I'm surprised that Auntie Moira, with her Kandyan background, and her interest in village life and village rehabilitation, et cetera, et cetera, hadn't heard it as a child, the way you did.'

Latha admitted that she, too, had wondered a little. Had Moira been feigning ignorance as a means of flattering van Kuyk?

'Dead right,' Tsunami replied. 'I think she's capable of anything to get what she wants.'

Feigned or not, there was no doubt that Moira's strategy was working: van Kuyk, delighted by his rapt audience, enacted every part of the tale.

'So Andarē called all the officials of the Court together, and asked them to enter an anteroom in the Palace. When they had all taken their places, he called the artists and craftsmen who were working in the Palace, the gardeners who were tending the flowers in the pleasure gardens, the cooks in the royal kitchens, the elephant keepers in the stables, everyone you can think of, and asked them to join the officials.

'"Any room left in there?" he cried.

'"No, Andarē!" they replied. "We're so crowded here that we can't even breathe!"

'"Very good!" said Andarē. He squeezed into the room himself, and with the greatest difficulty, pushing and shoving – like *this*! – he closed the door. And then, after a few minutes, the people in the room heard the sound of approaching *bera* outside. Dum-dada, dum-dada, dum-dada, dum-dada . . .

'"What's happening?" they cried.

'The sound of the drums grew louder, louder, louder, so loud that the people in the room were nearly deafened by the sound. At last the drums sounded outside the door, and with a final flourish, they stopped.

'"Here comes the King!" cried the royal heralds. "Make way for the King!"'

Moira's eyes were wide, and they were fixed on the storyteller.

'And then what happened?' she said. The tone of her voice was childlike, expectant.

'When they heard that the King was about to enter,' van Kuyk went on, 'everyone in the room, from the front rows to the back, shrank back a little out of respect. A little, a little, just a little, not very much because to step right back was impossible in that crush, and lo and behold! What did they find? *There was room for one more person in that packed and crowded room!*

'"You have proved your statement, Andarē," said the King to the jester, and gave him two villages to reward his wit.'

'Oh, what a truly wonderful story!' breathed Moira ecstatically. 'And how well you tell it, Gerry!'

'Flattery,' Tsunami whispered, 'gets Auntie Moira everywhere. There'll be no holding her now.'

Indeed, van Kuyk seemed quite as ready to receive flattery as his guest was willing to offer it. Taking advantage of his genial mood, Moira lost no time in reviewing the paintings that were leaning against the studio walls. She began her task of coaxing him to donate two – why not three? – large canvases as a personal gift to the Art Gallery.

'You are a national treasure, Gerry,' she said. 'Nothing less. You should be represented in our national collection by examples of your best work –'

It soon became evident that she had her eye on a particularly vivid painting in which a young woman, scantily draped in a crimson cloth, and seated on a swing, had placed a delicate foot in the hand of her dark-skinned lover so that he could adjust the bells on her anklet.

'You can't have that one, Moira,' van Kuyk said. 'I have a buyer for it already, a Fulbright professor from Dayton, Ohio.'

He laughed with mischievous glee.

'One wonders, does one not, what his friends and colleagues will make of it!'

He seemed immensely amused by the thought of one of his erotic paintings in a living room in the American mid-West. He seemed even more amused when his statement produced a vigorous complaint from Moira, about barbaric Americans who came out East and splashed their money about, buying up the country's priceless art treasures.

'What can a picture like this mean to him!' she said indignantly. 'What would he know of our culture? Why can't he find himself a pin-up picture of Betty Grable, instead of stealing our art? Because that's what it is: stealing.'

'No, it isn't,' van Kuyk replied. They had evidently had similar discussions before, and it was obvious that he enjoyed teasing Moira. 'The people who steal art works are people who hope to get them free.'

Doesn't she *see* that he's provoking her? Latha thought. Is she *totally* impervious to insult?

'Dr Whitehouse is an academic, on an academic's salary. He's no millionaire. But he's not an ignoramus, either. Whitehouse knows a good painting when he sees one, and he's prepared to pay for it. I'm an artist, Moira. I live by my brush. I appreciate his attitude. A very worthy man.'

'The trouble is that our people don't get a chance to see your paintings, when you keep them hidden out of sight in a miserable place like this, and show them only to foreigners.'

Moira pouted prettily.

'This is all such nonsense, hiding yourself away from everybody who can appreciate you. I know you believe that the only true life for an artist is a life lived away from the city, far from the maddening crowd—'

'By God, Moira, what a pleasure it is to hear Gray quoted out here in the wilderness! And quoted so accurately!'

'—but you're wrong, Gerry. If only you would accept our invitation, and come to Colombo . . .'

She broke off. Ran Menikē, who had accepted Moira's gifts from Alexander and taken them to the kitchen, had now returned. She brought with her a brass tray on which were arranged steaming cups of tea and a china plate piled high with pancakes that had been rolled and stuffed with sweet, spiced *panipol*.

'Girls, why don't you come over here and have something to eat,' van Kuyk called. 'This has been made especially for you.'

But Tsunami, at the far end of the studio, had discovered a picture of a small boy with a catapult which had caused her just then to exclaim with pleasure. Moira, remaining seated, gave Ran Menikē an order.

'Take the tray over there to Tsunami *hamu*,' she said in Sinhala, 'or her tea will get cold.'

Latha heard the command, and the tone in which it was delivered. She grew hot with embarrassment.

Once a servant, always a servant, I'll bet that's how Moira Wijesinha sees it.

Returning to the table herself, she took a pancake from the tray.

'Delicious,' she said, and then, speaking directly to Ran Menikē:

'Thank you.'

Her thanks were acknowledged simply, with a gentle smile. There was no trace on Ran Menikē's face of annoyance or resentment at the casual way in which Moira had treated her.

'That's my son Sanjiv,' she heard van Kuyk saying to Tsunami. He had noticed nothing of what had just passed.

'I plan to match it with a picture I painted years ago – I have it somewhere, I've just got to find it – of a boy flying a kite.'

'I'm sure I know the picture you mean, Uncle Gerry,' Tsunami said. 'And if you want to know where it is, I can tell you. It's hanging at Lucas Falls. In the hall, near the stairs.'

'Of course! That was where I last saw it. I remember now that Rowley bought it at my first exhibition. Well, Tsunami, you can tell your father he can have this one too' – he smiled wickedly – 'but at a price. These things have trebled in value, you know. Art must be paid for.'

Moira seemed anxious to change the subject. The boy with the catapult was dismissed without further ado.

'I wish,' she said petulantly, 'you would employ an agent, Gerry, to handle the business side of your life. An artist shouldn't hawk his own work. It isn't . . . nice.'

'Don't I know it!' Van Kuyk spoke with feeling. 'But whom can I trust? Any one of those dealers in Colombo who write letters to me every week would take a fat commission every time they make a sale. No, I'll have none of that. I sell a painting when I need the money: to repair the roof, to pay my doctor's bills, to put food on the table . . .'

'But, *Gerry*—'

'It may not be "nice" to say so, Moira, but that's the truth. We don't have the right kind of organization in this country to protect an artist's work. I have given away too many paintings in the past for nothing: I'm told they're fetching high prices in Colombo.'

He paused, and turned away.

'You won't get anything out of me without paying for it.'

'Now, now, Gerry, I didn't come all this way to "get something out of you",' Moira said patiently. 'I came out of admiration. I came out of respect. Respect for the king, like the courtiers in your story . . .'

Their argument, which seemed often on the brink of degenerating into a slanging match, ended half an hour later. Moira had succeeded in persuading the artist to accept half his originally quoted price for three very striking canvases. Examining the paintings she had selected, Latha had to agree with Tsunami's judgment that Moira had come a long way since Rowland had introduced her at Lucas Falls to the ballet dancers of De Gass. Gerard van Kuyk did not look pleased, but, as Tsunami told Latha later, he probably had no energy left to protest.

'I told you, Latha, she has that effect on people,' Tsunami said, as Moira clicked open her handbag, took out a cheque-book, and wrote out a cheque. 'She has that effect on *me*. After a bit, you ask yourself: what's the point? Is it worth it? And then you give up, give in, and let her have her way.'

'She *hasn't* had her way,' Latha whispered back. 'She wanted to get them free, and he hasn't let her.'

'Only because he's as bloody-minded as she is,' Tsunami said. 'Sorry to destroy your illusions, Latha! He's an artist and a great creative genius, and all that, but he knows his own worth. Auntie Moira tries to make out that he needs expert advice on pricing, but he's done all right by himself so far. The problem is that he hasn't a clue about investing money. Auntie Moira, on the other hand, knows exactly what those three paintings would fetch if they were sold in Colombo, and what should be done with the money. The price she's paying is nothing compared to what they're worth, and she's pleased as punch that she's got such a bargain for the Art Gallery. *If* they're for the Gallery . . .'

Moira, while making her farewells, repeated her invitation to van Kuyk.

'We look forward to seeing you in Colombo, Gerry,' she said. 'I am *sure* you will be coming to us soon.'

'Why don't *you* come up to Kandy, and set up as an art dealer, Moira,' van Kuyk responded acidly, folding up the cheque she had handed him, and putting it in the pocket of his embroidered cotton *kurta*. '*You* have a talent for it. A little art shop near the *Daladā Maligāwa* would be just the thing, wouldn't it? You could sell my pictures to tourists, along with brassware and lacquered cigarette boxes – and get, I hope, better prices than you gave me today.'

'Oh, Gerry!' trilled Moira joyfully.

Doesn't she see how annoyed he is?

'What a compliment! And I thought you'd never ask!'

III

Children of the future age,
Reading this indignant page:
Know that in a former time
Love! sweet love! was thought a crime.

William Blake, 'A Little Girl Lost' (1794)

What is love? 'Tis not hereafter;
Present mirth hath present laughter.
What's to come is still unsure.
In delay there lies no plenty,
Then come kiss me, sweet and twenty.
Youth's a stuff will not endure.

William Shakespeare, *Twelfth Night*, Act II, Scene III

1

L'AFFAIRE MANAMPERI

'Dearest Thaththi. Stop. Something terrible is happening here. Stop. Tsunami and I need your advice. Stop. Can you please come up to Peradeniya right away. Stop. Best make the trip by car. Stop. If not possible please send a telegram re your arrival time. Stop. Will meet you at New Peradeniya Station. Stop. Love Latha.'

Herbert had 'made the trip' in his car, cogitating furiously all the way as to what could have made Latha send him such an urgent telegram. The 'something terrible' sounded personal, unconnected with the academic problems about which she had written him a letter ten days ago, and which, he thought guiltily, he had still to answer. Well, it must be personal, or why should his daughter and his niece consult him? The telegram sounded, he thought, like an S.O.S. Recalling his wife's fears about the dangers to young women of life on a residential campus, Herbert feared the worst. Had Tsunami . . .? Had Latha . . .? Usually adventurous in his thinking if not in his actions, he actually feared to go further.

'Not in the Common Room, Uncle Herbert! Let's go somewhere outside, where we can talk without being overheard,' Tsunami said firmly, as soon as he had arrived at Sanghamitta Hall and the two girls had answered the usual summons of 'Latha Wijesinha! Tsunami Wijesinha! A visitor for you-ou-ou!'

Herbert inspected them both closely, but could find nothing amiss. Tsunami, he was pleased to see, seemed perfectly healthy, and was certainly as pretty as ever. Latha, though she seemed worried and anxious, was clearly in what Herbert regarded as her 'usual form'. Well, if it wasn't a sudden, steep deterioration in the health of one or the other, what could possibly be the problem?

Over lunch in a secluded corner of the Peradeniya Rest House – no time, Latha said, for lunch at the Queen's, and anyway, neither of them had any appetite – Herbert heard the story of what he was always to remember as *L'Affaire Manamperi*.

Yesterday afternoon, Tsunami told him, she had walked up the hill opposite Sanghamitta, to lunch with a classmate resident at James Peries Hall, and had witnessed an extraordinary scene. The refectory had been filled with students, talking and laughing as usual, when the Warden walked into the room, and stepped up to the dais. With her was the student she had identified to Latha and herself the previous year as a rural student of inferior caste, a young woman Tsunami had perceived to be totally blind. That blindness, formerly evident only to a careful observer, was now very obvious as she held on to tables and benches on her way up to the dais, and stumbled up the steps she could not see.

'Silence!'

At the sound of Mrs Lobelia Raptor's voice, everyone in the refectory stopped talking. Late-comers tiptoed in and took their places at the tables, careful not to let a book fall or a bench scrape on the floor.

'I want you to look at this student,' the Warden had boomed, pushing the blind girl sideways until she was standing in the centre of the long platform.

'This is Padma Manamperi. I want you all to look at her closely. Up to this day she has been one of you, a member of this Hall, receiving opportunities for social and intellectual advancement that would have raised her high above her lowly origins. From today she is an outcast, an outsider to our life and activities here. She has brought this situation about – Manamperi! Stand up straight! – through her own wickedness and low breeding. This young woman has disgraced herself and our University. She has brought shame upon our religion and our nation. Do you want to know what she has done? I will tell you. She is pregnant.'

A muffled exclamation swept the refectory. The Warden looked pleased with the effect her words appeared to be having. She raised her hand for silence, and resumed:

'And she has had the impudence to seek medical help for her condition from the University's own clinic! Naturally the Medical Officer, who is a highly respectable family man, brought the matter to my attention at once, and I have taken action. You will all be relieved to know that she will not remain here much longer to contaminate our Hall with her immorality, and ruin our reputation for good and virtuous conduct. She has been expelled from James Peries, and will shortly be expelled from this campus, the only student to have been punished in this way since the inception of the University. I have sent a telegram to her parents, informing them of their daughter's disgraceful behaviour. I have ordered them to come here from their village immediately, and remove her from this Hall. She will remain in her own room, under lock and key, until they arrive. No member of this Hall is to visit Padma Manamperi, speak to her, or encourage her wrong-doing in any other way. I trust I have made myself quite clear.'

Having delivered this speech at the top of her voice, Mrs Raptor had gripped the student by her elbow, and walked her to her room on the second floor, scolding her all the way.

'It couldn't have been worse,' Tsunami added, 'if Padma had been handcuffed.'

'Didn't she defend herself against these charges?'

'She didn't say a single word. Just stood there. But she didn't cry.'

'Perhaps she had no tears left,' Latha suggested.

'Where is she now?' Herbert asked.

'In her room at James Peries. I checked, just before we came here. It will be some time before her parents arrive. The village is far away, apparently, and they wouldn't be able to afford train tickets. They'll be on a bus.'

'I suppose, Latha, that you wired me because you both think I can do something about this,' Herbert said.

'Well, can you, Thaththi?' Latha's appeal carried an urgency that Herbert found hard to withstand. 'You know so many people,' she added, 'maybe you know someone who can help?'

'I spoke to Pater and to Auntie Moira on the phone last night,' Tsunami said. Her voice was devoid of expression.

'I'd thought Auntie Moira might be able to talk Mrs Raptor round. She knows her quite well – they're on a couple of committees together. But Auntie Moira told me that she couldn't possibly come up to Peradeniya for such a trivial matter. She said that a senior minister in the Cabinet had passed away last night, and she had an appointment with the hairdresser today because she and Pater had to ride in the motorcade at the funeral tomorrow. Pater came to the phone, too. He said the Minister's death may involve a reshuffle of ministries, so he has to be in Colombo or he may miss out on the post he wants.'

'The point is, Thaththi, whatever we do will need to be done quickly and very quietly,' Latha said. 'The James Peries students will gossip, of course, but as long as the University doesn't support Mrs Raptor in making a public spectacle of Padma, the gossip will be short-lived. She could perhaps leave Peradeniya, and then apply for re-admission in a year or two. We thought of asking Dr Springdale to intervene, but we're not sure Dr Springdale could possibly take on Mrs Raptor – she's too gentle and civilized, Mrs Raptor would simply walk all over her.'

'There are one or two members of the teaching staff we could have asked to talk to Mrs Raptor,' Tsunami said. 'But they're both on leave, and anyway, they're only tutors. Mrs Raptor's sure to pull rank if she's challenged.'

'Hold on,' Herbert said. 'Wait a minute. Who's your Vice-Chancellor? Isn't it Eustace Pereira? He'll be the one who makes the final decision.'

He reflected a moment, then asked:

'Where's the Department of Engineering?'

Late that same afternoon, an ancient Ford came chugging up Peries Hill with two people in it. At the wheel was Dr E.O.E. Pereira, Professor of Engineering and Vice-Chancellor of the University of Ceylon. A man of simple habits and unostentatious tastes, Professor Pereira kept no chauffeur and did not use a university vehicle. His own little car was well known on campus: it was much loved by his Engineering students, who had frequently conducted their experiments on it, and declared it to be held together only by a combination of putty, string, and their Professor's engineering skills. Mrs Pereira, hijacked for the afternoon by Professor Pereira's cricketing classmate Herbert Wijesinha, was in the passenger seat.

Mrs Raptor had been informed that she was about to receive a visit from the Vice-Chancellor. She had had her binoculars trained on the road leading from the Lodge, and when the Pereiras arrived she was standing at the Hall entrance to receive them.

'Welcome, welcome, Vice-Chancellor!' bellowed Mrs Raptor jovially. 'You do us a great honour.'

'Good afternoon, Lobelia.'

Eustace Pereira disentangled his lanky body from the little car, and inclined his head in his customary courtly manner.

'I understand you've had a spot of bother in your Hall.'

Mrs Raptor put both hands to her head in a gesture expressive of sorrow and despair.

A spot of bother?

Unspeakable deceptions had been visited on her Hall by students who were walking incarnations of Lust and Immorality, students who were showing no signs of repentance or remorse. Professor Pereira listened patiently to her litany of accusations. He nodded from time to time as the Warden described the wrongs she had suffered.

'I see,' he said at intervals. 'Yes, I quite understand. It has been a difficult time for you. Yes, yes indeed. Yes. With a little time and good will, Lobelia, we should be able to solve this problem . . .'

When the Warden ran out of breath, he made a request.

'Now, Lobelia! I would like, if I may, to see this student, Miss – er – Manamperi, is it? I would like, with your permission, to speak to Miss Manamperi.'

'Certainly,' said Mrs Raptor. 'I will take you to see her immediately. Spare no words when you talk to her, Vice-Chancellor! Perhaps this visit of yours will teach the wretch to see the error of her ways.'

She waddled up the staircase with Professor Pereira in tow. Their progress was watched with interest by the Hall students, who were crowding the upper landings and hanging over the banisters. As she went past them, she delivered a warning:

'Let this be a lesson to you, too!'

Unlocking a door, she flung it open. On an unmade bed, Padma Manamperi sat motionless, her blind eyes turned towards the open window.

'Stand up, Manamperi! Stand up immediately!' barked Mrs Raptor. 'The Vice-Chancellor has come to see for himself this student who has disgraced the University's good name . . .'

Padma rose to her feet, and turned in the direction of her interrogator's voice.

'Miss Manamperi,' said Professor Pereira gently. 'I know your name, but you don't know mine. Let me introduce myself to you. I am Eustace Pereira, Vice-Chancellor of this University. I understand from what Mrs Raptor has told me that you are preparing to leave the campus.'

His understanding was instantly corrected by the Warden:

'She has been *expelled*, Vice-Chancellor! Let there be no doubt about that!'

Eustace Pereira ignored the interruption.

'I understand,' he went on, 'that your parents have been contacted, and that they are coming to Peradeniya to take you home. It's unlikely, I think, that they will get here before tonight, so I would like to invite you to wait for them at the University Lodge, as the guest of my wife and myself. My wife is here. She is downstairs, in the car. If you are agreeable to my suggestion, Mrs Pereira will come up here to your room, and with the help of some of your friends, she will be happy to pack a suitcase for you. The rest of your things can be sent on later to the Lodge.'

Padma Manamperi dropped to the floor without a word, and attempted to place her forehead on Professor Pereira's instep.

'Now, now, you don't need to do that, my dear,' he said hastily. 'It really isn't necessary.'

He raised her up, tucked her arm under his, and escorted her down the stairs.

According to some students who had stood spellbound in the doorway while this was going on and who now made way for Professor Pereira and Padma Manamperi to pass, Mrs Raptor's jaw had dropped open at the Vice-Chancellor's words, and had had some difficulty readjusting itself. Tsunami was among the eager listeners to whom the same witnesses described later developments at the Hall. Padma's parents had arrived at Peries Hall late that evening in a distressed and distracted state. The Warden was unable to see them, having retired to her quarters with a headache, and they were directed by a Hall servant to the University Lodge. Herbert

Wijesinha, who had been invited to dine that night at the Lodge, was present when they arrived there.

Herbert had stayed overnight at the Rest House, and was able to bring Latha and Tsunami up to date on subsequent events over lunch the following day.

'Waiting in a locked room for your parents to come and take you away in disgrace is a very different thing,' said Herbert, 'from having them visit you at the University Lodge and be treated by the V.C. and his wife to tea, cake and cucumber sandwiches. I'm sure Padma Manamperi, poor child, found it so. Eustace carried off the thing perfectly, of course. Being a Burgher, he isn't accustomed to the common politenesses of our people, so he was a little embarrassed by the girl's way of showing her gratitude. But, quite instinctively, he did the right thing. And he wasn't putting on a show, you know, courtesy comes naturally to Eustace—'

'He's a hero!' exulted Latha. 'And so are you! Oh, Thaththi, how ever did you think of it?'

'I didn't "think" of it, I just remembered a news item I'd read in a paper last week, and acted on it. I hoped it would work. I'm glad it did.'

'I wish I could say, Miss Wijesinha, that they were in high spirits when they left,' the Vice-Chancellor told Latha when he met her at a Hall function later that week. 'But it wasn't the kind of situation that encourages high spirits. However, Miss Manamperi summoned up a smile, and thanked my wife as she went away, and we made a point of telling her parents that we hoped there would be no recriminations and scoldings on the way home. I don't know whether she knows how much she owes to your resourcefulness and concern. When she learns of it – and I shall make sure she does – she will be very grateful.'

Eustace didn't mention it to you, wrote Herbert from Colombo, when the dust had settled on *L'Affaire Manamperi*, and life for Latha and Tsunami had resumed its normal course,

> *but he's contacted the baby's father. He's a Peradeniya student, a naïve young fellow, the pair of them seem to have been unaware of the existence of such a thing as birth control. Or perhaps they had no access to it. Anyway, Eustace has made it clear to the lad that in the child's interests an early marriage will have to take place. On that will depend the young man's being allowed to remain on campus, and his wife's re-admission next year – to another hall of residence, of course. If he fails to face up to his responsibilities, he won't be able to sit the examination, and he'll get no degree. Strong-arm tactics, you will doubtless say, but necessary in my opinion. And undertaken in* caritas, *not in the spirit of the Warden of James Peries Hall . . .*

A happy ending to that little adventure, Herbert thought with satisfaction as he folded his letter to Latha and put it in an envelope. He was glad that he had been able to bring such an ending about, but was disturbed at the same time to consider how large a part chance had played in the turn of events. Chance had taken Tsunami to Peries Hall on that particular day. Chance had suggested to Latha that her father might be able to help. Chance, operating through shared schooldays and a mutual love of cricket, had made Eustace Pereira, scholar and gentleman, his friend. A chance glance at a newspaper had brought him crucial information regarding the identity of a Vice-Chancellor. And chance, nothing but chance, had ensured that the Pereiras were at the Lodge that weekend, and not at their son's up-country estate.

And, while on the subject of chance—

If Latha and Tsunami had not concerned themselves in the affair, and made that unfortunate girl's problems their own – which they need not have done, after all – she'd have been thrown to the wolves, punished for her naïveté and her ignorance. That Warden of hers would have personally seen to it that she was made to suffer . . .

Herbert paused to reflect for a moment on the frequency with which bullies like Lobelia Raptor seemed to pop up in public life these days, and the rarity in it of Eustace Pereiras. He was aware, like all readers of the daily papers, that many young women in Padma Manamperi's particular situation, driven to desperation by fear and shame, and depressed by being insulted at every moment by neighbours and family members, killed themselves by swallowing insecticide, weed-killer or acid, or by eating poisonous herbs.

And by other, simpler, means of self-destruction . . .

Herbert remembered Eustace's description of his meeting with Padma Manamperi at Peries Hall. She had been seated alone and unsupervised beside an open second-floor window, gazing out into a void she could not see, with nothing to look forward to but punishment and lifelong social disgrace.

'. . . And deprived by that monstrous woman,' Herbert said angrily to himself, 'of anyone to keep her company, to counsel or to sympathize.'

A dim memory tugged at his brain, of an anecdote of Rowland's about an Englishwoman he had known, a Governor's lady, who, years ago, had made a despairing leap into space. Back in the 1930s, it must have been, when Rowland had been an A.D.C. at Government House . . .

No one had been around to save *her*.

Herbert suddenly felt very proud: not so much of the part he had himself played in *L'Affaire Manamperi* (though that, he knew, would always give him satisfaction), but of Latha and Tsunami, the concern they had evinced for a young woman of a different community and unfamiliar background, the speed with which they had acted in her interests, and the discretion they had shown in a matter of confidentiality. He wondered what the future held in store for these two interesting young women, and hoped, with a rush of love for them both of which he had not known himself capable, that it would be equal to their deserving.

He stamped his letter, and placed it on the hall table, ready for posting. He had not yet answered the questions Latha had put to him about her problems in class. He would answer them in his next letter.

Or, maybe not.

More or less in the spirit in which he had placed his largest reference books on the lowest shelf of his library when Latha was a child, Herbert decided that they were questions to which it was probably best that she discovered answers for herself.

2

TUTORIAL

The tutorial rooms of Peradeniya's History Department are located on the second floor of the Arts Building. There are four such rooms in all, placed side by side along a corridor which sometimes becomes so noisy between classes that their solid wooden doors act as welcome mufflers of the sounds of hurrying feet and students' chatter. In the middle of each wooden door is set an elongated glass pane: a useful innovation which, though it denies privacy to a tutor who wishes to smoke a cigarette or otherwise relax, alerts him to the presence of students waiting in the corridor outside. He is able then to bring his discussion to a smooth close, rather than let the bell break in upon his train of thought.

The tutor whom the glass pane of Tutorial Room Two revealed to Tsunami's third-year History Honours class was a stranger. They had expected that their History tutor in their third year would be either tubby, genial Mr Justin LaBrooy or white-cassocked Father Ignatius Pinto, both of whom had taught them in their first and second years. But here was someone they had never seen on campus before – tall, broad-shouldered and richly dark of skin. His long legs, encased in belted blue jeans and ending in a pair of leather boots, were hoisted up on his desk.

'An American cowboy!' Tsunami whispered to Shirani Pathirana on first sighting the jeans and the boots.

And indeed, to glimpse a holster in their tutor's leather belt, or a silver star on his checked flannel shirt would not have surprised either of them. His deep-voiced drawl, too, when it rolled out a resonant 'Good morning!' to the class (for he swung his legs off the desk and clicked the door open as soon as he became aware that he was being observed), seemed to come straight out of a Western movie.

Dr Girishna Daniel Rajaratnam was, however, no new recruit to Peradeniya. Certainly, his doctorate (from Columbia University) was shiny and new, as fresh as his Fifth Avenue gear, and as American as his accent, so that it would have been easy to suppose him American-born as well as

American-educated. But though his students were unaware of it, the traditions in which their new tutor had been reared were those of Ceylon's ancient north, his home town was Jaffna, not Texas, and the sun that had burned his gleaming skin was the very same that shone more mildly on Peradeniya, and not some alien star. Dr Rajaratnam's family, one of the oldest and most conservative in the Jaffna peninsula, celebrated Thai Pongal in January and Deepavali in October in the traditional Hindu manner, with prayers and lights and feasting, but it had been quick to recognize the wisdom of sending its sons to the region's American missionary schools. There Daniel and his two older brothers, while successfully evading conversion to Christianity, had taken with enthusiasm to the life of the mind.

'An extremely gifted student with the potential to become an outstanding teacher.'

This had been the verdict of the headmaster of Jaffna College, on the youngest Rajaratnam to pass through his venerable institution.

'Have you considered an academic career for him, sir, in America?'

The idea had not previously occurred to Rajaratnam senior, but the more he thought about it the more he liked it. With this new objective in view, and entirely on the headmaster's advice, the lad had been sent to the University of Ceylon at Peradeniya rather than to Madras University, which would otherwise have been the family's first choice. (Both Girishna's older brothers had been sent to university colleges in India, where they had done very well: their graduation photographs, followed in due time by wedding pictures of the two young men with garlanded and bejewelled brides beside them, were among the family photographs on display in the Rajaratnam home.)

According to the headmaster, however, the world of education was changing its focus. The University of Ceylon, although still a comparatively youthful institution, was attracting to the staff of its Peradeniya campus some of the best brains in the world and was fast developing into the finest University in Asia. A good degree from Peradeniya, the headmaster had added, bringing to the subject all the authority of forty years' teaching experience on two continents, would provide Girishna with an instant passport to the multitudinous possibilities available in the West.

This was not at all what Girishna's father had wanted to hear. A 'Jaffna man' to the core of his conservative being, Rajaratnam senior distrusted and frankly despised the south (which he considered lax) and its majority community the Sinhalese, whom he considered decadent in their ways. He had, however, enormous respect for the headmaster of Jaffna College, whom he regarded (despite his American origins, for which he could not, after all, be held responsible) as a pundit in the time-honoured Indian tradition. He had bestowed the headmaster's surname on his youngest son; and in the end it was the headmaster's opinion that had carried the day.

'I am doing this against my better judgment, Sarojini,' he had told his wife on the day the decision had been made. 'I did not like to say it to Dr Daniel's face, but we named our son better than we knew at the time: truly, we are sending poor Girishna into the lions' den.'

Mrs Rajaratnam had soothed her husband's anxieties as best as she could, and calmed her own by offering puja to the goddess Saraswati before the image in the household shrine-room. She had also made a private vow on Girishna's behalf, using the traditional seven oil lamps of brass for *aalathi*, at the family temple. Name? What harm could come of a mere Christian name, especially when any malevolent effects it might have had over her son would be immediately dispelled by the stronger influence of his Hindu one? Did not Krishna, her son's namesake and his personal deity, vanquish his enemies, and dance in triumph on the serpents' heads? Good would overcome evil, she was certain of that. No harm would come to Girishna in the south: she was certain of that, too.

Events had proved her right. Her son acquitted himself with distinction at Peradeniya, winning the coveted Emerson Tennent Medal for History in his final year, and left for the United States where all his headmaster's predictions had been gratifyingly fulfilled.

And now he had returned to Ceylon in a golden glow of academic triumph and family approbation. Girishna's parents had received news of his brilliant successes abroad with satisfaction and pride. They were overjoyed to have him back again with his Ph.D. certificate in his briefcase; and if their son's American persona startled them a little – 'Call me Daniel,' he had said, on being greeted by an elder of the family, and had shaken the astonished old gentleman's hand instead of bowing down to the ground before him as he should have done – they did not tell him so. The Rajaratnams were practical people, and they would see to it that 'Daniel' was fixed up as soon as could be managed with a suitably dowried wife from a Jaffna family as much like their own as possible. And although, as his mother said sadly, it would mean resigning themselves to the inevitability of grandchildren with Yankee accents and uncivilized American values, they were even prepared to have him leave again in a few years' time for an academic career abroad.

As for Daniel himself, five years in America had turned a shy, gangling youth into a confident and personable man. He was pleased that his success had justified the money his parents had spent to send him to the United States and keep him there during his years of graduate study, and proud to know that his achievements had increased his family's status and reputation. He was aware, naturally, of his parents' long-term plans for him, for they made no secret of them: his was a mapped and charted destiny, set about with duties and responsibilities that could not be avoided by the son of an old and distinguished family.

Daniel had no objection to that. Indeed, he was rather glad of it: the existence of a higher plan seemed to give shape and purpose to what he suspected might otherwise quite easily become a purposeless, and even somewhat raffish life.

Daniel had developed a taste for Western ways of living during his years in the United States, and had discovered also that he was attractive to women. There was a strong streak of sentimentality in his make-up, too, which his father would certainly have regarded as a weakness, and which he therefore tried not to show. But his very presence in Peradeniya was evidence of it, for a return to teach in a small ex-colonial country like Ceylon was hardly a move that was likely to advance his career in America.

That return had been prompted by nostalgia for the University that had launched him into academe. At Peradeniya Daniel had experienced, for the first time in his life, a heady sensation of freedom. Although the Sinhalese people of southern and central Ceylon are jealously watchful of the reputation and good name of their daughters, they are much more tolerant when it comes to the conduct of their sons. The relaxed lifestyle and social flexibility of the south had been a revelation to the young Rajaratnam, who had been brought up under the strict supervision of an austere parental eye. And during his years in exile, amid the daytime frenzy of New York traffic, and on evenings shattered by the piercing whine of police sirens, it was not of sun-baked Jaffna and the peninsula's dry and arid climate that he had dreamed, but of the ease with which he had made friends among his fellow-students at University, both men and women; and beyond that, of Peradeniya's lush landscapes and fragrant, moonlit nights.

'Just one more year, that's all I need,' Daniel had told Dr Joan Springdale, Warden of Sanghamitta Hall, his parents' old friend. 'One more year in paradise. I can live on it for the rest of my life.'

He knew that his parents regarded his Peradeniya appointment as entirely temporary. So, he believed, did he.

Daniel's students knew nothing, of course, either of their tutor's family background or of the conflicting impulses in his nature. They responded enthusiastically to his exotic appearance and also to the impact of his informal 'Yankee' teaching style, which was very different indeed from that of the sedate, elderly gentlemen they had so far encountered on the Peradeniya staff. Daniel's academic reputation, which was soon generally known on campus, gave him additional glamour in their eyes. Here at last, said the men, was a role model worth having.

As for the women – especially the Tamil girls – in his classes, their new History tutor was young and unmarried; and although he was by no means conventionally handsome, even the least susceptible among them immediately recognized that Dr Rajaratnam exuded a potent personal magnetism which was impossible to ignore.

Tsunami certainly did not – could not – ignore it. Though all around her, as Latha had noted while reflecting on her own situation, Peradeniya students were falling enthusiastically in love, Tsunami's general attitude towards the men of her acquaintance had hitherto been one of polite, but quite genuine, indifference. Her striking good looks had ensured that she was attended throughout her first and second years at University by a train of humble worshippers. Attracting admiration on all sides, she had had no experience herself of sexual attraction.

The sensations that now overwhelmed her in Rajaratnam's intensely masculine presence came as a complete surprise. Not that the expression on her face gave anything away, to her new tutor, to her classmate Shirani, or to anyone else. She sat through his first tutorial with her Honours class without taking in a single word Rajaratnam was saying, and when the hour ended she took up her books and walked away without a backward glance.

'Anything wrong, Tsunami?' Latha inquired that afternoon, seeing her cousin staring blankly into empty space.

She could not guess that the space was not empty at all, but filled to capacity by the vibrant personality of the new History tutor. As far as Latha knew, there had been only one love in Tsunami's life up to that time: Ronald Colman who, though only five years younger than her father, had captured her cousin's heart in the darkness of the Himalaya, the old, bug-ridden cinema at Lucas Falls, where she had seen him play Sidney Carton in A *Tale of Two Cities*.

'Nothing's wrong,' Tsunami answered. 'The sun was very hot this afternoon, that's all. I seem to have some sort of a headache.'

'You'd have been welcome to borrow my sunshade,' Amali said. 'I don't have any afternoon classes, so I hardly use it.'

'I've got some Aspro tablets in my room,' Latha said. 'Give me a minute, and I'll go and fetch them.'

The last thing any of her friends would have suspected was that love had entered Tsunami's life.

'Love?' she had said once to Amali, Latha and Sriyani during one of their conversations on the balcony. 'It's just a figment of women's imagination. Men are put into this world to be walked on. Useful objects, occasionally well made, sometimes quite good to look at, but essentially carpet-like; and, like carpets, woolly around the edges. Do you fancy falling in love with a carpet? I don't.'

She had got into the habit of making statements of this kind, partly in order to reassure her father and her stepmother, who, like Latha's mother and aunts, tended to become restive when unknown young men drifted into her orbit at Peradeniya, and partly to impress or shock her friends. (Amali, for instance, was easily shocked.) Aware, too, of the campus tendency to gossip, Tsunami had decided early that one sure way to escape becoming a target for insinuations herself was to cultivate a reputation for remoteness. Better to be thought snobbish, she decided, than 'man-mad': there seemed to be no middle way.

If this is love, Tsunami now said to herself, it's not very comfortable.

As the days passed, she discovered that love, besides being uncomfortable, was not conducive to concentrated study. The young woman who had, until a fortnight before, regarded the men of her limited acquaintance with a severely critical eye which no gaucherie ever escaped, now sat in the University Library and gazed at the pages of reference books without seeing them, counting the hours that must pass before she once again entered Dr Rajaratnam's tutorial room.

When, in the week following, she did so, she happened to arrive a few minutes late, due to a last-minute and quite uncharacteristic impulse she had had to exchange the sari she was wearing for a prettier one. Her new tutor was not, on that day, in a particularly good temper: Daniel Rajaratnam had been disappointed by Peradeniya students' reaction – or lack of reaction – to his first lecture.

'Any questions?' he had inquired hopefully at the end of it, and had been answered with pleasant smiles . . . and a mystifying silence.

How different from his American students' response to the same ideas, he'd reflected wistfully. At Columbia he had been besieged at the end of the very same lecture with eager questions about *karma*, *samsara*, and the seeming absence in the Buddhist psyche of any sense of guilt. This last had been especially puzzling to students from the American mid-West, who could not understand how a system of morality could possibly exist without an acute sense of moral wrong-doing. Perhaps, Daniel thought, the silence that had met his explanations here last week had been brought on by shyness. He hoped his second lecture would have better results.

He was ten minutes into his lecture when the door opened.

'Excuse me, please,' said a clear, soft voice. 'I'm sorry I'm late.'

Daniel, who disliked being interrupted in the middle of a class when he was trying to concentrate, nodded irritably, his eyes on his notes.

'S'okay,' he said. 'Sit down.'

Barely glancing at the student who had come in late, he waved her into a seat. She found that the tutor was deftly 'recapping' the main points of the previous week's lecture. Of this Tsunami who, it may be remembered, had been lost in a dream of love while he was delivering it, had made no notes. She now paid close attention to what he was saying, and discovered that the lecture had been on the subject of rebirth: the first of four lectures

Dr Rajaratnam planned to give, which were to focus on philosophical concepts that had shaped the civilization of ancient India.

'Got all that? Fine,' said Daniel, closing the books, as it were, on the subject of rebirth. 'Let us now move on to a second set of philosophical concepts that governed the outlook of India's "Golden Age": in this case not so much of Buddhists, but of Hindus, ancient and modern. For you will find, if you ask your Hindu friends on campus how they think their lives will develop, that they will draw you a diagram in four parts, which exactly resembles the picture I shall describe for you now.'

A dozen pens recorded this statement.

'Hindu India based its view of human existence on the concept of the Four Stages of Life: four distinct stages into which a human life – any life – is naturally divided. These stages, although distinct from one another, are not separated in the Hindu mind, but connected. Each gives place naturally to the next, until an individual life is rounded and complete.'

'What about death?' Shirani asked Tsunami later, when the two girls were walking back to Sanghamitta Hall that evening. 'Wouldn't death create an interruption in this scheme, wouldn't it make a difference?'

'Death or divorce,' Tsunami had replied, with the nonchalance of one who couldn't care less, either way. 'You'd think so, wouldn't you?'

'Stage One,' Rajaratnam continued, 'is called *brahmacharya*.'

He uncoiled his long body from his chair, went to the blackboard, and wrote 'brahmacharya' on it with white chalk. Beside this, in parentheses, he wrote two more words: 'adolescent' and 'student'.

'An individual who is at the stage of being a *brahmacharin* loves learning, devotes himself to study, and treats his guru as his God.'

Daniel smiled – a trifle self-consciously – as he said this, and was rewarded with answering smiles from the students in the room.

'I knew it,' Tsunami said to Shirani that evening, 'he's used that line before, so he knows it works.'

She reflected with pleasure, but not aloud, that being in love does not necessarily cloud one's powers of observation.

'A *brahmacharin*,' continued Daniel, 'is typically very young. He is a student – very much like yourselves; and, of course, also like yourselves, he is strictly celibate.'

He paused again. The pause had been part of his usual performance at Columbia, since he expected the smiles of the men in his audience to turn at this point into a ripple of laughter, and he always allowed space for this interruption. His male American students had invariably cracked up at the mere idea of a world in which college students would remain 'strictly celibate'. Even the girls, Daniel remembered, had been amused, thus establishing a relaxed and congenial atmosphere, and getting his lecture off to a flying start.

It would be unrealistic, of course, to expect such a degree of sophistication from Peradeniya's sheltered and unliberated women.

The pause lengthened. There was no laughter from anyone, not even from the men. Daniel's harmless little pleasantry (usually so reliable) appeared to have fallen flat, and his words had been met once again only by silence and industrious scribbling.

What the hell is the matter with college kids in Ceylon? Don't they have a sex life?

With an effort, Daniel continued his lecture.

'Stage Two, in which the former student finds his occupation in life, marries, and becomes a householder, is called *grihasta.* It is a period of responsibility, for with his earnings the householder is now able to support the community and its religious institutions, as well as the family of which he is now the head—'

With irritation Daniel realized that he was delivering the dullest bloody lecture anyone had ever given a bunch of university students. The knowledge that he was delivering it caused him intense annoyance, for he was proud of the reputation he had earned among students at Columbia as a charismatic speaker. He added the word 'householder' to 'grihasta' on the blackboard, and looked around the class. He noticed that one of the students – that girl who had interrupted him at the beginning of the session by coming in late – was taking no notes.

'Forgotten your notebook, Miss?' he inquired icily.

'No, Dr Rajaratnam. I'm listening, not writing,' Tsunami replied.

'Is that so? And when, may I ask, do you intend to begin writing?'

'When I've had time to think about what you are saying.'

This, Daniel now remembered, was the same girl who had sat through his lecture the previous week without writing down a word of it.

'Good,' he said. 'I'll be interested to hear what you have to say when question time comes round.'

Tsunami smiled at him. She had, Daniel noticed, a particularly sweet smile. She made no effort, however, to take up a pen and begin writing. He continued his lecture.

'Stage Three,' he said, 'begins when the householder has achieved stability in life. He has prospered in his occupation, he has seen his children married and settled in households of their own, and he has no financial worries to trouble him. He now begins to give more attention to the spiritual side of his personality, to think about withdrawing from the rush and bustle of everyday existence, and focusing on the state of his soul. Some men at this stage would actually withdraw from social and family life, and seek sanctuary in lonely places such as forest caves where they could meditate in peace. The Sanskrit word for 'forest' is *vana.* Hence the name given to Stage Three: *vanaprastha.*'

On the blackboard, beside the word 'vanaprastha', Daniel wrote: 'Age 60–65.'

'Finally,' he said, 'Stage Three gives way to Stage Four – that is, if the individual in question happens to live that long. At Stage Four the former recluse becomes an actual ascetic, a *sanyasin*. He abandons his home, his family, his possessions, and everything else that ties him to the material world, and seeks spiritual fulfilment through fasting, meditation, prayer, and a variety of ascetic practices.'

Daniel proceeded to illustrate the contemporary relevance of Stage Four by relating an anecdote about a distinguished Indian colleague of his at Columbia, who had contributed a chapter to a book he had himself compiled. When the book was published and the time had come to distribute royalties, it was discovered that Dr Prasad, who had by then returned to India, had taken to the life of a sanyasin.

'My former colleague,' Daniel said, 'had resigned from his university position in Rajasthan. He had left Jaipur, and had substituted for his campus office a shady spot beneath a golden mohur tree on the banks of the Ganges.'

The golden mohur tree was a picturesque addition on Daniel's part – he liked to imagine its shining blossoms drifting from the branches and falling gently around a bearded, half-naked Rajendra Prasad, who would be seated on the ground, his eyes closed, immobile in meditation – but the tale itself was a true one. Every time Daniel had related it, the story had unfailingly inspired a flood of questions and comments from students in America. At Peradeniya, however, it seemed to be drawing a blank.

'Any questions?' asked Daniel desperately.

A single hand went up, a hand with an emerald-green bangle around the wrist.

'What happened to Professor Prasad's wife and his family when he left home?' Tsunami asked.

Daniel was prepared for the question. Some woman student in his classes at Columbia had invariably asked it, when he reached this point in his lecture.

'They stayed home, of course,' he said easily. 'And I directed to Mrs Prasad the royalty payments that were due to her husband. Any other questions?'

'Yes,' Tsunami said. 'I have another question.'

Daniel leaned back in his chair, took off his reading glasses, and looked at her for the first time.

'Shoot!' he said.

'I believe you said, Dr Rajaratnam, that there are four distinct stages into which a life – any life – is naturally divided.'

'That's right.'

'Does the concept of the Four Stages of Life apply to women's lives too?'

Daniel realized with dismay that he had been asked a question for which he had no answer ready. Did the concept apply to women? He searched his mind rapidly for references, and could find none.

Why hasn't this question occurred to me before now? Well, obviously, because it's a dumb, completely damnfool question. If it were not, I'd have thought of it before now; and come up with an answer, too. Of course I would.

But, as any sensible person could see, the question posited a situation that was totally untenable. How could the laws of Manu encourage respectable Indian housewives to abandon their domestic responsibilities and take, without so much as a by-your-leave, to the religious life? What would happen in their absence to their families, the care of which was, is, and always would be – quite rightly – the main focus of a woman's existence? It was unthinkable, and he would say so.

And yet, can I honestly present Rajendra Prasad's example as a blameless one?

Rajendra had abandoned academic responsibilities as well as domestic duties, leaving not only a sick wife at home, and a daughter unmarried, but his students floundering without the examination paper he had contracted to set for them . . . How would his own father cope, Daniel wondered, if his devoted Sarojini were to suddenly take it into her head to leave her familiar hearth and the comfortable home he had provided for her in Jaffna, and selfishly depart in search of a cave in which to meditate?

He looked up, and saw the beginnings of a smile on the face of one of his male students. Daniel glared at him, and the smile promptly vanished. In the growing silence, Tsunami helpfully elaborated on her question.

'It seems to me, Dr Rajaratnam,' said she, 'that the concept of the Four Stages of Life could apply to a woman. But only in special circumstances. It could apply to her only when, having lived a virtuous life as a wife and mother, she received a gold star for good behaviour by being reborn as a man.'

Someone in the class giggled nervously, then relapsed into silence. Daniel looked hard at Tsunami. Was this girl attempting to ridicule him? Apparently not, for he could detect in her expression no trace of insolence. She seemed absolutely serious.

'I – I believe you are quite right, Miss—?'

'Wijesinha.'

'You are perfectly right, Miss Wijesinha. The laws of Manu do not appear, as far as I know, to have made provision for women to live according to this concept.'

Well, I've done the right thing: I've allowed a student to put forward an original point of view, even though it's opposed to my own, and I've encouraged her to sustain it.

In Daniel's own undergraduate years, when the principle of *guru bakthi* had reigned supreme on campus as it did in the schools, a student who tried the kind of thing she'd just pulled would have been immediately reported to the Dean.

'Perhaps,' Tsunami said, in a conversational tone that made her sound more like a guest at a cocktail party than a student in a tutorial class, 'Manu didn't believe women were actually human?'

Daniel's self-satisfaction evaporated.

'Is that a question or a statement, Miss Wijesinha?'

'A question.'

'Well, I wouldn't go so far as to say that Manu actually excluded women from the human race,' he said. 'We mustn't be too hard on the old boy, must we?'

Describing this exchange later to Latha, Shirani Pathirana said it had been obvious that Dr Rajaratnam was playing for time. Tsunami had given him no help. Their tutor hesitated a moment, then capitulated.

'But I think you may be justified in . . . reaching such a conclusion.'

Okay, you've made your point, and I've accepted it: let's move on.

Daniel prepared to move on, but it seemed that his questioner was not quite ready yet to do so. She appeared to be turning something over in her mind.

'No,' Tsunami said at last. 'That won't do. It would be a logical conclusion, but it won't do. It wouldn't fit the period, would it? I don't suppose Manu ever thought about women at all, did he, Dr Rajaratnam? Except as cooks, or as housekeepers, or as part of the furniture in his house. He probably had five or six wives. Why would it ever occur to him that one of the five or six chairs he had in his house had spiritual aspirations?'

The bell rang as she asked this question, and the rest of the class, bored with an exchange in which they had played no part, got up to go. Tsunami rose to her feet, and so did her neighbour. Watching the two girls collect their books, Daniel realized that a third-year student had, by asking a single question, by rejecting the concession he had generously made, and by then introducing a theory of her own, effectively hijacked the discussion he had intended to control.

How did I allow such a thing to happen?

As the last of the Honours class filed out and a new group prepared to take their places, Daniel stepped out into the corridor: he needed a cigarette. As he lit up, he glanced down the corridor and glimpsed a flash of scarlet and green at the head of the stairs.

Into his mind there shot without warning a sudden memory of himself as a ten-year-old boy, dashing out of doors with his butterfly net. Just as he reached his objective and made his move, bringing the net down and across in the practised stroke that had won him so many prizes in the past, the exotic butterfly that he had seen alighting on a jasmine bush near the veranda rose into the air and danced out of reach.

The girl was still there, studying the notices on the departmental pinboard. Stubbing out the cigarette he had just lit, Daniel came up behind her.

'You left your pen behind in class, Miss Wijesinha.'

Tsunami turned round, surprised. She took the pen from him and looked at it.

'That's not mine, Dr Rajaratnam,' she said, and returned it to him.

'Isn't it? I could have sworn it was yours.'

'I didn't use a pen this morning,' she said. 'Don't you remember?'

Daniel walked back to his tutorial room. On his mind was imprinted an image of a pair of flashing dark eyes, and a manner as cool as ice cream. Well, her eyes and her manner gave nothing away, but the hand which momentarily brushed his had trembled . . .

It trembled. Definitely, it trembled. I'm sure of it.

He put his pen back in his pocket, and hoped that if Miss Wijesinha was still in the corridor, watching him walk away, she hadn't seen him do it.

Before beginning his second tutorial for the morning, Daniel checked the attendance list for the first. There was only one 'Wijesinha' on the list, so 'T. Wijesinha' would have to be the student who had come in late.

He returned to his bachelor lodgings at Mahakellē that afternoon in an extremely confused state of mind. A man who regarded himself as an acute analyst of his own motives and actions, Daniel was aware that it had been only the wish to meet this student (whose first name he didn't even know!) outside the context of the tutorial room and, if possible, arrange to meet her socially later, that had made him approach her in the corridor with his absurd question about a pen. He asked himself why he wanted to meet her socially, and came up with an excellent answer.

As a good teacher, I need to know what an obviously intelligent young woman like Miss T. Wijesinha thinks about subjects other than ancient India.

This was perfectly true.

But it did not explain why Daniel Rajaratnam kept a watchful eye on the glass panel in his tutorial room door for several days afterwards, hoping to see Miss T. Wijesinha pass by; and when she did not, attended an audition for the Varsity Voices on Ronald Marchmont's invitation, on the off-chance that she might attend it too.

3

MAHAKELLĒ

Ten miles beyond Sanghamitta Hall on the Galaha Road, set high on a picturesquely wooded mountainside, is the Mahakellē Staff Bungalow, a massive stone house with a magnificent garden. Both house and garden had been the creation of a British Major-General in the 1890s. The University of Ceylon has a lease on the property, which it thoughtfully offers as quarters to its unmarried academic staff. Ronald Marchmont had joined the group which was currently in residence there, with Peter Appuhamy, a dapper survival from the British era, to look after their needs.

Single women were officially welcome to stay at Mahakellē, but Marchmont found that his fellow residents were, without exception, bachelors like himself. Peter Appuhamy, who had been in sole charge of the bachelor establishment of a British superintendent of police at the time (as he liked to say) that the Empire closed down, liked to keep it that way. Only on one occasion had a woman taken up residence there: she was the female half of a married couple that had come to live at Mahakellē until a university bungalow became vacant. Her stay had been a near-disaster: the lady had taken it upon herself to examine Peter's account books, and had informed her husband and his colleagues that they were being robbed by an unscrupulous rogue. When questioned, Peter had handed in his resignation with dignity. He left his forwarding address with the Secretary of the Residents' Committee, however, and on the departure of the married couple to a staff bungalow on Augusta Hill at the other end of the campus, he had been promptly reinstated. He returned to his post at Mahakellē with his reputation intact, and a firm resolve that in future the sole female resident of the house would be the cat.

The easy-going bachelor atmosphere of Mahakellē Staff Bungalow suited Peter Appuhamy – and his 'young gentlemen' – very well indeed. He was an excellent cook, and the breakfasts he provided were substantial and delicious. Lunches and dinners during the week were no problem, for the residents tended to eat out, on campus or in Kandy, and it was only at the weekends, really, that Peter had much more to do than keep the wooden floors polished and the bookshelves dusted, and put fresh flowers in the vases.

At weekends, Peter came into his own.

'Peter's a pretty marvellous kind of chap,' Marchmont had told Dr Daniel Rajaratnam, the new resident who had recently been recruited to the History Department to teach Indian History. 'Magics things up out of nothing.'

'I've been told that his miracles don't come cheap,' had been the cautious response of Daniel, whose Jaffna background occasionally broke through his veneer of American sophistication.

'Nonsense,' Marchmont said cheerfully. 'You've been listening to rumours. I say we're lucky to have him. Now, where do you want these to go?'

They had met on the stairs a few days after Daniel moved in, and Marchmont had offered to give the new resident a hand with unpacking his books. The offer had been gratefully accepted: there were indeed a lot of books to be unpacked, Daniel thought ruefully, the accumulation of five years in the States. The only book-case in his three-room flat was already filled to overflowing, and four wooden boxes full of books and papers had still to be opened.

Marchmont tried the old-fashioned tasselled bell-pull that hung beside the mantelpiece, and a distant tinkle was heard from the kitchen downstairs.

'Ah, there you are, Peter,' said Marchmont when Peter appeared. 'Any chance of getting Dr Rajaratnam another book-case?'

Peter considered the question.

'A book-case in the garage there is, sir,' he said. 'But that book-case not good: shaking, shelves needing repair.' A phrase from the past, familiar to him from his days with the police superintendent, came back to him, and he nodded. 'Today itself,' he said, 'I will take the matter into custody. But for now . . . Please excuse me, sir.'

After twenty minutes Peter came back, accompanied by one of the Mahakellē gardeners, who was staggering under the weight of a dozen rose-coloured clay bricks in a wicker basket. The man set the basket down beside the window and disappeared, returning almost immediately with a stack of long wooden planks. Within minutes, Daniel's temporary book-shelves had been set up.

'See what I mean? The man's a magician,' Marchmont said. 'I rang him up at eleven o'clock from my office last Saturday and said, "Lunch for twelve on Sunday, please, Peter! Can you cope?" "Okay, boss," he replied; and when my guests arrived, he'd got savouries ready to serve with the drinks, and had laid on an absolutely magnificent banquet to follow. By the way, Peter, I don't think I remembered to thank you. That was a sterling effort on Sunday.'

Peter Appuhamy liked to be appreciated; he inclined his head graciously.

'Thank you, sir. No problem.' He looked across at Daniel. 'Anything else you are needing, sir?' he inquired. 'If not, I will go and see to serving afternoon tea.'

Marchmont looked at his watch.

'A quarter to four,' he said. 'I must be off, too. Choir practice at Sanghamitta with the Varsity Voices at five-thirty and I mustn't be late, because the Voices never are.'

'The Voices?'

'A choral group. Unaccompanied voices. Great fun, I think, and they seem to agree.'

'Who are "they"?'

'Mostly students so far. Very few of our colleagues seem to be interested, alas, though Professor van Loten drops in sometimes, and Titus Dupré too (if he isn't playing tennis). Oh, and your colleague Justin LaBrooy's become something of a regular, he's got a good tenor voice. Why don't you join us?'

'Sorry to disappoint you, Ronald. I'm no good.'

'I don't believe it. You've got a speaking voice like a sounding board. I am sure I hear a bass hidden in there somewhere.'

'Well,' said Rajaratnam, smiling. 'Maybe I do sing sometimes. Mostly in the shower. When the water temperature's right I can do a passable imitation of Paul Robeson . . .'

'I knew it!' Marchmont was jubilant. 'You're coming along with me this evening. Don't worry, you won't be on your own, there's a couple of other people auditioning.'

'Auditioning? What in heaven's name are you putting on? *The Gondoliers*?'

'A concert. It's just a little one, but it's our first, and it's shaping up well. You'll enjoy being part of it.'

'Out of my league, I'm afraid. Sorry.'

Marchmont was disappointed. His choir was short on male voices, and a good bass would have been a real asset. But he was not one to give up easily. Daniel was alone in the panelled dining room when Marchmont looked in on his way to choir practice.

'Thought I'd stop by to see if you'd changed your mind,' he said. 'And grab a cup of Peter's tea before I take off. Steadies the nerves.'

'May I ask why your nerves need steadying?'

'Culture clash, social conditioning, shyness, call it what you will. Some of the students just don't seem to give.'

'Give? Give what?'

'They don't seem to give . . . themselves. Between me and these kids, Daniel, there seems to be a great gulf fixed. And that's no good, you see: when you sing, you simply have to give everything that's in you, or you might as well abandon the whole thing and go home.'

'Your students,' Daniel told Marchmont, 'are probably nervous. Remember, you're a Brit, the imperialist bad guy they've read about in their history textbooks. They might be finding it hard to square the Ronald Marchmont they meet at choir practice with their image of Clive and Rhodes and Brownrigg.'

'Brownrigg? Who's Brownrigg? Oh, I know,' said Marchmont, remembering. 'That's the chap on a prancing horse, brandishing a sword above his head. At the entrance to the Queen's Hotel. "The Conqueror of Kandy." If anyone wants to put a bomb under that statue, I'd join the party.'

'There you are,' Daniel said. 'You have arrived at the heart of your difficulty. The students don't know what you think of Brownrigg, you see. They don't know you despise colonialism. If they did, Ronald, you'd have no problem. You must give them a chance to get to know you better.'

He stirred his tea, and reached out a long arm for another of Peter Appuhamy's scones.

'These are good, aren't they? The man's a genius.'

'What did I tell you?'

Marchmont lost no time in reverting to the subject closest to his heart.

'Getting back to the Varsity Voices: in all fairness, I have to say they aren't all unresponsive. Some of the Honours students who are in the Voices – Merrick Seneviratne, for instance, and the Wijesinha girls, and then there's a Miss Pathirana – they're willing to work hard, but they're relaxed about it. What I *really* appreciate,' Marchmont added, 'is the way they go along with me when I suggest we try new and difficult things.'

Daniel's cup remained poised in mid-air.

'Did you say Wijesinha?'

'Yes, there are two of them. Related, I believe, but I'm not sure. Not that it matters – everyone in this country seems to be related to everyone else! The one I know best is Latha Wijesinha, she's one of my own Honours students. Very bright indeed, we have great hopes for her. The other, Tsunami, is reading History, I think. Great fun and, incidentally, very good-looking – you couldn't possibly miss her if she's in one of your classes.'

'I rather believe I had a Miss Wijesinha the other day in an Honours class,' Daniel stated with careful casualness.

Yes, and I have been dreaming about her ever since.

He replaced his cup in its saucer and stood up.

'Well, maybe I *will* take a break. The rest of my unpacking can be put off for tomorrow. Perhaps I'll drop in on your practice this evening.'

'Why not come along with me right now? I'm taking the car.'

'Thanks,' Daniel said. 'You're very kind.'

As they walked together towards the garage, he asked:

'Buses not running this evening?'

'The bus service stops at seven-thirty,' Marchmont replied. 'The singers often go on beyond that.'

Ronald Marchmont had caused something of a sensation on campus by being the only car-owning foreign academic to use the Kandy bus service. He was quite unaware of his fame, hopping on to the buses at the Mahakellē bus stop, his books and papers swinging from his shoulder in a colourful handwoven bag he had bought at the Kandyan Art Centre, hopping off them at the turn-off to the campus with great agility, and attaching himself with easy informality to the stream of students making their way to the Library and the lecture theatres. Senior academics at Peradeniya deplored such undignified goings-on, especially in a British expatriate. A Cambridge academic, they said, should know how to keep his distance. The younger ones were amused: most of them assumed that Marchmont was riding the buses in order to chat up the women students. Daniel, aware that British academic stipends were far from generous, and knowing that the buses were crowded and uncomfortable, assumed that Marchmont was riding them to save money.

They were all mistaken: as no one but Tsunami Wijesinha knew, Ronald Marchmont was writing a novel.

'Amazing!' he now said to Daniel.

Stopping the car at the side of the road, he took a notebook from its sidepocket, and made a note. 'It would have been so much simpler to have a post put over there, saying *Bus Stop*, wouldn't you say? Instead, what have they got? *Motor Bus Halting Place.* What a country!'

'How are we going for time?' Daniel asked Marchmont, as they came up Sanghamitta Hill. 'I'd like to call on the Warden, if she's in. Dr Springdale is an old friend of my parents.'

Marchmont consulted his watch.

'We've got a quarter of an hour to spare.'

On inquiry in the front hall, they were informed that the Warden was in her office.

'My dear boy!' Joan Springdale was delighted to see Rajaratnam's tall figure framed in the doorway. 'I'd heard you were back. It's wonderful for us to have you on the staff. It must have been so tempting to stay on in the States.'

She shook Daniel's hand, greeted Marchmont warmly, and added: 'I'm glad you two have met. You're here for a Varsity Voices practice, I think, Ronald?'

'We're both lodging at Mahakellē, Dr Springdale. Just up the street from you.'

'A rather long street,' the Warden observed. 'Ten miles at least, surely? It's very kind of you, Ronald, to make the effort to come here every week. I appreciate it very much, and so do the students. Don't they, Miss Wijesinha?'

'We certainly do,' Latha said.

She rose from her chair by Dr Springdale's desk. Her regular weekly 'sub-Warden's chat' with the Warden had been just about to end when the two lecturers were announced. She prepared to leave.

'Don't run away, Latha,' Joan Springdale said. 'I'd like you to meet a new member of the academic staff. This is Dr Rajaratnam, who has just returned to us from Columbia. Daniel, let me introduce our third-year sub-Warden, Miss Latha Wijesinha.'

Daniel smiled politely at Latha.

Well, here's one of Marchmont's Misses Wijesinha. Where's the other one?

'Daniel's auditioning tonight, Dr Springdale,' Marchmont said, studiously avoiding his colleague's eye. 'Wouldn't you like to come and hear him?'

A few minutes after the Warden, accompanied by Latha and the two young men, had entered the Common Room which Sanghamitta Hall had dedicated to the Varsity Voices practices, Tsunami walked in. She glanced briefly around her, acknowledged the visitors' presence with a calm, unrufffled smile, and seated herself on a bench at the side of the room waiting her turn to perform.

She did not look again in Daniel's direction.

Well, the way's open now. I've only got to cross the Common Room floor, sit down on the bench beside the girl, and start a conversation.

After all, he wasn't there as a teacher or as an academic, he was just another hopeful, due to audition at any moment, just as she was. It would be perfectly natural for them to talk to each other. There was no reason in the world why anyone should think anything of it.

Of course it would certainly help things along if she would only glance at me once. A single glance, just to show she's interested.

For, despite appearances, instinct told him that she was. That cool remoteness, so different from the giggles and blushes with which most of the female students in his classes responded to a question from him in tutorials, was surely a pretence.

It's an act, I'm sure of it.

Her hand – he repeated this several times to himself – her hand, when she returned his pen to him in the corridor, had trembled at his touch.

Ever since that first tutorial, Daniel had amused himself in idle moments by visualizing the maddeningly composed Tsunami Wijesinha felled by the power of his lovemaking. He could imagine no sweeter sensation than taking her in his arms and melting her cool reasonableness (with which he found it so difficult to deal) into something much more manageable. He wondered whether she would maintain her remoteness in the face of a direct approach from him: he doubted it. No, she would be ecstatic, unreasoning, she would respond to his love-making from the depths of what he was convinced was a passionate nature, her mind emptied of everything but pleasure at his touch. She would not, he thought, be able to marshal arguments for and against the laws of Manu while her tongue was imprisoned in his mouth, his hands on her breasts, her bird of paradise plumage stripped from her body to make a couch for them both to lie on in the fragrance of a Peradeniya night.

Such fancies were not new to Daniel, and he had had plenty of experience in putting them into practice. So what had held him back? Why had he not done what, as he knew very well, he had come to Sanghamitta Hall to do? Why hadn't he spoken to Tsunami Wijesinha? It suddenly occurred to him that if he had, she might have given him a silly or stupid answer which broke the spell she seemed to have cast over him; it was unlikely, but she might have. And if she had, the whole difficult situation would have ended there and then: which would have been the best possible outcome. But he had *not* spoken to her. On the contrary, from the moment he had seen her come in until the evening's end, he had carefully avoided catching her eye.

Returning to Mahakellē after the audition, Daniel Rajaratnam reviewed his own actions with admirable objectivity.

There's no question about it. I conducted myself this evening like a lovesick adolescent.

His behaviour at the Varsity Voices practice, so comically inconsistent, had done no credit to his image of himself as a sophisticated man of the world. He could find no explanation for it. In America, the inhibitions planted in him by his upbringing had seemed blessedly irrelevant to his life on campus. He could deliberately set them aside there, as he might have done a book: for future reference, to be picked up again when he returned to Jaffna and his family obligations. In America, where he had not been dogged by contradictory impulses which made him say one thing and do another, he had pursued his objectives with a directness that, he had reason to believe, was fully appreciated by the various young women who had at different times shared his bed.

If I'd met a girl in one of my classes at Columbia about whom I felt the same way, I'd probably have slept with her by now.

Or he would, at the very least, be dating her with ardour and enthusiasm. So why not Tsunami Wijesinha?

Daniel had never been in love himself, but he recognized its symptoms. He was accustomed to awakening positive reactions in women, sure, and perfectly capable of responding in kind. But that didn't amount to 'love'.

As far as he was concerned, the sidelong glances of the Jaffna girls to whom his parents had introduced him on his return from the United States and the much franker interest of American women were two sides of the same coin. They were proof, equally, that whatever quality it was in him that attracted women was in good working order. He was flattered by female attention, and knew exactly how to deal with it.

But again, that wasn't 'love'.

Okay, let's forget about 'love' and other sentimentalities. Let's recognize that I'm in the grip of good, old-fashioned lust.

And for whom? For a girl whom chance and the history Honours timetable had thrown in his way.

I want, more than anything else in the world, to make love to Tsunami Wijesinha.

He had wanted it ever since she had calmly taken over his tutorial, and he had noticed how different she was from the other young women in the class. They giggled shyly, dropped their gaze when his glance fell on them, coquettishly adjusted the fall of their saris, and were continually touching and rearranging their hair. She, on the other hand, looked him directly in the eye as she asked and answered questions, apparently indifferent to the effect she had on him. Her seeming indifference piqued Daniel, who was not accustomed to it in the women he attracted.

For the first time in his life, Daniel felt the traditions that shaped his Tamil Hindu consciousness press with almost unbearable weight upon him, obstructing instead of advancing his hopes and desires. With an effort he pulled himself together. Common sense reasserted itself as he realized that in thinking of Tsunami Wijesinha as wife or even as lover, he was merely spinning fantasies. The position was simple and clearcut. Here, on the one hand, was Tsunami, a young woman from a conservative Sinhalese, probably Buddhist, family. There, on the other, was himself, Girishna Daniel Rajaratnam, Tamil by race, Hindu by religion. They were poles apart. The only thing they had in common was the English language. This was the reality. What did it matter that this girl presented contradictions in her behaviour that at once intrigued and disconcerted him?

As far as I'm concerned, and as my father would tell me if I asked him – which I have no intention of doing – Tsunami Wijesinha's out of bounds.

The reason for his inconsistent and contradictory behaviour during the evening at Sanghamitta now became perfectly clear to Daniel. It should have been obvious to him from the start that it was the natural outcome of his character and his upbringing. He was a man: it was natural that he should admire and, yes, desire a beautiful and intelligent girl. But he was essentially a man of honour, with a proper sense of duty to his family and his community.

I did not wish to start something that I knew I could not honourably complete.

Having arrived at this sensible conclusion, Daniel began immediately to feel better. He decided that he would put all thoughts of 'love' out of his mind, and concentrate on his research.

4

BALCONY TALK

Tsunami's evening did not go well.

'Your Dr Rajaratnam's quite something, isn't he!'

Sriyani had dropped in for coffee on the third-floor balcony.

'I looked in as I passed the Common Room after gym, Latha, to find out where this gorgeous baritone voice was coming from, and there the lot of you were, absolutely mesmerized!'

'Bass, not baritone,' Latha said. 'He's got a good voice, certainly, but nothing special: not as good as Merrick's, for instance. Anyway, he's not *my* Dr Rajaratnam. And we were *not* mesmerized!'

'No? Well, you certainly fooled me. I got the distinct impression you were all hanging on every note. Even you, Tsunami!'

Tsunami did not reply.

'I must say I liked the choice he made for his audition,' Latha said. 'I read 'The Foggy, Foggy Dew' a long time ago, in a book of American folksongs, but this is the first time I've heard it sung. It suited his voice perfectly. How many cups of coffee, people? Four?'

'Five,' Amali answered: 'Careful, Tsunami, you'd better not put your library books down near the Hanging Gardens, they might get wet.'

Amali had been watering the plants on the balcony. When she wasn't studying Economics and going to temple ceremonies, Amali had been transforming their shared balcony into a garden of flowers. She had only to look at a plant, Tsunami had said once, to make it grow: six clay pots on the balcony ledge which Amali had filled with earth and planted with petunias and rock violets made up the mini-conservatory that was proof of this statement. 'The Hanging Gardens', Tsunami called it. The petunias had already begun to flower, and trail their pinks and purples over the parapet wall.

'It's a little like sitting in a forest when I come to have coffee on your balcony,' Shirani said.

Sriyani agreed.

'Yeah, you feel as though one of those woodland creatures among the bushes and tree-roots in *Snow White* and *Bambi* – what were they? Chipmunks? Squirrels? – might peer out at you at any moment.'

She looked at the books Tsunami had brought back from the library on overnight reference. There were three, the maximum allowed to undergraduates.

'What's up?' she asked. 'You surely don't mean to sit up all night with these?'

Unlike her friends, Sriyani de Alwis was uncomfortable in the presence of books. Her room, which was at the far end of the balcony, was quite unlike theirs, being almost devoid of books and papers. A map of Southeast Asia decorated one wall, more for what it revealed of the nations participating in the Asian Games than for anything it did to advance Sriyani's Geography studies. The principal feature of her room was her collection of posters glorifying the sports stars of many countries, principally the U.S.A.

'Why did I come to Peradeniya?' Sriyani said once, responding to an unspoken question in Latha's eyes. 'I'm here for one reason, honey bunch, and one reason only: Peradeniya's got this country's only cinder track, and I wanted a chance to run on it.'

Powered by this unusual ambition Sriyani had got through the General Arts Qualifying examination at the end of the first year. Her friends had patiently taken turns hearing her rehearse the points she had noted down for mention in her examination answers. She had learned those points by heart until, she said, she could recite them in her sleep.

'Doesn't matter what the question is, I'll set every one of these points down in my answer. Can't let all this hard work go to waste.'

'Is that wise, Sriyani?" Latha had asked. 'Suppose the question you are asked focuses on something completely different? Something you haven't studied in detail?'

'Detail? I don't intend to study *anything* in detail,' Sriyani had returned briskly. 'And it's no good looking at me like that, Latha. It can't be helped: either I spend every day swotting in the library, or I train for the All-Island Athletics Championships. I can't do both. So I've worked out a strategy. I'll mention whatever it is the question asks as the first point in my answer, then I'll write "But", "but", "but", and bring in all the others that I've learned by heart. How can they possibly fail me? The main thing, as I see it, is to whack all the points down on paper as fast as I can, so that the examiners can see that I know them.'

Latha had sighed.

'Anyway, make sure you complete all your answers,' she had advised anxiously. 'It doesn't do to write *Ran out of time* at the end of an answer, and leave it unfinished.'

This was the 'strategy' Sriyani had adopted at the General Arts Qualifying examination, and had only just managed to scrape through.

'See it from the examiners' point of view. They can't award marks for points that aren't actually on the answer paper.'

'"The race",' Tsunami had quoted thoughtfully, '"is not with the strong but with the swift." I don't know who wrote that, or even whether I've quoted it correctly, but it seems relevant in your case, Sriyani.'

'Yeah, yeah, folks,' Sriyani had said. 'Thanks for all the expert advice. I'll be okay. You'll see.'

Her new strategy, unconventional though it was, had 'worked', and Sriyani was now in her third year. Latha joined her in turning over the books Tsunami had placed on her desk.

'*Ancient Hindu Customs and Practices*, *Family Life in Ancient India*,' Latha said. 'I thought you were writing an essay on the lead-up to Independence, Tsunami! What's happened to Gandhi, Nehru, Jinnah and Mountbatten? Why this sudden interest in ancient India?'

'Background,' Tsunami said.

She took her library books away from Latha and Sriyani.

'What about you, Latha? What's your first assignment like?'

'Oh, we're reading the Bible,' Latha said cheerfully.

'The *Bible*?' Amali was astonished.

'We were just as surprised as you are,' Latha told her. 'Especially as the Bible's not on our text list.'

At the first English Honours tutorial of the new term, Professor Everard van Loten had startled Latha and her fellow-students by inquiring how many Christians or Catholics there were in the class. Half the students present had reluctantly put up their hands.

'Buddhists?'

Two hands had gone up, one of them Latha's.

'Hindus?'

Three hands were raised.

'Muslims?'

One.

Latha said that the non-Catholics and non-Christians in the class had begun to fidget under this questioning, and look extremely uncomfortable.

'You're not accustomed to minority status, you see!' Tsunami remarked. 'A new experience, I'll bet, for some people. Now, as for me, Latha, I grew up with minority status.'

'And which minority, pray, are you a part of?'

'A very select little group. Intellectuals. Rationalists. People who think, people who question, people who don't accept everything they're told. Non-conformists.'

Latha, who knew that her cousin disliked what she called her meek conformism, ignored the barb, and went on.

'Well, some people in the class discovered that they disliked minority status very much. Merrick, for instance, who was sitting next to me, leaned over and asked me whether I would agree that "English Studies" at Peradeniya was merely another name for religious discrimination.'

'Well? And what did you tell him?'

'There was no time to tell him anything, because Professor van Loten had begun to speak. 'Please don't imagine for a moment that I'm bent on converting you!' he said. (Which was timely, because you could see that that was exactly what many people *were* thinking.) He was smiling, so I think he knew quite well how students were likely to react.'

'Can't blame them,' Sriyani said. 'With all this anti-Christian propaganda that's going around, everyone's edgy.'

'Anti-Christian propaganda?'

'Oh,' Sriyani said carelessly, 'xeroxed letters, urging true Sinhalese Buddhists to rid this country of aliens. Ship plantation Tamils back to India, they say, and Burghers back to the Netherlands, tell Western tourists to get lost, etcetera, etcetera. The boys were talking about it at the gym this evening. Apparently the letters are sent by mail. They're unsigned, and headed *Save our Motherland!*'

'My father received one the other day,' Amali said. 'He said it was obviously the work of a crank.'

'One would hope so,' Latha said slowly. 'But supposing it isn't? Supposing some organization's behind it? Some organization that wants political power, and doesn't care how it gets it?'

'Not in our country,' Amali said. 'Never in Ceylon.'

'Well,' Latha said, 'Professor van Loten made *his* purpose clear quickly enough. "You have all elected to study English Literature," he said, "and the study of English literature at Honours level requires *at the very least* a working knowledge of the English Bible. You will want to know why this is so." (He looked at Merrick and me when he said this, so he may have spotted us whispering.) "There's an excellent reason for it: the poets you will be reading this term – Shakespeare, Donne, Milton, Dryden, Pope and Johnson – were all brought up on the Bible. At every turn you will meet with Christian imagery and Biblical prose rhythms. And since not all of us are regular church-goers, and need to do some reading in order to get the most out of this course, I'd like every member of this class to have read certain texts in the Bible's Authorized Version before we meet again next week." And then he gave us a list of references. I must say, I'm feeling a bit lost. Don't know where to begin.'

'Let's have a look at that list,' Tsunami said. 'The Book of Genesis, Chapter One; The Book of Exodus, Chapter One; St Matthew's Gospel; St Paul's Epistle to the Corinthians; and The Song of Solomon. Well, you won't need to join the queue at the library, that's for sure, Latha. I've got my school Bible here. I don't think any of the pages are missing.'

'Thanks,' Latha said with relief. 'It would really be a help. This is just the beginning, you see. Next week it'll be St Luke's Gospel and The Acts of the Apostles.'

Tsunami fetched the Bible she had used at Ashcombe, and gave it to Latha. The blue cloth binding had been rubbed almost bare in some places, but although the text was printed on very thin paper, not a page was torn. Latha opened the book. Facing the title page was a brightly coloured picture of Pharaoh's daughter standing by a stream, retrieving a basket with a baby in it from a clump of rushes in the water. Beneath the title, surrounded by a garland of crayoned leaves, was the name and address of the Bible's owner:

Tsunami Alexandra Wijesinha
Form II, Ashcombe Anglican School,
Boyd Place, Colombo 3
Ceylon
The Indian Ocean
Northern Hemisphere
The World
The Earth
The Universe

'It may be a bit battered, I'm afraid,' Tsunami said apologetically. 'I used to write my homework on the fly-leaf and the blank pages—'

Latha found that this was indeed the case. She found also what she had not previously noticed, that the Egyptian princess's upper lip had grown a luxuriant red ink moustache.

'Oh, Tsunami!' she said reproachfully. 'Didn't you have a homework book and a scribbling pad?'

'Of course I did. Heaps of them. I just kept losing them . . .'

Although Tsunami set her reference books up on her desk that night, and sat down before them to study, she could not keep her mind focused on ancient India. There had been several occasions during the previous fortnight when she had come close to telling Latha and Amali about her feelings for Rajaratnam, but every time she had been on the point of doing so, she had thought better of it and stopped herself in time. She did not, she told herself, want to be laughed at or teased by the friends to whom she had imparted her earlier opinions on love. Latha would be kind, and even sympathetic, she knew. But what would Amali say?

Sriyani's right, I have been mesmerized. But only for a while. I'll get over it.

And, following the audition for Marchmont's concert, at which Rajaratnam had ignored her presence, she was glad that she had been discreet. Like everyone else in her group of friends, Tsunami was well aware that the politics of race, which had begun to contaminate the larger society outside Peradeniya, were manifesting themselves in unpleasant ways at Peradeniya. Latha had told her that several Sinhalese students at Sanghamitta who associated freely with Tamil or Muslim classmates had received threatening anonymous letters and insulting postcards in the mail. Tsunami came to a decision. She would stay out of Rajaratnam's way. And if his name came up again in the course of casual conversation, she would, as she had done that evening, deflect the discussion in other directions. Good sense told her that this was the safe and proper thing to do.

All the good sense in the world could not, however, prevent her thinking of him. Like it or not, Tsunami was deeply in love, in thrall to a personality unlike any other she had hitherto encountered, to a voice that echoed in her dreams, to words into which, despite all appearances and her own excellent sense, she read a message that she believed had been intended for herself alone:

One night she came to my bedside, as I lay fast asleep,
She laid her head upon my bed, and she began to weep.
She sighed, she cried, she damn near died,
Ah me, what could I do?
So I hauled her into bed, and I covered up her head,
Just to keep her from the foggy, foggy dew . . .

Latha later told Amali that keener observation on her part on the evening of the Varsity Voices audition might have enabled her to detect the chemistry between Tsunami and Daniel Rajaratnam at an early stage of its development. Clues had come her way, which she had missed altogether.

'If I'd picked up those clues and interpreted them correctly,' Latha said, 'I'd have done something about it. I'd certainly have advised Tsunami to end the relationship before it went any further.'

In entertaining such speculations, Latha showed good will and growing self-confidence, but also her naïveté in the area of human relationships. By the time Tsunami did finally confide in Latha and Amali, it was much too late for either of them 'to do anything about it'.

If, indeed, there is anything anyone can do to halt a moving avalanche or a killer wave once they have been launched upon their paths of destruction.

5

THE ROAD TO JAFFNA

'I wonder, Daniel, if you'd be good enough to explain something to me,' Ronald Marchmont said.

Daniel Rajaratnam, stretched at full length in the splendid planter's chair Peter Appuhamy had thoughtfully assigned to his sitting room at Mahakellē, put down his book and paid attention.

'Certainly.'

Marchmont came in, settled himself on a cretonne-covered window-seat, and lit a cigarette.

'I have a problem,' he said. 'And it's to do with students.'

'What, not again?'

'No, no, not the Varsity Voices. Other students. Students on the buses.'

It appeared that Marchmont, on his way into Kandy on the previous day, had found himself on a crowded bus.

'It was the usual Kandy crowd,' he said. 'Housewives with their marketing bags, a group of lads from Arunachalam Hall – obviously on their way to see that John Wayne film at the Regal – the usual Government clerk enjoying a weekend break . . . Well, the bus pulled up at the campus stop, and a group of girls got in, students going shopping, probably. Every seat was occupied, even the ones in front reserved for clergy. The girls weren't troubled by that, they cheerfully stood in the aisle, and strap-hung for a bit. I decided to get up and offer one of them my seat. I did so, and I'm sure I did it very politely, but – she refused to take it! And this even though our bus driver was a crazy sort of character, taking the bends in the road at such a speed that it must have been almost impossible for the girl to stand up in the bus and keep her balance. She didn't refuse politely, she simply turned her back on me and looked out of the bus window, while all her friends giggled, and I felt a first-class fool. Now, what I want to know is, was that girl shy, socially inept, or just plain bad-mannered?'

Daniel considered.

'I'd say she was one of the first two: shy, or socially inept. There's also the possibility that she didn't understand what you were saying.'

'Oh, come off it, Daniel! My accent's not that bad! I said, very clearly indeed, "Would you like to have my seat, Miss?" And as I said it I pointed to my empty seat. Nothing obscure about that.'

'Okay. Let's look at other possibilities. She might have thought you were trying to pick her up – or, as she would probably say herself, "get fresh" with her. So, as any nice girl would, she gave you the brush-off. And then, there's also the question of the other person seated on the end of the seat you were offering her. Who had been sitting beside you? Was it a woman?'

'Good Lord, *I* don't know! How can I possibly remember something like that? No, I remember now. It was one of the clerks. He was reading a newspaper. I remember because he'd just asked me whether I'd seen the latest Test scores.'

'Elderly?'

'No, middle-aged, I should think. Honestly, I can't remember. Does it matter?'

'Oh, it does, it does. If the person sitting beside you had been a woman, or better still, a woman with a young child, the girl would have thanked you and accepted your seat. She might even have done so if the person was obviously a granddad. But to voluntarily sit beside a man young enough to make a pass at her – that would never do! What would happen to her hitherto blameless reputation?'

'You're having me on, aren't you? Do you seriously mean to tell me that all these considerations whiz through the mind of a young woman who is merely being offered a seat on a bus?'

'Not consciously. And it's not that they've got sex on the brain. It's just a matter of conditioning. Tell me: did any of the men from Arunachalam emulate your good example? How many of them jumped to their feet to offer their fellow-students their seats?'

'Not one,' Marchmont replied. 'I thought it odd at the time. Is gallantry dead at Peradeniya?'

Daniel laughed.

'Not at all. It just functions in different ways. Mostly governed by an inbuilt familiarity with the rules. If you had been one of those students, you would have offered your seat to an elderly woman, or to a mature lady struggling to cope with kids and a shopping basket – but to a servant girl? Never. Or to a young woman of your own social class who can obviously stand upright, even in a swaying bus? Not on your life. Well, not unless she's a relative, or you're engaged to her, or there's a romantic attachment between you. You'd only get yourself talked about.'

Marchmont threw up his hands in mock despair.

'I'll never understand you people,' he said. 'And here I was, thinking that my ignorance of Sinhala and Tamil would be my main problem in writing my novel. If I can't begin to understand why you do the things you do, and why you don't do the things you don't do, how can I develop a single credible character?'

'We are a nation of walking contradictions,' Daniel told him. 'Accept that, and everything becomes clear. A man might be an astrophysicist of international reputation, but when a marriage is being arranged for his daughter, he will call in an astrologer to nominate an auspicious time for the wedding ceremony to take place. If you think that's ludicrous, here's another scenario. A man might want to ask a politician for a favour. He will call on the politician with a gift in his hand – that's traditional courtesy, by the way, it isn't a bribe. When asked if there is a reason for his unexpected visit, he will smile politely and say that the call has been made for no reason but that of respect. Then, at the moment of leave-taking, he will state his request.'

'I couldn't live with such hypocrisy,' Marchmont said.

'It's not hypocrisy, it's obliqueness,' returned Daniel. 'Our national characteristic.'

'Could *you* live with it?'

'I grew up with it,' Daniel said. 'But you're right. From what I've seen of you, I don't think *you* could live with it. But then, why should you? Are you thinking of settling here? Many Westerners do, you know; and not all of them are retired tea-planters.'

Marchmont reddened slightly. 'Of course not. I love this place, but I'm no Joan Springdale, to dedicate my life to it. It'll be back to Blighty for me, but I'd been hoping that it would be with a manuscript in my baggage—'

'Get around,' advised Daniel. 'See something of the island. Kandy and Peradeniya are beautiful, and the people here have a character of their own, but there are other places, and other people. Not so beautiful, perhaps, but once experienced, never forgotten. Have you seen the sacred cities?'

'Last year.'

When his plan to make the trip in the company of a Cambridge friend had fallen through – his friend's commitments had taken him in the opposite direction, to Germany – Marchmont had joined a British Council tour of Anuradhapura, Polonnaruwa and Sigiriya, ably conducted by a knowledgeable official from the Department of Archaeology. He had come back with an album of photographs, his mind filled with stone images of meditating Buddhas, with royal pleasure gardens in picturesque decay, with long-eyed, small-waisted women whose images, painted on a rock wall, had seemed to him to move to unheard melodies. He described some of his impressions to Daniel, who listened attentively, discounting Marchmont's inevitable enthusiasms but noticing that his pronunciation of 'Polonnaruwa' – a place-name on which most foreigners slipped up – was not at all bad. He's really trying hard, Daniel thought, and liked him the better for it. Maybe there's a local girl somewhere he's getting serious about . . .

'Good. I'm glad you had that opportunity,' he said aloud. 'And glad that you took it. Your impressions may not translate into fiction just now, but perhaps they just need time. And now, what?'

An idea occurred to him.

'Ever been to the north?'

'To Jaffna, you mean? No.'

'Would you like to go?'

'I don't know anyone there,' Marchmont said. 'An organized tour is all very well, but something became very clear to me on the trip I did last year, and that is, that to really get to know a place, you need to experience it quietly, accommodating yourself to its special rhythms, seeing it through the eyes of its own people, not in the company of outsiders.'

The tour coach had been filled with back-slapping visitors on short-term visas, brimming with beer and holiday spirits.

'The guide did his best, but it wasn't what I needed.'

Daniel rose, and stretched himself.

'Well, Ronald, here's an offer for you. I'm off to Jaffna in a week's time, to see my parents. I'll be driving up. Join me if you like, they'd make you very welcome.'

Marchmont opened his mouth to speak, but Daniel forestalled him.

'You would, of course, be staying in our home, as my guest – no, no, there's no point in protesting: my mother would not forgive me if I brought a colleague to Jaffna and we put him up at a hotel.'

'It's very good of you,' Marchmont replied. He reflected a moment. 'We'll be in vacation, won't we, so except for the fact that I'm going to have a few essays to mark while I'm on holiday, I've no one to please but myself. Right: I'm accepting your invitation herewith. When do you plan to leave?'

'Next Saturday. That suit you?'

'Yes, indeed.'

'Good.'

Daniel was pleased. Like many historians who take South and Southeast Asia as their field of interest, and are thereby constrained to study the effects of British colonialism in those regions, he did not care for the British on principle. But he had taken to Ronald Marchmont, liked him as an individual, and had warmed to his colleague's openness to new experience.

Besides, it was likely that Marchmont's company on this occasion would be especially welcome. He had had several letters from his mother, urging an early visit, and Daniel suspected that marriage plans for him were the prime reason for her urgency. (Discreet inquiries addressed to his father as to what, if anything, was afoot, had yielded nothing: either Rajaratnam senior knew nothing of his wife's plans, or he was affecting complete ignorance of them.) If his suspicions were correct, the presence in the household of a stranger, and a foreigner at that, might be a useful distraction.

Before leaving Peradeniya, Daniel paid Sanghamitta Hall a visit, having been invited to take afternoon tea with the Warden. Joan Springdale was pleased to hear that Marchmont was accompanying him to Jaffna.

'You're driving up, I suppose?' she said. 'Such an opportunity for Ronald to see the island; and he couldn't have a better guide. I hope you're taking him to see Francis Twynam's ponies?'

'Thanks for reminding me,' Daniel said. 'I'll build the ponies into Ronald's itinerary.'

A herd of wild ponies, whose progenitors had been brought to the peninsula from South Africa during the Dutch occupation of the north, inhabited the overgrown and neglected grounds of Old Government House, a building permanently connected in the local mind with a former British Government Agent of Jaffna. 'Francis Twynam's ponies' were a well-known feature of Jaffna town.

'When I was last in Jaffna,' said Dr Springdale, handing Daniel his tea, 'I tried to lure them with carrots and lumps of sugar. Tate and Lyle was still available then, and I still have a few packets, for special occasions like this one. (Which reminds me, one lump or three? Your papa, as I remember, likes his tea very sweet.) Anyway, it didn't work, they just tossed their heads and cantered away, always managing to keep just out of reach. Beautiful creatures. I remember young Colin Wijesinha telling me once that he'd tried to lasso one of them when the family spent a holiday in Jaffna—'

'Wijesinha? A relation of one of our history Honours students?'

Daniel had grimly put Tsunami Wijesinha out of his mind, and had survived several tutorials with the Honours class without losing his resolve to treat her with an indifference that matched her own. Now, against his will, her name had recaptured his attention.

'Yes, Colin is my godson, and Tsunami's brother.'

Daniel leaned forward, and helped himself to another piece of chocolate cake from the rose-patterned plate on the tea table.

Well, what do you know?

'So the Wijesinhas are not a Buddhist family?'

'They're Anglican. Well, Colin and Tsunami's branch of it certainly is. Very much C. of E., though I suppose the correct term nowadays is 'Church of Ceylon'. In spite of their mother having been a Hindu.'

Daniel's determination to waste no more time thinking about Tsunami

Wijesinha took an unexpected back flip, and vanished. He said casually:

'Hindu? But that's a little unusual, surely?'

'Oh, the marriage caused quite a sensation at the time. You can imagine. There was a lot of gossip about it in the newspapers. Everyone expected young men of Rowland Wijesinha's background to carry on family traditions and marry appropriately. But Rowland was absolutely determined: it was to be Helen Ratnam, and no one else for him. His family, as I remember, was none too pleased: a Hindu! and from India!'

That would certainly have been a shock for the local colonial bourgeoisie!

'And did she – er, did Mrs Wijesinha settle down happily in this country?'

'Oh, I'm sure she did. Very happily indeed. Five children. Such fun to visit, and to be with. They were a very happy family, before . . .'

Here Dr Springdale paused, and seemed somewhat agitated. Daniel waited. 'Helen was absolutely delightful, you see. Charmed everybody who met her. Tsunami misses her, I can see that plainly. And I miss her too. I – I was very fond of Helen.'

So her mother's dead, Daniel told himself. Perhaps there's a stepmother. He tried to imagine his own home without his mother in it, and a stranger in her place: he found the thought almost unbearable. Poor little kid, Daniel thought, she must have been through a hell of a time. He was filled with admiration for the dignity with which Tsunami bore her motherless state. All was now clear.

No wonder she seems so remote, so detached: obviously, the trauma of her mother's passing has left the poor child indifferent as a nun to everyone and everything around her.

Daniel's feelings for Tsunami underwent an immediate and profound change. He felt deeply ashamed now that he had made her the object of his sexual fantasies. It had been wrong of him, unpardonable in fact.

She's so obviously above all that sort of thing, she's pure, virginal, a saint . . . I shall prove myself worthy of her.

Perhaps he was the knight that fate intended should rescue Tsunami from her sad and neglected state. So her mother had been 'a Hindu, from India'! Perhaps they did have some important things in common, perhaps his dreams of happiness were not the stuff of fantasy after all.

Anxious to find out everything he could about the family background of his beloved, Daniel held on to his cup and requested a second refill. But the Warden, fearing, perhaps, that she had already said too much, could not be tempted. She resolutely abandoned the topic of the Wijesinha family, and ignored every attempt Daniel made to revert to it. For the remainder of his visit, their conversation focused on the subject of his imminent journey to Jaffna.

'My regards to your parents, please, Daniel,' Joan Springdale said. 'Sanghamitta cannot offer them the luxury of Mahakellē – unless I can manage to lure your wonderful Peter Appuhamy away from it. But our

Hall is not without its attractions. I hope I shall have the pleasure of meeting your father and mother again when they come to stay with you.'

A Hindu . . . and from India!

The Warden's words sang in Daniel's head. His long-deferred visit to his parents in Jaffna had just taken on an unexpected dimension. As he ran down the steps to his car, he felt his spirits soar. His father's bias against Sinhalese Buddhists did not, as far as he knew, extend to Sinhalese Christians. Add to that, Daniel told himself, the fact that the differences between Indian Tamils and Ceylon Tamils were so small as to be virtually negligible. Unwilling to waste precious time establishing whether this idea was true to the facts or merely wishful thinking on his part, he began to devise a description of Tsunami that was likely to win his parents' approval, given that the young woman he was proposing to marry was not a Jaffna Tamil. His account of the future Mrs Rajaratnam would have to be one that emphasized her mother's Hindu heritage.

Should I speak to my father and my mother separately, or tackle them together? Should I approach them on my own, or through someone else? Someone of their own generation, who is still young enough in spirit to welcome new ideas, and support mine?

He couldn't think of anyone suitable just now, he'd need a few days to think about it. He would, in any case, need to think out his strategy very carefully before he said anything at all to either of them. To show too much enthusiasm would never do: his father would attribute his enthusiasm to impulsiveness, to sentimentality and weakness. Better, perhaps, to create an opportunity, during his visit with Marchmont, to bring up the subject of marriage outside the Tamil community.

There's no harm in doing that, if I do it discreetly, and in a general way: in the course of a conversation, for example, about the increasing frequency of Sinhalese/Tamil marriages these days, and how they are creating better understanding between the communities . . .

Daniel was glad the road to Jaffna was a long one. He would use the time given him by the journey to think about the information Dr Springdale had given him. He needed to turn certain ideas over in his mind, and consider their implications before he made any kind of move. Marchmont would carry on talking about the virtues of the New Criticism, and never notice his silence.

At the very moment that her son was planning his journey to Jaffna, Mrs Sarojini Rajaratnam was standing in the doorway of her kitchen, surveying with the greatest satisfaction the array of vegetables, fruits, spices and condiments laid out on her kitchen table. She had picked out the fruit and vegetables in the market herself that morning. The spices and condiments had been washed, dried in the hot Jaffna sun, pounded into powder and bottled two days ago. They would all go into the chutneys and pickles she was making today in preparation for her Girishna's visit. She was looking forward to that for its own sake, naturally, but on learning that her son was bringing a colleague with him, and that the colleague was an Englishman, Mrs Rajaratnam had had to review her original plans. The meals she served would have to be bland – English people, she knew, had poor digestions, and did not appreciate chilli and garlic in their food – but having some of her savoury specials on hand would help spice up the dishes for everyone else, and keep her husband happy.

Mrs Rajaratnam was not entirely pleased by the fact that there would be a stranger in the house during this, Girishna's first visit home since he had taken up his teaching position at Peradeniya. There were important matters to be discussed within the family, matters in which a visitor could take no part. Ever since her son's return from the United States, Mrs Rajaratnam had been active in visiting far-flung relatives, gathering information and advice, and recruiting sisters, sisters-in-law, and close cousins in the search for a suitable bride. She now had a short list drawn up of satisfactory candidates, all of whom were from acceptable families. Several of them had been educated up to the Senior School Certificate standard: some had even sat for the examination and passed it, before they were removed from school. She could not, at this early stage, ask to inspect their horoscopes, but she had scrutinized their photographs carefully to make sure there were no hidden traps: no squints or hare-lips or disfiguring moles, for instance, that the photographer had artfully brushed out or corrected. When the young women appeared in person she would check for limps that the pleats of a sari had been draped to hide. She had, of course, already made sure that there were no earlier involvements that had fallen through for one reason or another, regarding which the families were keeping quiet. According to their sponsors, every one of the short-listed candidates could play a musical instrument. Some of them sang. All were excellent cooks, 'neat and clean and home-loving'.

Mrs Rajaratnam was not a mercenary person: she had not, for instance, allowed the lack of money in a candidate's family to blind her to the young woman's virtues and advantages. As she often said scornfully, she and her husband were above that type of thinking:

Ours is not, after all, a family that has risen to its present eminence through trade.

She knew that what matters most in a daughter-in-law is a gentle, docile nature and a sound family background: everything else, including even what the world calls education, is of secondary importance.

In preparing for her son's coming, Mrs Rajaratnam had gone further than many of her friends and relations generally did when they were planning marriages. She respected her son's intellect, and she knew very well that he would never be happy with a silly or ignorant bride. Accordingly, she had arranged social functions of various kinds at which her son would have an opportunity to talk with the young women she had arranged for him to inspect. She had also built adequate opportunities for innocent (but suitably chaperoned) conversation into every social function that he would be called on to attend.

The presence of a foreigner at such functions could, of course, turn out to be a distraction. On the other hand, she reflected, they could hardly leave Mr Marchmont out of them if he were living in their house: he would not, after all, wish to spend all his time visiting temples and beaches in Jaffna. Mrs Rajaratnam decided that since her husband was affecting ignorance of what had been on her own mind for several months, appearing to think that matters would fall into place of their own accord, entertainment of their guest could become his special responsibility.

Her husband had been just the same when arrangements had been under way for the marriages of Girishna's brothers. But those occasions had been easier to manage, since both their elder boys had been quite happy to accept her judgment. Neither of them had needed an opportunity provided for conversation. Observation from a discreet distance, a shy smile from the young woman his mother had chosen as she offered him a plate of sweets said to be of her own making, had been enough for each of them.

And quite right, too.

In her day, Sarojini Rajaratnam reflected, conversation between the two young people who were to be married had not been necessary: in fact, it had been actively discouraged. Her first sight of her own future husband had been across a large room crowded with relatives who were celebrating the homecoming of a recently married couple. She had been descending a staircase among a group of laughing and gossiping girls, had glimpsed this young man as he stood talking with her father and other elders, had liked what she saw, and had mentioned the fact to her parents. Discussions had then taken place between representatives of both families: Sarojini herself had not been informed of the outcome of those discussions until two months before the wedding. And even after that, verbal exchange had not been permitted until a few days before the marriage ceremony. Her future husband had, on the other hand, been present on an occasion when she had played the *veena* and sung several classical songs to the general acclaim of a small but discriminating musical group in Jaffna town, and that was, after all, much better than any private conversation they could have had, for her father had told her that the young man appreciated good singing just as much as he did. The language of music had said everything that needed to be said between them.

Besides, everyone knows that a pretty young girl looks even prettier when she is playing a musical instrument.

Well, things were certainly very different now. The young women of today were not content with a training in music and the domestic arts, they prided themselves on being 'advanced': a word that was not necessarily complimentary when used in Jaffna's more conservative circles. Sarojini was aware that some young girls from some very respectable Jaffna Tamil families were actually attending University in the south. This she did not approve of, though of course many good Jaffna boys, including two of her own, had been sent to India for their education. But then, India was different.

She heartily approved of most things Indian, but when it came to marriage Sarojini preferred the Jaffna way of doing things to the Indian. Dowries, for instance. The giving of dowries with daughters appeared to have gone out of fashion on the subcontinent, largely due to the influence of Gandhi over the hearts and minds of the people. As the mother of three sons, Sarojini hoped it would be a long time before such subversive ideas caught on in Ceylon.

This is not to say that Sarojini Rajaratnam was not 'progressive'. On the contrary, she was a great reader of the newspapers, and kept herself up-to-date on world affairs in order to participate in discussions with her husband and her sons. She treasured a courteous letter she had received from Jawaharlal Nehru, thanking her for her congratulations on a Congress Party victory.

'I take my hat off to you, sir!' Mrs Rajaratnam had written.

It was an interesting phrase to come from her pen, since Mrs Rajaratnam, an orthodox gentlewoman from Ceylon's conservative north, had never worn a hat in her life, and was never likely to wear one. But if Pandit Nehru had been amused by the phrase, he had forborne to mention it in his courteously worded reply.

Sarojini had brought her husband a dowry, the magnificence of which was still talked about in Jaffna when weddings were the subject of discussion.

Do you remember Sarojini's dowry? The saris, the jewellery, the ebony and calamander wood furniture, and on top of all that, the house property and land . . .?

Well, her father had been a rich man, and she was his only daughter. A tear came to Mrs Rajaratnam's eye at the memory of her late father, but she wiped it away with the end of her sari, called Sellamma to peel onions and garlic, and picked up her well-honed kitchen knife. This was no time to be giving way to sadness and sentiment. There was work to be done.

The identical thought – that there was work to be done – was in the mind of her expected guest, Ronald Marchmont, as Daniel Rajaratnam brought his car to rest in the porch of the Anuradhapura Rest House, where they were to break their journey and spend a night. Marchmont had stopped by the Department to check his letterbox on their way out of Peradeniya, and had found Latha Wijesinha's essay on *Persuasion* and Irwin Fernando's on *The Eve of St Agnes* waiting there to be collected. Good, Marchmont thought, he'd work on them while he was in Jaffna. Having university work of his own that he had to do would indicate to his hosts that he did not need to be entertained and amused.

Contrary to Daniel's expectations, their journey to Jaffna, far from being punctuated by literary chatter from Marchmont, was marked by long periods in which neither of the two men had anything to say. Both were deep in thought, and each appreciated the other's silence. Daniel hummed occasionally, and once he even sang – briefly – in his big bass voice, but Ronald did neither. He had a lot to think about.

Marchmont had prepared himself for the trip by reading everything he could find on the history of Jaffna, and hoped that opportunities would arise to get around a bit on his own and see things for himself. Having had plenty of practice during his tour of the Sacred Cities with the British Council, he was pretty sure he could conduct himself correctly in most situations. To remove his shoes before entering temples and shrines was now an automatic gesture with him, and he was no longer astonished by statues and carvings in holy places that showed lovers locked in voluptuous embrace. Marchmont had done his homework, he had read Coomaraswamy, and he knew that such images symbolically represented the union of the human and the divine.

The notes for his novel were in his suitcase, together with plenty of blank paper for notes and further writing. He hadn't formulated a plot yet, preferring to let chance and inspiration take him where they would. Better to observe, reflect, and only then to write, Marchmont thought. His experience with the woman student in the Kandy bus had taught him that human interaction in a society as complex as this could be bristling with traps for the unwary. Jaffna folk might think like southerners in most matters: on the other hand, they might not.

Safest to trust my Muse.

As they neared Jaffna, Marchmont noticed that every vehicle they encountered on the road was an Austin. He mentioned this observation to Daniel as his friend skilfully negotiated a way around a cow lying in the middle of the road, apparently deaf to all the pleas of the car's horn. Daniel smiled.

'Every model that the Austin Motor Company ever turned out,' he said. 'You'll find them all in Jaffna. From the earliest to the latest, from the famous 1920s models to the Sprite, the Sheerline and the Princess, you'll see them all here. One of my father's friends owns an original four-cylinder Ten. You may not believe this, but it's still roadworthy.'

'Doesn't anyone in Jaffna drive anything else but Austin cars?'

'Not if they can help it. My father doesn't trust any other manufacturing company, it's Austin for him, and always has been. The car he's driving now is a 1937 model, but he's in no hurry to trade it in. And there are many who would agree with him.'

'For heaven's sake, why?'

'For many reasons. The Austins are economical on petrol, that's important to the man from Jaffna: probably the most important consideration. Next, there are plenty of spare parts available – just look around you and see whether we pass any garages servicing anything but Austins.'

Marchmont obeyed. He could see none.

'Exactly. And best of all, every mechanic here knows everything there is to be known about Austins. The kids probably play with Austin spare parts from their Appa's garage as children elsewhere play with building blocks. Long before they've grown up, they've become experts.'

'How did this come about?'

Marchmont thought about Peradeniya and its dons, who were said to measure the value of an overseas Fellowship by its capacity to accommodate the price of a European car.

So, is yours a Volkswagen Fellowship or a Peugeot Fellowship?

That was a question regularly asked of academics poised for a field trip, by one of Peradeniya's more playful Registrars.

'It's the profitable side of colonialism,' Daniel replied. 'We were instructed by the British that British manufacture is the best in the world: nothing could beat it, certainly nothing from Germany, which was sure to be unreliable – like the Germans – and nothing from Japan, which was gimcrack at best, low-grade imitations of British originals. How long has Austin been in business, Ron? Do you know?'

'They started up in 1906,' said Marchmont, whose little car, now resting peacefully in the spacious garage at Mahakellē, was an A40 he had bought in Colombo on his arrival in Ceylon. 'In Birmingham.'

'Well, there you have it – the right address: Birmingham, famous throughout the Empire for high-quality manufacture. Hand out the same message over a period of fifty years, and people believe it implicitly. Southerners with Austins for sale drive them all the way up to Jaffna because they know they'll find plenty of buyers here, the conservative type of owner who wants a solid, durable car, and rates reliability over style. Buyers like my father.'

'So why don't *you* drive an Austin?'

'Because I've seen something of the others. Appa thinks I'm crazy to have bought this – "No second-hand value in a French car," he says. "A Renault Dauphine? Tchah! What kind of car is that? No one's going to want to buy it. You'll see!"'

'It's awfully comfortable, Daniel.'

'Don't I know it? It's a terrific car.'

How can we keep 'em down on the farm, Now that they've seen Paree?

The old tune went insistently through Marchmont's head. He began to hum gently to himself, and was still humming when the Renault purred smoothly between two woven palmyra fences and came to rest in front of a white-painted house. A middle-aged woman in a crisp cotton sari stood on the front steps, smiling a welcome.

'That's my mother,' said Daniel. 'She must have some sort of sixth sense – I've never got back home at any time in my life when she wasn't standing there, just there, on that very spot, waiting to welcome me home. Even when I was a schoolboy. My brothers say it was just the same with them.'

'A remarkable lady,' Marchmont agreed.

He recalled his own mother, a ciggy drooping from the corner of her mouth as she slapped his dinner on the kitchen table before leaving for the evening shift at the factory in which she had worked for twenty years. Remarkable women altogether, mothers. He checked his handloom shoulder-bag to make sure the wrapping of his gift for Mrs Rajaratnam hadn't got crushed during the journey, and joined Daniel on the veranda.

Marchmont had wondered what he should take with him as a gift to his hostess. He had been about to purchase an expensive leather handbag he had seen in Cargill's shop-window when Joan Springdale, happening by, had advised against it.

'Not at all the thing, Ronald,' she had said. 'The Rajaratnams are orthodox Hindus, you know. The wearing of leather may well be off-limits. Like the eating of beef, you see.'

She had paused a moment to consider.

'Something personal and guaranteed to please . . . I know! I know exactly what she would like best. Take her some Knight's Castile soap. Knight's Castile is the nearest England comes to sandalwood soap from Mysore, and she will appreciate that. Call over at Sanghamitta the day before you leave – I'll have it waiting for you.'

She had been as good as her word: four cakes of soap, gift-wrapped and tied up with ribbon, were waiting in the sub-Warden's office at Sanghamitta when Marchmont called round on Friday evening. With them was a note from the Warden which carried a postscript:

You may run into Tsunami Wijesinha in Jaffna. Her father's opening a new wing in the Jaffna Public Library, and she mentioned last week that she may drive up with him.

Marchmont's gift was a great success. Mrs Rajaratnam was pleased and touched.

'How did you know it is my favourite?' she wanted to know. 'I can't find it anywhere these days.'

Marchmont smiled enigmatically, and did not answer. He didn't think Dr Springdale would mind too much if he collected some gold stars for prescience. Mrs Rajaratnam hospitably indicated a chair on the veranda:

'Come, come, Mr Marchmont! Sit, sit, while I call him.'

She then disappeared, while Marchmont looked inquiringly at Daniel.

'Him?'

'My father,' Daniel said. 'My mother never speaks of my father by name. She would consider it impertinent.'

'I see.'

A-a-alfie! In his head Marchmont heard his mother's voice ringing shrilly through their semi-detached in Leeds. *Where the hell are you?* And yet she had loved his father dearly.

Mr Rajaratnam appeared, neat in a white cotton *verti*, a short-sleeved shirt and sandals. He embraced his son and shook Marchmont's hand.

'We are so happy to see you,' said he. 'While you are here, you must consider yourself in your own home.'

His wife stood a little way behind him, smiling her assent.

'Thank you very much, sir,' Marchmont responded. 'It's very kind of you both.'

His host advanced to the edge of the veranda, and surveyed Daniel's Renault.

'So it made the journey,' said he. 'Good. I didn't think it would. "We might have to drive out to Elephant Pass to rescue them," I told her. "That flashy car of Girishna's will never make it." All paint and no substance, these European models.'

He turned to Marchmont.

'What's your car, Mr Marchmont?'

'An Austin, sir, a second-hand A40 I bought in Colombo.'

Mr Rajaratnam nodded his approval.

'And it is giving you good service?'

'It certainly is. I've no complaints.'

'Have it driven up here when the time comes to sell it,' he was advised. 'You'll get a better price than you would in Colombo.'

'I will. Thanks for the tip.'

In the evening, Mrs Rajaratnam said, there was to be a small party to welcome their son and his guest. How small? Oh, very small. Only about eighty people . . .

Eighty people?

. . . yes, a very small party, only close friends and relatives, all of them people who enjoyed good music. Nothing formal.

But for the present, their programme was to be lunch, followed by the good rest she was sure they both needed after the long drive.

'I had hoped—' Marchmont began, then stopped himself.

He had hoped to do a bit of sight-seeing before lunch. He'd been about to mention this to Daniel's father when it struck him that he might be considered discourteous if he sloped off on his own within an hour of getting here. Perhaps it would be best to wait until after the meal.

The thought of sight-seeing was still in his mind when they sat down to lunch. The idea of starting his experience of Jaffna with a visit to Old

Government House, that relic of British colonial times with its herd of wild ponies, appealed to him. By the time the meal was drawing to a close, however, the lassitude brought on by a hot Jaffna day had combined with Mrs Rajaratnam's cooking to make Marchmont wish for nothing more than to stretch himself on the fresh white sheets on his bed. A few minutes' rest would be very welcome, he thought, closing his eyes and listening to the gentle creaking of an old-fashioned ceiling fan stirring the air overhead.

Around him, the house slept soundly in the drowsy warmth of a Jaffna afternoon. Everything was quiet, except for an occasional chirp from a bird splashing about in the ornamental Italian birdbath that stood outside his window: a gift, he had been told when he commented admiringly on its workmanship, from Daniel's eldest brother and his wife, presently resident in Rome. Now would be an excellent time to slip away if he wanted to. Daniel, who was occupying the room next to his, appeared to have vanished, and in their bedroom further along the shadowy corridor, Mr and Mrs Rajaratnam were probably enjoying an after-lunch siesta. Marchmont remembered the essays he had brought with him to read and correct but, try as he might, he could not marshal the energy needed to sit up, reach out, and extract them from the bag at the foot of his bed.

Consciousness gradually slipped from him. His last thought before sleep overwhelmed him utterly was that his plan to go sight-seeing that afternoon had been a thoroughly foolish idea.

One of the silliest I've ever had.

6

A MUSICAL EVENING IN JAFFNA

Marchmont had never seen so many pretty women in his life – at any rate, he had never seen so many of them gathered in one spot.

That spot was the large entrance hall of the Rajaratnam home, and it was filled with the shimmer of silk saris, the fragrance of flowers worn in hair that coiled like black silk or swung in braids, and the music of female laughter. Behind that music, Marchmont detected another plangent melody, and ran it to earth at last in a corner of the room in which a group of musicians, seated on a white cloth spread on the carpet, had begun to tune their instruments.

Soon they would begin to play; and Marchmont, to whom most of the instruments he could see were unfamiliar, was looking forward to hearing the sounds they would bring forth. There were some instruments that he recognized, having attended a concert given by Ravi Shankar in London – the *tabla*, of course, which you couldn't mistake, the *veena* and the *sarodh*. But what was the name of that drum, and that other instrument that looked rather like an accordion?

Daniel could not enlighten him. He did not share his parents' love of oriental music, and as a child had once seriously offended his father by describing the singing of a famous Jaffna vocalist as 'gargling'. He allowed Marchmont to make his own way among the guests, who seemed to welcome the questions of this polite, well-mannered young Englishman. He noted with amusement at one point that his friend went down on one knee to talk to the *sarodh* player.

Daniel himself was being kept busy by his mother, who made him cross and re-cross the room several times in order to talk to one group of guests or another. So artful were Mrs Rajaratnam's arrangements that it took Daniel some time to realize that this was an 'inspection visit' on a very grand scale. The realization, when it came, did not alter his manner. Aware though he was that in a day or two he would be presenting his mother with a proposal that would prove all her efforts to have been useless, he continued to stand and move at his ease, smiling down from his great height on one flowerlike face after another, listening attentively to all that was being told him by parents and relatives. One young lady had won high distinctions in all subjects in the Senior School Certificate examination, another concocted table arrangements from coral and seashells, the ulundu vadai made by a third melted in one's mouth, a fourth specialized in embroidery.

Several little girls, beautifully dressed and seriously intent on the task which Mrs Rajaratnam had set them, were handing round savouries and sweets arranged in rows on silver trays, while Mr Rajaratnam personally presided over the serving of drinks from a trestle table in the garden. The buzz of conversation grew louder, until it was suddenly broken into by a girl's voice.

'Ronald! How wonderful to see you! Why didn't you tell me you would be in Jaffna?'

Guests craned their necks, eager to identify the speaker, a person who was apparently on such intimate terms with the Rajaratnams' English guest that she had shamelessly addressed him by his first name before a room full of strangers.

'Who is that girl?' his mother hissed in Daniel's ear. 'I've never seen her before.'

Daniel had been stunned into momentary silence by the unexpected sound of Tsunami's voice. He spun round, and there she was, on the other side of the room, elegant in a crimson silk sari and perfectly at ease, holding out her hand to Ronald Marchmont: who was, Daniel noted with irritation, gazing at her with quite unnecessary enthusiasm. He turned away from this unwelcome vision and, with difficulty, found his voice.

'She's one of our Peradeniya students,' he said.

'What is she doing here?'

'She must – she must be here with the Minister,' replied Daniel, who had suddenly glimpsed Rowland Wijesinha at the other end of the room, in conversation with his father. 'Her father – look, he's over there, talking to Appa – is Minister for Cultural Affairs, so I suppose he is in Jaffna for some official reason.'

'Your Appa didn't tell me he had invited a Minister here this evening,' Mrs Rajaratnam said.

She was not pleased. She knew very well that private parties attended by politicians generally cease to be private.

'Everybody here is a music-lover,' she stated crossly.

'I'm told that Mr Wijesinha is a connoisseur of the arts,' Daniel said. 'So he's probably a music-lover, too, or Appa wouldn't have invited him.'

At any moment now, Ronald will tell her that I am here.

His father was looking in their direction, presumably pointing out his wife, and telling the Minister that there, standing beside her, was his U.S.-returned son. What if all these visitors came over at the same time, from different directions, to greet his mother? For then – then, great heavens, *she will be standing beside me, she will be meeting my parents, she will be a guest in my family home . . .*

He steeled himself to hear Tsunami's voice.

What will she say to me? How should I respond?

The buzz of conversation in the room had by no means ceased, but it seemed to Daniel that the whole world had fallen silent around him and that time itself had stopped. As in a dream he saw Marchmont take Tsunami's outstretched hand in his and kiss it.

The extravagant public gesture caused a further sensation. Children giggled, girls looked envious, fathers registered amazement, and mothers disapproval. The only people in the room who did not react in some extreme way were the Headmaster of Jaffna College, who smiled into his beard, the Minister for Cultural Affairs who came over with Mr Rajaratnam to be introduced to his hostess, and strangely, Tsunami herself, who continued to stand talking with Marchmont, apparently quite unruffled by her companion's gallantry.

So Marchmont had *not*, after all, pointed him out to Tsunami. He suddenly recalled how his friend had reddened when asked if he had any thoughts of making his home in the island. Interesting, he thought angrily:

She calls him 'Ronald' off campus, but it's always 'Mr Marchmont' at choir practice.

'Pretty girl,' Mrs Rajaratnam said somewhat grudgingly, observing Tsunami as she stood smiling up at Marchmont on the other side of the room. Through the turmoil of his thoughts, Daniel heard his mother inquiring:

'I suppose they are to be married?'

'Not that I know of.'

'But he—'

'In Europe and America, Amma, a kiss is no big deal,' said her Yankee son. He sounded furious, and his mother wondered what had happened to upset him.

'No different from shaking hands.'

Mrs Rajaratnam was shocked. Were Daniel's manners with acquaintances outside his home as relaxed as his friend's, she wondered. Was *he* in the habit, like Mr Marchmont, of kissing his students?

The sooner this son of ours is safely married, the better.

The orchestra appeared to have finished tuning up, and Mr Rajaratnam directed the spreading of snow-white sheets on the carpet for his guests to seat themselves. He announced that they were to enjoy a special treat:

Suhasini Rao, a classical singer from India, who was on a visit to Jaffna, had accepted his invitation to sing for the assembled company.

A pale-skinned, intense-looking woman in a white sari, wearing no ornament other than a gold *thali* around her neck, now took up her position beside the orchestra, and waited attentively for quiet. Tsunami subsided on to the floor, her silk sari spread around her in a pleated half-circle, and Marchmont, after a moment's hesitation, sat down cross-legged beside her. The little girls abandoned their trays, and began distributing sheets of paper among the seated guests. Marchmont took one, and found that it was typewritten in English.

'I think these must be the texts of the lyrics we're going to hear,' Tsunami whispered. 'There are quite a few people here who are expats, and have lost touch with the language. The idea is to help them reconnect. Pater tells me Mr Rajaratnam is passionate about music, and when he hosts a musical evening like this one, he likes to make sure everyone participates and knows exactly what's going on.'

Marchmont nodded, making a mental note of the fact that while Daniel called his father 'Appa', Tsunami appeared to call hers 'Pater', a term that was no longer used, he believed, even in England. Would he ever succeed in understanding the complexities of this society?

He looked around for Daniel, so that he could point him out to Tsunami. His friend was nowhere to be seen. Marchmont returned to his paper as the singer, standing now in the centre of a circle of listeners, turned slowly with her arms raised and her hands clasped, addressing herself courteously to every section of her audience. He listened carefully as the musicians struck their first notes.

That's a signal, that's the key, offered so that she can pick it up.

Since he could not access the language of her lyrics, he decided that he would try to distinguish each instrument as it came into play: he might then be able to respond to the singer's performance at the level with which he was most familiar, that of music.

Suhasini Rao produced a high, sweet note, following it with what seemed to be an arpeggio that carried her voice up and down the scale, and Marchmont studied his paper, attempting to work out a connection between what he was hearing and the words on the page:

I wait for my Lord in the silence of the night,
I wait for his presence to bring light to my darkness.
The moon covers her face in a veil of cloud,
The stars have hidden themselves:
Where is my Lord?
Why does he not come to me?

Marchmont realized that what he was hearing was not a love song but a hymn: or rather, he corrected himself, a love song *and* a hymn. One by one, the instruments took up the melody that the singer had sketched for them, and as they did so, some of the listeners began to keep time with movements of the head and feet. This, Marchmont thought, must be what Tsunami means by 'participating'. Caught up in the music, he was just about to try keeping time himself when, looking up from his typewritten sheet, he found the singer gazing directly into his eyes.

I have prepared a bed for my Beloved,
Soft with green leaves and the petals of new-blown roses,
Wine I have brought, and ripe pomegranates
For his delight.
But where is my Lord?
Why does he not come to me?

Marchmont had never before attended a private concert of Indian music. He felt himself grow hot with embarrassment as the singer fixed her gaze on his face. Her eyes looked deep into his, she appeared to be singing for him alone. His instincts urged him to look away, to look down at his paper, to look up at the ornamented ceiling, to look anywhere but at those glittering dark eyes gazing so passionately into his.

Why is she singing to me in this very private, intimate way, in a room filled with strangers?

Marchmont's urge to look away immediately was accompanied by a very English conviction that this would not be a polite thing to do. Unaware how to proceed, he did nothing: sitting absolutely still, hoping that he was not making a complete ass of himself, he gazed earnestly back at the singer.

'You did exactly the right thing,' an amused Tsunami assured him afterwards. 'If a singer happens to catch your eye, just look straight back at her until she moves on to someone else. If you had looked away from her at that moment, you could have broken her concentration.'

'Daniel should have warned me this kind of thing might happen,' Marchmont said.

'Is Dr Rajaratnam here?' Tsunami asked.

'Of course he is,' Marchmont replied in surprise. 'This is his family home.'

'I didn't know that,' Tsunami said. Her eyes searched the room. 'I can't see him anywhere.'

'He was here,' Marchmont said, 'until just a moment ago. But he told me once that he doesn't share his parents' taste in music, so maybe he made himself scarce when the instruments started tuning up. I really don't know where he can have got to.'

'You sound rather desperate, Ron! You'll survive the evening without him, you know.'

'Oh, I know. But I'll admit I was terribly embarrassed.'

'There was no reason to be,' Tsunami said. 'Suhasini Rao wasn't singing to you, personally. Didn't you see where she was looking?'

'Into my eyes,' Marchmont said, and blushed at the memory.

'Not at all. You may not have existed for her at all, except as a sort of shadow. She was looking inwards, at the image of Krishna in her heart.'

'I see,' Marchmont said. 'Thanks for telling me!'

Tsunami laughed.

'Why don't you have another samosa?'

Having reached the end of her stanza, Suhasini Rao had turned away from Marchmont, and focused her attention on another listener in the audience. Marchmont breathed a sigh of relief. Released at last from the mesmerizing spell of her regard, he looked around him. Her new target, a middle-aged gentleman with an embroidered shawl about his shoulders, was much more relaxed about the whole thing than he had been: tapping his toes and wagging his head, he was smiling with enjoyment as the music flowed around him.

And what marvellous music!

Able once again to concentrate, Marchmont closed his eyes and gave himself up to the pleasure of listening.

'You were enjoying yourself, Mr Marchmont!' his host said the next morning, approvingly. 'You appreciate good music!'

Ronald didn't deny it.

'Wasn't that Tsunami Wijesinha?' Daniel asked Marchmont casually, when the two young men were alone.

'Of course it was,' Marchmont replied, a little sharply. 'I was surprised that you didn't come over and talk to her. She's one of your students, after all.'

'She seemed very interested in talking to *you*,' Daniel said coldly. 'Quite preoccupied, in fact. I didn't want to interrupt your conversation.'

Damn! I shouldn't have said that: now Ron will imagine that I'm jealous.

A ridiculous idea.

After a short pause, during which he busied himself with looking for a map of Jaffna that Ron could use during his stay in the peninsula, Daniel found himself saying:

'Anything between the two of you?'

'Who? Tsunami Wijesinha and me? No, of course not, we're just good friends. We have a lot in common, you know. Pity she's reading history and not literature – she has a real feeling for words.'

'Oh?'

'Yes. She was explaining the texts of the songs to me, and doing it very well. She's so sensitive to language, and tremendously well read. I was impressed – and appreciative! Any problem with that?'

'Not at all. My mother was curious, that's all.'

7

WASTE

At breakfast, the morning after the Rajaratnams' party, Daniel's father had been in an exceptionally genial mood.

'That fellow Wijesinha,' he told Ron Marchmont over the *appam* and fish curry that constituted his favourite morning meal, 'knows something about music. Rare in a politician, and *very* rare in a Sinhalese.'

Well, *that's* an auspicious beginning, Daniel thought gloomily. He looked across the table at Ron who, by nodding agreeably, was doing the right and tactful thing. It didn't do to disagree with his father first thing in the morning, whatever you thought about what he was saying: that was a lesson Daniel had learned early in life, the hard and practical way. It seemed that Ron had learned it by instinct.

'That daughter of his, too. She actually speaks Tamil!'

Hullo! Here's an unexpected opening . . .

'Her mother came to Ceylon from India,' Daniel said quickly. 'Dr Springdale told me Mrs Wijesinha was Tamil, a very cultured person.'

Mrs Rajaratnam bustled in with a tray of vegetables and pickles, said 'No wonder! That explains it!' and bustled out again. She had declined to sit down with them at the breakfast table, preferring to serve the food herself.

'From India?'

Mr Rajaratnam was surprised.

'How did that come about?'

'I understand she had been a very gifted child artist, sir,' Marchmont said. 'Mr Wijesinha was touring India, saw her exhibiting her paintings at an art gallery in Bombay, and—'

'And that was that,' finished Daniel impatiently.

How has Ronald obtained so much inside information about her family history?

'Well, the daughter is a charming, intelligent girl,' Mr Rajaratnam said. 'And *you*, Mr Marchmont, are a fortunate man!'

The misunderstanding took a little time to resolve, during which the thread of the conversation, which had just begun to look rather promising to Daniel, was irretrievably lost. He decided that he would try to find it again in a few days' time, when Ronald should have gone sight-seeing on his own. In the meantime he suffered, with loving patience and great politeness, his mother's attempts to interest him in one 'suitable' Jaffna girl after another.

Realizing, by the fourth day of his stay, that she was unlikely to support the idea of his marriage to a Sinhalese, Daniel brought up the subject of Tsunami Wijesinha with his father. Although he did this discreetly and casually – so casually as to convey the impression that he was talking about a hypothetical case, rather than his own – the effect was shattering.

The presence within earshot of their English guest might have imposed some restraint on the old man, at least as regards volume of sound. But since Marchmont was well out of the house at the time the argument began, Mr Rajaratnam could let himself go. Daniel encountered, for the first time, what he had never before heard verbally expressed, his father's deep-rooted distrust of Sinhalese southerners.

He had never seen his father in such a state. Mr Rajaratnam's views (based on his experience of Sinhalese chicanery and duplicity over many years) appeared to be set in concrete. His vocabulary grew richer by the second, and it was obvious that nothing Daniel could say on the side of reason would have the smallest effect in changing his mind.

Mrs Rajaratnam entered the room when they were halfway through their discussion. On learning the subject of it, she challenged her son directly:

'You are not talking to your Appa of someone else's wishes, but of your own.'

Daniel could not deny it. Upon which, his mother burst into tears and accused him of trying to dishonour the family name.

'Have you asked this – this person to marry you?'

'I have not,' Daniel said.

'Well, we must at least thank God for that!'

'But I want to do so, Amma. I am sorry that you and Appa don't like the idea, but I feel sure that Mr Wijesinha will not refuse me when I speak to him.'

'Mr Wijesinha? That Sinhalese minister who was here the other day?'

'You may not have heard me say it, Amma, but Tsunami's mother is Tamil, a Tamil lady from India . . .'

'And a Christian!' his mother wept.

'She is not a Christian, Amma. Mrs Wijesinha is a Hindu.'

'Christian or Hindu, what difference does it make? The father is a Sinhalese. What have your Appa and I done, that such misery should come upon us! What sin have we committed?'

Mrs Rajaratnam declared that as she could never survive the sorrow and shame of having a Sinhalese daughter-in-law enter her house, she might as well drink poison or insecticide immediately and put an end to her life. Alternatively, she said, she would follow the example of the Mahatma and fast unto death.

She did not, in the event, carry out any of these threats, but her obvious distress so unnerved Daniel that he could not persist. The subject was abandoned, and was not resumed for the whole period of his visit.

Mr Rajaratnam was not present when the two young men made their farewells and left for Peradeniya. The eyes of Mrs Rajaratnam, who *was* present, her hands filled with parcels for Joan Springdale and delicacies for themselves, were red with weeping. Marchmont, sensitive to the increasing tension in the family, sensed that her sorrow must have its roots in something more than the fact that Daniel was ending a brief visit home.

The journey back to Peradeniya was marked by talk which, as far as Daniel was concerned, was of little consequence. He had left Jaffna in a sombre mood, and now hardly heard what his colleague was saying. Marchmont had succeeded in getting through the task of reading and marking his English Honours essays; and after one sideways glance at Daniel's grim profile as he drove, and another at the climbing needle of the speedometer, he was glad Latha Wijesinha's essay on *Persuasion* had provided him with a timely topic of conversation. Very little of his enthusiasm for her performance got through to Daniel, however, who stared silently through the windscreen as his Renault consumed the miles to Peradeniya.

For by this time Daniel was much too far gone, too deeply in love, to give up his determination to marry Tsunami. As soon as they returned to Mahakellē, he commenced an ardent courtship: ardent, that is, in terms of what Peradeniya permitted at the time. Which was not much, thought Daniel, remembering past flirtations at Columbia, and hampered, too, by the fact that Tsunami did not seem in the least aware of his feelings for her.

I might as well be invisible, for all the notice she takes of me.

Notes left on Tsunami's desk elicited no reply. Finding her seated in the reference library one evening, he had taken the desk next to hers. She did not seem to register his presence, and he had sat beside her, reading, for a whole hour without a word having been spoken between them until at last she had got up and left.

A parcel delivered to 'Miss T. Wijesinha' at Sanghamitta Hall was found to contain a beautiful Indian silk sari, but the note that had accompanied it disappeared before her friends could find out who had sent it.

'Just like my brother Chris,' Tsunami said carelessly at lunch that day, 'to send me a present and forget to put in a card.'

A flask of perfume, similarly delivered, was also a seeming casualty to Wijesinha male forgetfulness: on this occasion it was presumed by the top-floor balcony that the gift had been sent by Tsunami's father. Both sari and scent, securely parcelled and neatly labelled, were returned to Daniel's letterbox in the Staff Common Room the following week. Taking the parcel back to Mahakellē in his briefcase, Daniel looked for a letter or at least a message of some kind, hidden in the folds of the sari: there was none. His attempts to catch Tsunami's eye when he asked her a question in class failed dismally. She looked either out of the window or down at her desk.

Meeting with cool indifference in the tutorial and outside it, Daniel decided to call for assistance from the one student in Tsunami's class he believed to be free of the damnable inhibitions that seemed to beset the rest.

'Miss Pathirana, would you stay back, please, at the end of this class? I would like to discuss some aspects of your last essay with you.'

Shirani Pathirana, surprised, remained in her seat when the bell rang, while the rest of her class filed out. Daniel picked up her essay, sat down at the student desk in front of her, and (for the benefit of any person who might be observing him through the glass panel in the tutorial room door) began turning its pages.

'I hope you will not be offended, Miss Pathirana, by what I'm going to say. This is not about your essay at all, which is, I should say, very well-researched and a credit to you. What I want to say to you concerns your classmate, Miss Wijesinha. Please help me to tell her that I love her.'

Shirani was startled into complete silence. A fleeting suspicion crossed her mind that she was the victim of an elaborate practical joke devised by Messrs Marchmont & Rajaratnam, 'the Mahakellē Bachelors' as the top-floor balcony sometimes called the two young lecturers. But as Daniel continued to speak, gazing with obvious sincerity directly into her eyes as he told her of notes and gifts that had been returned by her friend, and messages that had gone unanswered, scepticism turned into sympathy.

'Who'd have thought,' she told Latha later, 'that the man had so much passion in him?'

Choosing her moment, Shirani said that afternoon to Tsunami:

'What do you think you're playing at, Tsunami? Do you want Dr Rajaratnam, or don't you? Decide one way or the other, and put the poor man out of his misery! He's hoping you'll send even an occasional glance in his direction, instead of treating him as if he doesn't exist.'

'I've decided to apply for transfer to Mr Labrooy's tutorial class,' was Tsunami's reply.

'Why?'

'Dr Rajaratnam confuses me,' Tsunami said. 'I don't know what to make of him. He ignores me totally one day, and sends me expensive presents and cryptic messages the next. Just look at this note. It arrived yesterday.'

She showed Shirani a half-sheet of paper covered with Daniel Rajaratnam's neat handwriting.

'So what? It's a xeroxed list of references for our next tutorial. I received one exactly like it.'

'Look closely. Look at the last item. Do you have *that* on your list?'

Shirani read the reference aloud.

'"See Robert Browning, *Dramatic Lyrics*, 'Life in a Love', Verse 1, lines 1–3" . . . I don't understand it,' she said. 'Why is he referring you to Robert Browning for a History essay?'

'That's just what I asked myself,' Tsunami said. 'So I looked it up last night, in a copy of Browning on Latha's shelf, while the rest of you were having coffee on the balcony. Do you want to know what the "lines" are? The first two are made up of just three words:

Escape me?

Never—

And the third line just beneath those two, is—

Beloved!

What am I supposed to do, Shirani?'

Shirani stared at her friend for a moment, then dissolved into laughter.

'Ooh, I *like* your Dr Rajaratnam, Tsunami! He may be feeling down, but he certainly isn't out, is he! How can you possibly resist such an approach?'

Tsunami made no reply. Shirani looked closely at her friend.

'Well, well, well! Do I detect a blush? Are we experiencing a flutter of the heart?'

'Do be quiet, Shirani, please! Someone will hear you.'

'Well, there's nothing cryptic about *that* message, if you ask me! You'd better give the matter some serious thought, sweetie, and please do it soon. As a favour to me. If he has to ask me to stay back after class another time so that he can pretend to check my essay, our classmates will be getting ideas about *me*.'

Daniel had appealed to the right person. Shirani contrived, without delay and with Dr Springdale's benevolent permission, an interview for him with Tsunami in the Warden's private sitting room at Sanghamitta. Matters must have been concluded to the satisfaction of both lovers during that interview, for during the remainder of the term Daniel and Tsunami found ways and means of meeting privately, on and off campus, safe from prying eyes.

'Lucky for Tsunami she's at Sanghamitta and not at Peries Hall,' Shirani told Latha later. 'One look down the throat of that leopard in Mrs Raptor's quarters, and poor Dr R might have run for his life.'

Latha, remembering Mrs Raptor's all-seeing binoculars and the efficient information system that had quickly carried news to her of the picnic she and Tsunami had enjoyed with Chris and Alexander by the river in

Teldeniya, advised her cousin that a public show of mutual indifference would help to deflect campus gossip.

Also helpful in this regard was Tsunami's timely transference to Mr Justin Labrooy's tutorial class. Latha and Shirani revealed to no other member of their close little group where 'our star-crossed lovers' (as Shirani insisted on calling them) met, nor how, in a world filled with curious and inquisitive people, they found the time and the place to make love.

Despite these successful strategies, the strain on Tsunami was obvious to Latha. In situations of enforced silence and pretended indifference, paranoia develops, emotions become more intense, and even the most intelligent lovers lose their sense of humour. When Tsunami confided to Latha that she and Daniel planned to marry at the end of her final year ('We may have to elope,' she said), and appealed for help in arranging some of their meetings on campus, she could not summon up a smile when Latha quoted Leigh Hunt's lines to her—

Stolen sweets are always sweeter,
Stolen kisses much completer,
Stolen looks are nice in chapels,
Stolen, stolen, be your apples . . .

There were moments when some of their fellow-students – Amali, for instance – came close to guessing the truth; as when she and Latha came late into Hall one evening after seeing a movie at the Arts Theatre, and ran into Tsunami at the head of the Sanghamitta steps. Her long black hair, usually so elegantly swept up, lay tumbled about her shoulders, and her beautiful blue and orange sari was carelessly draped, as if it had been put on in a hurry. Her lipstick was smudged, but her eyes shone like stars, and her arm, which brushed Latha's as the three girls walked together into the Hall, felt as hot to the touch as if she had a fever.

'Where on earth have you been, Tsunami? You missed a lovely film!' Amali said.

Tsunami said she'd been kept late at the gym, but, as Amali said to Latha later, it was odd that she wasn't wearing her track suit.

'Your Dr Rajaratnam's easily the sexiest man on campus,' Premani de Silva told Shirani and Tsunami, on another occasion.

'The fact that he's my History tutor doesn't make him *my* Dr Rajaratnam,' Shirani had promptly shot back, to save Tsunami the need of a reply. But Premani was not to be deterred.

'Come off it,' said she. 'Don't tell me it doesn't make a difference to have someone like that teaching you!' She poured milk into her coffee, and added:

'Such a *waste*!'

Tsunami, who had been lounging in a chair on the balcony, gazing up at the stars in their bright procession in the clear Peradeniya skies, said sharply:

'What do you mean, a waste?'

'Well, that he's a Tamil, naturally!' Premani laughed. 'His family's sure to get him hitched to some nice girl in Jaffna with a big fat dowry. What hope can there be for poor us?'

Premani was not, of course, serious in her mock-despair. Marry a Tamil! That was out of the question for a Sinhalese girl, and they all knew it. Latha, Amali and Shirani laughed at Premani's joke, as they had been expected to do. Tsunami said nothing: she did not appear to have heard the answer to her question. Latha could not see her cousin's face in the darkness of the balcony, but on the following morning she had to ask Mutthulakshmi to come in with her dustpan and brush to collect a tangle of shredded cotton that lay under her chair. Tsunami, sitting silent in the dark, had been tearing her handkerchief to pieces.

For the year was 1957. Ever since 1956, when the leader of Rowland Wijesinha's party had been swept to power on the strength of his promise to make Sinhala the nation's official language within twenty-four hours, politically inspired prejudice directed against non-Sinhala speakers, extending rapidly to Hindus, Christians, Muslims and ethnic minorities in general, Sinhala-speaking or not, had begun to infect the island's tranquil society. The situation in the country as a whole, and the profound shift that was taking place in race relations, was brought sharply home to Latha and Tsunami in their ivory tower at Peradeniya when Rowland Wijesinha was informed in an anonymous letter of his daughter's romantic involvement with a Tamil don on campus.

Infuriated by the news, and even more by the manner in which it had been conveyed, Rowland chose to forget the liberal inclinations of his own youth. He drove up to Peradeniya without prior warning of any kind, charged into the Warden's office, and insisted that his daughter pack her clothes and books, and leave the campus with him forthwith.

Things moved very fast after that. It seemed to Latha that a wheel had been set rolling down a steep hill and no one could stop it. Daniel Rajaratnam tried to contact Tsunami through her campus friends, but her family had seen to it that she was unreachable.

'Tsunami *hamu* on holiday with the Master and Madam on the estate,' said Raman when Latha rang up to inquire.

Rowland himself came to the telephone when Latha rang a second time, a week later. Tsunami would get in touch with her friends when she returned to Colombo, he said. His voice was unfriendly. Weeks passed by before one of Shirani's insistent telephone calls to Tsunami elicited a reply.

'She's abandoning our History honours class to marry a cousin of hers,' Shirani said crossly. 'A businessman.'

'*An arranged marriage?*'

Latha was horrified.

'More like a shotgun wedding,' Shirani said. '"I promised my father I wouldn't see Daniel again," she told me. Mr Labrooy is devastated. He shook his head in disappointment when I told him the news. I asked Tsunami straight out why she thought it necessary to give up her studies. You can continue with your degree as an external student, I said, you know perfectly well you're the best brain in our class. She'd been heading for a First, there's no doubt about that.'

'What did Tsunami say?'

'Not much. She was so choked up that I could hardly recognize her voice. "What's the point in going on with the degree?" she told me, "Nimal doesn't approve of university studies for women."'

Latha appealed to Herbert.

'Thaththi, *do* something! Speak to Uncle Rowland!'

Herbert did his best. But when he protested to Rowland that Tsunami should not be denied the chance to complete her degree, Moira (backed up by Tara) vetoed the suggestion. She was convinced, she said, that if Tsunami returned to university studies while Rajaratnam was still on the Peradeniya staff, 'all this nonsense will just start up again'. Besides, Moira said, it was Tara's opinion that Tsunami 'simply could not be trusted'.

'I'm sorry to say this, Herbert,' Rowland Wijesinha said. 'But Latha has been a bad influence on Tsunami. She had the power to influence her for good, and she did not use it.'

These were terrible words, and they lay on Latha's mind like weights of lead. She tried hard not to mind her uncle's remark, but she did, in fact, mind it very much. Did Ranil think equally badly of her? She was not sure she could bear it if he did.

Latha wondered whether Chris and Colin thought the same way, and consoled herself at last by remembering that they knew their sister well enough to know also that she had a mind of her own, and was not to be easily influenced by anyone.

8

FIRE ON THE MOUNTAIN

The abrupt end that had been put to Tsunami's love affair left Latha feeling depressed and miserable.

'Tsunami isn't allowed to speak to me now,' she told Amali. 'Not even on the telephone. I'm regarded as a criminal because I encouraged her love affair with Daniel.'

But Amali, who only a year previously would have been the last person to actively promote a cross-cultural love affair, adopted a different point of view.

'You must not let yourself think in that way, Latha,' she said firmly. 'Dr Rajaratnam isn't only a clever, gifted person, he's a good man. *You* saw that. Why didn't Tsunami's father see it? It's Mr Wijesinha and the family that's in the wrong. Why can't they see the right thing to do, and do it?'

'Because they think the way society thinks,' Latha replied.

She remembered the optimism she had felt in her first year at University, her conviction that the future of society lay in the hands of her own generation.

'Maybe we were too hopeful, too naïve. We were quite certain, weren't we, that we had all the answers!'

'We *did* have the answers,' Amali retorted, with a forcefulness that surprised Latha. 'We still have them. People just need to listen. Nobody can tell me Tsunami and Dr Rajaratnam weren't meant for each other. They're two people who really *deserved* each other. And society deserved *them*, society would have gained by their being together.'

It was a union that must have been to the advantage of both . . . but no such happy marriage could now teach the admiring multitude what connubial felicity really was.

Latha was amused and half-irritated by the facility with which her mind could find a quotation for every occasion. This is real life, not *Pride and Prejudice*, she reminded herself firmly, and said aloud:

'The Rajaratnams and the Wijesinhas didn't think so.'

'Did they give themselves an opportunity to find out?'

'No, they didn't. Tsunami told me that when Daniel put the idea to them, his parents closed their minds: they refused to hear anything more about it. And we all saw the way Tsunami's father reacted. I am not sure that the way Tsunami was treated by him, hustled off to Colombo against her will, shut up on an estate, denied access to anyone who could help her until she came round to his point of view – well, I don't know enough about the law, but isn't that a case of kidnapping?'

Isn't it what the law calls 'duress'? If I'd read about it in a Gothic novel, I wouldn't have believed it. I can hardly believe it has happened here, now, to Tsunami.

'I agree with you,' Latha told Amali. 'Most people would think this was just another campus romance, like all the others we see here every year. But Daniel and Tsunami – well, they're different. They're special. By separating them, their families have actually diminished our society. All of us are the poorer for what has happened.'

In the midst of Latha's tribulation, Ronald Marchmont's reaction to her essay on *Persuasion* was an unexpected source of consolation.

'You have not convinced me on the matter of Anne Elliot's character,' he had written in the margin of the essay, 'but I cannot fault your arguments.'

He had awarded her essay the grade of A++. For the rest of that week, Latha walked on air. Marchmont's praise increased a hundredfold her confidence in her own abilities. But she had learned a lesson from the events of the preceding weeks. Never again, she decided, would she let her preoccupation with literary fiction distract her from what really mattered: the reality of the lives around her.

To one person only did Latha confide her joy in her achievement.

Congratulations [Herbert wrote] *on finding yourself a teacher like Ronald Marchmont. Truly, a rare bird.*

Yet, in spite of Amali's spirited defence of the part she had played in the matter, Latha's feelings of guilt could not be easily overcome. She was convinced that she could have helped her vulnerable cousin by cultivating a better understanding of the society of which, whether they liked it or not, they were both a part. She had a sudden memory of Franz Goldman's warning, delivered so many years ago, to the children playing Monopoly at Lucas Falls:

It is lucky for her that Tsunami has her three strong brothers to protect her, a fine, sensible sister, and a loving cousin. You young people will have to look after this little girl. You must guard her interests, or she will be lost.

It was up to me, Latha said to herself. Ranil and Chris and Tara weren't here, so *I* should have cautioned Tsunami, *I* should have warned her that her relationship with Daniel Rajaratnam could only end in unhappiness for them both. How could I have failed her when she needed me most?

What was I doing? What was I thinking of?

Well, she could see it all too clearly now. She had been floating on a cloud of ignorance (or perhaps it was indifference?), too absorbed in her books and her essays and in Hall affairs, too secure in her small group of special friends, to observe what was going on in the real world. If Tsunami was now being pressured by her family into a marriage she did not want, she was paying for the mistake Latha had made.

Although she would have given a great deal to have been spared the task of breaking to Daniel Rajaratnam the news that Tsunami would not be returning to Peradeniya, he had to be told what had happened. Latha sought an interview with Daniel, and planned in advance what she would say. She would be brief, but leave him in no doubt that the Wijesinha family's decision was final.

Daniel heard her out in silence, standing at the window of his tutorial room, his back to her and his eyes on the hills beyond the campus.

'And her Honours degree?' he said, when she had finished. 'Have her family thought of that?'

'Yes, they have,' Latha answered. 'But they don't think her degree is important to her. Her sister says that Tsunami was just filling in time at Peradeniya, until she got married.'

'That,' Daniel replied, without turning round, 'is not true.'

'No, it's not. But it's what they choose to think.'

In the silence that followed, Latha marshalled her forces to take the next step. Somehow she must find the words to tell Rajaratnam that a marriage had been arranged for Tsunami.

It won't be a surprise to him: after all, he comes from Jaffna!

She hesitated. Better that he hears it from me, she decided at last, than that he should hear it from someone else, or read a marriage announcement in the papers.

'Dr Rajaratnam,' she said, 'I don't know how to tell you this, but Tsunami is about to be married.'

It had never occurred to Latha that men could weep. She was so shocked by the emotional storm her careful, sympathetic words evoked that she rose to her feet and, careless of whether or not she could be seen through the tutorial door by passers-by in the corridor, she joined Daniel at the window and placed her hand on his arm.

'It's an arranged marriage, Daniel,' she said. 'She doesn't have a choice.'

In the weeks that followed, it came as no surprise to her to learn that Rajaratnam's manner in class had altered. Shirani complained to her companions on the top-floor balcony that her History tutor had become off-hand and careless. His comments on students' essays were no longer constructive, they were scathing and dismissive.

'Goodness knows what he'll be like next year,' Shirani said. 'Even meaner than he is now, probably. And in our final year, too, just when we're going to need his complete attention. The only good thing now about his teaching is that he hasn't lost his sense of humour. Yesterday, though he knew perfectly well that many of us were impatient to get off early to the table tennis finals at Marrs Hall, he went slow. It was deliberate. The bell rang, and the boys in the class began to shuffle their feet and open and close their desk lids, the usual hint that it's time class ended, but the lecture continued. At last, without so much as looking up, he said dryly, "You needn't be in such a hurry . . . I have a few more pearls to cast."'

But Daniel's wit didn't make up, in Shirani's opinion, for the deterioration of his teaching skills.

'I used to look forward to his classes, but now I dread them,' she told Latha. 'If his heart's no longer in his teaching, he should go away.'

And as soon as the examinations were over, just before campus broke up for the Long Vacation, the astonishing news on campus was that Daniel Rajaratnam *had* 'gone away'. He had resigned from his post at Peradeniya, and accepted an appointment at an American University. This piece of news was quickly followed by another, equally surprising. He had married a bride that his parents had chosen for him, and had left with his wife for the United States.

'I suppose it was always on the cards that he'd do it,' Shirani said. 'Remember what Premani told us last year, when all the Jaffna girls in his classes were falling for Rajaratnam in dozens? "His family's sure to get him hitched to some nice girl in Jaffna with a big fat dowry." Well, they've done it, haven't they?'

'It looks like it,' Latha said. 'And you'll have to put up with a new History tutor in your final year, Shirani! However, I have one piece of good news, and I think it will cheer us all up. Tsunami is coming back to Peradeniya.'

'*What?*'

'It's a fact. I heard the whole story from my parents. My father says that when it came to the point, Tsunami refused point blank to marry the man her aunt had arranged for her. She said she had given her father her solemn promise that she would never see Daniel Rajaratnam again. That was enough: she wasn't going to marry if she didn't want to. Well, they couldn't *force* her, could they? Even Auntie Moira's not that medieval. There was a fuss about it, but the engagement to her cousin was called off. And when my father heard what had happened, he wouldn't rest until he'd talked Uncle Rowland into letting Tsunami finish her degree. Thaththa told me he isn't proud of the tactics he used, but in this case, he says, the end justified the means.'

'What did your father do? What could he have said to talk Mr Wijesinha round?'

'My father told Uncle Rowland that since Dr Rajaratnam was now married and permanently teaching overseas, Peradeniya was "safe" once again for Sinhalese girls!'

That pompous fool Rowland, Herbert told Latha, had actually taken this argument seriously.

'So we can be sure, Herbert,' he had said, 'that the campus is now free from danger?'

'As if love were some kind of disease or crime,' Amali said. 'Your father, Latha, must be a truly wonderful man.'

'He is,' Latha said simply. She remembered *L'Affaire Manamperi* and smiled. 'You know, Amali, I honestly believe my father can do anything.'

When Tsunami returned to Peradeniya in the second week of the new academic year, her friends by common consent spared her from any mention of the absent Daniel Rajaratnam.

'It's not as if we were still seeing him every day,' as Shirani said. 'We've no *reason* to talk about him.'

There were other, more pressing, matters to talk about, in any case, for when the new term began, it brought with it an unseasonable heatwave. The lawns surrounding Sanghamitta grew brown and dry, and from their balcony in the evenings, grass fires on the hillsides opposite the halls of residence were frequently visible.

'Those fires look plain dangerous, you know,' Sriyani said one evening, sipping her coffee and looking out over the balcony. 'I can actually see the flames. What if they spread?'

'The Marshals tell us there's no cause for alarm,' Latha assured her. 'Everything's under control, they say.'

'Well, I just hope the Marshals are right – I don't think I've seen any hoses in this part of the Hall grounds, and there certainly aren't any fire-extinguishers on the corridors. If anything were to happen, this Hall would become a fire-trap.'

'How do you think those fires begin?' Latha asked. 'Is someone deliberately setting the *patanas* alight?'

'Who would do such a thing?' Amali said. 'And why?'

'I think it happens spontaneously when the ground has become very hot,' said Tsunami. 'The grass becomes so dry that it catches fire of its own accord. When we were children – I couldn't have been more than five or so at the time – fires sprang up on the *patanas* below our house at Lucas Falls. It was a very hot July, and the grass on the slopes had become bone-dry. The fire leapt the gaps, and spread, and we watched it climbing up the hillside towards us. It was terrifying. Just like some angry animal on the rampage. Pater said later that he'd really thought the estate was finished. He didn't say so at the time, of course, just encouraged everyone to form chains and pass buckets of water along to the worst-affected spots. Ranil,

Chris and Colin joined in, with men and women labourers from the lines, and they all worked for hours to put the fires out, but they didn't succeed. Mercifully, a spell of heavy rain stopped the flames, but for days afterwards the fires went on smouldering. Every so often a flame would start up here and there on the damp ground.'

The rains were long in coming to the hill-country that year, and even the Mahaweli River, which flows by the Peradeniya campus, shrank between its banks. The grass fires on the hillsides continued to glow through the nights, a constant reminder to Latha of Tsunami's account of the fires at Lucas Falls that had continued to smoulder long after the flames had been officially extinguished.

Had Tsunami's feelings for Daniel Rajaratnam truly been stamped out? Tsunami never mentioned him in her conversations with Latha but, despite her silence, Latha had a shrewd idea that he was seldom far from her cousin's thoughts. She remembered that many years had had to pass before Tsunami had told her exactly what she thought of Franz Goldman.

And what about Daniel's passion for Tsunami? A member of a united, conservative Jaffna family, he had been prepared even to cut his links with his clan for her cousin's sake. Recalling the anguish that her news of Tsunami's impending marriage had caused Rajaratnam, Latha doubted that he would easily 'get over' so strong an attachment.

It suddenly occurred to Latha that Daniel had married and left the island just in time to make it possible for Tsunami to resume her studies for her Honours degree.

Was that coincidence, just a lucky chance? Or a deliberate decision? Even, perhaps, a lover's parting gift?

Despite Tsunami's claim to have ended the relationship, despite her promise to her father, despite Daniel's marriage and their physical distance from each other, despite the oceans that kept them apart, they might, for all she knew, still be in touch with each other.

Rather guiltily (for on no account whatever, Latha told herself, was she ever going to *spy* on Tsunami) she kept an eye on the Sanghamitta Hall letter-board for airmail envelopes with American stamps on them.

There were none.

9

MINISTER OF STATE

In his letters to Latha, Herbert wrote generally about books and people, rather than about public affairs. Sometimes, however, the two topics coalesced:

> *Last week I bought a book that has just been published for Buddha Jayanti Year. It has a very dramatic title –* Revolt in the Temple. *The author, who writes with passion, seems to be a real fire-eater, the main target of his animus being the Christians and Hindus of this country who, according to his reading of our history, have been consistently hostile to Buddhist principle and Sinhalese practice. I hope I'm not reading things into his 'message' but it seems to me that he is calling upon all right-thinking Sinhalese Buddhists to join forces in this special year, and mark the 250th anniversary of the Lord Buddha's enlightenment by repatriating all Indian Tamils on the tea plantations, and forcibly throwing every other non-Buddhist out of the country. (Which would mean, of course, Christians like me, all Tamils, all Burghers, and even, possibly, people like our neighbours the Ismails since they are Muslims.) Lots of references in the book to the heroic prince Dutu Gemunu who, you will remember, complained to his mamma that he couldn't stretch himself out comfortably in bed because he felt confined by the ocean at his feet and the Tamils at his head. One hopes that no one takes this man seriously, or your Thaththa will be drawn and quartered by militant Buddhist activists as an unpatriotic subversive . . . Only joking, of course . . .*

Having stamped and posted his latest weekly letter, Herbert returned home one evening from the Post Office to find Rowland Wijesinha's limousine parked in the little drive at the front of the house, and Alexander seated in the driver's seat, reading a newspaper. On seeing Herbert, Alexander put the newspaper down and sprang out of the car.

'Good evening, sir.'

'Good evening, Cassim. What brings you here?'

'The master is paying you and the madam a visit, sir. He's in the house, waiting for you.'

Herbert hurried up the front steps, to find Soma, all smiles, entertaining

Rowland in the veranda. A tray had been placed on the small occasional table, on which stood a bottle, a glass and a bottle-opener.

'Oh, good,' Herbert said, after the first greetings had been exchanged. 'Beer! Or would you prefer something a little stronger?'

Rowland declined the offer. He was going on afterwards to an official reception at Temple Trees, and needed to keep a clear head. Herbert was amused to see that his cousin, while abandoning Western dress in the interests of politics, had retained his taste for luxury. Rejecting the handwoven white cotton cloth that his colleagues, and even his leader, wore to official functions, Rowland had chosen to attire himself in gleaming white satin. Soma went indoors to fetch a glass for Herbert. When she returned she brought with her also a small bowl of roasted cashew nuts.

'So nice of you to visit us, Rowland Aiya,' she said. 'It gives us a chance to congratulate you properly.'

Rowland brushed her congratulations aside with becoming modesty, and helped himself to cashew nuts.

'It seems you're branching out in all kinds of new directions, Rowland,' Herbert said. 'I've just bought your book, *Man of Destiny*. First a cabinet minister, next an author, eh? Where will it all end?'

'At Temple Trees, I trust.'

Herbert was so startled that he very nearly dropped his glass. Had Rowland lost his sense of humour? Or had he completely lost his head? He had mentioned, with what seemed to be perfect seriousness, the official residence of Ceylon's prime ministers.

Rowland continued:

'If Wilmot can do it, why not I?'

Herbert raised his eyebrows.

'Why not, indeed!'

'Have you seen the material Wilmot's got to work with, Herbert?'

'I read the newspapers,' Herbert replied.

'Well, it's embarrassing, isn't it? I know Wilmot finds it so. Every time one of those johnnies who call themselves my cabinet colleagues opens his mouth, he puts his foot in it. "Thank God you're with me, Rowland," Wilmot said to me yesterday, when we were walking at Galle Face . . . Oh, did you know that we walk together every morning along the promenade, Herbert? Very early in the morning, before the sun comes up. It's quite dark at that time, no one about and a nice breeze blowing, and that's a good time for a confidential talk. Awful bore, of course, having Wilmot's bodyguards walking behind us all the time, frightful chaps, built like refrigerators and armed to the teeth, but it can't be helped, Wilmot says, it goes with the P.M.'s job . . . "You're the one man in my Cabinet I can rely on to conduct himself like a gentleman," he told me yesterday, "the only man I can trust not to make a damn fool of himself before the entire diplomatic corps."'

'You must find that very encouraging,' Herbert said.

He sipped his beer.

'But shall I tell you what *I* don't find at all encouraging, Rowland? All these reports I read in the papers of Wilmot involving himself with temple ceremonies for Buddha Jayanti. As a church-going Anglican, he'd be first in the firing-line if the Sinhala-Buddhist fanatics have their way.'

Rowland was amused.

'Nonsense, old boy, you shouldn't believe everything you read in the papers. All those *pirith* ceremonies and *bana* preachings and so on, that's just publicity for the press. The masses need to feel the P.M. is one of them, they need to believe that he thinks as they do. In actual fact, he's got the situation well in hand. Crafty devil, Wilmot, didn't know he had it in him. I mean, who'd have thought—' His voice was full of admiration. 'He's got a Tamil and a Thambi in his Cabinet to keep the minorities happy. A cosmetic job entirely, of course. He's got a rent-a-crowd of monks at Kelaniya, ready to put on a ceremony at the drop of a hat. And he's got the wife of the author of *Revolt in the Temple* lined up as the next Minister of Health as soon as the current one retires, which happens next month. And *she's* got a direct line to the *sangha*.'

'The *sangha*? What's the *sangha* doing in politics? I thought it was the first duty of monks to meditate, fast and preach.'

'You're seriously out of date, Herbert old chap,' replied his cousin. 'The present incumbent of one of this country's largest temples does everything *but* meditate, fast and preach. He's a thoroughly modern monk, into everything, especially the ladies. Loves his tum, too. The story is that he puts a fez on his shaven head at night, and goes in a curtained car to have his dinner at the Buhari Hotel. Wilmot put it rather wittily the other day. "My good friend, the High Priest, is a man of many parts: he fasts by day, and he *feasts* by night!" Of course, he didn't say that to the press. Only to me.'

'To be perfectly honest, I don't give a damn what the High Priest's doing with his time or where he goes to have his dinner,' Herbert said, 'as long as he isn't inciting murder and mayhem.'

Rowland's mention of *Revolt in the Temple* had reminded him of that book's intolerant, un-Buddhistic message, and he added:

'I don't mean to be alarmist, but it seems to me that our distinguished relative is playing with fire.'

'Don't give it a thought,' Rowland returned cheerfully. 'Remember, Wilmot's been playing the political game ever since he got back from Oxford. There isn't a card any of these chaps can play that he can't trump. And he's very popular. You've only got to look at the majority he came in with.'

'I'd rather not, if you don't mind,' Herbert said. 'The public are notoriously—'

'Oh, I know what you're going to say, Herbert! "The public are fickle, and the huge crowds that elected Wilmot yesterday could turn tomorrow into the mobs that will pull him down and tear him to pieces." Am I not right?'

Herbert shrugged, but did not deny it.

'Take my word for it, Wilmot knows what he's doing.'

Wonder what Rowland's here for, Herbert asked himself warily. Just to talk politics with me? I don't think so!

'To tell you the truth, Rowland,' he said, 'I'm more concerned about you than I am about Wilmot. I hope you know what *you're* doing, getting in with this crowd. It doesn't look at all like your scene to me.'

'Well, I agree with you. It's not. Not at the moment. Most of the party faithful haven't studied beyond the Fifth Standard. But the next election, Herbert, laddie, wait for the next election! That will bring in real talent, and then we'll see some good government.'

'I certainly hope so.'

Rowland looked about him.

'I see Soma's gone indoors, and left us to our own devices,' he said. 'Not much interest in politics, eh?'

'I wouldn't say that . . .' Herbert replied; and silently added: '. . . in her hearing.'

'Helen was just the same,' said Helen's former husband. 'Shouldn't blame them for it, really, I suppose. Got other things on their little minds, haven't they, as Ministers of Home Affairs!'

He smiled at his own wit, and resumed:

'Luckily for me, Moira's not like that at all. Dedicates herself heart and soul to my political advancement.'

'Glad to hear it,' Herbert said politely.

Rowland's casual dismissal of Helen had riled him even more than his earlier comment about Soma; but as usual, he did not show his feelings.

Rowland did not seem especially concerned about Soma's absence, for he continued:

'Gives me a chance to say what I really came to see you about, Herbert. It's about Tsunami.'

'What about her?'

'Moira and I are getting worried about her. Emotional ups and downs for which there's no explanation. There was the silly little affair she had last year with that Tamil don at Peradeniya, of course. But she's quite got over that, I'm glad to say. Tsunami's very fond of me, you know, Herbert. When I told her what damage a Tamil son-in-law would do to my political career, it made her sit back and think a bit. Also, I won't deny that I used strong-arm tactics! She had the fright of her life, I should think, when I told her what could happen to her boyfriend if she didn't toe the line and give him marching orders. I can see from your face that you think I went too far, Herbert – but what can one do? Our children have to wake up to the realities of life. Well, I think I can say that from now on, she'll be on the straight and narrow. Moira says so, and she's a good judge of character. Tsunami went up to Lucas Falls with me recently and seemed perfectly all right: happy, smiling, great company . . . That tutor of Latha's, Marchmont, was in Nuwara Eliya on holiday. We asked him over to dinner, and Tsunami charmed him so much that I thought he was going to ask me for her hand in marriage . . .'

'He's a good man, Marchmont,' Herbert interposed. 'A first-class teacher, I understand.'

'Moira says Tsunami was probably practising her skills on the fellow. According to Tara, she does that sometimes. But that good mood was short-lived, because she came down to Colombo for the last vacation, and you wouldn't have thought it was the same girl who'd accompanied me to Lucas Falls. She spent her time mooning around the house looking glum. And then, one evening, she flew right off the handle, as you might say. Insulted one of my cabinet colleagues at our own dinner-table—'

'Indeed?' Herbert was very interested. 'That doesn't sound like Tsunami. She's always had perfect manners, even as a child. What could have set such a situation off? Whom did she insult?'

'It was that silly ass, D.K. Beliwatte. She took exception to something he said. Nothing of importance, really, in fact, nothing more than I said myself a moment ago. Though I suppose he went a bit further than I did. Belly and I were discussing the ethnic make-up of the Cabinet, and Belly said he didn't think Wilmot should have given the minorities any representation at all, it would only give them ideas above their station. "The only good Tamil is a dead Tamil," Belly said. "And the same goes for Muslims and all that low-caste riff-raff that seem to be everywhere these days." Then, without any warning whatever, Tsunami went for him. Called him all manner of names.'

'What names?' prodded Herbert.

'She called poor old Belly a fool, an idiot, a politician without principles, told him he should resign from his cabinet post if he didn't know how to conduct himself in the national interest . . . and she said all this to his face, if you please! She asked him whether he knew for how many centuries Tamils and Muslims have lived in this country and called it their home, whether he knew that the Kandy Perahera in which he walked so grandly every year couldn't be held if so-called low-caste people didn't contribute their talents and skills to it—'

Good for her! thought Herbert, mentally applauding his niece. Well done, Tsunami!

'—so Moira and I thought the child might have been sickening for something. You never know what she might have caught at that Hall of hers, Moira tells me the place is chock-full of people from the villages, God knows what primitive ideas they bring with them to the campus about cleanliness and personal hygiene . . .'

'How did Beliwatte take all that?'

'Very well, I thought,' said his cousin. 'He sat stock-still for a bit, looking straight in front of him, you could see he was fuming – it was obvious he'd never been spoken to like that in his life – then he turned to Moira and said, "Very advanced ideas your daughter has, Moira." Pretty decent of him, I thought. Admirably restrained, but that's the old Kandyan way, his father was the same, I understand, perfect gentleman even when he tied a thieving servant to a tree and flogged the scoundrel till the flesh came off his back in strips. I know some among my cabinet colleagues who would have given their daughter a belting if she had dared speak like that to a guest. Moira was very upset – Belly is related to her, as you know, and she'd been thinking of his son – the boy whom I fixed up with a job at Hayley's – as a match for Tsunami. Well, obviously, that would be no go, now.'

'Rowland,' Herbert said, 'you know in your heart that Tsunami was right, don't you? It's just that it's not political sense to say it in the way she did.'

A short silence followed, which Herbert broke with a question.

'Well, *was* she sickening for something? Latha hasn't told us Tsunami has been ill or out of sorts.'

'No, thank the Lord, it turned out to be a false alarm. Touch of flu, probably. "Give her plenty of ginger and coriander," I told Moira, "that was Mater's remedy for cold and coughs: *inguru koththamalli*." But Moira seems to think it might be more serious. She tells me Tara believes Tsunami's met someone.'

'Who?'

'Good God, *I* don't know. But it struck me that maybe Latha does: we feel sure Tsunami confides in her. Of course, Moira might be quite mistaken – maybe Tsunami's classes aren't going too well, and that's upsetting her, though it's highly unlikely, you know how bright the child is. What I want to ask you, Herbert, in the strictest confidence, is: would you ask Latha to keep an eye on Tsunami? They were very close as kids – well, you know all about that – and I've no doubt they're just as close now. If anyone knows what's on Tsunami's mind, Latha does.'

'Now, look here, Rowland,' said Herbert. 'You and Moira told me not so very long ago that Latha had been a bad influence on Tsunami in the Rajaratnam affair. I understood your feelings at the time, and I decided to overlook it, but Latha took that remark to heart, you know, and she agonized about it for months. I can't see her agreeing to spy on Tsunami for you.'

He was glad to see that Rowland had the grace to look uncomfortable.

'I'm not asking her to *spy* on Tsunami,' Rowland said.

'And you wouldn't succeed if you did.'

While I've got the chance, I'll make the bugger squirm.

Herbert went on:

'As I remember it, their friendship involved vows of complete and utter loyalty. They might have pricked their fingers and written the vows in blood, for all we know. You couldn't get a bad word out of Latha about *anyone* in your family, then or now. Heaven knows Soma's sisters have tried hard enough for years.'

He didn't mention that Soma had tried as hard as anyone.

'Well, none of them cared much for Helen, did they? That's the ladies all over, bless their little hearts.'

Rowland looked at his watch, then rose from his seat on the veranda.

'I'd better be off, Herbert. Say goodbye to your lady wife for me.'

He clapped his cousin on the shoulder.

'It's been good talking to you, old boy. A heart-to-heart, eh? We must do this more often.'

At the bottom of the veranda steps, he turned round:

'Then you'll speak to Latha?'

'I'll think about it,' Herbert said.

'You know best,' Rowland said, and added:

'We hope Latha will pay a visit to Lucas Falls soon. Moira's made a lot of changes there: she'll be interested to see them.'

Alexander closed the car door on his satin-clad employer, saluted Herbert, and they were on their way. Herbert collected the tray and its contents, and went indoors, where Soma was waiting for him.

'What does he want you to speak to Latha about?'

'They'd like Latha to go up to Lucas Falls sometime soon, for a holiday,' Herbert replied, 'as she did in the old days.'

Soma sniffed, a sniff full of hidden meaning.

'I'm surprised he called it Lucas Falls when he spoke to you,' she said. 'They've changed the name, didn't you know? It's called Wijesinha Maha Walauwa now.'

Herbert did not know.

'Where did you hear that?' he asked.

'Never mind where I heard it, Herbie. It's a fact.'

10

LETTERS FROM COLOMBO

My dear Latha [wrote Paula Phillips]
Thank you for remembering our wedding anniversary. We did not celebrate the occasion in any spectacular way, our home isn't big enough for a party, but the friendship and support of our neighbours was a celebration in itself. I will confess that when Rajan and I first came to live here, I doubted whether we – or rather, I – would make a success of it. It was all so different from what I had been used to in my parents' home. But I have no doubts now, and feel more and more convinced that the journal Rajan has started is having a positive effect on public opinion.

By now you would be preparing for your Finals at Peradeniya. Our best wishes for your success in the examination. As you must surely know, I had the highest possible opinion of your abilities when you were at school, and if you will put your Hall responsibilities and extra-curricular activities aside for a while now and allow yourself time for concentrated study, I have no doubt at all that you will achieve the First Class that Rajan and I have always predicted for you.

Please come and see us while you are in Colombo. We've got a telephone now, so it should be easy to fix on a date.

Despite her good intentions, and the Phillipses' acquisition of a telephone, Latha had not managed to call on them while she was in Colombo. Tsunami's concerns had demanded priority. And now that she was back at Peradeniya, the affairs of the Hall loomed large.

At the start of their third year, Latha and Tsunami had noticed that their life at Peradeniya had a tendency to insulate them from what was going on in Colombo, and indeed, in the rest of the island. Latha had not expected this to happen, and she felt unhappy about the absence of news and information. But there was little she could do to remedy the situation. The newspapers destined for the student Common Rooms had invariably lost many of their pages before she could get to them, or they had been torn to pieces by students ripping out ads. Such 'news' as reached her did so by word of mouth, casually, between lectures and tutorials, for the radio in the third-floor Common Room was invariably claimed by students who camped around it, turned up the volume full blast, and sang along with Sinhala and Tamil pop songs all day.

'Do our little O-Fac darlings *have* to produce that awful, nasal *shriek*?' Tsunami inquired one afternoon, when the racket from the Common Room had been particularly oppressive. 'It's even worse than having Hema Gikiyanagē next door.'

Unfortunately, the remark was overheard by one of the O-Fac campers, a fan of Hema (who was now making a name for herself on the Commercial Service of Radio Ceylon). The word rapidly spread that Tsunami Wijesinha was a spoiled, upper-class brat whose English education had robbed her of the ability to understand or appreciate the culture of her own country.

'Rich and useless,' was the verdict of O-Facs and Marxists alike.

On Tsunami's birthday, among many cards and letters that appeared on the Hall letter-board and were opened by her at lunch time was one that Tsunami did not show Latha.

'Who's that one from?' Latha asked, as her cousin put the card away in her purse after glancing briefly at it, and returned to eating her meal.

Tsunami shrugged.

'Who knows? It's signed "From An Admirer",' she said carelessly, and Latha asked no further questions. There were many young men on campus who would have rated among her cousin's 'admirers', but who, as Sriyani had said once, would have had to be born again before they could hope for a glance from Tsunami.

Despite the magnificent birthday cake of Vaithi's creation that Alexander brought up from Colombo, which everyone on the balcony enjoyed, it appeared to the observant Latha that Tsunami was not her usual self that afternoon. Something, it seemed, had ruined the day for her. The other students, less perceptive, enthusiastically drank the health of the birthday girl in lemonade and orange barley, played Consequences with hilarious results, and couldn't have had more fun, Amali observed, if they'd all been six-year-olds again, and attending their first birthday party.

'Latha, do you think—' Tsunami said once, urgently, during these festivities, and then stopped herself.

Latha wondered what the question would have been that Tsunami had been about to ask, and wondered too whether it would have had some connection with the card from 'An Admirer' that her cousin had put away in her purse. There was no such card among those arranged on Tsunami's desk at her birthday celebration on their balcony. Latha remembered how her cousin's face had changed when she read it in the refectory, and wondered whether it had conveyed an insult rather than a compliment.

Poor Tsunami, it's not her fault that she's 'handsome, clever and rich', Latha thought, remembering the petty warfare that had been waged on students from Colombo schools in their first year, in the form of malicious anonymous messages, letters dropped from the Hall letter-board, and seats mysteriously unavailable on the Refectory benches.

This kind of persecution did not usually trouble Tsunami, who airily dismissed it as 'typical O-Fac', and not worth worrying about. But it troubled Latha. Joan Springdale had retired early in the year, and Latha could no longer rely on the Warden's advice in potentially explosive situations. Dr Springdale's successor, an eminent Oxford-educated scientist, was efficient, capable, and full of good intentions, but she was not known for tact or discretion. The new Warden confronted Hall problems head-on, and seemed to believe that the best way to solve problems was to cut straight through them. In such circumstances, Latha felt herself to be very much on her own.

Informed by Amali of what was being said about her cousin by the O-Fac 'campers', Latha directed her energies to mending fences with all the tact and skill she could muster. She believed, on the whole, that she was succeeding, and was thankful that she had a friend like Amali, who could provide insights into many things that would otherwise have remained hidden from her. It was only a week or two earlier that Amali had asked her balcony mates:

'Did you know that this is Buddha Jayanti Year?'

Answering Tsunami's inquiring look, she had explained:

'It's the two-thousand-five-hundredth anniversary of the Lord Buddha attaining enlightenment! That's why the whole country is celebrating.'

Tsunami had made no comment. Amali's statement, stemming from her regular association with the Buddhist Brotherhood on campus, meant very little to her. To Latha, however, it meant a great deal, for it recalled an earlier comment her father had made in a letter, on remarkable changes that had been taking place in the life of his cousin Rowland:

> *You may remember that your Uncle Rowland, disappointed by his failure to retain his cabinet post under the new government, switched sides some months ago. He now wears national dress and sits with the Opposition in Parliament, where he looks extremely uncomfortable, among a strangely assorted bunch of characters with whom he has nothing in common except – as I suppose – a determination to contest the General Election later this year. His leader is a relative of his (and of ours, though I don't think you've ever actually met him) and, fired by his example, your Uncle has discovered a new interest in Buddhism. This week's newspapers carried pictures of Rowland and Moira offering trays of flowers at the Daladā Maligāwa in Kandy. The fact that someone who Rowland thinks has what he calls 'the qualifications for leadership' – he says so in a fawning little booklet he's just had published which, needless to say, is the current jewel*

in my collection – may be the next PM if things turn out right gives your Uncle some kind of hope that he, too, might stand to gain by the change which everyone seems to think is inevitable.

Latha's mother did not write at all. It was from Paula Phillips, taking time off from her teaching to keep in touch with her former pupil, that Latha learned about the outcome of the events to which her father had referred:

> *Sinhala* [wrote Paula] *became, as you know, the official language of our country by an Act of Parliament that was passed two years ago. There was public rejoicing at the time, but the euphoria seems to be wearing off now. Many people we know resent the removal of English from its former position of supremacy; though, quite frankly, Rajan and I cannot see why. Even though we're both English teachers, we cannot sympathize with that point of view. It seems to us only right that the official language of a country should be the language that is known to the majority of its people. As long as English is well taught, and continues to be a means of communication between communities, and of contact with the outside world, and Tamil continues to be used in areas where Tamil speakers predominate, why should this bit of legislation be a problem for anyone? I'm sure you remember the courtroom scene in* The Village in the Jungle, *Latha, in which a debate as to whether an accused person is guilty of murder or not is carried on in English among the officials present, while the accused in the dock remains unenlightened as to what is being said, and what will happen to him. Well, the Official Languages Act of 1956 must surely change all that for the better.*

Rajan Phillips added a message to Latha, that his wife enclosed with her letter:

> *The new Government has come in with such a huge majority that the new PM can do virtually anything he pleases. Incidentally, I gather that he is a kinsman of yours, and that another of your relations is in line for a Cabinet post. Let us hope that this Government will not adopt the dynastic policies of the last one! Not that either of the two gentlemen concerned lacks talent or education, but it would be most unjust – and unwise – if the country is run by them as though it were a private estate, which was certainly the case under the previous régime . . .*

Tsunami had not informed Latha that her father had changed his political colours and his religion, and Latha, reluctant to give her cousin the impression that Herbert indulged in gossip about her family, did not bring the subject up.

She had been invited to spend a fortnight at Lucas Falls at the end of the first term. Perhaps Rowland and Moira would be there. Latha hoped so.

The idea of her Uncle Rowland offering flowers at a temple in national dress had created a picture in her mind that she found hugely entertaining. Perhaps, at Lucas Falls, she would have an opportunity to observe this comedy for herself.

11

THE VALUE OF THINGS

Tara's son Lohan was eating his dinner.

Latha could not help wishing that this ceremony could have been held earlier in the evening or, better still, in some other part of the house (like the room upstairs which had been once devoted to her Aunt Helen's painting and was now transformed into a nursery with a procession of Walt Disney cut-outs on its wall). But it was generally understood that the little boy wanted to eat his dinner in the dining room with the grown-ups, and it was also generally understood that this was a very special little boy, whose wants were not to be denied.

Lohan was attended by his ayah, a patient little woman named Podihami, who stood beside his high-chair throughout the meal. It was her responsibility to cut up the food on his plate into very small pieces, and feed these pieces to Lohan with a spoon, one by one. Lohan, a chubby child who looked as if he could have missed several meals without feeling a single pang of hunger, liked nothing better than keeping his uncomplaining ayah in a permanent state of unease. As the spoon neared his mouth, he would turn his face away at the very last moment, causing the food to spill down his embroidered bib, so that Podihami would have to prepare another spoonful. In between mouthfuls, he kept up a noisy monologue, some of it addressed to Tara who gazed at him adoringly from the head of the table, a position she occupied when Rowland or Moira was not present to take it.

Under these conditions, conversation among the adults at dinner became very nearly impossible. Latha gave up any hope of rational talk, and contented herself instead with observing her cousin Tara, whose management of the household she had not witnessed since Helen's departure from it. Tara was in her element. She had always accepted the deferential behaviour of servants as her proper due, and although she was clearly enjoying her own meal, she kept a watchful eye on the ayah to make sure that Lohan received every indulgence to which he was entitled.

'Eat, eat, *Hamu*!' Podihami pleaded, and Latha caught Tsunami's eye as Lohan, grinning mischievously, sent another spoonful of cereal to the floor.

'Isn't my precious hungry?' Tara cooed. 'Eat up your nice dinner, my treasure. The new cook prepared it specially for you.'

'Don't want it,' Lohan pouted.

'Eat it, sweetheart, just to please Ammi!'

'No, I won't!'

Pushing away his plate, Lohan got Podihami to help him down from his high-chair. Once on the ground, there were other enjoyments awaiting him, chief among them a shiny toy sports car that his grandfather had ordered from Hamley's of Regent Street as a special present on his second birthday.

'Car!' Lohan said imperiously, and a small servant boy obligingly brought the car into the dining room, and held it steady while Lohan climbed into it. The entire scenario was then re-enacted over dessert, Lohan driving his car around the dining table, and tooting its horn between mouthfuls of blancmange and stewed apple.

'What a little rascal he is!' Lohan's father beamed proudly, ignoring the fact that the car had cannoned into a table-leg and ricocheted from it to hit his shin.

'Boys are such little devils, Latha,' Tara said happily. 'You just wait till you have one of your own.'

Never, never, never! Or if I do, I certainly won't spoil him the way Tara is spoiling Lohan.

She had thought Lohan a beautiful baby, but now, observing his behaviour to the patient Podihami, she was convinced that if Tara and Tissa didn't take a firm line with their son, he would grow into an obnoxious little bully. She listened to Tara's tales of the cunning wiles she had used to trick Lohan into eating when he was a baby – 'Here's an aeroplane, darling! Look, *whoosh, whoosh*, it's heading straight for the aerodrome! But, oh my, why is the aerodrome closed? Let's open it, my angel!' – and wished she had the power to put Lohan on a diet of water and fruit juice for three days and watch his appetite return.

But Tara, pregnant a second time, was obviously enjoying the role of young mother. Aided by Moira's little army of women servants, she had made every detail of childcare into a ritual. (Tsunami told Latha that her brother Christopher referred to the ceremony surrounding his nephew's morning toilet, during which one ayah stood ready with a jugful of hot water, another with an armful of fresh towels, while a third carried the soap and talcum powder, and a fourth a china chamber-pot, as 'The Order of the Bath'.)

It did not escape Latha's notice, however, that when Rowland was in the house (which he visited for a few days during Latha's stay, stealing a brief holiday, as he liked to say, from affairs of state), Lohan's dinner was eaten upstairs. There he could not be heard by the Minister *Hamuduruwo*, even if he played his usual tricks on Podihami or threw a tantrum, as he was perfectly capable of doing if crossed. Moira, too, although she lavished teddy bears and miniature model cars on the little boy, was far too involved with her duties as Minister's lady to take on the role of a grandmother.

Tsunami distanced herself effectively from Tara's family life – 'Luckily,' as she told Latha, 'this house gives you the space to do it' – and although a conversation was out of the question at meals, the two girls had plenty of opportunities to talk during Latha's stay.

Rowland was pleased to find Latha in residence when he arrived on his visit. It was not long before he took his niece aside and asked her whether Tsunami had anything on her mind that had made her so moody and ill-tempered recently.

'Your Auntie Moira and I have both noticed it. So has Tara. I have been worried enough about it to speak about it with your father.'

'I know,' Latha said calmly. 'Thaththa told me you had mentioned something of the kind.'

Rowland looked at her expectantly.

'Well?'

'She isn't sickening for anything, you can be sure of that,' said Latha, who had been greatly entertained by Moira's fears, retailed to her by Herbert, that Tsunami might have caught some infection from her fellow-students at Sanghamitta. 'Her studies are fine, she's getting straight As in everything, she keeps up her tennis, works out regularly at the gym, and she's thinking of standing for election next term as Hall President.'

'Do you think she—' Rowland hesitated, then brought out the words in a great hurry – 'Would she be in – er – love, do you think?'

'I haven't seen any sign of it,' Latha replied.

And I know better now than to tell you, even if I had!

'She has heaps of admirers on campus,' she added, 'but that's not the same thing, is it?'

Rowland hesitated.

'What about that fellow Rajaratnam? Are they still in touch?'

Latha looked steadily at her uncle.

'I thought she had promised you that she would not see Dr Rajaratnam again. Don't you trust her to keep her promise?'

'Of course I do, Latha, of course I do. It's just that there's no knowing what an unprincipled scoundrel like that might not do to make her break it . . . And what about Marchmont? He caused a sensation during a visit we paid to Jaffna, with his attentions to Tsunami.'

Latha shook her head.

'She hasn't even mentioned to me that he was there. They are good friends, they have a lot in common, they like sharing a joke . . .'

'Sure that's all? He kissed her hand in public, you know.'

'Oh well, he's English,' Latha said, smiling to herself as she remembered her conversation with Tsunami when they were children, about the tendency of Neuropeans to kiss everybody. 'I don't think he's got the measure of our society yet. And he certainly wouldn't know much about Jaffna society.'

But Rowland was not entirely satisfied.

'Do you know, Latha, I wonder sometimes whether Tsunami understands the importance of her position: or, I should say, of *our* position. Democracy is all very well – in its place – but it's there to be used by us for the good of everyone, it's not there to govern *us*. I rely on you, Latha, to make sure Tsunami associates with the right kind of people—'

'And doesn't spoil the family name by linking it with a nobody,' Tara added.

Neither Rowland nor Latha had noticed the entrance into the room of Tsunami's sister.

'I've been hearing all sorts of stories about what she was up to last year at Peradeniya. Wasn't there a Tamil lecturer, a Jayaratnam or Rajaratnam or something, whom she was encouraging?'

Latha bristled, but she managed to answer coolly enough.

'If your informants are thinking of Dr Rajaratnam, who was her History tutor last year, Tara, they should also understand that he's married, and is currently teaching in America. He's a *brilliant* academic, absolutely outstanding, and he certainly thought very highly of Tsunami's work, but there's no romantic connection between them.'

'And there'd better not be!' Tara said firmly. 'That kind of thing is quite impossible, and the sooner Tsunami realizes it, the better.'

Tara had come in with a request: could her father possibly spare Alexander and the ministerial car? She was about to run out of the imported milk food that had been prescribed by her paediatrician for Lohan, and she needed to get some tins of it from the pharmacy in town.

'Take Alexander, take the car,' Rowland said at once. Although he had formerly refrained from letting his official car be used by members of his family, he never refused a request now that concerned his grandson's welfare.

'Why don't you come too, Latha?' Tara said. 'I have to look at some new curtains for the house, and you could tell me what you think about the designs. We can visit a bookshop on the way back, maybe?'

Latha was glad to escape from Rowland's insistent questioning, but she soon found that she had merely substituted one form of inquisition for another.

'I'm glad Pater spoke to you about – on that topic,' Tara began, as soon as the Lucas Falls gates closed behind them.

Raising a well-plucked eyebrow, she glanced meaningfully at the back of Alexander's head, and Latha remembered that Alexander not only spoke English, but had a special affection for Tsunami.

'Pater won't be around for ever, you know, and he wants to see each of us settled in life before he goes. Which means that we have to act responsibly, and show that we understand – well, that we understand what's what, if you see what I mean.'

Surmising, from the blank expression on her cousin's face, that she would need to be more explicit if Latha were to grasp her meaning, Tara elaborated:

'About the value of things, you know, the value of property, of estates and houses. It's important that these things should be properly protected and carefully maintained, so that they can be passed on to the next generation. Pater's worried about something that . . . our young relative once said to him, that if she ever had property to dispose of, she'd sell the lot and give the proceeds to charity. I told him she must have been joking, but Auntie Moira says no, she was absolutely serious.'

'Our young relative,' replied Latha, employing Tara's euphemism, 'is in the habit of saying things she doesn't really mean, entirely to shock the people she's speaking to at the time. You know that, and I know it, Tara. She's never discussed property questions with me . . .'

No, because you don't have any property, sweetie!

Aloud, Tara replied:

'Well, all I can say is, that remark of hers gave Pater a severe shock. Coming on top of an earlier incident in which she had insulted one of his colleagues, calling him a politician without any principles and a fool without the brains of a nit, it upset Pater so much that he developed a terrible headache. Auntie Moira called in Dr Lucien Gunasekera, and poor Pater has been diagnosed with high blood pressure. He's on regular medication now, but you can just imagine the strain of it all on them both. Our young relative's problem is, that she's so much younger than the rest of us that she's become thoroughly spoiled. She's never learned to be responsible.'

'May I ask you something, Tara?' Latha said. 'What was the subject of discussion when . . . when our young relative said what she did?'

'Auntie Moira tells me they were discussing the race and caste mix in the Cabinet,' Tara replied.

'I see. And does she know about Uncle Rowland's anxiety regarding the family property?' Latha asked.

Tara shook her head.

'I don't think so.'

'Well, it might help if you let her in on some of your . . . these family concerns,' Latha said. 'She's a thoughtful person, but if she's to be kept in the dark about things that everyone else in the family considers important, well, she isn't going to change her thinking, is she?'

'Why not?' Tara countered. 'Shouldn't it be obvious to her that sensible people must protect what is their own?'

'Not necessarily. By saying the things she seems to have said, she was acting responsibly and sensibly. From her point of view.'

'Latha! How can you say that!'

'What I mean is, she was acting responsibly in relation to national and social concerns,' Latha said.

'Are you telling me that my sister has become a bloody Bolshie?' Tara inquired.

'No. But she's developed an open mind,' retorted Latha. 'Don't you remember, Tara, what it was like when we were all children together at Lucas Falls? We could say anything and everything we liked, and your parents – especially your father, with his liberal views – encouraged that. It was one of the things I really loved about your family. I felt . . . *free* when I was with you.'

Tara looked at her pityingly.

'That was a long time ago, Latha,' she said. 'We all have to grow up.'

12

A HOUSE PARTY AT LUCAS FALLS

At first sight, Lucas Falls had appeared unchanged to Latha.

She had been looking forward to walking with Tsunami in the gardens which, viewed from verandas and windows, seemed as beautiful as ever. She had wanted especially to revisit Helen's 'Indian' garden, but at Tara's insistence she put these pleasures off for a later time. First, Tara said, Latha should make the guided tour of the house which was now offered to all visitors as a matter of routine.

It was not her intention to deliberately seek out faults and flaws, but Latha realized almost immediately, in the course of Tara's 'tour', that, despite outward appearances, the old house had in fact undergone many changes since she had last seen it. Helen Wijesinha's subtle embroideries, for instance, had completely disappeared; their replacement throughout the public rooms with representations of Sigiriya frescoes crudely executed in batik on antimacassars, cushion covers, and curtains stridently proclaimed the influence of her successor. The family photographs had vanished from the mantelpiece in the drawing room, along which there now walked a procession of ebony and ivory elephants. Above the mantelpiece, replacing a flower painting in watercolours by Helen that had hung there when Latha was a child, there was now a four-foot-high frieze in what seemed to be sculptured bronze, but on closer inspection turned out to be gilded *papier mâché*. It depicted Prince Dutu Gemunu in full battle regalia, kneeling at the feet of a woman with a crown on her head and very prominent breasts.

'This work of art was commissioned by Mrs Moira Wijesinha,' explained Tara, reading to Latha from a printed guide composed by her stepmother. 'It celebrates the historic moment in which the heroic prince solemnly promised his royal mother that he would go a-warring no more.'

'"A-warring"? Or "a-whoring"?' Tsunami murmured idly as she followed in the wake of her sister and their cousin.

This piece of irreverence earned her a glare from Tara, who obviously enjoyed deputizing for the absent Moira. The bedrooms had all been newly decorated in handloom material block-printed with a pattern of red and black elephants designed by Moira, and over the fireplaces hung painted devil masks from Ambalangoda. Amid this profusion of local cultural *motifs*, Latha was astonished to see on each bedside table a Gideon Bible.

'Auntie Moira put the Bibles there after her last trip to the United States,' Tara informed her. 'She says every well-appointed guest room should have one.'

'Like every well-appointed stately home should have its resident ghost,' offered Tsunami helpfully. 'Has Auntie Moira put anything in there about Lady Millbanke?'

'Don't talk nonsense, Tsunami,' Tara said. But she shut the guidebook with a snap, and went downstairs.

'Lady Millbanke? Who's Lady Millbanke?' Latha asked.

'A Governor's lady of yesteryear who flung herself from her bedroom window and broke her neck,' Tsunami told her.

'*What?*'

'Surely Colin must have told you all about Lady Millbanke when you were staying here, Latha? He used to enjoy terrifying visitors with stories about the house being haunted. I'll show you the window, if you like. It's right at the end of this corridor.'

It was only when Latha saw the window (now securely locked and barred) that she remembered having seen it before, when she was a child.

'I believe,' she said slowly, 'that Colin *began* telling me about the ghost, but Chris interrupted, and stopped him.'

'That'd be about right,' Tsunami said cheerfully. 'Chris probably wanted to prevent you staying up all night, worrying about it. If you want to hear the rest of the story, ask Pater: he was the Governor's A.D.C. at the time, so he knows all about the incident. As a matter of fact, *he* used to love telling visitors the story – he called it "The Defenestration of Lady Millbanke" – until Auntie Moira married him and put a stop to it. She wants Pater to sell Lucas Falls to a hotel chain, and she says that kind of talk would lower its re-sale value. You'd have to ask him when Auntie Moira is out of the way.'

So Moira Wijesinha regarded Lucas Falls as a hotel, Latha thought, rather than as the private residence it had been throughout its long history!

The familiar personalities of Raman, Vaithianathan and Alice seemed to have made as clean a disappearance as Helen's paintings and needlework. They had been replaced by an entirely new staff. In command was a person Latha dimly remembered having seen before, but could not place until she glimpsed him the following day on the veranda, giving instructions to the gardeners. She recalled then that she had last seen him years ago in the very same place – standing on the veranda, until invited to sit down – when he had called with a deputation to invite her Uncle Rowland to enter politics.

'Who is that?' she asked Tsunami.

'Pater's estate manager, Karunaratne,' was the reply. 'He's Ranil's estate manager, really, since Ranil advised Pater to take him on, and Karunaratne actually reports to Ranil rather than to Pater. Ranil says he's very efficient – knows the whole place like the palm of his hand and knows every worker on it by name. Maybe I didn't tell you,' she added, 'but after Pater went seriously into politics, Ranil took over the running of the estates.'

'How can Ranil possibly do that?' Latha asked. 'Doesn't he live in Colombo?'

'Oh, he's up here pretty often,' Tsunami said. 'Brings friends up all the time. My big brother enjoys playing lord of the manor, and all that. You'll see.'

A few days later, Latha *did* 'see'. A long-distance call from Colombo announced that Ranil was coming up for a few days.

'He'll be here at lunch time,' Tsunami said at breakfast. 'He's bringing some people with him. They're keen to get in some golf and tennis, if they can.'

It was nearly half past one on the next day, when four cars swept up the drive. The tall gates were flung open at their approach. Karunaratne himself was on hand to welcome them, and sprang forward to open the door for the 'Young Master'. A party of young women from the estate lines came forward with garlands of marigolds in their hands; and Latha, hoping to catch a glimpse of her cousin from the window of the bedroom she was once again sharing with Tsunami, saw Ranil, as sleek and athletic as ever, leap on to the front steps and bend his handsome head to receive a garland. A fair-haired girl wearing dark glasses and brief shorts joined him there and, turning, admired the view. Latha observed the expansive gestures with which Ranil pointed out to his companion various features of the landscape that she herself knew so well. He's like a king, surveying his kingdom, Latha thought.

As she watched, Tara and Tsunami appeared at the head of the steps to welcome their brother's guests: a merry party, twelve altogether, laughing and talking, and calling out apologies for their lateness to whoever might be listening. It was such a hot day, they said, and the sight of the waterfall had tempted them to have a dip in the river and explore the pools around the Falls.

They were immediately forgiven, of course, and the new chef, Vaithianathan's successor, was directed by Tara to serve lunch by two o'clock. Returning to the bedroom, where Latha was brushing her hair, preparatory to pinning it up, Tsunami announced that there were five young women in the party.

'Not counting Ranil's current girlfriend,' she said. 'You'd probably know most of them.'

'I probably wouldn't,' Latha replied; and in her disappointment at hearing the words 'Ranil's girlfriend', couldn't stop herself adding:

'I don't move in high society, you know.'

'High society!' Tsunami was amused. 'Oh, *they're* not "high society",' she said. 'They're just the usual Colombo party girls. They don't have much money but they love a good time, so they're ready to go out and stay out till all hours at the drop of a hat. There's a whole string of girls like that who make themselves available to our boys, and Ranil and his friends know them all! "What would we do without our good-time girls!" is what he says. "In a backwater like Ceylon, how else is a man to gain experience?"'

'Does Chris feel the same way?'

'I shouldn't think so. He doesn't see much of Ranil, anyway, and doesn't care much for his friends.'

Latha adjusted the pins in her hair, and asked, as casually as she could:

'What's Ranil's girlfriend like?'

'Her name's Ninette,' Tsunami replied. 'She works at the French embassy in Colombo. Keen to see as much as she can of the island before she goes back to France.'

Meeting Ranil's guests a few minutes later, Latha found that two of the 'party girls' she had glimpsed from the window were Eurasian, one Tamil, and two Sinhalese. Three of them, having attended Ashcombe, had a nodding acquaintance with Tara and Tsunami. The other two were from schools of which Latha knew nothing. All five were good-looking, very smartly dressed, and dauntingly self-confident. Latha thought she had met two of them before, and spent some time wondering where, until she realized that their faces were familiar from her reading of the weekend newspapers, in the Women's Pages of which they frequently modelled clothes and hair styles for local designers.

She looked at their short skirts, well-cut shirts and blue jeans with awe: there wasn't a hope that her mother would allow her to wear anything like that! She was struck by their informal, easy manners with the men in the party who were, without exception, old school friends of her cousin Ranil. They had all, it seemed, spent the previous evening together at a dance in Colombo that had continued into the early hours of the morning.

'O-oo-oh, I'm so *tired*,' one of the girls said, yawning. 'But these fellows wouldn't take no for an answer, even though not one of them was fit to drive after all that drinking. Daddy didn't like to let me come on this trip at all, but then Ranil promised us faithfully that he would be doing the driving. So then Mummy said "Go, child, go and enjoy, maybe you can get some sleep in the car."'

'And you did get some sleep, didn't you, Ramona?' asked Ranil, placing a genial arm around his guest's slender waist.

'Sleep? What sleep!' retorted Ramona pertly. 'With this fellow Nihal sitting next to me in the back seat, and nudging me every time I closed my eyes—'

'Nudging you, was he? Or squeezing?' asked a male voice.

'Just wanted to make sure you didn't miss the view, sweetheart,' said 'this fellow Nihal' hastily. He turned to Ranil.

'One thing, this tea country gives you spectacular scenery all the way up, machan! Mountains and valleys wherever we looked . . .'

'Yeah, and I bet you looked everywhere, didn't you, Nihal?' inquired the voice.

It belonged to rugger full-back 'Slim' Kodikara, who had acquired his nickname at College on account of the size of his massive thighs. 'Slim' had been the acknowledged wit of Ranil's class at King's, where he had specialized in the art of the suggestive *double entendre*. Everyone in the group laughed at his jest and, just as they had done in their schooldays, they took it up where 'Slim' had left off.

'With Nihal,' put in one of them, 'you can be sure no inch of territory's ever left unexplored . . .'

'Or unappreciated . . .'

'Just ask Ramona . . .'

'Meet our pal Nihal, friends, the world's *fastest* traveller . . .'

'Marco Polo has nothing on Nihal . . .'

Ninette from the French embassy was puzzled.

'So Nihal knows the countryside well?' she asked Ramona. 'He arranges tours of wildlife sanctuaries, yes? Can I book myself on one of your tours, Nihal?'

There was a fresh burst of laughter from all present. The puzzled expression on Ninette's pretty face drew more witticisms from the men.

'Any time, Ma'mzelle, you just say the word, he'll be there . . .' said 'Slim' Kodikara.

'Nihal's Express Tours departing every hour, on the hour . . .'

'Outstanding service guaranteed, on Nihal Express Tours *Un*limited . . .'

'Correction! *Up*standing, not *out*standing . . .'

Ranil raised a hand.

'Hey, hey, that's enough. Ladies present. You fellows don't know where to draw the line.'

He turned back to Ramona:

'Don't worry, there'll be plenty of time after lunch to get some sleep.'

'I wouldn't be too sure about that, Ramona,' said a grinning 'Slim'. 'In a cool, bracing climate like this, people must keep warm. They need each other's company, and time's too precious to be wasted sleeping. What do you say, Dolores?'

This remark drew another laugh from the men present. The girls shrugged their shoulders, exchanged knowing glances, and giggled.

'Now, don't you try any funny business after lunch, you hear?' said the girl he had addressed as Dolores, though the tone of her voice was far from chiding.

'No, you'd better not,' said one of her girlfriends. 'If you try anything, we'll tell everyone!'

Latha, who had been summoned to the telephone to answer a call from her father, had made a late, very shy entrance into the dining room, and so had missed most of the badinage. Her earlier feelings for Ranil had come back with unexpected force, paralysing her with embarrassment at the prospect of meeting again the cousin she had hero-worshipped as a child. She would be meeting him, she thought, not in the middle of a wedding celebration with crowds around them, but here, in the lovely old house in which they had spent so much time together, and which, as a result, held so many happy memories for her. She had wondered briefly as she descended the stairs to meet his guests, whether the Monopoly board was still stored in that chest beneath the four-poster bed in the spare room, and whether Ranil ever recalled the midnight kiss that had followed their card-playing on that never-to-be-forgotten New Year's Eve. Her cheeks burned at the thought that perhaps he did.

Everyone was already seated at the long dining table when she came in, and Raman's replacement was directing the serving of an entrée. He did this in a blinding glare generated by a glass cabinet at one end of the room in which shelf upon shelf of Venetian glass ornaments reflected a blaze of light from a double row of electric bulbs. Another of Moira's showy 'improvements', and a particularly vulgar one, thought Latha, but she was glad of it, because it forced her to keep her eyes down. Unwilling to look up and perhaps meet Ranil's eye – for she was agonizingly conscious of him, seated at one end of the table while Tara presided at the other – Latha did not realize at first that she had already met one member of the party.

Anupam Munasinghe rose, smiling, from his place at the table.

Did Latha remember him at all? His words implied that she must be surrounded by so many eager candidates for her attention that he could not reasonably expect her to recall their meeting. He claimed to be especially pleased to see her today, not having really had a chance to speak to her at Tara's wedding.

'There was such a crowd of people around you,' said he, regretfully, 'and you were so busy – so many duties to perform!'

Oh yeah? That was more than two years ago. If you'd really wanted to speak to me, there must have been many opportunities at the wedding. And what about afterwards . . . ?

Anupam exchanged his seat for a chair next to hers so that, as he said, they could continue a conversation that had ended much too soon on the last occasion of their meeting. He inquired politely after her parents' health, and asked how her father's book about his Government Service experiences was coming along. Latha caught a glint of amusement in Tsunami's eye as she answered Anupam's questions. She looked away immediately.

You're so polite. Much too polite. You can't possibly mean what you're saying.

But it seemed that he did. He recalled that she had been about to enter University when they last met, and asked whether Peradeniya had answered her expectations. He had visited Kandy and Peradeniya several times himself since then – 'It's so beautiful that I keep going back' – and on the last visit, his commitments in town having ended early, he had actually driven up to Sanghamitta Hall, hoping to call on her, but had been informed that she was out. Latha, who had never before encountered such concentrated attention from a member of the opposite sex, became very confused. She was aware that their protracted conversation was attracting the notice of every other person at their end of the table, and dreaded that Anupam might say something, however trivial, that would give away the circumstances in which they had met at the Capri.

He did not.

Latha breathed a sigh of relief, and the new chef's creations, which had seemed for a moment to turn to ashes on her tongue, magically regained their flavour.

'Hello, Latha.'

She turned with relief towards the familiar voice.

'Chris! So good to see you!'

'I've been up to Peradeniya recently too, Latha, did you know?'

Latha realized that her exchange with Anupam Munasinghe had not gone unnoticed by her cousin.

'Like my friend Anupam here, I missed you, but I ran into a curious character, a Mrs Raptor.'

'Oh, no!'

'What's the problem? She's an interesting person! Interesting . . . and interested.'

'I'll bet she was interested,' Latha couldn't help saying. 'Interested in finding out who you were!'

'Well, yes,' Chris replied, smiling. 'Now you come to mention it . . . She did ask me a lot of questions about myself, and my profession. Wanted to know what I was doing. "Minding my own business," I longed to say. But I didn't. I'm afraid my imagination ran away with me, rather: I told her I was a private detective, who occasionally worked with the C.I.D. She was absolutely riveted. Asked me about the cases I'd worked on.'

'And what did you say?'

'I told her that I'd helped to clear up the singular tragedy of the Atkinson brothers at Trincomalee,' replied Chris.

'You didn't!'

'Why not? I figured it was ten to one that she'd ever read Sherlock Holmes. And I was right. She hadn't. She believed me.'

Back once again in their bedroom, Latha endured Tsunami's teasing with dignity.

'And what was all that with the extremely glamorous Mr Munasinghe, may I ask?'

'I've no idea what you mean, Tsunami. I don't know him at all, really.'

'That wasn't the impression you both gave.'

'Well, maybe so. But it's the truth.'

'Who is he?'

Latha parried.

'I thought you knew everyone who was there.'

'For pity's sake, Latha, do you think I know all my brothers' friends? I've never seen him before in my life.'

'His parents are old friends of Amma and Thaththa,' Latha explained, as casually as possible. 'I've met him only once, and then only by chance.'

'He's *very* good-looking!' Tsunami said. 'Aren't you interested?'

'No, I'm not!'

'Then you won't mind if I have a shot at him? Didn't get a chance at lunch, because I was seated at Tara's end of the table. In any case, he only had eyes for you! Don't look at me like that, Latha, I'm only joking! He's probably as boring as the rest of Ranil's friends.'

It seems, reflected Latha, that Tsunami has quite got over her feelings for Daniel Rajaratnam. *Then you won't mind if I have a shot at him?* That didn't sound to her like the voice of a broken-hearted lover. Maybe, she thought, Mr Bennet had been right in his cynical opinion of the natures of young women! *Next to being married, a girl likes to be crossed in love a little now and then . . .*

When they went down to the drawing room that evening for pre-dinner drinks, Latha and Tsunami found the women seated in a circle at one end of the long room, talking clothes. At the other end, the men had congregated around an elegant cocktail bar which Latha recognized as a recent addition to the room. They were talking sport.

'We might as well get this over with at once,' Tsunami said. 'Come on, Latha, do your duty.'

Joining the women, Latha and Tsunami paid polite attention to a discussion of the relative merits of the 'Coorg' and the 'Mini', variations of the sari which were being promoted by two rival dress designers in Colombo, with whom their guests were apparently on the most intimate terms. The topics of fashion and rugger might well have carried everyone through until dinner was served, had not Ranil, as host and Master of Ceremonies, ordered the servants to place the chairs against the wall and roll back the drawing-room carpet for dancing. Latha watched with amusement as the girls preened expectantly, but continued their conversation. No one looked round. It was obvious to her they were waiting for the music to strike up, but they did not, perhaps, wish to seem too eager.

'Ladies, fair ladies! I must ask you please to . . . ahem, to *widen your circle*, to accommodate me . . .'

It was 'Slim' Kodikara, towering over the little group of women, first off the mark as usual with a loaded *double entendre*. In case its meaning had missed their understanding on its first utterance, he did them the favour of repeating it.

They giggled appreciatively, and obediently moved their chairs back to make room for him. 'Slim' sat down next to Tsunami, who gave him a glance of glacial disgust and promptly turned her back on him. She was aware that one of his sisters had already made discreet overtures to Moira, a preliminary to the marriage proposal that was almost certain to follow. I really can't stand any more of this, Tsunami said to herself. If only Ranil had waited until after dinner to propose dancing, she could have pleaded a headache and gone early to bed.

Tsunami's acquaintance with Daniel Rajaratnam had, if anything, intensified her habit of looking down with scorn at the men in her family's circle of relations and friends. Peradeniya had sharpened her contempt for swaggering ex-public school 'boys' like 'Slim' who, rather than study for the university entrance examinations or qualify for the professions, had used their College connections and sporting records to wangle niches for themselves in commercial firms or in the planting industry as soon as they left school. Their conversation bored her, revolving, as it did, chiefly around sporting fixtures in which she took no interest. As for their brand of humour . . .

She hoped 'Slim' had not joined the group of women with the intention of asking her to dance. It looked very much, however, as if he had. Well, she was not going to wait around to find out. As Ranil put the first record on the gramophone, Tsunami got up and made for the drawing-room door. Just as she reached it, however, she found her path blocked.

'Would you care to dance?'

She was given no time to refuse. Without prior warning of any kind, she found herself on the improvised dance floor, her hand clasped firmly in that of a stranger.

'You're Chris's sister, aren't you? I saw you at lunch, but I'd come in too late to be introduced.'

Tsunami was pulled into a close embrace. Accustomed to maintaining the gap of several inches between herself and her dancing partners that had been insisted upon by her dancing teacher to satisfy the nuns at Ashcombe, she attempted to disengage herself, and got nowhere.

'We are much too close,' she managed to say at last, as her partner spun on his heel and took her with him.

'Too close for what?'

'Too close for comfort.'

'I'm sorry. Is this better?'

'Much better, thank you. I can breathe a little now.'

Tsunami took advantage of her release to glance upwards, receiving an impression of dark eyes gazing down at her curiously from beneath straight black brows. She immediately looked hastily away again. Who *was* this? A new addition to Ranil's group of King's College friends? They went the length of the drawing room and back again without exchanging a further word. We can't go on dancing in silence, surely, Tsunami thought with alarm, and plunged desperately into conversation.

'Have we met before?' she asked.

'I met your cousin Latha a year and a half ago, in Colombo. My name is Sujit Roy.'

The name meant nothing to Tsunami. But she had recovered her breath and, with it, her poise.

'Welcome to Lucas Falls,' she said. 'Is this your first visit?'

'Yes,' said the unknown Mr Roy, executing a complicated turn which Tsunami, to her surprise, was able to follow without missing a step, 'but I gather most of the people here have been up before on your brother's invitation, at some time or another. This is your family home, Chris tells me. It's a very attractive place.'

'Well, yes, I suppose it is,' Tsunami said, 'though my father lives most of the year in Colombo now.'

Sujit Roy made no reply to this, so Tsunami chattered on nervously.

'My sister Tara, who is married, lives with her family in Colombo,' she said, 'and I'm at University in Peradeniya.'

Silence.

'Are you from Colombo, Mr Roy?' she asked. 'Does your family live up country?'

Silence.

'How did you meet my brother Christopher?'

Silence.

At last Roy said, as he swung her into another breathless turn:

'May I ask if you always talk as much as this while you're dancing?'

Tsunami stared at him.

'Usually,' she said.

'Now, why would you want to do that?' Roy asked. 'This is Sinatra. It isn't music to talk by. Although I must say you have a beautiful voice.'

Without losing a beat, it seemed, the music had changed. Her partner bent his head and put his lips close to her ear.

'Take it easy, little girl,' he said. 'Don't waste this marvellous music by chattering through it! And do me a favour – please stop clutching my shoulder, you might dislocate it.'

Little girl? Startled, Tsunami relaxed her grip, and Roy laughed.

'Okay, that's better. Now, don't talk, just lean on me and move to the music. Trust me, I won't let you fall.'

The first Sinatra song was followed by another one, and then by another. This is altogether too romantic, Tsunami told herself as Sinatra's finely modulated rendering travelled smoothly up and down the scale, against a backing of female voices.

'Economical on vocabulary,' murmured a voice above her head. 'Not to mention ideas.'

Tsunami could not help smiling at this unexpected echo of a thought she had often had herself. The record ended, and was succeeded by another. Immediately, the mood in the room changed, and as if in response to it, her partner drew Tsunami closer to him.

The new record Ranil had chosen was 'Sway', the popular mambo song by Pablo Beltrán Ruiz that she had heard a hundred times before, but never until that evening had its lyrics moved her in quite this way. Tsunami glanced about her, and saw that the other couples on the floor were as closely linked as she and Sujit Roy. Her brother Ranil had his hands on Ninette's slim hips, and he was gazing steadily into her eyes. One of the 'party girls' – Ramona – had removed her hand from its conventional position on her partner's shoulder, and had placed both her arms around his neck.

This, Tsunami told herself, as she moved to the pulse of the music, was not the way Mrs Ingleton had taught her to dance at Ashcombe – and it was certainly not the way Ranil, with the watchful eyes of their relatives fastened on him, had danced at Tara's wedding! She tried to free herself as unobtrusively as possible from her partner's embrace, but she was held too closely in the circle of Roy's right arm, fixed too firmly in her position by the lithe body that had fitted itself so perfectly to hers, for her attempt to escape his notice.

'Anything worrying you?' Sujit Roy asked, above her head. He sounded amused.

'No, nothing,' Tsunami replied quickly.

On one of their turns she had glimpsed Latha with Chris sitting beside her. They were looking at her, surprise written clearly on their faces. She smiled cheerfully up at Sujit.

'Nothing at all.'

'I'm pleased to hear it,' he said. 'One wishes only to be a source of happiness to the world.'

Ordinarily, Tsunami would have taken him up on a remark like that. Strangely, she felt no desire to do so. She closed her eyes and erased completely from her consciousness the presence of other dancers on the floor, and of Chris and Latha too. She would think about them later on, when the evening was over.

'Beautiful,' said Roy's voice softly in her ear, as they moved to the music. 'You're so damned sweet, I can hardly believe it.'

Sweet? 'Sweet' and 'cute' were words that were not in Tsunami's vocabulary, unless she was talking of children. Of course there were some exceptions.

'They're so *cute*!' she had sometimes said condescendingly, of the first-year courting couples who walked together each evening as the shadows deepened around Sanghamitta Hall. This stranger, who had actually dared a moment ago to address her – super-sophisticated Tsunami! – as 'little girl', had just described her as 'sweet'! Did he imagine *she* was a child?

She had no time to speculate further on the subject.

Someone dimmed the lights, a cool, close-shaven chin was placed against Tsunami's forehead, and her partner's right arm tightened around her waist. Gently but quite deliberately, his thumb began to circle the hollow of her palm. Intimate and deeply disturbing, the pressure of his hand on hers grew stronger and more insistent, waking a sequence of sensations in Tsunami that were neither 'cute' nor 'sweet', and stirring instincts in her that were altogether new.

The room seemed suddenly to have become very warm. This *cannot* be happening, Tsunami told herself. I'm imagining things. Since when have I taken to melting like wax because some guy holds my hand? Good sense told her that she should protest, and break away from Sujit Roy, but speech seemed to have suddenly become unnecessary and irrelevant. As for breaking away . . . curiously, that had become an impossibility.

She glanced up into her partner's face, hoping to find there a clue to what was happening between them, and saw that his gaze was no longer on her, but focused intently ahead, as if he were observing something very far away. With a sudden flash of understanding—

I believe he's forgotten that we're dancing, she thought. He's making love.

The shock of this discovery, and her surprise at the intense pleasure it gave her, caused Tsunami to miss a step. She stumbled, and might have fallen, had it not been for Roy's supporting arm.

'Are you feeling tired? Would you like to sit down?'

Now was her chance to bring the situation to an end. It would certainly not be the first time that she had walked abruptly away from boorish or boring dancing partners who had been introduced to her by Moira or Tara. On such occasions she had been perfectly indifferent to the offence she might be giving by doing so. Why, then, didn't she accept the proffered excuse, agree that she was tired, and leave the floor? Because, she told herself, Roy was neither boorish nor boring! Also (Tsunami was honest enough to admit this to herself) she didn't *want* the experience he had created for her to come to an end. Ever.

She threw caution to the winds:

'No,' she said. 'I'm fine.'

Well, she had missed her chance. She began to dread the moment when, once the evening was over, prudent and strait-laced Latha would tell her with her usual frankness just what she had thought of her behaviour on the floor.

'So what if he used dancing as an excuse to go too far?' Tsunami imagined her cousin saying. 'Most men would, if they're given half a chance. He wouldn't have done it if you hadn't allowed it!'

And she would have deserved such criticism . . . Then a new thought struck Tsunami. It came to her mind, entangled with memories of Daniel Rajaratnam.

How far was 'too far'?

Sujit Roy was obviously a man of experience, at ease with the world in ways that the shy young men among her campus friends were not. She had never danced with Daniel, not even at a Colours Night celebration on campus, and she had no means of making a comparison. What if this kind of intimate dancing was something everyone in Sujit Roy's social circle did, something that was casually produced for the pleasure of every partner, no matter who? What if physical closeness, which had meant so much to her with Daniel, and was now playing such havoc with her own peace of mind, meant nothing at all to Roy?

Tsunami made a second attempt to disengage herself, with no result except that Roy held her closer still. She decided that he was sending her a clear signal, so clear that she could not pretend she did not understand it. But what kind of experience it foreshadowed, and how she would respond to that experience, she was unsure. She was certain only of one thing: she was not going to walk away from it.

Coming upon this unsuspected dimension to her own character made Tsunami slightly dizzy. Thankful that no one else in the room could see into her mind, she dropped her gaze, made no more attempts to free herself from Sujit Roy's embrace, and gave herself up wholly to him and to the music.

'Well, well, what a flirtatious little sister I seem to have!'

It was Ranil, dancing past them with Ninette in his arms. He winked broadly at Tsunami, and when he spoke he did not trouble to lower his voice.

'And what will Pater have to say about *this*?'

Across the room, Tara heard Ranil's remark and stiffened visibly. Chris had informed his sisters that he would be bringing two friends up to join the weekend party at Lucas Falls. One of them – Anupam Munasinghe – Tara had met earlier in the evening, and approved of.

'It's easy to see your friend Mr Munasinghe's from our kind of background,' she had told Chris. 'You should encourage him to call on Pater and Auntie Moira in Colombo. It's about time Tsunami met some decent people.'

Chris had smiled, but had made no reply.

Sujit Roy, however, having driven up from the south coast in his own car, had arrived late at the Falls, and had not yet been introduced to Tara. As the dancers stood together in pairs, waiting for the record to change, Tara looked Roy up and down. He was certainly very presentable. A great improvement on that scruffy, bearded ruffian from the campus who had visited Tsunami in Colombo. (The faithful Paul, who had called on Tsunami during the last vacation to give her early news of her Special History examination result, had been snubbed mercilessly by Tara for his pains, and pointedly ignored by Moira.) Tara took in Sujit's height, his good looks, the ease of his manner, and the cut of his evening clothes. She recognized immediately, as Tsunami had not, that such a degree of stylish sophistication could not possibly be home-grown.

She shifted her gaze to her sister. Tsunami, Tara noted, was drifting in her partner's arms as if she were lost in a dream. Her eyes appeared to be closed.

That man dances much too well, Tara thought. I don't trust him.

She decided that it was her duty to question Chris about the unknown Mr Roy at the earliest opportunity, and get some answers.

'Excuse me a moment,' Chris said to Latha. 'I'm going to cut in on Roy, and ask Tsunami to dance the next one with me. Ranil can be a bit heavy-handed, sometimes.'

Latha observed her cousins dancing together, her pleasure a little damped by a niggling disappointment that Chris had not thought of asking *her*. At the other end of the room, Sujit Roy picked up a glass from the bar and raised it to her with a smile before he drank.

He really is extraordinarily good-looking, Latha thought. She wondered why she had not noticed this fact when she had met Roy with the Munasinghes in Colombo. Which reminded her: what had happened to Tsunami's earlier plan to 'have a shot at' Anupam? Under the spell cast by Sujit Roy, Tsunami seemed to have forgotten all about him! Latha glanced around the room, and could see no sign of 'the extremely glamorous Mr Munasinghe'. Perhaps Anupam didn't care for dancing? She seemed to remember that while Sujit had danced with Shalini Munasinghe during the evening they had all spent together, Anupam had preferred conversation.

Latha politely returned Sujit's smile, and looked quickly away, hoping that neither he nor his friend Mr Munasinghe would think of moving in her direction: she had no desire to recall, or have them recall, the evening they had spent in each other's company at the Capri. She was saved from this possibility by the music, which came to a finish just as Raman's replacement appeared at the end of the long room, to announce that dinner was served.

'Sujit Roy,' Tsunami said to Latha late that night, 'is really quite nice.'

Now, there's an interesting statement! Latha thought. And it's been made by a girl who's spent a good part of the evening in the man's arms . . . She glanced quickly at her cousin. Tsunami seemed wholly preoccupied in searching the floor for something she had dropped.

Latha continued folding her sari. She hung it up in the wardrobe, and with careful casualness replied:

'He's certainly a very . . . experienced dancer.'

Tsunami didn't seem to have heard her.

'Such a change,' she went on, 'from Ranil's usual set of ghastly friends.'

Latha made no reply.

'He says he knows you.'

'Not really,' Latha told her. 'He's a friend of Anupam Munasinghe's. I met them both together, on the same occasion.' She did not say what the occasion had been, and added only: 'I remember he told me he was in Ceylon to study boat-building.'

As Latha spoke, she remembered the magical vision she had had at the Capri, of the storied isles of Greece, of blue sea and sky, and white houses on vine-covered hillsides. She wondered whether Sujit Roy had come any nearer to realizing his dream.

'What are you looking for, Tsunami?'

'One of my turquoise earrings. I felt it fall a moment ago, and it must be here, somewhere.'

'Look for it in the morning,' Latha advised. 'It's so late already.'

'It's my lucky earring, Latha. I *have* to find it. I want to wear it tomorrow.'

In the bedroom he was sharing with Anupam Munasinghe in the opposite wing of the house, Sujit Roy kicked off his shoes, stretched himself out on the elephant-decorated counterpane, and closed his eyes. Anupam looked down quizzically at his friend.

'And what, may I ask, was that all about?' he said. 'That shameless exercise in full-on seduction?'

'It was nothing of the kind!'

Roy opened his eyes and looked reproachfully at Anupam.

'And anyway, where were you to take note of it? Just when I needed my guardian angel to advise or intervene, he'd vanished into thin air.'

'Don't change the subject! You know I don't dance if I can avoid it.'

'Well, where *were* you?'

'I was doing what I do best,' his friend replied. 'Observing carefully from the sidelines. And frankly, I'm not at all sure that I liked what I saw. As my old school history book said of Viscount Torrington in 1848, you were using a machine gun to shoot down a mosquito.'

'Who was Viscount Torrington?'

'A nineteenth-century Brit in Ceylon. Forget Torrington – I'm talking about Chris's young sister. She acts sophisticated, but she's only a child, Sujit: much too young and inexperienced to play casual sexual games.'

'I'm aware of that.'

'So, what's your excuse? That you couldn't help yourself? That argument is as old as Eden, and it's not an honest one. Shaw put it better. He called dancing – the kind of dancing *you* were doing – "a perpendicular expression of a horizontal desire".'

He received no reply.

'Am I to understand that what I observed was *not* casual?'

'Maybe it began as a game, but that wasn't how it ended. It became . . . something else. It became special.'

'And will it still be special tomorrow? Next week? Next month? You know what your track record's been like, my friend.'

'Forget about the past. This is different.'

Anupam smiled.

'Is it? Well, I hope you know what you're about. The Wijesinhas are an old family, and I'm told they don't welcome strangers.'

'They'll have no option but to welcome *me*!'

'You sound very sure of yourself.'

'I am. And I'm very sure of *her*.'

'What! After ten minutes on a dance floor?'

'A lot can happen in ten minutes between a man and a woman. If they understand each other . . .'

Yes, I suppose it can, Anupam Munasinghe thought a little enviously, remembering an acutely uncomfortable evening in Colombo during which his parents, ignorant as yet of their son's homosexuality, had strained every nerve to arrange a match for him with Latha Wijesinha. When they told him the day after their evening at the Capri that they wished to send a formal proposal of marriage to Latha's parents, he had refused. And then, he had told them the reason for his refusal.

Thank God for Shalini! Anupam thought. His sister had helped him weather the tempest that had inevitably followed the disclosure, for the first time, of what his parents might have at times suspected but had never known for certain.

'My precious son!' his mother had wept.

His father, distress plainly visible on his face, had managed to put an arm around Anupam's shoulders and embrace him.

'I don't need consolation!' Anupam had cried. 'I don't want forgiveness or pity! I want you to be glad for me!'

'*Glad?*'

'Shut up, for goodness' sake,' his sister had whispered. 'Don't get into an argument about this. Leave them to me.'

Anupam looked across at Sujit, now sleeping soundly in the bed opposite, and gave thanks, not for the first time, that he had been granted – just when he had needed it most – such loyal support in a sister and a friend. His relationship with Sujit Roy, sexually uncomplicated in their schooldays, when they had been brought together only by common interests in study and sport, had proved itself a lifeline for Anupam when they found themselves plunged together into the stream of sexually active student life in Cambridge. Surrounded there by men for whom he simultaneously felt attraction and fear, dreading embarrassment, and conscious that his very nature exposed him to attack, Anupam had found protective colouring for himself in Sujit's undoubted success with women. He had done it, he sometimes thought, in much the same instinctive way that a puny boy at a public school might attach himself for his own safety to the biggest and most powerful rugger player in his class.

Sujit had shown a sympathy for his predicament that Anupam knew he would not find in any of the young Ceylonese men who were at Cambridge in his time. He knew it, because at first he had looked tentatively to them for understanding, and had been disappointed. They regarded homosexuality as a pastime of their schooldays, something to be abandoned as they reached manhood and marriage, and to be sniggered about ever after. The jokes they made about classmates and masters who had been 'that way inclined', and who had 'made passes' at them on the sports field or in the class room, made Anupam shudder and flinch when he thought about what he would have had to endure if any of them had ever guessed the truth about himself.

Love had certainly come Anupam Munasinghe's way during his Cambridge days, but very occasionally, and never in any form that looked as if it might become permanent. Just before he and Sujit went down, however, Anupam had met a stranger at a concert, a member of another Cambridge college, with whom, for the first time, he had allowed himself to hope that things might turn out differently in the future.

Anupam gave himself up to memories of a fortnight he had spent in a little seaside hotel near London, just before he took up his post in Bonn, with the lover who, following their second meeting, was a stranger to him no longer. He had thought despairingly that they might never meet again, and had prepared himself for the end of happiness. But the Fates had been kind: they had been able to renew their relationship; and life, Anupam thought, was altogether better now. Now that the chasm in the centre of his existence was filled with regular letters and occasional meetings, he could work, he could concentrate, he had time for other people and other friendships. He could, for instance, act as Sujit's 'guardian angel' when called upon to do so, advising him with absolute sincerity, and without a trace of the envy he had, admittedly, sometimes allowed himself to feel in the past.

Anupam could now recall with amused detachment an evening at an hotel in Washington when, dipping idly into the Gideon Bible in his room because he'd had nothing else to read, he had come upon a verse in the Book of Proverbs that had seemed at that time to sum up his personal situation exactly. He switched on his reading light and looked for the Bible he remembered having seen on his bedside table that afternoon. Turning to Proverbs, he ran his finger down the margins of several pages until he found what he was looking for:

> There be three things which are too wonderful for me, yea, four which I know not . . . The way of an eagle in the air; the way of a serpent upon a rock; the way of a ship in the midst of the sea; and the way of a man with a maid.

The way of a man with a maid . . .

Fleeting images of the evening that had just ended moved behind his closed eyelids: Ranil and Ninette, Nihal and his Ramona, Kodikara and Dolores, and now Sujit and Tsunami. All of them lovers, all of them possessed, though doubtless in varying degrees, of that 'wonderful' secret that he would never know. Anupam believed he had seen the 'way of a man with a maid' expertly demonstrated by Sujit on the dance floor that very evening.

Meeting Latha Wijesinha a second time, observing her as she talked and laughed with her cousin Chris, he had realized how attractive she was. university life had matured her, given her poise and self-confidence. But he had also realized that, however charming she might have become, however poised and self-confident, she was not for him.

Unless . . .

Anupam thought about the several married men of his parents' generation whom he knew to be practising homosexuals, some of them the respectable fathers of seemingly happy families. He had sometimes wondered, observing them 'from the sidelines' as they downed their whiskies and sodas in Colombo's clubs, narrowed their golfing handicap, and dutifully showed up at weddings and funerals with their wives and their children in tow, whether the lives of men and women in such marriages consisted of pretence or compromise.

Could he live with an arrangement of that kind? Could he keep up a lifetime of diplomatic deceit with an intelligent and sensitive wife whom he liked and respected, but could not love? He imagined, as in a scene from a play, a marriage proposal being sent by his father to Latha's parents, *and being accepted by them.* Could such a scenario become even a distant possibility?

Anupam closed the Bible and switched off the light.

The world was certainly full of wonderful things and of wonderful girls. It was a pity they were too wonderful for him.

In her room at the end of the passage, Tara was writing a letter:

Dear Auntie Moira,

I have some very good news for you and Pater. I really think I have found the right person for Tsunami – at last! He has come up to Lucas Falls for the week-end with Chris, and I am sure Chris would vouch for him. I could not, at that early stage, and with so many people there, ask too many questions about his family when he was introduced, but I understand that his father, Dr Siri Munasinghe, is a London-trained doctor. Anupam is in the Ceylon Overseas Service (educated at Harrow and Cambridge), VERY presentable, and seemed to get on well with everybody. He was very sweet with little Lohan, who took to him at once!

Even Tsunami, who, as we know, turns up her nose at every proposal anyone brings for her, would definitely consider this one.

In any case, it's about time Tsunami settled down into a solid, respectable marriage. I've always thought that sending her to Peradeniya was a serious mistake on Pater's part. The university has put all kinds of unsuitable ideas into her head. Besides, the girls she meets there are not her social equals, and though the men are completely useless as marriage prospects, there's always the danger that someone as emotional and irresponsible as Tsunami could suddenly lose her head over one of them. Which, as we saw last year, was exactly what happened. Fortunately, Pater managed to put a stop to that, but I'm not sure that Tsunami has learned her lesson.

In fact, while we were dancing last night to some of Ranil's records, there was a point at which Tsunami had me really worried – however, I think it was just a passing fancy and doesn't amount to anything.

I have suggested to Chris that Anupam Munasinghe should be encouraged to call on you and Pater in Colombo. You can judge for yourself then, and see what you think of him . . . I understand that he has a sister of whom he is very fond, and he has struck up a close friendship with Chris, so close that they're already almost like brothers.

Altogether, the family seems an ideal one with which to be connected – they're just like us!

Your affectionate niece,

Tara

13

LORD OF THE MANOR

The clock downstairs struck five, and Ranil Wijesinha considered that it was time he got back to his own room. Ninette was still fast asleep, her blonde hair spread out over the pillow, and he turned the door knob very softly so as not to wake her.

Karunaratne was waiting for him when he walked out on to the veranda. 'Your coffee is on the tray, *Hamu*,' he said. 'Shall I bring the car round?'

Ranil considered.

'No, I'll walk to the muster. You can wait for me there.'

Bowing and scraping, smiling and rubbing his hands together as usual, Ranil thought irritably. A real-life Uriah Heep! Karunaratne was a good office manager, but he suffered to an inordinate degree from what his brother Chris called 'the *walauwa* mentality'. Not that Ranil objected to a proper degree of humility from servants – that was part and parcel of local tradition, after all – but Karunaratne's brand of Heep-like obsequiousness was a bit too much to take at five-thirty in the morning, even for Ranil.

Five-thirty, and coolie women with their shawls wrapped around them against the chill air, and baskets strapped to their backs, were already making their way down the hillside from the lines. As he passed by with long strides, his stick in his hand and his bull-terrier leaping beside him, they salaamed and quickly edged sideways, out of his way. Ranil always enjoyed the early morning walk to the weighing sheds where the muster was held. It gave him a chance, he said, to take note of improvements on the estate, to observe the point at which a new well had been dug on his orders, to check whether the new drains had been competently cut.

But better than all of that, he admitted to himself that he enjoyed the submissive cringing of the estate workers, the sensation of power that walking up here alone gave him. So, he thought, must it have been with the British planters who had been his father's predecessors at Lucas Falls, the knowledge that they owned all the land as far as the eye could see. And all the people.

A table had been set out in front of the weighing shed, and a chair had been placed behind it. The estate ledgers were open at today's date, and a dipping pen lay ready to his hand, with a bottle of blue-black Quink beside it. This was all as usual, exactly as it had been done in the old days, when his father and Franz Goldman had walked down to the muster together. Ranil took his seat, and glanced up and down the lines of workers. He was planning to bring another, much smaller, party up to the Falls in a few months' time. His guests would all be male, but there would be no King's College men among them. Almost all the party would be businessmen with political connections, city people eager to partake of that particular type of entertainment which was known in the island as 'Plantation hospitality'. When the workers' names were called today at the muster, Ranil would be able to see for himself what kind of talent Karunaratne had been able to round up for the pleasure of his guests next month.

As the 'young master' of the estate, Ranil was entitled in theory to the pick of the crop: Karunaratne acknowledged this unwritten rule by catching Ranil's eye questioningly whenever some particularly shapely beauty stepped out of the line to claim her pruning knife, the badge of her occupation as a worker on Lucas Falls Estate. He had only to nod, and a cross would be pencilled against the girl's name. A discreet message would later be sent to the coolie lines that she was required that evening for 'service at the house'. That was the way it had been done in British times, and it was still the current practice.

As an adolescent schoolboy occasionally deputizing for his father, Ranil had sometimes amused himself with pretty girls he had encountered when walking the estate roads. But he had not had them brought to the house. And he had refrained altogether from using his manorial privileges following an incident that had occurred while he was still at College which had very nearly landed him with a paternity case. Without a word said to Rowland, the plaintiff had been bought off by Karunaratne's predecessor with a hundred rupees to satisfy her father's honour. That old rascal had salaamed, and touched Ranil's feet when the 'gift' was given. The woman had miscarried, anyway, and Ranil had been let off the hook.

Following Rowland's entry into politics, the situation had altered. The management of the estate was now in the hands of his eldest son, and Ranil, though he knew that he could do pretty much as he liked, was never forgetful of his family's reputation and his own. Outside the estate, he was careful to restrict his sexual adventures to women of his own class, women like Ninette and her like, who were sophisticated enough to know how to stay out of trouble. By next month, however, Ninette would have returned to France, and rather than spend two lonely nights on his own at Lucas Falls while his guests enjoyed themselves, Ranil thought he might well be in the mood to join in the revels. There would be no good-time girls at the next house party to carry tales back to Colombo, and no relatives to disapprove. Chris and his two friends would not be invited, Tara and her family would be back in Colombo, and Tsunami and Latha would have returned to Peradeniya. Not that he had to explain his actions to any of them, but their absence would reduce the chances of unnecessary complications.

Ranil reflected on a particular complication that had recently been presented by Tsunami. On the last visit his sisters had made to Lucas Falls, Tsunami had decided to take an early morning walk, and had encountered her brother's companion of the previous night returning to her quarters in the coolie lines. This should not have happened: the women of the estate were under strict instructions to approach and leave the house on such occasions by a special side entrance, an entrance that in Helen's time had been called 'the garden door'. (A screen of hibiscus along the path leading to it prevented their being seen from the windows or from the veranda.) But the girl had not been properly instructed, or maybe Ranil himself had been careless.

Tsunami had mentioned the meeting to him at breakfast, her gaze levelly meeting his own. Fortunately they had been alone, Tara being still occupied upstairs with her son.

'This happens every night, does it?' Tsunami had asked him.

Bloody cheek!

'Only when something special has to be prepared for the following morning, and they're short-handed in the kitchen,' Ranil had replied, calmly helping himself to the dishes on the sideboard. 'Karunaratne arranges for someone from the lines to stay over.'

'So Karunaratne makes the arrangements, does he? I see.'

Her tone had been casual, and the subject had never come up again, but ever since then Ranil had felt uncomfortably that he was under surveillance. He wondered whether Tsunami had mentioned the incident to Latha. He thought it unlikely although, reflecting on the events of the previous day, he believed he had sensed a certain chill in his cousin's manner to him which could result from knowing more about him than was good for her.

Dear little Latha! It would be a pity if her hero-worship of him were to take a toss, the child would never get over it. He had spoken with some severity to Karunaratne about the incident, and had been careful himself to permit no repetition of it for the duration of his sisters' visit.

Strict rules were of course observed when a house party of the kind he was planning for next month got under way. The women from the lines were not permitted to fraternize with the house servants while they were up at the house, or visit the servants' quarters; and they had to be off the premises before five o'clock each morning. From the guests, too, certain niceties were expected: a generous tip to the estate manager to show appreciation of special services was welcome, and it was made very clear that no violence of any kind would be tolerated.

This last injunction was especially necessary, since the knowledge that they were accountable to no one while they were on the estate had a tendency, occasionally, to go to the heads of some of the visitors: especially those who were not, as one might say, to the manor born. One or two of Ranil's more reckless associates had been tempted in the past to carry things a little too far, thereby creating serious problems, since the dispensary on the estate was not equipped to deal with anything out of the ordinary. Ranil had noticed that Karunaratne now made a point of removing from the guest bedrooms any objects or curios that could be misused by a rampaging visitor: the old planters' whips, for instance, those interesting relics of a colonial past which hung coiled on the walls of some of the rooms, were thoughtfully placed under lock and key in the estate manager's office before the guests arrived.

'Better be safe than sorry, *Hamu*,' Karunaratne had cautioned Ranil, his face impassive.

And, of course, the man was quite right. To convey a weeping and injured young woman to the hospital in town in the early hours of the morning in the estate car was obviously out of the question because of the publicity that would result in a township where every vehicle was known and gossip was everybody's meat and drink.

As the last of the tea pluckers took her orders for the day and left the weighing shed, a discreet cough beside Ranil indicated that Karunaratne had something to say.

'Yes, what is it?'

'*Hamu*, I think you said that Mr Tissa Palipana would be one of the next house party.'

'Yes. He has been here before. What of it?'

'We might have to make some special arrangements to accommodate Mr Palipana this time, *Hamu*.'

Tissa Palipana, the spoiled younger son of one of Rowland's cabinet colleagues, was known for his hot temper, and had also acquired a reputation for tippling of which Ranil was aware.

'Do you mean we should provide extra drinks? I won't have any drunken brawling at the Falls, Karunaratne.'

'I was thinking of some other things, *Hamu*. The last time he was here, Mr Palipana told me how he had recently taken a young woman with him to Yala, where he had stayed at one of the circuit bungalows. In the night, he had come out into the veranda with the young lady, and called for a pot of curd and a half-bottle of *kithul* treacle, which the bungalow-keeper had supplied.'

'So what?' Ranil inquired. 'We should have no difficulty supplying him with curd and treacle here.'

Karunaratne coughed again.

'The young lady was naked, sir. Mr Palipana daubed all the curd and treacle on her body, and then he spent a long time licking it off. When he had had enough, he beckoned the watcher of the bungalow, who had been walking around some distance away, and invited him to lick off the rest of the curd . . .'

'And did he?'

'Yes, *Hamu.* Mr Palipana laughed as he told me this story, and said the watcher will vote for his party for the rest of his life.'

'I *think,*' Ranil said carefully, 'I *think* we had better keep curd and treacle off the menus while Mr Palipana is here. We don't want him getting any ideas . . .'

'No, *Hamu.* And there is another matter that you should know about. Mr Palipana carries a gun these days.'

'How do you know he does?'

'It's common knowledge, *Hamu.* When he dines in a hotel or a club in Colombo, Mr Palipana is asked, when he comes in, to leave any weapons he has with him at Reception. I think, *Hamu*, you might have a word with him when he arrives, and take any weapons of his into your own keeping *before* he retires for the night. Also, it might be a good thing if I put the key to the estate gun cabinet into the safe while he is staying here. It would be difficult for me to refuse, if a Minister's son demanded it.'

'You're right. Good thinking, Karunaratne. I'll keep it in mind.'

Six-thirty in the morning, and from the kitchens came the distant sound of a pestle pounding rice into flour for the preparation of breakfast. Latha, who had almost forgotten what that sounded like, since Podina, her parents' household help, had adopted the practice of serving traditional breakfast dishes at dinner time, stretched luxuriously in bed, and listened for the sounds she knew would soon follow, the ring of metal on brass as curtains were drawn back by a maid servant's hands, and the chink of china as trays of early morning coffee and tea were carried to the guest bedrooms.

'What a lovely life you lead up here, Tsunami!'

She was aware that her cousins' life of leisure was only possible because of the wealth that maintained a staff of servants, but that didn't make it any less pleasant.

'Care for a walk before breakfast?'

'Why not?'

Other people had had the same idea, it seemed. As the two girls turned into the avenue, Anupam Munasinghe and Sujit Roy came towards them.

'You're up early!'

Since Tsunami and Sujit did not seem disposed to say anything, the burden of making conversation devolved on Latha, who seemed to be the only one of the four with nothing on her mind but the beauty of the morning. On this theme she rhapsodized for some time – How far had they been? Had they seen the new season's roses? What did they think of Arabella Lucas's famous garden? It was always at its best at this time of year, and especially at this time of day, before the sun heated everything up. Did either Anupam or Sujit have an interest in landscape gardening?

She was nobly supported in this effort by Anupam, until they both ran out of things to say about avenues and herbaceous borders.

'I'm told there's an Indian garden hidden away somewhere here, at the far end of an avenue,' Sujit Roy said at last. 'We were hoping to find it, but we seem to have lost our way. We should probably have explored another avenue, not this one.'

'I know very well where that is,' Latha said eagerly. 'It's my favourite place in the gardens.'

Then she remembered the alterations that had been made in the house, and added:

'It may not be there now of course. It was a long time ago that I last visited it with Auntie Helen.'

'The Indian garden's still there, Latha.'

Tsunami had spoken at last.

'Changed, of course. Like everything else.'

'I would like to see it,' Roy said. 'Would you take me there?'

Although Latha had been the one to claim knowledge of the Indian garden and to express enthusiasm for it, his question was addressed directly to Tsunami.

Anupam glanced at his watch.

'I have to get back to the house,' he said. 'Awful bore, but I'm expecting a phone call this morning from the parents, and I'd like to be there when it comes through.'

Latha hesitated, and Anupam added:

'If you'd be kind enough to come with me, Latha, it would prevent my getting lost a second time. Besides, my mother would love to speak to you.'

Sujit watched the pair turn out of the avenue and disappear from sight before he turned to his companion. She spoke before he did.

'Latha would have made you a better guide than I could, you know,' Tsunami said. 'She spent much more time with my mother in the garden than I ever did.'

'It doesn't really matter,' Sujit replied. 'It's your company I want anyway. If I had not met you just now, I would have searched every inch of this place for you until I found you. There's something I have to give you.'

'Oh? And what can that be?' Tsunami was at her most casual.

'An apology. My friend Anupam tells me I owe it to you. For my behaviour last night.'

'Whatever did you do? *Do* tell me!'

'My friend tells me that I went too far. And too fast.'

'I see. Is there a regulation distance and speed laid down for these things? I wasn't aware of it.'

'Don't make things difficult for me, Tsunami.'

Sujit stopped walking, and took both her hands in his.

'You know perfectly well what I'm talking about. Don't pretend.'

'I'm not pretending. Everyone on the floor last night was doing exactly what you were doing.'

She took her hands away, and continued along the path.

'What *we* were doing, I should say . . . I don't remember trying to stop you.'

She had turned her face away from him, and he could not see her expression.

'You sound amused,' Sujit said, 'and you like to sound experienced, but whatever you might say, I'm almost certain that you're not as sure of yourself as you make out. I say "almost" because I don't know you very well . . . yet. Anupam accuses me of manipulating and confusing you last night. He says I was wrong to act as I did. I thought about it later, and I believe he was right.'

'Quite the little conscience, isn't he, your friend Anupam?' Tsunami said.

'He's my best friend,' said Sujit simply. 'I've known him since we were both schoolboys, and his advice is usually reliable.'

'What makes him such an expert on other people's affairs?'

'I suppose one's able to observe other people pretty accurately when one's . . .'

'Uninvolved oneself?'

'Something like that. But look, I don't want to talk about Anupam. Tell me the truth, Tsunami, have I created a problem for you? With your family?'

'Because Ranil said what he did to me? Oh, no. He's hardly in a position to criticize other people's conduct. If there's a problem, it will be with Tara. She's bound to tell my father, and she'll use heavily loaded words like 'misbehaving' and 'shameless' and 'unstable', which will get him thoroughly upset. But Chris will speak up for me. So will Latha. I'll be back in Peradeniya in a fortnight's time, anyway. And by the week after that everyone'll have forgotten about the whole thing. Even Tara.'

'You sound as if you've been through it all before.'

There was a short silence before Tsunami said:

'Yes, I have.'

Sujit said:

'Well, I'm glad you told me. Can I ask: is it over now?'

'I don't know. I think so. Anyway, I know what my family's like. No surprises there.'

They walked a little distance before Sujit spoke again.

'I want to point out,' he said, 'that a short while ago, you made a serious mistake. You told me: "Everyone on the floor last night was doing exactly what you were doing."'

'Why do you say I was mistaken? That's how it seemed to me.'

'Appearances can deceive. *No* one was doing exactly what I was doing. They can't have been . . .'

'Why not?'

'They weren't in love.'

Tsunami said:

'And you're telling me that you are?'

'Don't you know that I am, Tsunami?'

'How can I be sure? You don't know me at all, you don't know how I think, how I feel . . . In any case, love's not something I want to get involved with again.'

She frowned, and added:

'It's not something that I have any reason to believe in, either.'

'There was a moment last night when I could have sworn that you did believe in love. That you *were* sure: of both yourself and me. Was I wrong?'

Tsunami was silent.

'We don't have much time,' Sujit said. 'At any moment someone else who wants to see the garden will come round that bend. This is what I want to say: I don't know where this path is leading us, or where we are going, but I for one would like to make a fresh start.'

Tsunami looked at him questioningly, and said nothing.

Sujit continued:

'A new beginning. With you, but somewhere else. Somewhere quite different. As if we had never met before, never been introduced . . .'

'We never *were* introduced,' Tsunami reminded him.

'Exactly. We should start again, correctly this time, formally—'

'—With a proper introduction—'

'—With no music to . . .'

'—To – how did your friend Mr Munasinghe put it? – to manipulate and confuse us . . . Well, certainly not *that* music,' Tsunami said. 'I was thinking it over last night, and I believe my brother chose those records quite deliberately. He intended to create a particular atmosphere.'

'And he did: an atmosphere conducive to seduction . . . But he didn't do it for your benefit, surely!'

'Oh, no. Ranil's *much* too selfish to think of me! For his own benefit, of course. And possibly for his old College friends. Men like horrible "Slim" Kodikara . . .'

Sujit tried not to smile. He had caught the look with which Tsunami had greeted Kodikara's ill-judged pleasantry the previous evening: it was the kind of look, he had thought at the time, that she might have given a slug, had she found it on her plate of salad.

'Even Kodikara,' he suggested mildly, 'might have some hidden virtues.'

'You think so, do you?' Tsunami snapped. 'They're certainly hidden from *me*. And you'd better walk on the other side of this path, we're almost within sight of the dining-room windows.'

'Another beginning,' Sujit said thoughtfully, as they made their way back to the house. 'Yes, I think it can be arranged.'

Four days later, Moira Wijesinha received a letter from a stranger:

Dear Mrs Wijesinha,

My husband Siri and I are planning a little dinner party for a few young people, to celebrate the return home from London of our daughter Shalini. We have decided on Wednesday next week as a suitable date. Your niece Latha, whose parents are old friends of ours, will be one of our guests, and we should be very happy if Tsunami and her brother Christopher can also join us.

If Chris is not available on that day to escort Tsunami our son Anupam (whom you might remember as one of a little group of Chris's friends who joined in to help at your daughter Tara's wedding) will arrange to call for her and will also see that she gets safely home.

Would you let me know as soon as possible if the date is convenient? Yours sincerely,
Annabelle Munasinghe

14

DINNER PARTY

'What beautiful flowers you've sent me, Sujit!' Annabelle Munasinghe said. 'Come with me into the dining room, and tell me whether you like what I've done with them.'

Sprays of red and white carnations, set off with delicate ferns, centred a table laid for twelve.

'I hope you approve?'

'Superb, Mrs M.,' said her guest. 'As usual.'

'If you're wondering where Shalini is, she's still unpacking. Anupam isn't back from work yet, but if you'd sit down for a moment—' (instead of pacing around the room like a caged tiger, she very nearly added) – 'I'll tell Shali you're here.'

'I should apologize,' Sujit said, 'for having arrived too early. I finished up at work, then found myself unable to settle down to anything, so I thought I'd come early and make myself useful. Provide transport for a stranded guest, perhaps . . . something like that?'

'You would certainly be making yourself useful if you could help me with these seating arrangements. I have the place cards here. Now, let me think – if Anupam and Shali are to be seated at either end of the table, where shall I place Latha Wijesinha and her cousins? There are two, aren't there? Christopher and . . . and . . .

'Tsunami.'

'What an interesting name, Tsunami . . . Do you know either of Latha's cousins, by any chance?'

Sujit looked hard at his hostess, but she avoided meeting his gaze.

'Oh, I forgot, you've met them both recently, haven't you, and Latha too, Anupam mentioned that to me. So you would know whom they'd be most comfortable with.'

'What about yourself and Dr Munasinghe? Aren't you joining us?'

'Oh, we are, we are. But this is the children's party, not ours, and I've placed Siri and myself opposite each other at the middle of the table.

Then we'll be within kicking range of each other, if either of us says the wrong thing.'

'Have you ever been known to say the wrong thing, Mrs M.? You've never once said the wrong thing in all the years I've known you, so I can't see you beginning now.'

The front door bell rang.

'See who it is, Jayatissa,' Mrs Munasinghe called.

But as the servant went to the door, she followed him.

'No, I'll see to it myself . . . Here, Sujit, would you take these place cards and set them out? I'm sure you'll do the right thing by everyone.'

Shalini came into the dining room, and kissed Sujit briefly, in comradely fashion.

'Good to see you, friend.'

'Your mother is such a tease,' Sujit said.

'Is that so? You poor boy . . . What's she been saying to you?'

She looked at the cards in his hand.

'And what's this you're doing?'

'Your mother asked me to—'

'Mum likes to pretend she's such an innocent! You didn't tell her, did you, that putting you in charge of the seating arrangements on this particular occasion would be like putting the fox in charge of the chicken-run?'

'I'm afraid I don't know what you mean.'

'Only joking. Come on, show me where you've placed her!'

'In the middle of the table. Just across from your father. That's where she wanted to be.'

'Not Mum, idiot! Your girlfriend.'

'My girlfriend? Oh, *she's* at the head of the table, where she ought to be, since this party's in her honour.'

Shalini swooped on the card he had placed in its holder at the head of the table and examined it closely.

'But that's my card, not hers! Who's teasing now, Sujit? Oh, come off it. It's not like you to be embarrassed! But don't worry: I know all about the grand pash – Anupam told me. Where's Tsunami Wijesinha sitting?'

'Here, as it happens. Next to me. But she's not my girlfriend. And there's no *grand passion*.'

Shalini ignored this.

'She's nice, I gather . . .?'

'Very nice.'

'And you're totally besotted. I'm so glad, Sujit. It's about time – you've been playing around far too long.'

'Latha,' Christopher Wijesinha said, later that evening.

'Yes, Chris?'

'I'm glad I've had the chance to take you home. Such opportunities don't often come my way.'

'I'm sorry you'll have such a long drive back.'

'It doesn't matter. We have a lot to talk about.'

'We do?'

'About Tsunami, for instance.'

'What about Tsunami?'

'Well, you did notice that Sujit Roy's driving her home tonight, didn't you? I'd thought I was to be responsible for you both.'

'I'd thought so too. But plans sometimes change . . . I don't think the transport arrangements for this evening were engraved in bronze.'

'You're very calm and composed about it, I must say! Pater and Auntie Moira will hit the roof if they're still up when Tsunami arrives, and they see she's the only passenger in Roy's magnificent chariot—'

'Don't worry about it, Chris. Auntie Moira will probably think it's Anupam Munasinghe who's bringing Tsunami home. And isn't it true that Auntie Moira's all for encouraging Anupam, even though she hasn't met him, and doesn't know his family? Tsunami told me so.'

Chris gave a reluctant laugh.

'Yes, Tara sent Auntie Moira a glowing report on Anupam even before she left for Colombo. I don't think she could have mentioned—'

'Sujit Roy? Oh, I'm sure she didn't, unless she mentioned him in the most negative terms. He's from India, you see, and therefore not to be taken seriously as a suitable match for her sister. Anupam Munasinghe, on the other hand, would strike Tara as eligible in every way, and someone to be encouraged . . . I saw the same thing happen when my mother met Anupam and Sujit together a couple of years ago – Amma focused all her attention on Anupam, and ignored Sujit altogether. Whereas . . .'

'Whereas, it's Sujit who is the real source of danger, isn't it?'

For some reason he could not explain, Chris felt irritation rising in him.

'Wasn't that what you were going to say?'

'Certainly not! I wasn't going to say anything of the kind. Why should Sujit be a source of danger? Why shouldn't he admire your sister? It's only natural that he should. Take a good look at Tsunami, Chris! Is it possible *not* to admire her? In any case—' and here Latha paused, and looked directly at her companion – 'what's wrong with Sujit being from India? Uncle Rowland didn't let Auntie Helen being from India stop him marrying *her*!'

Chris was silent for a short while. This was an outspoken, confrontational Latha he did not recognize, a very different person from the gentle girl whom he had thought he knew so well. He said:

'Look, Latha, don't get me wrong. I like Roy. But whether I like him or not is hardly the point. You saw him at Lucas Falls, with Tsunami. And you saw them together tonight. I think we're both aware that he's going – may well have already gone – much further than admiration. And that's what's making me thoroughly worried, since Tsunami might never have met him if I hadn't brought him as my guest to the Falls. I'll be held responsible for whatever happens, you see . . . when Pater comes to know of it.'

'Why should Uncle Rowland object?' Latha's voice was cool now, and her manner seemingly careless.

Chris hesitated for a moment, then decided to take the plunge.

'Pater would say, if challenged, that times have changed, that what was perfectly acceptable in the Ceylon of the 1930s is no longer so in the 1950s. You and I, of course, would say that if times have changed in such a way as to make someone like Roy unacceptable, then they've changed for the worse. But Pater has become a politician now, and he thinks on political lines . . . However, leaving Pater out of this for the moment, and racial differences too, I shall feel responsible! There's quite a gap between the two of them; I don't mean only in years, though there's that, too. But Roy's much older than she is, and very experienced, and Tsunami – well, I honestly don't know whether my sister knows anything at all about life. Or love. Can you tell me? Has she ever been in love? I mean, *really* in love?'

Doesn't Chris know about Daniel Rajaratnam? Where was he last year?

Latha said, carefully choosing her words:

'She's got heaps of admirers on campus, Chris, but I don't think she returns the feelings of a single one of them. If she does, all I can say is that she keeps it very quiet.'

'By now,' Chris said, 'according to all the experts, Tsunami should have been falling in love about once a fortnight! Tara did, at her age – before she married, it was a case of one love this week, another one the next. Tsunami's quite different. She speaks so scornfully of men and marriage! I used to think it was just a pose, but there have been times, you know, when I've wondered whether she *can* love . . .

Latha told Chris now what she had never confided to anyone: Tsunami's championship of a blind student in her second year and her furious rejection of caste and racial prejudice when she met it in the shape of the Warden of Peries Hall. At last, after much hesitation, she spoke to him of Daniel Rajaratnam.

'Last year,' Latha said, 'Tsunami was engaged to a Tamil don on campus. I thought you would know all about that, because Uncle Rowland put pressure on her to break up the relationship. He forced her to leave Peradeniya, and wanted her to marry someone else, one of Auntie Moira's relations.'

'This is the first I'm hearing of any of this,' Chris said. 'And I can hardly believe it. If I'd been told this story by someone else, or read it in a novel, I *wouldn't* have believed it. *Pater?* Force an arranged marriage on Tsunami? Impossible!'

'I think the real pressure may have come from your aunt Moira,' Latha said. 'And from Tara.'

'Why didn't Ranil do something to stop them?' Chris asked. 'Pater would surely have listened to him.'

Latha hesitated.

'Whether Ranil knew anything about what was going on, I really don't know, Chris. What I do know is that Tsunami's feelings for her fiancé went very deep at the time, and I am not sure whether she's got over them yet. She does a great job of covering up . . .'

'Always did,' said Chris.

'Yes. I don't know about love for any particular person, Chris,' Latha ended, 'but the people I've told you about, and the situations they were in, represented issues about which she feels very strongly and deeply. Tsunami found herself defending . . . justice, and . . . and freedom, and the individual's right to choose. Those are things that matter to her.' She paused, then added quietly: 'They matter to me, too.'

Chris said thoughtfully:

'Has Tsunami ever mentioned Franz Goldman?'

'I've only heard her mention him once.'

'What did she say?'

'You won't like this, I'm afraid! She called him a bastard.'

'She's not forgiven him, then?'

'I don't think so,' Latha said. 'And I don't think she's forgiven Auntie Helen, either.'

'She can't,' Chris said after some reflection, 'have a very high opinion of men or of marriage. Which might explain . . .'

'What?'

'Never mind. I won't pretend to a knowledge of psychology that I haven't got. I just have a . . . a premonition, let's say, that Tsunami's about to fall very hard for Sujit Roy. If she hasn't done so already. Do you agree?'

'It's possible.'

'But how can you be so calm about it? She's only just met him! She knows nothing about him—'

'May I ask you a question, Chris? How much do you know about him?'

'Only that he's established a very successful business, building catamarans and motor boats out at Hambantota. And that he plays a first-class game of tennis.'

Latha smiled.

'I was asking about his character, Chris, not his business background and his sporting skills! But, all right: I'll ask about his business record: Has he cheated anyone in his business affairs? Does he practise discrimination in hiring staff and personnel? Has he wriggled his way out of a contract? Has he let anyone down?'

'Not that I know of. In fact, he's got a very good reputation, I'm told, in business circles.'

'Well then, I may know more about him than you do!' Latha said. 'Anupam told me that Sujit handed over his share of the family fortune to his sisters because he wanted to make it on his own.'

Chris whistled.

'Does Tsunami know about this? It's just the kind of gesture she'd consider brave and noble.'

'Well, *I* think it's rather noble, too, if you want to know!'

'Has she said anything to you about him?'

'Just that he's a pleasant change from Ranil's friends.'

'And that's true enough! Well, it may be that I'm worrying unnecessarily. But, listen to me, Latha, if I'm right, and a romance does develop between them, could you possibly try to discourage it?'

In the darkness of the car, Chris did not at first perceive the force of his cousin's reaction to his words. He went on:

'For the sake of the family, for Tsunami's sake. At least – at least, try not to actively promote it! Please don't turn away from me – I believe you have a lot of influence with my sister.'

'You're wrong, Chris. I have none. Tsunami asks my opinion from time to time, but she follows her own star, she always has. You talk about "family", by which I suppose you mean mostly your father, Ranil and Tara. But isn't it *Tsunami* we're talking about – doesn't she have a choice in what kind of life *she* wants to live?'

Chris hastened to mend his fences.

'You misunderstood me,' he said. 'I'm not my father, nor am I my brother Ranil. They – and even Tara – would certainly tell you that Tsunami, being a girl, doesn't *need* to have a choice, since her father and her brothers are there to decide things on her behalf.'

'Oh, so *Ranil* knows best what's good for Tsunami, does he? And for me? And, no doubt, for all women?'

There was a passionate scorn in her voice as she mentioned his brother that Chris had not expected to hear. Latha continued:

'. . . I know perfectly well that if I try to stop Tsunami going in a particular direction, it will have no effect at all. So, just as long as she's alert to the difficulties ahead and is not doing herself any harm, I go along with her ideas, *and I don't betray them*!'

Chris heard the slight break in her voice, and placed his hand on her arm.

'I didn't mean to upset you, Latha. Are you very angry with me?'

'No.'

'We're friends again?'

'Yes, of course.'

'Good friends?'

'Yes. But I can't make the promise you want me to make, Chris. I don't have an option, do you see? My relationship with Tsunami is based on trust. That's the way it's always been.'

Chris sighed.

'Okay, Latha, I won't press you. You're very wise, do you know? You don't worry, you don't speculate, you just take life as it comes. You'd manage to stay calm and composed in the middle of an earthquake.'

'Would I?'

'I'm saying not only that you would, but that you do! I wonder what you'd be like if you ever fell in love. *You've* never been in love, have you, not with a real person!'

It was a statement, not a question, Latha thought, and it didn't need a reply.

15

MOONLIGHT

When the telephone rang in Rowland Wijesinha's house the following morning, it was answered by the Minister's secretary.

'Three seven one six? Mr Rowland Wijesinha's residence?'

'This is his secretary speaking: do you have an appointment with the Hon'ble Minister?'

'This call is for Miss Tsunami Wijesinha. Is she in?'

'Please hold the line, sir. I'll see if I can find her.'

'Hello?'

'Tsunami?'

'Yes.'

Silence.

'Aren't you going to say anything more than "yes"? You said much more than that to me when I drove you home last night.'

'It's a little difficult . . .'

'You're not alone?'

'No.'

'Damn.'

Silence.

'Well, at least, last night was a beginning. I was formally introduced to you. And by no less a person than Dr Munasinghe. What could be more respectable and correct?'

'What, indeed.'

'Who's that on the telephone, Tsunami?'

'Someone who was at the Munasinghes' dinner party, Auntie Moira. A friend of Chris's.'

'What does he want?'

'He has a message for Chris.'

'Tell him Chris is out.'

'I'm sorry, but my brother Chris isn't at home just now. Would you like to leave a message?'

'Yes. I'd like to leave a message. For Chris's sister. What's the next step for us, Tsunami? Tell me. Do you want me to go on?'

'Yes.'

'Any letters for the post, Latha? I can take them along for you. I'm walking past the post office.'

'I'm just about to write a thank-you note to Mrs Munasinghe,' Latha said. 'She took a great deal of trouble arranging that party.'

'Have you finished writing it?'

'I haven't started yet. But it'll only take a moment.'

'It's University Colours Night next month,' Tsunami said, wandering casually into Latha's room from the balcony, where she had been making coffee. 'Were you thinking of going?'

'No,' Latha replied. 'I've never been to a campus dance, there's no one who knows me well enough to ask me. Were you?'

'Some of the lads at Arunachalam Hall – Sriyani's track and field crowd – have asked me to join them. But I haven't said yes or no yet. I might say yes, if you'd join us. With a partner.'

'As I've just told you, Tsunami,' Latha said patiently, 'there's no one who knows me well enough to ask me.'

'*You* could ask *them*,' Tsunami said. 'Why don't you?'

'Oh, Tsunami, I couldn't do that!'

'Why not? Auntie Soma would have a fit! Isn't that it?'

Latha did not answer.

'Well,' said her cousin, 'Auntie Soma doesn't have to know about it, does she?'

She glanced at Latha's face, and suggested:

'*We* could do it. You and I. With Sriyani, of course. We could organize tickets for a group, six or eight people, to go together as a party. No one could possibly object to that.'

'No, perhaps they couldn't,' Latha replied slowly. 'But whom would we invite on campus to make up a party? None of the men in my English class dance. I'm sure of that!'

'We don't *have* to invite people from Peradeniya,' Tsunami said, and added, with seeming indifference, 'There must be heaps of people in Colombo who might like to come. If they're invited. People who, as your beloved Mr Darcy said on a memorable occasion, it wouldn't be a punishment to stand up with!'

Latha laughed, but she looked closely at Tsunami.

'Like who?'

Tsunami shrugged.

'Oh, I don't know . . . Anupam and Shalini Munasinghe, for instance. My brother Chris might be interested, don't you think? One or two of his friends . . . And Sriyani might have some suggestions.'

Was Tsunami's indifference genuine, or was it put on? Latha could not be certain. What her cousin had said sounded like a broad hint, a definite push in a certain direction.

One or two of Chris's friends . . .

Did Tsunami have Anupam Munasinghe in mind? Or someone else? What Latha had witnessed at Lucas Falls suggested that her cousin had fully recovered from her broken engagement to Daniel Rajaratnam. But had Sujit Roy actually *replaced* Daniel in her affections? Their friendship had never accommodated girlish confidences; and Latha's experience in the case of Daniel had made her wary. If the family had objected to Daniel, what would they say to Sujit?

Latha remembered her own recent words to Chris:

Justice, and . . . freedom, and the individual's right to choose. Those are things that matter to her. They matter to me, too.

Dear Auntie Annabelle [Latha wrote],

I would like to thank you and Uncle Siri for a very enjoyable evening on Wednesday. I am sure my cousins Chris and Tsunami will be writing to Shalini with their thanks.

Tsunami and I are back on campus now, and we are wondering whether Shalini and Anupam would like to join our party at University Colours Night on Saturday the 15th of next month. Colours Night is the social highlight of the campus year, and they would, I feel sure, enjoy it.

My parents ask me to send you and Uncle Siri their affectionate regards.

Yours sincerely,

Latha Wijesinha

P.S. Perhaps Anupam's friend Mr Sujit Roy would like to come up too? Please let me know, so that I can reserve the right number of tickets. LW

Latha wondered, as she stamped the envelope, and gave it to Tsunami to post, whether she was doing the right thing. Not the right thing by what Chris had called 'the family', but the right thing by Tsunami?

At the dance that followed the Colours awards, she observed her cousin carefully. So did many others, who had never seen Tsunami Wijesinha at a university dance before, and were consumed with curiosity as to the identity of her unknown partner. In the Common Room at Sanghamitta Hall the following morning, excitement ran high.

'*Tsunami Wijesinha . . .!* Mr Sujit Roy to see you . . .! *Tsunami Wijesinha . . .!* Mr Sujit Roy to see you . . .! *Tsunami . . .*'

'Sorry about that, Sujit! It's our local intercom. Give me a moment to get my breath back . . . My room's three floors up . . . and I ran all the way . . .'

Sujit regarded her with amusement.

'Eager to see me, eh? Now, that's good to know.'

'Not a bit of it, don't give yourself airs! I was just eager to save you embarrassment. If I'd known you were going to call this morning, I'd have warned you not to give your name. Then it would have been merely "A visitor for you!", and you could have remained anonymous.'

'Does this happen every time someone comes to see you?'

'I'm afraid so, Sujit. Privacy doesn't get high priority around here . . . What's that little book? It's very pretty.'

'My appointments diary. This year's diary is a present from my sister. Bound in handloom cotton, very fashionable at the moment in Bombay.'

'You have a sister!'

'I have three.'

'How little I know about you, Sujit. You have three sisters, you keep a diary—'

'Of course I keep a diary! I'm a methodical, hardworking businessman. I have to keep my appointments in order.'

'What appointments do you have today?'

'Just one, but it goes on all day. An all-day conference. With a Miss T. Wijesinha.'

'I'd suggest, if you don't mind, that you stop looking at me like that. There are too many interested people looking at us . . . What's this?'

'A souvenir of last night. A flower from your hair.'

'It'll fade. Look, it's fading already!'

'It'll be all right. I'll press it between these two pages. And I'll tape it in place later, so that it won't ever fall out again.'

Sujit replaced the tiny spray of jasmine in his diary, closed it, and put it away.

'Tsunami—'

'Where are Chris and Anupam?'

'At Ramanathan Hall, I fancy, sleeping off last night's exertions. Chris has a friend there, who put us up last night.'

After a short silence, Sujit continued:

'It was a wonderful evening, Tsunami.'

'So Colours Night was worth coming up for?'

'You know that wasn't the reason I came up. But it was a bonus. Where are Shalini and your cousin?'

'Taking it easy upstairs. Like the others.'

'No interruptions, then. Good. I want to talk. We need to make a plan, you and I.'

'Now?'

'What's wrong with now? We have the world to ourselves.'

'Up to a point,' Tsunami said. 'You may not have realized it, but there are at least a dozen people sitting in this Common Room, and a dozen more hanging over the stair-rail, who are looking you over and wondering who you are. And the Warden of Peries Hall, who has no love for either me or Latha, has a pair of powerful binoculars. Rumour has it that her gaze can pierce concrete.'

'Let it. I've got the car outside. I'm taking you out of here, to a place where there are no walls, no barriers, no intercom, no spies, no tell-tales, no monitored telephones . . .'

'It sounds like heaven. But where would we ever find a place like that?'

'Trust me,' said Sujit Roy.

Later that day:

'A lazy afternoon, on a mountainside high above the world . . . It *is* heaven,' Tsunami said. 'Clever Sujit.'

'Just an ordinary Rest House, British vintage, circa 1925. Made quite extraordinary by your being here with me.'

'How's your diary going?'

'Filling up nicely with Tsunami-days. To make it a reality, I'd better take up residence in Kandy or Peradeniya for a month. What do you say?'

'Not a good idea. I have an examination looming . . . oh, and there's nowhere you can build boats here, unless you buy the Kandy Lake.'

'True. All right, we'll re-schedule. Pre-exam, post-exam . . . When do I call on your father?'

'Let's not think about that.'

'It's got to be done, Tsunami.'

'Does it? Why can't we go on as we are? At least for a while?'

'Is that what you want?'

'Yes.'

'All right. If you say so.'

Presently, Sujit Roy said:

'And this evening?'

'This evening,' Tsunami said, 'I thought we might go to a movie.'

'Where? In Kandy?'

'No, at the Arts Theatre. They're showing a film I haven't seen since I saw it with Latha and Chris ages ago. At Lucas Falls, when we were children. Nelson Eddy and Jeannette Macdonald in *Maytime*. Lots of lovely singing. A bit out of date, of course – do you mind?'

'Does it really matter to you what film we see?'

'No, not really.'

The fragrance of Queen of the Night rose like incense around them as they emerged from the theatre, and joined the student couples walking slowly back to the Halls in the moonlight.

'I am amazed,' Sujit said.

'By what?'

'By the fact that, while spending three years in a magical place like this, a place that makes such an all-out assault on one's senses, you haven't fallen in love before now.'

'But I have,' Tsunami said. 'I told you. Remember?'

Sujit said:

'I have chosen to forget everything you have ever told me up to last night. Here beginneth a whole new story. *The Legend of Tsunami and Sujit.*'

They had reached the steps at the top of Sanghamitta Drive, and now paused in the darkness, facing each other.

'Goodnight, Tsunami!' said some first-year students, slipping past them into the lighted circle of the Hall entrance.

'Goodnight!' Tsunami answered mechanically.

A few couples still lingered in the shadows.

'They're like us,' Sujit said. 'They don't want to say goodbye.'

Tsunami remembered suddenly how she and Daniel had often stood there, on that very spot, spinning out their farewells. The breeze freshened, causing the leaves to rustle around them, and she shivered in her thin silk sari.

'This,' she said resolutely to Sujit, 'is where I say goodbye. As you can see from the way everyone's standing around, men aren't allowed beyond this point. Warden's orders. In a few moments, Sergeant-Major Banda will turn up to see you safely off the premises.'

'Noted. Kiss me.'

Tsunami did not appear to have heard him. She touched Sujit's shoulder lightly, and turned to go, but was detained. He put his arms around her and gently turned her face to the moonlight.

'Kiss me, Tsunami.'

'I can't. Not possible. It'll be all over the Hall tomorrow—'

'Nonsense. Just look around you. No one's giving us a glance. They're minding their own business. Fully occupied with their own affairs. Kiss me.'

'There. Good night, Sujit.'

'Not like that.'

'Like this?'

'No. Like this.'

As the Hall porter came towards them, torch in hand, Tsunami slipped out of Sujit's arms, ran up the steps, and vanished.

'Fine moonlight night,' remarked the porter. 'Sorry, sir. Time to go.'

'Banda, is it? Goodnight, Banda.'

'Goodnight, sir.'

16

GERARD VAN KUYK, ARTIST AND LOVER

Moira Wijesinha was planning a party. This was by no means a rare occurrence where Moira was concerned, but the occasion was a very special one, and required the hostess's most careful attention to details.

'*In honour of Mr Gerard van Kuyk*,' the invitations read.

They were embellished with a drawing by van Kuyk of a naked girl with her arms around the arching neck of the sacred *hansa* of Indian legend. Moira had requisitioned the services of the Ministry's secretaries, and with their assistance invitations were sent to everyone she knew in the island's artistic and cultural circles who had some connection with van Kuyk. They were also sent to many people who were not known to have any such connection, but whom Moira wished to get to know. Members of the '49 Group with whom van Kuyk had exhibited his early paintings naturally received Moira's invitations; and also invited were members of the Arts Society, selected officials in the Ministries of Culture and Education, heads of Colleges in Colombo and the outstations, Colombo Museum officials, leading physicians in Colombo, members of the Bar, the Vice-Chancellor of the University of Ceylon and chosen members of his academic staff, officials at the British Council, the Alliance Française and the United States Information Service, all the Embassies and High Commissions, editors of all the national newspapers, the Prime Minister himself . . . The list was a long one, and Rowland's secretaries (he had two, one at the Ministry, and the other at his Colombo residence) added more names to it every day.

Mr Ivan Ganesan, senior librarian of the University of Ceylon at Peradeniya, who was known to be working on a definitive bibliography of the artist, received an invitation to the Wijesinhas' party. The invitation included his wife. Aware that Ranjini would enjoy visiting the capital (something she did very rarely), he gave the invitation a few days' serious consideration before deciding, finally, that he would not accept it. His reasons were many. Ganesan owned a little Volkswagen Beetle he had purchased by means of stringent saving during a research stint in London, and he cherished it with a love too deep to permit his driving it in the maelstrom of Colombo traffic. Add to that the unattractive prospect of travelling from Peradeniya to Colombo by bus: he had recently recovered from influenza, and doubted his ability to cope with the vagaries of the Colombo–Kandy bus service in his present state of health. He had just picked up his pen to write a polite refusal when chance brought Latha Wijesinha to his office to request help with an elusive reference.

When Latha saw van Kuyk's beautiful bird-lover on Ganesan's desk, she instantly recognized the invitation for what it was: her parents had received a similar one.

'Mr Ganesan, Tsunami and I are going down for her aunt's party,' she said. 'My father has offered to drive us to Colombo and back. Do please join us. I know he would like to meet you.'

Almost immediately, Ganesan changed his mind. Not only was the offer of a ride to and from Colombo in the comfort of Herbert Wijesinha's roomy Morris too tempting to refuse, but he foresaw, knowing Herbert by reputation as a reader and collector of books, that the three-hour journey would almost certainly be enlivened by book-talk. There was, besides, a question that he very much wanted to put to Latha's father.

'I understand, Mr Wijesinha,' said the librarian, as Herbert steered his Morris off the Peradeniya bridge and on to the Colombo road, 'that your family is well acquainted with Mr van Kuyk. Especially these two young ladies.'

Engaged in cataloguing the artist's paintings and drawings for an exhibition of his works in Colombo, Ganesan had come upon a sketch of two young girls in Indian dress titled *Radha and her Confidante await the coming of Krishna*.

'Your names were in the subtitle,' Ganesan explained over his shoulder to Latha and Tsunami. 'I made a note to myself that I should ask you how that had come about.'

He listened with careful attention to the two girls' account of the van Kuyk family's visit to Lucas Falls in the 1940s. Herbert, who was hearing of that visit for the first time, wondered yet again at the strength of his daughter's determination to keep to herself all information relating to Rowland's branch of the family.

'May I be allowed to see your autograph album some time soon?' Ganesan asked Latha. 'When we are back in Peradeniya, perhaps? Or in Colombo, if that is where it is? I would like to photograph it.'

Herbert stopped at a wayside stall to buy mangoes and a pineapple for Soma. The transaction took a little time, and Ganesan made use of the opportunity provided by the car's being temporarily stationary to whip out of his pocket a set of library cards held together with a rubber band, and make notes of what he had been told. He then inquired:

'I suppose you know that Mr van Kuyk has moved his residence to Colombo?'

He was amused by his companions' amazed reaction to this news. Ivan Ganesan, they were to discover, enjoyed surprising people. Latha and Tsunami had regarded the librarian as a very sedate and even pedantic individual, erudite and dignified. In the relaxed atmosphere of Herbert's car, encouraged by the rapt interest of his audience, his dignity dissolved. To Herbert's delight, Ganesan turned out to be, not only an intimate friend of Gerard van Kuyk over many years, but an inspired storyteller and a wickedly mischievous gossip.

'Would you like,' he said, 'to hear about the manner of Gerard's departure? I can promise you, it's quite a tale.' Turning to his wife, Ganesan added:

'Ranjini, it's you who should really relate this story.'

Eventually, they related it together.

One evening, Ranjini Ganesan began, just as they were finishing dinner in their campus home on Augusta Hill, there was a knock on the front door. Gerard van Kuyk was standing on the doormat, agitated and excited:

'Ivan, old friend, can you give us a bed?'

By 'us', said Ganesan, interrupting his wife's narrative, van Kuyk was referring to himself and Lalita Das, a woman who had recently come into his life. The wife of a wealthy Bombay businessman, Lalita fancied herself as a patron of the arts. No sooner had she met the painter and viewed his work, than she had claimed to recognize in van Kuyk the genius with whose life Fate intended her to link her own, and whose career she had been born to nurture.

'Lalita Das whisked Gerard off to India, financed exhibitions of his paintings in the art centres of Delhi and Bombay, arranged a tour of south India for his benefit, and finally returned with him to Ceylon, leaving her husband behind in Bombay. She had come, she said, to look after Gerard's business affairs. With her appearance in Sapumalwatta, Gerard's household became a *ménage à trois*—'

'Except,' Ranjini said, 'that the three sides of the triangle weren't quite equal because Lalita—'

'Who was a Bombay socialite,' interposed her husband.

'—had no intention whatever of taking any responsibility for the running of the household. So Ran Menikē became a servant to Gerard and Lalita. She looked after them and cooked for them with all the devotion she had up to that time lavished on Gerard alone.'

'But,' continued Ganesan, 'though Ran Menikē accepted Lalita's presence in the house without complaint, the menfolk of the village of Sapumalwatta weren't going to put up with that! They had accepted and even welcomed Gerard into the village as the chosen mate of one of their own community, but they now sent a deputation to inform him of their refusal to allow an interloper from India to treat "their" Ran Menikē as a servant in her own home.'

'Well,' Ranjini Ganesan took up the tale, 'in the darkness of the night, large stones thrown by invisible hands crashed on to the roof of Gerard's house—'

"—Slaughtered crows,' Ivan Ganesan said with relish, 'were found hanging from the doorposts at dawn, their blood dripping on the steps . . .'

Correctly interpreting these events as warnings of violence to come, Gerard had sought sanctuary with his friends on the Peradeniya campus.

'*Old friend, can you give us a bed?*'

Now, said Ganesan, and his eyes twinkled behind his spectacles as he reached this part of his tale, Gerard discovered that friendship has its limits.

One old friend simply refused point blank: he had two young daughters, he said, who were in the habit of addressing Gerard and Ran Menikē as 'Uncle' and 'Auntie'. How was he to tell them that there were now *two* 'Aunties' in 'Uncle' Gerard's life, not one? He had hurried Gerard out of his house before the racket he was making awakened the children.

Another old friend, manager of one of Kandy's oldest and largest hotels, refused, for high moral reasons, to allow Gerard and Lalita Das accommodation in his establishment. ('The old hypocrite! Told me I could bring my wife to his hotel but not my mistress,' Gerard had told the Ganesans furiously, 'when everyone knows that any British lecher with a tart on his arm can book a room in his bloody hotel any time he likes, and no questions asked.') Ivan and Ranjini Ganesan, extremely hospitable and, fortunately, childless, had been third on Gerard's list, and had proved a better bet than either of the first two. They had responded sympathetically to his appeal, Lalita was summoned from the taxi in which she had been waiting outside their garden gate, and she and Gerard took up residence in the Ganesans' spare room.

During their first night at Augusta Hill, Ranjini Ganesan had been wakened several times from her sleep to supply Gerard and Lalita with flasks of hot black coffee to sustain them through what was evidently a night of vigorous love-making. When morning came, an exhausted Ranjini had been wearily preparing *roti* and *sambal* for the household breakfast when Gerard emerged from the spare bedroom.

'Looking, if you please, as fresh and jaunty as any bridegroom!' said Ranjini crossly. 'And he hailed me with: "Greetings, Ranjini! Why are you working so hard on this beautiful morning?"'

Lalita, who had followed Gerard out of the bedroom, carrying their bedclothes in her arms, nodded to Ranjini as she passed by, but did not offer to help her in the kitchen. Instead, she and Gerard had taken their blankets and pillows out into the garden and spread them comfortably on a stone garden seat at the edge of the lawn. Surrounded, as in a bower, by Ranjini's carefully tended ferns and flowers, Gerard and Lalita had proceeded to make love.

'Quite as if,' Ranjini said picturesquely, 'they had been Radha and Krishna in the Garden of Vrindāvan in the time when the world was young.'

It was unfortunate, Ivan Ganesan continued, that the garden seat overlooked a public road along which school children walked every day to school. Not that Gerard minded an audience of small boys and girls, squinting through their fingers against the early morning sun in order to take in a spectacle the like of which they would probably never see in a lifetime . . .

'Not that Gerard minded any kind of audience, really,' the librarian added. 'You may say what you like about Gerard van Kuyk, but he's no prude.'

Behind him, Latha and Tsunami rocked with silent laughter while Ranjini, smiling to herself, gazed out of the car window. Ganesan turned around in his seat and surveyed them all with great satisfaction. It was just as well, Herbert thought, keeping a straight face in the interests of propriety, that Soma wasn't there: she'd have shut Ganesan up pretty fast if she had been. The librarian would have been on his best behaviour, and he would have missed hearing this story.

Now began, Ranjini Ganesan said, one of the most difficult periods of her own life as van Kuyk and Lalita's sojourn in the Ganesan home, which had been supposed to last only until Gerard found alternative accommodation for the two of them – 'just a day or two, no more,' Gerard had assured his old friends – stretched into weeks, and then into months. A few days after their first arrival, at about eleven o'clock in the morning, when Ivan had left for the University Library, Ranjini had had a visit from Ran Menikē. Gerard and Lalita were still asleep.

'Resting after the night's hard work,' Ranjini said acidly, and added: 'Fine thing to be doing – at his age!'

Ran Menikē, who had come all the way from Sapumalwatta by bus, asked her not to wake them. She was happy and thankful, she said, that Gerard and Lalita had found accommodation in Ranjini's house, because Ranjini and her husband were trusted old friends of Gerard's. She knew, of course (as who did not?), that Ranjini was a very good cook, but Gerard's digestion had been giving him trouble recently, so she had brought cooked rice and some of his favourite vegetable curries along 'for Gerard and Lalita'. Saying which, she uncovered an array of small clay pots.

'Did they eat the meal that Ran Menikē had brought?' Herbert asked.

Through his mind raced ancient tales of charms and poisons, used by vengeful women through the ages to punish their faithless lovers.

'Lalita refused to eat any of it,' Ranjini said, 'and she warned Gerard not to touch it. But Gerard never could resist Ran Menikē's cooking. He ate up everything Ran Menikē had brought, and—'

'Fell violently ill?' asked Latha.

'—and suffered no ill effects whatever!'

'Ran Menikē must be a very unusual person,' Latha said.

'Extraordinary,' said Herbert.

'My wife,' said Ivan Ganesan, 'is very frank and direct, and if she disapproves of something, she comes right out and says so. On this occasion she wasn't just disapproving, she was furious. "How," she asked Ran Menikē, "can you possibly be concerned about the health and welfare of a man who has treated you so shabbily?"'

Ranjini said that Ran Menikē had given her a remarkable answer:

'Please don't think badly of Gerard,' she had said. 'You see, Ranjini, Gerard is a great artist. He is a free spirit, not an ordinary person like you and me. Artists must be free to create, to live life in their own way.'

Latha thought about the quiet woman she had encountered at Sapumalwatta, the living embodiment of a rural idyll. Ran Menikē, whom Moira Wijesinha despised as a nobody, an ignorant villager, had proved herself a truly loving woman, devoted to her man. But Gerard, that world-renowned artist supposedly possessed of an artist's delicate sensibility – what had his affections been worth?

Sigh no more, ladies, sigh no more,
Men were deceivers ever . . .

Love, Latha thought sadly, how long does love last? She and Tsunami thought themselves knowledgeable and sophisticated. But what did they know?

At last, continued Ivan Ganesan, van Kuyk realized that residence at Augusta Hill, however convenient to his needs in the present crisis, was not conducive to his art.

'Deprived of his palette, his easel and brushes, unable to return to Sapumalwatta, Gerard wandered around the house and garden—'

'—getting on my nerves—'

'—monopolizing the conversation at dinner—'

'—scandalizing the neighbourhood—'

'—until Lalita Das took matters into her own capable hands—'

'—bought a house in Colombo—'

'—and moved herself and Gerard into it—'

'—and there he lives now,' Ganesan concluded, 'slaving away at his easel from morning till night, turning out paintings for which Lalita makes sure he gets top prices. Making up for lost time, she calls it. He is surrounded by sycophants and art dealers, and sees nothing of his old associates—'

'—They're bad for his concentration, his gaoler says—'

'—has no time for a companionable drink with friends as he did in the Sapumalwatta days—'

'—because it's bad for his health—'

'—and eats into his bank balance . . .'

No concern for Ran Menikē disturbed Moira Wijesinha in Colombo, where preparations for her party were in full swing. Moira had been delighted by the news that her dear Gerard had finally settled in Colombo: it was what she had urged him many times to do, and the party she was throwing in his honour reflected her wish to celebrate his presence in the capital. Admittedly, Lalita Das had seized the role Moira had coveted for herself of guardian and promoter of the island's acknowledged genius, but Moira was pleased by the fact that, under Lalita's influence, Gerard had given up his earlier nonsensical notions about putting down roots in a Kandyan village. He had done at last what he should have done a long time ago: he had left the bucolic crudities of Sapumalwatta and Ran Menikē behind him for good, in order to live among people like herself and Rowland (and of course Lalita, too) who genuinely appreciated his work, and knew what was what where art was concerned.

Lalita Das, for her part, had been happy to leave behind her the provincial life of Kandy and the irrational hostilities of its rural neighbourhoods. She hoped she had done so for good. She was now very busy indeed, organizing an exhibition of van Kuyk's paintings at the Art Gallery and writing letters to publicists and art dealers at home and abroad. She had recognized a kindred spirit in Moira, but did not trust her too far, keeping a watchful eye on van Kuyk to make sure that he kept those valuable paintings coming in a steady stream, and did not give any away to opportunists who stopped by hoping, on the strength of an old friendship, to pick up a drawing or a painting on the cheap.

'That wretched, bloody woman! Keeps poor Gerard chained to his easel,' complained one old associate of van Kuyk's, who found the door shut in his face when he called in the hope of a comfortable chat with the artist of the kind they had both enjoyed in pre-Lalita days.

There was no doubt about it: Lalita Das's personality was a powerful one, and her control of van Kuyk was total. Under her influence, according to Ivan Ganesan, the style and subjects of van Kuyk's paintings had changed. Out went the innocent rural idylls of old, in came sophisticated, long-waisted temple dancers, their wrists and ears hung with gold and jewels. Though Lalita was no longer in her first youth, she was, in her way, a strikingly beautiful woman, possessed of the long eyes of heroines in the Ajanta frescoes and a slender, voluptuous body that van Kuyk celebrated in painting after painting during what art critics were beginning to call his 'Colombo period', sometimes in oils, but nowadays more often in the brilliantly tinted acrylics that Lalita procured for him from America.

17

SUJIT ROY

'I'm a methodical, hardworking businessman,' Sujit Roy had told Tsunami a few weeks after they had first met.

It had been no more than the truth; for until he saw her walk into the dining room at Lucas Falls, his attention had been entirely focused on establishing himself in the commercial world of Colombo, getting his company off the ground, and making his way in a new society.

Life had treated Roy well, and he did not see any reason why it should not continue to do so. When Anupam Munasinghe described his friend to Latha in 1954 as working to a life plan which involved sun-warmed days cruising the Mediterranean in boats of his own manufacture, the remark had been partly made in jest. But by 1958, jest had become reality. Admittedly, the isles of Greece with which Sujit's imagination had played as a boy had been replaced by the beaches of southern Ceylon, but his dream of combining a life's purpose with 'messing about in boats' had been achieved in good measure. A boatyard he had established in the sea coast town of Hambantota to further his dream had prospered. Motor boats and small pleasure craft of his design and manufacture were to be seen on Bolgoda Lake and in bays and inlets around Galle and Trincomalee. Vessels that had been commissioned by enthusiasts overseas had been dispatched to Europe and America, and had begun to attract more commissions. His affairs were moving so well that eventually Sujit had abandoned his dreams of Greece, added to his land holding in Hambantota, and begun considering a venture into the export trade.

It is not surprising that Ceylon had bewitched him, and made him alter course. Poised on the cusp of Europe and Asia, the island's manifold attractions have spun their enchantments through the centuries, capturing numberless unwary travellers who had been originally bound in other directions. In the 1950s, Ceylon had all the colonial charm of Bombay and Singapore, without the burgeoning population of those cities and their overcrowded thoroughfares. Roy found English-speaking, Westernized

Ceylon very much to his taste. He acquired a small but well appointed office in the Fort of Colombo, and owned an attractive modern flat in Cinnamon Gardens. The city's way of life was sufficiently like that of the Bombay in which he had grown up to seem familiar, yet it possessed a style of its own that pleased and attracted him.

He had not as yet achieved the millionaire status which Shalini Munasinghe had playfully predicted for him, but in post-war Ceylon money was readily made by those who had faith in themselves and adequate funds to start with. Sujit was very comfortably off. He drove a gleaming new Opel Kapitan, one of the first to make its appearance in the capital, and he was spoken of in business circles as 'a coming man'. Once he had decided to establish his company headquarters in Colombo, his acquaintance with the Munasinghe family had been a great asset to him. Dr Munasinghe and his wife knew everyone worth knowing in the capital, and their friendship opened many local doors to Sujit that might otherwise have remained shut to a newcomer.

In the meantime his Cambridge background, his sophistication, and his obvious financial success brought him invitations to every social event of note in Colombo, while his sporting prowess guaranteed his popularity with local clubmen. The golden opinions of such solid citizens carry weight. Sujit found friends wherever he went, and Christopher Wijesinha, a keen tennis player himself, put him up for membership of the C.L.T.A.

At Cambridge, as in Bombay, Sujit's approach to romance had been as direct and straightforward as his approach to everything else. He had grown up as the only male in a household of women, and like many wealthy young Asian men in that position, was accustomed to getting what he wanted. He had fallen briefly in and out of love a few times, but he made no secret of the fact that he liked being single and had no wish to 'settle down'. His mother and his sisters hoped that he would do so as soon as possible, preferably in India of course, but they had been firmly told that though he had established no relationship outside marriage which was important enough to be taken seriously, he did not want a marriage arranged for him. His sojourn in Ceylon had confirmed this attitude. Until the day that he met Tsunami at Lucas Falls, marriage had not entered into his calculations.

All that was now changed. The man who had never believed in 'love at first sight' knew in the few moments of his first meeting with Tsunami that the world had altered for him, and that his life was developing a new dimension. He had not intended to fall in love; and he had not expected, once in love, that he could ever become so quickly and so deeply enmeshed. But now the unbelievable, the unintended, and the unexpected had occurred. Sujit could not get Tsunami out of his mind. And since, characteristically, he considered time wasted in which he was not advancing one or more of his various projects and had no intention of wasting it on irrelevancies, he decided that the best and most sensible thing for him to do was to bring matters to a satisfactory conclusion as rapidly as possible, so that their attachment to each other could be officially recognized and an engagement announced.

Sujit did not foresee any difficulty in accomplishing this aim. And so, when Anupam warned him that the Wijesinhas were an old family that might not welcome strangers, Sujit casually dismissed the warning. He had heard on his own account (a sarcastic observation, this, from a man-about-town in Colombo who didn't share Rowland's political views) that Rowland Wijesinha was completely out of touch with modern life.

'A dinosaur, an eccentric survival from a Victorian novel,' Sujit's informant had grumbled, calling for another G. and T. at the Orient Club. 'Ridiculous idea of the P.M.'s, giving Wijesinha a Ministry. What does *he* know about politics?'

'In that case,' Sujit reasoned, in a discussion he had had with Anupam, 'Minister Wijesinha should certainly approve of me! I mean, just look at me, my friend: an ideal son-in-law. My intentions – perfectly honourable; my character – pure as the driven snow . . .'

'More or less,' interposed Anupam.

Sujit ignored the remark and continued:

'. . . My company books can bear the closest inspection, and I can support a wife so that she lacks for nothing. Besides, Tsunami's no longer a child. She's a young woman with a mind of her own, who will soon be a graduate with a career of her own. And once she's told her family that she's willing to put up with me, and she will, of course, say so when I ask her to do so, I can't see why anybody should object to our getting married. Can you?'

Anupam made no further attempt to dissuade him, and Sujit accordingly suggested to Tsunami that she should seek an interview with her father as soon as possible.

At this point, however, he met with an unexpected obstacle. To his surprise Tsunami first discouraged the idea, then she stubbornly rejected it. When he asked her if she preferred that he should call on Rowland himself, she said she did not want him to do so. Her attitude surprised and perplexed Sujit. Didn't she see that her reluctance was effectively barring the way to securing what they both wanted? He had considered that her earlier attachment, of which she had frankly and honestly told him, was now a thing of the past. With characteristic self-confidence he had believed that no memory of it lingered in her mind which he could not obliterate. But now he was not so sure.

Perceiving, however, that there were tears in her eyes as she begged him not to take the matter further, Sujit said no more.

But of course it was impossible to let matters stand as they were. There were limits, after all, to his patience. While Tsunami devoted herself to her books in the weeks preceding her final examination, Sujit mentally reviewed their relationship to find out if he could what difficulties, hitherto unforeseen, lay in his path, and how he could remove or circumvent them.

The only indication he had received that there might be any difficulties at all was a remark Tsunami's elder brother had made to her when he saw them dancing together at Lucas Falls.

'Well, well, what a flirtatious little sister I seem to have!' Ranil Wijesinha had said.

He had smirked as he said it, and had added:

'I wonder what Pater will have to say about *this*!'

Tsunami had affected unconcern, but Sujit, who had been initiated by three sisters into the mysterious workings of the female mind, had seen through her pretence easily enough. She cared all right. She had been hurt by the taunt and, for reasons he could not understand, seemed to be fearful of its consequences. What consequences might there be? Did she fear her father's displeasure? For what reason? She was over twenty-one, and could surely do as she pleased.

There was no telling, of course, what tyrannies might not exist within the closed circle of a conservative family. Regretting the earlier, open display of interest on his part that must have provoked her brother's remark, Sujit Roy began to realize that he might have been mistaken in so carelessly brushing off Anupam's warning. Ranil's words had sounded to him at the time like good-natured, brotherly teasing: he wondered now whether they had contained a hidden threat.

It looked as if he would have to tread carefully. Impatient by nature, the need for caution in a matter that he regarded as entirely personal and private annoyed and irritated Sujit, already deeply perplexed by Tsunami's refusal to speak of him to her father. Didn't she understand that it was creating an intolerable situation of furtiveness and secrecy when everything between them should be open and honest? Most disturbing of all, it contradicted in a very confusing way the ardour with which she responded to his wooing.

Deprived of regular contact with Tsunami by her wish that their relationship must be kept under cover, Sujit had resorted to dwelling in his imagination on the moments of their physical closeness, a private indulgence that he could not very well share with Anupam. Such moments had been few but significant. At the first of their private encounters, his overtures had been shyly accepted by Tsunami rather than welcomed, the kisses that succeeded them had seemed to surprise rather than please her.

Recalling Anupam's early reminder of her youth and inexperience,

Sujit had controlled his impatience, mastered the stir of his blood, and proceeded to court his lady gently but with persistence. He had received his reward. Gradually, it seemed to him, her hesitations vanished, to be replaced at last by a flow of passionate feeling that was everything he could ever have hoped for. At their second meeting, during which they had talked as much as they had touched, and laughed as much as they had talked, Sujit had been enchanted by the sinuous female mind that revealed itself to him, delighted to discover how much they seemed to have in common, and amazed by his own good luck in meeting such a marvellous girl. If only, he thought, such blissful moments could occur more often . . .

And then Sujit remembered: until their engagement was made public, he was wishing for the impossible. For he and Tsunami had been able to share such meetings of true minds only twice since they had first met: once in the privacy of his car, when he had driven her home from the Munasinghes' dinner party, and the second time at the up-country Rest House to which they had escaped together from the prying eyes that surrounded them on the Peradeniya campus. 'This is heaven,' Tsunami had said on the second occasion; and that, thought Sujit, was exactly what it had been. His memory of the lustrous afternoon they had spent together lingered in his mind very much as *rasamalai*, saturated with milk and the sweetness of honey and cardamom, lingers on a true Bengali tongue.

Whenever they were in the company of others, however, the atmosphere changed between them with dramatic suddenness, and the 'heaven' of intimate understanding remained frustratingly beyond his reach. Tsunami, obviously on edge and anxious, spoke little to him or to anyone else. She seemed even to avoid him, and was so nervous in his presence that she could hardly meet his eyes.

Sujit told himself that the contradictions in Tsunami's behaviour would disappear when her wish to marry him had been brought out into the open and accepted by her family. With three sisters of his own, all of whom were now married, he was perfectly familiar with the constraints imposed on young women by conservative families intent on guarding their reputations and the family name. But, he told himself, times were changing. However ancient and conservative the Wijesinha family was, it must be prepared to change with them. In any case, it was obvious that an end must be put immediately to this ridiculous situation in which every telephone call was monitored and a mature young woman could not go anywhere without a chaperon at her heels.

And since the young woman he had set his mind on was clearly not ready to confront her family with a statement of her wish to marry him, it was evident to Sujit that, whatever she said to the contrary, he would have to take the necessary steps by himself.

'I understand you're in Colombo for the van Kuyk celebration tomorrow,

Latha. Do you think you could give me half an hour before you return to Peradeniya? Tomorrow afternoon, perhaps?'

Latha met Sujit Roy by arrangement at the British Council Library, one of the few places in Colombo in which a young man could talk with a young woman for more than five minutes in the 1950s without setting rumours circulating of an imminent engagement. On the afternoon that they met, there were very few people about: most of the Council's staff and its regular readers were jammed into the lecture theatre, where a visiting British academic was speaking on the subject of Elizabethan stage conditions. Sujit and Latha had the library almost to themselves.

'I'm really grateful, Latha, that you made the time. I know you're in the middle of exam revisions, and you don't want distractions just now . . .'

'It's quite all right, Sujit, the van Kuyk celebration's a distraction in itself. Until Auntie Moira's party is over and done with, neither Tsunami nor I will be able to think about exam revision or anything else. What did you want to speak to me about? It sounded urgent.'

Sujit drew up a chair for Latha at a table near the window, and sat down opposite her.

'I'm here to ask for your help.'

'With what?'

'You're the only person I can talk to about this openly, and I think you're the only person who will tell me the truth.'

'I'll try. What do you want to know?'

A short silence followed, and Latha said:

'It's about Tsunami, isn't it?'

Sujit looked at her gratefully.

'Yes. I don't know how much she's told you about . . . us, but I know she must have told you *something*. That invitation to Peradeniya for Colours Night might have been her idea, but the letter which suggested that I join the party was written by you.'

'I'm beginning to think,' Latha said, smiling, 'that I'm developing a very devious mind. As soon as someone tells me something shouldn't be done, I think up ways of doing it. Not the right attitude for a law-abiding citizen.'

'Did someone tell you that I shouldn't be allowed to see Tsunami?'

Latha bit her lip, and hesitated.

'Not in quite that way. Not as an order. More as a warning: I was . . . advised, let's say, that I should think very carefully before encouraging her interest in you.'

'Who advised you? It was her brother Ranil, wasn't it?'

Latha shook her head.

'Tara, then?'

'Neither. It was Chris.'

'*Chris?* I didn't realize he was hostile to me.'

'He isn't. Not the least little bit. Chris is just concerned for Tsunami's happiness. He doesn't want to see her hurt. Neither do I, and he knows that very well. Hence his warning, delivered in the car on our way back from the Munasinghes' dinner party.'

'Good Lord, did I make my interest in Tsunami as obvious as that?'

'Of course you did.'

'It's the fault of this damned inquisitorial society,' Sujit said. 'It makes one paranoid. My apologies if I'm saying the wrong thing, Latha, but I don't know how people can act normally or naturally when they are surrounded by people who are watching their every move, thinking the worst, and reporting on it.'

In a country like this, where every man is surrounded by a neighbourhood of voluntary spies . . .

'Wasn't it like this for your sisters in India?'

Sujit considered.

'No, as a matter of fact it wasn't. They married as soon as they left boarding school.'

'So they didn't go to University?'

'College, we call it. No.'

'Well, there's your answer, Sujit. Your family did the traditional thing – married the girls off before they had time to see the great world! You would have been at University overseas, how could you have been aware of what was going on at home? In Uncle Rowland's family, Tara actually *wanted* to marry early and have a house of her own, she wasn't interested in University or a career. Tsunami resisted . . .'

'And met me.'

Latha hesitated.

'We-ell . . .'

'It's all right, Latha, you don't have to be so discreet! I know about that earlier attachment. Tsunami told me, right at the start. But that's all over now. And I understand he is married.'

'Yes. He is. Well, Sujit, what do you want me to do about it?'

Sujit looked at his companion with respect.

'You're very direct, aren't you?'

'I have to be. Time's short, and I should be at home right now. Getting ready for Auntie Moira's party.'

'All right. Here's my problem, Latha. I want to marry your cousin. I want to marry her soon. Tomorrow, if possible.'

'You can't. She has examinations next month.'

'Immediately after her examinations, then. I want to speak to her father and lodge a formal proposal.'

Latha interrupted him.

'That would get you nowhere. Uncle Rowland would simply show you the door. You need a . . . a go-between, someone who is known to both parties and is trusted by both, someone like a family elder, who would make the proposal on your behalf. In my parents' day, apparently, it was done through professional marriage-brokers.'

'They still use professional marriage-brokers in India. A horrible system.'

'I agree. But you can't deny that it's useful. If the marriage fails, both sides can blame the go-between. My father quotes a local saying: *Seven thunderbolts await the unsuccessful marriage-broker*. He quotes it when he wants to discourage my mother from arranging a marriage for me!'

'Your father,' said Sujit thoughtfully. 'He would be Mr Rowland Wijesinha's first cousin, wouldn't he?'

'Not so close. More like a second or third cousin.'

'Is he on good terms with Tsunami's father?'

'I'd say so, though Thaththi privately thinks Uncle Rowland's politics are a huge joke. I'm afraid my father doesn't take Uncle Rowland very seriously. And he doesn't care for Auntie Moira, mostly because she supplanted Tsunami's mother, whom my father admired very much. Why do you ask me that question?'

'I was wondering—'

'Whether my father would be your marriage-broker?'

Latha laughed, imagining Herbert in the role.

'Actually, he'd do it very well. Though I know someone else who would just *love* to do it – my mother! On second thoughts, though, I wouldn't advise that, Amma can't stand Auntie Moira, and it shows. In any case, neither of my parents would really do – they don't know anything about you.'

'That,' Sujit said, 'can be easily remedied. With your help, Latha. *You* would speak up for me, wouldn't you?'

He's really very charming, Latha thought. I can quite see why Tsunami . . .

She said:

'Yes, I would. I like you, and I believe you love Tsunami, and will take care of her. She needs looking after, Sujit. Someone who knew Tsunami very well told Chris and me many years ago, "You must guard her interests, or she will be lost." But my opinion wouldn't carry weight with Uncle Rowland. He regards me as a child. What does Tsunami say about your speaking to her father?'

'That's part of the problem. *She* doesn't want to talk to him about marriage, and she doesn't want *me* to do it. Whenever I bring up the matter, she changes the subject. She doesn't realize it, but it's driving me crazy. Sometimes I wonder whether she really cares for me.'

'I can hardly believe *that*. She doesn't talk about you, even to me, but I can assure you that if I wasn't certain of her feelings for you, I'd have taken Chris's advice and stayed out of your affairs.'

'Then why, for heaven's sake, is she taking this attitude? I don't want to act without her consent, but she leaves me no option.'

Latha considered.

'I understand the way you feel, Sujit, but if I were you I wouldn't rush her. A lot of things have happened in Tsunami's family, you know, and to her, too . . . She needs time to come to terms with some of them. You'd need to go slowly, in any case: if you and Uncle Rowland don't have a trusted friend in common, you'll need to impress my father, and that might take time. He thinks the world of Tsunami, and he wouldn't help you with Uncle Rowland if he didn't think you worthy of her. On the other hand . . .'

A sudden idea had occurred to Latha.

'The Munasinghes are old friends of my parents. If Dr Munasinghe can bring the two of you together, introduce you to my father, and say the right things about your character and background and so forth, things might work out more easily. Especially if he can provide accurate information about your bank balance . . . Auntie Moira has a sincere respect for money.'

Sujit said: 'Latha, you amaze me.'

Latha pushed her chair back, and rose.

'Didn't I tell you, Sujit? I'm developing a very devious mind.'

Latha reflected that Sujit Roy, of whom she had had hardly any opportunity to form an opinion before she encountered him at Lucas Falls, was certainly turning out to be a determined lover. His telephone call to her on the day after the Munasinghes' party had worried her mother, perplexed her father, and intrigued the maid servant Podina, who had answered the telephone.

Soma did not approve of Sujit at all. She remembered him as 'that irresponsible young man from India' who was avoiding his family responsibilities in order to follow a foolish dream: worse, she suspected him of having influenced the Munasinghes against pursuing a connection with her own family. She was seriously perturbed by his telephone call. Latha, she recalled, had declared that she liked him – more, she had actually said she admired him!

'Look here, Latha, your mother is getting very anxious. She and I both want to know: what does this young man *want*?'

Herbert usually resisted the temptation to ask his daughter intrusive questions, feeling that she faced enough of that kind of thing from her mother, but Soma had worn him down.

'Sujit Roy? He's . . . let's say he's a Maharajah on *shikar*,' Latha replied, laughing. 'Oh, don't worry, Thaththi, I'm not the quarry he has in his sights! He just wants me to act as his gun-bearer.'

When Latha arrived with her parents at the Wijesinha house, they were greeted by an elated hostess. Moira Wijesinha, resplendent in green and gold silk and a spectacular emerald necklace, was floating along on the glittering surface of her party, triumphant and happy. Her careful planning had paid off handsomely. Her house was fragrant with expensive flowers, glittering with lights, and crowded with cultured and fashionable people, all of them talking at once, and at the tops of their perfectly modulated voices, about art and music. She had heard herself and Rowland praised by the Prime Minister, no less, as 'cultural icons of the new Ceylon'. And to crown it all, their guest of honour, clad in an elegant embroidered *kurta* of fine linen that Lalita Das had bought for him in Delhi, was behaving himself with perfect propriety. Lalita was at Gerard's side, pointing him towards all the right people. (It was quite extraordinary, Moira thought, how quickly the woman had grasped who exactly was who in Colombo's cultural world.)

She made the circuit of the room, mentally checking off people on her guest list. Mr and Mrs Ivan Ganesan, previously unknown to Moira, had greeted Gerard like old friends. Indeed, it had turned out that they *were* old friends of his. (Moira had at first doubted this, Mrs Ganesan being so simply dressed that she had wondered if they were gate-crashers.) Dr Siri Munasinghe and his wife, also previously unknown to Moira, were accompanied by their son and daughter, the son being presumably the young man of whom Tara had written so enthusiastically. Moira watched as Chris and Tsunami joined the young Munasinghes, taking Herbert's daughter with them. Tsunami's looking very good, Moira thought: that sari suits her. Or maybe it's love? She had noticed that young Anupam Munasinghe was paying Tsunami a good deal of attention, and she beamed upon them with satisfaction. Tara was right – they made an attractive pair. And here was her good friend Michelle Feuillard now, kissing her moistly on both cheeks: dear Michelle, who had foretold a brilliant future for Moira by reading her fortune in the Tarot cards, who had introduced her to the handsome astrologer who now guided her every move; Michelle, who had so helpfully initiated her into the mysteries of correct French pronunciation! Moira smiled to think how naïve she had been in this important area of cultural knowledge until she had met Michelle at a French Embassy reception, and begun taking lessons from her.

There seemed to be some excitement at the doorway. People were falling back, creating a passageway through which Yvette Hashmi was walking in, wearing a crinoline of frilled and flounced taffeta, with her adoring millionaire husband Omar walking three paces behind her as usual. Behind the Hashmis came a posse of photographers, and behind them flocked still more guests.

Rowland, of course, was as usual at the centre of a group of political people, holding them absolutely *riveted* with his anecdotes. The perfect host. Though it was a pity, of course, that the island's parliamentarians were so crass and uncultured, knowing nothing at all about art and music, so that poor Rowland had to limit his range to political jokes. Something the P.M. said provoked a roar of laughter from the men surrounding him, which increased in volume when Rowland wittily capped it. And there were Herbert and Soma: Soma – oh, dear! – on the fringe of things as usual, out of her depth, of course, in this kind of company, and Herbert – inevitably – with his fingers lovingly curled around the stem of a brimming glass.

Well, despite a few such flaws – which could not be helped, after all – it was altogether a lovely party. There was dear Kirthi, there was Yrol, there was that recently married friend of Tara's whose name Moira didn't know – Darlene? or was it Noreen? – who had made a point of getting her businessman husband to buy two of Gerard's new paintings, there were Miriam de Saram and Ena de Silva, Harry Pieris and Richard Gabriel, Sakuntala Rajagopal and Christine Blackler, Q.C. Ramanathan and his daughter Sushila, Jeanne Pinto and Lucien de Zoysa . . .

It was already clear that the occasion was a smashing success, and Alagi Muttucumaru's catered supper hadn't even been served yet! Moira looked forward to hearing the gasps of surprise and delight that would arise around the table when her guests saw Alagi's salmon mousse, unmoulded on to an oval mirror in the shape of a *veena* (a delicate compliment, this, to dear Gerard's 'Indian period'). Which reminded her – what had happened to the music she had planned for the party?

'Music has charms,' Moira had remarked to the Indian High Commissioner, 'to soothe the savage beast. I want to hire some good musicians for our party, but I just don't know where to turn for information . . . Can you help, Mr Desai?'

Mr Desai had been a little doubtful as to what beast Mrs Wijesinha had in mind. He concluded at last that she, as the wife of a politician, must know that there would be several people among her guests tonight who were undeclared enemies of her husband or herself. Certainly, Indian music had a sweet and soothing quality, and if there were to be savage beasts about with jealousy in their hearts, soothing music would be a useful antidote to their hostility. He had responded to Moira's appeal by telling her about a group of skilled musicians who performed regularly at High Commission functions. She had seized on his suggestion with enthusiasm. Besides, there would be a foreigner present who was devoted to Indian music: Mr Ronald Marchmont, a visiting professor at Peradeniya, had taken a good deal of trouble explaining to Moira the difference between the *veena*, the *tabla* and the *sarodh*.

It is so impressive, Moira thought, the sheer variety of talent and the depth of sensibility represented here tonight! She hoped that everyone present realized that it was only at a home like hers that they could experience such a fascinating mixture of cultures.

The musicians did not seem to have arrived yet. But luckily, neither had Mr Marchmont. No, she had been mistaken. There he was, on the other side of the room, talking to Sushila Ramanathan. Well, that was all right, she would keep him busy until the musicians had been found. With a small sigh of exasperation (but not a very loud one, because she was feeling so blissfully happy) Moira looked around for Ranil or Tara to send in search of them.

'Latha baba,' said a voice at Latha's elbow.

'Why, Alice! How are you?'

'Come, baba, come to this side, too much talk here, I want to ask you a question,' said 'Old Nokomis', and beckoned Latha towards a little chamber adjoining the reception room which had been fitted up to Moira's design as a powder room for female guests. Into this they retreated, and Alice asked her question.

'Latha baba, is it true that my lady is coming home?'

Helen! Returning to Ceylon! Could it be possible?

'I don't know anything about it, Alice. Where did you hear this?'

'Ali Cassim told me, baba. He had heard it from Master Chris.'

'Let's go and find Chris right away, Alice – I want to know why he hasn't told *me*!'

IV

All things have second birth;
The earthquake is not satisfied at once.

William Wordsworth, *The Prelude* (1850)

Ah, love, let us be true
To one another! For the world, which seems
To lie before us like a land of dreams,
So various, so beautiful, so new,
Hath really neither joy, nor love, nor light,
Nor certitude, nor peace, nor help for pain;
And we are here as on a darkling plain
Swept with confused alarms of struggle and flight,
Where ignorant armies clash by night.

Matthew Arnold, *Dover Beach* (1867)

1

SHAKESPEARE

Separating the Galle Road from the waves of the Indian Ocean, and overlooked by the old colonial splendours of the Galle Face Hotel, is an open expanse of treeless turf known as the Galle Face Green. Along the entire length of the Green is a strongly built walkway from which occasional flights of steps lead down to the beach below.

A stone monument erected halfway along this promenade informs the world that a British Governor dedicated the Green a hundred and fifty years ago to 'the recreation of Colombo's ladies and children', and from that time to this it has been a favourite location for family enjoyment. The practice of strolling on the Green began in colonial times, when British soldiers in their scarlet and white uniforms would march out of the army barracks in the Fort to drill on the grassy turf, and the citizens of Colombo gathered to watch the spectacle and listen to the martial music of the band. Later, after the army high command shifted its quarters elsewhere, elderly British residents of the Galle Face Hotel began to take their daily constitutional along the promenade, and the Green itself became the city's favourite playground.

The heat of the tropical sun makes walking on the Green after ten o'clock in the morning extremely uncomfortable, and the hidden presence of rocks and boulders in the surf discourages any but the most foolhardy sea-bathers at every time of the day. But by four o'clock in the afternoon, the burning heat of the tropics has diminished, the grass has ceased to bake in the sun, a steady sea-breeze has begun to blow, and Colombo comes out to play.

After four o'clock in the 1950s, kite-sellers would appear, and vendors who sold ice cream in little tubs with wooden scoops, hot spicy vadai and cashew nuts in paper bags, and roasted peanuts in twisted paper cones.

When Latha and Tsunami were little girls, their parents had often taken them for evening walks on Galle Face Green. That was the time of the day the Wijesinha children loved, when the sun would go down, leaving behind it a sky shot with streaks of orange, rose and gold. With its departure, the street lights of the Galle Road would come on, one by one, and as if in response to them pinpoints of light would show on the horizon, where cargo ships waited in line for their turn to enter the harbour. The waiting children would break their grass rings and make their wishes. A natural home for innocent pleasures, the Green is dear to Colombo's young, and has always been so.

But not more dear than it is to the city's senior citizens. They choose the early morning hours to visit the Green for their daily constitutional, for at that time the breeze, having begun to blow out to sea with the retreating tide, is not so strong. It is a pleasant walk, with a hint of adventure about it, for at six o'clock in the morning the skies are still dark, with fugitive stars dotted here and there, the sea waves can be made out only by their foam-tipped edges, and three massive cannons planted at intervals along the promenade, facing out to sea, remind walkers with a sense of history of times when the city of Colombo required defending from foreign invasion.

There is no cause for alarm now, however, for the Colombo Municipality has planted elegant street lights along the length of the promenade to discourage hawkers, pickpockets and professional beggars who might otherwise make themselves a nuisance to walkers on the Green. A police post established halfway along ensures that anyone who tries to do so will be arrested and summarily punished. Security on the Green in the early hours of the morning has been a top priority of the Colombo police ever since Ceylon's first Prime Minister fell from his horse and died while exercising on Galle Face Green. Horse-riding at Galle Face as a form of exercise for the rich and powerful fell out of fashion after that, and horses are no longer to be seen cantering on the greensward. The walkers, however, continue to take their constitutionals; and among the walkers who regularly made their appearance on the Galle Face promenade in the 1950s were two eminent persons: Mr Rowland Wijesinha, Minister of Cultural Affairs, and his cabinet colleague Mr D.K. Beliwatte.

The morning following the Wijesinhas' reception in honour of Gerard van Kuyk was cloudy and wet. Rowland remarked on this to his companion, adding his hope that the rain had extended itself to the hill country, where it might have brought some relief to estates that were in the grip of an unprecedented drought. Beliwatte, who, like Rowland, had inherited extensive property in the Central Province, agreed. They were in agreement on most things, most of the time: the slight estrangement between them that Tsunami's comments had caused some months previously seemed to have been completely forgotten, and Rowland, perceiving that light rain during the night had left pools of moisture on the tarred surface of the promenade, drew Beliwatte's attention to this hazard.

'Take care, Captain, that you don't slip in the water. The country can't afford to lose you.'

Rowland, who had called Beliwatte 'Belly' throughout their schooldays at King's, had dropped the nickname when they became cabinet colleagues, and now addressed him tactfully as 'Captain', a title Beliwatte greatly preferred. It was a comforting reminder of the glorious days of his youth, when he had captained the College at cricket, and both Wijesinha and the present Prime Minister, Percy Wilmot, then a lad of seventeen, had played in the team and had looked up to him as a hero.

Now, of course, both Rowland and Beliwatte were players on Wilmot's team, an instance of the way life sometimes surprised one with an unexpected turn and turn about. Beliwatte recalled that Rowland had been a useful bat, not brilliant, but always reliable on the field; equally so when he was off it, using his persuasive powers to fend off a challenge to his captaincy from some ambitious nobody with delusions of greatness. When Rowland was playing with the idea of entering politics, Beliwatte had praised him to Wilmot as a sound man who could be depended on to see things from a right and reasonable point of view, and to speak out boldly at cabinet meetings. Once in the Cabinet, Rowland had undertaken, not infrequently, to fly a kite on behalf of the P.M. by enunciating policies that might not have looked well if they had been uttered directly by Wilmot himself. His Oxbridge background and his successful legal career had made Rowland impressively articulate, and the *yakkos* from provincial schools who unfortunately still predominated in the Cabinet tended to retire, awed, as soon as Minister Wijesinha began to speak in the House.

It was a pity, thought Beliwatte, skipping nimbly around a pool of water on the walkway, that King's had gone down so much since their time at College, admitting the sons of men from God only knew where, on the strength of nothing but high marks in the entrance examination. When it came to leadership, it was not brains but breeding that really counted. Everybody knew that; although, in these democratic times, nobody could actually say so. And now he and Rowland were embarked in partnership on the adventure of governing the country. Beliwatte had not been to Oxford or Cambridge, and did not aspire to scale the political heights, but he knew that great leaders require loyal lieutenants, and it was as Wilmot's right-hand man that he was determined to make his contribution.

Take the question of education, for instance. It was absolutely crucial to the welfare of the country that the men who were in charge of things should have had the right type of education, the training (on the field and off it) that fitted them for responsibility.

Or take the national economy. The island's economic welfare depended on the continued success of its tea plantations, and the gradual replacement of the outgoing British planters with strong, solid young men from schools like St Alban's in Colombo and All Saints' in Kandy boded well for the industry. Trained by the British, the new planters followed tradition, standing no damned nonsense from their Tamil labour, and guaranteeing by their hard work and their healthy outlook on life that shareholders in Lipton's and Brooke Bond's received very satisfactory dividends.

Or take the country's health resources. Obviously, more hospitals were needed, with the population growing at the speed of light, but Ceylon's medical facilities were the best in Asia, and the island's physicians and surgeons, trained in London and Edinburgh, among the best in the world. They could cope. And they *were* coping. It annoyed Beliwatte that ever since the granting of Independence had confirmed the island's status as a free democracy, anti-social elements had been doing their utmost to disrupt the harmony of life in the virtual paradise he and his class had inherited from the British. He was getting very tired of listening politely to people who wanted English and Classical Studies phased out of the schools to make room for the study and use of the island's indigenous languages; people who wanted Western medicine replaced in the hospitals with the filthy potions and smelly ointments of *ayurveda*; people who wanted to shut down the tea estates, and to replace them with the lots of small farmers who saw no point in cultivating anything but yams, brinjals and chillies . . .

On these and a multitude of other issues, Beliwatte found Rowland Wijesinha a reassuring sounding-board that returned to each of his own strokes a comforting echo. Rowland had made a public speech the other day that put the Tamil agitators in their place – and very good of him it was to do it, too, considering the fact that his own family had Indian Tamil connections. Beliwatte, who was related on his mother's side to Moira Wijesinha, wished heartily that her husband's first marriage had never taken place. In the present climate of opinion, such connections affected the popular mind and tainted even the best of men with a hint, however slight, of unsoundness. And a successful politician could not *afford* to be unsound: he became a liability . . .

'Do you believe in horoscopes, Rowley?' Beliwatte inquired, as they reached the police post on the promenade, and were accorded a smart salute by the sergeant on duty.

'All this stuff about planets and stars and good and bad periods? I've been warned that I'm about to enter on a very unlucky period in my own life—'

Rowland advised his colleague to ignore such doom-sayers. He made a rule, he said, of ignoring them himself. But then, he was a modern man, with an educated, liberal outlook on life. Moira, on the other hand, having been brought up in the traditions of an old Kandyan *walauwa* (Beliwatte nodded, acknowledging this respectful reference to his own and Moira's ancestry), well, *she* thought differently on such matters. And one had to placate the ladies, after all . . . Moira went about the whole thing in a very practical way, said Rowland. There was an astrologer in Colombo whom she consulted as regularly as she got the doctor chappie to check her pulse and heart rate, and he had not, as far as Rowland knew, ever given her bad advice. She had had him cast horoscopes for all the children—

'Did he cast one for you, too?'

Rowland was a little embarrassed.

'I said very firmly that I didn't want one cast for me, but Moira had given Ratnapala the details regarding the date and time of my birth, and as a result, I now have a horoscope. I don't know what's in it – I don't *want* to know – but she has had it read, and she keeps me informed if there's danger lurking anywhere . . .'

'Danger?' said Beliwatte.

The word made him nervous, and he struggled not to show it.

'Well, that of course could mean anything from a car accident to a cold. No point in worrying about such things.'

'No point at all. And in any case,' Rowland rejoined, suddenly visited by a happy inspiration, 'if the stars *were* preparing some . . . unpleasantness for you or the P.M., Captain, don't you think they'd give us prior notice of it on one of these morning walks of ours?

When beggars die, there are no comets seen;
The heavens themselves blaze forth the death of princes . . .'

'Ha! *Julius Caesar*.' said Beliwatte appreciatively.

He was not a scholar, but he knew the play well. Due to his small stature and smooth, fair complexion, he had often played the female lead in school plays, and he had played Calpurnia when King's put on *Julius Caesar* in his last year. (In the previous year, he'd played Miranda in *The Tempest*, and before that, Celia in *As You Like It*.) 'Princes', eh? Recalling his schoolboy triumphs on the cricket field and on the stage made him feel much better, and the ominous predictions of his horoscope slipped from his mind. The two gentlemen walked on in companionable silence to the end of the Green, turned, and began walking back towards the Galle Face Hotel.

The bodyguards walking a few paces behind them turned also, and fell into step.

Six forty-five.

One by one, the lights along the promenade clicked off. Far out at sea, a ship's fog-horn hooted.

Events of the previous evening had left Anupam Munasinghe restless, and the echoing sound of the fog-horn woke him from an unquiet slumber.

Sleep was out of the question: he wandered out on to the balcony, and stood leaning on the balustrade, looking down on the street below where the only cars to be seen still had their headlights on, and a few early cyclists were riding to work. The dawn light gradually grew stronger, and Anupam could hear the sound of muffled voices and the dull rhythm of a rice-pounder as the domestics of the Soysa family next door prepared breakfast for the household. In a few moments, he knew, the familiar rituals of his own home would begin. Sure enough, within seconds he heard the familiar chink of china as a tray was placed outside his door, but he did not look round, for just at that moment a car he knew well drew up beneath his balcony, a dog barked, and a flock of crows rose out of the trees in the small park opposite and flew, cawing, into the sky.

'You're up early,' Sujit Roy remarked, joining Anupam on the balcony.

'So are you. What brings you here, may I ask? Coffee's on a tray outside, help yourself.'

'Thanks.'

Sujit brought two cups out onto the balcony.

'What brings me here so bright and early? Business meeting in the city. Thought I'd drop in on the way.'

'Draw up a chair and join me,' said Anupam.

They sipped in a silence that Sujit was the first to break.

'Well?' he asked. 'How did things go last night?'

Anupam smiled.

'I wondered when you would ask me that question,' he said. 'It was a good party. A very grand occasion, in fact. The organization was superb, and the food was first-class. The whole affair did credit to the hostess.'

He paused, and then added casually, as if it was an afterthought of little consequence:

'By the way, you will be interested to know that I met Chris and Tsunami's father last night.'

'Oh? That would have been interesting.'

'It was.'

'Well?' Sujit said impatiently, as another silence seemed about to succeed the first. 'What's Minister Wijesinha like? One hears such contradictory reports.'

Anupam burst unexpectedly into rapid speech.

'I want you to understand that I went prepared to like him, Sujit. I'd told myself that with a son like Chris, he was bound to be a good sort. And I wanted *him* to like *me* – I wanted that for your sake, if you see what I mean, as well as for my own. He'll need proof that your friends – and Chris's, too, of course – fitted in well with the family . . .'

Sujit, who was always alert to changes of mood in the friend he had come to regard over the years as a brother, instantly perceived in Anupam's manner certain familiar symptoms of distress. He noted his anxiety, his unnecessarily frequent allusions to Christopher Wijesinha.

Oh, Anupam! We're back to Square One, back again on the old, sad path of unrequited passion.

Sujit had seen Anupam through several such situations, and he wondered now whether Chris was aware of the feelings he had aroused in his friend. Evidently not. Sujit had developed at school and at University a certain technique for helping Anupam cope with crisis, a strategy that combined pretended obtuseness with very real sympathy. Accordingly, he gave no indication of his awareness. Mentally filing this most recent perception away for future reference, he returned to the matter under discussion.

'Well, it's quite obvious to me that *you* didn't like *him*, Anupam. May I ask why not?'

'I'm still trying to work it out. He's a very good host and all that, intelligent, well-read, tells a good story, thoroughly hospitable, but . . . Well, I regret having to say such a thing of your future father-in-law, but it's just that he's such a pompous ass! Very different from his cousin Herbert.'

'Who's Herbert?'

'Latha's father.'

'Come on, let's hear what happened. What did you talk about?'

'In accordance with my calling, I scouted around for something diplomatic and non-controversial to say that would give the Minister an opportunity to shine. I remembered the library at Lucas Falls. You may remember that I spent a lot of time there while you were engaged in rushing Tsunami off her feet . . . and I'd noticed that three whole shelves were devoted to crime fiction. So I'd asked Chris which member of his family was the Dorothy Sayers fan. He told me it was his father.'

Sujit considered this.

'Well, there's nothing wrong with that as a conversation starter! From all I've heard, Mr W. is a bit of a fop: he probably sees himself as Lord Peter Wimsey. I don't suppose he wears a monocle, but for all we know, he may have a grey topper lurking in his wardrobe . . . You could have exchanged profound thoughts on the great detectives, Anupam!'

'Certainly. And that's exactly what we did. He was *delighted* to talk about the great detectives! Poirot, Jane Marple, Wimsey, all the way back to Father Brown and Sherlock Holmes. Knew his stuff, too. Then he asked me if I didn't think Sayers was the finest crime writer of them all. That's when I made my mistake. I said I admired her ingenious plots, her eye for detail, and her invention of a main character who is compassionate as well as clever.'

'Sounds fine to me.'

'Yes. And then, like a damned fool, I ruined my opportunity. I brought in a "but". I said I could forgive Lord Peter his aristocratic origins because, unlike most members of his social class, he has a brain. But it was a great pity, I said, that Sayers's fine novels are almost unreadable today because they contain so many insulting racist expressions. So many of her characters, I said, are referred to routinely as "niggers" and "Jew boys" and "dagoes"—'

'Well, you're perfectly right. They are.'

'It was Sayers's only weakness, I said. And as soon as I'd said that, Mr Wijesinha went off the deep end. Absolutely and completely. Read me a lecture then and there on the necessity of developing a proper sense of life's realities. Told me there was no point in being idealistic and burying my head in the sand, the world was full of criminal characters, most of them niggers and Jews, and every writer who drew public attention to the fact deserved the Nobel Prize. He ended by telling me that Tamils are the Jews of Ceylon, that they're invaders from India, that they're here entirely on sufferance, and that if they continue to demand equal rights with the Sinhalese, they would someday be taught a lesson they would never forget . . .'

'I wonder what the old boy will say when he learns that his daughter wants to marry an invader from India!' Sujit said.

He did not seem in the least affected by Anupam's story.

'Go on, I'm listening.'

'His attitude took me totally by surprise, Sujit. Mr W.'s got quite a reputation here as an intellectual, a cultured, sophisticated person who has an open-minded view of the world. I'd thought that presenting him with a subject like crime fiction to talk about would bring out that side of him. I was discussing Marjorie Allingham and Ngaio Marsh with Chris the other day, and we had a thoroughly enjoyable talk. I never expected his father would be so—'

'And how did this very instructive conversation end?'

'Oh, Mrs W. came along and hurried me off to be introduced to the guest of honour. Van Kuyk was having the time of his life, surrounded by a circle of devotees to whom he was holding forth on the meaning of Life and Art. I was glad to join them. Look, I'm terribly sorry, Sujit. I've put my foot in it, haven't I?'

'Not a bit of it. Diplomat or not, you can hardly be expected to spend your life trying to find areas of agreement with everyone. What *I'm* wondering is why he reacted in such an extreme way to what you said about Sayers . . . Do you think it could have had something to do with the past? Some experience he's had that he doesn't normally talk about? You do know, don't you, Anupam, that Tsunami's beautiful mamma ran off with a German Jew? Someone named Fritz – or possibly, Franz – Goldman?'

'Well,' his friend said reluctantly, 'I wasn't going to mention it, but people of my parents' generation still talk about the affair, and when they do, they do so in capitals. My father refers to it as The Great Elopement. It was *the* sensation of the 1940s, apparently. I checked Mr Wijesinha's official biography, to learn what I could about his family: there's no mention whatever of his first wife. She's never been back since, according to my parents. Has Tsunami talked about her to you?'

'No. She's never mentioned her mother,' Sujit said. 'It appears to be a blank area. We will eventually talk about her, I suppose, and even about The Great Elopement, but not just yet, it seems.'

'What about Chris? Has he mentioned it?'

'Oh, Chris told me about it as soon as he realized that I was planning to become his brother-in-law. Maybe he wanted to put me off!'

'That's highly unlikely,' Anupam said severely. 'He was just being honest and straightforward with you.'

'. . . Which would be much more like the Chris we know. You're perfectly right. I take back the aspersion. Anyway, Chris is in touch with his mother *and* Mr Goldman: he's the only member of the family willing to forgive and forget, apparently. His brothers and sisters act as though she had never existed.'

'Maybe they take their cue from their father. Having met him, and seen him in action, I'm willing to bet that he can harbour quite a grudge.'

'According to Chris, Mr W. behaved very decently when Tsunami's mother went away,' said Sujit.

'Well, of course he would! He'd feel he owed it to his dignity, and to family honour and all that. But underneath, would he have forgiven her? It must have been a terrific blow to his vanity. And if he hasn't forgiven her, that might go a long way to explaining his fury on the subject of Jews . . . Because that's what it was, fury . . .'

Anupam was struck by a new idea.

'Oh, God, Sujit, he may even have thought I'd brought up the subject deliberately, wanting to needle him and watch him react. I am *so* sorry!'

'Forget it, friend,' said Sujit Roy.

But Anupam could not 'forget it'.

That evening, Soma Wijesinha looked up from her sewing, and raised herself slightly in her chair. She had heard the garden gate click, and craned her neck in order to see who had arrived.

'Who's this coming up to the house, Herbie?' she asked.

Herbert put aside his newspaper.

'It's Siri and Annabelle's boy,' he said. 'Mr Incomparable.'

'Good afternoon, sir,' Anupam Munasinghe said pleasantly. 'Good afternoon, Mrs Wijesinha. Is Latha in?'

Soma regarded Anupam with undisguised pleasure. Her disappointment at the failure of what Herbert still privately called 'the Munasinghe fiasco' had not dispelled her hopes of him as a son-in-law.

'Please sit down, Anupam, I will go and see,' she said.

Latha *was* in, and Soma knew it, but it would never do to seem eager.

'Duwa? Where are you?'

Latha was not physically far away, but she was spiritually and mentally in another universe, having recently acquired a glass-fronted book-case that had unexpectedly taken her father's fancy at an auction sale. He had made Latha a present of it, and she, delighted to have somewhere at last to house her personal library, was spending her last days in Colombo arranging her books.

'What's this? *Another* book-case?' Soma had complained, when a furniture van bearing the legend 'Vandersmagt and Son, Auctioneers' delivered Herbert's purchase at the Wijesinhas' door.

'Where are we going to put it?'

The book-case had eventually been given a place in the corridor next to the veranda. With it there had arrived four sets of fifty book-plates which Herbert had had specially prepared for Latha by a friend of his who owned a little printing press in Maradana. *Latha Wijesinha – Her Book*, said each book-plate in elegant black cursive script.

'Can put some nice decoration just below the words?' Herbert's printer friend had suggested. 'Something suitable for a young lady – a Sigiri fresco, perhaps, or a lotus flower? Can do. Or can have this drawing, a village girl with a water pot. How you like?'

A true artist, the printer was delighted to work on a project as attractive as this, when he wasn't producing the brightly coloured wrappers for Sunlight Soap and Island Coffee from which he made his living.

'Just the words, thanks,' Herbert had said hastily.

Bringing her books together for shelving, Latha had been pleasantly surprised by the extent to which her library had grown, combining books given her by her parents with books bought out of her own pocket-money, and with Collins Classics in black leather bindings lettered in gilt, the prize books she had won during her years at Amarapāli Maha Vidyālaya. Added to these were the books purchased by way of a sheaf of vouchers made out for generous sums, that had been given her as birthday and Christmas presents over the years by relatives who didn't know what else to give to a book-obsessed niece. She had exchanged the book vouchers at K.V.G. de Silva's and the Lake House Bookshop for the items on a short list that had been drawn up at her request by Ronald Marchmont and Rajan Phillips. These were the books, they told her, that no serious student of English literature should be without. Altogether, it was a handsome collection, and she was proud of it.

Having spread the floor around the book-case with sheets of newspaper, Latha had settled down to her task and had soon become deeply engrossed.

She was using her book-plates for the first time, and found her progress hindered somewhat by the activities of a lively puppy (also recently acquired) which was making little rushes at the piles of books she had carefully stacked on the newspaper. Engaged in keeping the puppy in check while assigning the books to their proper places, Latha did not hear her mother's call. It was only when Anupam's elongated shadow fell across the cement floor of the corridor that she registered the presence of a visitor.

'You startled me, Anupam!'

'I'm sorry, I didn't mean to interrupt. I can see you're busy.'

'No, no,' Latha said. 'It's only that I—'

'Perhaps I can help?'

Latha, who had jumped to her feet in her surprise at seeing Anupam, sat down again. The puppy, happy to discover a new interest, began investigating the turn-ups of the visitor's perfectly creased trousers.

'You certainly can,' she replied briskly.

'What you could do, Anupam, like a good fellow, is to keep this puppy in order while I go on with sorting my books. He's cute, but he's in my way. If you help me, I can be finished soon, and then I can get us both a cup of tea.'

Anupam made a grab for the puppy, but it scampered away.

Outside, on the veranda, Herbert and Soma looked at each other. *Like a good fellow?* Since when had Latha been on terms of such easy familiarity with 'Mr Incomparable'?

'He's pretty quick!' Anupam said, securing the puppy at last.

'He's house-trained, so don't worry, he won't make a little pool around your shoes,' Latha said.

Anupam smoothed down the puppy's ears.

'He's an Alsatian, isn't he?' he said. 'What's his name?'

'We haven't got around yet to naming him. You've got to be very careful when you're naming pets . . .'

'Why's that?'

'Well, partly because everyone in the household needs to be able to pronounce the name. And then you have to keep in mind what they'll look like when they grow up.'

'But you know what *he'll* look like. Handsome. Like every other Alsatian.'

'Yes, but if we didn't know? Just imagine what the result would be if we named that character in your lap "Cuddles" or "Cutie-pie" on the strength of his beautiful, big brown eyes, and his blunt nose, and his floppy ears, just because he's so little and—'

'Fubsy?'

'Exactly.'

Latha looked at Anupam with new interest.

'Oh, so you like Kipling, do you?'

'Naturally. Bagheera and Baloo are my favourite fictional characters.'

'There's no "naturally" about it! One of my tutors at Peradeniya can't get over the fact that I enjoy Kipling. He's English, with progressive ideas, and he thinks that as an ex-colonial I should hate the old imperialist with a hatred as bitter as death. *I* think that's an unreasonable attitude. It's the words that matter, not the imperialist ideology—'

Anupam said:

> '*Oh, hear the call! – Good hunting all*
> *That keep the Jungle Law!*'

'Exactly,' Latha said. 'Could anyone with a feeling for language resist words like that?'

'No. I agree with you,' Anupam said. 'And you'll have no problem with this little fellow if you name him "Raja" or "Caesar". He'll grow up looking appropriately regal, wait and see. There'll be no fubsiness then.'

Latha stood up.

'Give me that puppy, Anupam, and I'll take him back to Podina in the kitchen. Why don't you take my place, and see how you make out with the book-plates?'

When she returned, she found Anupam reading.

'This is such a fine collection, Latha,' he said. 'And all of them are yours, I see.'

'All mine!' Latha said proudly.

She looked at her books with satisfaction.

'I've been gloating all day.'

'It's easy to tell, you know, from looking at your books, exactly where your affections lie! All the Augustans – Dryden, Pope and Johnson; some of the Romantics – here's Keats, here's Byron . . . Where's Austen?'

'Top shelf, on the left. Her surname begins with "A", after all.'

'Ah, here she is. All six novels, present and correct. But from what I hear, Austen would be on the top shelf of any library of yours, even if her surname had been Zachariah.'

'Who told you that? It sounds like Chris.'

'It wasn't Chris. And from the same source I hear that you will, in a few weeks' time, graduate from Peradeniya with a First Class . . .'

Latha was annoyed.

'You've been talking to my tutor, Mr Marchmont.'

Anupam spread his hands.

'*Mea culpa, mea maxima culpa*. Your cousin Tsunami introduced me to him yesterday, at that reception her father gave for Mr van Kuyk. Naturally, we talked of you.'

'He had no business discussing his students' work with strangers!'

'Ah, but I'm no stranger, am I, Latha! I represented myself to him as a friend of yours. Was I wrong?'

There was no reply.

Anupam changed the subject.

'What a superb copy of Shakespeare's *Sonnets*. I wish it were mine.'

'It's a present from my father. He ordered it out specially for me, from Blackwell's.'

Podina emerged from the kitchen with a tray on which reposed two glasses of Orange Crush and a small plate of cheese biscuits. She put the tray down on a small table at Anupam's elbow, and began to dust Herbert's grandfather clock with a checked cotton duster. She then began to dust and polish the chair beside it.

Anupam turned a page.

When in disgrace with fortune and men's eyes
I all alone beweep my outcast state,
And trouble deaf heaven with my bootless cries,
And look upon myself and curse my fate,
Wishing me like to one more rich in hope,
Featur'd like him, like him with friends possessed—

'How beautifully you read poetry!' Latha said.

She meant it. Anupam read with such deep feeling that she could, she thought, have listened to him for ever. The unselfconscious admiration in her voice made the young man glow with pleasure.

'How beautifully you listen!' he replied.

He was tempted to read another sonnet aloud to her, but thought better of it. She was leaving for Peradeniya in three days' time, and the task on which they were engaged had to be completed before she left. He was glad he had had those second thoughts when Latha added:

'The trouble with a job like this one is that it's such a temptation to . . . to stop doing it and read the books instead. Don't you think so?'

Anupam took the hint, closed the *Sonnets*, and put the book back on the shelf. Podina, having thoroughly dusted every piece of furniture in the room, and finding no further excuse to linger, returned to the kitchen.

'That is such a sweet-faced young gentleman,' she told Soma. 'It's sinful, *aney*, to see how our Latha baba orders him about. He does just what she says. She told him to stop talking and stack the books, and he did it right away . . .'

'What was he talking about?' Soma asked quickly.

'Just books, lady,' said Podina. 'Fancy that! So much talk, and only about books!'

2

MR FIX-IT

'I really do think, Miss, that you've got the wrong man,' Herbert Wijesinha said, retreating from the earnest gaze of the journalist who sat before him, her pencil poised and her note pad at the ready. 'It's my cousin, Mr Rowland Wijesinha, who can give you the information you need. He's the politician in the family.'

'But, sir, you're the person who's writing the book!' said the journalist.

She was on her first assignment for her newspaper, and was determined to make a success of it.

'Book? I'm not writing any book,' said Herbert. 'Where ever did you hear of such a thing?'

The journalist checked her notes.

'A Mr Munasinghe told us, sir, that you know more about current affairs in Sri Lanka than any other person in the country, and that you base your knowledge on years of experience. He told us that you have kept *detailed records*.'

Herbert smiled.

'If your Mr Munasinghe is the person I think he is,' Herbert said, 'he's a diplomat. Which means that it's his job to say nice things about everyone. I'm not writing a book, I'm just scribbling notes about my experiences in Government service. It's a way of passing the time. There must be any number of people like me – dinosaurs – who are doing the same thing. Believe me, Miss, I'm nobody special.'

The journalist was disappointed.

'You see, sir, we can always interview politicians. As a matter of fact, their secretaries are always ringing my editor up, announcing press conferences they want him to attend, and ceremonies at which they are scheduled to give speeches that they want reported. But Mr Munasinghe told us that you were different, that you have information no one else has, and he advised me, if I possibly could, to meet *you*.'

'*Kindly tell your friend Mr Incomparable* [wrote Herbert in his next letter to Latha] *that when I next meet him, I'll have something to say to him.*'

But he did not deny, to himself at least, that the journalist's visit and Anupam's praise of his political acumen had pleased him. He went into his library, and surveyed with satisfaction the scores of manila folders, each neatly labelled, that lay on his shelves. One day, he said to himself, yes, I *will* write that book . . . At the moment, however, there were other things on his mind. He was expecting a visit from Sujit Roy at four o'clock that afternoon, having chosen a time when he was certain that Soma would be out, visiting one of her sisters.

Safer that way.

Ever since Latha had mentioned Roy's request to her father, Herbert had made it his business to find out as much as he could about the person he thought of privately as Tsunami's *burra sahib*. According to Latha, the man he was about to interview was the only son of a wealthy business family in Bombay. Which translates, thought Herbert, who had observed the success of Indian entrepreneurs in Ceylon, as a warning to us all: Here is a lad who is used to getting his own way! But it seemed that Roy was prepared, too, to work hard for his achievements. Herbert had heard a fair amount about the success of Roy's boat-building venture from a card-playing crony who liked to spend his weekends boating on Bolgoda Lake. He had found out the address of the company's Colombo office, had had one of his friends pay it a discreet visit, and had taken note, not without a small twinge of envy, of the splendid car that Roy drove around town. Obviously, Herbert concluded, there was no shortage of funds there!

Nor, it seemed, did Roy lack supporters. The Munasinghe family, he'd heard, had done a lot for him. The general consensus among Herbert's friends at the Orient Club was that Roy, in addition to being a good sportsman, was a good sport: he was pleasantly spoken, unpretentious in spite of his wealth, and prompt in paying his Club bills.

So far, so good. Surprising, though, that with all these advantages, some enterprising mamma in India hadn't captured him yet for her daughter. Herbert wondered why: Roy's personal background was something, he decided, that he would have to bring up in the course of their interview. He wasn't looking forward to it, a man's private life was his own affair. But Herbert wasn't going to be a party to letting Tsunami suffer a second disappointment. It was hard enough that the child's first love had been sent packing by that bitch Moira, but a philandering husband would be the last straw . . .

The latch on the front gate clicked, and Sujit Roy came walking up the drive. He had evidently left his car on the street outside. Herbert looked at his watch. Four o'clock, on the dot. He rose to greet his visitor, and offered him a chair on the veranda.

'Cooler out here,' he said. 'Like a beer?'

Sujit had brought a briefcase with him, which he placed on the little stool beside his chair. Unlike many businessmen Herbert had encountered in the course of a long career in the Customs, who were inclined to spend a long time discussing quite unrelated matters before taking up the problem that had brought them to him in the first place, he wasted no time on polite preliminaries.

'I want to thank you for seeing me, Mr Wijesinha, and I hope I won't take up too much of your time.'

'Not at all, don't give it another thought,' said Herbert, who had nothing more weighty on his evening's programme than a book he had bought at Cave's that morning. 'I'm no professional marriage broker,' he added, 'but it's a pleasure for me to do anything I can for Helen and Rowland's children.'

He looked with some trepidation at Sujit's briefcase, from which its owner had begun to extract several files and folders.

'I've never done this kind of thing before, sir, and I wasn't sure what you'd want to know. But I thought you would definitely need some information about my business prospects, so I've brought you the lot. Company records, completed projects, plans in progress . . . You don't have to return them, by the way, you can go through them at your leisure.'

'Thanks,' Herbert said, and meant it. The papers, as Sujit removed them from his briefcase, looked like a formidable pile.

'These are copies that I had specially made for you. And for Tsunami's father.'

Well, Rowland's name and Tsunami's had now been mentioned. Taking his cue, Herbert stepped into the opening provided.

'Have you ever met my cousin Rowland Wijesinha?'

'No. But as soon as I hear from you that you approve of what you've read, and that you've passed the papers on to Mr Wijesinha, I'll make an appointment to see him.'

He's got it all planned, down to the last detail.

'I hope you will speak for me, sir. Latha encouraged me to hope that you might.'

This is moving too fast for me. Time to bowl him a googly.

'What can you tell me about yourself, Mr Roy, apart from details about your business? You have, if I may say so, a very impressive personality. My niece is notoriously hard to please, and I imagine from the fact that she's consented to marry you, that you can be very attractive to women. So I owe it to her to ask you frankly: do you think you have it in you to make Tsunami a faithful husband?'

Let's see how he deals with that one!

Sujit hesitated a moment before he spoke.

'I'm twenty-nine, Mr Wijesinha, and I've been around. Cambridge provided many opportunities, and I won't deny that I took up a good many of them. But I can assure you that Tsunami is the only woman in my life, and I can promise you on my honour that she always will be.'

'An honest answer,' Herbert said. 'Thank you. If you had not been able to give me that frank assurance, I can tell you, just as frankly, that our conversation would have ended right here. May I ask how much she has told you about her family?'

'Not very much. She seems very reticent about her parents.'

Herbert nodded.

'That figures,' he said.

'But there's a biography of the Minister, which I've read. I know her brother Christopher quite well . . . and, of course, the family itself is very well known. People talk about them a lot in Colombo.'

'Yes, I suppose they do,' Herbert said. 'Well, I have another question for you, Sujit. From what you've heard and read about the Wijesinhas, do you think you'll fit in?'

'I don't see why not, sir. Mine is not an ancient family, but Tsunami's brothers and I have a lot in common, education, sport, and so on. And no one can possibly say that I have my eye on a dowry. As those papers will show you, I have more than enough money of my own. Tsunami will want for nothing, when she marries me.'

'*When*', Herbert thought: not '*if*'. He had never before encountered such confidence in a young man. He found himself wishing that he'd had half Sujit Roy's assurance when he was courting Soma. His father-in-law, now in his eighties and in excellent health, still had the power to terrorize his large family. There were times, Herbert thought, when Soma reminded him very much of her father . . .

'Mr Wijesinha, may I ask you a question?'

'Certainly.'

'I would really like to know a little more than I do now about Tsunami's mother. Part of my interest is that Mrs Wijesinha apparently came to this country from an Indian family, possibly one quite like mine. That doesn't often happen, does it, in Ceylon? Yet the Minister's biography doesn't even mention his first wife's name. And of their five children, only one is in touch with her: and that one is Christopher, not Tsunami. I don't want to know what Mrs Wijesinha did that has made everyone shut her out—'

'You wouldn't need to dig very deeply if you did,' Herbert replied dryly. 'It's common knowledge that Helen Wijesinha left her husband and eloped with a European Visiting Agent.'

'Yes, I've heard the story,' Sujit said. 'But I've heard it in various versions, very few of which are complimentary to her. I am not a fool, and I know enough of life to guess that there's more to it than that Mrs Wijesinha was promiscuous, or acted on impulse. Or even that it was a grand passion. Why she did it doesn't matter a jot to me. I have also heard Mrs Wijesinha described, by a friend who knew her well, as an admirable, very gentle lady. I understand from Chris and Latha that Tsunami resembles her mother in appearance (while her elder sister Tara doesn't), but I want to know whether Tsunami resembles Mrs Wijesinha in other ways. In other words, I want to know what she is really *like*. Latha says that if anyone could tell me that, it would be you.'

Herbert took a deep breath.

'Helen Ratnam . . .' he began.

The wall-clock in the dining room had struck seven, and the day-time traffic on the main street had stopped before Herbert became aware that darkness had fallen. Soma would be back soon, she was probably on her way home already. He got to his feet, and switched on the veranda light.

'Thank you very much, sir,' Roy said. He placed the papers he had brought on the veranda table, beside their empty glasses. 'I appreciate your frankness.'

'A pleasure,' Herbert replied laconically. 'You wanted information on a favourite subject.'

'Soma,' he said, later that evening, 'do you remember that character at Tara's wedding whom everyone called "Uncle Eric"? Natty grey suit and a white flower in his button-hole? Do we have an address for him?'

'No,' said Soma, 'but I know where he can be contacted. At the Pagoda Tea Rooms in the Fort. Why, Herbie? What do you want "Uncle Eric" for?'

'Remind me to telephone him at the Pagoda tomorrow, and ask him for some tips.'

'*Tips?*' Soma asked. 'What for? Are we giving a party?'

'I need to brush up on my technique. What with people descending on me in droves, seeking information and assistance, it seems, my dear, that your husband has become the new Mr Fix-It of Colombo.'

3

CHRIS AND TSUNAMI

'I don't want to meet her,' Tsunami said. 'You seem to have forgotten that she cheated on Pater, but *I* haven't forgotten it. She let Pater down. She deserted him, and she deserted us. She and I have nothing to say to each other.'

'There may not be another opportunity like this for a long time, sis. She's on her way to visit her family in Delhi, and they're not coming back this way.'

'Oh, so he's with her, is he?'

'Of course he is. He considers himself responsible for her, he wouldn't let her make that long journey on her own, any more than Roy would—'

'Does she know that Pater is in the middle of a political crisis, and that the last thing he'd want is publicity that rakes up past events? Especially *those* past events! Does she know I've got my Finals in two weeks? Does she *care*?'

'For God's sake, Tsunami, be sensible. Of course she cares. She wouldn't want to meet you if she didn't care. You and Latha. No one else, she told me. Not even Ranil or Tara or Colin. She hasn't come here to embarrass Pater or Auntie Moira, in fact she's done everything she can to make herself totally invisible while she's here. I've arranged a couple of rooms for them in a quiet boarding house down a side street in Wellawatte, where they'll meet nobody they know. She's not interested in shopping or sightseeing, only in meeting you. And they'll be away and gone before you get back to Peradeniya.'

'I just can't see Franz Goldman blending into a Wellawatte landscape,' Tsunami said. 'He'd stick out like a sore thumb.'

'Nothing of the sort. He makes a very passable Australian tourist, in his shorts and socks and dark glasses, with a camera slung round his neck. No solar topee now, of course, he wears a cloth sun hat. But he hasn't changed much, and neither has she. You'd enjoy seeing them both again, you know.'

'I wouldn't bet on it,' Tsunami said.

After a short while, she placed her hand on her brother's arm, and pressed it.

'I appreciate what you're trying to do, Chris. But it won't work, it just won't work.'

Chris heard the catch in her voice. He returned her pressure on his arm, and said nothing.

'What does she want to talk to me about? Marriage? She's hardly the person to give anyone advice on *that* subject! In any case, she'll be wasting her time. I'm not at all sure I *want* to get married.'

'What's the matter? Cold feet? They *are* apt to become a bit chilled when you're "standing with reluctant feet, where the brook and river meet", or so I'm told. It's a passing phase, it seems, and the tootsies soon thaw out. Or have you changed your mind about your *sahib*?'

'Stop it. Don't turn everything into a joke: it's not a laughing matter. And it's nothing to do with Sujit, at least not yet. It's to do with marriage itself. I'm not sure I want it.'

'Good Lord, Tsunami! This is *not* the impression you've given me. It's certainly not the impression you've given Roy. In fact, unless I'm greatly mistaken, he's already halfway to lodging his claim with Pater . . .'

'I know. I've told him not to.'

'You didn't think he'd take you seriously, did you?'

'Why not?'

'Because, my dear idiot, it doesn't make sense. Anyone can see with half an eye that you're both crazy about each other—'

'That's just the trouble. We're not seeing straight. We haven't really discussed anything yet. He doesn't know anything about us, about *me*. He's just taken everything on trust, and I'll be a big disappointment to him. I know I will.'

'Tsunami,' Chris said patiently, 'Sujit is not a little child. He's been around, he knows the world a great deal better than you do. I can't see anything disappointing him, in fact I can't see anything even *surprising* him! So, come on. What is it? Out with it, Tsunami. What's your dark secret? Share it with me, I won't tell!'

'It's not something I want to talk about, frankly. And believe me, you wouldn't want to know.'

'I *do* want to know,' Chris said stoutly. 'You're obviously in a state about something, and by keeping it to yourself, you're not going to be able to solve it. If it's something you don't want to discuss with me, why not talk it over with Latha?'

'No. She'd tell me not to be silly.'

'Oh, no, she wouldn't. Why don't you try it and see?'

'Chris,' Tsunami said at last, 'I'm so frightened.'

'What of? Getting married? What's there to be frightened of? People get married all the time . . . So they tell me.'

'People like me shouldn't . . . they shouldn't get married.'

'Why not? What do you mean, people like you?'

'People like me and . . . and my mother. Don't you see? Some day I'll do to someone else what . . . what *she* did to Pater. I've done it once already, you know about that, don't you, Chris? What if I do it a second time, supposing I do it to Sujit? I'm no good, you know. I've probably taken after her, thoroughly untrustworthy, thoroughly unreliable. *Like mother, like daughter* – that's what people say, don't they?'

'Who dares to say any such thing?'

Chris, who had never seen Tsunami cry, gazed at her bewildered.

'Everyone. *Everyone* says it.'

Tsunami's shoulders shook with the violence of her sobs.

'People like us shouldn't marry. Anyone who takes us on is asking for trouble.'

'You've got it all wrong, Tsunami,' Chris said at last. 'You're wrong about yourself, and you're wrong about our mother, too. If you've taken after her, you should be proud and happy that you have. Better that than—' he stopped, and produced a handkerchief. 'Here, take this and blow your nose. *Hard.* Now, come on, be sensible. She's here, she wants to see you. Why don't you meet her halfway on this? I'll be there too, if you like. Just get it over. You can work out your personal problems later.'

After a while, Tsunami said: 'Anyway, where do you suggest we meet – if we do meet?'

Chris hesitated.

'Well, that poses something of a problem. I'd thought of asking Uncle Herbert for the loan of his library, but there would be Auntie Soma to contend with. I can't guarantee that she'll be out, and even if she is, that servant of theirs will be sure to tell her when she gets back . . .'

'No, that won't do,' Tsunami said firmly. 'Letting Auntie Soma know anything about it would be like putting a notice in the *Daily News*. What's wrong with the boarding house?'

'It's a bit run down and shabby. Not really our mother's style, Tsunami. Nor yours. I chose it to serve a special purpose – anonymity – and it won't do for a reunion. I had to make a quick decision, and I have. I'm taking my little sister for a drive tomorrow morning. The official story is that we're going down south, for a beach picnic and a swim, to clear the cobwebs before your Finals. How does that sound to you? Convincing enough for Auntie Moira?'

'Lovely, big brother. Don't make it too enticing, though, or she'll want to join us.'

'That's much better,' Chris said. 'I thought for a moment back there that you'd forgotten how to smile.'

'But remember, Chris, I've got to be back by tomorrow night, because

Uncle Herbert's offered to drive Latha and me up to Peradeniya, and we'll need to make an early start.'

'How early?'

'*Very* early. Half past four or earlier, Latha said.'

'Hell!' Chris said. 'I wanted to meet Latha before she left Colombo, and now there may not be time.'

Tsunami was puzzled when an unfamiliar car appeared at the gate the following morning. Her brother opened the door for her.

'What's happened?' she asked him. 'Whose car is this? Why's Alexander driving us? Where are we going?'

'I'll answer those questions in order: my car's not big enough to accommodate us all. This one's been hired for the occasion from a small firm Alexander recommends – it's too small to have the company name on its doors, so it's less conspicuous. Alexander's driving it because he wants to see Mother again, and pay his respects. Also because, by borrowing Alexander, we can all be fairly certain Auntie Moira stays back in Colombo. And I'm taking you to Hambantota, so that you can have a look at Sujit's boatyard. Might as well get to know your own property ahead of the day, don't you think?'

There was a muffled sound from the driver's seat.

'He's a good organizer, your big brother, Tsunami baba,' said Alexander. 'Very bossy today. I'm thinking he wants to get you off his hands as soon as possible. And safely married.'

They had circled the Wellawatte roundabout, and reached the top of Arethusa Lane.

'Does she know about . . . Sujit?'

'Well . . .' Chris hesitated. 'She's had a hint or two from me. I had to tell her *something*, you know. Couldn't let her meet you totally unprepared. Besides—' he said more cheerfully, recovering his composure as the car came to rest before a small front door with the number '57' on it, 'you might both be glad of something to say when you run out of things to talk about.'

Alexander alighted, and pressed the bell. The front door opened almost immediately. He removed his cap, held the car door open, and Helen got in.

Tsunami had often wondered what would happen if she ever met her mother again. Who would speak first? What would she say? What would the answer be? What would happen next? If Mother and I were Europeans, Tsunami thought, we'd kiss. That's what people did in movies, when they were reunited after long separations. All differences melted away in the warmth of that friendly hug she had often witnessed on the screen, and among her parents' Burgher and European friends. When Tsunami had been a child, kissing had been a natural thing to do within the family.

But after her mother went away and her father remarried, it was as if a high wall had been erected between herself and everyone else in the universe. Tsunami sometimes wondered why this should have happened, and why the wall should be so difficult to climb over.

Helen Wijesinha's children had speculated endlessly about the circumstances of their mother's departure, each of them following a different line of thought.

Had their mother loved Franz Goldman better than she loved Pater? (Colin) What could have made her so unhappy that she'd had to leave the family? (Chris) It must have been brought on by something they'd done, mustn't it? (Tsunami) Could life with Franz Goldman possibly compensate for everything their mother would lose as Rowland Wijesinha's wife? (Tara) Did she not feel shame or guilt at having betrayed her husband? (Ranil) They all knew that their discussions had only skimmed the surface of things, but at least they had been able to open up to one another, and discuss what was in their minds.

As the years passed, and life brought Helen's children other things to think about, these discussions had gradually petered out, and had finally stopped. Ranil was preparing to succeed his father as a man of property, Tara's young family claimed her attention, Colin and Chris were finding their way through school and University, and Rowland himself had entered politics, encouraged and supported by his new wife. Helen and her elopement seemed to have faded from the memories of all her children except two. Christopher, studying in Australia, had sought Helen and Franz Goldman out in their self-imposed exile, and obtained answers to some of his questions, although what those answers had been he did not seem to think it necessary to say. Tsunami's anger, unappeased by the small victories that were occasionally won at school and University by her wit and her sharp tongue, appeared to have gone underground. Her feelings were still in turmoil, and all too frequently they left a trail of destruction in their wake.

There existed an issue between Helen and her youngest child which Tsunami could not bring herself to discuss with others, not even with Latha or Chris. An envelope addressed to her had been on the letter-board outside the Hall refectory on the afternoon of her last birthday, and Tsunami, taking it in to lunch with her, had opened it at the table, and read the card it contained. The refectory had been rapidly filling up with students on their way to afternoon lectures, and Latha had been opening her own mail.

> *Don't think your silly airs and graces & your familys lies has fooled anybody* [the card had begun, wasting no time or space on polite preliminaries]. *Your mother is nothing more than a shameless adultress Tamil bitch, and your so-called 'father' is a fool.*

She left this Cuntry because he bribed her to go. He could not put up with the disgrase. It is a Good Thing that she has left Ceylon with her German boy-frend because we dont want peple like that here. Like mother like daughter. You better get your Indian boyfriend to take you back to India with him. That is where you belong, or in some other foren cuntry. There is no plase for you hear.

Tsunami's impulse at first glance had been to tear the spiteful, ill-spelled thing to pieces, and scatter the fragments on the refectory floor, but she had not done so. Instead, conscious that her every action was quite probably being covertly watched by the sender of the message, she had resisted the temptation to search the crowded tables for the culprit. Taking her cue from her father's admirable restraint all those years ago, she had given nothing away. Later, she had carefully hidden the card where no one could find it.

Later still, she had asked herself whether the sender of the card could be someone known to her or known to her family. The spelling suggested a writer whose first language was not English. But then, Tsunami reminded herself, recalling the detective novels she had pored over in the library at Lucas Falls, a poor education could always be simulated by a clever writer with malice or murder in his heart. But *was* the message a malicious lie? Her heart turned over at the thought that it might be based on fact.

She searched her memories of Helen and of Franz Goldman for give-away signs of an illicit relationship. Failing to find any, she fell next to scrutinizing her own reflection in the mirror. As a child, Tsunami had been fond of Franz Goldman, whose genial personality had created some of the happiest moments of her life at Lucas Falls. The anonymous card caused her to fear him now as a spectre who might spring out at her at any moment from its hiding place in the features of her own face. She looked for a photograph of Goldman in the family album, and found a snapshot taken by Chris of a picnic at the Falls in which the Visiting Agent was included. This she brought up with her to Peradeniya, and obsessively searched Goldman's cheerful face for tell-tale similarities with her own.

People often said that Ranil, Tara and Chris, with their height and their impressive, dark good looks, took after their father's side of the family. Colin and Tsunami, on the other hand, were thought to resemble their mother. But was there some feature of her appearance that she did not share with Colin? Something foreign and elusive that she could not herself perceive, but which proclaimed itself to others?

The anonymous card achieved, in fact, what all such malicious acts are intended to achieve: it threw its receiver into a fever of emotional anguish. Tsunami began to mull ceaselessly over the past, seeing it as a region scarred with pits and chasms, the largest and most menacing of which was a suspicion (later growing into a sorrowful conviction) that beneath the calm of the happy family life they had all taken for granted, there had been an absence of love. Some day, Tsunami had told herself, she would find out the truth about her own identity. She would not *seek* an opportunity to do so, but if one came her way she would not avoid it.

As for the elopement, if ever it chanced that she should meet Helen or Franz Goldman again, she would extract an explanation. (It was not, after all, *her* responsibility to explain or offer excuses, it was theirs.) She would not reproach her mother on her own or her siblings' behalf.

And on no account would she cry.

To do any of those things would show that she had been deeply hurt. She was grown up now, and grown-ups do not indulge in tantrums and recriminations. She would be courteous and polite. Above all, she would be *distant.*

In keeping with these sensible resolutions, Tsunami regarded with an air of cool indifference the elegant stranger who placed a hand over hers on the leather seat of the car.

'So I suppose it's true,' she said with a casual shrug, 'that Franz Goldman is my father?'

4

HELEN AND TSUNAMI

Whatever Helen had expected from her daughter she had not expected this. She was shaken, but she remained calm.

'No,' she replied. 'It is *not* true. And I am not his wife.'

Later, she would remember vividly the passion with which her daughter, cradled in her arms, had given way at last to the pent-up feelings of years. In front of them, Alexander sat steady as a rock, his eyes fixed on the road ahead, as Helen recognized in the adult Tsunami her own vanished self, the artist of extraordinary gifts who had disappeared by stages during her life in Ceylon. When she first heard from Chris of Daniel Rajaratnam's courtship of her daughter, Helen had marvelled at the boldness with which Tsunami had defied her family's expectations. She knew that she herself could never have engaged so fearlessly in a confrontation of which she could not know the outcome. Brought up to defer submissively to the opinions and wishes of others, Helen had given way throughout her life: first to the rule of her parents, then to that of her mother-in-law, and finally to that of her husband, until it had at last been brought home to her that only in escape lay her own survival.

Not that any of these people who laid down the rules by which she lived her life had meant to be repressive or would ever admit to having been so. Helen often reminded herself that her parents had wished only for her happiness, that her mother-in-law wanted only that she should be happy in her new life, that even Rowland (despite all evidence to the contrary) loved and needed her. But it was not long before memories of actual scenes she had shared with these several persons, and words that had passed between them and herself, edged their way to the forefront of her consciousness. She had attempted to retreat from her disappointment in her marriage into the companionship of her children and the management of her household. This, she understood from the confidences of her friends, was what all married women did if they were too young to find consolation in playing bridge or mahjong at the Women's International Club, or too old to seek it in a love affair. Helen, whose mind was not focused on men or on mahjong, could not find such consolation.

But she could have borne it all, she thought, had it not become clear to her that her husband's personality was changing. What had happened, she asked herself sometimes, to Rowland's intelligence? To his quick wit, which had been so much a part of the personality that had attracted her when they first met? To his ability to think for himself? The country had begun to move towards an insular nationalism, and it disturbed Helen to see how eagerly her husband identified with it. Rowland's entry into national politics relegated his Indian wife to the position of an outsider. He was surrounded by flatterers; and the more they flattered him, the more it pained Helen to observe how readily he accepted their opinions as a national norm, and submitted to the claims they made on him. At last she could hardly recognize the man she had married in the pompous, self-opinionated bore who dominated her life.

The friendship of Franz Goldman, which had at first been rather like a still oasis in a desert of isolation and loneliness, a source of quiet refreshment, quite suddenly changed its character. There came a day when, during a loudly political luncheon at which Franz had been present, Rowland's casual dismissal of his wife and his patronizing allusions to what he called her 'political naïveté' had been harder to bear than usual. A half-hour after her husband's associates had left the house, Helen retreated with relief to the veranda, and to a canvas that was still on her easel, of a picture of figures in a landscape that she had half completed a fortnight earlier. It was a recreation in oils of a childhood memory she treasured: a riverside picnic with her sisters. Seeking distraction from her melancholy thoughts in a landscape distanced from her in time, Helen examined what she had accomplished so far. Satisfied, she picked up her brush and her palette and prepared to take her composition further.

So absorbed had she been in her thoughts and her painting that Helen had not been aware that she was being observed until, from his chair in the Lucas Falls veranda, watching her as she painted, Franz had said, in words that had eerily echoed her own thoughts at that precise moment:

'Why don't you leave him, Helen?'

Startled into almost dropping her paintbrush, Helen had doubted at first whether she had heard him correctly.

'I can help you do it,' he had added. 'If you will let me.'

Helen could hardly believe that someone had perceived her unhappiness without condemning her for it. She might have responded to him immediately, then and there. But Tsunami and Latha had come in laughing from the garden, with a basket full of antigonon buds they wanted to make into necklaces for the princess in a play that Tsunami was writing, and the moment for confidences was over.

A few days later Helen received a declaration: not so much of love as of loyalty.

'I know you do not love me,' Franz said to her, 'but it does not matter. I have observed you, Helen, for many months now, even years – indeed, it would surprise you to know how long I have been watching you with pity, as you drag out your existence here! Do you know of what you remind me? Something I once heard said by an actor in a stage play: "Oh! How many torments lie in the small circle of a wedding-ring!" Well? Is it not true? I know that for you what was once a happy home has turned into a Belsen.'

The comparison had shocked her.

'Please don't exaggerate, Franz. It is nothing of the sort.'

'Is it not? The prisoner in chains, the routine labour, the limited view, the mental torture, the lack of hope, the daily humiliations, the loss of freedom. Are not these the features of the concentration camp? It is true that the warder in your case is guilty not of sadism but of crass stupidity. He is insensitive, not cruel. But, much as I used to like your husband, I do not think him capable of change. No two words about it, ma'am, you will have to make a break for it.'

This sounded so much like one of Franz Goldman's jokes that Helen did not take him seriously until he added:

'And let me tell you this: you will never escape if I do not arrange it for you. Rebellion is not in your nature.'

'How can I agree to this?' she had asked him then. 'They'll never keep you on at Rothschild's.'

'Of course. I know it. I would have crossed the line so clearly marked "No Trespassing", eh? But I will be all right. The world is a large place. There are other things that I can do besides planting tea.'

After a slight pause Franz had added:

'But for you it is different. If *you* leave your marriage and your family, you will need a man beside you. This country is not kind to single women.'

Very soon afterwards, the decision had been made. Franz Goldman gave notice to Rothschild's that he was going home to Australia on six months' leave. His travel plans were finalized, his passage (on the P&O liner, S.S. *Stratheden*) reserved. One November evening, while at dinner with the Wijesinha family, he announced that he would be driving to Colombo the day after tomorrow, and leaving for Perth on the following day. Helen had looked up and, over the arrangement of carnations and ferns on the dining table, she had met his eyes. A day later, very early in the morning, he drove up to the gates of Lucas Falls in his big Humber, and found her waiting for him.

Seeing the hurt Tsunami had tried so hard to hide, Helen realized how naïve she had been, to regard the act of leaving Rowland as a private and personal decision involving no one but herself.

Naïve? I was unforgivably selfish.

What had been her excuse? That she would not be missed by a husband for whom she had ceased to be important. Rowland, she had told herself, hardly noticed whether she was there or not – unless, that is, she had done something which irritated or annoyed him. His attention had shifted to the advancement of his political career.

Helen had known that her departure would arouse a good deal of gossip in Rowland's family for a while, but, forgetting the nature of the society into which she had married, she had believed that time would put everything to rights again. She had not realized the intensity of the sorrow and bewilderment it would cause her children.

The boatyard, when they reached it, was humming with activity, and the sound of saws and machinery provided some distraction for them both. Its owner was nowhere to be seen, but Chris introduced his mother and his sister to Sujit's foreman, who took them on a tour of the building. Mr Roy's orders were that lunch was to be served out of doors, the foreman said. Everything was ready. The visitors had only to give the word.

'Where's Chris disappeared to?' Tsunami asked. 'He's supposed to be organizing this picnic.'

'He told me he had a couple of telephone calls to make,' said Helen. 'He asked us to begin without him.'

'A good example of his elephantine tact,' Tsunami said. 'Leaving us together to talk things through . . . What's happened to the butter?'

'Here it is, hiding beneath the bread rolls.'

'A far cry from our picnics by the Falls. Do you remember those picnics, and how Chris and Ranil used to wolf down most of Vaithi's *lamprais*?'

'Young men's appetites,' Helen said; and added, *apropos*, it seemed, of nothing in particular, 'Chris tells me you are thinking of getting married. To the young man who owns this boatyard. Such an interesting place – so much activity! Is he really from India, Tsunami?'

'He is.'

'I would like to have met him, but I don't think there will be time. Does your father approve?'

'He hasn't been told of it yet. But I'm very much afraid he won't. And what you have just told me convinces me of that.'

'What will you do if he doesn't approve?'

'Frankly, I don't know. But then, I don't even know whether I want to get married at all. Fancy becoming another Tara! I don't think I could bear it.'

'Be careful what you do with your life, my darling Tsunami. It's too precious to waste.'

'There seem to be so many traps along the way,' Tsunami said. 'If other people don't make them for us, we seem to lay them for ourselves. Isn't that true?'

'It must look like that to you. But many people make happy marriages. I'm sorry that my experience with your father hasn't been a very good advertisement for marriage.'

'Not encouraging, perhaps, but then, maybe not everyone changes as Pater has done. We were all there while it was happening, but we didn't *see*, we didn't realize what it meant for you.' She paused, and added: 'At least, I didn't, but I think Latha did, though she didn't say anything. And the outcome has been a good one, hasn't it? You seem so happy now.'

'I *am* happy. Or, so as not to tempt the gods, let us say that I am as happy as anyone can hope to be in this imperfect world. I'm painting again, you know, Tsunami! In a small way, of course. I joined an artists' group soon after I settled in Sydney, and once I'd regained confidence and produced a respectable body of work, Franz arranged for an exhibition of my work at a Balmain art gallery. That went very well, there were enthusiastic reviews – and every painting sold! And now there's another exhibition coming up, this time in Melbourne.'

'And Mr Goldman? Is *he* happy?'

'I think so,' Helen said. 'I hope so. And both he and I would be so pleased if you'd call him Franz, Tsunami. He's . . . an old friend of yours, after all.'

'I know. I seem to have wasted a lot of time hating him for taking you away from us.'

Helen laughed, then grew serious as she remembered the words on the anonymous card that Tsunami had described to her.

'Tell me frankly, Tsunami – did you believe what that card-writer said of me?'

'When I saw Pater described in that card as "your so-called father", it was a terrible shock. I didn't know what to believe. It could so easily have been true, you see. For if life turns out so badly that it can't be borne any longer, it would be natural, wouldn't it, to look elsewhere? But that's my adult reaction. When I was little, I thought we'd done something so wicked or hurtful that you didn't want us any more.'

'It is a great relief to me to have met you,' said Helen. 'I'm very grateful to Chris for having arranged it.'

The sun was high in the sky, and Helen suggested that they should go indoors, to the cool shade of the boatyard, where work had ceased while the midday meal was in progress.

After a silence that lasted some time, Tsunami said:

'What about your meeting with Latha, Mother?'

'I believe Chris is arranging something for me there, too. He tells me it can be done, if he takes me back to Colombo immediately, and we don't linger on the way.'

'Aren't we returning together?' Tsunami asked in surprise.

'I don't think so . . .'

'Here comes your transport, Tsunami,' Chris called, as Sujit Roy's Opel rounded the corner of the road and pulled up before the boatyard gates. Chris went up to the car, and shook hands with the driver.

'Good timing, Sujit. You must have driven like the wind.'

Chris always had such a sense of the dramatic! Helen thought, as the two young men began to walk towards her.

Roy looked up. Seeing Helen for the first time, he brought his hands together in *namaskaram*.

'Well, that was a bit rushed,' Sujit said, as the hired car disappeared from sight with Alexander at the wheel. 'But adequate. I must say I give Chris top marks for organization, Tsunami. Your brother's wasting his talents running a laboratory, he should be running the country.'

'Can I ask you what you think of my mother?'

'What can I say, based on a half-hour's acquaintance, that would be worth listening to? I'd heard quite a lot about her—'

'From whom?'

'From your Uncle Herbert, Latha's father: I gather he's a great fan of your mother's. And I was prepared to be totally bowled over by her, of course, having first met you.'

'Be serious, Sujit. It means a lot to me that you should get on with her.'

'Why?'

'Because you may not like my father very much. You have to get on with at least *one* of my parents, haven't you?'

'Well, it would be a good thing to get on with both of them, if that were humanly possible. But if it isn't, it isn't. There's no *have* to about it, dearest. However, since you want so earnestly to know my thoughts on the subject, they are as follows. First. Your mother is, bar one, the most delightful woman I have ever met. Second. She showed great good sense in choosing you as a daughter. Third. Your father did not, I regret to say, show equally good sense when he allowed her to leave him. You may be absolutely certain that I, since I am a *very* sensible person, will never permit *you* to leave *me*. Fourth. Mr Goldman is fortunate to have the honour of being your mother's friend. Fifth. Despite all the horror stories I've been told about bossy mothers-in-law, I shall have no objection to your mother visiting us, with or without Mr Goldman, after we are married. That enough for you?'

'Yes. For the present.'

They drove on in silence for a few minutes before Sujit asked:

'What's the matter?'

'Nothing, really.'

He drew up at the side of the road and, picking up the hands that were lying idly in Tsunami's lap, he turned them upwards and kissed their palms, one after the other.

'Is it because I mentioned getting married?'

'Yes. No. I was thinking of Franz and my mother. I saw her for the first time today as he must have seen her for so many years at Lucas Falls. She was in enemy hands, Sujit, just as he'd been once, as a child in Hamburg. No wonder he felt compassion for her.'

'Well, you know now that he's a good man besides being a lucky one.'

Sujit let in the clutch, and the car purred into motion once again.

'But the question presently before this committee doesn't concern Mr Goldman. The question is: What is to be done about *you*?'

'About me?'

'Too many tears in your beautiful eyes, Tsunami. Something must be done to get rid of them. It's been a specially happy day for you, and it calls for a special celebration. What shall it be? Name it. Your every wish is my command.'

Receiving no reply, he continued undeterred:

'Thanks to your brother's excellent management, we have a whole evening before us, and seventy miles of long, straight road. This, you will admit, is a rare occurrence in a comparatively small country, and it shouldn't be wasted . . . Especially when we have a chariot like this one to ride in . . .'

Silence.

'You're depriving me, you know, of the greatest joy in life.'

'What's that?'

'Riding in a fast car with a pretty woman.'

'What nonsense!'

'Nonsense? Watch your language, girl. No less a man than Dr Johnson said that.'

'I don't believe you. How could he possibly have—'

'Well,' Sujit conceded. 'He didn't actually mention a *car*. In his time it was a post-chaise. I have it! Why don't I give you your first driving lesson? I will, of course, make sure that you arrive home safely at the end of it. What about it? Are you ready to change places with me, and take the wheel?'

Tsunami said nothing.

'No? What a pity. There's a superb new 1,488cc engine turning over so sweetly in here – you'd have loved it. I do. Never mind, you can play with it another time. Straight on to Colombo, then?'

A sparkling vision of blue-green ocean and windswept palms slid past.

'Or, on the other hand . . .'

Sujit suddenly swung the steering wheel to a forty-five degree angle, bringing the car to a standstill facing the waves. Slipping the gears into neutral, he gently released the brake. The Opel moved smoothly forward until Tsunami heard the crunch of sea sand beneath its tyres.

'This looks like a good spot,' Sujit said, and turning to his companion, he placed her hands on his shoulders and tilted her face to his. 'With scenic effects specially laid on – a blue sea, golden palms, and a glorious sunset that's due to switch itself on—' he glanced at his wrist-watch – 'in precisely twenty minutes. What more can one ask?'

'I love you, Sujit.'

'There's a fisherman's hut at the far end of the beach, with a catamaran moored beside it. But apart from that, we seem to be on our own, with no distractions of any kind. By far the best way to be, I'm sure you'll agree . . . What, for heaven's sake, are all these buttons and ribbons for? . . . There, that's better.'

'I love you.'

'Very noisy, these waves pounding on the sand. I didn't quite catch what you said.'

'I love you.'

'Yes, that's what I thought you said. Could you keep on saying it, please? I find it very inspiring.'

5

FINAL EXAMINATIONS

At half past four on a Monday morning, Latha and Tsunami left Colombo on what was to be the last trip to Peradeniya they would ever make as university undergraduates.

'But will you be able to get us there in time, Thaththi?' Latha had asked when Herbert offered to drive them up. 'We must be in the Hall before the bell rings. It's a *rule*.'

She isn't usually as edgy as this.

Herbert picked up Latha's bag and Tsunami's and put them in the car.

'Of course you'll be there in time,' he said. 'Trust me.'

Podina appeared in the veranda, yawning, with a thermos flask in each hand, and stood beside Soma on the steps to wave them on their way.

'Now I want you to be very, very careful,' Soma Wijesinha had instructed her daughter. 'Keep an eye on your father all the way, and watch for the moment when he starts stroking his hair back from his forehead. That's a sure sign that he's getting sleepy. Then, Latha, make sure he stops the car immediately, and make him drink a cup of coffee before he starts driving again.'

Tsunami had curled up on the back seat of the car, her head pillowed on a cushion that Soma had thoughtfully provided. She seemed to be asleep. Latha, from whose eyes sleep had been effectively driven by her mother's instructions, sat bolt upright beside Herbert, making sure that his hands were steady on the steering wheel, and watching the road ahead for oncoming traffic. She was relieved to see that there weren't many vehicles on the Kandy road at that early hour, just the occasional lorry laden with sacks of grain, fruit or vegetables, bound for the markets in Colombo.

They drove through silent villages, which showed no sign of life beyond an occasional green glint as Herbert's headlights picked up the half-open eye of a stray dog sleeping by the roadside. It was still dark when Latha said:

'Thaththi, I think it's time you had a break, and we had a cup of coffee all round. What about it, Tsunami? Would you like some coffee?'

There was no reply. Tsunami was fast asleep. Herbert pulled up at the side of the road and got out of the car to stretch his legs, while Latha unscrewed the cap of a thermos flask. The coffee was hot and milky, and tasted of cinnamon.

'Just the way I like it,' Herbert said, and asked for a second cup.

Dawn was breaking as they drove in to Ambēpussa, the mid-point of the journey to Kandy and Peradeniya. Just as Herbert prepared to make the ascent to the Rest House, a soft voice spoke in Sinhala from the back seat of the car.

'We can get off here, sir, thank you.'

Surprised, Herbert stopped the car with a jerk, and he and Latha turned around, to find two diminutive boys in blue shorts and white shirts, with satchels on their shoulders and a small plastic drink-bottle strung on a cord around each neck, seated quietly on the seat beside the sleeping Tsunami. One of the boys opened the car door, and they jumped down into the road.

'Thank you, sir, thank you, madam,' they said in unison, and took off in the direction of a school-house that Latha now saw for the first time through a slight early-morning scattering of dew.

'Where did they spring from?' Herbert asked.

'They must have got in when we stopped back there for coffee,' Latha said. 'They must have thought we were offering them a ride.'

'Resourceful types,' was Herbert's only comment.

Well, they're going to need all the resources they can muster, poised as they are on the very brink of the precipice of higher education . . .

'Any coffee left?'

It was Tsunami, waking up and looking around. She had not noticed the two children who had soundlessly kept her company in the back seat for five miles of winding road.

'Coffee? We can do better than coffee,' said Herbert heartily. 'Prepare for a feast of *indi-appa*, my children, with a *kiri-hodhi to* make your mouths water, and *pol sambol*, and if we're lucky and that rascal of a Rest House keeper has done his stuff properly, a luscious chicken curry or an *ambul thiyal* . . . Hoy, Appuhami!'

'Sir, sir!' cried the Rest House keeper, flying out to welcome this favourite customer.

'Everything ready?'

'All ready, sir! Just the way you ordered in your telegram.'

It was a quarter to seven when the car began its ascent of Sanghamitta Hill.

'Fifteen minutes to go,' Latha said. 'We'll make it. Thank you, Thaththi.' She did not take the Hall rules lightly, and did not care to give anyone, even her father, the impression that she did.

'Oh, Lord,' Herbert groaned, as a familiar blue bonnet came into view. '*Beware the Jabberwock, my son, The jaws that bite, the claws that catch! Beware the Jub-Jub Bird, and shun The frumious Bandersnatch* . . . Any chance of slipping past her without being seen?'

'Not a hope,' Latha said gloomily, as Lobelia Raptor bobbed up to the car beneath her yellow umbrella.

'Good morning, Mr Wijesinha!' she yodelled cheerily. 'I see you are chaperoning two young ladies!'

'Good morning, Mrs Raptor,' Herbert said.

He courteously lowered the window on his side of the car. Quick-thinking Tsunami had put her head down on her cushion and was feigning sleep, but Latha could not escape the Warden's observant eye. Making a great effort, she managed a polite greeting. It was amazing, she thought, that Mrs Raptor seemed actually delighted to see them. Could she possibly have forgotten all about *L'Affaire Manamperi*?

'You will find your good Warden waiting for you,' Mrs Raptor informed Latha. 'Like me, she is an early riser. Early birds catch all the worms, isn't it!'

She continued on her way down Sanghamitta Hill, and Herbert pulled up at the front steps.

'If your revered Aunt Bertha were here, Latha, she'd tell you that seeing the Jabberwock first thing on a Monday morning will most certainly wreck your luck for the week, and probably send your examination performance down the drain,' he remarked.

'No fear, Mr Wijesinha. It would take more than a sight of Mrs Raptor to rob Latha of her First,' said Sriyani de Alwis, appearing beside the car as the Hall bell began to ring. She had been looking out for them, and now helped with the luggage.

'So, Tsunami! What news?' she asked, as soon as they were on their balcony.

Tsunami, with an effort, recalled those parts of her recent experiences that could bear retelling.

'It was a good party,' she said. 'But the best thing about it was the trip to Colombo. Mr Ganesan turned out to be a great storyteller, he kept us entertained all the way there, and would probably have done the same on the way back if the V.C. hadn't offered him and Mrs Ganesan a ride back to campus.'

'Latha? What about you?'

Latha took a moment to consider.

'I met an old friend,' she said, 'and I made a new one.'

'A boyfriend?'

'No. Sorry to disappoint you! But a really good friend. And I own a library of my very own.'

'Okay. Now, hear *my* news!'

While they had been in Colombo, Sriyani, it seemed, had been getting engaged.

'Well, well, never did I think you'd be the first on our balcony to get engaged and married, Sriyani,' Latha said. 'I thought yours is a life dedicated to athletics.'

'It is! I am! Wait till you hear . . .'

A distant cousin of Sriyani's, whom she had not met since they were both children, had picked up a newspaper one day and, turning first to the Sports Page ('as all right-thinking people do,' Sriyani said), had seen there a press photograph of Sriyani taking the four-hundred-metre hurdles in fine style at the Western Province Athletic Meet. He had immediately telephoned her parents, and requested permission to call on her at Sanghamitta. They were now engaged to be married.

'And that was that?' Latha said, laughing. 'How beautifully simple! So tell us more. I realize he's a sports fan, but there must be more . . .'

'"*A sports fan*"? What are you talking about? Pratap is an *athlete*, my dear child! Putt Shot and Discus Throw. *Great* muscles . . . He's representing Ceylon at the Asian Games in Jakarta next month, and since the exams will be over by then, I shall be there to cheer him on.'

The days slipped by. They were filled with study, study, and nothing but study, Latha lamented to herself, as she moved between her desk in her bedroom and a desk in the University Library, making summaries of lectures, re-reading notes, and checking references. Tsunami took time out from study to play an occasional game of tennis, and appeared to spend a fair amount of time writing letters, but Latha, who had no such pleasant distractions to introduce variety into her day, read until her eyes ached, slept, and read again.

Tsunami and Shirani's first examination and Amali's were scheduled for the morning of the first day of the examinations, Latha's and Sriyani's for the afternoon of the second.

'The exams, Sriyani! Will you be able now to concentrate on the exams?' Tsunami had teased their friend.

'With your combined help, yes,' Sriyani said. 'I've been cramming like crazy while you've been away. And now I have an incentive, you see . . .'

'Getting married, do you mean?'

'Well, yes, that too. But . . . oh, I haven't told you yet, have I? I've been offered the post of Sports and Athletics Director here, right here, if I get through my exams. Brent Leawood is retiring next year.'

Latha spent an evening 'hearing' Sriyani's planned answers, and was happy to congratulate her on her progress.

'Well done, Sriyani! A hundred per cent score on that last question paper! No doubt about it, you'll be fine!'

She was at lunch in the refectory on the first day of the examinations, when Amali appeared beside her in a pitiable state of nerves.

'I don't know what's the matter with me, Latha! I couldn't concentrate on anything I was reading yesterday, *nothing* made sense, I had such a terrible headache that I went to the Warden for help. She gave me two tablets, told me to take them after dinner, and go to bed.'

'Very good advice. It was probably just what you needed, a good night's sleep.'

'But I slept so soundly that I didn't have time to revise *any*thing, and I nearly missed the examination. I got there so late that I got a very nasty look from the invigilator . . .'

'Never mind the invigilator. Did you answer all the questions, Amali? Did you finish the paper?'

'Did I? Yes. Yes, I did. I suppose the *pirith nool* our temple priest gave me to wear during the examinations must have been working to keep evil influences at bay.'

Latha noticed for the first time the strand of white thread tied around Amali's wrist.

'Amma told me it would be sure to protect me. Do you think it did?'

'Of course it did. Why don't you visit the Hindagala Temple and offer some flowers? That will be like saying "thank you", and it'll make you feel settled in your mind. Tomorrow's exam will be just fine, and the next day will be even better than that. Just wait and see if I'm not right.'

The trouble with handing out Oriental Balm to all and sundry, thought Latha, was that she couldn't express to anyone the fears that were clutching at her own heart. She had politely refused her mother's suggestion that she should visit the Gangarāma Temple while she was in Colombo, and hear *pirith* chanted or listen to a sermon from the chief priest, a well-known scholar. No rites and rituals for me, Latha had told herself: if I make it, I'll make it on my own. She hoped now that there had been no 'evil influences' about at the time to overhear that foolhardy resolution.

The next day dawned bright and clear. Alone in the corridor, Latha stepped out on the balcony and tried to give her mind to study, but she found it impossible to concentrate. A One-For-Sorrow landed beside her on the balcony rail, flicked its elegant black and white tail, and hopefully inspected one of Amali's flower pots.

'An early bird in search of its worm,' thought Latha, recalling Mrs Raptor's greeting on Sanghamitta Hill.

Why did it have to be a One-For-Sorrow that I see first thing this morning?

Where, Latha asked herself moodily, was that magpie's partner, who could have made it Two-For-Joy? Nature itself seemed to be conspiring against her by sending inauspicious omens along to depress and plague her.

So foul and fair a day I have not seen . . .

She panicked immediately, remembering reading somewhere that English actors avoid quoting *Macbeth* before a theatre performance for fear of bad luck. What had brought those doom-laden lines into her head?

The bell rang announcing lunch. Latha did not feel like eating anything, but she went to the refectory, sat down at one of the long tables, and forced herself to eat a spoonful of country rice and dhall. Nothing seemed to have any taste.

'Well,' Tsunami said, coming into the refectory with Shirani, 'we've survived the first onslaught. Your turn this afternoon, I think?'

Latha nodded. She filled her glass with water, and drank it.

'Any letters?'

'I didn't check.'

Shirani went away, and returned with a sheaf of letters in her hand.

'One for me, and one for Tsunami, and four for you, you lucky thing! People wishing us luck, no doubt.'

She was ripping an envelope open as she spoke.

'I know mine won't be from Sujit,' Tsunami said. 'He's coming up this weekend, which will be *much* nicer than a card . . . Yes, it's from Chris. Okay, now open yours.'

'Not now. I'll look at them when I get back.'

Tsunami looked at her steadily.

'You're all worked up, aren't you? Relax, sweetie. You know you're good. You know you're *very* well prepared. How can mediocre brains like van Loten's, and even Marchmont's, think up any questions that *you* can't answer? It's just not possible.'

'They're *not* mediocre,' replied Latha faintly. 'How can you say such a thing, Tsunami!'

'Of course I know they aren't. But you've got to *believe* they are, Latha! Just for the three hours that you're writing the paper. Now come on, open up your letters.'

'This one's from my parents, wishing me luck. This one – oh, how nice – is from Paula and Rajan Phillips. This one – oh, look, I've got one from Chris, too . . . And this one . . . Tsunami, it's from Anupam Munasinghe.'

'Is it, indeed! And what does he have to say?'

'Oh, just two or three words . . . Heavens, look at the time! I'd better make a run for it, or I'll be late for the exam.'

Latha sat at the desk assigned to her in the examination hall, and calmly watched the Chief Invigilator, a lanky young man who taught Economics in first year, handing out answer books. She thought about the card she had received from Anupam.

Good Hunting, Latha!

How curious, she thought, that three little words on a card should have had the power to alter her mood so completely. When the invigilator came up to her desk, she asked him for four answer books, and wrote her index number neatly in the designated space.

The voice of Paula Phillips sounded in her head.

'Now remember, Latha, that for each paper you will have *three hours* in which to answer *four* questions. Think about that. It means you will have *forty-five minutes* in which to answer *each* question. It seems like a lot of time. But remember, that's only in *theory*. In *practice*, there will be some questions on the paper that will suit you better than the others. In order to work out which they are, allow yourself ten minutes at the start and use those ten minutes to read the paper slowly and carefully through to the end. Don't rush it, *read* it. It will be time well spent. Place a tick against the four questions you want to answer, then number them one, two, three, and four, in the order in which you will write the answers. My advice is that you write your best answer first, spending a whole hour on it if you want to, but not more. Then your second best, then your third. But in choosing your fourth answer, you must choose carefully. You may not have any special liking for the author or the text. That's not important. It's the nature of the *question* that's important, for you may have left yourself only ten or fifteen minutes in which to write the answer, and you need a question that can be dealt with in point form if necessary, *for you must not on any account leave an answer unfinished . . .*'

The hands of the clock on the wall of the examination hall stood at three minutes to two o'clock, and question papers were being distributed by the invigilators. Seated at a desk across the way from Latha's, Irwin Fernando glanced about him before picking up his paper, and took note of the deliberateness with which his classmate laid her fountain-pen across the top of her desk, straightened her answer book, and checked her wristwatch against the clock on the wall.

'You can give up any hope of that First, putha,' he said to himself. 'She's going to *skin* the paper.'

On the stroke of two, the Chief Invigilator said:

'You may now begin writing.'

Latha picked up the paper. She read the first question, and wanted to jump to her feet and shout for sheer joy. Checking the impulse to start writing immediately, she read the paper through to its end. As she read, her panic vanished as if it had never been, and a steady, focused determination took its place.

Good Hunting, Latha!

Very well, Latha thought. On with the chase.

She picked up her fountain-pen (a present from Herbert), uncapped it, and began to write.

6

FEELING FESTIVE

'It's a good thing our exams are being spread over two weeks,' Tsunami said. 'Gives us a little breathing space between each one. I see you're wearing your blue Manipuri tonight.'

'I'm feeling festive,' her cousin said. 'I need a break, and heaven bless Ronald Marchmont for providing one. Just check the hem, Tsunami, as I turn around very slowly – is the hem even all round, and is the height all right?'

They were dressing for an evening party for final-year honours students, hosted by the 'Mahakellē bachelors'.

'Perfect. Here's a safety pin, that'll keep it moored. Remember there's a flight of steps to negotiate at the entrance. You don't want to trip over that hem! So you're feeling festive, eh? Hence the flower in the hair, I take it?'

Latha laughed and said:

'It's marvellous, to be dressing up again for a party. I feel I've been doing nothing else but reading and writing, reading and writing. You, too, Tsunami. I think it's time we both had a little fun.'

She sat down before her mirror, and reached for her hairbrush. Tsunami sat on the bed, and watched Latha as she pinned up her hair.

'You do that so expertly now, Latha!'

'I've had plenty of practice . . . Hey!' Latha leaned forward, and scrutinized her cousin's reflection in the mirror. 'You're wearing a *pottu*!'

'Like it?'

'It looks wonderful. It makes you look so much like Auntie Helen, Tsunami. I remember pleading with her to wear her *pottu* all the time. But she never did.'

'That was because Pater didn't like her doing it. There were so many things Pater didn't like, weren't there?'

'What does he say about you wearing one?'

'He'd probably throw a fit if he saw me tonight. I certainly wouldn't wear it in Colombo. Selvie let me have this one, from her supply.'

Selvamani Chelladurai, a fourth-year engineering student, had had her marriage registered in Jaffna earlier in the year. She would be formally married when the examinations were over. Meanwhile, Selvie was enjoying collecting her wedding trousseau.

'She's got whole sets in red and black, and sequins, too, that she bought in India. She offered me a choice, but I don't feel quite ready yet for sequins.'

Latha said: 'Sujit would probably like it very much, if he saw you tonight . . .'

'Really, Latha, surely we can make up our own minds as to what we wear or don't wear. I'm wearing a *pottu*, not because I want to please other people, not even because I want to please Sujit, but because I know it suits me. And because I'm happy and relieved that that first exam went so well!'

'All right, all right. My mistake. At what time are they calling for us?'

'Don't worry, we've heaps of time. Seven o'clock, Ron said, and it's only six-thirty now. Are you taking that fan? It's very pretty.'

'Well, it's a warm night,' Latha said. She fluttered the fan, and curtsied to the mirror. 'Isn't it gorgeous? Did you know that there are whole chapters on "The Proper Management of the Fan" in eighteenth-century books on etiquette? This one's a present from my father.'

'Very nice. Uncle Herbert does everything right!'

'By the way,' Latha said, 'you do know Sujit has called on Thaththi, don't you? And that Thaththi is about to put his case to Uncle Rowland?'

'Yes. I know. I told Sujit not to.'

'For heaven's sake, why? You do want to marry him, don't you, Tsunami?'

In the silence that followed, Latha saw that her cousin had turned her head away, and was looking out of the window at the darkness outside.

'Well, don't you?'

'I don't know, Latha. There are times – times when we are together – when I feel sure that I do. I even feel glad then that Pater broke up my affair with Daniel, because if he hadn't, I'd never have fallen in love with Sujit. But there are other times when I feel I'm not fit to marry *anybody*. How do I know that, having let Daniel down the way I did, I won't do the same thing to Sujit? I've—'

'Come on, Tsunami, this is not making sense. You didn't "let Daniel down", the two of you were literally forced apart—'

But Tsunami was not listening to her.

'—I've made so many mistakes in the past, I don't want to make any more. Because the mistakes I make don't just affect me, they involve *other* people . . .'

'Don't cry, Tsunami. You'll ruin your *kohl*. Here's a handkerchief. Cheer up. You heard me? Cheer up. *Immediately!*'

While her cousin dried her eyes, Latha appealed to logic.

'Look, why in the world should Uncle Rowland object to Sujit? He found a bride in India himself, for goodness' sake! He can't possibly object to your doing the same thing. You've all got heaps of aunts and uncles and cousins on the Indian side. Tara wouldn't have "objected" to being left a fortune by your Indian aunt, would she? Well then! Your marrying Sujit would be just as if you were marrying one of your Indian cousins. That's reasonable, isn't it? I reminded Thaththi that that was an argument which Uncle Rowland wouldn't really be able to get past . . .'

Tsunami shook her head.

'It's no good appealing to *reason*, Latha. That's the point. Pater's become absolutely unpredictable. What he says and does depends on the political situation at the time, and from what I've heard, the political situation just now is very dodgy indeed.'

'When have you had time to read the newspapers?' Latha asked with interest. 'I'd really like to know, because *I* haven't. Both you and I have had our noses buried in books for the last four weeks.'

'It's not what I've been reading in the papers, it's campus talk. Paul was up here two days ago, and he told me that three of his Tamil classmates have withdrawn from the examinations. Their parents had insisted that they accompany them to Jaffna. According to Paul, they've been scared by pamphlets they've been receiving, warning them to leave the south before the end of May, for if they don't, they will be killed, and their houses and businesses burned—'

'What nonsense! We're not living in Nazi Germany or in Little Rock, Tsunami. Such things don't happen here.'

'I'm only telling you what Paul told me. The father of one of his classmates is a businessman in Polonnaruwa, and the elder brother of the other is a lawyer in Kegalle. They're closing their houses, shutting up shop, and leaving.'

'I don't believe a word of it. Thaththi would have written to me about it, if any of this was to be taken seriously.'

'Maybe Uncle Herbert doesn't want to worry us, especially with the examinations going on. Maybe, Latha, he doesn't even *know*. The newspapers don't say a word about these pamphlets, and people in Colombo don't know or care what goes on in the provinces.'

Latha took a deep breath, and changed the subject. She said encouragingly:

'Uncle Rowland may be a politician now, but he's still a reasonable man. He wouldn't be swayed by political gossip – because that's all it is, you must see that. Anyway, he surely won't try to kidnap you again, would he? Not in the middle of your exams!'

Tsunami didn't seem sure of that, either.

'How do you do it, Latha?'

'How do I do what?'

'How do you stay so calm in a crisis, and see things so clearly?'

Latha made no reply. Her own situation at the moment was hardly enviable, she thought: her mother seemed to be doing her best, with the tacit approval and assistance of Mrs Annabelle Munasinghe, to arrange a match for her with Anupam. It was only by exerting her will to keep at her books and her notes that Latha was managing to cope with her mother's energetic activities.

Your Thaththi gets on so well with Anupam! [Soma had gushed, in one of her rare letters to Peradeniya.] *When we had people to dinner last week, and I wanted to invite other young men, your Thaththi asked me: 'Why aren't we inviting Anupam, Soma?'*

It was true that her father's letters never failed to mention Anupam, usually in connection with a visit the young man had paid to the house, or a book Herbert had discussed with him. Although he tended to refer to him jokingly as 'Mr Incomparable', it seemed to Latha that Annabelle had become her mother's best friend, and Anupam her parents' most frequent visitor. Latha described this turn of events to Tsunami, only to be told:

'Well, what are you complaining about? I'm not at all surprised. Anupam's really fond of you, Latha. Sujit says so, and he should know. Anupam's his closest friend. And you like him, don't you? You've told me you do.'

'Of course I like him,' Latha said. 'I like him very much. But I don't love him. Not – well, not the way you love Sujit. How can I marry him?'

Marchmont's car had arrived at the Hall entrance. Shirani was waiting for Latha and Tsunami on the steps, and they could not continue their talk of the Munasinghe family. When they reached Mahakellē, they found the party in full swing. Peter Appuhamy was in attendance, serving trays of *hors d'oeuvres* and pouring out drinks. He showed no sign of ever having met Tsunami before that evening – perhaps Daniel Rajaratnam never brought her here, thought Latha; and then remembered Tsunami's warning to her about the flight of steps at the entrance to the house. So she *had* been at Mahakellē before, and Peter was either forgetful, or he was being very discreet . . .

The conversation at the party, as if by general agreement, avoided the subject of examinations altogether. Marchmont announced that he had had recent news of the Rajaratnams: they had moved from their apartment in New York to a house in New Jersey, since Daniel's wife was expecting a child in June. Did Tsunami and Shirani wish to write to their former tutor? If they wanted to send the Rajaratnams a card, Ron would be happy to pass on the New Jersey address.

'I've just passed the address on to Peter. He'd got very fond of Daniel while he was here, and was sorry to see him go.'

Professor de Saa had put some of his Spanish records on the radiogram, in the hope perhaps that the rhythmic beat of castanets would lighten the mood of his student guests, and help everyone relax. Latha, who had never been to a Mahakellē party before, wondered what effect the alcohol that was circulating so freely might be having on her teachers. Certainly, the men *were* drinking rather a lot. She had heard Mrs Titus Dupré hint darkly once that the bachelors who lived there got up to all kinds of amorous shenanigans: maybe, Latha thought with amusement, she'd said so because she was annoyed by their failure to invite her to their parties! She sipped the sherry that had been put in her hand, and hoped that Marchmont himself would be sufficiently sober to drive them back to the Hall when the party was over. What would they do if he were not?

The same thought seemed to have struck Shirani. She had prudently attached herself to Rosamond, Arnold Castilian's elegant wife, who worked with Ivan Ganesan at the University Library.

'Mrs Castilian drives her own car. If the worst comes to the worst, and Ron Marchmont and Arnold are both out for the count,' whispered Shirani, 'we could ask Mrs Castilian to take us home. Do you think you could ask her?'

'Sure,' Latha whispered back.

She didn't tell Shirani that she was greatly entertained by the sight of several people she had only known so far in the formal atmosphere of the lecture hall letting their hair down to an unexpected degree.

'I'm sure she'll say yes.'

Tsunami wandered over to them, and bent down beside Latha.

'Have you taken note of Ron Marchmont's surprise guest?' she asked softly, under cover of re-fastening the buckle of her shoe.

Sushila Ramanathan, former Campus Queen, recent law graduate, and now a member of a Colombo law office, was seated across the room, a radiant Marchmont hovering over her like a watchful hawk.

'Just look at the poor idiot,' said Tsunami pityingly. 'Besotted.'

Further observation was not possible. Arnold Castilian, who seemed to be in remarkably good spirits, seated himself next to Latha, and amused himself by mischievously inquiring whether she had chosen a topic for her Ph.D. dissertation yet. Considering that it was well known on campus that he had never completed his own London University thesis, he was full of good advice for her on the subject of choosing a subject and devising a title for it.

'Always remember the useful words "Aspects of",' said Castilian. 'Those two little words put you in control, you see. If you were to describe your project as' – he plucked a title out of the air – '*Idiom and Orthography in the time of Johnson*, let's say, you'd never finish it. You'd find yourself having to cover the whole caboodle. But if you were to describe it as "*Aspects of* Idiom and Orthography in the time of Johnson", well then . . .'

The Castilians did, in fact, drive the girls home, but not because Marchmont was incapable of doing so. When they left, pleading their need of an early night as their excuse, the party looked set to go on until morning. The music had changed, and dancing had begun. As she stood at the top of the Mahakellē steps, waiting for Arnold Castilian and Rosamond to drive up, Latha looked back.

Marchmont and Sushila Ramanathan were doing the Charleston.

'Tell me more,' Tsunami said, the next day. 'I want to hear all about Anupam Munasinghe. What has Auntie Soma been up to?'

She showed no sign of her emotional outburst of the previous evening, and made no reference to anti-Tamil pamphlets, to the Rajaratnams, nor even to Marchmont, except to hope that Sushila's charms wouldn't have befuddled him to such an extent that he wouldn't have his wits about him when he was marking her cousin's examination answers.

'Amma's taken to writing letters to me,' Latha said. 'She, who was always too busy to write! And her letters are all about Anupam and his family. They're a "good Buddhist family", she tells me, "the right caste and everything", he has "literary tastes" and "loves reading", just as I do, so what more can I possibly ask? In her last letter she said his mother wants to take me to "their family temple", and introduce me to the Chief Priest there, who apparently guided Anupam in tracing his first letters in a sand tray, and still loves him like a son. It seems that when Anupam was about five years old, a new image of the Buddha was installed in the temple, and the Munasinghe family were not only in attendance on that occasion, but they presented the image with its sapphire eyes.'

'Oh, Latha!' Tsunami said. 'Sujit hasn't told me anything about all *this*. Maybe he doesn't know.'

'Maybe Anupam doesn't like to talk about it,' Latha said. 'But his mother certainly does.'

'Will you go to the temple and meet the Chief Priest?' Tsunami asked. 'It'll be almost like getting married.'

'I don't see how I can get out of *going*,' her cousin said. 'You know what my mother's like. But I can tell you one thing for sure – getting married doesn't come into the equation. I don't want it, and I'm almost certain Anupam doesn't want it either.'

'I don't believe you,' said Tsunami.

7

SUJIT'S PROPOSAL

Sujit Roy did not like being kept waiting. He always made a point of being punctual himself, suspecting that people who waste the time of others do so because they need, for some reason, to assert their own importance. On this occasion he had had forty-five minutes to take in every detail of the anteroom to Rowland Wijesinha's sanctum in the Ministry of Cultural Affairs before the way was opened to the man he had come to see.

He had given a good deal of thought to the way he wanted his interview with Tsunami's father to go. His own natural impulse was to come directly to the point, openly state his feelings for Tsunami, and request her father's consent to their marriage.

It had become clear to him, however, that something more would be required.

The descriptions of Rowland Wijesinha that had come his way in the clubs of Colombo had been, as he told Anupam, confusing and contradictory. It occurred to him that the man he was about to interview seemed to possess as many different aspects as a Hindu deity has arms. Which of these manifestations was the correct one? Which of them should he address?

On one occasion he had heard Tsunami's father described as hopelessly out of date, 'like a character in a nineteenth-century novel'. Anupam himself had called the Cultural Affairs Minister a pompous ass. And yet, Sujit had also heard Rowland Wijesinha described by one person as a cultivated, modern-minded individual, by another as 'the only man in the Cabinet you can truly call a gentleman'. The last two descriptions he considered distinctly encouraging. He believed that whatever initial objections Rowland Wijesinha might have to his daughter's union with 'an outsider', reason and good sense must win such a man over in the end.

'Good morning, good morning! What can we do for you?'

The Minister was in an excellent mood. The question was accompanied by a genial smile and a gracious wave of the hand towards a leather-covered chair on the other side of the ministerial desk. Sujit mastered his irritation at the delay there had been in admitting him, took the seat indicated and observed that his own business card was lying face-up on the blotter between them.

Well, he knows who I am, and why I'm here.

'Thank you for agreeing to see me, Mr Wijesinha.'

'Not at all, not at all,' said Rowland.

He picked up the card his secretary had placed before him, and glanced at the logo on it, a line drawing of a catamaran riding a wave. Holding the card between his finger and thumb, Rowland looked his visitor up and down. Extraordinarily well turned out, he thought: for a business man. Doubtless one of the new breed of Indian entrepreneurs – and certainly a welcome change from the old-style sari-shop Borahs and Parsis and Thambis, with their flapping draperies, betel-stained smiles, sandalled feet and bad shaves. Rowland, who believed that clothes (as well as manners) go a long way towards making the man, and preferred a crisp aftershave to the attar of roses dear to many male hearts in the orient, warmed towards his well-groomed visitor.

Probably looking for a Government loan to start a business venture, or maybe expand one. Well, nothing wrong with that: these enterprising johnnies whose activities brought in Government revenue deserved a helping hand and an encouraging pat on the back. The question he had asked the fellow had become Rowland's standard opening gambit when called upon to interview unknown businessmen:

What can we do for you?

It struck, he believed, exactly the right note, blending courtesy and condescension. But why had the chap come to the Ministry of Cultural Affairs? Wasn't he in the wrong place?

'A pleasure,' Rowland added vaguely.

Sujit studied the man seated opposite him who, up to that moment, he had seen only in press photographs. A handsome face, he thought, recognizing in it an older, somewhat time-worn version of Ranil Wijesinha. The Minister's national dress, he noted, was snow-white and perfectly starched, a rarity among politicians, who tended too often to look like bundles of old clothes put out for the *dhobi* to take away in a wash-basket. To Sujit's observant eye, however, there was something about it that suggested fancy dress: he suspected that the Minister would have been more at home in a European-style suit. The hands which still held his business card were smooth, and the nails were fastidiously manicured. Never done a day's real work in his life, thought Sujit, who spent three days of his working week in hands-on activity at the Hambantota boatyard. Certainly we have here something of a fop!

'I believe, sir, that your cousin, Mr Herbert Wijesinha, has spoken to you already, regarding my proposal . . .'

Herbert? Herbert? Rowland asked himself. Why's the fellow talking about Herbert? What did Herbert have to do with boats and businessmen? He thought for one terrible moment that his cousin had got himself into some scandalous scrape at the Customs Office. Got nabbed smuggling something in, by any chance? No, that didn't sound like good old honest Herbert. On the other hand, it was only the other day that one of Rowland's cabinet colleagues had been hauled over the coals by the P.M. for just such a misdemeanour . . . If Herbert had been up to something, it wouldn't do if the press got hold of it . . .

The word 'proposal' stirred a vague memory in his mind and he looked at Sujit's card again. Roy. Sujit Roy. He now remembered Herbert mentioning the fellow's name to him . . . talking him up as if he were the answer to a maiden's prayer . . .

A moment passed before realization dawned on Rowland.

Good God, he thought, it's that impudent rascal who's been making up to that silly child Tsunami. He'd got Herbert to act as his *kapuwa* – Herbert having obviously fallen for slick talk and a smooth, sophisticated manner. As had Tsunami. Well, thought Rowland, one could make allowances for an inexperienced, naïve little girl, but Herbert, a grown man, had no excuse for such stupidity. It was transparently clear that this nobody was hoping, through Tsunami, to storm the citadel of class and privilege . . . He thought he could wangle his way into the world of the *walauwa*, did he? . . . The nerve! A damned fortune-hunter, no question, maybe even a crook looking for a politician's nod to put through a shady business deal . . .

'. . . We thought we should wait until after her final examination to put the matter formally to you, sir . . .'

Formally? *Formally?* So she'd already agreed to marry the scoundrel, had she, and had sent him along to get Daddy's official seal of approval on her arrangements? Not a word to him beforehand that there was anything like this in the wind. Rowland seethed inwardly at such wanton disregard on Tsunami's part of a father's proper role in a young woman's affairs.

'. . . I want to assure you, Mr Wijesinha, that I'm very well able to . . . You must have seen the files relating to my business affairs . . .'

But Rowland had heard enough.

'Files?' he said. 'Files? If you're talking about that bundle of paper my cousin Herbert Wijesinha handed to me the other day, I'll tell you what I did with it. I put the lot into the waste-paper basket.'

'I beg your pardon?'

Sujit's air of disbelief riled Rowland.

'You do *not* have my pardon, nor will you have anything else of mine. Give up any hope you might have had of that, my lad! I can see very well what you are about, please don't imagine I was born yesterday. You have taken advantage of an inexperienced, immature child, and you should be ashamed of yourself. How dare you come pushing your way in here, to promote yourself to me? Did you really think that a nobody like you, a jumped-up fortune-hunter of all things, would be tolerated *for one moment* in the Wijesinha family?'

'I think you have misunderstood—'

But Sujit was not permitted to go on.

'Misunderstood? You, Mr Roy, had better understand this: you do *not* have my permission to make your proposals to my daughter, much less marry her. Do I make myself clear? I regard it as an impertinence on your part to have sought this interview with me. Kindly leave my office immediately.'

'But—'

'No "buts", please! I don't want to hear any explanations. There is nothing more to be said on the subject.'

Rowland Wijesinha pressed the bell on his desk, and his personal assistant came in.

'Show this person out, Francis.'

His encounter with Rowland Wijesinha had taken rather less than ten minutes, but it left Sujit angry, and smarting from the experience. Not only had the material he had so carefully prepared been rejected unread and he himself dismissed without a fair hearing, but he had been personally insulted and treated as if he were a common criminal. He had expected pride, even some snobbery, to be directed at an 'Indian invader' by the conservative head of an ancient clan. But he had not been prepared to meet arrogance and irrationality on so majestic a scale.

It's an old family. I understand they don't welcome strangers.

The full significance of Anupam's diplomatic understatement was now brought forcefully home to Sujit. It was to protect him from a humiliation such as the one he had just experienced, he concluded, that Anupam had delivered his warning, Tsunami had tried so hard to prevent his calling on her father, and Latha had urged him to enlist the services of a go-between. No wonder Mr Herbert Wijesinha had been so cautious on the subject of his cousin, no wonder Helen Wijesinha had been so reticent, and Christopher as silent as the grave. He'd had warnings enough, from sympathetic friends as well as from impartial strangers, and he had disregarded them all. He had only himself to thank for the collapse of his hopes of a pleasant, and ultimately successful, interview.

At the same time, and annoyed as he was by Rowland's treatment of him, Sujit admitted that part of his irritation arose from the fact that, yearning to retaliate, he had been restrained by principle and training from giving as good as he'd got. He was furious at having been unjustly called a fortune-hunter by Rowland, but he knew also that he could never have brought himself to reply in kind.

And tell me, Minister, by what chicanery did your ancestors acquire their wealth?

Impossible! He could not have said such a thing to Tsunami's father, whatever the provocation. Nor would he have stated in his own defence that, far from having designs on his fiancée's property, he had turned down a fortune left to him by his father, and had made a second one by his own efforts.

There was one aspect of Rowland Wijesinha's behaviour which had unexpectedly aroused an affectionate memory in Sujit, and helped for that reason to calm his feelings. A lesser man, he thought, might have stumbled and stuttered in fury, before descending at last into bluster and incoherence. Whereas Rowland's impressive command of invective – and in English, too, that language which has been well described as the language of business and insult – had reminded Sujit of his own father. The late Mr Amarjit Roy, a well-educated bilingual gentleman of the older generation, had earned universal respect for his ability to swear picturesquely in either one of three languages – English, Bengali or Hindi – for twenty minutes at a stretch without once repeating himself or stopping for breath. Sujit remembered the impression his father's talent had made on a Cambridge friend of his who had called on the old man in Bombay.

'I heard your father before I saw him,' Harry Osborne had told Sujit, laughing at the memory. 'I was just paying off my taxi when I heard this terrific racket . . . The taxi-driver and I walked round the corner to find out if there was a riot taking place that he hadn't heard about, and there was this gentleman in an elegant linen suit, standing on the steps of a big building which I later understood to be his office, and he was haranguing – I'm sorry, but there's no other word for it, Roy, absolutely *haranguing* – a meek-looking individual in *dhoti* and *kurta* who was standing on the step below him. I couldn't, of course, understand what was being said, but I could tell that he was in a tearing rage. "What's he saying?" I asked my taxi-driver, a Sikh. The taxi-driver replied: "Gentleman very angry." "I can see that," I said. "But *why* is he so angry?" The taxi-driver listened carefully for a while, and then he told me: "Other person, he gentleman's chauffeur. Gentleman angry with chauffeur because car is dusty. Chauffeur have not washed it." It was a hot, dry day, and in the city, where some massive construction work was going on at the time, everything in sight – buildings, cars, a white marble statue of Queen Victoria, even the odd tree – was grey with dust. "What's the point of washing a car," I pointed out, "when in five minutes' time, it will be covered once again with dust? Why get so worked up about it?" The taxi-driver considered the question for a moment, and then he shrugged his shoulders and said: "He Bengali."'

Sujit recalled the spectacular flow of invective he had witnessed from Rowland Wijesinha that morning, and wondered whether there was any substance in the theory, which he had heard occasionally put forward over sun-downers on the Mount Lavinia Hotel's terrace when race relations had been the subject of discussion, that the Sinhalese race had originated in Bengal. He remembered that his late father's anger, quick to flare up, had been usually of short duration.

'Like a soda bottle when you shake it up,' his mother had said once, smiling at the memory of her late husband. 'He would fizz for a while, then he'd settle down.'

Sujit wondered whether this might be true also of Rowland Wijesinha. Given time, would he, too, 'settle down'? And how much of his father's effervescent temper had he himself inherited?

Driving up alone to Peradeniya the next day, Sujit considered the problem presented by Tsunami's father. Rowland Wijesinha was obviously a much more complicated character than he had imagined him to be. The descriptions of him which had come his way had fallen short of the truth because each described only a single aspect of the man whose opposition seemed to be now the main obstacle in the way of his achieving his desire.

And Sujit Roy had no intention of giving up that desire.

8

BOTANICAL

When Tsunami greeted him at the entrance to Sanghamitta Hall, she was smiling.

'I don't have to ask,' Sujit said. 'Obviously, your examinations are going well.'

'*Very* well. I couldn't have hoped for a better paper yesterday. I just hope I did it justice! If I didn't, I shall doubtless hear all about it from the internal examiners before too long. Latha loved her Practical Criticism paper, too.'

She laughed.

'Latha told me that every one of Ronald Marchmont's papers so far has had something in it about love and romance. In the Shakespeare paper, a key question hinged on the meeting of Ferdinand and Miranda in *The Tempest*. In the Practical Criticism paper, the question asked for an analysis of David Copperfield's proposal to Dora Spenlow . . . It doesn't take half an eye to see the man's in love.'

'Who's the girl?'

'Sushila Ramanathan, a lawyer. She was at the party that Ron and the other Mahakellē bachelors gave in our honour on Saturday. They seem very attached to each other. I hope they don't run into trouble from her parents.'

Tsunami sounded so downcast as she said this that Sujit took his eyes off the road to look down at her for a moment. He decided to change the subject if he could. His moments with Tsunami were too precious to squander on negative thoughts.

'Well, good luck to him!' he said easily. 'And it's Latha's good luck that he's been here to take her classes during this all-important final year—'

'That's true.'

But Tsunami sounded unconvinced. She hesitated, then said:

'I know Ron quite well, Sujit. I wonder what he would do if the love affair were broken up by her parents, and Sushila married someone else. I suppose he'd go back to England, wouldn't he? What would be the point of hanging around?'

'What, indeed! And that reminds me: now that your examinations have only a little way to run, don't you think you and I should decide on a date? Three months from now? That's the standard period of an engagement, so they tell me.'

He had debated whether to tell Tsunami of his meeting with her father, and had decided against it.

Not now. Later. Bad news, like discussions of other people's unhappy love affairs, can always wait.

He stopped the car at the gateway to the Botanical Gardens, and took a plaid rug out of the boot.

'Usual place?'

'Yes.'

Their meetings in Peradeniya, continually plagued by the consciousness of fleeting time, by her need to beat the seven-thirty bell at the Hall, and by his to avoid at morning and evening the worst traffic times on the Kandy–Colombo road, had been from the beginning always so brief that they had also been very tense. At any rate, Sujit thought so. For him, their sedate, supervised walks beneath the balconies of one hall of residence and in full view of another had been exquisite torture. Their relationship had moved faster and further since its uncertain early beginnings, and he wanted more. His possession of a car was, of course, a great help, since it occasionally gave him an opportunity to take Tsunami away from the campus. But even with that advantage, which undergraduates did not have, very rarely could he enjoy the luxury of an entire day spent in her company, since it was necessary to drive a fair distance in order to escape the surveillance of watchful, curious eyes.

The Botanical Gardens at Peradeniya, only a few minutes' drive from the University, had not seemed to him at first to be a viable possibility for their meetings, due to its great popularity with locals and visitors alike: on any day, and especially at weekends, there were crowds everywhere in the Gardens. Or so it had seemed until, on a slightly overcast Sunday afternoon, he and Tsunami, abandoning the cleared pathways and tarred drives for a walk along the river bank had accidentally discovered what had since become their 'usual place'.

As a general rule, nobody ventures very far into the Gardens, people prefer to keep to the manicured lawns with their graceful garden seats, within easy reach of the Orchid House and its exotic blooms. They like to walk along the winding borders of crotons and colias that picture postcards have made familiar to locals and visitors alike. The deep, moist grass on the river bank, a likely hiding-place for snakes, tends to discourage the timorous visitor, and on that first occasion it would have discouraged Sujit too, had he been in any mood to think about it.

But he was not; and as he went further and further into the shadows of the trees with Tsunami's hand in his, stopping every few yards to draw her close to him and kiss her, so long and so ardently that at times they had to stop walking altogether, the impulse to make love to her became so urgent that he had stumbled blindly on through the grass, hardly knowing where he was going, until at last they had come upon a stand of huge trees by the river, with roots so massive that they were like enclosing walls. Overarching branches, heavy with blossom, provided a fragrant canopy beneath which they could not be seen, even by people walking along the pathways above.

In later years Sujit often looked back to that magical day and gave thanks that a kindly fate had arranged such a sanctuary, and led him to it. For the 'usual place', with its perfumed silence and its curtain of green leaves, cast its tranquil spell over all their subsequent meetings, replacing their anxieties with joyful confidence in love and in each other.

Today being a weekday, there were not many visitors about in the Gardens. They passed a party of schoolgirls, demure in white uniforms and purple ties, who were examining rare blossoms in the Orchid House and sketching them under the supervision of their Botany teacher. The girls giggled as Sujit and Tsunami walked by, and followed them with curious eyes until a bend in the path hid them from view. We were like that at Ashcombe, Tsunami remembered, we were always wondering about couples we glimpsed on the way to church, speculating about what they did in private, wondering what *it* was like . . .

'Here we are,' Sujit said. 'There's dew on the grass, but the rug will fix that. Come here.'

He reached for Tsunami's hand, and pulled her down on to the rug beside him. From the path above came the sudden sound of voices: the speakers must have been quite near although, muffled by the dense screen of trees, they sounded as if they were a great distance away. Tsunami's eyes were fixed on his, questioning.

Sujit shook his head.

'Don't worry,' he whispered. 'No one can possibly guess we're here, if we don't talk.'

And sigh only occasionally . . . very, very softly . . .

He took her in his arms.

'I don't intend to talk. Do you?'

The dew had evaporated from the grass, and the sun, shining through the leaves of the trees above them, had moved a little higher in the sky by the time Sujit lay back on the rug and contemplated Tsunami as she unwrapped sandwiches and poured out lemonade. He had never in his life, he thought, seen such a perfect day.

'Sujit . . .'

'M-m-m?'

'I wish we could stay here for ever.'

'Here? In this place?'

'Yes. And in this moment of time.'

'Never grow old, do you mean? Tsunami, lovers have made that wish for centuries, though they know it can't come true.'

'That isn't what I meant. I was thinking how lucky we are, not only to be young and in love, but to be alive in such a time of peace, in such a happy, prosperous country. When I was reading all those Ancient History texts this year, I realized that people who lived in past times were hardly ever at peace, they could never be sure that right in the middle of a meal, or when they were asleep in their tents, or milking their cows, a party of marauders wouldn't ride in from somewhere and lay everything to waste around them, looting and killing, burning everything in sight—'

'You're thinking of Attila the Hun, aren't you?'

'Yes, but it happened in every age and in every country, didn't it? It happened in Scotland. It happened in India.'

'Yes.'

'If we could only choose a moment, and hold on to it for ever . . . Someone should invent some way of slowing down the passage of time, so that when a spell of perfect peace and happiness occurs, like this one, it can be made to stretch for centuries . . . Sujit?'

'Did you say something?'

'There's no urgency about it, is there? Getting married, I mean?'

Sujit sat up.

'What do you mean, "no urgency"? My dear girl, have you any idea at all what this waiting is doing to me? It's driving me crazy. I can't sleep, I can't eat . . .'

'"Can't eat"? You've just demolished two massive sandwiches . . .'

'. . . I talk nonsense to my friends . . .'

'You're talking nonsense now.'

'That's because you're here beside me. Whenever you're near, I can't think straight. I babble.'

'Be serious, Sujit. Term ends next week and Latha and I go back to Colombo. We won't be able to meet here after that. And we have such a lot to talk about.'

'We do. I promise to be rational later. But not just now. Put those sandwiches away and come here to me, Tsunami. I want to take the pins out of your hair.'

'Don't lose them.'

'Of course I won't lose them!'

As Tsunami's hair, released from its hairpins, tumbled down upon her shoulders, Sujit caught his breath, then buried his face in its fragrant waves.

'If you had any idea what seeing this waterfall does to me, you wouldn't ever pin it up. I could swim in it for ever.'

He picked up a thick, wavy lock and kissed it.

'I may decide, you know, never to give your hairpins back . . .'

'Sujit!'

'Sh-sh-sh! Someone up there might hear you. Here are your hairpins, safe in my shirt pocket. Now, Tsunami, what are you going to give me to make me return them?'

9

NIGHT JOURNEY

Night was falling as Sujit filled up his petrol tank in Peradeniya and checked the oil and water levels in his car. He had left his return to Colombo a little too late, and knew that it would be dark long before he got back to his flat, but he didn't mind that. He enjoyed the long night drives during which, his mind filled with thoughts of Tsunami, with memories of her voice, her touch, the fragrance of her hair, he could give the car its head without the distraction of the day-time traffic that clogged the roads.

He lit a cigarette, settled back luxuriously in his seat, and pointed the Opel Kapitan towards Colombo.

There seemed to be some sort of festival on tonight, for village after village was illuminated with lamplight. Clusters of men, their sarongs tucked up for comfort, had gathered outside the taverns to smoke, drink, and discuss the business of the day. Sujit slowed down as he approached a village. There appeared to be more than the usual conviviality in the air. People seemed unusually excited: newspapers were being handed round in the tea-shops, and in one village a man surrounded by a group of eager listeners was reading aloud from a printed sheet by the light of a swinging kerosene lamp. Sujit drove into Warakapola and stopped beside a wayside stall from which a radio, its volume turned up full blast, was pouring Sinhala popular songs into the night.

'Sir?' called the owner of the stall, and several of his customers stepped out on to the road to gather admiringly round the Opel.

Sujit wound his window down.

'Do you sell Gold Flake?' he asked in Sinhala, and when the stall-holder replied that he did, Sujit held up a finger in the gesture of the one-cigarette smoker.

He had recently been smoking too much, and by purchasing his cigarettes in ones and twos rather than by the packet or the tin, he was trying to break himself of the habit. He could not, of course, buy single cigarettes in a city store, but the owners of little stalls and street-corner boutiques didn't object to a customer buying a single cigarette at a time. A small boy dressed in shorts and a banian came running out to the car with a saucer on which reposed a single Gold Flake cigarette. Sujit took it, and placed two ten-cent coins in the saucer.

'Just look at this fellow!' said a voice from among the crowd of men surrounding him. 'Drives a luxury car, but he's too mean to pay Sediris *mudalali* the price of a packet of cigarettes.'

Sujit knew he had been misunderstood. Two years spent working side by side with Sinhalese carpenters and craftsmen in his Hambantota boatyard had accustomed him to the Sinhala language and taught him, besides, a good deal about the set of the Sinhalese mind.

'If he's mean with money, he must be Demala,' said someone else. 'A Demala planter from up-country.'

'That's right! *Anyone* can see he's a Demala,' said a third voice.

Sujit was amused. He shook his head.

'I am not Demala. My *gama* is Bombay,' he said.

The crowd became interested. A citizen of Bombay who uses the Sinhala word *gama* when speaking of his own hometown is a rare phenomenon. As Sujit lit up, the bystanders murmured their appreciation of his German-made cigarette lighter.

'Must be a film star, what else, if he comes from Bombay?' one man said. 'Looks just like Dev Anand.'

The Indian film idol's name was promptly relayed from the front to the back of the crowd. Almost immediately, a tall, burly man stepped out of the lamplight and joined the men standing around the car. He was swaying slightly, and held a half-filled glass in his left hand.

'So, so, let's see. Where is this Dev Anand?'

'Ask him the question! Ask Dev Anand the question in the newspaper!' called someone at the back of the crowd.

'No point in asking him anything. What would he know? He's a foreigner from Bombay.'

The Opel purred into life, and some of the men standing around it stepped back.

'Ask him the question anyway – let's see what he says!'

The man with the glass of arrack stood swaying beside the car. He placed a hand on the door handle, and bent forward towards Sujit.

'You speak Sinhala?' he said through the window.

His speech was slurred.

'Yes.'

'Good. So tell some Sinhala, will you, for us to hear. We are listening.'

His words were mild enough, but the tone of his voice carried a curious suggestion of menace. Sujit decided to ignore it: the man was drunk. He smiled, and let in the clutch. His interrogator did not remove his hand from the door handle.

'Tell him to sing a Sinhala song,' someone suggested

'Yes – see if he can sing "Namo Namo Matha"!'

At the mention of the island's national anthem, Sujit decided that the time had come to withdraw from the conversation. It was only too clear that several members of the crowd had been drinking and, as he had had occasion to observe in Bombay, the most innocuous situation can develop very quickly into a full-scale street riot when language, religion or politics comes under debate. Besides, he was alone in the car, and he had no ambition to end his life in a roadside ditch.

He began to wind up the window, and said in Sinhala, as the window glass reached the halfway mark:

'Time to be going!'

No one moved.

'*Gihin ennang*,' he said pleasantly.

He had used the universal Sinhala farewell. Appeased by the courtesy, or perhaps astonished that it was a foreigner who had offered it, his adversary released the door handle and stepped back. Sujit released the brake and the car slid forward.

But as the Opel moved away, a massive blow connected with it that shook the car and rattled its windows. The man had struck at Sujit, with the closed fist of his right hand, a blow which, if the reinforced glass of the window had not obstructed it, would certainly have broken his jaw.

The telephone was ringing in his ground-floor flat as Sujit let himself in. Chris Wijesinha's voice at the other end of the line was agitated.

'Everything okay, Sujit? Are you all right?'

'Of course I'm all right. Why, what's the matter?'

'Stay where you are, and don't go out again, whatever you do. I'll come to you.'

When Chris arrived, he brought a printed paper with him.

'You'd better read this. There's rioting all over the city. Didn't you see any crowds as you came into Colombo? Or hear the shouting?'

'No,' said Sujit. 'Everything was quiet.'

Chris sighed with relief.

'Thank God. That means they're concentrating on another district. Well, it gives us a little time to get organized. Where's Victor?'

Sujit's servant, a youth of seventeen who had been fast asleep on his mat in the veranda, showed himself in the open doorway.

'Tell Victor to shut that front door and pack a suitcase for you, Sujit. And while he's doing that, get together any papers or documents you have in the flat. You'd better come to us. Where's your passport?'

'Here. In my safe.'

'Good. Bring it with you. You don't want to lose that if there's any kind of unpleasantness.'

'Unpleasantness? Would you please tell me what's happening?'

'Something so extraordinary that I can hardly believe it. Oddly, it has its beginning in something that seems – on the surface, at least – quite ordinary and reasonable! You're probably aware of the closing-down of the Royal Naval dockyards in Trincomalee?'

Sujit nodded.

'Yes. I've just taken on some of the retrenched workers at Hambantota.'

'Tamils?'

'I believe so. Yes.'

'Well, your new recruits are probably members of four hundred or so displaced Tamil families. Under the Government's plan, these labourers from Trinco were to be taken to East Padaviya for settlement. Last night a bunch of Government labourers in Polonnaruwa, all of them Sinhalese, convinced that they had to defend their plots of land from a Government-sponsored Tamil invasion, went on the rampage. Maybe they were responding to some ancient race-memory of actual, historical invasions from south India, or it's possible that this seemed to confirm the unease they had already been feeling about the obliteration of "Sri" signs, who knows!'

'Sorry, Chris, I'm not with you. What "Sri" signs?'

'Federalist politicians in the North have been looking for a way to symbolize their struggle for linguistic equity. Some months ago they hit on the idea of having their supporters obliterate the Sinhala "Sri" from signposts and public notices, as a message of protest. These things, coming together as they did, seem to have tipped the scale in favour of violence. The Sinhalese labourers got it into their heads that they had a duty to defend their motherland from marauding Tamils, and started looting Tamil homes, raping Tamil women, and beating up Tamil labourers and public officers. Apparently they were absolutely confident that the police wouldn't interfere. The Tamil labourers in the Polonnaruwa sugar-cane plantation fled when they saw the crowds approaching, and hid themselves among the sugar-cane. The hoodlums in the crowds set the sugar-cane alight, and flushed them out. As they emerged, screaming for mercy, all of them – men, women and children – were cut down with grass-cutting knives and *kathi*, or smashed to a pulp with heavy clubs. The violence has spread to Colombo now, there are groups of men patrolling the streets – our streets! – with knives and clubs in their hands, stopping people in cars and on bikes, and ordering them to speak a Sinhala sentence. If anyone fails the test, or dares to refuse, he gets beaten up, or stabbed—'

'What happens if someone they intercept *can't* speak Sinhala? Colombo is full of foreigners, after all!'

'Well, if they're obviously foreign – tourists, for instance – no one would bother about them. It's the Tamils they're after. How's your Sinhala?'

'You needn't worry about me – I can cope . . . In fact, I *have* coped already, this very evening.'

He described the incident outside the Warakapola tea-stall to Chris, who stared at him, then laughed.

'Good Lord, Sujit! And I've been ringing you every ten minutes for the last two hours, to make sure you were aware of what was happening, and to tell you to stay indoors!'

'I'm beginning to think, from what you've just told me,' Sujit said, 'that though my Sinhala passed muster this evening, I was lucky to get away when I did. For other reasons. Things were beginning to look fairly rocky back there.'

After a moment's thought, he suddenly said: 'We'd better ring the Munasinghes, Chris.'

'Why? *They* don't need warning, they're Sinhalese.'

'That's true: the parents would be safe. But Anupam and Shalini have lived in Britain all their lives. I wouldn't bet on either of them being able to speak a coherent Sinhala sentence. Or, if it comes to that, to sing a Sinhala song – that's what *I* was ordered to do! Have you ever heard Anupam speak Sinhala?'

Chris considered.

'No, I haven't. But he doesn't need to.'

'Exactly. None of us needs to, because everyone around us speaks English, even the servants. Anupam could manage a Sinhala phrase or two, I suppose, if he's ordering a drink at the club. But if he's stopped in the street by a crowd of people brandishing knives and clubs, and commanded to converse in Sinhala, I can assure you that Anupam will . . . well, he'll definitely have a problem.'

'Anupam and his sister will have to be careful,' Chris said. '*Very* careful, because if they're caught up in an angry crowd, no one's going to waste time working out who they are, whether they're Sinhalese or not. It'll be a case of strike first, ask questions later . . . Look, let's put our heads together, and work out a plan of action. Think of your friends, think of any Tamil or Indian business associates you have. Jot down the names of people we should ring up . . . I'll use this pad, shall I?'

'Go ahead.'

Chris took a fountain-pen out of his shirt pocket, and sat down at Sujit's dining table. His agitation fell away as practical considerations took the place of anxiety.

'What did you mean,' Sujit asked him suddenly, 'when you said "You'd better come to *us*"?'

'Why, come and stay with our family, of course, until all this blows over, and it wouldn't matter any longer if you're taken for a Tamil.'

Sujit said:

'That might take a long time . . . Perhaps it would be better if you gave your invitation to Anupam, Chris, rather than to me. He needs it more than I do. And, all things considered, he'd be more welcome in your home than I would be.'

'Nonsense! What are you talking about?'

'I called on your father this morning with a proposal of marriage. He promptly showed me the door. As a matter of fact, Latha had warned me that he might . . .'

Chris heard Sujit's account of the morning's interview with Rowland without uttering a word. When it was finished, he rose and placed a hand on his friend's shoulder.

'I am *so* sorry, Sujit. I don't know how to apologize.'

'Don't even try. Your father acted according to his lights, and I according to mine. It was a pity that, having come together, the two of us generated more heat than illumination . . . The main point is, having just thrown me out of his office as a fortune-hunter, would your father take kindly to my insinuating myself into his home as a guest? I think not!'

'It's good of you to take it like that.'

'No other way to take it. But it was a kindly thought on your part. I appreciate it.'

The telephone rang, startling them both. Chris motioned to Sujit to stay where he was and answered it.

'Latha? It's Chris here. I'm sorry you couldn't get me at home, I've been out most of the day . . . Yes, and then on the phone for most of the evening . . . Ever since the news broke, in fact . . . Where are you calling from? Peradeniya? That's good, that's a relief. Stay right there, don't move out of the Hall . . . Are the two of you all right?'

He listened for a few moments, then said:

'Fine. Give it to me, I'll go there right away and check on them for you. Meanwhile, would you call your parents?'

There was a pause, during which Chris took the writing pad back from Sujit and wrote down names and an address. He then said, in response to a question from Latha:

'Tell Tsunami not to worry, he's in no danger. He's here, with me, and it might interest you to know that his Sinhala is probably better than yours and mine . . . Oh, all right! Better than mine, then . . . No, Latha, I *don't* think it would be a good idea for the two of you to come to Colombo, you're much safer up there in your Hall than you would be here. Besides, the Colombo road may be blocked . . .'

'Tell Latha,' Sujit interrupted, 'that she and Tsunami must on no account travel by train.'

He had been overtaken suddenly by a memory that had haunted his dreams during his Cambridge years. His daily journey to school in Bombay had involved a train journey from a railway station constantly crowded with commuters. That was how he knew that what he had seen while waiting on the platform one sultry afternoon for a hawker to pour him a glass of *lassi* had not been his private nightmare but a public one, shared with thousands of other people who would, like him, carry for ever more the images of slaughter which haunt every Indian who lived through Partition in 1947. As a passenger train from the new state of Pakistan came into the station, the waiting passengers, anxious to get home, surged forward eagerly, then drew back terrified as a door swung open, and a thick, red liquid began to drip from the compartment floor on to the steps of the train. As they watched in horror, the red stream overflowed on to the platform below. Through the open door of the compartment a sickening stench swirled out into the hot afternoon. Sujit had been eighteen when the first trains carrying their burden of hacked and bleeding Hindu bodies had rolled into Bombay.

'Who knows,' Sujit said, 'when someone in Jaffna or Trinco will remember what happened in India, and take revenge by sending a train-load of dead Sinhalese to Colombo . . .?'

Chris relayed Sujit's message to Latha, omitting the last part of the sentence.

'No, no, it hasn't happened, but Sujit fears that it *might* happen . . . Such things have happened elsewhere. Yes, certainly they might happen here, Latha, once rumours of atrocities on both sides get going . . . if someone's bright enough to think of it, and in the mood for murder . . . I'll ring you tomorrow morning.'

Chris put the telephone down.

'I've got to make a quick visit to Mount Lavinia, Sujit. I have to check on some Tamil friends of Latha's who live there. I suggest that you keep the doors and windows of this flat locked while I'm gone, and switch off all your lights – some of these self-appointed heroes might think of making house calls . . . But I'll come back here afterwards. I'd like to stay the night in your flat, if that's okay with you.'

He paused, then added:

'You may be glad of the company.'

'Hold on a minute,' Roy said. 'We'll go together.'

10

EXODUS

It's written in Ingreesi,' Seelawathie had complained. 'How to understand?'

The sheet of paper Seelawathie brought to Paula Phillips for explanation was printed in bold black capital letters. When it arrived on her doorstep, Seelawathie (whom Paula had been teaching to read and write English with the aid of her small son's Grade 2 reader) had tried to decipher its message. Unsuccessful in her attempt because, as she said, the words were too long, she had taken it to Paula next door for translation as she did all Government communications in English: it might, after all, contain some important message about election meetings, water cuts or rubbish removal in the neighbourhood. In this way Paula and Rajan had received their first intimation of what was to come.

THIS IS A WARNING TO TAMILS, ROMAN CATHOLICS AND BURGHERS!!

Your good times are over. Your oppression of the Sinhalese people is at an end. After three centuries of cruel exploitation by foreigners like you, this ancient land is throwing off its chains and asserting the claim of its Sinhalese Buddhist majority to rightful and unquestioned rule.

If you have not yet made preparations to leave the country, you are advised to do so immediately. Leave before the 28th of this month, or you will be killed one by one or in groups by hand bombs, shooting or stabbing. Don't think that you will be safe as we have enough petrol to make living torches of you all, and monuments of your houses.

Be warned. Death is at your doorstep. Act now, for we are resolute in our struggle for freedom from Tamils and other aliens. Our sacred cities and our capital city must be made one hundred per cent Sinhala, without any foreigners or non-Buddhists allowed to live in our midst and corrupt us.

DON'T DELAY, FOR THE RESULT OF DELAY WILL BE DEATH.

A practical joke, Rajan had said, when his wife showed him the pamphlet. A particularly nasty joke, certainly, devised by someone with a very warped sense of humour, but undoubtedly a joke. Witch hunts, pogroms and Final Solutions happened in other countries, not in Ceylon, a land of rich ethnic diversity where pleasant, smiling people were always ready (as the tourist brochures with their glossy photographs showed) to extend hospitality to visitors from other lands.

Having made this positive assessment of the situation and (he hoped) quieted Paula's misgivings, Rajan made a point, over several days, of casually stopping by the homes of some of his Sinhalese neighbours for an evening chat after work. He learned for the first time of a rumour that had been circulating in the area for some weeks about the imminent start of a project initiated 'at the highest levels' that was designed to cleanse the country, once and for all, of unwanted and dangerous elements. A date for the start of this project had yet to be announced, and in the meantime strangers had been 'dropping in' at his neighbours' houses on casual visits. These visitors talked a great deal about the project, reminding everyone how necessary it was to Ceylon's international image as a free and independent nation that she should demonstrate the purity of her racial inheritance and the uniqueness of her role as the defender of Buddhism. Was it not an insult to that inheritance, they inquired, that the electric fans, refrigerators, cookers and other material goods that were to be found in the houses of wealthy Tamils, Burghers and other foreigners had been bought at the expense of poor, unemployed Sinhalese who could not afford such luxuries?

In the absence of any reports in the newspapers, the rumour had grown and spread. People had discreetly begun to hoard stocks of grain, oil, pulses, tinned foods and other dry goods, not because they expected violence – of course not – but just in case shopkeepers put up their shutters without warning, or happened to run out of supplies. Rajan himself did not believe the rumour until one of his neighbours, a Sinhalese whose son he had tutored in English and Mathematics for the Senior School Certificate examination, unaccountably turned his back on him at the local Co-operative store. When an elderly Sinhalese couple who lived three doors away from the Phillipses' home decided to take an extended holiday on their son's tea estate up-country, they did not ask Rajan as they usually did on these occasions to oblige them 'by keeping an eye on the house' in their absence: they sought the help of another (Sinhalese) neighbour instead.

These were seemingly trivial incidents, but they depressed Rajan and worried his wife. They seemed to contradict the belief by which Rajan lived, and which Paula had adopted as her own: that the spirit of co-operation and mutual respect which they worked to develop in their little community was too strong to be eroded. She became so nervous after reading Seelawathie's printed pamphlet that when Rajan asked her where she kept worn-out dusters and handkerchiefs, and proceeded to carry the dozen or so that she gave him to their empty garage, alarm bells rang in her mind. Exploring, she found containers filled with paraffin and petrol stacked against the garage wall, and a dozen empty soft-drink bottles. When Rajan got back home from his English classes at St Alban's that evening, Paula mildly inquired why they were storing petrol when they didn't have a car, why they needed paraffin when they didn't own a paraffin lamp, and what the ginger beer and Orange Crush empties were doing in the garage when they should have been returned to Elephant House for replacement.

She knew the answer to her questions before she asked them, but she asked them anyway, hoping that she had been mistaken. There must, as she told herself, be some rational explanation: if there wasn't, her peace-loving husband must be heading for a nervous breakdown of some kind. He gave her an explanation, but Paula didn't regard it as rational. And as she was aware that Rajan possessed neither knowledge nor experience in the making of explosives, she was very glad indeed when the car that pulled up at their front door delivered, not a crowd of bloodthirsty ruffians brandishing crowbars, torches and knives, but two quietly-spoken young men, one of whom introduced himself as Latha's cousin, the other as her friend.

During their drive to Mount Lavinia along a road littered on both sides with debris and the charred and smoking ruins of Tamil-owned houses and small shops, Chris and Sujit had agreed on the account of the situation that they would give Latha's teachers.

'We're not,' Chris said, 'in the business of frightening people.'

'No. On the other hand, we do want to get them to safety.'

'Of course. But not if it means circulating *more* rumours.'

'They should, however, be aware of the facts. They sound like highly intelligent people, they'd want to know the extent of the threat to life and property.'

'Well, *we* don't know that yet, do we?'

'When we do.'

'And till then?'

'Oh, I'd suggest we play it by ear . . . We should be guided mostly, perhaps, by what we think Mrs Phillips can bear to hear . . .'

'And what her husband needs to know . . .'

When they reached Mount Lavinia, Chris was still shaking with anger at the information, gathered on the way, that police officers on duty in the Pettah had looked the other way when a Tamil shopkeeper, pursued by a jeering crowd, had fallen on his knees beneath a *bo* tree at a street corner shrine and begged for mercy, only to be cut down and killed, but he said nothing about it to Paula and Rajan. Nor did Sujit think it necessary to pass on to them the information that an angry gang of hoodlums in

Panadura had stormed into a Hindu temple and, failing in their attempt to burn it down, had hustled the officiating priest out of the *kovil*, barred the heavy temple doors against him, thereby preventing any idea he might have had of seeking refuge within its sanctuary, poured petrol over him, and set it alight.

'So I suggest, Mrs Phillips,' said Chris, when he reached the end of his edited account, 'that you pack a couple of suitcases, and prepare to leave with us as soon as possible.'

'Oh, I don't think that's at all necessary,' Rajan said immediately.

Paula, who had got up to leave the room, sat down again.

'May I ask, sir,' Sujit inquired, 'how you will defend your home if it is attacked? The crowds on the Galle Road appear to be targeting Tamil-owned homes and businesses.'

'This is my house,' Rajan said, 'and I have no intention of moving out of it and hiding in the hills for fear of a bunch of thugs and looters. If anyone comes *here* with hatchets and knives, I'll give them a very warm welcome . . . with Molotov cocktails.'

Chris and Sujit looked at each other.

'May we see?'

They followed Rajan to the garage, where they respectfully inspected his apparatus of defence.

'Very impressive,' lied Sujit. 'Judging by what we've heard, though, you'd be outnumbered about sixty to one.'

Chris added: 'It would be no dishonour to leave.'

They pointed out that Paula's presence in the house would complicate matters rather than assist them since, in times of war and social disturbance, women were invariably the first objects of violence.

Neither Paula nor Rajan were willing to hear these arguments.

'In any case,' Paula said, laying her hand on her husband's arm, 'it'll never come to that. Not *here*.'

She was sure, she said, that their Sinhalese neighbours would fight off any attackers:

'They would never let anyone hurt us.'

Chris looked at his watch.

'I suggest that you rethink your strategy, Mr Phillips,' he said. 'And Mrs Phillips, you had really better pack those suitcases. There isn't much time left.'

Chris spoke more sharply than he had intended. He hoped that when he called Latha the next day, he would not have to tell her that he had failed to grant the only request she had made of him in years.

The discussion appeared to have reached a stalemate. Nobody moved. It was only when Seelawathie ran into the house through the back door with the news that a crowd of men from their own neighbourhood, armed with axes and clubs, were approaching the lane, intent on thieving and looting, that Paula made her decision. Fifteen minutes later, with two suitcases packed at the last moment with what she described as basic essentials (these included the manuscript of an English Literature textbook that she and Rajan were currently writing), and holding her little son by the hand, Paula locked up the house, entrusted the keys to Seelawathie, and followed her husband into the back seat of Chris's car.

'Go with God, dear madam,' Seelawathie said to Paula. 'Goodbye, sir. Goodbye, *baba*.'

Tears were running down her cheeks as she waved them goodbye and went into her own house.

The Galle Road was deserted when they drove along it. The crowds had gone elsewhere, leaving heaps of burning rubble behind. A cloud of grey smoke hung in the air.

'We're in your hands now, you know,' Rajan Phillips said to Chris. 'A couple of refugees in our own country. Are you sure you really want such a liability?'

He smiled as he spoke, but beneath his easy manner the two young men could hear the anguish of bitterness and disappointment. Chris made no reply. Behind him, Paula sat in silence, her son's head in her lap.

At the Dickman's Road junction, Chris turned right, drove on for a few minutes, and pulled up in front of a modest house set at a little distance from the road. As they climbed out of the car, and Chris and Sujit lifted the two suitcases out of the boot, a light came on in the porch and a familiar figure stepped out onto the veranda.

'We live in interesting times,' said Herbert Wijesinha. 'I think a drink is indicated, don't you? Soma! Our guests have arrived.'

11

A STATE OF EMERGENCY

During the first four days of the race riots of 1958, Paula and Rajan Phillips, who, with their small son, were occupying Latha's empty bedroom as her parents' guests, had no way of finding out whether their own home in Mount Lavinia was still standing. Rumours flying from the north to the south and from the east to the west of the island and back again, wreaked destruction and laid waste in all directions as each community in turn, learning of fresh horrors, avenged its losses, real or imagined. When murderous mobs, calling themselves Sinhalese patriots, began to patrol the streets of Colombo in broad daylight, slaughtering anyone they suspected of harbouring fleeing Tamils, and burning their homes, Herbert Wijesinha locked and bolted the door of the Phillipses' bedroom, and told the maidservant Podina pleasantly that if she breathed a word of their guests' presence to anyone – anyone – he would skin her alive or personally deliver her to the rampaging thugs.

On the fourth day of the riots, while from Kalaweva to Nalanda people's houses were in flames, the Ceylon Army awoke from its slumber and made some unimportant arrests in the North, chiefly of young men who, armed with brushes and pots of paint, were alleged to have been seen blacking out the Sinhala letter *Sri* on signposts and the number-plates of cars.

On the fifth day, shortly after noon on the 27th of May, an Emergency was declared, and a dawn-to-dusk curfew was imposed by the Government as a method of quelling the rioters' worst excesses. This came as a welcome relief to people whose nights had previously been spent in anxious watching, and it stanched, to some degree at least, the flow of blood.

The curfew was accompanied by governmental censorship of news broadcasts on Radio Ceylon, and a strict clamp on news reports in the papers. Herbert Wijesinha, whose habit it was to walk down to the tea-shop at the street corner every morning to buy his daily paper, found that the early-morning tea-drinkers he met there were a better source of information than either the newspaper or the radio. Rajan did not, of course, advertise his presence in Herbert's house by joining his host on this daily pilgrimage, but when Herbert returned home with his paper they both, like their fellow-citizens, studied its every page. Both became adept at reading between the lines composed by journalists frustrated by the censorship laws, whose grim humour was to become one of the permanent contributions made by the Emergency to the nation's literature.

Irritated by the absence of genuine information in the heavily censored newspapers, Herbert Wijesinha retired to his library and took down from its shelves a selection of the manila folders he had devoted throughout the years to politics and politicians. In times of despair and depression, he told himself, one's spirits needed a lift. He was confident that the posturings of public men, carefully and accurately recorded by his own unforgiving pen, would feed his imagination and fire his energy.

The curfew might even give him the time and opportunity he needed to write the book for which he had been so long collecting material.

How curious, then, and how disappointing, that on opening the folders and looking through the clippings and cartoons he had collected, and the biographies he had painstakingly compiled, it was disgust that Herbert felt and not enthusiasm. Astonishingly, he seemed to have lost his appetite for political gossip.

He looked at his watch. Seven o'clock. In an hour, Soma would have dinner on the table, and he would have to show up, at least out of courtesy to her and to their guests.

Sitting down at his desk, Herbert gave a new folder a heading, and began to write.

EMERGENCY 1958

What we are going through now is, I very much fear, Stage One in an inevitable process: the ultimate disintegration of our world. Nothing more, nothing less. Of course the armed forces and the police will eventually restore some semblance of order, and the beasts that now rage through our streets will crawl back into their swamp. But we cannot expect that they will be content to remain there for long. The age of our innocence is past. Life, as we have known it, is ending, and we must do our best to make sense of what remains.

As intelligent and thoughtful people, should we not have sensed the earthquake coming? Could we not have taken steps to prevent it by correcting the fault-lines in our society? Tectonic plates have been shifting beneath the calm surface of our lives, and to our shame we have ignored them, or refused to recognize them. Will we recognize them in the future? I think not. One newspaper devoted two pages yesterday to attributing what it calls 'our present troubles' to the evil influence of stars and planets. 'The nation is going through a bad period', says the paper's astrological expert, and places the blame for our ills fairly and squarely on Saturn. The mere idea that the causes of those ills might be found in ourselves, and in our reluctance to revise the fateful conditioning of the past, is, of course, bound to be unpopular. Only to be expected. Nobody would be ready to consider such a possibility, much less grant it.

If someone – I, for instance – were to tentatively suggest that, in searching for causes, we might do worse than look into our own prejudices, and our past conduct towards our fellow-men, I haven't the least doubt that within twenty-four hours any such suggestion will be shot down in angry letters to newspapers. I would be called a traitor to my race, and accused of communal motives in purveying such unpatriotic sentiments . . .

'What Herbie is writing so much about, I don't know,' Soma complained outside the library door, causing Herbert to start and drop his pen. 'Dinner is ready, Herbie!'

'Coming, my dear.'

'The book going well?' inquired Rajan Phillips as Herbert took his place at the table. Rajan had been using his own 'curfew time' to work on the English literature text he was writing jointly with Paula.

'Made a start today,' Herbert said. 'Can't say I've got very far, but it's something. Odd thing, though: it's not at all the kind of book I'd planned to write.'

'Oh? So what is it?' Paula was interested.

'I suppose you could call it a journal. My very own Journal of the Plague Year.'

Nobody asked any further questions, and it was not long before Herbert shifted the subject of conversation to something quite unconnected with the Emergency.

Human kind, as Latha Wijesinha wrote, quoting Eliot while she was answering the Modern Poetry question paper at her final examination in 1958, *cannot bear very much reality*.

12

GOOD ADVICE

'These are such sad and worrying times,' Mrs Munasinghe said to Herbert and Soma. 'We've become so nervous that I don't allow Shali to go anywhere on her own, in case she outstays the curfew or runs into ruffians armed with sticks and stones. She can still sing some Sinhala nursery rhymes she learned as a small child, but that's about as far as her knowledge of Sinhala goes. Anupam's just the same, but, thank goodness, he has Chris Wijesinha keeping a lookout for him, and they're both staying at Sujit Roy's flat. According to Chris, Anupam's perfectly safe there.'

'I believe,' Soma said, 'that this would be a very good time for Anupam and Shalini to visit the temple and listen to the monks chanting *pirith*. It will calm their minds and yours, Annabelle. A *pirith* thread around their wrists will be sure to protect them. And Venerable Vachissara will give them good advice.'

Herbert allowed himself the thought that a good many of the 'ruffians armed with sticks and stones' who were currently beating up Tamil people all over the city, and putting their shops and houses to the torch, probably had *pirith nool* tied around their wrists, too. But he saw that Annabelle's distress was genuine, and he kept his irreverence to himself.

'Why doesn't Latha visit the temple, too?' Annabelle Munasinghe suggested. 'It might help her exam results.'

A visit to the Munasinghes' 'family temple' was accordingly arranged for the following Saturday. Shalini cried off at the last moment, but Latha, demurely clad in the white garments required of devotees, duly removed her sandals at the entrance to the building, and entered the image-house with Anupam. Each carried an offering in the form of white frangipani blossoms, arranged in a cone woven from fresh green leaves.

'When you have placed your flowers on the altar, Anupam, you must prostrate yourself before the image, and then find yourself and Latha a place with the other devotees, to listen to the chanting of the monks,' his mother instructed him. 'When the chanting is finished, the monk will tie white thread around your wrists for your protection, and he will bless you. Auntie Soma and I will wait for you at the *vihara* entrance. The Chief Priest is expecting you.'

Why such detailed instructions? Doesn't Anupam know how he should conduct himself in a Buddhist temple?

Schooled at Amarapāli M.V., and accustomed to accompanying her mother and her aunts to the Vajirarāma Temple, Buddhist rites and the order in which they are to be performed had been second nature to Latha for years. How much truth could there be, then, in her mother's assertion that Anupam came from a 'very good *Buddhist* family'?

In fact, by the time he and Latha walked across the immaculately swept courtyard to the *vihāra*, British-educated Anupam had come very close to abandoning the whole project. It was all very well for Latha, he had thought irritably as they laid their flowers at the feet of the golden Buddha image with its heavy-lidded sapphire eyes and listened to the chanting of the monks, the ritual was familiar to her, probably almost automatic. But these were rites which did not come naturally to him, and he had no understanding of their significance. The simplest action appeared to be fraught with meaning that to him seemed pointless and incomprehensible.

Just when he had been about to place his flowers on the altar, Latha had startled him by grabbing his arm.

'Use your *right* hand, Anupam, or use them *both*! But not the *left*.'

He had obeyed her curious command without asking her to explain it, but he had done so resentfully; and Latha, who by this time had come to know Anupam's moods quite well, sensed that he was annoyed. She saw him recoil and very nearly turn away when one of the monks who had chanted *pirith* approached him with a spool of white thread and tied a double strand of it around his right wrist.

He's longing to remove it! And I'll bet he will, once he's out of here.

Anupam hadn't liked leaving his shoes at the temple entrance, either.

'Don't worry, no one's going to steal them!' Latha couldn't help whispering teasingly.

Anupam scowled in reply.

The Chief Priest was waiting for them. Venerable Vachissara Hamaduruwo was seated on a carved, cane-bottomed couch at the far end of a large room, fanning himself with a pleated palm-leaf fan. The skin of his face and of his bared shoulder, half covered by his yellow robe, was smooth and unlined, despite his eighty years. He inclined his head courteously as they approached him, and smiled approvingly when he saw the white threads on their wrists.

'Good, good. Very good,' he said in English.

Anupam looked about for a chair to sit on, but there was none. He and Latha remained standing before the monk until two young novice monks came forward, and placed low stools at either side of the couch.

'No one, not even a King or a President, can take a higher seat than a monk, or sit on an equal level,' Latha told him later. 'It's a *rule*.'

And it's a rule everywhere in the Buddhist world, Anupam! You're a diplomat – but it's obvious you've never had a posting in Thailand or Burma.

This is all such utter nonsense! Anupam thought. And yet Latha seemed to accept it all without question or protest.

Venerable Vachissara had a soft voice, so soft that both young people had to strain their ears to catch his words. His old eyes looked at Latha kindly, but appraisingly, through horn-rimmed spectacles.

'I have heard very good things about you, child,' the monk said. 'I hear that you come from good Sinhalese stock, and that your mother's family is one that has protected the *sangha* and the *dhamma* through many generations. I hear that you are gifted and clever in your own right, and that you have taken your examinations at the University. So you are at a point in your life when you must make some important decisions. Am I right in thinking you have come to me for blessings and advice?'

Latha replied, using the traditional forms of address, that she would receive with respect and gratitude anything he would say to her.

'I understand, my son,' the monk said, addressing Anupam, 'that your friend here is hesitating between two choices in life. Should she choose the life of the householder? Or the life of the scholar? The two are not incompatible, both are virtuous, both can bring her great happiness. I myself chose the second, and have never regretted my choice: the greatest blessing of the scholar's life is the knowledge that in translating the ancient Pāli texts, one is advancing the true philosophy of the blessed Lord Buddha. Its satisfactions are therefore considerable, although sometimes there are disappointments along the way. The path of a householder, on the other hand, and especially that of a wife, has no obscure passages. It is an easy path, perfectly clear and straight . . .'

Oh, yeah? Shall I tell you, Venerable, about my cousin Rohini? She's a young wife who proposed to hang herself and her husband from the roof of their house on Vesak day, in lieu of paper lanterns . . .

She had no time to develop this subversive line of reflection, for it seemed that the Chief Priest had more to say.

'. . . with no room for disappointment, since her husband is the light of her existence, and all her actions can have but one end in view, his welfare and the welfare of his family.'

At this point the Chief Priest paused so long that Latha, under the impression that he had reached the end of his homily, opened her lips to thank him formally in reply. Before she could begin to do so he took a deep breath, closed his eyes, and continued, in a musical chant:

'Without informing your husband, do not with hasty steps go out of your house.

'Be as a servant to your husband's relatives and friends, and treat your servants alike in sorrow or in gladness. If you become rich, do not show unbecoming pride or ostentation.

'Sweep your home and your garden constantly, and do not tolerate the sight of dirt or rubbish anywhere in your dwelling. At daybreak and evening, do not fail to light lamps in your house.

'When your husband returns to the house after a long journey, welcome him gladly and, without ordering a servant to wash the dust from his feet, do it with your own hands. Do not stand in the doorway of your house, looking idly at the passers-by. Do not be indolent in the work of your household.

'Lie down to sleep after everyone else in the household, and be the first to rise at dawn. When your husband awakens, be near him for his security! Always consider what will be profitable, now and in the future, do not be wayward, do not breach the bond of affection, never overrule your husband's wishes.

'When your husband is enraged, do not speak harsh words, but generate kindly compassion in your mind; and even if his affections have wandered elsewhere, do not think of another marriage . . .'

The Chief Priest broke off in mid-chant, opened his eyes, and smiled sweetly at Latha.

'I hope you will make allowances for an elderly person like myself,' he told her. 'I live out of the great world. The advice I give you on married life is taken out of our scholarly books, and it is possible that what I say to you may be . . . a little out of date.'

Latha smiled back at him, and made no reply.

Describing this meeting later to her father, she confessed that Venerable Vachissara's blithe assertion that a husband must necessarily be the light of a wife's existence had made her yearn to contradict him.

'I wanted to tell him about Rohini and Ravi,' she told Herbert. 'Do you remember that Vesak visit we paid them, before Ravi died?'

'I remember it very well,' said Herbert. 'But, to be frank, Latha, I hoped you had forgotten it! Did you tell him what Rohini said?'

'Of course not! He's such a charming old gentleman. It would have upset him too much to learn what goes on in the real world. And I didn't tell him that I'd spotted the source of his good advice, either – that would have upset *and* embarrassed him!'

Latha had perceived, when Venerable Vachissara was halfway through his homily, that he was quoting from the poet Sri Rahula's *Kavyasekara*, presumably because he had no original advice to give her.

'It sounds to me,' Herbert said, 'as if your behaviour at the temple has been exemplary. I'm very proud of you.'

What if the Chief Priest had been unable to instruct Latha in the proper duties of a modern wife? There was nothing anyone could teach his daughter about the graces essential to a female scholar.

Ironically, the temple visit had reactivated Soma Wijesinha's hopes of making a match between Anupam and Latha.

'I wish you had been there to see them, Herbie!' she exclaimed. 'Dressed all in white, like a bride and bridegroom on the wedding *pōruwa*, with white flowers in their hands.'

'Did our Latha look happy or scared?'

'Happy, of course! Why should she look scared? What has she got to be scared of?'

'Oh, nothing,' Herbert replied, and did not mention a visit he had had from his niece, Tsunami, while Soma and Latha were at the temple.

'Uncle Herbert,' Tsunami had confided, in the appealing way that had always touched him when she was a little girl, 'I was worried before, but now I'm terrified. Sujit went to see Pater about our getting married, Pater turned him down and made the most awful scene. Sujit doesn't mind so much about that, but how can we marry if Pater objects? Sujit says he doesn't care what my father, or anyone else says, he's made up his mind. He says we're getting married, no matter what.'

'Quite right! I'm glad to hear it.'

'But – *Uncle Herbert*!' Tsunami cried. 'What am I to do?'

No wonder Latha is so protective of this fragile child. Go carefully now, Herbert! She's not as worldly as she pretends to be . . .

After a moment, Herbert said:

'What about your mother, Tsunami? Is your mother agreeable to your marrying Sujit?'

'Yes, she is. She's met him, and talked with him. She told me afterwards that she thinks he's right for me, and I for him . . .'

Wonder just what Helen told Sujit . . . I'd like to have heard that conversation!

'Well, then, there you are! Sujit seems to have given up on your father's ever seeing sense, but you obviously care about getting parental permission – which, by the way, is very nice to hear, Tsunami! And now that you have your mother's permission, surely you can relax and stop worrying?'

He patted her shoulder affectionately.

'If your father doesn't give his consent, Soma and I are here to look after you, not to mention Latha and at least two of your brothers. You are of age now, child, and no one can stop you marrying Sujit if you wish to.

Not that anyone's going to try – I have the impression that Sujit, in his present mood, is unstoppable . . .'

Tsunami was smiling.

'You always manage to see the funny side of things, Uncle Herbert.'

'On the contrary: I'm being perfectly serious and sensible. As regards money, you both will have more than enough to live on—'

'It's not money I'm worried about,' Tsunami said. 'It's marriage itself – I'm so frightened of it. I know everybody says that it's a happy state, and a blessed state, and every magazine and novel tells you that a girl should regard getting married as the thing to aim for in life – that, and bringing up a family – but just look at my mother and father, Uncle Herbert, what kind of marriage did *they* have? There are so many people we know, who have ended up so miserable, they don't just wish they'd never got married, they wish they'd never been born . . . Suppose Sujit and I end up like that? How could I possibly bear it?'

Herbert studied his niece.

'Now, look here,' he said. 'It's no good thinking like that. For one thing, you're exaggerating. There are lots of happy marriages around.'

'Name one,' Tsunami said.

'Well,' Herbert said at last, after several minutes' thought, 'there's us. Your Auntie Soma and myself. We're all right. Each of us has changed a bit from what we were when we met, but it hasn't made any difference. People grow older, they change. That's life, Tsunami. You have to *expect* change.'

'What if Sujit changes? What if he becomes like . . . like Pater?' Tsunami said.

Herbert laughed.

'Not in a million years,' he said. 'To become like Rowland, a man has to have some very special character traits. Or else he must develop them. From what I've seen of him, your *sahib*'s missed out on the lot. You don't need to worry about that. And you don't need to worry about your novel, either. You can go right ahead, and give it a happy ending.'

'Latha told you about that, did she?'

'We talk a lot about books, Latha and I,' he answered. 'Naturally, we talked about yours.'

'Uncle Herbert,' said his niece. 'how long have you and Auntie Soma been married?'

'Let's see . . . It'll be twenty-six years on the nineteenth of June,' Herbert said.

'And you've always been happy? No regrets? No disagreements? You *must* have a secret! Why don't you tell me what it is? To let me in on a secret like that would be better than a wedding present. Besides, you'll be doing literature a service: I can use it in my novel.'

'Oh, we have many, many disagreements,' Herbert said. 'As Latha may have told you, we argue all the time. But you're right when you say that we must have a secret. We do. When your Auntie Soma and I reach a point when it's obvious to us both that agreement is impossible, there's a very simple solution. She goes her way, and I . . .'

'Yes?'

'I go her way.'

13

OPINIONS AT THE S.S.C.

Extract from the *Daily News*:

MYSTERY SHOOTING OF CABINET MINISTER

In the early hours of the morning of the 11th of June, an assassin's bullet brought about the death of the Hon'ble Mr D.K. Beliwatte, Minister in the present Government. The tragic incident occurred on the promenade at Galle Face Green, Colombo, in the darkness before dawn. The Minister had been taking his usual morning constitutional on the Green in the company of the Hon'ble Mr Rowland Wijesinha, his cabinet colleague. Mr Wijesinha was taken by ambulance with injuries to his neck and shoulder, to Burdan's Hospital, where he remains under close observation.

The building nearest to the spot on the promenade on which the Minister fell is the Galle Face Hotel. Whether the Hotel is close enough to that spot for the fatal shots that killed Mr Beliwatte and injured his colleague to have been fired from one of its windows, is yet to be determined.

Two bodyguards had been in attendance on the two Ministers; and with security so tight during the Emergency, both at the Hotel and on the Green, it is considered unlikely that anyone could have approached the two Ministers on foot without being seen.

A possible explanation for the tragedy has been offered by Mr Calistus Nidikumba, Secretary to the Cabinet, that the Minister was accidentally felled by a bullet which had been intended for his colleague. It is well known that Mr Rowland Wijesinha is not sympathetic to what is known as the 'Tamil cause', the demand presently being put forward by politicians from the North for equal representation with the Sinhalese in the House of Representatives. He had recently made a controversial speech on the subject in Parliament. Police inquiries are proceeding.

Despite the early hour, tidings of the shooting on the Green had spread like a *patana* fire in July. Even before the first ambulance, its sirens blaring, arrived at Burdan's Hospital, a large and excited crowd had gathered outside the hospital gates. When it was seen to be closely followed by another ambulance, equally noisy, the crowd outside the hospital trebled in size and its excitement rose to fever-pitch.

The prospect of viewing one dead Minister would have attracted a multitude in Colombo at any time, but the possibility of viewing two was irresistible. A stretcher bearing Rowland's injured and bleeding body was wheeled through the hospital's swing doors. As it hurtled along the corridors and into the Intensive Care Unit, his voice could be heard protesting feebly:

'No special treatment for me, please, no special treatment . . .'

But his protests were in vain, for Moira had entered the Unit.

'*No special treatment?* What are you talking about?' she demanded of a cowering nurse who had dared to repeat Rowland's request. 'Don't you know who this patient is? *This patient is the Prime Minister's cousin!*'

At the sound of her voice, all barriers fell. Moira was very well known on every level of the hospital's three floors, for it was at Burdan's that she accumulated the political credentials of compassion, posing once a week for the press cameras in her capacity as a cabinet minister's wife, folding bed sheets, distributing spectacles, advising dietitians, even – on one occasion – smilingly assisting with admissions.

While Rowland lay in his hospital bed, being lovingly nursed by his wife and recovering slowly from his injuries, public attention fastened on the wide-ranging implications of D.K. Beliwatte's death.

'This bally Emergency is the bloody limit,' said 'Slim' Kodikara, downing a whisky-soda at the Sinhalese Sports Club. 'Couldn't even give the old bugger a proper send-off.'

Everyone present agreed. As the Emergency had not yet been lifted, and large gatherings of people were forbidden in public places, the passing of D.K. Beliwatte had been marked by a private funeral, which only members of his immediate family were permitted to attend. This had ruled out the usual *tamasha* that surrounds a politician's funeral, and greatly disappointed Beliwatte's fellow-stalwarts of the King's College O.B.A., who would otherwise have attended the funeral in force, together with members of those two other noble bodies of men, the Boy Scouts Association and the Ceylon Kennel Club (Beliwatte's hobby had been the breeding of pedigree bull-terriers).

Equal representation for Tamils and Sinhalese in the House of Representatives! It was the opinion of the drinkers at the S.S.C. that no Sinhalese worthy of the name would stand for such an arrangement.

These bloody Tamils had been getting above themselves lately. They needed to be taught a bloody lesson, said 'Slim' Kodikara, and he, for one, was bloody glad that the people themselves had taken matters in hand during the recent riots, and all but wiped the bloody buggers off the face of the bloody earth. The Emergency had stopped them temporarily, of course, but before it was imposed they had bloody well managed to make their point. They had done so, at any rate, in Colombo, and if they wished to carry their heroic battle into other parts of the country, Emergency or no bloody Emergency, they certainly had *his* bloody support.

'Hear! Hear!' said other patriots clustered around the bar.

Next, everyone took up the topic of the Beliwatte assassination.

Did anyone have any theories as to who had done it, and why? What about the talk going round that the fatal bullet had been intended for Rowland Wijesinha? Probably a figment of a journalist's imagination – those chaps at Lake House would do anything these days to sell their bloody papers.

But if it wasn't, and the bugger in the assassin's gun sights *had* actually been Wijesinha, now if that were the case, well, all 'Slim' Kodikara could say was that it was a thoroughly bad bloody show. Wijesinha, as everybody knew, was a harmless chap, a sportsman and a gentleman, if ever there was one, and bloody generous too: his name was on the College rolls, and on the donors' lists of just about every bloody public school in the island. A thoroughly sound fellow, in fact. If that bullet had found its mark it would have been a terrible thing for his children, and of course for Mrs Moira Wijesinha, a very cultured lady who was devoted to her husband.

But who would want to kill Rowland Wijesinha? Someone must have had a motive, and it was to be hoped the police would succeed in ferreting it out.

Ah, but the theory that the victim had been killed by mistake could well have been put forward by the police themselves to shield the real culprit. Had anyone thought of that? Everybody knew that honesty and integrity were things of the past in the police force these days.

How had it been done?

The obvious answer, someone said, calling for another tot, was that the gunman had pretended to be an early-morning jogger on the promenade. He must have run up to old Belly from the opposite direction, shot him at close range, and run off along the promenade before the bodyguards or Wijesinha became aware that anything untoward had happened.

'Impossible!' said someone else. 'The curfew was on. At that time of the day he'd have been stopped on his way to the Green by a patrol car, and asked to show his pass. Even if he'd managed to get to the Green, he'd have been stopped by Belly's bodyguards, or at least by one of the officers at the police post on the promenade.'

This earned a smile from one of the speaker's drinking companions.

'Ever been walking on the Green in the early hours yourself, machan?' this friend inquired. 'The chaps in the police post are so sound asleep that you'd have to let off a bomb under their bloody chairs for one of them to hear you.'

When Ranil Wijesinha happened to drop into the club to renew his subscription, the discussions took a new turn. People crowded round him.

How was his father recovering in hospital?

Did Ranil intend to run for old Belly's vacant seat in the House at the next election? He was urged to do so. The country needed men like him in positions of real power.

Ranil shook his head.

'Too much to do,' he said.

It was understood that, as a result of his father's incapacitation, many urgent matters had devolved on him as the old man's right-hand man. Besides, he could not abandon his responsibilities in connection with the Wijesinha estates. And there was another reason:

'In any case, there'll be a much better candidate than myself coming forward for Paranapitiya. The P.M.'s persuaded my aunt to stand for election.'

Extract from the *Times of Ceylon*:

A NEW VOICE IN POLITICS
THE P.M. SAYS: 'I KNEW SHE COULD DO IT!'

Large crowds gathered on Sunday to hear Mrs Moira Wijesinha, wife of Mr Rowland Wijesinha, Minister for Cultural Affairs, address an election meeting in Bathalapitiya, her ancestral village, located in the district held until recently by her relative, the late Mr D.K. Beliwatte. Our outstation correspondent writes that Mrs Wijesinha, in accepting nomination for the seat left vacant by the murder of Mr Beliwatte, had done so with great reluctance. A typical Ceylonese lady of simple tastes, shy and retiring by nature, Mrs Wijesinha said that her time is fully taken up at present with the care of her husband, who is still in hospital, recovering from his wounds. Her principal interest has never been in politics, but in a quiet family life, although in recent years she has ventured sometimes into public life to support her husband's cultural initiatives. A very large proportion of the audience was made up of women of the Bathalapitiya electorate, anxious to demonstrate their sympathy for the Beliwatte family, and curious to see how Mrs Moira Wijesinha would conduct herself in her new role.

A delighted Prime Minister told our correspondent after the meeting: 'I knew she could do it!' He said that Mrs Wijesinha's grasp of political issues and public affairs had impressed him greatly from the time he first met her at her wedding to the Hon'ble Mr Rowland Wijesinha. Her performance today had proved that his judgment had been correct. He had every confidence that she would show herself to be a capable and responsible leader.

In a brief interview that Mrs Wijesinha granted to reporters, she confessed that she had never considered a career in politics for herself, having thought only of assisting her husband's work as a parliamentarian and cabinet minister. In fact, Mrs Wijesinha said, she had learned everything she knew about politics from her husband, whom she had married soon after completing her education at that exclusive institution, the Girls' High School, in Kandy. It was only because of her family connection with her uncle, the late Mr D.K. Beliwatte, that she had accepted nomination for the seat he had formerly occupied in Parliament. She would not, otherwise, ever have come forward for any seat but her husband's.

'My entry into politics was, strangely enough, foretold some months ago by our family astrologer, who told me that he had read a brilliant career for me in my stars. It will be my pride as well as my duty, in the future, to implement the policies my late uncle held dear, which his untimely death has prevented from coming to fruition.'

When a journalist from the *Ceylon Observer* telephoned Ranil Wijesinha to request an interview, Ranil had expected that their discussion would focus on his aunt Moira's political future. He was mistaken. The journalist had a new theory to explore concerning D.K. Beliwatte's assassination.

'But why should you think I can help you?'

The journalist hesitated.

'Some aspects of my theory, sir, are a little . . . sensitive. At least, your father the Minister may think so. But as he is in hospital, and unable to grant me an interview, I thought I should consult your good self before I turn the piece in to my editor for review.'

Ranil, who had been about to dismiss the journalist, changed his mind. 'Let's have a look.'

He read the draft through twice:

INVESTIGATIONS INTO MINISTER'S MURDER
DID THE ASSASSIN APPROACH BY LAND? . . . OR BY SEA?
MYSTERY VISITOR

Since the possibility has now been ruled out that the shot which killed Minister Beliwatte a fortnight ago was fired from a window of the Galle Face Hotel, other theories are being explored. One such theory is that since tight security would have rendered approach from the landward side almost impossible, the Minister's assassin might have made his approach from the sea.

'A small motor boat would have served the purpose well,' your reporter was told by Detective Inspector Sherlock Ralahami, who is working on the case. 'In a suitably small craft, a person with knowledge of the tides could have avoided the rocks, and moored on the beach below the promenade. A small boat would not have been noticed there, especially in the hours before sunrise.'

With regard to possible reasons for the murder, it has been suggested that the killing, previously thought to have political overtones, might have resulted from a personal reason. In that connection we can reveal that some days prior to the murder of his colleague, Mr Wijesinha received in his office at the Ministry an unknown visitor who brought with him a proposal for his consideration. The exact nature of the proposal is not known, though it has been suggested that it related to a Government loan, and acquisition of Government property. The Minister is said to have found the proposal unsatisfactory, and rejected it. The disappointed petitioner, seeking revenge, could have shot the wrong man.

'Interesting,' Ranil said at last.

'Thank you, sir.'

'What's this about an unknown person visiting my father? Anyone particular in mind?'

'Some suggestions have been made, sir, but they have not yet been followed up.'

'Well, I can tell you straight away that this is the first I've heard of any unauthorized person visiting my father. Nobody can see the Minister without first making an appointment. His secretary will have a record of all of those.'

'A letter from you, sir, would help a lot.'

Ranil smiled. He knew Francis Gonpala, his father's personal assistant, a stiff-necked civil servant if ever there was one. Francis would have promptly choked off all inquiries, especially those made by inquisitive journalists.

'That isn't a problem. But I should like to see the piece before it goes to press. Make sure that I do.'

'Yes, sir. Thank you, sir.'

The report was printed, and created a wave of speculation. Two days later, the journalist requested a second interview with Ranil. His theory had crystallized. The difficulty, he told Ranil, was that investigation of it would involve members of the influential Wijesinha and Beliwatte circle of family and friends. The editor would most definitely refuse to finance defence costs if a libel action were to be brought against the newspaper on account of it, and the journalist would then be out of a job.

'If you would just look through my draft, sir . . .'

INDIAN MAGNATE HELD FOR QUESTIONING

The visitor who called at the office of the Minister for Cultural Affairs, Mr Rowland Wijesinha, a few days prior to the murder of his colleague, Mr D.K. Beliwatte, on Galle Face Green on the 11th of June, has been identified as Mr Sujit Roy, an Indian national, owner of a shipping company based in the Southern Province.

This paper understands that Mr Roy has been a visitor at Lucas Falls, Mr Wijesinha's hill-country estate, and enjoys close personal relationships with his children (two of whom, Mr Christopher Wijesinha and Miss Tsunami Wijesinha, have been visitors to his company's premises, together with their mother, Mr Rowland Wijesinha's former wife, Mrs Helen Goldman).

'Sure of your facts?' Ranil asked.

'Yes, sir.'

'If what you say here is true, you've certainly done your homework. You've told me things that even *I* didn't know . . .'

The journalist was pleased.

'However—' and Ranil drew a line through the final paragraph – 'I think you had better leave your draft report with me for a few days. Can you do that?'

The journalist was disappointed, but he knew better than to protest.

'Certainly, sir. I have a copy.'

The publication of the news report, even in its truncated state, created a sensation at the S.S.C.

'Anyone know anything,' someone wanted to know, 'about this fellow Roy who owns a shipping company in the South?'

'I know him very well,' volunteered a fellow-drinker. 'Drives a Cadillac.'

'No,' a friend corrected him, 'he drives a Chev—'

'Rubbish!' said a third. 'He drives an Opel Kapitan. Saw him the other day at the C.L.T.A, and had a good look at his car.'

'Ask 'Slim' Kodikara about him,' someone said. 'Bugger knows this chap Roy well. They were fellow-guests at Lucas Falls a few months ago. They were invited up by the Wijesinha boys.'

'Any truth in the story?' someone asked 'Slim'. 'Could Roy have been angling for a loan?'

'Not likely!' was the answer. 'The man's feelthy rich. He's hardly the kind of person to pursue a minister for a Government loan.'

'Totally cock-eyed reporting,' was the opinion of another member of the group. 'Everyone knows Rowland Wijesinha's looking for a buyer for Lucas Falls.'

'Place like that eats up money in repairs and maintenance,' said someone sagely; and someone else asserted that he knew for a fact that the old man had had to mortgage other property in order to keep things going.

Several rounds later, a new theory had developed to resolve the mystery surrounding D.K. Beliwatte's murder. The businessman, whoever he was, had put in a bid for the old ancestral. Wijesinha wasn't having any of that, and told him so. And poor old Belly had been accidentally bumped off as a result.

'Wijesinha property in the hands of Indian business?' as 'Slim' Kodikara said. 'What did our pals in Polonnaruwa and Panadura go to all the trouble of rioting for? You have to be bloody kidding.'

14

FAMILY CONCLAVE

When Tsunami came down to breakfast, she was surprised to find her brother Ranil seated in her father's place at the head of the dining table. Tara, at Ranil's right hand, was presiding over the coffee pot, and Moira was nowhere to be seen. Probably visiting Pater at Burdan's, Tsunami thought; although it was just as likely, these days, that she would be at an election meeting.

Chris wandered in, followed almost immediately by Colin.

'Hello, everyone.'

For all the Wijesinha children to be in the family home at the one time had by now become such a rare occurrence that Tsunami could not help wondering what had brought it about

'Going shopping with Auntie Moira, Tara?' she said. 'And Colin, it's a bit early in the morning for you, isn't it?'

Ranil looked at his watch, and put down his coffee cup.

'Nine o'clock, on the dot,' he said. 'Thank you for your punctuality, everyone. Especially Tara and Colin. I appreciate it.'

Goodness, how pompous Ranil sounds! Where does he think he is? In a company office? And who does he think he is? Chairman of the Board?

'As I mentioned,' Ranil went on, 'there is urgent family business to be discussed.'

'Oh?' Tsunami said. 'No one mentioned any meeting or family business to me. Should I be here? I'll take my cup of coffee out on to the veranda, if you like.'

'Sit down, if you please, Tsunami,' Ranil said. 'The matters to be discussed concern us all.'

Tara evidently thought some explanation was called for.

'Ranil asked me to be here at nine o'clock,' she said.

Ranil stated:

'I sent messages to Tara and to Colin, because they don't live in this house, and they would need to make special arrangements to attend. Since you, Chris and I actually live here, Tsunami, and we're all usually down to breakfast by nine, I didn't consider it necessary to inform you.'

'What about Auntie Moira?' Colin inquired. 'If it's urgent family business, shouldn't she be here?'

'There are certain matters that are best discussed first among ourselves,' Ranil replied. 'I shall be speaking to Auntie Moira, and of course to Pater too, about those matters. But later on. Eventually. And maybe, if our own discussions go well, there won't be any need to involve them at all.'

He looked around the table at his siblings, then drew a folded piece of paper from his pocket.

'This is the draft of a journalist's report on the Beliwatte murder. It has not been published, and it will not be published until I give the writer my permission to print. I have had it held back because I want you all to be aware of what this report might mean for our family. Have a look at it.'

He handed the paper to Tara.

'Read through it carefully, please, before you pass it on. And look particularly at the last paragraph.'

The paper went the round of the table, while Ranil poured himself another cup of coffee. When it came back to him, he turned to Tara.

'Well?'

'Is it true that Mother is in Colombo?'

'She isn't here now,' Chris replied. 'But she did visit Colombo some months ago, on her way to India to see her family. While she was here, she met Tsunami, Colin and Latha.'

'Did she bring Goldman with her?'

'Yes,' said Colin. 'I met them both. They're fine.'

'Really? How interesting,' Ranil said. 'I'm sure we're all glad to hear that good news. And why, may one ask, were Tara and I not included in this meeting?'

'She didn't ask to see you,' Chris answered simply. 'She—'

'Oh, so you were the go-between, were you, Chris?'

Tara had taken a few moments to digest this news and its connection with the draft she had just read.

'And I suppose it was you who introduced Sujit Roy to her, and encouraged her to visit his wretched boatyard? I suppose you even took her there? My *God*, Chris, you really are the limit! What were you thinking of?'

'I thought it was necessary for Tsunami to see Mother again. And for Mother to meet the man Tsunami's going to marry.'

'You are mistaken,' Ranil said. 'They are *not* going to marry. Pater has forbidden Roy to have any contact with Tsunami.'

'Well, thank heaven for that, at least,' Tara said.

She turned on her sister.

'What is the *matter* with you, Tsunami? Do you *have* to plunge this family into crisis after crisis? No sooner have we all recovered from one of your love affairs, than we have to cope with another.'

'Sorry, Tara, I'm not with you,' interposed Colin. 'What are you talking about? What crisis? What love affair? I thought we were discussing a news report about the Beliwatte murder. Why does nobody in this family tell me what's going on?'

'Your sister Tara, Colin,' said Ranil in tones of ice, 'is talking about the fact that Tsunami has got herself involved, not just once but *twice*, with men who are not welcome in this family. They are unwelcome because . . . because they are not socially acceptable persons. I don't have time this morning to go into all the sordid details – you can ask Tsunami for them later, if she is not too ashamed of herself to give them to you. The point that we must all decide now is what we are going to do *as a family*, about the damage which publicity of the kind represented by that paper I passed around can do to Pater's political future. And to Auntie Moira's, too, of course. That journalist's investigations link us with a *very* shady underworld—'

'And they link us by *name*,' interrupted Tara furiously. 'The *disgrace*! It suggests that Lucas Falls – *Lucas Falls!* – is a haunt of criminals and smugglers and murderers . . .'

'Only if it is published,' Ranil said. 'We won't need to worry about that – I'm determined to keep that paragraph out of the papers, even if it takes a hefty bribe to do it. What concerns me much more, I must say, is the way the press may use the Beliwatte case to drag the story of Mother's elopement with Goldman back into public view in order to sell newspapers. That's the kind of thing people love to read, and the kind of situation they love to speculate about. *Why* did she do it? Did Pater treat her badly? . . .'

'Yes,' said Tsunami, speaking for the first time. 'And all those other questions, too – Are the children his? Or are they Goldman's? You don't mention that, Ranil. Why? Doesn't it worry you? It fascinates other people. Maybe you think the question doesn't affect you and Tara and Chris, because you were all born before Franz Goldman came to Rothschild's, that it only affects Colin and me. I suppose that's why you've all been talking about me, *discussing* me, as if I weren't even in this room. But the public speculation doesn't need to stop there, does it? If Mother was the kind of woman they'd like to think she was, *none* of the children need be Pater's, she could have been sleeping with every man who came to the house . . .'

'Okay, sis, don't upset yourself,' Chris said quietly, taking Tsunami's hand. 'As far as I am concerned, that journalist can print what he likes. We all know what Mother was – is – really like, and nothing anyone says can change that. In any case, there isn't anything in this piece that is untrue or fabricated – Mother *did* visit the boatyard at Hambantota, Sujit *did* come to Lucas Falls as my guest, and he *did* call on Pater at the Ministry, to ask his permission to marry Tsunami. He called on him by appointment. There was nothing underhand or furtive about it, Colin, whatever has been suggested just now, and if I may say so, Ranil, you are completely out of order to suggest that Sujit is . . . what did you say? "Socially unacceptable". The only error I can find in the draft is that the writer describes Mother as "Mrs Goldman". That's not correct. She has not married Franz.'

'*What?*' Tara could not believe her ears. 'But everyone says . . .'

'Yes, "everyone says". But I've met them both in Sydney, and I can assure you they are not married. Good friends, yes, companions, yes, but not husband and wife. For the record, Tara, Mother still signs her name as Helen Wijesinha.'

'Does she, indeed!' said Ranil. 'I wonder whether she has any legal right to do that. She should call herself "Helen Ratnam", isn't that what women do when their husbands divorce them? They go back to their own family name. This may sound harsh to a sentimentalist like you, Chris, but I can tell you frankly that I, for one, have no desire to have Mother's name linked with mine. There are some countries in the world where women are stoned to death for adultery. Not that we have to look to the Middle East for examples. In Mother's own country – India – the punishment in some rural communities for a woman who does what Mother did is public rape. We are, I believe, more civilized and compassionate here. Ostracism will do. When Mother left Pater for Goldman, she established herself as a woman of loose moral character, and that makes her the kind of woman with whom none of us should have anything to do.'

There was silence for a moment around the table. Then Colin said:

'Don't you talk about Mother like that.'

He got up from his chair. His spectacles had misted over, so he had to hold on to the backs of chairs as he walked around the table to seat himself beside Tsunami. Ranil watched him with undisguised amusement.

'Thank you, Colin. I'm sure we all appreciate that very valuable contribution to the discussion.'

'And here's a contribution from *me*,' said Chris. 'You've just suggested that stoning a woman to death for sexual misdemeanours is a just punishment, Ranil. Do you think it's wise to be quite so ready to pass judgment on the subject of Mother's so-called moral failings? Are you, for instance, so much above reproach that you can afford to throw the first stone?'

Ranil ignored Chris's question.

'Well, we certainly know now where we stand, don't we, in relation to this situation, and in relation to each other. Tara and I on Pater's side, and the three of you against him.'

Tsunami said:

'That's not true, Ranil. I've supported Pater through everything, even when he married Moira, and she made him send Tara and me to boarding school. That wasn't easy. I made a promise to him that I would end my engagement to marry Daniel Rajaratnam, and that I'd have no further contact with him: I've kept my promise. That's not been easy, either. But on *this* matter, I'm not going along with him. It's unreasonable of Pater to forbid me to marry Sujit, and if you and Tara want to tell tales to him that I said so, you can go right ahead. I don't care.'

'You'll care all right,' Tara said viciously, 'if Pater dies of his injuries, and you find that he's cut you out of his will. I'll bet you didn't expect that, did you? Well, that's what he did when he found that you wanted to marry this nobody Roy, and disgrace the family name. He was furious when he heard about it. Auntie Moira and I thought he was going to have a stroke. It was all we could do to prevent him going up to Peradeniya again, ill as he was, and dragging you back to Colombo as he did the last time. Then Auntie Moira pointed out that he shouldn't distress himself unduly about it – "For all you or anyone else knows, she's Goldman's daughter," Auntie Moira said. "Why should *you* care whom she marries?" That actually calmed him down a bit. I put in a word too. "Tsunami will see sense," I told Pater, "when her exams are over." Then Auntie Moira suggested that he should call the lawyer, and write a proper will, to make sure that if anything happened to him, the property he had inherited should go to his own children, and not to someone else's—'

'Excellent idea,' Ranil said. 'Keep things in the family.'

'Besides, as she reminded him, her astrologer had read your horoscope, Tsunami, and he'd warned Auntie Moira that your stars are hostile to Pater's . . . Well,' Tara continued, 'I thought that after Roy had been sent packing, and the dust had settled on the whole affair, Auntie Moira and I would talk Pater into writing another will, reinstating Tsunami. If Tsunami behaved herself, that is. Well, that's just not on any more. I've had enough. Rajaratnam was bad enough, but *this* . . .! I'm writing you off, Tsunami, it's obvious that you don't have a clue about the meaning of family values and don't give a damn for family tradition. And when you find yourself alone in the world without any family support, and deserted by one of those feckless individuals you're so fond of associating with, maybe you'll have learned something from the realization that you've deserved every bit of it.'

Tara had run out of breath. She pushed back her chair, and rose from her seat at the table.

'I'm sorry, Ranil, I can't afford to waste any more time on this nonsense. I'm leaving.'

Her siblings watched her go, and they heard her car start up on the drive before anyone spoke again.

'Well, that's that,' Ranil said. 'I regret that Tara spoke to you as strongly as she did, Tsunami, but now you know exactly what your position is with regard to the family, and with regard to the family property.'

He looked around the table.

'You may not be aware, everybody, that I, as Pater's eldest son, am the executor of his new will. In the event of his dying as a result of his injuries which, naturally, I sincerely hope will not happen – I shall, of course, be scrupulously fair to all of you. But I warn you all that Pater's wishes as regards his own possessions must come first with me. On no account will I go against those wishes, whether it's Tsunami who is concerned, or anyone else. As regards the journalist's draft that I showed you, I shall do my best in the family's interest to persuade him to drop that final paragraph. Does anyone else have anything to say? No? Then I think we may regard this meeting as closed. Thank you very much.'

'Oh dear, have I just missed Tara? What a pity!'

Moira bustled into the dining room with her arms full of paper folders. She dumped them on the dining-room table, and spread the contents over its polished surface.

'I need Tara's advice on these proofs for election posters. They've got the colour of my sari wrong *again*!'

She looked around the silent table.

'What brings you all together here this morning? What's the matter with you all? Why is everyone so quiet?'

There was no reply.

'Has the hospital been in touch? Is there some news of Rowland?'

15

THE MARRYING KIND

'Auntie Soma,' said Tsunami, 'may I please come to stay?'

Soma nearly dropped the telephone.

'What's the matter, child? Has something happened? Has your father passed away?'

She put her palm over the receiver and called:

'Herbie!'

'No, Auntie. Pater's all right, though he's still in hospital. It's just that I'm leaving home."

'*Leaving home?* What are you talking about? (*Herbie!*)'

'I'll tell you all about it when I get there,' Tsunami said. 'But will it be all right if I come? Today? Immediately?'

'Herbie, where *are* you, for goodness' sake! Tsunami's leaving home. She wants to come and stay here, with us!'

Herbert took the receiver from his wife.

'Certainly you can come, Tsunami. Any time. Most welcome. Shall I call round and collect your things?'

'No, it's all right, thanks, Uncle Herbert. Chris will drive me over.'

'Wonder what's been happening at the Wijesinha Maha Walauwa,' Herbert told Soma as he replaced the receiver. 'Something fairly earth-shattering, from the sound of it.'

'I thought first that Rowland must have died,' Soma said, 'or that Ranil or Chris had had an accident. I thought, actually, that she wanted us to come over there, but mixed up the message because she was upset.'

She went to the dining-room door and called:

'*Podina!*'

'I'll get Latha's room ready for Tsunami right away, Herbie,' she said, when her domestic appeared. 'Come, girl, we have work to do.'

As she disappeared with Podina, her husband heard Soma say:

'*That poor child!*'

With the lifting of the curfew and the ending of the Emergency, Paula and Rajan Phillips had returned to Mount Lavinia with their son, and Latha's room was quickly prepared by Soma for its new occupant. Even so, her spontaneous sympathy for her husband's niece was already giving way to her usual curiosity by the time Chris drove up with Tsunami sitting beside him and several suitcases in the boot of his car. She listened with rapt attention to Chris's account of the meeting Ranil had called that morning, and was prompt to apportion blame where she thought it was due.

'It's all that Moira's doing,' Soma said. 'What business has *she* to interfere in Rowland's family matters?'

'May I suggest, Auntie Soma,' Chris said, 'that as we only heard Tara's account of what happened to make Pater write Tsunami out of his will, we shouldn't be too quick to judge Auntie Moira harshly. Tara told us this morning that Auntie Moira suggested it, but it's much more likely, in my opinion, that Tara suggested it herself. Just ask yourself, Uncle Herbert, who would stand to gain from a new will which laid down that Pater's property was to be divided equally among four children, rather than five? Ranil, Tara, Colin and I, that's who! Not Auntie Moira, she's only got a life-interest in one estate . . .'

'You have a lawyer's mind, Chris,' said Herbert. 'I'd hire you to represent me any day.'

'I know the terms of Pater's original will, that's all,' Chris replied simply. 'We all do – it was no secret, he's talked about it often enough! Tara wasn't in line for anything major, since she'd already received property as part of her dowry. Lucas Falls was to go to Ranil, the rubber and coconut properties in Weligama and Chilaw to me, the tea estate in Kadugannawa to Colin, the Colombo house to Tsunami, paddy lands to us all . . . I would bet that in a new will, written on Tara's advice, Tsunami would be totally excluded, and – since you can't really divide a house among four people – she would be replaced by Tara. I grew up with Tara, and I know the way her mind works. Auntie Moira may be silly and frivolous, but she's not greedy, and she doesn't *grab*. Whereas *Tara* . . .'

'So what will Tsunami do about money?' Soma wanted to know. 'The child won't have two cents to rub together. If Rowland stops her allowance—'

'Don't worry, Auntie Soma, Colin and I will look after Tsunami's finances – at any rate until Sujit takes over.'

'"Until Sujit takes over"?' Herbert's voice showed his astonishment. 'What makes you believe Tsunami would put up with being a dependent wife, Chris? *I* think she'll be keen to find herself a job as quickly as she can. Luckily there shouldn't be any difficulty about that, not with the Honours degree which I suppose she's in line for . . .'

Chris looked doubtful.

'Unless Ranil blocks her prospects for a decent job. He's quite capable of it, I fear. *And* he's got a lot of influence: people wouldn't like to cross him—'

'Yes,' Soma said, 'but what about her inheritance? What about her property? Couldn't she take the matter to the Courts, and say she was cheated?'

'She certainly could,' Chris said. 'But she won't. Tsunami doesn't care about money and property, you know. Never did. You could see that in her even as a child, when we were playing Monopoly. I saw it in her again this morning. She didn't turn a hair when Tara told her Pater had written her out of his will. But when Tara told her that Pater had done it *because he believes she isn't his daughter* . . . That's what did it. That's when she decided she was going to marry Sujit, no matter what. Even if Pater regrets what he's done and keeps her allowance going, Tsunami will probably return it. She told me she couldn't bear to spend another day in his house.'

Fascinated by the insights she was receiving into the inner workings of Rowland Wijesinha's family life, details of which had hitherto been kept so private and so well hidden from her, Soma had to be almost physically restrained by Herbert from plaguing Tsunami with questions when she finally appeared on the veranda, having unpacked her suitcases.

'This is so kind of you both,' Tsunami murmured. 'But I can assure you that you won't have to put up with me for very long. I'll be moving soon into Sujit's flat.'

Soma was shocked.

'But how can you do that, child, when you aren't married to him! What will people say? It's not nice. Far better you stay here.'

'I honestly couldn't care less, Auntie, what people—'

'Don't give it a thought,' interrupted Herbert cheerfully. 'We're getting quite used to putting up refugees and runaways, aren't we, Soma? I'm thinking, in fact, of putting our address and the facilities we offer on the National Refugee Register . . .'

Latha, who had been visiting the Phillips family in Mount Lavinia, returned home that evening in very low spirits. Paula and Rajan, it seemed, were planning to emigrate. They had applied for their passports and visas, and had brought home from the British High Commission a dozen pamphlets and brochures giving details of low-cost housing, primary schools, and teaching opportunities in the North London area.

Latha's first reaction to the news had been utter dismay. What had happened to the ideals which had motivated her teachers in the past, and which she had adopted as her own? Had Paula and Rajan completely abandoned their hopes for a new society, given up on the people, once their trusted neighbours, who had betrayed them? Well, of course, she told herself, they had every reason to feel disillusioned. Hunted out of their own home, thrown on the mercy and charity of strangers . . . Emigration was obviously the wise thing to do, she could see that. What if 1958 happened again, and Chris was not around to rescue them?

But all the reasoning of which she was capable could not prevent Latha from feeling that her best friends were deserting her, and then feeling angry with herself for harbouring such selfish thoughts.

Her mood brightened considerably when she went into her room, and found Tsunami sitting on her bed.

'I'll spare you the details,' her cousin said, 'except to say I've got a new perspective on Ranil and Tara. The main thing is that I'm here, free and independent, living with people who care for me. Even your mother, Latha! I'd always thought Auntie Soma didn't like me much at all, but I must have been mistaken.'

'I think Amma believes that by having you to stay here with us, she's saving you from a fate worse than death,' said Latha. 'That must make her feel good. She'll suspect Sujit of the worst possible intentions until the moment comes when he actually puts a ring on your finger and makes an honest woman of you.'

In the kitchen, Podina, too, was feeling good. A drama which seemed to contain all the elements of a popular Sinhala film was unfolding before her very eyes, and Podina, a dedicated film fan, was properly sympathetic to the injured heroine who had fled from her persecutors to seek sanctuary in the house. When Sujit arrived the next day in his gleaming chariot to see Tsunami, the maid-servant brought a tray of ginger beer and orange barley out to the lovers seated on the veranda, and was thrilled to see the hero pick up the heroine's hand and kiss it. She could not, however, be completely happy: something important was missing.

'What is happening about our Latha baba?' Podina asked Soma. 'Where is that sweet-faced young gentleman who used to come here so often, Madam?'

With the ending of the Emergency, Anupam had, in fact, ceased to call on Herbert and Soma. Latha herself had not seen him since they had gone to the temple together and met the Chief Priest. It seemed, she thought, that the visit had had an effect on Anupam that was the very opposite of what his mother and hers had hoped for. This idea amused her, and so did her memories of his awkwardness in performing the simplest acts of temple-worship. Poor Mr Incomparable!

I really shouldn't laugh at him, but how can I help it? If he does come to see us, I must be very careful not to mention the temple . . . or flower offerings . . . or shoes!

To her great surprise, she discovered that she didn't really care very much whether Anupam called to see her or not.

A question rather similar to Podina's had been in Tsunami's mind too. She had been longing for some time to ask it, but the time had never seemed right: Soma or Herbert seemed to be always within earshot. But there came an evening at last when Tsunami got her opportunity. Just as Latha joined them on the veranda, Sujit recollected a book which Anupam had asked him to return with his thanks to Herbert. As he went down the drive to retrieve it from his car, Tsunami turned to her cousin.

'Latha,' she said, 'are you going to say yes when Anupam asks you to marry him?'

'That question will never be asked,' Latha replied. 'At any rate, not by him. By his parents, perhaps. But not by Anupam.'

Tsunami looked at her in surprise.

'But I'd thought – with your visit to the temple, and all that, Latha – I'd thought the engagement would be announced any day now.'

'Oh, I'm sure it would have been, if his mother and mine had had any say in the matter, but fortunately the decision has been ours, not theirs. I like him very much, as you know, Tsunami, but there just isn't between us that – that *chemistry* I saw working between you and Sujit at Lucas Falls. He knows it too. Neither of us, it seems, is the marrying kind.'

'What nonsense! That might be true of Anupam, but I'm sure it's not true of you! What do you think, Sujit?' she asked, as he came back up the steps with Herbert's book. 'You know Anupam better than either of us. Latha says he's not the marrying kind.'

Sujit made no reply. It seemed that he had no views on the subject. Later, when they walked together to his car in the gathering darkness, Tsunami put her question to him once again.

'Is that true, Sujit? That Anupam's not the marrying kind?'

Sujit hesitated before he replied.

'Anupam has talked so much about your cousin to me,' he said carefully, 'and he likes her so much, that if he *were* what you call "the marrying kind", Tsunami, I'm absolutely certain that Latha's the only girl he'd want to marry.'

'I would so like them to get together,' said Tsunami. 'It seems to me they're perfect for each other.'

'Does it?'

'The trouble is,' Tsunami said, 'that we'll never get a word out of *her*.'

Her cousin had never been one to discuss her private feelings with others, Tsunami told Sujit, and here was yet another example of her reticence. Though one might have supposed, she added a little crossly, that as theirs had been such a long and intimate friendship, Latha would have made an exception in her case.

16

CELEBRATION AND MOURNING

Arrangements for the state funeral which marked Rowland Wijesinha's passing brought his children together for the first time since Ranil had called them all together to discuss 'family matters'.

Tara, arriving with both her sons and a troop of women servants, made the Colombo house her headquarters for the duration of the first part of the mourning period, which would extend, according to custom, for a month, ending with an alms-giving in Rowland's memory.

Chris interviewed Raymond's, the family undertakers, regarding the funeral arrangements. Rowland's wish, well known to his children, for a simple and austere ceremony in keeping with Wijesinha family tradition, was, however, quickly overridden by his grieving widow. Moira insisted that every moment of the ceremony should be recorded on film. Given Rowland's eminence, not to mention her own, those moments would one day become priceless archival material.

'We must not forget to plan for the future even as we grieve for the past,' she announced, in a manner so much like Rowland in one of his more pompous moods that Chris wondered whether she had been taking lessons from his father.

Ranil and Tara chose the music that would accompany Rowland all the way up to his cremation; and on the day before the funeral, fifty workers from Lucas Falls arrived by coach under the supervision of Karunaratne, the estate manager, to surround the coffin with white lotuses from the water pools of the estate.

Rowland, the focus of all this attention, had been brought home from Burdan's Hospital to lie splendidly in his polished mahogany coffin, dressed (by Raymond's) in the picturesque costume of an eighteenth-century *mudaliyar*. Lighted torches were placed at his head and feet, and all night long family retainers holding ornamental *sesath* banners aloft took turns to keep vigil around his body. When Herbert arrived with Soma and Latha to say his last farewells, he could not help admiring the magnificence of his cousin in repose, and wished ruefully that he had had reason to respect Rowland more while he was alive.

'We must choose a nice epitaph for the gravestone,' Moira told Herbert. 'Something that tells everyone what he really was. Do you have any suggestions, Herbert aiya?'

Unbidden, a verse sprang fully formed into Herbert's head:

A weak but harmless dilettante,
He lived, and should have died,
Had Vanity not turned his head
And Politics his hide.

Ambition took him by the hand
While Power stole his sense
Of what was right and what was wrong –
He died in violence . . .

'I'm really sorry, Moira,' Herbert said. 'But I cannot, for the life of me, think of anything suitable. For me Rowland was – he was . . . beyond definition.'

Moira's hands were clasped and her eyes were shining.

'Oh, but that's perfect. "*Rowland Wijesinha – A Man Beyond Definition*" . . . Thank you, Herbert aiya! I knew I could depend on you.'

Beyond the gates of the late Minister's house, crowds began to gather from nightfall on the day before the funeral. Colombo loves a splendid occasion, and all the way from the funeral house to the cemetery at Kanatte, the streets would be crowded with people eager to witness the passing of the cortege, which they knew would be followed by a slow procession of limousines bearing the late Minister's colleagues (the Prime Minister himself among them), diplomats and members of the Wijesinha family.

'It would be best, don't you think,' Chris had said, 'for us to have Tsunami picked up from Uncle Herbert's and brought here so that we can all leave together for Kanatte? At what time shall I ask Alexander to call for her?'

He moved towards the telephone.

Tara, who had been directing Podihami in the proper ironing of the white sari she planned to wear to the funeral, looked up.

'Tsunami is certainly not travelling with *us* to Pater's funeral, Chris,' she said flatly. 'People who see her with us in Pater's car would receive a completely false impression – they would imagine that she's a member of the family.'

'That wouldn't be a false impression,' Chris replied. 'She *is* a member of the family.'

'No, she's not.'

'Of course she is. She's your sister and mine—'

'*But she isn't Pater's daughter*,' Tara said. 'That's the point you seem to keep forgetting. As far as I am concerned – and I'm sure Ranil would back me up on this – Tsunami is an outsider, with no claim whatever on any of us. She certainly has no right to travel in the family car, with Auntie Moira and me.'

'Ranil aiya!' said Colin helplessly. 'Auntie Moira!' He looked from one to the other. 'What do you say?'

But Moira, it seemed, had nothing major to contribute to the discussion.

'These are matters for you children to decide,' said she. '*I* don't want to interfere in matters that don't concern me. Besides, I have other things to think about.'

Ranil summoned Karunaratne from the veranda, where he was supervising a dozen young women who were hard at work, opening out the tightly closed petals of lotus buds.

'I want you, Karunaratne, to take charge *personally* of traffic arrangements at Kanatte tomorrow,' he said.

'Yes, sir—'

'By which I mean that the only vehicles permitted to enter the gates will be – write this down, and show it to any policeman on duty who challenges you – the Prime Minister's car, the Ministers' cars, the Master's own car (which Alexander will be driving, and in which Madam will travel with me, Tara *hamu*, and our two brothers), and cars which you know belong to members of the family.'

'Yes, sir.'

'You know every one of us personally, so it's up to you to prevent any mistakes being made. Do you understand what I am saying? *No unauthorized persons*. Is that clear?'

'Yes, sir,' Karunaratne said. 'No outsiders to be allowed at the Kanatte ceremonies—'

'Or in the house,' interposed Tara.

'Have you both gone quite mad?' Chris said hotly. 'How do you suppose Tsunami's going to attend Pater's funeral?'

'I can't say I've given the matter much thought,' said Ranil. 'But now that you mention it, I don't suppose she'd want to, would she?'

He lit a cigarette, and drew lazily on it.

'If she does want to attend Pater's funeral, I'm sure she can make her own arrangements. After all, there are plenty of taxis . . . and buses.'

'I wanted to hit him then,' Chris told Latha, 'but Tara was looking so triumphantly at me that I wouldn't give her the satisfaction of knowing she'd caused an all-out brawl in the family—'

'—And a very good thing you didn't,' Latha said. 'I imagine you're a great deal fitter than Ranil is, but a fight with him wouldn't have achieved anything, except that you'd both have arrived at the funeral with bleeding noses and black eyes. Now *that* would certainly have given people something to talk about . . .'

Almost against his will, Chris smiled.

'You're very good for me, Latha,' he said. 'Would you consider—'

'Oh, yes! I'm very good at advising other people!' she replied. 'Not so successful in solving problems of my own, though.'

'Latha—' Chris began, but what he had been about to say was drowned in a clatter from the kitchen.

'Madam! *Madam!*' shouted Podina.

She erupted into the room, waving a red and white soap wrapper.

'I've found it! The picture of the Lifebuoy son!'

The noise she was making brought Herbert out of his library.

'Bring me the other pictures you have, Podina, let's make sure there's no mistake.'

There was no mistake. Father, mother, son and daughter, the Lifebuoy family was complete. Podina laid them out on the dining table, and produced the entry forms that had accompanied the wrappers she had been collecting. Herbert selected one and filled it out for her, before handing it to her to sign.

'Now, Podina, make a copy of what I have written, using one of the other forms,' he said, 'and keep it in a safe place. If questions are asked, that will be your proof. And then, child, we shall take it to the Post Office, and post it to the Lever Brothers Company. But we shall send it by Registered Post, so that you have a record and proof of posting. It will be safer that way – you don't want the form lost in the post, or stolen, isn't that so?'

Podina certainly did not want her precious entry lost or stolen. The vision of the sovereign gold necklace and earrings that were about to come her way brightened her eyes, and made her catch her breath.

'Can we go to the Post Office today, sir? *Now?*'

Herbert considered the question. He had not considered going anywhere that day. In all the excitement surrounding Rowland's funeral and the turmoil surrounding Tsunami's predicament, he was the only member of the family who remembered that they had not only a death to mourn, but a triumph to celebrate: his daughter's First Class university degree. The death of Rowland Wijesinha had created such a furore in his family, that the results of the University of Ceylon's final examinations, which brought Latha a First Class in English and Tsunami an Upper Second in History, had been completely overshadowed.

It was plainly evident, however, that no one would enjoy any peace of mind until Podina's set of Lifebuoy family portraits was safely on its way. Better do it today, he thought, than tomorrow, when every street will be choked with funeral crowds.

'Yes, we'll go now. And on the way back we'll stop at Green Cabin to buy *lamprais* and *biryani*. Join us for dinner, Chris. And of course Sujit will be here, too. It will be a real celebration!'

Soma was about to protest at this unwarranted extravagance, but Herbert stopped her in mid-sentence.

'Can you really see Podina cooking us a decent meal tonight, Soma? I can't. She'd need to come off Cloud Nine first. And that may take her some time. Come, child. Get that form ready, and we'll go and post it.'

17

MOVING ON

It seemed to Latha that everything around her was changing rapidly, and that she was changing with it. Hard on the heels of the news of her examination success had come letters from Sriyani de Alwis and Amali Kiriella. Both sent apologies and regrets. Neither of them would be able to attend Tsunami's wedding: Sriyani because she would be in Thailand on the day of the wedding, attending the Asian Games in Bangkok in her official role as University Sports Director.

'I'm sure you'll be amused to learn,' wrote Sriyani, 'that I shall have another responsibility at the Games, as official chaperon to our nation's women athletes! What do you think of that? It amuses *me*! Our kids are so fit and tough – especially our relay team – that any one of them could send a man into flight with her little finger if he tried to get fresh with her. Are we still living in the Middle Ages, or what?'

Amali's response, on a plain white card, announced that she was about to be ordained as a novice nun in a Buddhist meditation centre in her hometown of Kurunegala.

Latha went to Kurunegala to meet Amali before she took her final vows, and was greeted at the door of the Kiriella house by Amali's mother, a quiet, soft-spoken Kandyan lady.

'Amali will be so happy to see you,' Mrs Kiriella said; then immediately corrected herself. 'Of course, we must get used to calling her Sister Nivedita now – I keep forgetting.'

Latha had known, of course, that there would be differences now in Amali's way of life, but the first sight of her friend's shaven head took her by surprise.

Oh, Amali! Your beautiful hair!

She was glad, later on, that she had managed to suppress the words before they were uttered. It would have been so completely the wrong thing to say to Amali at such a moment. She learned quickly that there were other topics too that she must avoid mentioning. Within the first ten minutes of their meeting, Amali informed her that she had asked her parents not to inform her of her final examination results. Latha, who knew that Amali had obtained a First in Economics, took the hint, made no reference to her own success, and avoided the subject of examinations altogether.

Her friend's bedroom, into which Mrs Kiriella had led her on arrival, contained a minimum of furniture: a cupboard, a writing desk, two chairs, and a mat rolled up against a wall, on which, presumably, Amali slept at night. There were no pictures on the wall, and – which was unusual for Amali – no flowers anywhere to soften the austerity of the room, not even a bowl of flowers before the Buddha image that stood on a simple corner pedestal by the window. Latha had brought a gift with her, a small sandalwood image of a meditating Buddha. She had seen it in an antique shop in Colombo, and had been drawn to it by the tranquillity of its expression. Amali took the little statue from her immediately, with obvious pleasure, and placed it on a bracket above her writing desk.

Latha had wondered, on her journey by train to Kurunegala, whether the path Amali had chosen should be the path she should follow herself, a life free of worldly distractions, and the continual need to think about money and a career.

Getting and spending, we lay waste our powers.

The tranquil atmosphere of Buddhist monasteries had always appealed to her, and she had often thought that the learned monks of Vajirarāmaya must lead a satisfying life, dividing their time between meditation and study. Since love and marriage were clearly not about to come her way, why should she not take up a way of life for which she was surely fitted, the life of a scholar-nun?

Pope's Eloïse had chosen the life of a nun. Well, had she *chosen* it? Or had it been thrust upon her by circumstances, and the formidable will of her erstwhile lover? Latha recalled, as her train chugged in and out of the track's numerous tunnels, how Eloïse's predicament had touched and intrigued her when she read Pope's poem in her second year at Peradeniya. To have said a last, sincere farewell to all the joys of love, and to have locked herself up in a nunnery for years – that, Latha had thought, was sad enough. But then, the moment when, by sheer chance, letters from Abelard's hand had come into her possession! What letters Eloïse had written to him then! In words and phrases that cried out her undying love for him – only to be answered by Abelard with stiff, formal chiding for giving way so weakly to thoughts that had clearly been put in her mind by the Devil himself.

Latha had laughed and cried over the poem, cried at the tragedy of love first thwarted and then unrequited; and laughed at the strategy adopted at last by this witty woman to keep her former lover in play as an angler tempts a fish – sending him letters disguised as theological queries to which she claimed to require urgent answers: urgent, because only his brilliant mind, she told him, could supply the solutions essential to save her soul from jeopardy . . .

But a Buddhist nunnery in modern Ceylon would surely be very different, she thought, from the medieval Roman Catholic abbey in which Eloïse had locked herself away from the world. She had met Buddhist nuns during her schooldays, cheerful, jolly ladies, most of them European, who seemed to get a tremendous amount of enjoyment from the lives they had chosen. And why not? Latha visualized the satisfying life she would lead if she followed their path and Amali's . . .

There'd be a library filled with books, and myself in the midst of them, a member of a company of like-minded scholarly women and girls, translating ancient texts into English, unlocking the secrets of olā leaf manuscripts . . .

There were very few books, however, in Amali's room. Those that Latha could see were Buddhist texts. On the writing-desk was a copy of the *Dhammapāda*, which had been given to Amali by her father, and which Latha remembered from their Sanghamitta days. There were, besides, a number of small booklets on the techniques of meditation. Amali told her she had given away her Economics textbooks to a student at her old school who was sitting the university entrance examination that year. She asked after Tsunami, and seemed pleased to hear that her wedding to Sujit Roy was imminent, but she was not, Latha suspected, particularly interested in hearing about the arrangements that were being made for it.

By the time she made the return journey, Latha had changed her mind about the satisfactions of life in a nunnery. There was no doubt that Amali had been pleased to see her again, and she was glad for that reason that she had made the visit. But, despite her efforts, she was no longer at ease in the company of her friend, and she missed the Amali she had known at Peradeniya.

Latha found a letter awaiting her in Colombo that confirmed her melancholy impression that unforeseen and undesirable change had become the new *motif* in her life. Ronald Marchmont, writing to congratulate her on her First, had also decided, it seemed, to take an alternative path. He had been due to return at the end of the year to Cambridge in order to complete his doctoral degree. That was all over now: he had abandoned his Ph.D. studies, prevailed on Sushila Ramanathan to marry him, and taken a position as Choir Master at St Paul's School in London.

So many delightful changes, one after the other! [Marchmont wrote] *Some, of course, more delightful than others!! For behold in me now, Latha, Ronald Marchmont the married man!!!*

Latha read Marchmont's letter aloud to Herbert, who said:

'Make allowances for the excessive use of exclamation marks, duwa.

You can't expect flawless punctuation from a man who's just got back from his honeymoon.'

But don't let my irresponsible example deter you from what I truly believe to be your destiny [Marchmont had added, becoming suddenly very serious]. *I've been in touch with Professor Wheelwright at Girton College, and I am certain there will be a place for you there, should you decide to apply for it, as I earnestly hope that you will.*

The invitations to Tsunami's wedding had been sent out in the names of Herbert and Soma Wijesinha, and the marriage was to be registered in the living-room of their home. It would be, as Herbert said, a true 'home-and-home match', for Christopher was to give the bride away, Latha was to be her bridesmaid, and Colin had been asked by Sujit and Tsunami to act as groomsman. Two of Sujit's sisters arrived from Bombay a few days before the wedding day, bringing with them the skilled artist who would attend to painting the bride's hands and feet with henna in patterns of leaves and flowers.

The wedding day, when it dawned, was bright and clear, with no hint of rain. A good thing, Soma Wijesinha said, for the house could not have accommodated the large number of guests for whom chairs had been arranged in groups in her garden.

'How do I look?' Tsunami asked nervously.

She stood before Latha's dressing-table mirror in her *choli* and petticoat, her arms held stiffly away from her as her cousin folded the pleats of her wedding sari and tucked them into her silver waist-chain.

'Gorgeous,' Latha said. 'You know you do. Now turn around – *slowly* – so that I can drape it properly over your shoulder.'

The stiff Indian silk, heavy with gold embroidery, was difficult to drape, but Latha managed it at last.

'Where are you spending your honeymoon?' she asked, as Tsunami sat down before the mirror, and opened the florist's box on the dressing-table. 'Or is it too early to ask?'

'Oh, didn't I tell you? We'll have three days in Yala, then we're flying to Bombay to spend four days with Sujit's family, and then, Latha, *then*, a whole blissful week in a houseboat on the Dal Lake in Kashmir.'

'Lovely. Let's get these hairpins firmly moored so that your flowers stay in place. There, it's done! What do you think, Amma?'

Her mother had come in with Annabelle Munasinghe, both of them anxious to view the bride and offer advice.

'So beautiful!' Soma said, and added: 'You look just like your mother must have done on her wedding day.'

Latha saw tears rise to Tsunami's eyes, and handed her a handkerchief just before they fell.

'The perfect bridesmaid,' Tsunami said, managing a smile. 'Yes, I know, Latha! It's not a good idea to smudge my *kohl*.'

'It could have been such a beautiful double wedding,' Mrs Munasinghe said wistfully. 'If only things had been different . . .'

Latha detected something very like reproach in Annabelle Munasinghe's voice and expression, and pretended that she hadn't heard the remark. Here too, she thought, was evidence of change, for she had heard from Shalini that her brother had been posted by Foreign Affairs to Washington, and would be leaving the island directly after he had carried out his duties as Sujit's best man at the wedding.

Moving among the guests in the garden, following the ceremony, Latha met Alexander, Raman, Vaithi and Alice. Although Ranil and Tara had pointedly ignored the wedding invitations Herbert and Soma had sent them, all the servants Latha had come to know so well at Lucas Falls had somehow contrived to be present to see their favourite married. She also noticed that staff from Sujit's Hambantota workshop had attended the wedding in force. While she was making sure that generous supplies of wedding-cake were distributed among them, Chris came across the garden towards her, bent down, and whispered in her ear:

'What's Karunaratne doing here, Latha? Did Uncle Herbert invite him?'

'Certainly not! Where is he?'

'Over there. Near the *araliya* tree.'

Latha looked in the direction Chris had indicated, and saw the familiar face of the manager of Lucas Falls. He seemed to be deep in conversation with Alexander. Karunaratne looked up and, catching Latha's eye, smilingly put his hands together in greeting. He seemed unaware of her hostility.

'Quite the family retainer, don't you think?' Chris said.

It occurred to Latha that although Tara had not indicated by word or gesture that she was even aware the wedding was taking place, it was possible that she had, even at the last moment, undergone a change of heart towards her only sister.

'Perhaps,' she said, 'Tara has sent him over with a wedding-present?'

'Highly unlikely,' Chris said, and added: 'I don't trust that man, Latha.'

It was growing dark by the time Sujit and Tsunami were ready to leave. As Colin held the door of Sujit's car open for her, Tsunami turned and, bowing to the ground before Herbert and Soma, touched the feet of her uncle and aunt. Latha, whose hands were filled with confetti, forgot to throw it as she remembered Tsunami's words to her years ago, when they were children at Lucas Falls.

WE don't bow down to anyone.

Soma lifted her niece up, and kissed her. Herbert was so taken aback and moved by the unexpected gesture that he could not speak, even to say goodbye.

As Sujit and Tsunami drove away amid showers of confetti and rose petals, Anupam Munasinghe came over to Latha's side to say goodbye.

'I hear you're going to Cambridge in September,' he said, taking her hand in his.

'I haven't made my mind up yet,' Latha replied, wondering who Anupam's informant had been, and deciding at last that it must have been her father. 'They've offered me an Assistant Lectureship at Peradeniya. It's only a temporary position, but I'm very tempted to accept it.'

'May I make a suggestion, Latha?'

'Go ahead. I'm listening.'

'Don't accept it,' he said. 'Put your idealism aside, and go to Cambridge instead. You'll love it. And Cambridge will appreciate *you*.'

He always contrives to say the right thing: a perennial source of good advice! But what is he really telling me? That my own society doesn't appreciate me? That there is no place in our island now, for people like myself . . . and him?

Latha wondered briefly at a perverse fate that seemed to constantly bring the two of them together at moments when each was proposing to travel in a different direction.

'Have a safe flight tomorrow,' she said. 'Keep in touch.'

'You surprised me today, Tsunami,' Sujit said, as the coast road from Colombo unfurled before them, a yellow ribbon in the headlights of the car. 'I didn't know that your family used that traditional gesture.'

'What traditional gesture?'

'Bowing down before your uncle and aunt. I remember my sisters bowing like that before our parents, when they married. But it doesn't come naturally to me.'

'It doesn't come naturally to me, either,' Tsunami said. 'I surprised myself. I've never done it before, and I hadn't had any intention of doing it today. It was impulse, pure and simple – I felt suddenly that I wanted to thank my uncle and aunt for everything they've done for me, and that's the way it came out. Not in words. Some long-ago race memory, probably. What's that sound, Sujit?'

A mysterious rattle had made Sujit wonder too. He pulled up, checked the back of the car, and sighed.

'Your brother Colin's struck again,' he said, throwing a string of tin cans into the back seat. 'He takes his duties as groomsman seriously, doesn't he? . . . I suppose I should count myself lucky that he hasn't scrawled *Just Married* in indelible ink on the back of the car. Though I suppose the dew would have washed that off eventually.'

'Dew?' Tsunami said. 'I'd thought it was a shower.'

'It's dew all right,' said Sujit. 'It's later than it seems.'

Memory plays unexpected tricks on you, Tsunami thought. She took the chamois cloth her husband handed her, and wiped the windscreen, which had misted up.

. . . And the only, only thing I did that was wrong,
Was to keep her from the foggy, foggy dew . . .

'A penny for your thoughts?' Sujit said.

'Oh . . . nothing much.'

'Well, here's one of mine. As it's already very late, Tsunami, it might be a good idea to break journey at Hambantota. What do you say?'

'Where would we stay?'

'Well, we have two choices. We could stay overnight at Hambantota Rest House before travelling on to Yala tomorrow. Or we could, of course, go to the boatyard, there's a room fitted up there that I use when I stay overnight.'

He hesitated, and added:

'It's a bit on the primitive side, I'm afraid. The bed's a single bed – though that would not, I imagine, bother either of us tonight . . .'

. . . So I hauled her into bed, and I covered up her head,
Just to keep her from the foggy, foggy dew . . .

Engaged in shaking confetti from the folds of her sari, Tsunami did not appear to have heard him.

'Not such a good idea,' Sujit decided. 'Besides,' he added, 'the staff's probably still celebrating in Colombo, so there'll be no one there but the security guard. I'll just have a word with him and then we'll go on to the Rest House. That suit you?'

He swung the car off the main road, in the direction of his property.

'That was quite a crowd at the turn-off,' he said. 'Surprising, since it's so late – did you know it's nearly midnight, Tsunami? Wonder where they're all heading?'

The crowd seemed to increase as he drove on. Everyone seemed to be walking fast, or running, in the same direction in which they were going.

But there was no glare in the darkness to tell them what had happened. The flames had had time to die down, and a stiff breeze from the sea had blown the smoke away. It was only as they reached the gates that Sujit and Tsunami saw what had attracted the noisy crowd gathering on the road, which increased by the minute as news spread through the area, and more and more people rose from their beds though it was nearly midnight, and rushed to see for themselves the charred, blackened and still smouldering ruins of what had once been a flourishing boatyard.

18

CHRIS

The wedding guests had left, except for a few family elders seated on the veranda, who looked as if they were preparing to spend the rest of the evening in conversation with Herbert and Soma. Latha bade them all a polite goodnight, and went back into the house with Chris, who went straight to the refrigerator and poured her a glass of iced coffee from the jug Podina had thoughtfully placed there.

'Laced with brandy, I believe,' he said. 'According to Uncle Herbert's directions. Drink that, it'll do you good, Latha. You're tired. And I think you're emotionally exhausted.'

Latha took a sip, and sighed with pleasurable relief.

'It all went so well! And Tsunami looked so *happy*!'

Chris watched her as she unpinned the spray of flowers in her hair and set it floating in a bowl of water on the dining-room table.

'They'll still be fresh tomorrow,' she said. 'I'll press them when they're dry. A souvenir of Tsunami's wedding day.'

'Here's another souvenir for you,' Chris said. He took the rosebud from his button-hole, and added it to the jasmine in the bowl. 'Though I don't know whether it would take kindly to pressing.'

The sight of the flowers floating together awakened in Latha a sudden memory of a verse they had often sung together as children at Lucas Falls.

Rosamalai pichcha malai yanawa vathurē
Darling-gē dhakunu athē magē pinthurē . . .

The rose and the jasmine float together on the river,
and in my sweetheart's right hand is my own portrait . . .

When she glanced up at Chris, she found that he was looking questioningly at her, and she knew that he was thinking of the old song too.

'Latha—'

Latha interrupted him.

'A letter from Ronald Marchmont arrived this morning, Chris, and in the excitement of the wedding, I forgot all about it! You *must* let me read it to you before you go.'

She put down her empty glass, and disappeared into her bedroom. Chris, who had had no intention of 'going' anywhere, settled himself comfortably on the sofa, and stretched his long legs before him. He knew that since his departure to Britain, Ronald Marchmont had maintained a correspondence with a few of his Honours students at Peradeniya, Latha among them. Latha, who often read Marchmont's letters aloud to her father, sometimes showed them to Chris and Tsunami. A lengthy discussion often followed, which was greatly enjoyed by them all. Chris was interested in Marchmont's view of life, and agreed with his sister and his cousin that the Englishman was an entertaining correspondent. Very well, he decided now, what he had to say to Latha could wait: at least it could wait until she had read him her former tutor's letter.

'It was on my dressing-table, still unopened,' Latha informed him.

She had returned to the sitting room, a blue air-letter in her hand.

'Why don't you have some of that coffee yourself, Chris, and sit back and enjoy Ron's letter? You know he always sees the funny side of things, and this letter will be even more cheerful than most – he's probably writing to congratulate Tsunami.'

It seemed to Chris that Latha was much more talkative than usual.

She's positively chattering! Why doesn't she look me in the eye? Does she know what I'm about to say to her?

No doubt her agitation was due partly to the wedding. But he sensed that her reluctance to give him an opportunity to speak was due to her fear that, once the words had been said, and his feelings for her were out in the open, their affectionate, comradely relationship would never be the same again.

Well, she'd be right about that: it'll become something far, far better . . .

Chris glanced around the sitting room and noticed, not for the first time, its small size and the shabbiness of its furnishings. The upholstery on which his hand was resting was threadbare beneath his fingers. He breathed a deep sigh of contentment as he imagined the comfortable life he would make for Latha, free of the petty economies and material deprivations she had borne without complaint throughout her childhood and adolescence.

He had observed Anupam Munasinghe making his farewells to her, and had made a point of meeting Anupam immediately afterwards. He had shaken the man's hand and wished him a safe journey to Washington with sincere satisfaction. He thought with pleasure of the future he himself would now share with Latha, a future free of the constraints and doubts that had dogged him up to now. He would be free for evermore of comparisons with sophisticated Cambridge-educated diplomats, free to get out from under his elder brother's everlasting shadow . . . His own way was clear at last.

Latha slit open the flap of the letter and began to read aloud. Chris had been looking forward to being entertained, and his concern was great when, after a couple of paragraphs about the editorial work Marchmont was currently undertaking for Oxford University Press which was, he said, keeping him intellectually occupied in the midst of the bliss of married life, Latha's reading slowed down and finally stopped.

'What's the matter?' he asked. 'I hope it's not bad news?' 'No. Well, not exactly.'

'You can tell me, Latha.'

'Read it for yourself, and tell me what you think.'

Last Monday [Marchmont had written] *I had a pleasant surprise, literally bumping into no less a personage than Everard van Loten on the steps of the BM Library. Naturally, we pushed off and had a cup of coffee together . . . and an iced cake, of course! His famous sweet tooth is still what it was at Peradeniya. (Though he told me wistfully that he misses his rice and curry – Emma van Loten, great cook though she is, apparently doesn't rise to such heights!) Van Loten was his usual charming, affable self; but it was obvious to me that he has been deeply disturbed by the events that necessitated your recent Emergency. My reason for saying so is that I think it could only have been great distress of mind that would have led him to abandon the subject of the book he is writing about Ceylon and say to me, quite suddenly:*

'You know, Ronald, I don't believe race relations there can improve. As long as both a caste system and racial hatred are built into the consciousness and the upbringing of the young, the most we can hope for is an attempt to control their consequences.'

He spoke a little later of the fine students he had taught at Peradeniya (including yourself!) but did not seem hopeful of their chances of generating change.

'Education, as one thinks of it,' he told me, 'will have to start with parents and grandparents, as well as with infants.'

I hope that this letter will not upset you, Latha. It is not intended to do so, only to pass on the considered opinion of a great man – probably the greatest educationist you or I will ever meet . . .

'Well, it's certainly not an *amusing* letter this time, is it!' Latha said, attempting a smile.

'No. Marchmont is telling you the truth, as he sees it. It's the letter of a sincere friend.'

'It's not what I want to hear . . . just now.'

She thought of Anupam's farewell advice to her, then put the memory firmly out of her mind. Professor van Loten, Ronald Marchmont, and Anupam Munasinghe were mature, experienced men who knew the outside world as she did not, and she conceded that their opinions could not be ignored. But what if her own ideas and her personal experience contradicted what they had to say?

She believed that society could change. *She* believed that her own generation still had the power to redress the wrongs of the past, and bring about a just society.

Chris watched the changing expressions of his cousin's face, and searched for the right words to set her mind at rest.

'Try looking at it this way, Latha,' he said at last. 'Professor van Loten, great man though he is, is not infallible. Ronald Marchmont, even in the few years that he was here, came to love and understand this country. But though they loved it, they both chose to leave it. Ask yourself, Latha, would exiles ever forecast a prosperous future for the land they have left behind?'

'That's not fair, Chris! You're suggesting that their opinions are coloured by a mean, ungenerous spirit—'

'I'm doing nothing of the kind!'

'—but I was a student of theirs, and I can tell you, they are just not *capable* of such an attitude—'

'I never said they were!'

'No, but you implied it—'

'No, no. Listen to me, Latha! I was pointing out that ours is a complex society, so complex that it may be beyond one man's capability to fully understand it. However intelligent, even *brilliant*, that man might be—'

The telephone shrilled in the passage.

'Answer that, will you, duwa?' Soma called from the veranda.

Latha rose from her seat beside her cousin, and went to the telephone. She was away from the room so long that Chris got up and followed her. He found her clutching the telephone table, the receiver pressed to her ear.

'It's Tsunami, Chris,' she said. 'There's a lot of noise on the line, and I can't hear her very clearly. But I think there's – there's been an accident.'

Chris took the receiver from her trembling hand.

'The boatyard burned down?' she heard him say. 'Where are you speaking from? Are you and Sujit all right? Where are you staying tonight?'

Herbert had come in from the veranda, and was standing beside Chris.

'If they're at the Hambantota Rest House, tell Tsunami to get the Rest House keeper on the phone,' he said. 'I'll speak to him, I know old Rasiah very well. He'll look after them.'

Chris relayed this message, and added:

'Tell Sujit I'll be over there first thing tomorrow. We'll talk it over when we meet.'

He gave the telephone to Herbert, and went back with Latha to the sitting room.

'Sujit's boatyard at Hambantota has been completely burned down,' he told her. 'Nobody knows how it happened, no witnesses can be found who saw anything suspicious. The police think it was an accident.'

'An accident? But there are security people at the boatyard,' Latha said. 'Even if many of them were in Colombo, celebrating at the wedding, there would have been *someone* there.'

'The wedding!' Chris exclaimed. 'So that's why Karunaratne was here this evening . . .'

'Karunaratne? What has he got to do with it?'

'. . . Didn't you see his smug smile, Latha? He was planted here, to make sure that if anything occurred to hold up proceedings in Colombo – if Sujit and Tsunami decided to leave early, for instance – Ranil's men in Hambantota could be alerted by telephone, told to get on with the job quickly and clear out, or call off the exercise for another day . . .'

'Exercise? What exercise? I'm sorry, Chris, but I don't understand you.'

'The delivery of my brother Ranil's wedding-present to his sister and his new brother-in-law,' replied Chris furiously. 'Come to think of it, putting off delivery for a later date wouldn't have made the point properly, would it? In order to really hurt Sujit and Tsunami, the damage needed to be done on the wedding-day itself. Perfect timing, typical of Ranil! With the entire staff on holiday or celebrating the boss's wedding in Colombo, and Sujit's security guard effectively put out of the way by Karunaratne's team of rough-necks, what was there to stop them burning down the boatyard?'

His conversation with Tsunami over, Herbert had joined them in the sitting room.

'Hold on a minute, Chris,' Herbert said. 'You're going too fast for me. There's no proof that Ranil has anything to do with it. He's miles away, in Nuwara Eliya, this weekend.'

'Of course he is, Uncle Herbert. Why should he waste his time in Hambantota, when a few hundred rupees in the right hands can get these things done by means of a simple bribe?'

Latha placed a restraining hand on her cousin's arm. This was a Christopher she didn't recognize.

'Let's be thankful,' she said quietly, 'that nobody lost their lives. If your theory is right, Chris, and there were people about with instructions to harass Sujit as he drove in to Hambantota, he and Tsunami could both have been attacked and killed. People have done worse things in the past than burn a boatyard, when they wanted to avenge an insult to their family honour. Tsunami's well aware of that; and Sujit would know it too – I'm sure it's just the same, probably worse, in India.'

'So what will Sujit do about this?' asked Chris. 'Will he just shut up and say nothing?'

'He's called in the police, of course,' Latha said, trying to collect her thoughts. 'Tsunami told me that was the first thing he did. He telephoned the police station from the Hambantota Rest House. To their credit, they arrived within twenty minutes. Then Tsunami rang us. She says there will be a police investigation immediately, they'll interview witnesses, and then—'

Chris laughed a bitter laugh.

'Called in the police! A police investigation! With Auntie Moira a minister in the Cabinet and Ranil her right-hand man? Even if they manage to find a witness – which I think is *very* unlikely – the police will be bribed to say they can't find sufficient evidence to convict, and the inquiry will be dropped.'

'You're so cynical, Chris,' Latha said. 'Things can't possibly be as bad as that! They're bound to find someone who saw what happened. Tsunami told me that a very big crowd had collected at the boatyard.'

'They won't find anyone anywhere who would have seen a thing or have the guts to report it, even if the security guard had been tied up in front of their very eyes,' said her cousin. 'I sit in on cases of arson every week in the District Courts. I assure you I know what I'm talking about. I am *not* being cynical!'

Latha was silenced. With a quick glance at her, Chris changed the subject:

'Let's hope Sujit has insured his property.'

'Oh, he *must* have insured it,' said Latha. 'He's a very successful businessman.'

Chris nodded.

'He's a very successful businessman who's also given to taking risks . . . No, I think it's up to me to act.'

'You?'

Latha was genuinely surprised.

'Yes, me! Why, Latha, do you think I can't deal with the situation? Are you proposing to call on Sir Ranil the Pure-in-Heart for help?'

Chris sounded so angry, so unlike his usual easy-going self, that Latha drew back from the argument and said no more.

'As Tsunami's eldest brother, Ranil should take charge: of course he should. But he won't. He'll just say it's nothing to do with him. Or if he *does* act, he'll do it in such a perfunctory way that it will be worse than useless. So, as I said, it's up to me to let the people responsible know that they can't get away with it. And I'll pay Ranil back, with interest . . . I'll pay him back in kind.'

'*In kind?*'

Latha was horrified.

'By doing what, for heaven's sake? What are you talking about? Are you proposing to burn down Lucas Falls? Please don't do anything rash, Chris.

Leave Ranil alone. Our laws are there to protect us when things like this happen.'

On a sudden inspiration, she added:

'Who knows? It may all work out for the best. Now that this has happened, coming on top of the Emergency, Sujit might give up the Ceylon operation altogether, sell the property, and re-start his old dream of building boats on an island in Greece. Life on the Aegean would suit Tsunami just fine . . . perfect for writing fiction . . .'

Her attempt to make light of the situation was not successful. Chris didn't seem to be listening.

'Ranil must not be allowed to get away with it,' he said. 'I really think, you know, that he's going mad. And when a dog goes mad, it has to be put down.'

'Now, look here, Chris,' Herbert said, 'pull yourself together. Your suspicions may be completely unfounded.'

'Uncle Herbert—'

'Listen to me for a moment, before you do anything rash. The place may have burned down accidentally – electrical wiring that wasn't properly earthed, or a half-smoked cigarette or *suruttuwa* tossed into a pile of wood shavings, these things happen – or else, some member of Sujit's staff might harbour a grudge against him or his company. If, on the other hand, your theory is correct, and Ranil *is* responsible for doing this, it certainly sounds as if he's losing his marbles. In which case, he'd need to see a psychiatrist. But if *you* go on like this, and keep talking the way you're talking now, well, then I shall have to concede something I've denied all my life, that most old families are crazy, and the Wijesinha family is crazier than most.'

With this, Herbert went off to bed.

Latha was relieved to see that her father's words had calmed Chris down considerably. As her cousin showed no sign of leaving, she crossed to the radiogram. Perhaps music would help put things back on an even keel.

'What about some Satchmo, Chris?'

There was no answer.

Latha chose an Armstrong record from her father's jazz collection, and Chris, who had been pacing up and down the living-room floor in a manner that Latha found extremely unsettling, sat down beside her to listen. But his change of mood did not last longer than a few moments. It was evident to Latha that he was still upset, for he turned to her and said, without any preamble:

'It's always been Ranil, hasn't it, Latha, for you?'

'What on earth do you mean?'

'He's always been two steps ahead of me in everything I've ever wanted to do. Taller, better-looking, a better degree, the glamour boy of College cricket, I should have known I'd never have any chance with you – you've been in love with him since you were twelve! So much in love with him that you didn't even notice me whenever he was around – I've loved you for years, but you don't even notice me *now*—'

'Chris, please stop this. You're talking nonsense. Please stop—'

'—I thought for a time that Munasinghe might wake you up out of your dream of love for that rotten scoundrel – for that's what my *wonderful* brother is, whether you want to know it or not, rotten through and through. Munasinghe's a decent sort of chap, if I couldn't have you, I didn't mind his being the one you ended up marrying, but even *he* didn't succeed . . .'

'Chris, listen to me, please. You'll regret tomorrow morning that you ever said these things to me. There's no point in upsetting yourself for the sake of someone who isn't even there . . . I'm going away, you know, quite soon, and—'

'You're *going away*?'

'I'm going to England, Chris, to Cambridge. I wasn't sure of it before, but I'm certain now. I'll be away for years. Three whole years – just think about it! Anything can happen in three years, and the best thing that can happen is that—'

'Yes, yes, I know. The best thing that can happen is that I'll meet someone else who really loves me, and I'll get married! And we'll all be good friends, and live happily ever after. Isn't that what you were going to say?'

Latha did not reply.

'It's no good, Latha, I'll never care for anyone else, so don't waste your breath: that argument's not going to work. It'll never work as long as I'm alive and you're single, whether you're here, or in England, or anywhere in the world . . .'

Latha sat still on the sofa for quite some time after Chris had left the house, before she became aware that the radiogram had fallen silent. She got up and put Herbert's record carefully away in its sleeve, and placed it in the record rack with the rest of her father's collection. Podina had long gone to bed. Latha locked and latched the front door, switched off the lights, and went to her room.

But she had heard too much that night to settle easily to rest. Sleep was a long time coming, and even when it did it could not stop her tears.

19

PLANTATION HOSPITALITY

Dearest Duwa [Herbert wrote]
I have been hesitating some time as to whether I should send you the paper I have enclosed with this letter. It is a certified copy of a document filed with the records of the District Court of Colombo, which I was able to obtain on the strength of my being a member of the Wijesinha family. A truncated and Bowdlerized version of it appeared in the newspapers last month, and even in that form attracted (as you will understand when you read the original) an enormous amount of public attention. Your mother's sisters were, as you can imagine, especially scathing in their comments.

I surmise that this baptism of fire was what Chris meant when he told us that Ranil deserved to be repaid 'in kind' for his grim wedding-present to his sister and his brother-in-law, the burning of Sujit's boatyard in Hambantota. Certainly, Ranil's reputation has been so well and truly scorched by this document, and Tara has got herself so irrevocably identified with him, that I believe the marks they both carry will take a very long time to heal.

Let's turn to happier things: Tsunami writes us from Mykonos, where, as I am sure you must know, Sujit runs a highly successful ferry-boat service on the island, and builds small pleasure craft as a leisure activity. She thinks her novel-writing needs intellectual ballast, so she's set herself to study Greek history and civilization. I'm the one who gains from this, because she discusses some of her discoveries with me and, I rather think, with Ronald Marchmont in London.

It would be interesting to know whether anyone has sent her a copy of the newspaper version of the document I'm sending you. She'd tell you that the Greeks have a word for what her brother Christopher has done: philotimo. I looked it up in Britannica *today, where it's defined as a sense of 'honour' or 'pride' pervading one's feeling for family, community, and nation, and carrying with it a duty not to bring shame or dishonour to one's group.*

Strictly between ourselves, Latha, I do not take as gospel truth the claim made in the penultimate paragraph of the document I'm enclosing that the author's 'only motive in submitting this statement is that of wishing to see justice done'. Others, of course, who do not know of Christopher's devotion to you, will take that assertion at its face value. I personally believe that the document is the product of a veritable cocktail of motives: one part public spirit, certainly, but definitely one part revenge for what was done by her sibling to Tsunami; one part, probably more – although you may not like to hear this – a determination to push Ranil, once and for all, off the pedestal he has occupied for so many years in your affections; and as we must not forget, a sizeable dash of philotimo.

Your affectionate
Thaththa

Enclosure:
A statement submitted to the Police presently inquiring into the circumstances surrounding the events of 23rd September 1962 in the case of the Crown v. Chelvathy Vellasamy of Lucas Falls Estate, Province of Uva, in Ceylon:

In rehearsing the facts of this case as I know them, it is necessary to go back beyond the events of the twenty-third of September to certain matters that were set in train very much earlier. Some of these matters relate to a place, the well-known and very beautiful hill-country tea property named Lucas Falls in the Province of Uva that was, until 1959, owned by the late Minister for Cultural Affairs, Mr Rowland Wijesinha. Some of them relate to personalities: in particular, the personalities of the late Mr Wijesinha himself, and of his eldest son, Mr Ranil Wijesinha, the present owner of the property.

Lucas Falls estate resembles our country in having been for many years, and in being still, a home to many different kinds of people. The family that owns and controls the property, like the political party that holds power in our country, is Sinhalese, and therefore part of the island's majority community. But the workers on the estate are predominantly Tamils whose ancestors were brought to the island from south India by the British as indentured labour in the last century, and who have lived at Lucas Falls for several generations.

Another point of similarity is that a large proportion of the estate labour force consists of women, on whose skill and delicacy of touch depends the quality of the tea plucked at Lucas Falls, and marketed at the tea auctions of Colombo and London; while I believe that most people who know Ceylon would agree that the island's womenfolk, who bear the burden of running its households and bearing and bringing up its children, are among its most valuable assets. It is an interesting fact, and one we should take note of in the context of this case, that although our land depends for its prosperity on the day-long work of women at almost every level of society, those women are mostly unpaid (or are paid very little) for their labour. They are seldom granted the status of heads of their households, and are consequently helpless before the law.

It has occurred to me that in many ways the events that occurred at Lucas Falls estate on the twenty-third of September reflect and symbolize certain unfortunate aspects of the national character, in particular our exaggerated respect for custom and tradition, our readiness to defer to our superiors, and our casual treatment of those we have come to regard as our social inferiors.

Consider first the personality of the late Mr Rowland Wijesinha. A member of an ancient and respected family, Mr Wijesinha was a well educated landowner whose interests went beyond the management of his inherited estates to the spheres of art and culture. He took a special interest in our country's history and the part played in it by his own family, often expressing his admiration of the steadfast way in which certain personalities of the past had kept up the country's time-honoured traditions. One of these personalities was an ancestor of his, a Gate Mudaliyar of the Southern Province, who refused his patronage to a great Sinhala poet of the sixteenth century and drove him out of his presence because the poet had dedicated his work to Saraswati, Goddess of Wisdom, and not to himself. Another was a Kandyan nobleman of the last century to whom Mr Wijesinha was distantly related on his mother's side, who is said to have punished a servant found guilty of stealing coconuts from his estate by having the thief tied to a tree and personally flogging him until the flesh came away from his back. It is also said of this particular nobleman that in his household certain codes governing the dress of domestics were strictly observed: any servant or slave, male or female, who dared to appear before him or serve at his table with the upper half of their body covered was reprimanded and whipped. Such conduct, which does not appear to have been general, might seem severe, even barbaric, to us when we hear about it today, but those who observed such traditions did not doubt that they were entirely within their rights in doing so. Mr Wijesinha is known to have actually approved of the traditions I have cited above as being not merely acceptable, but in keeping with our country's customary laws.

I wish to make it clear that the late Mr Wijesinha is not known to have himself imitated the actions of these historical figures. Nor did he practise a good many other customs that were, and are still, regarded as traditional and customary in some parts of our country. For example, it is well known that here, as in other parts of Asia and in Europe and South America, landowners of the colonial era exercised manorial and seigneurial rights over the workers on their properties, especially in relation to sexual matters. In British times, and even in our own, if a Government official stayed overnight on a property such as Lucas Falls as a guest, the owner of the property might assign to a female member of the household staff the duty of keeping the visitor company, and ensuring that he passed a pleasant night. So accommodating in this respect were the coffee and tea planters of the past that the practice of entertaining guests in this particular manner has come to be euphemistically called 'Plantation Hospitality'. Despite Mr Wijesinha's deep respect for tradition, however, he is not known to have exercised seigneurial rights over the workers on his estate, nor is he known to have provided 'Plantation Hospitality' to the many guests who visited Lucas Falls.

When Mr Wijesinha passed away in 1958, the victim of a tragic accident, the property passed to his eldest son. Mr Ranil Wijesinha is an outstanding sportsman, and a popular personality. He has a wide circle of friends, many of whom he invites to house-parties on his beautiful estate. He takes pride in keeping up family traditions, and is pleased to extend generous hospitality as his father did before him, paying attention to every detail that will advance the comfort of his guests.

Care for the comfort of one's guests is, of course, a virtue and not an eccentricity. And in Mr Ranil Wijesinha's younger days, i.e., before his father's death, his concern took a pleasant and attractive form: for example, he would take the trouble to choose with care the dishes which were to be served during his guests' stay, the recorded music that was to be played when ballroom dancing was to be on the programme, even the flowers that were to decorate bedrooms and public rooms. Such domestic details are usually the concern of the lady of the house. But Mr Wijesinha was then, and still is, a bachelor who lives for the greater part of each year in Colombo, and the estate is run on his behalf by Mr Sajith Karunaratne, his estate manager. Mr Karunaratne acts under his master's instructions to see that the household runs smoothly. The estate is, or has been until recently, a credit to Mr Karunaratne's efficiency.

Following the death of his father, however, Mr Ranil Wijesinha's concern for tradition appears to have taken an unusual turn. This need not surprise: old families are known sometimes to harbour foibles and eccentricities. Inheriting his father's wealth and his Epicurean tastes, Mr Wijesinha wishes to conduct his private life as his ancestors conducted theirs 'in the olden days'. In following this fancy he has recently made it his pleasure and duty to actively revive many old customs that his late father respected in theory but did not observe in practice. The events of the twenty-third of September demonstrate that Mr Wijesinha's liking for tradition is being carried so far at present that it could be said to have become a danger to society.

On the twenty-first of September last year, a group of visitors arrived at Lucas Falls to spend a weekend on the estate, and Mr Karunaratne had received instructions beforehand as usual, as to the preparations that were to be made for their reception. There were no ladies in the party, the group consisting only of ten males between thirty-two and forty years of age, all of them without exception Mr Ranil Wijesinha's close friends and professional associates. A programme had been devised by their host according to which his guests would, during their stay, have the opportunity to play tennis and golf in the townships of Bandarawela and Nuwara Eliya, visit a nearby wildlife sanctuary, and picnic by a magnificent waterfall in the neighbourhood. On the evening of the twenty-third of September, the last night of their stay, the guests and their host were to enjoy a special celebratory dinner in the dining room of the Lucas Falls house. The practical details relating to this programme, which had been planned by Mr Wijesinha with the special interests of his guests in mind, were arranged as usual by his estate manager.

The beauties of the house and gardens of Lucas Falls, a show-place that is frequently photographed and has been the subject of many articles in newspapers and international journals, are well known. Mr Wijesinha, who has in recent years demonstrated a marked interest in Ceylon's history and traditions, has been adding to his late father's library at Lucas Falls first editions of certain early publications that have lately come on the market. Fascinated by the illustrations and plates in these books, he has had multiple copies made of some of them, which he has had elegantly framed. And as part of the preparations for his weekend house-parties, Mr Wijesinha has been recently giving instructions, not merely that the linen in his guests' rooms should be changed daily – for that was always done, in any case – but that the *pictures* in those rooms should be changed also! When his guests retired after dinner each night, he wished them to discover over the mantelpiece in their bedroom a picture different from the one that had hung there in the morning: a picture specially chosen to hint at or depict the pastimes and pleasures that awaited them on the next day. He intended these changes to provide a topic of conversation among the guests, and create in addition an atmosphere of pleasurable anticipation.

On the twenty-first of September, the day preceding the planned picnic, the picture selected for display was a nineteenth-century print showing Dunhinda Falls. On the twenty-second, the day preceding a visit to a wildlife sanctuary, that picture had been taken down and replaced by a print showing elephants in the Yala wilderness. On the twenty-third, which was the day of the celebratory farewell dinner, the picture chosen by Mr Wijesinha was an illustration from a famous book published in 1681, Robert Knox's account of his experiences as a prisoner for twenty years in the court of the King of Kandy. I am submitting with this statement a copy of that picture, which shows a richly dressed Sinhalese nobleman seated on a carpet on the ground, deftly pouring a stream of liquid, possibly coconut or *kitul* toddy, into his mouth from a spouted bottle. Standing beside him is a woman with a dish in her hands from which she is serving him with a spoon. The fact that the woman is naked above the waist suggests on the one hand that the scene is an intimate, domestic one depicting a householder and his wife. On the other hand, since in times gone by domestics were forbidden by custom in some noble households to clothe themselves above the waist, the woman holding dish and spoon might just as probably represent a servant or a slave.

According to Mr Karunaratne, who was standing by the sideboard throughout in the role of steward, conversation at the dinner table that evening was dominated by a lively discussion of the significance of this picture. One or two of the guests jokingly asked their host whether the picture indicated his intention to announce his imminent engagement to some fortunate lady. This Mr Wijesinha denied. All the servants handing the dishes at his table being male and fully clothed, and there being no wife or female friend of Mr Wijesinha present, the guests concluded that the picture related in an uncomplicated way to the dinner they were consuming in their wealthy friend's home, the half-naked representation of the female figure being the result of artistic licence on the part of the engraver. The main meal having been served, the empty dishes were removed from the table, and the servants withdrew from the room.

It was at this moment that the significance of the picture chosen by their host for his guests' last evening in his house was most graphically demonstrated. A procession of twelve young girls came into the dining room, carrying small silver dishes of fruit and sweetmeats which they placed on the dining table before taking up their positions beside the chairs of the guests. These young women were attractively clad in colourful silk body-cloths, fastened at the waist. Above the waist, they were completely naked.

After the first gasp of astonishment, the guests (gentlemen who pride themselves on their sophistication, and who regard themselves as men of the world) laughed, and gave their host a round of hearty applause. The general consensus of opinion around the table was that under Mr Ranil Wijesinha's rule, the time-honoured traditions of the hill-country relating to domestic life were being duly and correctly observed at Lucas Falls. This certainly seemed to be the case, for the twelve young women did not break into a song and dance routine (as they might have done, had they been merely entertainers hired for the occasion from a city night club) but busied themselves, in the manner of well-trained domestic servants, with setting out fresh glasses for the guests, which they filled with wine, whisky and arrack. The serious drinking of the evening now began, the guests' enjoyment of this part of the entertainment being naturally augmented by the close proximity of so much beauty and bare flesh, and by the willingness with which the young waitresses met their every requirement.

To the disappointment of some of Mr Wijesinha's guests who had visited Lucas Falls on earlier occasions, 'Plantation Hospitality' had not been offered them on the nights of the twenty-first and twenty-second of September. The ambiguous illustration from Robert Knox's book in their bedrooms that morning, however, and the appearance of a dozen submissive and half-clothed young women to serve them in the dining room that evening, seemed to indicate that at least on their last night at Lucas Falls, this omission would be made good. Stimulated by the physical presence of so many pretty young women, Mr Wijesinha's guests looked forward eagerly to the pleasures of the night to come. It is possible that, in their excitement, some of them drank too much. Certainly, their talk (which was in English and Sinhala, languages they believed were unfamiliar to the young women who were serving them, all of whom were drawn from among the estate's Tamil labour force) became unnecessarily free. Having apparently been instructed by the estate manager on previous visits as to what their behaviour should be towards the estate's female staff, the guests refrained at first from touching or brushing against the waitresses, but as the evening went on their actions became less restrained, and their speech, by stages, grew openly offensive. This was especially true of one of the guests, Mr Amrit Palipana.

Mr Palipana, the son of a Minister in the present Government, perhaps assumed that the good fortune which had placed him where he is had also guaranteed him special privileges. He had some basis for this assumption, since Mr Karunaratne had seen to it, on his employer's instructions, that he had been assigned the best of the guest bedrooms at Lucas Falls. A special request, sent beforehand to his host, had also secured for Mr Palipana not just one young woman to see to his comfort that night, but two. The Minister's son had inquired, as an afterthought, whether it could be arranged that the two young women assigned to look after his needs were sisters: a curious fancy that Mr Ranil Wijesinha, for reasons best known to himself, had apparently wished to indulge. He had instructed his estate manager to do what he could for this favoured guest; and Mr Karunaratne had been able to oblige.

As his statement to this Court indicates, Mr Karunaratne takes pride in loyally serving his master, and on this occasion he was pleased to inform Mr Wijesinha that he had managed to find two pretty young girls on the Lucas Falls estate, Chelvathy and Rukmini Vellasamy, who were not only sisters, but sixteen-year-old identical twins. Delighted to find his smallest whim catered for in such a highly satisfying way (the twins were positioned on either side of him at the dining table, their eyes modestly on the ground), Mr Palipana removed his tie and loosened his shirt-collar, revealing the mat of curly black hair that decorated his chest. He leaned back lazily in his chair, and indicated to Rukmini that he would like a piece of *puhul dosi* put into his mouth. When she had shyly obeyed him he indicated to Chelvathy that he wanted his glass refilled.

'A thorn between two roses, Amrit?' said one of Mr Wijesinha's guests acidly.

Palipana didn't mind being teased. This, he may have thought, sensing that he was the envy of every other man at the table, was certainly the life! Exhilarated, he began to talk too loudly, drank too much, and eventually went too far. He stretched out an arm and pulled Rukmini Vellasamy on to his lap. Planting his lips noisily on her neck, he fumbled with one hand at the clasp of the silver waist-chain that secured her cloth. With the other, he proceeded to fondle her naked breasts.

'*Adey!* Like nice, juicy *jambu*!' said Mr Palipana admiringly, and giggled.

Now, the young woman who was being publicly mauled and humiliated in this manner is no experienced 'Lady of the Night'. She and her sister are the younger daughters of a respectable worker on Lucas Falls estate. They have both been formally promised in marriage to men of their community; and inquiry reveals that although some of the other young women present that evening had participated, by their employer's order, in 'Plantation Hospitality' provided discreetly to his male guests on earlier occasions, she and her sister had not. Rukmini and Chelvathy Vellasamy had been told by the estate manager that the 'service at the bungalow' for which they were required that evening would merely involve waiting at table. Nothing had been said to make them suspect that they would be expected to do so without decent covering on their bodies. On the contrary, Mr Karunaratne had promised that their clothes for this special occasion would be provided at estate expense, and would include ten glass bangles, a pair of silver anklets and a gold chain each (which would make a welcome addition to their respective dowries). If the evening ended late, they had their master's permission to sleep overnight in the servants' quarters, where middle-aged Thangamma, one of the female cooks, would look after them. If it ended early, they could go home.

Mr Palipana's uncontrolled behaviour had now made it clear, even to this pair of innocents, that they had been deceived. One of the twins, distressed at what was happening to her sister and fearful of its outcome, attempted to intervene. She daringly tugged at Mr Palipana's arm in an effort to make him release the girl.

'Let my sister go! She's ill, she must be taken home!' Chelvathy whispered, in her halting Sinhala.

Mr Palipana, registering the urgency of her tone but too far gone to understand what she was saying to him, smiled down the table at his host.

'My God, machan, where do you find talent like this? This kid's so bloody keen to get in on the act that she can't even wait till I've finished with her sister . . .'

'You're too drunk to cope with either of them, Amrit, much less both. Come on, be sensible and let that girl go. Karunaratne will help you to your room.'

'Exshellent idea,' said Mr Palipana. 'Firsht class idea. To my room. Hear that, girls? Off we go!'

Retaining his grip on Rukmini, he staggered to his feet.

'Come along, baba!' he said to her. 'Forward! Quick march!'

Looking round, he extended a helpful hand to her sister.

Instead of taking the hand held out to her, Chelvathy threw herself at Palipana, and with all the force she could muster, slapped him across the face. Karunaratne rushed towards them, grasped both the girl's hands, and pinioned them behind her back.

'What do you think you are doing?' he muttered fiercely in her ear in Tamil. 'Don't you know who this gentleman is?'

'That is nothing to me,' Chelvathy replied. 'Tell him to let my sister go, or I'll tell my father—'

Karunaratne laughed.

'You'll tell your father? Silly girl, your father is the person who sent you both here. He has been well paid for it. As for you, you have a job to do. Now do it! Leave your sister alone, ask the master to forgive you, and get back to your work.'

Palipana's knowledge of Tamil is minimal, but he perceived that all was not well with his two ladies.

'Whatsh the matter, baba? You feeling shy? Want to keep company with your little sis? Daddy undershtands. Just you both come with me, Ka – ka – karunaratne and I'll look after you. Nothing to worry about. We'll do right by you, won't we, Karu?'

He turned back to his host.

'Nice big bedsh you have in the . . . in the old ansheshtral, Ranil, old man,' he said approvingly. 'Plenty of room for ush all.'

By now they had the attention of everyone in the room. The carefully planned evening was in ruins. Ranil Wijesinha rose to his feet, furious.

'What's the meaning of this? Karunaratne, I'll see you afterwards. Meanwhile, take that girl to the kitchen, give her back her belongings, and see that she goes home.'

He had spoken in Sinhala, but was immediately understood by Chelvathy.

'I will not go home!' she screamed at him. 'Not unless my sister comes with me! Tell that man to let her go.'

Palipana, perhaps realizing that matters had come to an impasse where one of the twins was concerned, decided to concentrate his attention on the other. He clasped Rukmini tightly round the waist and, ignoring her attempts to free herself, he began to walk her to the dining-room door.

Seeing Mr Wijesinha sit down again in his chair, showing no signs of interfering on her sister's behalf, Chelvathy struggled out of Karunaratne's grip and snatched up a dessert knife from the table. She ran towards the couple, stood squarely in front of Palipana and, before anyone could stop her, plunged the point of the knife into his chest.

And on that very knife-point her life story may well end. She will stand in the dock in a few weeks' time, with more than a dozen witnesses, some of them from families that are among the most respected in the land, to affirm the fact that on the night of the twenty-third of September last year, Chelvathy Vellasamy committed murder, killing the man who she believed was about to rape her twin sister. She does not deny the charge, and indeed has said in her statement to the Police sergeant who arrested her that she is glad to have performed the deed in defence of her family's honour and her sister's.

In concluding this statement in Chelvathy's defence, I would refer once again to the inequity of the law where women, especially women without wealth or high status, are concerned. The accused in this case comes from a humble background. She and her family have neither money nor political authority to buy her the expert legal advice that might swing the balance in her favour. I submit that she is innocent of the charge of murder, and I believe also that certain others deserve, at this moment, to be standing in her place in the dock, since it is on their irresponsible and unashamed exercise of power that the blame for this tragic event should be laid.

As I am in possession of information about the Wijesinha family that no person but a member of it can supply, and since there is no one willing to defend Chelvathy Vellasamy's action but myself (an individual who has no official status in this case and who has indeed only recently completed his legal studies), I state my readiness to give evidence at the official hearing, if I am asked by the Courts to do so. While declaring a personal interest in these matters since I am myself a kinsman of Mr Ranil Wijesinha, I wish to state that my only motive in submitting this statement is that of wishing to see justice done.

I am confident that Chelvathy's case is a just one, and trust that it will not be prejudiced in any material way by the fact that my method of presenting it might have been inexpert and the approach I have taken to it unconventional.

(Sgd.) Christopher Wijesinha. B.Sc., L.L.B.

20

A PROPOSAL AND A PROPOSITION

Christopher Wijesinha heard his uncle Herbert before he saw him.

'Mrs Katugaha,' said the familiar voice as Chris climbed the steps to the open veranda and, finding no one about, walked into the *sala* unimpeded. 'Mrs Katugaha, what is this you are telling me? I informed you three months ago that I would be needing a new gas cylinder for our cooker, and you assured me that you would see about it. "My wife and I live out of town now, and I cannot be running to Colombo for a replacement when the gas runs out: I need a spare," I said. And you said, very kindly: "A new gas cylinder will be ready and waiting for you, Mr Wijesinha, without fail." That was what you told me three months ago, in September 1962. It is now December, and now, Mrs Katugaha, you are telling me something very different?'

Chris pushed open the half-open door of his uncle's library.

Herbert Wijesinha's back was towards the door and his feet, elegantly crossed at the ankles, rested on the top of his carved rosewood writing desk. His attitude, as he held the receiver to his ear, was that of one listening to the music of the spheres.

'But, Mrs Katugaha, why should I write to the Minister to complain? Her Excellency is, by all accounts, a very busy lady. Yes, she does happen to be a relative of mine – though by marriage only, Mrs Katugaha, by marriage only and she does happen to be the Minister of Home Affairs – but is that any reason why she should be bothered with my difficulties in purchasing a new gas cylinder? My dealings are entirely with you and your company, not with the Minister.'

A pause ensued, during which Herbert listened indulgently to what seemed to be a complicated explanation.

'You tell me it's a Government regulation that your company must distribute new gas cylinders only to newly married people? When was this regulation made?'

More explanations.

'So, Mrs Katugaha, what you are telling me is, that in order to qualify for a new gas cylinder, it is Government policy that I divorce my wife and marry again?'

Chris sat down very quietly in a chair beside the study door, which was now wide open. His uncle gave no indication that he had heard anyone come in.

Can it be that the old boy's enjoying this? It would drive me nuts.

'Mrs Katugaha,' went on Herbert, 'I have a problem with what you are telling me. You see, I don't really *want* to divorce my wife, since we are very happily married, and she has looked after me well for many years. However, a thought has just struck me. I have never seen you. But although I am no longer a young man – in my fifties now, but I assure you, in full possession of all my faculties, including my sense of hearing – you sound to me like a very beautiful woman. Perhaps, if I *could* see you, Mrs Katugaha, I might reconsider my position.'

This suggestion was received with peals of musical laughter.

'Please don't laugh, Mrs Katugaha. Have pity on me. I am perfectly serious . . . and I need a new gas cylinder. What is that you say? I have a nice sense of humour? I have to have a sense of humour, Mrs Katugaha, to deal with your bloody company. Forgive the language, madam, passion overcame me just then . . . The new gas cylinder will be delivered tomorrow? Thank you, Mrs Katugaha. You have been most kind and helpful. And remember, my offer still stands.'

Herbert replaced the receiver, and removed his feet from the top of the writing desk. He spoke without turning round.

'So, what are you waiting for, moron? Put my cup of tea down.'

'Sorry, Uncle Herbert. It's not Vaithi with your tea. It's only me.'

The swivel chair spun round, Herbert jumped up with an agility that belied his years, and embraced his nephew.

'Chris! Why didn't you let me know you were coming?'

There was a slight pause.

'How long have you been sitting here?'

'Long enough to hear your proposal of marriage to Mrs Katugaha. Congratulations, Uncle.'

'On what? On getting a new gas cylinder? That's the way things are these days, my boy, you know it as well as I do. The shops are full of imported rubbish no one needs or can afford to buy, and when it comes to the necessities of life or supporting local industries, you have to go down on your knees to everybody from the counter clerk upwards.'

'Or propose marriage. You seemed, if I may say so, to be thoroughly enjoying yourself.'

Herbert smiled.

'Yes. Well. You've got to get your entertainment where you can find it, haven't you? Not much of it to go round these days. The newspapers carry nothing but pictures of over-dressed society women parading their clothes and jewellery – though that's not funny, it's obscene, makes you want to throw up – and politicians laying foundation stones for hospitals and libraries that everybody knows will never be built . . .'

'Which reminds me – how's your book going, Uncle Herbert?' Chris inquired.

'Oh, it's getting there, it's getting there. Trouble is, who would want to know the political views of a dinosaur like me? Plenty of people rushing to the papers with theories on how to stop ministers taking bribes, how to fix the economy . . . I wrote to a newspaper with some ideas on the subject, but they took absolutely no notice of my letter. Didn't even print it . . . But never mind all that now. Have you had something to eat?'

'Yes, thanks. I had lunch on the train.'

'On the *train*? Where's your car?'

'The battery's flat. It's beyond charging, they say, and the suppliers won't be able to find me a new one until next week.'

'I see. Just like our gas cylinder. But lunch on the train – Good God, Chris! We can do better than that.'

He picked up the telephone receiver.

'Vaithi!'

An order was given for an elaborate dinner.

'What, no crabs in the market? Nonsense. Take the car, and go and *find* them. Go down to the beach front if necessary. Crab curry, yellow rice, dry fried potatoes, cadju curry, the lot . . . Got that? For how many? For four, you moron: myself, madam, Mr Christopher, and your good self. Think I'd deprive you of crab curry, especially when you've cooked it?'

Chris was impressed by his uncle's domestic arrangements.

'A telephone connection to the kitchen, Uncle Herbert? It's a novel idea.'

'Had it installed last week. I advise you to do the same. Only way to live, dear boy. Only way to live. I take the day's menu very seriously, and so does Vaithi. His father taught him well, and he's a good cook – in fact, I'd go so far as to say he's a great one. Trouble is, these hotels, Chris! Springing up everywhere like mushrooms. If one of them ever got to know about young Vaithi, they'd offer him a chef's hat and three times the salary I pay him. If he lived overseas, he'd certainly be on TV, running his own show. It's been my principal aim in life, since I retired from the Customs Department in 1961 and we came out here, to keep young Vaithi in blissful ignorance of the outside world, so content with life in this peaceful backwater, out of the line of fire, that he'd never think of leaving us.'

Chris could not resist.

'Forgive the question, Uncle Herbert, but may I ask if he's content to be regularly addressed as "moron"?'

'Certainly he is. Perfectly content. Thinks it's a polite form of address, I believe,' Herbert said. 'Roughly equivalent to "maestro".'

'English was never his dad's strong point,' observed Chris, remembering the old days at Lucas Falls.

'No, and it isn't his, either. And now, let's get you settled. What about a bath and a change of clothes? Meet me on the veranda at six-thirty, and we'll have a drink on the Q.T. before Soma joins us for dinner. I've been advised to go slow on the booze, but it's not as though we see you every day.'

Over their pre-dinner drinks, Chris outlined a proposition for his uncle's consideration.

'Would you be interested, Uncle Herbert, in joining an independent panel that would monitor and report on the conduct of public institutions? There's a small group of us, like-minded folk, who think something could be done by working together, since it is obvious that individuals, working on their own, haven't a chance of succeeding against . . .'

'Against the monolith of state and institutional lethargy?'

'Precisely. My associates and I haven't got beyond the planning stage as yet, and we would value your experience of Government service in setting up a structure and getting it working. And after that, in keeping us on track . . .'

Herbert smiled.

'You see me in the role of human gad-fly, do you, Chris?'

'Think it over, Uncle Herbert.'

Herbert thought it over. He thought of the inefficiency and irresponsibility that had become features of everyday life in the country he loved, he thought of the tales of individual greed and corporate corruption that formed the staple of the daily papers, he thought of the shameless lies and meaningless platitudes that passed for public debate, and he sighed. He glanced at Chris, in whose eyes he had detected the unmistakable light of idealism, and wondered whether his nephew and his friends understood that the task of ridding the country of a half-century of accumulated filth was an impossible one.

There were, of course, several organizations that had recently sprung up, which claimed to be actively cleaning up public life. The best publicized of these was the Sri Lanka Institute for Moral Enlightenment, under the chairmanship of the P.M. himself. Under its patronage, the Sri Lanka Association for Peace, the Sri Lanka Association for Sinhala Heritage, and the Sri Lanka Association for the National Development of Ethnic Rapport were very much in the news. Herbert read of their activities in the daily papers with the cynicism that had now become a habit with him, and wondered what S.L.A.P., S.L.A.S.H. and S.L.A.N.D.E.R would ever achieve under the auspices of S.L.I.M.E.

Why doesn't Chris just turn his back and walk away? Because he's still young, still energetic enough to fight battles, to be in love.

But why, for heaven's sake, did Chris want to involve him?

Battling the country's ills would be like cleaning the Augean stables, and I know only too well that I'm no hero. The only things we have in common, Hercules, old lad, are the first three letters of our names . . .

And then Herbert remembered his still unfinished book, and the many hopes and plans he had had that everyday events had overtaken. He hadn't achieved much on his own so far – a few little victories here and there, certainly, but nothing on the scale that might have been achieved if he had worked with a committed team. He refreshed his nephew's glass and topped up his own.

'You do realize what I shall be giving up if I join you and your high-minded pals, Christopher? I shall have to abandon the cynicism that has sustained me all my life. I shall have to begin actually *caring* about what is happening in our country. A terrifying thought, indeed.'

'Yes, it is,' said Chris. 'But I've never known you to be afraid of anything.'

'Well,' Herbert said at last. 'I'll be proud to join you. And I promise you I'll give it my best shot.'

There was a short silence. Chris put down his glass and said slowly:

'I'm glad of that, Uncle Herbert. More glad than I can say. Because you'll find that your colleagues in this enterprise include people you know very well.'

Herbert looked up, surprised.

'Who?'

'Latha, for one.'

'*Latha*?'

'She's coming back,' said Chris. 'And there's something else she may not have told you yet, but I don't think she'd mind too much if I tell you first. When she comes back, it will be to be with me.'

Herbert very nearly dropped his scotch and soda.

'Good Lord!' he said; and added:

'My apologies if I sound amazed, Chris, but I'd thought it was all over between the two of you.'

'There have been times when I thought so too,' Chris admitted. 'But I've never given up hoping. And I've never given up asking.'

'*She's coming back to be with me . . .*' Herbert said reflectively. 'That's a novel way of saying you're getting married.'

The question hung between them in the air. At last, Herbert forced himself to ask it.

'Well, isn't it? You *are* getting married, aren't you? Don't misunderstand me, Chris, I am delighted to hear this news, but I wouldn't be doing my duty if I didn't ask you, in the proper traditional way, just what your intentions are regarding our daughter?'

'Strictly honourable, Uncle Herbert! I'd meet Latha at the airport with the marriage licence in my pocket, if she'd let me. But she won't. She says marriage must wait until she's completely independent. And until her book is published, she won't be. It's been so hard getting her to this point that I don't want to say anything that might make her change her mind.'

Herbert said:

'I don't know what her mother will say to the idea of her only daughter living in sin, but you both have my congratulations, Chris. *And* my support. One hundred per cent. But I shall leave it to you to break the news to Soma.'

At dinner that night he was in a celebratory mood, so much so that his wife looked sharply at him across the table.

He's always happy when Chris comes to see us. But tonight something's happened. Has he had a tot too much?

'Let's have young Vaithi in and compliment him on his cooking, Soma,' Herbert said genially. 'This yellow rice is really first-class – better, even, than his august father's.'

Encountering a plump cardamom pod in a mouthful of rice, he rolled the pod on his tongue, and savoured its discharge of high-octane pleasure against his palate. The flavour of cardamom, especially when it had melted in the process of cooking into no more than an exquisite rumour, a mere hint of its own presence, had always held a high place on Herbert's list of the supreme joys of life. Across the dining table, his wife smiled a smile of relief. So it wasn't an extra drink that had done it, Herbert was just high on good food.

'What's next on tonight's menu?' persisted Herbert, determined at all costs to avoid the topic of Chris and Latha.

Latha and Chris . . .

'We have some really good curd and honey,' Soma said.

'There you are, Chris, curd and honey, the king of desserts—'

'Have you heard from Latha recently, Chris?' his aunt inquired.

'Latha? Oh, yes, she writes . . . sometimes,' Chris said casually. 'And I write to her . . . Occasionally . . .'

Soma sighed.

What is the matter with this daughter of ours, I just don't know.

21

LETTERS TO LONDON

Christmas Day 1963

Christopher paid his usual monthly visit to us a few days ago [wrote Herbert, in his regular weekly letter to Latha]. His usual excuse for coming to see us is that he wants to hear my views on one political issue or another. I keep up the fiction, and we sit and talk politics until he asks – again, as usual – whether we've heard from you recently. I have always supposed that he does this, hoping that one of these days he'll get lucky, and we'll tell him you're expected home. But on this occasion, as I've no doubt you are aware, it was he who had good news to impart. A Christmas gift, of the best kind . . .

What he had to tell me has made me very happy, duwa. I shall write again in a day or two, after I've examined it from all angles myself, and have found the right words with which to express my feelings. But your mother had best hear it from you, rather than from me.

On his last evening here, Christopher stood his aged uncle a drink at the S.S.C. It was a pleasant enough way of passing the time – they had put up some lights and polished the brass to mark the season, and all the usual suspects had been rounded up as in *Casablanca*, they were holding up the bar, and talking sport and political gossip. There was plenty to talk about in the way of politics – as you know, your Aunt Moira is our new P.M. A few people were there of my own generation, seated sedately in the Club armchairs – like me, they're all waiting around 'in the Departure Lounge', as one of Ranil's former classmates, a massive plug-ugly called Kodikara, graciously put it when he strolled over to talk to Chris. He must have thought I'm deaf as well as elderly, and hadn't heard him, but I *did* hear him, quite clearly. Once Kodikara had worked out who I was – in particular, that I am the father of Chris and Ranil's distinguished cousin Dr Latha Wijesinha – he favoured us with his considered views on women's education.

'Bloody silly, in my opinion, all this nonsense about giving our women university degrees. With all respect to you, sir, what the hell is your daughter going to do with hers? I met her a couple of years ago – she was with your sister Tsunami, Chris – and both of them were studying for exams at Peradeniya! I ask you – couple of bloody smashing girls like that, what do they need exams for? Learn to sew, cook, play the piano, run the house and whack the bloody kids when they need a whacking, that's all that life requires of them, isn't it? What do *you* say, sir?'

I replied that these days 'our women' might require a little more out of life than that. For instance, I said, they might like to read; and through their reading, find out something about what's going on in the world . . .?

'What for?' quoth Kodikara. 'My sisters read far too much already. They read *Who* to find out who's sleeping with who in Hollywood, they read the Sunday papers to find out who's wearing bloody what in Colombo, and they read the obituaries in the *Daily News* every day, so that they know whose bloody funerals they'll have to attend that week anywhere in the island. Surely that's enough?'

While he was here, Chris passed on to us something that he may not, with all that has been happening in his personal life, have remembered to tell you. The big news in his branch of the Wijesinha family (apart from the doings of Prime Minister Moira, who's going from strength to strength, demonstrating that she has what it takes to stay at the top in our brave new world) is that his brother Colin has enlisted in the army. You know, duwa, Colin must have pulled quite a few strings to do it, since his vision is far from 20/20. To be honest, I hadn't thought Colin capable of such patriotism. Apparently he feels he owes it to his country to join up. It's a case, I suppose, of that poem of Moore's you used to love so much—

The minstrel boy to the war is gone,
In the ranks of Death you'll find him.
His father's sword he has girded on,
And his wild harp slung behind him . . .

Though of course Colin's no longer a boy, and his father's sword was never anything but an ornamental one, part of a Mudaliyar's fancy-dress. I don't suppose Colin himself has ever played a note in his life, on a harp, or a piano, or anything but a mouth organ.

'The ranks of Death' . . . yes, well, Colin will be lucky if he survives the conflict that everyone seems to think is looming. If we have a repetition of the emergency of 1958, the best outcome we can hope and pray for is a rapid end to a useless war . . .

You will be interested to know that a brand-new hotel has come up on Sujit's burnt-out site. Right on the beach at Hambantota, with 180 degree views of that marvellous bay, with its white sands and fishermen's boats. The owner is the same hotelier who built the Sapphire Reef Hotel in Galle.

He'll make a packet out of it, of course, for tourists are pouring into the new hotels all along the south coast, thinking this country is Paradise. Well, it is . . . Or was.

And now, Latha, I come to something that Christopher does *not* know, but which closely concerns you. I was summoned last week to Temple Trees, for an interview with Her Excellency herself. After I had been ushered into her presence by an impressive gent in an all-white outfit with a crimson and gold sash and white gloves – I had thought that kind of thing went out with the British, but I was obviously mistaken – your Aunt Moira sat me down on a carved ebony couch, and offered me a scotch and soda.

'I want to talk to you about Latha,' she said.

She informed me that she has been considering various candidates for the position of Sri Lanka's Ambassador to France, which has recently fallen vacant. Not one of them, she said, could be relied on to do us credit on the international scene. One had picked his teeth at a diplomatic dinner, with a safety-pin borrowed from his wife; another (formerly an attaché at our High Commission in London) stained the Buckingham Palace wall-paper every time he blew his nose, a third could barely write, let alone write French, a fourth chased women. At this point I began to wonder whether Moira was leading up to a suggestion that *you* should enter the diplomatic service, duwa, and represent Sri Lanka abroad. I was about to tell her that what she was suggesting sounded to me very much like nepotism, when I remembered that she very probably doesn't know the word, so I didn't bother. But I need not have been concerned, for it turned out that your aunt is pursuing another idea altogether. She's decided that Ranil is to be the nation's choice.

'*Ranil?*' I asked Moira. 'For *Paris*?'

Moira looked me straight in the eye.

'Can you think of anyone in the party who is better fitted for an ambassadorial role?' she asked me.

'Besides, Ranil needs to get away, he's still suffering, poor boy, from all the publicity that terrible court case attracted. Why they allowed it to come to court at all I don't know, when they could so easily have hushed the whole thing up from the very beginning. It was just an accident, after all, a trivial argument involving a couple of nobodies, young Palipana and that silly coolie woman from the lines. But after Christopher deliberately disgraced the family by sending a formal submission to the Court, making a *mountain* out of an *ant-hill*, and painting his elder brother as a procurer and a pimp, besides being stark, staring mad, what could they do? And after all, Herbert, Ranil is our nephew: however much disgrace he has brought upon our family, we can't just *flush* him away, can we? In any case, he needs steadying. He needs to settle down. He needs to get married. And my astrologer says that his stars are auspicious right now for wedding arrangements to be made.'

'Who would have him?' I asked her.

If your Aunt Moira had been a cat, the fur on her back would have bristled. As it was, she answered me briskly enough:

'There are *plenty* of nice girls around, of very good background, who would be *delighted* to marry into our family, Herbert. But why should we look so far? I was talking the matter over with Tara and my good friend Michelle Feuillard, and Michelle suggested that Latha would make the perfect wife for a diplomat in Paris: she is good-looking and elegant – well, we all know *that* – and she speaks and writes excellent French, so Michelle tells me. Besides, *we* know Latha doesn't get into political arguments as Tsunami did – so upsetting, that used to be, for poor dear Rowland!

'And another point in her favour, according to Tara, is that Latha knows all about good food. She'll know which wines to serve with what, she'll get her chef to serve wonderful savouries at Embassy receptions, and she'll throw D.P.L. dinner parties in Paris that will do our country proud.

'But most important of all, Herbert, *I* know that Latha has been brought up well by you and Soma. *I* know that she is a modest, sensible girl, a sweet, *simple* girl who doesn't expect too much from life. She practically grew up with Ranil, so she must know all his little weaknesses, and she'll make allowance for them. Latha's like the Queen, she knows that a wise wife turns a blind eye to her husband's little *piccadillies*.'

A tall young army officer, buckled and belted, came into the room at this point with a message for the Prime Minister, saluted smartly, and delivered a sealed envelope to Moira. She took it from him, and gave his broad, khaki-clad shoulders a long, appraising stare as they disappeared through the ornate doors. Then she turned back to me and smiled at me very sweetly.

'Good bod, no?' said Her Excellency.

Moira told me then that she has discussed the matter with Ranil, and he has asked her to send us a proposal of marriage. *I* told *her* that your future is your affair, not ours, and that any proposals should be sent to you direct.

So there you are, Latha, you could have a future before you as a diplomat's wife, should you want to change your mind as regards Christopher and accept Ranil's proposal instead. I will resist the temptation to give you my own opinion on the matter, apart from saying that I believe, with all my heart, that you have already made the right choice in deciding to make Chris your life's companion.

Whatever you decide, duwa, will be all right by me. And on my own behalf, my dearest daughter, I must tell you how glad I am that you are coming back. It's the right decision for you – I know you too well to think that a life outside this country could ever hold any permanent attraction for you. And despite what Kodikara and his kind believe, people still read books here, they don't just pass the time listening to the Commercial Service and reading *Who* magazine.

When you come back, Latha, you can help me finish my book. If you had put off your return much longer, it would have been a case for me of 'up stumps and back to the pavilion'.

We're growing old, your mother and I, and I miss you.

'I just love the flat,' Shalini said. 'It's perfect for me: size, location, everything. And Anupam will be able to stay here when he has to be in London, instead of putting up at a hotel. It's very kind of you to pass it on to me, Latha.'

'Not at all,' Latha assured her. 'I'd have had to give it up anyway, once I decided to leave. So go ahead, enjoy the flat! I would have regretted leaving the books, but now that I know they're in your hands and your brother's, it doesn't feel too bad. Tell Anupam I've left my copies of Shakespeare's *Sonnets* and *The Jungle Book* behind, especially for him.'

Shalini looked at the inscription on the fly-leaf of Latha's Kipling.

'"He travels the fastest who travels alone" – I take it there's a message there for Anupam, Latha!'

'Yes . . . There's the door-bell, I think the taxi's at the door.'

'Have you got everything? I'll forward any letters that come for you – and that reminds me, I haven't given you your mail. These arrived this morning.'

Latha took the letters from Shalini, and turned them over.

'Next month's rental – that'll be yours from now on, Shalini. An invitation to Independence Day celebrations on the fourth of February at the High Commission – I shall have to miss that, I'm afraid. What's this?'

'Doesn't it look impressive!' Shalini said. 'I couldn't help noticing that it carries the crest of the Prime Minister's office.'

Latha opened the ornate envelope, and glanced at the contents.

'There's no time to answer it now,' she said. 'It's not important, anyway.'

She put the envelope in her coat pocket, kissed Shalini, and picked up her suitcase.

'You're travelling light,' Shalini observed. 'That little case doesn't look as if it weighs anything at all.'

'Everything I need is at home.'

'Don't forget to give our love to Uncle Herbert and Auntie Soma,' Shalini called down the stairs as her friend paused, her hand on the knob of the front door. 'And to Chris.'

'Will do.'

Latha got into the waiting taxi, and waved to Shalini.

It was not until she was rummaging for her pen in order to fill out

Immigration and Customs forms at Heathrow that Latha remembered that she still had Ranil's letter in her pocket. Sitting in the Exit lounge, she read it through once again before she tore it up, together with Moira's covering letter, and dropped the pieces into a bin on her way to board her plane.

COPYRIGHT ACKNOWLEDGMENTS